Simon M. Zayas was born in Tampa, Florida. His ancestry is rooted in northern Spain.

At seventeen, Simon entered a monastery in Pennsylvania, obtaining a B.A. degree. Later, in Toronto, he obtained a Master of Divinity degree. In 1984 Simon was ordained a Roman Catholic priest.

Simon's first assignment as a priest was in Rome in administration for twelve years, traveling extensively worldwide, exposed to different cultures, languages and politics. He also served as a priest in New York City, various parishes in Texas and finally in Mexico City.

Now retired, this is Simon's first novel, Book One of a trilogy.

For Silvia Marie, my mother, who kept me safe in her womb and sacrificed for me.

"Mama", gracious, surest friend, who loves me and has always believed in me and still does.

Simon M. Zayas

The Air That We Breathe – Book One

Leicester

Austin Macauley Publishers
LONDON · CAMBRIDGE · NEW YORK · SHARJAH

Copyright © Simon M. Zayas 2025

All rights reserved. No part of this publication may be reproduced, distributed, or transmitted in any form or by any means, including photocopying, recording, or other electronic or mechanical methods, without the prior written permission of the publisher, except in the case of brief quotations embodied in critical reviews and certain other non-commercial uses permitted by copyright law. For permission requests, write to the publisher.

Any person who commits any unauthorized act in relation to this publication may be liable to criminal prosecution and civil claims for damages.

This is a work of fiction. Names, characters, businesses, places, events, locales, and incidents are either the products of the author's imagination or used in a fictitious manner. Any resemblance to actual persons, living or dead, or actual events is purely coincidental.

Ordering Information
Quantity sales: Special discounts are available on quantity purchases by corporations, associations, and others. For details, contact the publisher at the address below.

Publisher's Cataloging-in-Publication data
Zayas, Simon M.
The Air That We Breathe – Book One

ISBN 9798895430347 (Paperback)
ISBN 9798895430354 (Hardback)
ISBN 9798895430378 (ePub e-book)
ISBN 9798895430361 (Audiobook)

Library of Congress Control Number: 2024923091

www.austinmacauley.com/us

First Published 2025
Austin Macauley Publishers LLC
40 Wall Street, 33rd Floor, Suite 3302
New York, NY 10005
USA

mail-usa@austinmacauley.com
+1 (646) 5125767

This novel could not have been written without the encouragement and support I continually received from those around me. I am indebted and grateful to so many family members and good friends for this but I especially want to thank: Alejandro De La Torre, Silvia C. Zayas, Raoul Enrique Zayas, Karen Maria Zayas, Lisa A. Hembry, Mercedes De La Torre. I also want to thank Miss Weenie my faithful dachshund companion who very often sat and slept on my lap while I wrote during the many long hours of night until sunrise. "Mamushka", I miss you beyond words, my little girl.

Table of Contents

Prologue	11
Chapter One: Letting Go	14
Chapter Two: The Sword	46
Chapter Three: Lost and Abandoned	77
Chapter Four: Trusting	110
Chapter Five: Learning the Ropes	145
Chapter Six: Sexual Awakening	189
Chapter Seven: The Seminary	245
Chapter Eight: Toby	278
Chapter Nine: The Sexual Revolution	324
Chapter Ten: Coming of Age	359
Chapter Eleven: The Heart	398
Chapter Twelve: The Night of the Long Knives	432
Chapter Thirteen: Finding One's Voice	470
Chapter Fourteen: Kevin	515
Chapter Fifteen: "Stay with Me"	549
Epilogue	585

Prologue

"Bore Olam," the demon Ashmedai whispered disdainfully, one of his thorny brows grazing the pavement slightly as he bent forward exaggeratedly, in feigned adoration.

"You bow so gracefully before Me when it suits you," the Creator of the Universe said from His throne of gleaming lapis lazuli above the cherubim. "It's almost convincing, if I didn't know you so well."

The demon's brilliant eyes glanced sideways, not daring to make eye contact. "Oh yes, Ancient of Days, you certainly do know all things."

"Tell Me, what mischief are you planning now?" The Eternal Father stared at the tortured creature below Him.

"Mischief? Me?" The demon asked nervously. "No mischief here."

"Ashmedai, Ashmedai, don't toy with Me." The demon cowered and trembled at the mention of his name from the lips of the Almighty. "I'm only too well acquainted with your unfettered, foul behavior."

The vile creature's serpentine tail flinched and twitched behind him as he answered seductively, "My Lord, being the lusty beast that I am, well, You should know my nature." He curtseyed and then added mockingly, "After all, You created me."

Bore Olam thundered angrily, "I most certainly did NOT create you as you are now! I did not create in you what you have become by your own design!" He paused and said, "I created you as My emissary, an angel, clothed in My majesty. I created you as sheer goodness and light, but you chose another path. You rebelled and became something repulsive, unholy and dark!" He stretched out His arm and pointed at the squirming demon. "You rebelled against Me!"

The demon's lips curled up cynically as he hissed, "Seems to me like You have a perennial problem with Your creatures, n'est-ce pas? And humanity, in particular, seems to have followed my lead over the centuries. I seduce so many souls, so easily. Things haven't quite worked out as You planned, have they?"

"Mind your wretched tongue, Beast!" the Omnipotent God retorted. He considered the deplorable fallen angel crouched before Him. "You fool, you think you know everything but in your hubris, you fail to realize that you don't hold all the pieces of the puzzle. Only I do." Then He added, "If you seduce humanity, as you claim, it's only because I permit it for a greater good in the long run."

"It seems to me—"

The Almighty cut the demon off, "You itch to take My place and sit on this throne. That is at the root of your rebellion." His gaze was steady upon the demon as He spoke. "You now wander aimlessly, through barren wastelands without a clue of who you were meant to be, but once in the beginning…yes…once, I created you in love for such lofty splendor near this very throne."

The demon cringed closer to the pavement and voicing his subservience, cried out in anguish and genuine misery, "Domine! Kyrios! Hashem!"

Bore Olam rubbed His weary eyes slowly and sighed into the vast and infinite halls of eternity that spread out before Him in every direction of space and time. "The Divine Plan, My Plan, is never outdone even in the face of rebellion." He looked at the demon with compassion and said, "Let me tell you a story, Ashmedai, a story about a creature I have loved since the moment of his conception in his mother's womb, when I breathed My Breath into him. I created him in My own Image and destined him to stand before Me, in the presence of the Angels to offer the only fitting Sacrifice acceptable to Me. Yet, this creature was weak and remains so. Weak, to the point of rebellion, of deceiving himself into believing that he too, held all the pieces to the puzzle. He was often unable to distinguish between what is actual weakness and what is true strength. It wounded and bruised him terribly for a very long time and could have destroyed him completely except—"

The demon interrupted and looked around, snickering like an unruly child, "You speak of Larry, don't You? Or should I say…Simon? Ha, ha, ha." The demon waved his scaly arms in the air dramatically and then held his three heads, mimicking bewilderment, as if he was beyond confusion, shaking them wildly. "Larry Simon, Simon Larry! Larry, Larry, Simon, Simon! Which one is it?" Ashmedai straightened up and did a little jig as he sneered with raspy laughter and cried out obscenely, "Oh, I've had my eye on him for quite some time. That golden boy of Yours is so easily given to lustful things and every kind of excess. He is sidelined at every turn by things that glitter and is quite fond of his fellow men. Well, the ones that are easy on the eyes, that is. He's the innocent child who always wanted to be faithful and pure but then…he lost his way." He added sarcastically, "So very tragic, wouldn't You agree?"

Gravely, Bore Olam answered the haughty, tawdry demon, "Yes, he rather reminds me of you, except of course, that we both know your story of rebellion and how pitiful you ended up." The demon bent low and dared not speak further. "But I haven't yet told you his story. Don't you ever wonder what became of him after he got away from your clutches? Ashmedai, listen now to what I am about to recount for you."

The demon moved away slowly from the spot where he had been below the throne and slithered into the shadows. "I'm not so sure I want to hear the sordid tale of Your boy, but if You insist…if You command me to do so, I suppose I can hear it from here." There was perfect silence for a moment and then the demon added faintly, "May it please You, My Lord, if You must recount the tale. I'm listening. I'm all ears."

Bore Olam closed His eyes. Then He began His narration, choosing His words carefully, "There was a terrifying incident, nay, an almost unbearable trial that unfolded for this boy long ago. You see, it was a hideous nightmare that had to take place, in a squalid room, very, very far away from here…"

Chapter One
Letting Go

If you board the wrong train, it is no use running along the corridor in the opposite direction.
Dietrich Bonhoeffer

The nightmare is always the same. The images that come to Simon never change but lately he has perceived that they have intensified. As he sleeps, the nightmare unfolds in perfect clarity. Tonight is no exception.

Simon appears to be alone and enveloped in endless darkness. He feels profoundly lost. He sees himself as he was when he was an emerging young man of 15 years. He is physically naked and is aware of his vulnerability which makes his nakedness psychological as well. His boney, bare feet are cold as he steps on great slabs of frigid stone. In front of him, in that endless darkness, he can barely make out what appears to be a long winding corridor. It is pitch black except for distant flashes of light. It reminds him of lightning and thunder when a threatening storm is approaching from the distance. Every now and then, the flashes of light allow him to see how cavernous the space really is.

Far away he can hear the unmistakable sounds of human sighs and groans which seem to him to be more about anguish than pleasure, but if asked, he would not be able to say which it was. He realizes that he is not alone and in his supposed solitude, this distresses rather than consoles him. He also hears something constantly moving near him in a kind of circle, slithering and dragging itself with difficulty due to its enormity. The real horror that overtakes him is the realization that he is being closely watched.

"Oh, God, where am I?" he whimpers to himself. "I want to go home." There is no way for him to explain why he's in this dark place. He can't even remember how he got here. He shivers in the cold abyss of shadows and his devastation runs so deep within him that he cannot even take solace in tears.

In the distance a torrent of water endlessly runs freely and he is reminded of a bathroom shower. Slowly, he warily continues to make his way down the twisted path. In an instant, he knows that he is not only being closely watched but that he is being hunted. That horrid thing means to devour him. As he thinks of this, nausea overtakes him and he bows down, opening his mouth to vomit. This depth of fear is alien to him and it takes hold of his mind like a deadly spell.

An unmistakable guttural sound close by causes Simon to turn his head and look behind him. He squints but it is all a sea of darkness to him. Then suddenly, the guttural sound turns into a grotesque and distorted, high-pitched laughter. He feels completely exposed and knows in his heart that the raucous laughter is mocking him. His naked boy's heart beats rapidly in his chest as he walks faster and listens to the ghastly echoes all around him. He has an unshakeable premonition that something dreadful is about to reach out from the utter blackness and leave him badly wounded.

"Run!" He screams to himself. "Run, Simon! Now! Hurry! Run and get out of here before it's too late! Run as fast as you can away from here!" He bends down and aims his head into the deep unknown ahead, ready to sprint away from the harm that challenges him. At first he thinks he can run freely down the corridor as fast as he needs to but he soon learns that everything is moving insanely slow for him. His legs ache like never before and yet, he knows that if he doesn't run fast enough the huge slithering menace will reach out from the dark and take him. Without warning, a blinding explosion of light bursts forth to one side of him and for the first time he sees the form of the Beast wielding its massive, monstrous head. In that brief moment of luminosity Simon takes in the enormousness of the perverse creature who has been circling him. He feels incredibly small. He does his best to run but he knows he cannot escape. He cannot outrun the evil that is closing in. "Keep running!" he desperately screams to himself.

In his innermost heart, he knows it's too late. Time has run out. Right in front of him, he sees the slithering beast crouched on its robust haunches ready to pounce. It is positioned there in the middle of the corridor, hunched and swaying methodically back and forth on its muscular, meaty thighs in a calculating manner. Simon can sense its hunger and desire. The same raucous laughter that had mocked him and the sound of the torrent of running water are now deafening in their proximity to him. He is keenly aware of the proximity and ferocity of an approaching storm and understands that it will envelope him very soon unless he can escape. The Beast is ready to take him and approaches slowly at first. It takes its time. Its gleaming eyes are fixed on Simon. In his anguish, Simon instinctively cries out, "Mama! Papa! Help me! Help me!", but no help comes. He is utterly alone, abandoned and lost.

Simon closes his eyes tightly ready to receive the impact of what is coming. Then, suddenly, everything changes and he is acutely aware that all is eerily quiet in the corridor. He waits a second longer before opening his eyes knowing that the slithering beast will be there. In the blurred shadows, however, it appears that the Beast has taken flight and in its place a man dressed in an elegant robe stands before him. It is difficult for Simon to see clearly in the shadows but the face of the man is familiar to him and he trusts him. Hopeful that not all is lost and that somehow, this man has come to save him from imminent danger, Simon reaches out cautiously to the man.

In his heart of hearts, he dares to hope that this man who stands before him has slain the Beast that meant to devour him. His semblance appears to be kind and the older, bald man standing in front of him comes forward and into focus. He is smiling warmly. Simon would swear that he knows this man. He believes even more now, that this man is trustworthy. In the far reaches of his memory, he remembers that he has trusted someone very much like him before. Standing very close to the naked youth, the older man says in a raspy whisper, "Simon, dear boy." The roar of the torrent of running water abruptly blasts in the dark corridor and Simon is seized with panic. He can feel the storm embracing him. Great drops of water echo in his ears and he understands with horror that it has arrived in all its fury. The constant drone of running water is also familiar to him. He knows that the face in front of him and the voice he has just heard are connected to it.

The cloaked man moves in closer now and Simon steps back as he hears him say. "Simon, dear boy, come to me. I won't hurt you. Trust me. I am here to help you. Don't be afraid. You know well who I am." Yet something is profoundly not right. Simon struggles within himself because he can't fully recognize the man.

Then recognition sets in and Simon screams desperately within himself, "Run, Simon, run!" He turns abruptly from the man and tries to run in any other direction into the darkness, but he knows he can't get away. His feet are anchored in place and he cannot move. All at once, everything around him shifts uncontrollably and he understands to his horror that he is in the man's powerful embrace. He feels a hand slither across his chest and grab his bare shoulder like a vise. Then another hand slides rudely down his abdomen and settles upon his exposed, shrunken penis. The bald man moans as he begins to obscenely fondle Simon.

Another powerful bolt of light detonates and Simon sees that the man is totally different now. He is bloated and naked. He snarls at him like a ravenous dragon intent on feeding. Simon can smell the man's needy, hot breath as he closes in on him. The rough tongue of the Beast brushes Simon's chin, as he grunts. "Look what I have for you, my dear boy!" He screams into Simon's face as he lifts his hand from the boy's shoulder and places it roughly behind his neck. He pushes Simon's head toward his own erect penis and Simon notices how out of proportion and monstrously huge it is, almost like a caricature. The man howls, "Look at this, you naked little slut!"

In his panic Simon closes his eyes tightly wishing to be somewhere else, wishing that all of this would just go away. The Beast grabs him by his hair and jerks his head painfully upward toward his own. Once again, Simon can feel the warmth of his breath on his own face. The man savagely clutches him and pulls him onto his sweat drenched chest, crooning, "Come to daddy." Panting in anticipation, he holds Simon's head away from him still clutching his hair and tilts his own bald head to one side as he admires his catch. Simon is aware that the naked man is now wearing only a ski mask over his face. Spittle flies from his crooked mouth as his tongue darts crazily from side to side like a serpent. The guttural sounds coming from him echo in the corridor and he groans and growls hoarsely in his pleasure. Simon shudders and braces himself for the bad thing that he knows will now happen to him.

He stares into the man's eyes and in an instant Simon recognizes the voice and the face! He knows perfectly well who the man in the ski mask is. The man knowingly stares back at the boy through the two eyeholes of the mask. His shark-like, bottomless eyes widen and then begin to brighten. Then, they turn dark. The naked man wearing the ski mask is completely visible to Simon now. The darkness around him has ceased. A dim overhead lightbulb has been turned on. In the yellowish, sickly glow of the bulb, Simon sees the man throwing his head backward bellowing deeply, "Come here, you little shit! Give yourself to me, you little whore! I've had my eye on you for far too long!"

Simon pulls back, and in their struggle the man screams at him in a high-pitched voice, "Come here so that I can fuck you good like you deserve!"

Simon hears himself cry weakly through tears, "No, Father! No! Please, you are a priest. A priest of God! I'm Larry, your altar boy. I've served your Mass so many times." But Simon is no match for the man. He pounces on the boy like a wild animal in heat and mounts him forcefully. He is ready to begin his merciless penetration.

"Please, God, stop it! Please, dear God, come help me!" But God is silent and appears to be absent. Simon wonders in those desperate seconds, "Where are you, my God? Why have you abandoned me? Where is your love for me?"

Simon can hear the faint rumbling of distant thunder. As the violent storm moves elsewhere, away from him, his desperate begging and his cries to the Almighty fade away. Simon rises quickly to the surface of consciousness. His feverish sleep and nightmare are no more. The cobwebs left from sleep that were so real, disintegrate and he wakes up panting. He looks around and sees his familiar bedroom and knows he's in his bed. It's always the same; shame and guilt wash over him. Under the covers, he feels himself go from warmth to damp coldness. He has wet his bed again and is soaked in his own urine. The nightmare leaves him shivering for many reasons. This night has been no exception.

+ + + + +

Simon rose and knelt on the floor beside his bed as he had done since he was a little boy. He made the sign of the Cross and after blessing himself, thanked God for the beginning of a new day. It was a boy's prayer, simple and straightforward and even now as a man, this uncomplicated dialogue with God remained intact. It was an unchanging ritual that began every day. It was something that gave him comfort because it was always the same. Simon didn't like things to change. Yet today as he knelt in his urine-soaked underwear, he felt himself changed, different in a way he could not explain. Guilt crept into him as he knelt before God. How many sins had he committed in his life? He desired so much to be acceptable to God. Since he was a boy he wanted to be worthy to stand in His presence and serve Him as a good priest, mostly, to offer the acceptable Sacrifice on the altar in the sanctuary of the temple.

He had told his kindergarten teacher, a young nun, "Sister, when I grow up I want to be a priest!"

He was five years old and must have given the nun great happiness because Sister took a photograph of him on that day in 1961, dressed in his starched white shirt and bow tie, holding a big black Bible. Simon knelt there by the side of his bed, holding on to the precious memory of himself as a little kid. He recalled that photograph and how he had used it for his ordination announcement over twenty years later.

Still, there was that other part of him since he was a boy. That other part of him that was just as pronounced. His other, darker self. The self that schemed, manipulated and lied in order to obtain. It was the part of himself that was curious without bounds. The part of himself that at times he couldn't completely control. Simon knew even as a boy that he was always ready and willing to "pay his five cents to look into the forbidden box of curiosities". Things that sparkled and glittered amused him beyond words, but mostly the forbidden called out to him insistently. He knew that only too well. And then there was that other, deeper thing, the "feelings" deep inside that he could not voice out loud to anyone, not even in the confessional on Saturday afternoons, because he knew it was forbidden to do so. Lord Alfred Douglas had put it so succinctly in the words, "it was the love that dare not speak its name". His father had been very clear on many occasions that being a certain way, or having certain "feelings" were an abomination and not manly at all. Simon felt that his father could see this hidden nature in him better than anyone else and therefore, as a boy he always felt exposed, unacceptable and judged by his father. He had been taught that having those feelings and worse, actually being that way, was to be perverted and therefore, repulsive and a degenerate. Yet, as he grew and discovered the first pleasures of the flesh, he could not stay away. It was strong like a magnet that pulled him to it and in honesty, he hadn't wanted to run from it. He remembered when he was four years old, in kindergarten, how he had stumbled upon such a thing. The memory now came into perfect clarity in his mind.

In a small lavatory at the kindergarten, behind the lunch room that had only one toilet in it, he had discovered something marvelous. The door to the lavatory could be easily latched inside by climbing up onto the toilet. Once the door was secured, he would carefully step down and turn on the hot and cold water to get it warm. There was a soap dispenser there that was like a white, pale glass bottle shaped like a dome that held a yellow-greenish liquid soap that made great suds. He had washed his hands often in this place and one day discovered a delightful secret. Without hesitation, he would pull up his t-shirt and taking the warm water and soap, would treat himself to rubbing his belly with it. It felt amazingly pleasurable to him at that young age and he engaged in the practice often during his kindergarten days. When he was done feeling good, he would dry off with a wet paper towel, climb up on the toilet again to unlatch the door and step down. Finally, in order to complete the deception, he would flush the toilet to make it sound and appear from beyond the door, that he had in fact a legitimate reason for locking the door. Somehow in spite of his age, he knew it was depraved and decadent and that if he were caught there would be shit to pay, but he engaged in it anyway because it felt natural to him and gave him pleasure. That memory of a four-year-old scheming had often made him smile.

Yet, he was not smiling now. These memories filled him with anxiety. The belly rubbing was nothing compared to the stubborn feelings and thoughts that had gripped him later on as an adolescent. These feelings he could not deny nor shake off quite so easily, feelings that had only gotten stronger as time passed and puberty set in with a vengeance. As he grew, he had tricked himself into believing that he had made some kind of peace with it. However, as he developed, he struggled between his spiritual side and his hedonistic side; a wrestling match between the fantasy of who he wanted to be and who he realized he had actually become. He was exhausted playing the different roles of who he supposedly was, spent in trying to keep everyone convinced of that charade. For so long he had kept the farce up. He often thought of himself and his efforts like the man he had seen one evening, while watching the Ed Sullivan Show with his grandparents. The poor guy's shtick was fascinating to watch and Simon had never forgotten it. The man had several billiard sticks secured to a base and on top of each was a rotating porcelain dinner plate. The shtick consisted in manipulating the plates and keeping them all rotating at once, never letting them fall off. It was exhausting to watch. Simon identified with the image because he had spent most of his life doing much the same thing. He lived in several worlds of his own creation depending on who he was with. He was very careful that no one discovered the truth. That was the pathetic shtick he had created for himself and he presumed that this was the only option open to him. His father's judgement weighed heavy on him and he surmised that being his true self was simply not an option.

He had not slept well the night before and felt exhausted kneeling there on the floor. He tried to place himself in the presence of God but his mind was racing. He felt different this morning. He felt changed. It was as if a fever had broken within him at some point. Something was afoot, unfolding in his life that would require him to wade into unchartered waters. A door had unexpectedly creaked opened somewhere within him. He felt wary. When did this happen? The nightmare stood in his memory like a distant sentinel and then faded into the darkness. Why did he feel different? He hadn't felt anything when he slid into bed the previous night. He thought to himself that it had been like that for him, you go to bed completely fine one night and wake up with a pain in your foot or leg in the morning without any explanation.

He bowed his head and held it in his clasped hands as he was accustomed to do when he prayed. "Dear God, where are you? Speak to me." He again waited for God to speak through images that often made their way into his thoughts with amazing clarity. He tried to make a mental representation of God but he was unable to hold onto it. He waited patiently but it seemed that God was silent for today. The seconds passed and he became aware of the stench of stale urine and sweat that emanated from him.

Once again, he remembered the nightmare from the previous night. He desperately needed to shower and come clean. He thought that God might still speak and waited for some answer. None came. Nothing came to him except the memories that flooded his thoughts and wanted so desperately to break in. The urge to give in to those memories was overtaking him. Then a thought came to him with great clarity, a thought he had never considered. Maybe, had God indeed been speaking to him all along?

As he knelt there by the side of the bed, he held on to this thought before it broke up and scattered. Could it possibly be that God had been speaking to him all along through the repetitious nightmare? It had never occurred to him. He knew the awful history of the nightmare but perhaps there was a deeper message. "What are you trying to say to me?" He wanted desperately to see himself in life as pure and innocent as the boy in the nightmare who trod the dangerous path down the corridor. Wasn't he a fragile victim? A part of him still believed that entry into God's presence demanded complete purity. Were we fully responsible and held accountable for the things that pushed and shoved themselves into our lives? Were we defined by the things that overcame us? He had been taught that only the holy, untarnished soul could stand in God's presence and give the Almighty what He expected.

As he knelt by the side of the bed, his perception grew and he could not deny that God had somehow been speaking to him all along through that hideous, frightening dream. There had to be a deeper message. As he wondered what it was, a voice opened up within his tortured soul. It was an ancient voice from the realms of endless days. He was unaware that he had lifted his face upward in response to it.

"Why do you run from Me?" The voice was crystal-clear in his psyche and was equally troubling to him. Simon was startled by it. He closed his eyes and tried to concentrate. His skin was covered in gooseflesh. The voice persisted, "You smell like piss and sweat! You smell like a filthy goat! Is that how you want to be? I have spoken to you since I first knitted you in your mother's womb. I have sent you so many signs since you were a boy so that you could be strong and understand. At first, you understood but then you slipped away. Until you let go completely and surrender to Me and come to Me, you will live in a constant storm of your own making."

Simon replied from the deepest part of his soul, "Let go, you say! But how do I let go? How? I don't know how."

"You know how, you just don't really want to let go. You don't really want to change your pain for joy. You want to keep the charade going because you're afraid. You are afraid to trade in the self-made image of yourself for the image of you that I have created."

In his soul, Simon rebelled and vigorously protested, "That's untrue, that's unfair…"

"Is it really? You can live in a shit-hole of your own making if you prefer. A lot of people do. They insist on being unhappy because that way they keep me distant and convince themselves that they are in control. You have spent most of your adult life doing this. The nightmare I often send you at night is meant to rattle your cage. It's supposed to make you understand a fundamental truth you seem to have forgotten. It's time for you to be honest with Me which means, being honest with yourself. It's up to you."

Simon hesitated. Was he going mad or had he genuinely arrived at a pivotal point in his life, albeit, one that he had not expected. In his exhausted soul, he managed to respond to the ancient presence within him. "You say 'let go' and 'be honest', but You would never want me if You knew who I really am. You expect and demand so damned much. You would run from me if I asked You to accept me as I am, as I have become."

"I already know who you are. And I'm busting your balls now because of who you think you have become. Don't get lost in becoming anything. Just focus on who you are now."

Indignation sprung up in Simon and he retorted bitterly, "You called out to me when I was innocent. I gleaned that only perfection would do for You. I understood Your requirements. But I fucked everything up along the way because I'm weak and don't possess all the cards. Now You tell me to 'let go'? You have the gall to tell me to 'let go'! Will You catch me if I let go? Or will I free fall into nothingness? Will I suffocate in nothingness and spiral down into that complete darkness that wants to devour me?" His heart beat rapidly in his chest and Simon waited for a response but no answer came. He waited.

As the seconds turned to minutes, a childhood image came to him. It was Professor Marvel from Omaha, a supposed wizard from a fictitious circus long ago who really didn't have any supernatural powers. The scene was from a movie he knew so well since he was a boy. He now imagined himself in the scene of the man's cozy gypsy-like covered wagon. Outside the wagon, danger was on its way. The sky was becoming very dark, dead leaves were flying everywhere and the twister was almost upon them though inside, everything felt safe. There he was, sitting next to the kindly old wizard from Oz, who wore a wizard's bejeweled, silk turban. Suddenly, the circus wizard said to Dorothy, "The crystal has gone dark."

Simon knelt there waiting but he knew the conversation with God was over. The crystal had indeed gone dark. He waited for God to speak, but He did not. He waited some more. His hands had become clammy and his face was hot and damp. Once again, his own pungent stench drifted up to him and he began rising on one knee to go shower when he remembered he had not finished his prayer. He knelt once again and as he had done all of his life, he prayed for those he loved most and concluded by praying for the dead as he had been taught by the nuns. He got up and thought only of cleansing himself of the foul residue left behind by the nightmare.

As he showered, he heard the restless thunder outside. It rumbled several times in succession, as it came closer. Storms could get nasty all of a sudden in Texas and Simon hurried to rinse off and get done. He thought about that other storm which had been brewing for so long in him. 'Let go', God had commanded. As water from the shower cleansed him, Simon asked himself, "Should I go to Confession on Saturday? Is that how I need to let go and come clean? Is that what God wants from me?"

A great flash of lightning detonated, tearing through the bathroom. It was immediately followed by a booming bolt of thunder outside. Then without warning, the divine voice thundered within him, "No!"

"No?" Simon turned off the shower and stepped out to dry himself. "No?" How else would he 'let go' and be honest with who he really is unless he went into a confessional and confessed his sins? How else could he come face to face with himself in God's presence? His "cage" was already rattled beyond belief when he blurted out earlier, "How? Tell me how?" Simon closed his eyes and cried out like he had never done before. Standing naked, he cried out again, "How dammit? Tell me! How am I supposed to let go?"

"Say it!" The voice pierced his soul.

"Say it?" Simon repeated the words slowly. "Say it." Then he asked, "Say what?"

"Tell the whole world who you are and what you have done, by first telling yourself. Realize and look at the untold suffering you have endured and that which you have meted out to others because of your self-delusion. Reveal it all to the whole world and by doing so, be aware of what you are revealing to yourself."

Simon blurted out in disbelief, "Tell the whole world? Are You fucking insane?"

"This is your epiphany, Simon. Don't you realize that? It's a singular moment of revelation for you."

Simon opened his eyes and screamed out, "My what? This is my epiphany? My fucking epiphany? I'm supposed to pour out my bleeding heart to the whole world? Do You really expect me—"

"This is your epiphany," the voice repeated calmly within Simon. It went to the core of his being and even if only briefly, for the first time in a very long time, fear gave way to hope within him. Several moments of silence passed and meekly, Simon asked, "How do I tell the whole world?"

God whispered gently, "By telling yourself first."

In an instant, Simon knew. The image that he perceived in his mind popped up out of nowhere, unannounced. What Simon grasped at that moment was completely absurd to him. He waited but nothing else came. He stood there dumbfounded by what he was contemplating. The image of the thought that came to him made no sense.

Dripping wet, Simon shivered because of his nakedness and he instinctively reached for the towel to dry himself. As he did so, he considered what had just come to him and what he must do. It seemed completely ridiculous. He had been told in no uncertain terms to "let go", but he had not been told how to do it. Or had he? This thing he must do, was it from God or was it some crazy shit his mind had conjured up?

He could not explain the bizarre conviction that filled him nor the clarity of how he was to proceed. He hadn't ever thought about what he now seriously contemplated. He simply knew it was what he must do. It was that simple. He had come to the crossroad. He remembered the voice that had said it was time. After drying off, he dressed in his black cassock and looked at himself in the full length mirror in front of him. "It's time," he said softly.

He went outside and walked quickly along the familiar stone path. Powerful winds had descended from the low lying, threatening clouds. Faded leaves shaken violently from the fragile limbs of the pear trees swirled around his shoes, some of them clinging desperately to the hem of his cassock. The day had just begun but it was shrouded in shadows rather than light. Simon knew in his heart that this day was about facing what was coming. His epiphany had come without warning this morning. He cautiously considered that he needed to embrace. He remembered from his days in the seminary that God's grace was about receiving strength and understanding and that it could come to any one, at any time, in any form. It could be as innocent as a sunset, or a flower or a dog's tail beating against the floor. It could come on the clouds of Heaven in a blaze of light or through a cornfield thick with green leaves. It could even come through a comforting mug of steamy hot 'café con leche' on a frigid morning. And then he further realized that it could even come through a macabre, ghoulish nightmare. It didn't matter how it came to us or how bizarre it was. It was meant to make us new again, wasn't it? Grace came directly from God, right? It wasn't something that one could muster or fake.

As he walked hurriedly, he was caught between finally addressing the mess in his life or running far from it. As the storm undoubtedly closed in all around him, he was now practically running for shelter. Years before, he had taken advantage of an old garage building which stood at the back of the family property he now had use of. There he had created a sacred space as he had done before, as a boy, a safe place where he could encounter God to his liking. Even though someday he might be forced to leave the active priesthood completely, Simon would always offer the Sacrifice of the Mass privately because he understood that he would be 'a priest forever'. This sacred space he had created on the family property, where he lived, would serve that intimate encounter with God. For now, he continued to serve as a priest sometimes in various parishes but he knew that his days were numbered for this. Too much had changed in the Church and the old persecutions never really disappeared.

The chapel Simon had built was a refuge for him. There he found solace from his wounds. He fully believed that when he had been ordained a priest, his soul had been indelibly marked forever. Simon held on tightly to the priesthood he had been given by God. It was something he refused to give up even if the day came when he could no longer serve the Church in a public way. For many years now, it seemed to him, the Catholic Church had morphed into a new religion, very unlike the traditional one he still venerated and believed in since he was a boy. It was his right to be a priest and to stand before God to offer an acceptable sacrifice as priests had done before him for centuries. After all, he had been called personally to do this. God knew the truth. Even though he had wandered far, he would always still be God's priest nor matter how flawed he had become. Nothing nor anyone could ever change that truth. Simon believed that once God had consecrated a priest, it could not be undone. God would not take back the consecration He had confected.

The heavy oak doors of the chapel awaited him under the shelter of a low, sturdy roof, and he entered quickly. It was as if he had entered a sacred womb where he was protected and loved. Red lamps filled with oil, burned brightly, unmoved by the menace of the approaching storm outside. The flames, safely ensconced in the hanging glass globes reminded him of the Creator of the Universe who was present there. Simon looked at the golden tabernacle on the altar and remembered the voice that had spoken to him that morning. The voice hadn't spoken to him with such clarity in a very long time. It was Him. Simon had no doubts about that. God rested within the tabernacle and Simon had the sense that his arrival there was noticed. A bright flame of fire danced merrily within a hanging lamp right above the tabernacle to signal God was home.

The first heavy drops of rain had begun to fall outside. In an instant, the fury of the oncoming storm was released and Simon could hear great gusts of wind and rain beating against the chapel roof. He approached the sacred presence and genuflected, opened the heavy metal gate of the altar rail and ascended the steps there. Genuflecting once again before the tabernacle on the altar, he lit two candles and prepared the missal. He stepped down and genuflected again to the divine presence, slipping away behind the altar. Entering the sacristy he washed his hands and prayed according to the ritual. Then he began to vest for Mass, saying the necessary prayers for each sacred garment: amice, alb, cincture, maniple, stole and chasuble. Fully vested in stiff, Roman vestments, he placed the black biretta on his head, took the veiled chalice and made his way to the sanctuary where God awaited him. Removing the biretta from his head, he genuflected again, climbed the steps and silently, placed the chalice on the altar, opened the missal and stepped down. All his actions were precise and without flaw, as demanded by the rubrics he had so well learned. The violent storm raged outside as Simon stood before the altar. Softly, he uttered the immemorial Latin prayers in the darkness, "In Nomine Patris, et Filii and Spiritus Sancti. Amen. Introibo ad Altar Dei…" He always felt God close at this moment. He knew he was far from being alone and it was usually as he stood there on that spot and later climbed the steps up and into the altar of God that he remembered what an old priest, Father Cornelius, had once said to him when he was an altar boy, "Do you know what happens on the altar when a priest begins the Sacrifice of the Mass?"

"No, Father."

"Myriads of angels gather all around the altar just before the Mass begins. Myriads and myriads of angels, all gathered in layers around the altar. When the Sacrifice of the Mass is going to be offered on an altar on earth, it's like a magnet that attracts angels. Do you know why?"

"No, Father."

Father Cornelius had leaned carefully on his cane and had bowed closer to him, explaining, "In Heaven, God is eternally surrounded by myriads of angels who adore Him day and night. When the Sacrifice of the Mass is offered on an altar here on earth, the angels come to adore the same and only God who comes down from Heaven to be here with us even while remaining in Heaven. Isn't that marvelous? God is never far from us and in this way, we can never be far from Him if we approach Him."

"Yes, Father, even though we can't see the angels, they're there, right?"

"On my, yes, that's right. Wouldn't you say that's a wonderful gift?"

Simon had no doubts that God was now here and that myriads of angels were all around him. Feeling close to God was something Simon desired with every fiber of his soul. As far as Simon was concerned, so much had taken place in his life that had put that proximity in peril. Yet, he thought about God's voice this morning. It seemed to him that God hadn't given up on him no matter the mess he'd made.

Standing there in his priestly vestments, Simon remembered what one of the nuns at school had taught him as a boy, almost whispering because of the weight of what she was teaching him. "Separation from God is the absolute worst punishment we can bring upon ourselves. It throws us into the pall of nothingness and sheer desperation. It happens when we sin, when we turn away from the light. But be clear, child, we bring the separation upon ourselves."

Simon knew that some kind of separation from God had happened to him. After all, since he was a young adult, and then as a priest, he had been living several lives at the same time, each life carefully separated from the other. It was a sham he had worked so hard to keep in place. A shtick just like the man with the billiard sticks and the rotating plates. Yet, he had to admit that God had never left him completely during that time. God had always pursued him ever since he was a child. He had enjoyed an exceptionally close relationship with God his entire life even when he himself was responsible for the marked strain in their relationship. There were others too that had crossed his path, beginning with God's Mother and some of the saints. He always thought that his Guardian Angel deserved a medal for not running away from him. He often thought of this constant companion as exhausted and panting, trying to keep up, his angelic tongue dragging out of his mouth like a threadbare, old necktie. These spiritual advocates were always there for him even when he would run away and hide. The unconditional love of God impressed him the most. He understood it in a theological way but found it much more comforting to know that God simply pursued him out of love. God had even extended a special calling to him. It was a lofty calling, the loftiest of callings. His belief in God was deeply rooted in him since the days when he was a boy and his mother would read the Bible stories in bed to him and his brother Bobby. Simon could not deny that he had sometimes wandered away from God far worse than King David and was badly bruised in his soul because of it. He was convinced that the wounds in his soul were of his own making, recalling what the voice had said to him this morning, "You can live in a shit-hole of your own making if you prefer. If you do, that leaves Me out." It was basically what the nun had said as well.

The sound of the wind and rain brought him back as he stood in the sacred place and he felt guilty for giving in to his distractions there. He bowed and climbed the steps into the altar of God. In a venerable gesture, he leaned down and kissed the marble stone containing the relics of martyrs and recited the prescribed prayers. He believed that God would soon descend and be present upon the sacred stone of relics. Yet, so many thoughts raced through his mind as he tried to concentrate on this mystery.

His mind's eye was filled with an image of a passage he had read in the Book of the Prophet Ezequiel. It tells of when God left the temple because it had become unbearable for Him to remain there due to people's insincerity and sin. Simon knew that God was saying the very same thing to him now. It wasn't that God had jumped ship, but that Simon had pushed God out, and off the ship. Lost in thought, he considered the epiphany he had received just a few hours before and it all seemed less freakish the more he thought about it even though he couldn't deny his doubts. He was convinced that he needed to tell the world and that he couldn't simply confess these things in a dark confessional to a priest. For his own sake, however, he understood now that he needed to do more. The voice had been clear on that.

A blaze of lightning tore through the sanctuary and a great crackle of thunder shook the tiny chapel. Simon looked up at the tabernacle, and remembered the distant flashes of light in the nightmare, exposing the form of the slithering beast and all that had taken place. An ocean of painful memories flooded his heart and he was overcome with grief, wondering how so many things had soured in his life's plan? Fragments of his hubris and lust spun around in his head. God had been calling to him night after night for how long? It was clear to him now that the repetitious nightmare was really the wake-up call.

He faced the tabernacle and asked outright, "What have You been trying to say to me? The nightmare and the things that caused it were beyond awful. Why would You allow those things to happen? Why did You abandon me?"

The familiar voice rose up in him, "I've never left you. I've never left your side even if you were convinced I had. Even now, I'm here for you as if you were the only creature I ever created."

"But I felt very much alone and abandoned that night. I had to run deep within myself in that awful place because there was nowhere for me to go. No one came to answer the cries of help I uttered. No one came. You didn't come to save me!" Simon was unaware of his tears.

"You felt alone and abandoned but you weren't alone. I was very much there. I'm always there with you."

Simon was stunned. The repetitious nightmare stood in his memory as well as the events that had caused it. Why had he not been able to grasp the message? He could barely whisper, "Help me to understand, then, because I don't. Help me to let go." As he stood there dressed in the silk spun, golden vestments, he thought about what he must do. The same crystal-clear, bizarre image popped up once again. Surely, he thought to himself, I'm going mad.

Simon closed his eyes. Would God really catch him if he trusted Him? He knew if he was to 'let go' it would be now. Any coherent thoughts left him and he found it difficult to concentrate. He wondered if he had gone completely batty, yet he knew he hadn't. God had once revealed to a great prophet that "the one who believes (in God), does not worry, does not flee, does not try to figure things out on his own". Simon tried not to worry even though what he contemplated he must do made no real sense to him. He waited and stared at the tabernacle. He was indeed worried.

He sighed and closed his eyes again. He would do this. He would tell the whole world who he was. He would shout out his truth in his own way and 'let go' of the lies and the fears. He would throw himself into God's arms. God had promised that then he would be free. Simon stepped forward and put his hands on the altar. He moved his face to the tabernacle and muttered, "I will tell the whole world who I really am in this way on the condition that You will be there with me, listening to everything that I say. I have this thought that I cannot shake. It keeps coming to me with greater clarity each time. I…I…can't explain why the idea is so steadfast in my mind, but it is. It won't go away. Did You plant it there? Tell me, please, that this crazy idea comes from You." Simon waited but no answer came. Finally, desperately, he said, "I…I will do it. I will do it on my flesh. That is how I will do it. My skin will be the vellum upon which the truth will be proclaimed. It will record everything. This is how I will obey You and face myself even if I do not fully understand what I am willing to do in order to obey You."

He stood there for a very long time, waiting for an answer. He had only been told that it was time to 'let go' and reveal who he really is, what he had really done. The voice hadn't said how he was to do it but only that he must trust. Simon shuddered recalling how he planned to do it. He waited for a response. He expected a rebuke. But no answer came. The crystal remained dark. The seconds ticked away and the voice said nothing. Or did it? Simon stood up and stepped back, his gaze never leaving the tabernacle. He begged, "Say something." And then he realized that he had already received an answer. He repeated the Latin proverb to himself: "Qui tacet consentiret." He smiled, knowing that God's 'silence gave consent'. It was done. The pact was established at that moment and Simon was resolved to 'let go'. Tranquility washed over him and for the first time in a very long time he felt as if a very heavy burden was being lifted from him.

+ + + + +

Several days passed and Simon considered his resolve. He had decided that he needed to begin. That part was huge for him but he needed now to do more. He needed to find someone, the one who would record his sins, his truths onto his skin. Simon had no idea how to find a tattooer that would be up to the task. He had to admit that he was nervous about how to go about it and knew that those closest to him would scoff at the idea of him, a priest, getting tattoos. Many folks think that those who bear tattoos belong to a sordid part of society even though nowadays it seems that more and more people are getting tattooed. He was resolved to move ahead with the idea even though he was incredibly nervous about it. He would ask the tattooer to put his first tattoo on his upper arm so that when necessary, he could conceal it. Simon didn't need anyone to tell him that the church people would not approve of their priest having tattoos. He had heard enough of them after Mass on Sundays speak in hushed tones about so-and-so's son or daughter who had "cheapened themselves", saying, "It's disgusting, you know! And they say it's very painful. Why would anyone want to suffer that kind of pain and mutilate their bodies? It has to be unhealthy, it just has to be! What is in that ink anyway and where does it go? I'll tell you where it goes! It goes to the liver and the kidneys and I wouldn't doubt it if it affects the heart. I just don't understand it, Father. How could God want that? How could He not punish those who put their own health in peril?

Good health is a gift from God. Isn't getting tattoos against Almighty God's Law?" Simon would smile and wait patiently until the tirade was over. He told himself that these were good people of another generation simply incapable of understanding. Sometimes, though, when the ranting got particularly vicious he wondered about their degree of goodness.

In any case, when he could get a word in, he would say gravely, "Those are good questions. I'll have to consult the bishop about it but I don't think that God has any problem with it."

"You're too kind, Father. It's the stuff of wayward sailors, Father! And drug addicts and prostitutes. Convicted murderers covered in tattoos from head to toe are sitting in prison cells this very minute. It's all just another sign of the end of the world. And those homos have a lot to do with it too. Just drive past the gay bars over there in Dallas down on Cedar Springs Road and you can see them out and about. So many men and young boys all painted up looking like some kind of stained glass window! It's horrible! Why would anyone mutilate their bodies like that? Don't they believe that they are temples of the Holy Ghost?"

Sometimes Simon would lose his patience and say irritably, "Perhaps they do understand that! Maybe that's why they do it. Temples are sacred places with plenty of stained glass windows that are ablaze and visible for everyone to see when light streams through. Isn't that so? Temples need to be more beautiful than any place else because the Holy Ghost dwells there! Maybe folks with tattoos are letting some of that light out for others to see. Maybe they shine because they know a few things about themselves that others don't." Simon would always be met with blank expressions. No one ever said another word after his troubled discourse.

More days passed and Simon thought about searching for a tattooer. He kept saying to himself that just as soon as he finished "this" or "that" he would go, but the days passed into weeks. He hated to say it but the church people's comments intimidated him and created doubt within him. He feared that they would reject him if they knew he was about to become a living stained glass window. He knew that there was a tattoo shop down on the gay strip because he had passed it many times as he drove in his pickup truck across town. Next door to it was a piercing shop. He had never had any impulse to go inside either establishment but now all that had changed and he was increasingly drawn to the place where he could receive what he needed. It was simply known as "The

Tattoo Shop" from the sign that hung on the façade over the door. It had two huge picture windows partially decorated with mirror decals and outlined in fluorescent red lights that burned day and night. A great red awning provided some shade over a cement bench just outside the entrance. Simon finally decided to make his move and picked up the phone one afternoon after he and Jack Daniel's had sat together for a good long while in his bedroom.

A young female voice answered. "Tattoo Shop. May I help you?"

"Uh, yes, I was…am interested in speaking with someone about getting a tattoo…well, a series of tattoos, I mean I have an idea for what I want but—"

The voice cut him off, "Yeah, yeah, okay. You wanna see Mark. He's the best. He's also the owner."

"When, uh, is he available so I can begin? Can I just walk in and ask for him?"

"Ha, ha, ha," the voice shrieked into the phone, making Simon jump. "Oh no, baby doll. You gotta make an appointment. This isn't Burger King. Ha, ha, ha. Mark's the best in Dallas. He's also the owner," the voice repeated.

"Well, when can I see him?" Simon asked trying to mask his anxiety which was turning into anger. "When is he free to speak with me?"

"Lemme see the book. Hang on." The phone was set on the counter and Simon could hear a radio playing in the distance. He could hear a cow bell clanging and wondered what that could mean. Pages ruffled back and forth. Finally, the phone was picked up again. "Ok baby doll, you are in luck. He just got a cancellation. He can see you on the third, that's…sixteen days from now. Name?"

"Sixteen days!" Simon was trying to control his nerves and cried out. "That's a lifetime away! Can't I get to see him sooner?"

"You should count your blessings, baby doll. The wait to see Mark is usually a couple of months unless he's working on a large piece or you're a friend. So are you interested or can I hang up?" Simon was shocked that anyone would speak to him that way. The voice finally asked again, but this time it was short with him, "Name?"

"Name?" Simon asked in confusion.

"What's your name, baby doll?"

"Oh right!" Awkwardly, he stumbled along, "Uh my, uh…"

"What's your name, you do have a name, right?"

"Uh, yes, sorry. My name is uh…Very Rev…I mean, uh…Simon." He closed his eyes and shuddered to think he was actually doing this. What was he signing up for? He shuddered.

"Simon! Okay Simon, I gotcha down to see Mark on the third at twelve noon."

+ + + + +

It was a sweltering August day and the Texas sun was merciless as he parked his Ford-150 not far away and approached the shop. Simon wore a pair of cut-offs and a white t-shirt. On his feet were his worn, Converse black high tops. Outside, two young men were sitting on the cement bench. One was an unshaven, heavy set guy wearing shorts and a sleeveless t-shirt. He had brightly colored tattoos on both his arms but mostly on his legs. His ears were pierced in numerous places. The other guy was skinny with piercings but only a few tattoos. Both men were smoking in silence as Simon approached. They eyed Simon carefully as he got closer. The skinny guy was heavily pierced on both ears with what appeared to Simon to be at least fifteen or more pieces of jewelry. He had three or four tattoos but they were done in black without any colors. Simon thought to himself that piercing was obviously the skinny guy's main thing.

"Hey guys, hot enough for ya?" Simon said, expecting some kind of response. Neither men spoke as they stared at him. He felt embarrassed and not for the first time asked himself why he was going through with his. He pushed open the front glass door of the shop and was greeted by the sound of a large cow bell attached to the top of the door. A sign on it swung and rocked back and forth as he let go of the door and went inside to the frigid air conditioned shop. The sign read: No children allowed!

The tattooed, handsome young man behind the counter at the shop was reading, rubbing his beard as he concentrated. He was sitting in a high chair leaning up against the wall on two of the chair's metal legs. In his hand was a tattered, yellow paperback. He looked up briefly at Simon as the door opened and then looked down as he had been before. Simon approached the bearded young man and with a nervous smile said, "Hey man, how's it going? I'm here to see Mark." The man neither looked up nor acknowledged Simon.

The door flew open and the cow bell clanged into life again, making Simon jump at the sudden intrusion. Two girls in their early twenties giggled to one side of him as they clung to each other and swayed, obviously nervous about being in a tattoo shop. Simon understood their apprehension perfectly. They pointed at the framed drawings of vintage tattoos that adorned the walls whispering secretly to each other. There followed another burst of nervous giggles that filled the small sitting room. The heavily tattooed guy behind the counter looked at them and then met Simon's eyes. "Fucking freaks," he said out loud, not caring if they heard him. He put one hand up to his temple as if it were a gun and held it there. His hands were tattooed right up to his nails. Intricate tattoos covered his muscular neck from his beard down, like a close fitting high collar of the Victorian period. The ink went from under his Adam's apple all the way to his ear lobes and wrapped around the back of his neck. A prominent gauge nose piercing hung between his nostrils. His demeanor was arrogant and definitely hostile. "Fucking freaks!" he repeated as he pulled the imaginary trigger of his hand gun and pressed it into his temple. He then went back to his reading. The two girls kept giggling and pointing. They clung to each other like Siamese twins. One kept her free hand cupped over her mouth in an attempt to stifle her wild guffaws.

The other one pointed at a vintage tattoo of a sleek bird flying over a heart and turning her head to the irritated young man behind the counter, asked in a quivering voice, "How much does that little birdie cost?" The irate young man never looked up from what he was reading and never answered them. This silence sent a fresh ripple of giddy laughter through the two girls who looked at each other in exaggerated disbelief.

"Get the fuck out of here, bitches!" He bellowed at them, as he moved away from the wall and straightened in his chair.

One of them said, "What a fucking asshole," and the giggling exploded all over again.

All of a sudden they ran for the door and were gone. Silence descended upon the room. Simon was about to speak when once again the door of the shop was violently thrown open and the cow bell clanged crazily as it announced another patron.

"Hey, Billy, I got an appointment with Mark for two o'clock," he announced loudly to the disinterested receptionist. The newcomer looked around and then dropped himself rather than sat on the broad red leather couch in the center of the room. The couch skidded to one side and creaked under the unexpected weight but held up just the same. The man was large and tall, in his thirties with an unkempt blond beard. His scuffed and soiled work boots were untied and he wore a massive t-shirt that failed to contain the lower overhang of his impressive beer belly. Once again, the tattooed young man behind the counter kept to his reading and didn't look up nor acknowledge the announcement.

Simon remained in front of the counter where he had been all along trying to take in all the activity around him. His apprehension index had risen considerably and was growing when suddenly a pair of saloon-like doors swung open to the left of the counter. Simon saw that behind it was a long hallway and several doors leading to workrooms. The arrogant receptionist's demeanor did a 180 degree change as he looked up. Standing there was a thirty-something tall man in a black baseball cap with no logo. He walked through the swinging doors and stood behind the counter. He looked at Simon standing there and nodded a greeting in his direction. The man wore a faded t-shirt and comfortable looking shoes. Simon saw that in contrast to all the others, this man only had one tattoo on his arm. It was of a dragon. The man's hair was cut short. The obnoxious receptionist threw the ratty book aside and got to his feet. In a dreamy voice, he asked, "Hey, Mark! Hey dude, how's it hanging today? Did you just get in?" If you had seen Mark on the street, you could not have guessed that he was a tattooer and owner of a tattoo shop.

Mark reached over and shook the receptionist's hand. "Yeah, dude just drove in. It's hot as balls out there. You get lunch already, Billy? Or is everyone out for lunch? Looks pretty empty back there."

To Simon, Billy was now transformed before his eyes into what appeared to be a timid little boy. He clutched his elbows as he nervously rocked to and fro, on his red Converses. "Yeah, dude, everyone is out. They should be back in a sec. No dude, I didn't get lunch yet. What you want me to order? Was waiting for you to arrive." Then he beamed a warm smile from ear to ear and pointing at Mark, added, "'Cause you the man."

Mark ignored the accolade and said without much interest, "Chinese sounds cool."

"Chinese it is! I'm on it." Mark turned toward Simon and stretched out his hand. Billy looked at Simon and said, "Hey Mark, this guy here must be Simon. He's got a noon appointment with you."

Mark smiled to himself and then shook Simon's hand tightly. "Hey, Simon, how's it going buddy? I'm Mark. Welcome to the shop."

"Thanks, Mark. Thanks for seeing me." Simon was impressed by the tattooer's warm demeanor.

"You bet," Mark said absently. Billy had put a form letter in front of Simon for him to sign. Mark said, "It's just your agreement to get a tattoo and that if you bleed to death in here, or have a massive seizure because we cut one of your veins, it's not our fault." He and Billy laughed and Mark added, "Only kidding, dude, but we do need your consent. We'll also need to copy your driver's license."

Simon took out his wallet nervously and pulled out his driver's license. He handed it to Billy trying to keep a steady hand. His nerves were on high red alert. Simon filled out the form while Billy had taken his driver's license. Suddenly, Billy held the license up in the air and dramatically blurted out, in a loud voice, "Hold on! False identification here! What the fuck is going on?" Mark approached and took Simon's driver's license into his hand and studied it carefully. Billy, looked over his shoulder directly at Simon and said sarcastically, "You said your name is Simon when you called in your appointment. What the fuck is this? Whose identification is this, dude? There's no photo on this so how can I tell it's you? It says Larry Zayas. I don't see Simon Zayas anywhere. What you tryin' to pull here?"

Simon felt his face redden. He hadn't thought of this. His mind raced as he tried to come up with a simple explanation. Finally, he said nervously, "My legal name is Larry Zayas, just like the license there says. It's a long story but I'm called Simon. It's a kind of…of a religious name I was given a long time ago and always use." It sounded to Simon like it had all come out wrong. He added meekly, "I know it sounds complicated but it's really me, I swear it is."

Mark gently pushed Billy away and said, "It's cool, Billy. Just file it all away as Larry. It's clear to me that Simon is just some kind of nickname, no big deal." Mark looked up at Simon and smiled. "We just need to file this information. It's basically bullshit but we gotta abide by the law." Billy looked at Simon suspiciously but wasn't about to contradict Mark. The tattooer gave Billy the driver's license to copy.

When all the paperwork was done, Mark turned around and said, "Come on back, Simon, and let's see what you got." With that, Mark walked through the saloon-like doors and Simon followed him down the corridor. Billy took out his phone and ordered lunch. Then he sat back on his chair behind the counter, leaned against the wall and took up his reading again.

From his slouched position on the red couch, the big burly man spoke out, as he turned toward the reception area, "Hey, Billy, dude. I got an appointment for two o'clock with Mark!" Once again the receptionist ignored him completely.

Simon was struck by the way the tattoo shop was organized. As he followed Mark down the hall they passed several workrooms. Each had a cushioned table in the center of the room like those used for massages and one room had what resembled a dentist's chair as well. In one room there was a large poster that hung on the wall displaying a baseball bat. Under the bat was the caption: Pain Is Free Here. There were various sketches on tracing paper of intricate tattoos. Some were destined for large tattoos covering entire arms. Other drawings were for complete backs or thighs. At the back wall of each workroom were cabinets and Simon assumed they held all the supplies of the trade. He was struck again by how cold the temperature was inside the shop.

Mark turned and entered the last room at the end of the corridor. It was a spacious room filled with personal works of art. Two walls were covered almost from floor to ceiling with the same tracing paper Simon had seen in the other rooms. These sketches were amazing because of their intricate details and size. Pointing to them, Simon asked, "Have all of these sketches become tattoos?"

Mark had opened one of the drawers in his cabinet and was taking out a sketch pad and pencils. He gently dropped them on the cushioned table in the center of the room. He looked up and asked, "Sorry, how's that?"

"Have all of these sketches become tattoos already or are they future projects?" Simon was intrigued by the beauty of the art.

"Some have already been done but most of them are pieces I'm tattooing presently."

"Wow, your work is impressive."

Mark sat back in his swivel stool which had wheels on it. He glided back behind him and opened a drawer as Simon glanced over the third wall. It was completely covered with trophy plaques Mark had received for his work over the years in various places. Mark pulled out a square eraser and moved back to the table, still seated on the stool. "Thank you," he said and gestured for Simon to sit on top of the cushioned table. Finally, he asked, "So what can I help you with today, dude?"

"As you can see, I have no tattoos," Simon said nervously, trying to keep an even, relaxed tone that he feared would betray him, "but I'm here to change that. My life journey has been complicated. Recently I had an experience that made me decide that I would like to get several tattoos. I don't really have any order in mind and I'm not even sure how they can be sketched. I am clear about one thing, though. All the tattoos I will ask you to create for me will be my secret symbols of important people and pivotal events in my life. I want to speak through my tattoos to the world. I envision that my tattoos will be the way I will be known in a world where I can't be known as I really am. I need the tattoos to be my way of expressing what I cannot voice aloud, at least not right now. Does any of that make sense? I want my tattoos to speak the truth about me in the midst of my deception. I'm coming clean. I don't want to hide anymore."

Mark chewed on the back tip of his drawing pencil as Simon finished his verbal dissertation. He was looking directly at Simon when he said, "Yeah, dude, I'm not really sure I get all the ins and outs of your life experiences. Sounds kinda deep to me and I'm not really interested in finding out your personal shit. Don't get me wrong, I know your personal life is important to you but I'm here just to do the tattoos." The room went silent and then Mark said, "Anyway, we can talk about your stuff as we go but let's talk about the first tattoo you're wanting. Do you know exactly what you're looking to get?"

Mark's blunt remarks took Simon by surprise and he felt mistreated somehow. As a priest, he had never been treated with such a lack of grace. His doubts about getting a tattoo blossomed in his heart but he pushed ahead regardless of how he felt and in a small voice said, "Well, I was thinking about this." Simon stood up and took out his wallet. His hand shook as he removed a small card from within one of the folds and handed it to Mark, saying, "Well, I was thinking about this for the first one. It's a symbol for the Immaculate Heart of Mary. It's a Catholic symbol for the heart of the Mother of God. It contains these symbols here for purity and love but also these roses and this sword piercing the heart. It's from a prophecy. Sometimes there are several swords but I'd prefer just the one." Then he added, "The flames around the heart and on top are important, so are the lilies."

Mark studied the holy card. "Very cool! It will make an awesome tattoo. Can you leave this with me?" Mark was looking intently at the holy card of the heart. "Oh yeah, this is great, Simon. I've seen this kind of Catholic art before and it looks great with vibrant colors. It'll make an impressive tattoo."

Simon relaxed a bit, feeling that somehow he had said the right thing in the unfamiliar setting he now found himself in. "I was thinking about getting it on my shoulder, up here." Simon gestured to his right shoulder.

Mark frowned. "Why there?"

"Well, I thought it would be a good place to start," Simon was lying.

Mark put the holy card down and clipped it to the pad with a paperclip. He wrote down a few things and then looked at Simon directly, asking, "This is your first tattoo, right? Why hide it? Show it off so the whole world can see, just like you said. You said you decided it's time to speak to the whole world and not hide anymore, right? I say you put it here, on your right inner arm, that way you can see it all the time and others as well."

Simon considered all of this and could not deny that at that moment all he wanted to do was just run out of there. Yet, he had come this far and was not turning back in his resolve to come clean with the world. He looked at this stranger named Mark and opened his mouth to say something but nothing came out. He wanted to say that none of this made sense to him. He desperately wanted to cry out and say he was afraid and not entirely convinced about what he was beginning to do. Simon thought about the heart tattoo and all that it represented to him. He realized that he was still on a fence and he hated his hesitation. It was time to begin. He finally spoke up and said, "Ok, you're the boss, Mark. Let's put it here on my right inner arm." Simon wanted to say more to Mark but held back because Mark had said clearly that he wasn't interested in people's personal shit. He thought that perhaps he had said too much already. Simon knew that if this was really the way to get free and live in the truth, then he would need to be completely honest with Mark. Simon supposed that somehow, it would all work out even if he hadn't the slightest idea how that would happen. There was so much he still wanted to hide about himself but he also knew that now he would have to give this stranger some details of his life in order to best record it. He wondered how he was going to communicate his personal shit. He pushed the intimidating thoughts away.

He glanced around the room and noticed a framed, vintage print hanging on the wall in between the numerous sheets of sketches that were taped on the walls. It appeared to be from an old magazine. Simon read the date at the bottom of the page along with the word "Puck". Mark saw him staring at the print and said, "It's a satirical Victorian cartoon taken out of Puck magazine. It shows a corrupt 19th century U.S. presidential candidate receiving a bath from his two secretaries. The politician's body is covered in word tattoos and each word tattoo is listing his alleged crimes. The two dip-shit secretaries are frantically trying to scrub away their candidate's crimes. Politics never change, huh? Bastards are always trying to hide their shit." Simon thought about the tattoos he would receive. He would carry them for the rest of his life. His tattoos would speak the truth about his life, his crimes and his triumphs. He would never erase his tattoos. Perhaps someday he could voice out loud, what they said in silence.

Billy appeared at the door of the room, carrying a bag and the room was suddenly impregnated with the steamy aroma of Chinese food. He handed the bag to Mark and said, "Enjoy! Hope it's what you wanted."

Mark looked at Simon and said, "Sorry dude. Lunch got here. I'm starving."

"You go ahead and eat. I think you have another appointment after me. I'm almost done anyway."

"Thanks dude." He set the bag on a side table. "Yeah, there's a two o'clock but he's always way early. It's only like twenty to one now. We got plenty of time. Let me look at my calendar and see when you can come in for your first tattoo." He pulled out a binder full of notes and appointment notations. He turned pages and studied his notes. Finally, he said, "Okay, how about three weeks from now? That would be three Fridays from today at three o'clock?"

"Yeah that sounds perfect. Thanks." Simon barely took in that it would be three more weeks before he could get his tattoo. He was far more interested at that moment just to leave the place and get to the safety of his home.

"I'll draw the heart kinda like what I'm seeing here, with a few changes. If I have any questions I'll give you a call. What's your number?" Mark took one of the pencils and added Simon's name and phone number in the appointment book. He slammed the book shut and tossed it aside. "Cool! Well, I look forward to working with you dude. I think I might do those roses free hand once we start the tattoo but we can see it here when you come in. Any other questions?"

"Not really, just grateful that you're doing this for me. It's intimidating getting a first tattoo. To be honest I never thought I would enter a tattoo shop and request one. It's a long story."

Mark had opened the brown bag containing his Chinese lunch and took a hungry bite out of a greasy egg roll. He held up another egg roll to Simon who declined with a wave of his hand. Mark shrugged and laid the second eggroll down. He swallowed what was left of the eggroll he had held. Simon noticed a marked difference in Mark's tone of voice as he said with interest, "So tell me, Simon, what's your story? Do you live around here?"

Simon asked himself why the tattooer was now interested in 'his shit'. Nevertheless, he said, "I live about fifteen minutes from here on the other side of the Trinity River."

"Do you come down here often, I mean, to this part of town, this neighborhood?"

"Yeah sometimes I do. Meet friends, grab a few beers. It's from those times that I noticed the tattoo shop but as I say I never thought I'd be coming in here. Life sort of led me here."

Mark took the second egg roll and ate it while he looked at Simon carefully. He felt that Mark wanted to say something to him and this made him feel uncomfortable. Not knowing what to do, he said, "Well, I guess I'll let you eat and get ready for your next appointment."

"Can I ask you a personal question, Simon? You don't have to answer it if you don't want to. I'm just curious." Mark was wiping the grease off his chin and from his hands with a paper napkin he had pulled out of the bag.

Simon froze from head to toe. He didn't know what to say. He felt pressured by the request and sensed that his face had reddened. He felt cornered by Mark's words. He wasn't used to anyone prying into his private life but more than that, he wasn't used to giving out personal information to strangers, especially this kind of information, prefaced this way. So he chose to make a joke out of it. He said smiling, "Well, that depends on the personal question."

Mark turned in his swivel stool, and put the appointment book, pad and pencils on the table behind him. Then he said, "It's just that this is the gay old neighborhood. When Billy brought me my lunch he looked at you and winked at me. It's a little game we play here in the shop. With his wink he was asking me if I thought you were gay. I don't think you caught me shaking my head slightly in the "no" response. He's gay himself, even though he looks straight and acts like a tough ass to scare people. He thinks everybody is gay." Mark chuckled and added, "So, I guess my question is, are you gay or not?"

Simon sat there, trying to process the question that had just been hurled at him and his hearing went berserk for a split second. It was as though a huge, shrieking freight train was traversing at high speed through his head between his ears. He thought his head would burst. He had never been asked that question so directly by anyone, ever in his entire life, let alone a perfect stranger. It was something he never saw coming. He was there to negotiate the beginning of a new chapter in his life and that chapter had to do with being truthful and letting go. God had made him see that. But Simon had become a master of deceit. He was usually not accustomed to telling the complete truth about himself to others, and not even to himself. He was so weary of the hiding and making up stories. He was tired of keeping all the plates rotating atop the billiard sticks. In a moment of courage, he said without hesitating, "Yeah, Mark, I'm gay. I don't look gay and I don't act gay but I'm very gay. Very few people know that truth." Then he added, "I fool a lot of people, all the time." This last admission struck a chord and saddened him.

Mark playfully slammed one of his fists into the palm of his other hand and cried out, "Damn, I was wrong. I can't believe it. Never would have thought you were gay 'cause you look butch. Don't get me wrong, dude, it's all very cool. Just a little game Billy and the rest of us play here with our clients. Being in the gay neighborhood a lot of our clients are gay. Even though I'm a straight guy, I'm usually right but this time I got fooled." Mark was laughing to himself.

Simon tried to muster up a bit of laughter but none of it amused him. Still smiling broadly, he managed to say, "It's cool, no problem." At that moment, he remembered when he had been in kindergarten and had seen a book cover that fascinated him. It depicted a strong young man named Gulliver. Sitting there in the tattoo shop he could remember clearly how excited he had gotten when he'd seen the image of the muscular young man on the cover. Gulliver had no shirt on and the bare-chested man wore tight trousers and rough looking boots. He had flowing black wavy hair and was lying down on the dusty ground struggling to get up while a great number of tiny men bound him with ropes. They had pinned their prize and Simon thought to himself that they were about to have their way with him. More than fifty years had passed since that morning in kindergarten and he could still see the book's cover vividly. It was his earliest memory of being sexually attracted to men.

Marked finished his lunch and gathered up all the wrappers and napkins he had used, shoving them into the brown paper bag. Simon realized that he had already told this stranger a secret that few others knew. They would be spending many hours together in the future and Mark seemed to be a curious man by nature even though he had said otherwise. Simon knew there would be other intimate questions. God had said to him, "You want to keep the charade going because you're afraid." There was no doubt in his heart about that. He knew that he was very afraid but he also knew he wanted to heal from his wounds. Simon felt badly bruised. He was reluctant to spilling his guts to just anyone except God in the confessional through the priest but now there was this stranger in this shop. He would need to open up. He looked closely at Mark who had put his hand over his mouth and belched. For some odd reason, hearing Mark belch like that made him seem very human and down to earth. He impressed Simon as being a good, upfront kind of guy. Strangely, he felt at that moment that he could trust him. He knew it was now or never and said very calmly, "There's something else I need to tell you, Mark. It's important that I tell you now as we begin to work together."

Mark looked up at Simon. "What would that be?"

Simon threw himself into the moment and said softly, "Yep, I'm gay, Mark, and I'm a Catholic priest as well."

Mark stared at Simon with a stunned expression on his face and in a hushed tone of disbelief asked, "Really? You're not shitting me, right?"

"Yeah, it's true. It's not the kind of information I carelessly throw around for obvious reasons. I just thought you should know."

"Dude, you mean you are a Catholic priest like of the pope and exorcisms and holy water and all that?"

"Yeah, I am, Mark."

"Well, fuck, I never expected that. Gay and being a priest." Mark looked pensive. At last he said, "Now some of the things you've explained to me about why you want your tattoos makes better sense. I didn't mean to put you off, it's just that I get all kinds of loonies in here and, well, I had no idea where you were coming from when you first spoke."

Simon was relieved that he had been honest with Mark and had trusted the man, even though he was full of anxiety. Strangely, he was feeling free.

Another weight had been lifted. The telling of a truth had given him a deep sense of freedom. "I'll explain some more when I come in for the tattoo, that way you'll understand better."

"Cool, I look forward to it," Mark responded. Simon had stepped off the cushioned table and Mark stretched out his hand. Simon took it into his own in a handshake. Mark smiled broadly. "I appreciate your honesty, Simon. I can imagine it wasn't easy to come clean with that. Gay and a priest. Don't think I've ever had a client in here like you, but who knows. The world is a big place." Mark put his hands behind his back and asked, "Will the tattoos follow the course of your life, or something like that?"

"Something like that."

"Well, we all have stuff in our lives, dude. All kinds of stuff. Nobody escapes from any of that." Simon knew it wasn't going to be easy for him to pour out everything but he was determined to do so. Mark accompanied Simon down the hall toward the two swinging saloon doors. As they neared the exit, Mark said, "Look forward to seeing you soon for your first tattoo, dude." He stopped and lowered his voice. Then he said, "Sometimes we think we are alone in our messes but we don't have to be if we don't want to. We are never really alone. I dunno, I've come to that conclusion. It just seems that way. I can imagine that all of us share many of the same heartaches even if the details are way different."

Simon shook his head in agreement, but at that moment, he could only think about his recurring nightmare and what his life had really become.

Chapter Two
The Sword

Some of us think holding on makes us strong, but sometimes it is letting go.
Herman Hesse

The moment finally arrived for his first tattoo. It was midafternoon and the heat was stifling. Simon was glad he was wearing flip-flops, cut-offs and a short-sleeved cotton shirt. He was well aware of a deep-seated nervousness within himself as he climbed down out of the cabin of his truck and walked toward the tattoo shop. He knew that on this day he was beginning to take the first steps in a new direction. But there was also something else that tugged at the far corners of his mind which he couldn't exactly explain. He felt intensely erotic and this filled him with guilt. As he approached this new chapter in his life, he couldn't help but think about the tattoo process and the ink he would soon receive in his flesh. Simon was about to bare his body to the penetrating stabs of a cruel needle and the image filled him with both apprehension and sexual fascination. It would be there forever. He admitted to himself that he was definitely erotically charged. What kind of wild ride had he agreed to?

Simon reached the tattoo shop and saw that Mark was sitting alone outside the shop on a low brick wall that encased the tiny courtyard there. When he saw Simon approaching he jumped down and extended his hand.

"Hey Simon. How's it going, buddy?"

Simon tried to hide his nervousness and sound cool and collected as he said, "Sorta ready for my tattoo!" It came out too loudly and he gave himself away.

"Why 'sorta', dude? Is something wrong?"

"No, no, nothing's wrong." Simon blurted out. "It's just that I'm nervous I guess."

"You'll be fine, you'll see. Let's go inside."

Simon followed him inside the cold, air conditioned shop, down the now familiar corridor and into Mark's workroom. The cushioned table upon which Mark worked was already prepared for Simon, his next client, to lie upon.

"Simon, you can go ahead and get up here," Mark said, indicating the table.

"Do I need to take off my shirt?"

"Naw, we're putting the tattoo on your arm, right? Just roll your sleeve up a bit just in case." Simon was completely taken aback as Mark nonchalantly reached out and confidently took Simon's bare right arm into his hands. The feel of the man's touch on his skin was electrifying and unexpected. Mark did not seem to take notice of Simon's heightened emotions and simply indicated the spot he intended to work on. "Right here, correct?" Mark asked.

Simon cleared his throat and said, "Yeah," but then he added, "I had thought maybe a little higher, toward my shoulder."

"I really think it will look better here, buddy, lower." Once again, Mark indicated the place just above Simon's wrist. "Remember, dude, you wanna come clean and show the world, not hide."

"Ok." It was all Simon could manage to say since Mark had not yet let go of Simon's arm, continuing to turn it to one side and then another, looking closely. It felt good to Simon to be touched by this stranger who already knew some of his secrets.

"Go ahead and sit up here for me," the tattooer said, as he sat down on his swivel chair and faced his work station. Simon climbed onto the cushioned black leather table and lay his head down on the little pillow, folding his arms comfortably behind his head. He stared at the bright fluorescent lights on the ceiling wondering what was coming next. Mark was opening drawers at his work station table, looking for something and apparently found it because he waved it in the air to no one in particular. He set down a disposable razor and turned around saying, "Go ahead and sit up, buddy." He turned around again and put on disposable purple colored nitrile gloves in silence. He tore sections of paper towels from a huge roll and placed them to one side. Lost in his own thoughts, Mark unrolled a thin sheet of plastic from a roll, and fixed it onto his worktable with scotch tape. Simon watched as Mark assembled several small plastic cups the size of thimbles. He noticed that the tattooer put a dab of Vaseline under each one before setting them in place on the plastic film checking to make sure that none moved. He opened a cabinet door and looked at the numerous bottles of brightly colored liquid that were stored there. He selected several out of the cupboard and set them down. Uncapping them, he filled each small plastic cup with a different colored ink and left one unfilled. This last was saved for a clear liquid Simon was unable to identify. Finally, Mark opened another drawer and pulled out an odd looking metal pistol covered in a plastic bag. A long electric cord extended from one end and Mark plugged it into the wall. He pulled the trigger and the pistol-like gadget momentarily whined loudly. He turned it off and set it down. Then, into the same drawer he reached and took out a slender white envelope with green lettering. Simon could see it said 'warning' across the bottom and was sealed. He tore it open and removed a long, shiny stainless steel needle which he inserted into the pistol. He set it down again on the plastic film. Mark swiveled around in his stool and faced him. Simon knew it was time to begin.

"Ok, dude. Here's the card you left with me last time." Mark took the holy card of the Immaculate Heart of Mary that Simon had given him and set it to one side behind him. "Here's the drawing I made." Mark held up a sketch on what appeared to be very thin paper. "It might look incomplete to you but I'm going to put in the details as I go, directly on your arm, okay? It's gonna look awesome! Would you let me see your arm again?" Once more, Mark touched Simon's bare skin as he had done before. Something again stirred in Simon that was unmistakably sensual. He heard Mark announce, "Ok, we're ready to start."

Simon was beyond words at this point and surrendered himself to Mark, drying the palm of his hands quickly on his cut-off jeans.

Mark saw this and smiled. "Clammy, huh? Just keep your arm steady for me right now." The tattooer held up the sketch of the heart tattoo making sure it was in the right position. Then he studied it closely. The thin tracing paper crinkled as it stretched easily over Simon's skin.

"Does that look good to you there, in that position?"

Simon looked, then hesitated, and finally said, "Actually, I had imagined it would be in this position." He took the drawing and turned it completely around. "Like this."

"Oh?" was Mark's response. "Dude, you want it upside down?"

"Well, it's upside down to you but to me it's right side up. I'd like it this way so that I can see it in the right position. It's important for me to be able to see it in this position."

"Gotcha! I see what you mean. Ok, cool. Is the size okay? I think it is."

"Yeah, it's perfect." The flimsy tracing paper lying on his arm gave Simon his first glimpse into what the tattoo would look like on his arm. He was impressed. Mark carefully took the fragile paper bearing the image of the heart and placed it to one side. He applied a sudsy solution on the spot where the tattoo would go. Taking the razor, he began to shave Simon's considerably hairy arm. Simon was startled to see the razor remove so much black hair. He had never shaved his arm before. Correct that, he thought to himself, he had never had another man shave his arm before. The razor reminded him of a small plow removing thick debris from an overgrown field of weeds. He felt embarrassed and said, "I know, Mark, I'm a fucking hairball! Sorry!"

Mark chuckled to himself. "Wait till you get tattoos on your thighs, legs and chest. I can see that I'm going to need a lawnmower." Simon peered down at his furry legs and thighs and said nothing. Mark continued, "I can't apply the sketch unless your skin is smooth. You hairy dudes gotta get shaved. No biggie. The fur will grow back." Then he looked up with a crafty smile and a mischievous gleam in his eyes. "Trust me, dude, I'm not getting off on this, ha, ha, ha!…or am I? ha, ha, ha. When was the last time a straight bro shaved you?" Simon burst out in nervous laughter and not knowing what to say, never answered. When Mark had shaved the entire area where he would work, he wiped it clean with a wet paper towel and straightened up. Simon gazed down at the bald spot on his arm, not liking his momentary, new appearance.

The tattooer meticulously took the thin paper and once again placed it where they had agreed. He got up and put the drawing into a machine that resembled a photocopier. He pressed a button and a sheet of tracing-like paper rolled out of the other end of the machine. He took a pair of scissors and cut the excess noisy paper around the sketch of the Immaculate Heart. Simon was surprised to see that the copy was done in dark purple lines.

Mark wet another paper towel and wiped the bald area on Simon's arm. He took the purple sketch and carefully placed it just above his damp skin. Then he gently pressed down on it to make sure it was in contact with the skin. Simon could see that it was a tricky procedure that required precision and patience. Once the purple ink on the paper touched his damp skin and Mark slowly lifted it, Simon saw that a purple lined image was transferred perfectly on his skin and began to dry quickly.

"Damn, I'm good," Mark said to himself, smiling as he congratulated himself. "That is a perfect transfer even if I say so myself. If the sketch isn't placed right where it needs to be then it's gotta be wiped away completely and reapplied, and that, dude, is a real bitch. This is especially true when the tracing is done on a complete leg or arm because you're talking elbows and kneecaps." Then Mark asked, "This is right where you want it to be, correct?"

"Yeah, right there." Simon admired the purple sketch imprinted on his arm. It was beautiful to him.

"Don't worry about these blank spaces here, I'll do those right on your skin with the needle. Go ahead and lay back like you were before and put your arm right here where I can work on it."

Simon looked intently at the image on his arm. The time was upon him to begin proclaiming silently the many painful secrets he held in his wounded heart. The Creator of the Universe had told him the best way for him to heal was to be honest. Simon knew he had to come clean and so, he was ready to begin even though this idea of tattoos still baffled him. Why had this seemed like the best way to proceed? He had no idea why this had occurred to him but he trusted his instinct. He had already gone too far and felt he could not turn back now. He cringed as he imagined what came next in this bizarre process. Pain from wounds and bruises in his soul would be healed by pain in his flesh. He braced himself to endure the physical pain that awaited him, to receive the long stainless steel needle that awaited him. He remembered that pain was free in this place.

Mark had turned around and had taken the tattooing gun into his hand. The long needle was in place. He dipped it into the cup with the clear liquid and pulled the trigger. The machine burst into life as Simon heard the shrill whining of the tattoo gun again. It was a dreadful sound that filled the room, high-pitched and menacing. The cruel needle was dipped into a cup of black ink. The tattooer turned toward Simon and without fanfare, simply said, "Okay, dude, here we go." With his left hand, Mark took hold of Simon's arm and held it firmly. He put the needle where it needed to be and pressed it into Simon's flesh. Excruciating, piercing pain bit Simon's flesh as if a razor blade was dissecting his arm in two. The acute sensation he experienced was that his flesh was being sliced open, and he remembered a long ago afternoon in high school science class when frogs had been dissected completely in half and left wide open. Unbearable agony shot through him all the way to his core and overtook him completely. He could think of nothing else except the long silver needle in the tattooer's hand. The tattoo gun continued to whine loudly and the needle mercilessly penetrated him relentlessly with calculated disregard, intent only in depositing its ink deep under Simon's skin.

Simon braced himself during those first excruciating minutes hoping with every fiber of his being that the intense pain would quickly subside but it didn't. Cold sweat broke on his forehead and down his spine. He could feel the back of his shirt cling to his skin as the minutes ticked slowly away. Mark worked without speaking and Simon lay there hanging on, trying his best not to arch his back nor swat away the tattooer's hands. He almost wanted to scream out, "Fuck! It's too much! Stop it!" but he was well beyond that point. He held on and concentrated. At that moment, he thought about Jesus being tortured and receiving His terrible wounds.

Then when it seemed Simon could bear no more, the tattooer stopped and lifted the tattooing needle in order to take more ink. He looked at Simon and asked, "You doing okay, buddy?"

"Yeah, I'm good," was all that Simon managed to say. He lay there for what seemed like an eternity and little by little he embraced the pain, thinking that those initial few minutes were certainly not for the faint of heart. In a kind of mental mantra he admonished himself to endure and to bear. Only in this manner, as he lay there, Simon was able to draw strength from the pain. The pain he was enduring was enabling him to endure and to bear. Obviously the pain had not lessened, but he recognized that he had taken back control of himself.

Simon made an effort to relax and felt the tension in his back and legs stiffen. Mark sensed the shift and asked once again, "You doing okay?"

"Yeah. I think those first minutes were the worst. I'm good."

"So tell me, dude. Why did you choose to start with this heart tattoo? What's the meaning of it? It's a great image for a tattoo. I can't remember what you called it." He drew more ink from the small thimble like cup and continued outlining the tattoo in black. Mark held onto Simon's outstretched arm tightly.

Simon did his best to concentrate on Mark's question and avoid thinking about the unbearable pain. "It's the Immaculate Heart of Mary, that's what it's called. It's a Catholic devotion. It symbolizes human love for God. There's another devotion in a similar symbol called the Most Sacred Heart of Jesus. It's like the other half, so to speak. That other heart symbolizes God's love for humans." Mark continued working and Simon felt that conversing with Mark helped him manage the searing pain. It was so tempting to give in to the stinging sensation he felt on his arm, but he held on. The damned needle seemed so eager to keep biting into his flesh. Without looking up, Mark asked, "I'm not religious but traditional Catholic art in general is really fascinating to me. Why the sword in this heart and the roses? What does it mean?"

"This heart symbolizes Mary's love for God in her own life. Even though she was Jesus' mother, she was still completely human. The sword represents the pain and sorrows that came into her life. The sword is the bad stuff in life that pierces our hearts and leaves us so badly bruised and devastated." The persistent needle in Mark's hand did not let up. It whined endlessly as the tattoo took shape. It reminded Simon of his own sword. "The roses are the joys, the good stuff. It's all like a story about her life experiences, good and bad, recorded in her heart. It's how she dealt with everything. She was able to accept both the roses and the sword because she simply let go of her plans in favor of what God planned for her. She didn't flee from the sword but instead, she let go of her fear of the deep wounds it would bring her. And the acceptance of the sword brought her painful wounds, indeed it did, but also something way more important. It brought her strength."

"Wow, that's some heavy shit…" A pause followed and Mark quickly corrected himself, "Uh, sorry, I mean, some heavy stuff, dude. I like it. So why did you choose to have it as your first tattoo?"

"I chose it because that's where I want to start figuring out the confusion in my life. I need to clearly understand the good and the bad in my life and not run from the bad stuff anymore." Simon weighed his words and finally said, "Remember that old 1930s movie, The Hunchback of Notre Dame?"

"Yeah, that's some bad ass film. It was with Charles Laughton. He kicked ass in that movie. He was awesome in Witness for the Prosecution, too, with Marlene Dietrich and Tyrone Power. I fucking love that film." Saying this, Mark kept his eyes on his work as he smiled and wiped away the excess blood from Simon's arm.

"Well, there's a scene at the end of that movie that struck me even as a kid. It's when the hunchback is way up high on the façade of the cathedral and he's crying his eyes out because way below, the people of Paris are having this fucking huge party. The handsome dude, Gringoire, got the pretty girl, Esmeralda. The hunchback loved her and wanted her for himself. But he was ugly."

Mark stopped his work and looked up. "Yeah, I remember that scene." He drew more ink and continued his work.

Simon was lost in the scene of that movie now and what had enthralled him as a boy now took hold of him again. "The hunchback grabs on to one of the stone gargoyles as he's looking down at the crowd. In his pain he says to the gargoyle: 'Why was I not made of stone like thee?'" The words caught in Simon's throat and he feared the onslaught of emotion that was ready to pour out. Mark continued working and when Simon got himself under control he said, "I knew as a kid what the hunchback was feeling and why he wished to be made of stone. When you're made of stone, you feel no pain." Then he added, "Jesus' mother, though, embraced the pain because it made her strong instead of being weak. She faced her wounds instead of running from them. That's the kicker about the sword in her heart as opposed to the one I carry." He sighed and said, more to himself than to Mark, "Fuck, I have so much yet to learn and own up to."

Mark concentrated on Simon's tattoo and without looking away from his work, he barely whispered, "Yeah, I get the sword now." The only sound in the room was the tattoo gun digging into Simon and slowly revealing the striking image of the heart, roses and sword. Simon was lost in his thoughts, and the tattooer in his work. Mark sat back and taking a fresh wad of paper towels, gently wiped away more blood off Simon's arm. He examined his work and reloaded the needle with more ink. Without looking up, he asked, "So I'm understanding that you've always been a religious guy, or am I wrong?"

"I've never really considered myself to be religious in the strict sense. When I was a kid, religion was certainly frowned upon at home, but I'll get to that later. Still, though, I've always been drawn to God. When my mom was a kid, she grew up in a home without religion and yet, she searched for God on her own as she grew into adolescence. Her faith in God became something very personal and she passed this on to my brother Bobby and I. Mom instilled in us an uncomplicated faith. Religion wasn't necessarily important but faith and union with God were. She often talked to us about the Bible stories and made them come alive. These were the days before air conditioning and we sat out on the front porch a lot at night. Mom made God real to me."

Mark said, "I never had that. Makes me kinda jealous, but go on."

"One of my earliest memories is actually about God. I realized He had noticed me too since I was a little kid and was seeking me out. I'll never forget it. It was when I discovered that God was like 'right there'. That was the first time I can remember God coming to me. I must have been four or five but I remember those things really clearly." As he said this, Simon recalled another early memory, a violent one, though, that took place at the beach. God had been present then too, but in a frightening way. It had taken place not long after that first powerful encounter with God. Simon almost gave in to that terrible memory when Mark's voice jolted him away from it.

"That's intense, Simon. Like I said, I'm not religious. I didn't grow up in a religious, church-going family. In fact, as a teenager I thought the whole religion thing was bullshit. Religion is so often used for all kinds of bullshit by all kinds of people." Simon remained silent. Mark continued, "I remember that I once wanted to let my hair grow out long when I was like fourteen years old and my old man said no. He said it was a bad thing. I was totally pissed and argued that if it was such a bad thing, why did Jesus have long hair? Do you know what that bastard told me? He said that Jesus had long hair because in those days scissors hadn't been invented yet! Damn, what a load of bullshit. Using religion to control people, what pathetic bullshit, all fucking lies." Mark sat back and asked, "So where did you have those first experiences of God? In church?"

"Actually, no, Mark. In fact, it was under the house."

"Huh? What the fuck?"

"Yeah, it was under my grandfather's house. Like I was saying, religion wasn't encouraged at home. I never went to church until I decided that I wanted to be an altar boy. Since we were Latin, the Catholic Church always loomed close by but we never attended church except for family weddings or baptisms. My dad had issues with the Catholic church that I never really understood."

"But you became a priest! Didn't your folks have anything to do with that?"

"Well, they did, but not like you would think. We always lived in the same house with my great grandparents and grandparents, Mom's side of the family. They were Spaniards and didn't have much regard for the Catholic Church. In fact, they were quite anti-clerical calling the Church 'fascist'. I remember conversations about priests and nuns as being way negative."

"Really?"

"Yeah, conversations about the Church were usually pretty loud and heated with a good measure of vulgarity thrown in by the men folk. I guess it all came from the difficulties the family had suffered in Spain prior to the civil war there and the news they had received in the 30s when the terrible war broke out. The civil war in Spain was some very, very bad shit. Yet, when scary lightning storms would suddenly break out, as they often still do in Tampa, my grandmother would close the curtains, put us all in bed with her and every time a bolt of lightning exploded, she would pray loudly: "Santa Barbara! Santa Barbara!" My brother and I were encouraged to repeat the incantations. That was Mom's side. My dad's side were totally different. They were Cubans. My dad was born in Havana. Most were party animals and took a much more relaxed tone when it came to life and religion. I remember they weren't church goers but everybody wore gold religious medals and religious pictures hung everywhere in their house. I was always mesmerized as a kid, by a massive portrait of the Sacred Heart of Jesus that hung in my Cuban grandparent's house."

"Sounds like even though your folks really weren't into church, you always seemed to be drawn to spiritual things."

"Yeah, I guess that's a good way to put it. We were all baptized Catholics but that was about it."

Mark shook his head as if remembering something. "Dude, I grew up in a house with none of that. But go on."

"I guess my folks had something to do with my curiosity about God in the sense that religious things were all around us. It was cultural to be Catholic."

"So if you hardly went to church and didn't talk about God, how was it that you first got the idea that God was near you, seeking you out?"

Simon lay there with his sore arm completely extended and thought back. It was his earliest memory of being aware of the sacred. No one had needed to tell him that God had been there.

"My first encounter with God, that I can remember, was, as I said, under my grandfather's house. All the old houses in Florida were built on pier and beams and there was sometimes almost three feet of free space under there. Growing up, there was a rule at home, well, one of many that my grandfather was adamant about: never play under the house. Of course, whenever the adults weren't looking, I would play under the house. I loved going under there by myself. It was cool, shadowy and had plenty of room to accommodate my small, slender frame. From time to time, it also yielded untold treasures."

Mark smiled as he looked at Simon's arm, turning it from side to side. "Ah, so you were scheming and breaking rules even as a little fucker." He said this as a conclusion, not a question.

"I suppose that's pretty accurate, yes." Simon relished in the memory that was unfolding in his mind. "It was easy for a little kid to get under there. For me, it represented the entrance to another world, a secret world of mine that I didn't have to share with anyone else. Looking back now, I'm certain now that my awareness of God started there, under that house."

"So you kept a lid on it. Smart move, little guy. Otherwise it was over."

"Yeah, exactly! Under that house, not in a church, is where I really met God for the first time. It made me feel safe and happy when I was there. Sometimes I would invite Bobby, my brother who was a year or so older than me, but usually I'd go alone."

Mark turned Simon's arm to one side and said, "Could you hold your arm this way just a bit? Yeah, thanks. Go ahead, I'm listening."

Simon was lost in the memory now and the burning pain in his arm had given way to his thoughts. Not really completely aware that he was speaking out loud, he said, "One day I was there alone, digging in the near darkness when all of a sudden, the rubble and loose dirt produced a treasure. It was a small, pale blue statue of what appeared to be Mary, the Mother of Jesus, no more than four inches high."

"How did you know that? I mean, you were just a kid that didn't go to church," Mark interrupted.

The question startled Simon and he asked, "How's that?"

"How did you know that it was Mary, the Mother of Jesus?"

"Well, like I said, we did go to church sometimes for weddings and baptisms. It was from going on those occasions and seeing the stained glass windows and statues that I figured it out that day. I had asked my mother who the lady was in those places in church. Mom had explained it to me and I remembered the lady in the Bible stories my mom had read to us about Jesus being born and all. I remember how excited I became when I found the statue because it had to do with God. I have no idea how I knew but at that moment I knew it had to do with God and that fascinated me. I can still remember how special I felt that something like that could happen to me. I felt like, there, in my grimy little hands, was something, like, very close to God. And the idea came to me that God had put it there for me to find in order for me to find Him.

But just as suddenly I had another thought: I must keep it absolutely secret from everyone in the house or there would be shit to pay. I knew how the adults felt about religious things. So I took the little statue and put her into my pocket as I shimmied out from under the house. I locked myself into the bathroom at the back of the house so that no one would see. In awe, I took the lady from my pants pocket. I looked at her closely. She was beautiful even though she was very dirty. She also had a great piece of metal screwed into her back right between her shoulders. I thought that it had to be painful for the lady to bear that. Carefully I removed it and washed the gaping wound delicately. I looked at her face and she was smiling at me. I washed the rest of her and wondered where I could keep her. So I asked my grandmother for one of my grandfather's medicine boxes. I'd put her there and hide her someplace."

Mark was applying color now to the tattoo. Simon could not see it but as he told the tale of the beautiful lady under the house, Simon thought to himself that a symbol of her heart was being stamped into his flesh forever. "I'm listening, dude. So where did you hide it?"

"Once I washed it and had the medicine box, I put the lady inside. Our front porch had three great brick pillars which supported the roof. On top of the pillars was a crevice. When no one was looking, I climbed on the porch railing and safely hid it in one of the pillars. No one could ever guess that it was there. I would visit her often. It was something God had given me and I knew somehow that I had been chosen for it. It made me feel special." Simon hung on to that thought until the glare of the bright lights on the ceiling brought him back to the present.

Mark had swiveled around in his chair and was rinsing the needle. "I can't imagine being able to remember stuff that far back. I'm really not an asshole but that's some weird shit for a little kid." He suddenly stood up as he removed his gloves and threw them into a wastebasket. "I've got to go take a leak, Simon. You need to take a leak or whatever? You can get up and stretch if you need to."

"Naw, I'm good, Mark. Not needing to go. I'll be ok right here."

"Ok, I'll be right back. I just need to check something at the front desk too. I won't be long."

Simon closed his eyes as Mark left the room and thought about their conversation. He had never really shared so many details of his life with a perfect stranger until now and held on to this curious thought for a moment.

The place on his flesh where the tattoo was appearing, burned. Simon held up his arm and couldn't believe what he saw as he contemplated his first tattoo. It wasn't finished yet, but the bright red of the heart stuck out so much that Simon thought it looked three dimensional. It was a painful way for him to tell the world who he really was but Simon was pleased with himself as he lay there. He wondered if God had taken notice.

He closed his eyes and thought about that other early memory of God that had tried to push itself in a few moments earlier. It was a frightful memory. It had been a powerful experience like his earliest memory of finding God under the house but it was way different. It had been an alarming experience that had filled him with the fear of being left alone and abandoned. It had shaken him then to think that God could have forgotten him.

As he lay there waiting for Mark, Simon allowed his thoughts to drift and he allowed the terrible memory to open up within him. With clarity, he could see himself and his brother Bobby on the shore of the beach. They must have been five and six years old respectively. It had rained without stopping since early morning that summer day and the beach was deserted except for them. The two brothers had taken a walk to the beach together, without the adults knowing about it. The sand beneath their feet was hard and tightly packed. Feeling free and happy, they gazed out upon the vast, angry sea before them. Clouds, thick with oncoming rain, were dark and menacing. The serene morning breeze had been calm when they had left the adults behind but by the time they stood on shore it was replaced by a gusty wind which was beginning to pick up all around them. Then the wind picked up and began to sweep the empty beach. The boys were unaware of the coming storm as they tried to outdo each other in collecting seashells. The clouds above them seemed to press down closer and the water at sea was becoming choppy. Something unseen seemed to beckon them to wade into the warm gulf waters. The brothers stepped merrily into the water unaware that after a rain storm there is usually a very strong undercurrent. The adults had explained all of this numerous times but the sea before them did not appear dangerous at all. The water rushed in to meet their toes and hugged their ankles and then fiercely drew back out hurriedly. The action was repeated again and again as they went a bit further into the sea's embrace. In rushed the luscious warm waters of the gulf and out again it went. The wind was cooler now but the water was enticingly warm and so without much thought they went in further until the water reached their knees. They were thrilled to be there. Simon could see the entire scene as he lay there in the tattoo shop. It was as if invisible hands were luring them into the sea. They didn't realize the horror that awaited them.

The memory of that day so overtook Simon, that he was no longer in the tattoo shop but knee deep in the sea with his brother Bobby. His skin erupted in gooseflesh.

In a matter of mere seconds the boys realized that they were far from shore and their feet no longer touched the sandy bottom. Somehow, they had been taken away. They were no longer laughing as they saw how far from shore they were and how fast they were being pulled out to sea. Then everything got confused and blurry from that point on. The sheer recollection of that moment had caused Simon to ball his hands into tight fists as the scene unfolded in his mind.

He had tried desperately to hang on to Bobby even though he realized it wasn't possible for him to so. His legs were getting tired and awfully heavy as he tried to tread through the churning current beneath him. Seagulls screeched and flew crisscross above their heads as if warning them of terrible things to come. And then he had spiraled down into cold and darkness as he was pulled under the murky sea water in one great powerful tug. From beneath the waves, he looked up and could see his brother through the hazy, glassy transparency of seawater. Bobby was to one side, above him, at the surface of the water madly moving his legs in an attempt to stay afloat. Somehow Simon managed to break free from the insistent tug on his small body. He rocketed toward the surface, wagging his head up out of the water, his eyes red and burning from the sea salt. With a raspy voice he screamed out to his brother in a desperate wail, "Bobby!"

They were both choking and coughing, white as ghosts. The sea took no compassion on them but moved hungrily, intent on devouring them. In a split second Simon realized they were being dragged out to sea far from shore. He understood that the sea was famished and meant to consume them. They would be taken deep down into darkness and death.

There in Mark's workspace, Simon swallowed dryly as he recalled how raw and swollen his throat had become from swallowing the salt water. He had cried out in his ever growing panic to Bobby who screamed something unintelligible back at him. Panic was thick in his brother's throat. Something terrible was going to happen to them. "Bobby, help me!" But his older brother could not hear him because he was in his own anguished struggle to survive. In this way they were carried out further and further into the sea.

At that moment in the churning water, Simon thought about Mama and Papa and his grandparents. He thought about Becky, his dog. The waves were immense now because of their distance from shore. Everything seemed to be spinning out of control as they were tossed about and became a blur. Exhaustion was rapidly replacing any real strength at this point and his limbs burned badly. He was barely able to breathe and each time he was pulled down, his rise to the surface became more difficult. At some point, he could no longer pinpoint his brother's whereabouts.

Simon had no recollection as to how or when his father arrived on the scene and saw the danger they were in but in any case his father had swam out to where they were. Simon remembered how his father's strong arm had felt around his small waist as he drew him up and out of the water. In his other arm he already held Bobby who was coughing and screaming something that he did not understand. The current, however, had grown stronger beneath the three of them and they could feel the sea's continued pull at their feet. "Papa, help us!" It was clear to Simon that something very bad was about to overtake them when he saw his father being pulled down. His father was there trying to save them but he was no match for the sea's strength. The three of them were about to drown.

In the last few seconds before Simon was torn out of his father's arm by the sea, he became aware of a fourth person. And then he saw him. Swimming toward them was a beautiful young man with eyes that shone like great fiery lamps. His build was slender and not muscular but he was very powerful. In one graceful scoop, he gathered up the three of them. He moved quickly and gingerly in the raging waters that were determined to swallow them up. When the beautiful young man touched him, Simon felt like he was hanging on to a sturdy steel pillar or a great solid rock firmly jutting out from the hideous waters. His brow was thick and furrowed but there was no expression of anger in his blazing eyes that shone with nothing less than splendor and infinite goodness. The powerful young man was determined and swiftly, without saying a word, the stranger gathered the three of them up in his powerful arms. He delivered them to safety on the deserted shore. Frightened and spent, the three of them had collapsed almost lifeless, coughing and catching their breath. Slowly it dawned on Simon that the beautiful young man with the look of blazing fire in his eyes was gone. Badly shaken and confused by the close encounter with death, the two brothers began to cry when they saw their father's face streaming with tears. He made no sobbing noise but through tears stared fixedly and silently up and down the beach. Where had the young man gotten to? None of them said anything but Simon knew that God had saved them and that the beautiful young man who had pulled them out of death's grip was none other than an angel sent by God. As a little boy on that beach, he knew once again, that he was special to God.

Noise erupted in the corridor as Mark made his way back to his workroom, calling out sarcastically, "Simon, dude, are you asleep? Awful quiet back here. Let's knock that tattoo out and get you on your way."

Simon lay there still affected by the compelling memory of that day on the beach. He was aware that Mark had entered the room and smiled at him when the tattooer sat in his swivel chair and said, admiring his work, "Damn, I'm good." He turned Simon's arm up in order to get a better view and added, "Almost done. You doing okay, dude? You look white as a sheet."

"I'm doing good, Mark." Simon sat up in the cushioned table and was awestruck when he took a closer look at the tattoo. "I...I can't...believe it! It looks like it's going to jump off my arm! Thanks, Mark! Gee...it looks fantastic, man."

Mark beamed with confidence and said, "Let's get to it."

Simon closed his eyes as he laid his head back down on the small pillow, bracing himself for another dose of free pain. The impressive event on that day at the beach which he had just recalled was proof to him that God had always been very much aware of him. To an outsider, it would seem like a fantasy story, a tale of magical events propelled by imagination. Some might even label it pure, unadulterated bullshit. Simon however, knew it had been real. Finding the lady under the house and being saved by the angel had been very real indeed. They were not events to be scoffed at.

"I'm going to tattoo the roses on now and after that we are done, Simon!"

"Awesome!" The needle began to pierce his flesh again.

"So tell me, Simon, you were how old when you knew you wanted to be a priest?"

Simon now understood much better, how the tattoo procedure worked, aside from enduring the sadistic needle. Conversation between the client and the tattooer was essential to making the entire process bearable and complete.

As a result, it occurred to Simon that he and Mark would get to know each other to some significant degree. Getting a tattoo was not something that was done quickly but rather, took several long hours. Mark's question didn't fill Simon with apprehension as his questions had done before. A bond was being established between himself and his tattooer. Calmly, he answered, "I must have been around five. That's when I told the nuns at school."

"So you went to Catholic school? Shit, that must have been an experience. I've heard all kinds of crazy shit."

"Oh yeah, plus me and my brother went to school with the nuns when they still wore all the flowing habits."

"Habits?"

"The flowing black robes and the long veils with stiff white linens around their faces called wimples that covered them up almost completely. They are called 'habits' or 'religious habits'. The priests used to visit the school often, dressed in their black cassocks and high, starched white collars and cuffs. I was in awe of the nuns and priests. My brother Bobby was more in fear of them and would shit his pants in their presence." Simon smiled to himself as he remembered. "Anyway, like I was saying, I told the nuns I wanted to be a priest. I loved most of the nuns I had as teachers."

"Shit, dude, you told the nuns at school? Sounds to me like you were trying to gather up brownie points. Did they love it when you told them?"

"Oh fuck, yeah. This one nun was real happy when I told her. She was young and beautiful. Some of the nuns seemed pissed most of the time, but not Sister Mary Agnes."

"But at home it wasn't quite a celebration, huh? I'd guess it was like the proverbial turd in the punchbowl."

"No, it wasn't received well at home."

"So you wanted to be a priest at five and your family was like, hating the whole church scene?"

"Yeah, I guess that's about it."

"Damn, Simon, you were a radical! Bitch, you were paving your own way! I like that."

"I never really thought about it that way. I kinda thought of myself as a victim and not a radical."

"A victim? I don't think so, dude. You must have had big cojones even as a little kid to face up to your family and say you wanted to be a priest."

"Well, I didn't actually announce it that way at home, I mean, the nuns knew because I had told them and a couple of priests later on, but at home only my Mom knew. I was about twelve years old when I officially told my Mom." Mark was immersed in his work and said nothing. "But I did know enough to realize that it impressed people outside my family because they totally knew that being a priest was something special."

"What do you mean?" he asked without emotion.

"I was awed by the nuns. It was the last days of a Catholic Church that has for the most part disappeared today. But like I was telling you, in those days the nuns at our school still wore the traditional long habits, complete with white cuffs, gold colored buttons, odd looking laced up black shoes, black nylon stockings, long black veils, stiff starched linen around their heads and necks, and long rosary beads that clinked as they walked. They also wore a large crucifix around their necks that rested on their breasts. Well, on the front, you know what I mean."

Mark shot Simon a sideways look, complete with crooked smile, saying, "Fuck, that sounds way out there. Those women taught you all dressed up like that? I mean, they were your teachers dressed up like that every day at school?"

Simon thought Mark's surprise was funny. He chuckled to himself and said, "Yeah. It was normal to us." Simon thought Mark's astonishment kind of humorous.

Mark went back to work, saying, "Go ahead, I didn't mean to interrupt. It just sounded weird to me. All my teachers just wore regular clothes to school."

"One day, not long after I arrived at the school, the nun we had for sixth grade class, Sister Mary Thomasine, asked for volunteers among the boys in our class to help move a trunk upstairs at the convent. A new teaching nun had arrived and her things needed to be taken to her room. It was an opportunity to go into the nun's space where no one was ever allowed to go. Sister Thomasine already knew I wanted to be a priest because I had told her too. She was one of the older nuns. My raised hand was rewarded with acceptance and it was on that day with three other kids, that I noticed the chapel off to the left of the foyer as we were allowed inside the convent. I remember it as a place with little light except for a lamp here and there. The waxed wooden floors creaked as we went in. Waiting to be told what to carry upstairs, I had stood back a little and noticed the chapel behind me. I had moved in enough to take a good look. It too was dark and mystical and I knew that God was in there, inside the tabernacle that sat squarely on the altar of the chapel. The nuns had told us as much. I reasoned with myself over the next few days that if God was so close to me every day on that altar in the nun's convent at school, how could I keep from going there and being with Him?"

"The nuns had a housekeeper who answered the door while they taught at school during the day. She shopped for their food at the supermarket and prepared their meals. She was a kind lady named Bernice, short, round and jolly with beautiful skin the color of brown sugar. One morning, I gathered all my courage and knocked on the convent door. Bernice came to the door in her white apron and asked, Good morning, young man! Good Lord, what is your name, son?"

"My name is Larry, ma'am, Larry Zayas. I'm in Sister Mary Thomasine's class. I helped move a trunk upstairs the other day with some of the boys."

"Is that right? And how can I help you today, Mister Larry?"

"When I grow up I want to be a priest and well, I was wondering if I could come in and see the nun's chapel for a little while? We are on morning recess now, so there's time." Bernice's face lit up and laughing to herself, she unlatched the screen door saying, "You gonna be a priest someday? That's wonderful! Sure you can come into the chapel! Come on in and make yourself at home in the Lord's house." She swung open the screen door and I stepped once again into the coolness of the darkened foyer of the convent, with its waxed hardwood floors and smell of candles.

Mark listened as he worked but said nothing.

"My visit that afternoon would be the first of many visits I would make to that chapel because Bernice always let me in after that day. Sometimes I would go there during our morning recess or at lunch time. When my parents were late in picking us up after school, I'd knock and be let in."

"So you were making connections, huh?" Mark laughed to himself without looking at Simon.

"I suppose you could say that. It did get me in a good way with the nuns."

"I'll bet. And what about the priests? Were you a favorite with them?" Mark asked this with a hint of sarcasm. Simon was put off by the tone in his voice and feigned ignorance, asking, "What do you mean?"

"Well, I guess I wonder if some of the priests were interested in you?" Again, Simon felt ill at ease and sensed that there was more to Mark's question, suspecting where he was going.

"What do you mean, Mark?"

Mark hesitated only a little and then asked, "When you were getting all brown nosey with the nuns and the housekeeper, were you an altar boy, Simon?"

The mention of being an altar boy momentarily transported Simon away from Mark's loaded question. It swept him completely away from what he suspected was Mark's vile insinuation and he said, "In those days, when I was a twelve- or thirteen-year-old boy at the school and going into the nun's chapel, God was waiting there for me. Honest, I could feel it. It was in that place where I thought many things through regarding myself, my family and my life. It was in those moments when many things occurred to me. I was a kid but I was already at an age where I was thinking about my future."

"I remember the day I began to wonder about becoming an altar boy and serving God at the most sacred place on earth, I mean, the altar. I knew the Mass was complicated and in Latin but I also knew I could learn what I needed to know. Since the day it had occurred to me, in the nun's chapel, the thought really took over in my head. I could imagine myself up on the altar wearing sacred clothes: a cassock, a surplus and gloves. I would also have the privilege of processing in with the priest into the altar of God. I would be allowed to stand in the sanctuary with God's priests. No one else but them and the altar boys were permitted to be there because it was holy ground."

"I had felt close to God since I was five years old, but it was becoming more intense for me as I turned thirteen. Now the chance of being an altar boy made this closeness with God even more serious. It was for me clearly the place I most wanted to be because it is sacred and the dwelling place of God."

Mark stopped tattooing and his tone had changed considerably. In a gentler tone, he inquired, "You really did believe all that, didn't you?"

"I did. I still do in many ways but in those days it was all crystal-clear to me. All of it."

"So did you become an altar boy?"

"Yeah, I did. I remember I spoke to my parents about wanting to be one. I got their permission and my mother took me to the church office to put in my request to be trained as an altar boy. My father gave it no importance or at least that's how I felt. My brother Bobby certainly didn't care. He once put a sign on his door on Sunday morning which read 'No, I do not want to go to Mass.' But my mother understood. She supported me all the way."

Mark had stopped working and looked at Simon directly. He hesitated somewhat and finally asked in the same tone he had used before, "So I need to ask you, Simon, I know the nuns loved you because you wanted to be a priest someday, but how about the priests? Did they show any appreciation because you wanted to be a priest? I mean, were you a favorite because you were an altar boy? I hear priests are fond of altar boys, especially the young cute ones?" An uncomfortable silence hung in the room like something wet and putrid. It was a grotesque question put forward in the most jarring manner. Simon was simply stunned by the repulsive question, as a flood of memories poured into his heart and mind. He said nothing. Then Mark asked the question Simon was totally unprepared to answer, "Did you ever get fucked by a priest in those days, Simon?"

Simon glared at the man sitting in front of him. "Damn you, Mark, that's quite a question!" In his embarrassment, anger rose up within him and Simon was utterly stumped. When he ultimately attempted to give a mature answer to the loathsome interrogation, nothing came out of his mouth. He was highly guarded and decidedly pissed. Silence momentarily hung in the room between them.

Mark finally let out a chuckle and changed his tone again. "Sorry if I came on too strong. Shit, I never get to ask a question like that from not only a Catholic guy but a Catholic priest! I'm sorry if I pissed you off, dude. Just curious."

Simon said nothing as he gathered his thoughts and wondered if he had time to begin to answer that question. It was not an easy question for him to answer and his response could not be given easily. Mark continued his work quietly and Simon finally asked him, "How are you coming along? Is the tattoo almost done?"

"Yeah, dude, it's almost finished and it's awesome. Just a few details and we should be done in half an hour or so. The roses are turning out to be one of my best pieces of art, honestly."

The unpleasant silence once again draped the mood in the room and clearing his throat, Simon replied cautiously, "Getting back to your question, Mark. It's huge, man." Simon chose his words carefully, not knowing exactly how to phrase what he wanted to say. "I told you when I met you that I need to be completely honest with you. No bullshit. It's how I'm trying to be completely honest with myself. Your question isn't an easy one for me to answer and quite frankly, it scares the fuck out of me, but I will try."

Mark didn't look up as he said, "I probably have no right in asking you that. I'm sorry, dude."

"Well, you have no right in asking me but, it's a legitimate question, Mark. There were and have been and always will be some sick fuckers within the ranks of priests." Simon paused. "But not all of them. I'll try my best to answer your question but first, I want to start by telling you about the good priests, the really good, holy ones I have known. Is that cool?"

"Fair enough, buddy."

"I already told you why I decided to become an altar boy in the first place. I became an altar boy in the days when altar boys had a lot to do at the altar, unlike the farce it usually is today in many churches. And so a day finally arrived when I was told to present myself at the parish church at 6:00 am for Low Mass. There would be two seasoned altar boys who would be serving Father's Mass. They would teach me what to say and do. Our parish church, The Most Sacred Heart of Jesus Church, is an old, Romanesque style, traditional Roman Catholic Church in downtown Tampa."

That morning, I arrived around 5:30 am. I had gotten up really early and my mother had walked with me to the corner for the bus going downtown. Remember, in those days it wasn't dangerous for a kid to get on a bus by himself when the sun wasn't out yet. Anyway, when I got there I entered through the sacristy door where one of the older priests was preparing the missal for Mass. It was Father Michael and he looked towering to me dressed in his impeccable black cassock. He greeted me kindly and told me to put on my cassock for Mass. I had no idea how to put on a cassock. Father Michael was a formidable priest. He had a head of pure white hair perfectly combed. To me he was the very essence of the priesthood. I wanted to be like him and the other priests there. On this particular morning, he was scheduled to offer the Sacrifice of the Mass. It was getting close to six o'clock and the other two altar boys had not arrived. Probably because he did not recognize me and sensed my fear, Father Michael asked me softly, "What is your name, son?"

"My name is Larry, Father. Larry Zayas." I barely managed to answer in a weak voice. I wanted to bolt from the sacristy.

"Is this the first Mass you will serve?"

"Yes, Father. I'm very nervous." The elderly priest looked reassuringly into my eyes and said, "No reason to be nervous, Larry. I'm sure the other boys will be here shortly."

"The big clock on the wall ticked away the minutes and soon it was almost time for Mass. The other two boys never arrived. The priest showed me how to put the black cassock on. I buttoned all the buttons and he helped me with the surplus and the white gloves. I was completely mortified because I had no idea what to do out on the altar. Then Father Michael said, 'Go and light the two small candles on the altar,' he pointed toward the sanctuary and I followed his gaze. 'There, on either side of the tabernacle.' I had seen the other boys do it so I knew what I had to do."

When I returned, he gestured to a cord that hung beneath a cluster of brass bells near the door that led to the altar and said, "Now ring the bells, Larry, to let the people know that we are coming out to begin the Sacrifice. Pull on the cord." I extended my hand nervously and pulled on the cord. The bells chimed loudly and echoed throughout the church. All at once the creaking of pews and the rustle of a packed congregation getting to their feet echoed throughout. The church was packed at six in the morning for Mass on a weekday! Like I said, Mark, it was a different time then.

Father Michael was fully dressed in his priestly vestments and wore the biretta on his head. As if sensing my dread he said to me. "Don't worry about what to do, Larry. This is your first time, just look at me all through the Mass." Then he took the veiled chalice with his left hand and bowed gracefully toward the crucifix above the vesting table saying, "Procedamus in pace. In Nomine Christi. Amen." Dude, I was so worried about not knowing how to respond to the priest at the altar because it was all in Latin.

We went out on the altar and everything sorta went by in a blur. Right after that first Mass with Father Michael, after he bowed to the crucifix once again in the sacristy and said, "Prosit", I knelt for his blessing. After the blessing, he said, "Thank you, Larry, for serving at Mass this morning and congratulations on your first time."

I said, "Thank you, Father. I'm sorry I messed up so much."

"It's fine, you'll learn the Latin responses in time. Remember never to speak anything to anyone. Not one word to me nor any other altar boy, except the proper responses when you are serving at the Sacrifice. When we go out there and into God's altar, we are speaking with God, not men. When we are on the altar, we speak only to God. God listens to everything we say."

I said, "Yes, Father. Thank you, Father. Father, can I tell you something?"

"Yes of course, what is it, Larry?"

"When I grow up I want to be a priest." Father Michael looked at me and then bent down a little putting his right hand on my shoulder as he said, "Is that right? It takes many years of hard study and there are many temptations along the way. You must pray and stay close to God. That's the surest way of being a good priest." He straightened up and reached into his cassock. In his perfectly manicured hand he held out a holy card. "I will pray for you, child. I will pray that you will be faithful to God's call. It's a serious calling, you know, and not for everyone. I want to give you this. It's an old poem a priest once gave me when I was an altar boy about your age. It has helped me to remember my calling throughout the years."

"Thank you, Father." I was stunned that the priest himself had given me something of his own, something holy. I stared at the image on the card. It depicted a young priest with hands uplifted in prayer at an altar. On the other side was a poem. From that day on, I knew the words of the short poem by heart.

"You know something, Mark, I knew then that I wanted to be a priest more than ever and to be a priest like Father Michael. It fascinated me to be a part of that whole sacred event on the altar, when God comes down from Heaven and is present and can be touched, seen and consumed. As a kid I had a very clear understanding of what a priest was to me. They represented God because God had chosen them from among men to bring Him down from Heaven upon the altar. What impacted me most about priests was that their vocation was different to all the other vocations men and women chose. A priest did not so much choose his vocation but rather said 'yes' to God who had chosen him. The priest received his call directly from God. This is what the nuns had drilled into us and I believed it."

"There were six priests at our church and of all the priests there, three of them impressed me the most. They were Father Cornelius, Father Francis and Father Michael. These were the older priests. Father Cornelius was probably the elder of the three men. He was tall, gaunt and frail, and he walked with a cane. He had white hair that looked as if it was difficult to comb. He was kind and timid. His threadbare cassock was always immaculate but mended and shiny. He had worked many years with the poor and discriminated in the south. I remember that he always wore a kind of shawl over his cassock which made me think he was really old. He seemed truly holy to me and I was in awe of him at the altar because of the way he offered the Sacrifice with such reverence."

"Father Francis, on the other hand, was balding and had a rather stern look. It wasn't exactly a scowl but he certainly wasn't jolly. I can't remember him ever smiling except for the day I told him I wanted to be a priest. In those days all the priests wore their cassocks which truly set them apart. Father Francis had the reputation for being too serious and standoffish but to me he was the kind of priest I wanted to be someday. He died at the altar during Mass one morning which only added to the mystique. I always admired his distance and aloofness because I did not consider the priests to be like the rest of men. And of course, there was Father Michael who I already told you about. These three priests were good priests, authentic priests. They impressed me."

"What attracted me most to the mystery of God, the Sacrifice of the Mass, the priests and the sacred space where it all came together, was the fact that it was unchanging. The Mass was the same as it had been for centuries. God came down on the altar at the same time when the same prayers were uttered in Latin. Holy Communion was done in the same way as it had been done for centuries. It was our religion, our faith. I accompanied the priest up and down the Communion rail and then back again with the paten. People knelt as the priest announced eternal life and blessed them with the Sacred Host before putting it on their tongue."

"All the way from one end of the altar rail to the other, just before Communion was given, a long, white linen cloth was rolled out. People didn't touch it, but the linen was under their clasped hands. The linen was there to catch any fragments of God's Body in case it fell from the paten the altar boy held out under each communicant's chin. No one but the priest could touch God because only their hands had been consecrated to do so. After Mass it was the custom to kneel before the priest in order to receive the same blessing from him. All of this never changed and did not appear it would ever change. But it did and it hurt me big time to see it crumble and end as it had been."

"It was horrible when at first it began to change little by little. Then most of it suddenly did change in 1969. I was thirteen years old and could not understand it. At school the nuns raised their habit's length, the veil shortened and eventually the entire habit and veil and the nuns themselves would be gone. The priests no longer wore their cassocks and Fathers Cornelius, Francis and Michael had all gone to Heaven. The Mass wasn't in Latin anymore. It was in English now and the ritual had been changed enough to make it unrecognizable. The bells were gone. People talked in church before Mass and sometimes there was even loud laughter. It was crazy."

"At one point, everyone shook hands and patted each other on the back as they hugged and laughed. I didn't know it then but many more changes were on the way that made these changes seem like nothing. Communion now looked like people standing in a cafeteria line and I wasn't needed to hold the paten for the priest anymore in case any particles broke away from the Sacred Host. Of course, the white linen cloth was never rolled out anymore. In fact, in time, people were not allowed to kneel anymore for Communion and they were given the Sacred Host to touch in their hands. Guitars took the place of the organ."

"The new altar boys did not ask the priest for the blessing after Mass and the younger priests did not seem particularly interested in giving one. I couldn't figure out what had happened and I wondered why something so true, beautiful and perfect had to end. It really didn't make any sense to me then and it doesn't now. Like I said, it hurt me. Why did it have to end? Why did they take it away?" Then he murmured, "In some places, it still exists as it was."

Simon drifted away in thought as Mark put the finishing touches on his first tattoo. He wondered if Mark had understood anything about what he had said, especially that not all priests were perverts. He hoped he had explained it well. Yet he was haunted by other thoughts. Dark thoughts sprang up in his mind and something in him feared that he had somehow caused the inappropriate behavior and abuse he had received from other priests. He felt very guilty about that. The priests he had admired so much had given him every reason to want to be a good priest himself but as a boy he had in time realized that not all the priests were good and holy like Father Cornelius, Father Francis and Father Michael.

Mark mumbled to himself and turned off the tattooing instrument. He admired his work on Simon's arm as he said, "Take a look, buddy. We are done here! Damn, it looks awesome!"

Simon sat up and extended his arm. His first thought was 'Awesome indeed!' He stared at the shiny, brightly colored tattoo of the Immaculate Heart of Mary. It seemed to be aglow with the radiant fire depicted all around it. He noticed his arm was red all around the tattoo and that it was somewhat swollen. "Is it normal, Mark? I mean, that my arm's swollen like that and the skin around it is so red?"

"Oh yeah, totally normal, not to worry. Put this on it for a few days after you shower. That way it won't get infected." He handed Simon several packets of anti-bacterial ointment. "You'll heal up just fine in a few days. If you have any questions, though or if it looks funny after a few days, gimme a call or stop by and I'll take a look. But you'll be just fine. Dude, it looks really so, so fine!"

Simon agreed, "It sure does, Mark! Thanks!" He was more than ready to go home. His entire body ached, especially his back and legs, not to mention the stinging he felt on his flesh.

"Let's go see Billy. You can pay him. Since this is your first tattoo, and like you said, the first of others, I'll give you a break with this one. It will be two hundred fifty dollars."

He swabbed Simon's arm with a medicated paper wipe and then applied ointment. Finally, he wrapped Simon's arm in plastic film. Simon straightened up and admired the tattoo. He spoke his words too quickly as he anxiously asked Mark, "When can I see you for my next tattoo? I want it in a hi-hi-hidden place." He blurted it clumsily in an attempt to get it out. Then he added, "Once and for all. I want to put it where no one can ever see it and won't ask me about it. But it needs to be done and said, once and for all." He was trying to be strong now and pushed forward but it was very difficult for him to talk about the painful memories of the abuse. He realized he had not expressed himself well and suddenly felt naked. At that moment, Simon did not know how to deal with the shame that rose up in him.

Mark was throwing his work gloves into the trash can when he said, "Sorry, but I'm not getting you, dude. I thought your tattoos are about putting it out there for you and the whole world to see. Now you wanna hide it? What's up with that?"

Simon felt as if he had been unmasked and cornered. He managed to respond, "I know it sounds weird, but I can't get into it now." Simon felt terribly ill at ease and really needed to leave. "I'll come when you're free. I'll bring you my, my…my drawing and I'll explain then, okay? I'm still trying to figure out how…how best to sketch what I…w-want." He was stuttering now. He had to leave.

"Whatever you say, buddy, no pressures, okay? I'll be here." Mark grabbed his appointment book and ruffled the pages back and forth somewhat nervously, finally saying, "Usually I like waiting at least three weeks from one sitting to the next, but if it's going to be somewhere else on your body other than your right arm, then we don't have to worry about this one healing up before we start another one. Are you free to come in this week sometime and drop off the art work? You can discuss it then with me, okay?"

"Yeah, sure, but wh-wh-what day?" He felt he was losing ground, as if he were sliding down a slimy, moss-covered shaft.

"Any day is cool just before we open at ten, so if you come around twenty to ten, I'll open up for you and we can discuss it, okay buddy?"

"Okay...okay, that works." His brow broke out in a thin sheen of cold sweat.

"And for the appointment, how about the twentieth at twelve noon?" Simon considered it and said, "Yeah, the twentieth at noon is good...yeah...that's good."

"Okay, I'm writing you down for then." When he was done, he looked up and asked, "Is your next tattoo about the same size as the one I did today? Or larger?"

"Not really sure, Mark."

Mark sensed his reluctance and said, "Dude, no worries, we'll figure it out when you come over, okay? Chill man, it can't be that bad."

Simon opened his mouth but didn't know what to say. With an effort, he answered, saying, "Ok, I'll be by in a couple of days."

"Okay, dude, you got it. I'll write you in for roughly the same space of time on the twentieth. We can adjust the time after we meet this week. See you then, man." Mark shook Simon's hand and was surprised to feel a damp note that Simon pressed into his palm. He shook Simon's hand and then saw that it was a folded fifty-dollar bill. He looked at Simon thoughtfully and said, "Dude, thanks. I'm very grateful for the tip!"

"Just a tip of gratitude. Your work is incredible. I'll be wearing it for the rest of my life."

Mark patted Simon's shoulder gently and led the way to the front of the shop. Billy was reading and stood up nervously as Mark pushed through the saloon-like doors. He told Billy what Simon owed and then disappeared through the swinging doors. Simon noticed that there were several people waiting. He paid his bill quietly and walked out of the shop. Something gnawed in the pit of his gut and he felt somehow changed. He looked at his tattoo and understood something fundamental about himself that he had long ago pushed way down deep inside.

An old memory now came to him with great clarity and Simon remembered one morning long ago when he was in Sister Mary Thomasine's sixth grade classroom. He was eleven or almost twelve years old. It was a typical sticky, Floridian day and the fans overhead in the classroom ceiling, were on high speed. The older nun was teaching her students about the dignity of the priesthood. Sister Thomasine impressed Simon with her conviction and no-nonsense way of speaking. Sister believed every word she was saying. She was draped in the old habit and would turn her head stiffly from one side of the classroom to the other being confined as she was by her heavily starched headpiece. She held her arms out in front of her as if she were conducting a great invisible orchestra and moved them with determination as she spoke. Suddenly she lifted a large black Bible from her desk and opened it to where she had placed a marker. Simon noticed how the bright sun streaming through the tall classroom windows reflected off the gold colored buttons of her stiffly starched cuffs. Sister was in full throttle now as she engaged her pupils. All eyes were on the nun and everyone sat on the edge of their seats as she commanded in a thundering voice, "The Letter to the Hebrews! Children, where in the Bible do we find this letter?"

With one voice, everyone answered, "In the New Testament, Sister!"

"Yes, dear children, that is correct!" And without comment, Sister began to read in a tone that left no doubt in Simon's mind that it was truly God speaking through the inspired text, "Every high priest is selected from among the people and is appointed to represent the people in matters related to God, to offer gifts and sacrifices for sins. He is able to deal gently with those who are ignorant and are going astray, since he himself is subject to weakness. This is why he has to offer sacrifices for his own sins as well as for the sins of the people. And no one takes this honor on himself but he receives it when called by God, just as Aaron did!"

Sister looked around the classroom with penetrating scrutiny. The proverbial pin could have been heard dropping even as the only sound were the ancient fans twirling crazily above their heads at high speed. Sister walked into a row of neatly arranged desks and standing in front of Simon's desk, added in a booming voice, "And God says in another place: 'You are a priest forever in the order of Melchizedek'!" She slammed the big, black book shut, and everyone jumped. Placing the Bible on her massive wooden desk behind her, Sister demanded to know what the words meant. "What does it all mean, children? Think! Put your thinking caps on!"

Everyone sat enthralled by the nun's imposing presence and the room stood still, cloaked in reverent silence. Sister continued, "A priest is a man, yes, but a man who has become God's ambassador! The dignity of a priest is greater than the dignity of emperors or of any king in this world! Why? Why is this so, children? Think!"

No one dared to answer. Then Simon raised his small hand. The nun's face glowed in anticipation of the answer as Sister stiffly gestured 'yes' with her veiled head and gave him permission to speak, saying, "Go ahead, Larry."

Simon spoke up cautiously that moment but with conviction, "It's because the priest alone receives the power to change bread and wine into the Body and Blood, Soul and Divinity of Our Lord Jesus Christ on the altar."

"Yes!" Sister proclaimed as she clasped her hands tightly together and gave a kind of little jump looking up in a display of genuine gratitude. Her face was radiant with joy. She had taught her lesson well. Lowering her voice Sister continued, "You know, Saint Francis of Assisi said long ago, many centuries ago, that if he saw a priest and an angel in his path, he would first bow to the priest and kneel before him to kiss his hands because only the priest has the power to change bread and wine into…?"

The entire class erupted, "The Body and Blood, Soul and Divinity of Our Lord Jesus Christ!"

"Yes, yes, dear children! Yes, that is absolutely correct and true! The angels, even though they stand before God in His very presence cannot change bread and wine into God's Real Presence. They do not have the power! But the priest does! Only the priest has that power. He has the supernatural power given to him by God!" Sister looked lovingly at Simon sitting in rapt attention before her. She looked directly at Simon more than anyone else in the classroom, and said, "Now, children, this power comes from God. We know this from God Himself, through this Letter to the Hebrews. This power is also a sacred duty. I would like to know what the sacred duty of a priest is." As Sister said this her eyes continued to be focused on the student she knew wanted to become a priest someday. Simon raised his hand and Sister gestured again for him to proceed. "Go ahead, Larry."

"The sacred duty of a priest is to offer the Sacrifice, that is, the offering of the Body and Blood, Soul and Divinity of Jesus on the altar at Mass so that God can forgive our sins."

There was a short, stern knock on the heavy oak door just before it swung opened. Even Sister Thomasine was thrown off and had no time to respond to Simon's correct answer. Everyone present, including Sister, gasped in surprise as Father Michael entered the classroom. No one expected him and his arrival was greeted with joyful gratitude. The students got quickly to their feet next to their desks, and everyone automatically greeted the priest as they had been taught, saying, "Good morning, Father Michael."

He seemed to glide in his cassock as he approached the center of the classroom. Simon sat enraptured by the unexpected presence of the priest. He knew Father Michael possessed the divine power and was now fully aware that God had also called him, a simple boy from Tampa, chosen from among men, to be a priest someday. Simon still remembered how the hair on his arms and neck stood out from his skin in a natural response as he sat in class that long ago morning. That morning, Simon understood more clearly than ever, that he had been chosen by God Himself to possess the sacred, supernatural power that Father Michael possessed. Someday he too would offer that Sacrifice to God, first for himself and then for all others.

Now outside that Dallas tattoo shop, so many years since that classroom event, he held the image as long as he could. Walking toward his truck, Simon smiled to himself remembering that day in Sister Thomasine's class. His smile faded considerably however, when he climbed up into his truck and took a good, close look at his first tattoo. It was the first installment of coming clean with himself. His first proclamation to the world as he felt God had instructed him to do. He thought to himself that certainly there had been many roses in his life. But then, there had also been a terrible, piercing sword he had never expected.

Chapter Three
Lost and Abandoned

Some wounds run too deep for the healing.
J.K. Rowling

He awoke feeling guilty. This filled him with anxiety as if someone in authority had caught him red-handed in the act of something dirty and perverse. It clearly wasn't logical to feel this way but Simon couldn't help the shattered feelings he held within himself. He felt spooked. It was what Seth, one of his best friends in the priesthood used to say to him when they were young seminarians and on one of their "tell-all" walks together. Seth would say, "Today I feel a little crazy and scared."

As he drove to the tattoo shop to see Mark that morning, Simon was rattled by the way he acted the last time he saw Mark. He had even stuttered and to his recollection, he hadn't done that in years. He paused at a red traffic light not far from where he would meet Mark. How was he going to approach the subject of his next tattoo? This whole tattooing endeavor was totally "out there" but what he planned to do today went way beyond even that. The memories swirling around in his head were too awful to focus on. As he waited for the light to turn green, he wasn't completely aware that he was mercilessly gnawing on the nail of one of his thumbs. He was thinking about how this day had begun.

He had awakened in the early hours while there were still shadows from the night before and everything in his bedroom was cloaked in endless darkness. The first thing he felt was the cold wetness that made him shiver in his accustomed loneliness. The stench of urine and stale sweat were like two familiar, unwanted lovers, vile bedmates whose presence he certainly did not desire. He had gotten up and stripped his bed of the wet mess he had done. Then he had showered and stayed under the hot spray for a long time. As he dried off, it felt good to be rid of the stench and the desolation that the nightmare had left. Yet, he could not shake the shame and the guilt he wore around his heart like a tight, ill-fitting suit. On this morning, his heart ached once again. He definitely felt "a little crazy and scared".

He was early for his appointment with Mark who had last said for him to stop by and bring the sketch a little before the shop actually opened. Simon parked his truck and walked to the glass door where the "closed" sign hung in its usual place. Using the tip of his keys, he pecked away on the glass. No one stirred inside and no lights came on. He saw his reflection in the mirror facing him from within and suddenly wondered what the hell he was doing in this place again. Just a few weeks ago, he didn't even know it existed and here he was again. Maybe this whole tattoo-thing was nothing more than bullshit. Maybe it was just another fantasy in his long list of schemes to run from himself rather than face the truth about who he had become.

He was reminded of those Saturday mornings long ago when, as a boy, he would go into a darkened confessional and kneel. Simon knew only too well what it was like to wait outside a confessional in church. The priest would finally appear without greeting anyone. Then he would disappear into his niche within the confessional, ready to hear all the muck and excuses for why Catholics had royally failed at being good. It was different when, as a priest, Simon heard other people's confessions. It was easy then, to be detached and simply listen and give absolution. But as a penitent going to confess one's sins, it was quite another scenario. Simon had approached the sacramental confessional all his life, since he was a little boy and the dread he felt then was exactly what he felt at this moment. Now he was coming again to this other kind of confessional, to lay down on a cushioned table in the middle of a brightly lit room and spill out his sins to another man whom he barely knew. He had scandalous, awful things to confess this morning and he had no clue how to begin.

It suddenly hit him like a bag of bricks and he said to himself, "What the fuck am I thinking? Why am I going to spill my guts to this guy who I don't even know? Who the fuck is Mark, anyway? He's no priest with the power to forgive and to heal, right? He doesn't deserve to know this shit anyway. No one needs to know. It's best buried and forgotten." Simon felt deflated as he realized that it no longer comforted him to bury and forget. All the bad stuff floated to the top like so many pieces of shit in his miserable existence.

Simon turned in haste from the glass door he had been so eager to enter. He had to leave and he must do so quickly before Mark showed up. This whole thing was a stupid mistake. He had imagined God's voice telling him what he must do and he still had a chance to flee. The little courtyard outside the shop was a quick run toward the parking lot and the blessed safety of his truck.

He almost congratulated himself on his prudent decision to leave when he heard the unmistakable clanging of the cowbell behind him and the familiar voice calling out, "Yo, Simon, dude, I'm here, man!" Simon jerked around to see Mark waving and holding open the glass door. "I was out back. Sorry, dude, I was setting stuff up. Come on in, let's look at your sketch." The mere mention of the sketch made Simon's skin crawl. He walked forward as if a magnet drew him against his will toward the dreaded confessional.

He managed a fragile smile. "Hey, Mark. How's it going?"

"Going great, buddy. Let's get inside and check out your stuff."

Simon searched Mark's expression and tone attempting to read any sign of hesitance or rejection, but found neither.

As they entered the shop Simon felt cornered and out of place, when Mark said "I've been thinking about you these last few days since you were here for your heart tattoo." He reached out and spontaneously took Simon's right arm where the tattoo stood out brightly. Casually, he held Simon's arm turning it this way and that, examining his art work. "Definitely one of my best pieces, dude. Totally free hand on your skin. Damn, I'm good!" Mark's hold on Simon was firm and confident. He looked up at Simon and said, "I just want you to know that you should feel no pressure from me while you are here, okay? I get it that this next piece is a difficult call for you and if you feel you want to take more time to think about it, that's very cool with me." He smiled and added, "There's no need to rush something so permanent. Take all the time you need." Simon felt his shoulders were all bunched up around his neck and his muscles ached as he stared at Mark with nothing to say. Mark continued, "I sorta got the idea that it's a bitch for you to talk about it. Am I right, buddy?"

Simon could feel the heat of shame burn across his face and wondered how red his skin appeared, admitting, "Yeah, it's a real bitch, Mark, a fucking bitch but I need to do this, I need to come clean." An old scene from his adolescence flashed wildly in his memory as he resolved every week to come clean with the priest on Saturday afternoons in the confessional. It was a bitch to tell the priest how many times he had masturbated and had to admit that "yes", he had pleasured himself even after it was made clear to him that blowing your load by yourself was offensive to God. It had been a bitch to face it week after week, especially when the kind old priest was replaced by another, less gentle soul who prodded and questioned and wanted to know the details. Yet, he just as clearly recalled how refreshed he felt afterward and how his soul breathed easily once he confessed and was cleansed.

Standing there in the reception area of the shop, with only Mark standing before him, Simon hesitantly took out a folded piece of drawing paper from his pocket and held it out to Mark. His hand barely trembled but Simon knew that if he held onto the creased piece of paper much longer, his shaking would betray him. He extended his hand toward Mark's and the tattoo artist took it.

Mark walked over to the counter and unfolded the sketch, spreading out the creases with his hands. Almost without thinking, Mark whispered more to himself than to Simon, "What the fuck?" He stared at the sketch before him then turned around and looked at Simon who drew close to the counter. As he gazed upon the familiar image, Simon's skin crawled and the ghastly memory was briefly roused in all its brutality. Mark stared at the sketch as he took it in both hands, asking "What the fuck is it, dude? What does it represent?" He didn't take his eyes off the unsettling image. "That's some scary, weird shit."

Simon eyes misted briefly but his voice was steady. "It's fucked, man. It's some crazy bad, weird shit that went down many years ago when I was a kid, around fifteen years old. Very bad, in fact. Never mind."

Quickly, Simon reached out for the sketch intent on putting it away but Mark pushed him away. "Naw, naw, c'mon, tell me, what the fuck is it?"

Then Simon said softly, "I told you last time that I would answer your question even though it scared the shit out of me." As he said this Simon recalled the dusty, dark confines of the suffocating confessional back in his parish church, with its worn-out cushion tearing up your kneecaps and the latticed screen between you and the priest on the other side.

Mark admitted, "Yeah dude, listen, maybe I had no right to…"

Simon cut him off nervously saying, "I told you it was a legitimate question and that I would do my best to answer it." Simon's agitation was pouring out of him as he spoke. Mark stared at him as he listened. Simon had not expected such a reaction from Mark and cautioned, "You'd do well to throw my sorry ass out of here. You don't need to do this tattoo, Mark. I know it's way fucked. You most probably don't want to listen to all my sordid, weird shit, either. I don't know what I was thinking even bringing this sketch to you. Hell, I don't even know what I'm doing in this place."

"Look, Simon, I don't want you to feel like you have to talk about all this shit if you don't—"

Simon cut him off, "You asked me if I ever got fucked by a priest when I was a kid…you asked me that! You fucking asked me that, dammit!" The undertone of rage in Simon's voice puzzled both men for different reasons and Simon lowered his voice, "Sorry, man. You asked me the damned question and I need to tell you. That's why I'm here. I fucking need to tell somebody face to face, not just the whole fucking world at large. You, anybody. It's bad shit I've buried for years and carried deep within myself." Then in a much sadder, pathetic tone, he added, "You wanted to know, man. You fucking wanted to know."

Mark was frowning now as he took one last, long look at the image Simon had drawn and finally broke the tension in the room by saying, "Okay, Simon, let me work on the details a little. I think the hands can be made to look more like gnarled claws and this arm reaching out here could be raised in a mocking gesture, kinda like he's holding a lamp up high. Did you sketch this, man?"

Simon felt worn out like an old dishrag. "Yes, I did."

"I get the vibe, dude." Then he added, pointing to the image, "That ski mask is some creepy shit." He paused but finally uttered, "Did some fucker…?" Mark was in mid-sentence when he looked up from the paper in his hands and saw the expression of horror on Simon's face. It was a grimace somewhere between despair and humiliation.

Simon simply said, "The tattoo you will give me, Mark, is my answer to your question."

The two men stood there in that very public space unsure of what else to say. The cowbell clanged behind them as the glass door swung open and Billy entered the shop. "Hey Mark! How ya doing, my man?" He completely ignored Simon as he passed them and disappeared quickly through the swinging saloon-like doors on one side of the room. It was ten in the morning and the shop was opening for a new day of business. The unexpected intrusion was enough to put away the hideous silence that had sprung up between them.

Mark put the sketch away in one of his front pockets and said in a pleasant voice, "Okay, buddy, I'll work on this and will see you in a couple of days on the twentieth at noon, cool?"

"Yeah, Mark, thanks. I'll be here." Simon felt drained. Down the hall and way in the back of the shop the unmistakable sound of urination could be heard pouring forth from what sounded to Simon like a great water hose.

Mark called out, "Close the fucking bathroom door, Billy! Damn, how many times do I have to tell you?" Mark was shaking his head in mock disbelief. "Nobody wants to hear you pissing like a fucking water buffalo, especially me."

The door could be heard slamming but not before Billy mumbled a halfhearted apology far down the hall, "Sorry."

"That fucking Billy, he's like a kid." He paused and looked at Simon. "All will be good, Simon. See you next week." Simon shook his extended hand and walked out the door of the shop. He felt as if a very fragile, partially broken part of himself had been gently taken from him by the man who remained at the counter. As Mark passed through the swinging saloon doors his hand went to his pants pocket where he had put the sketch. He could almost see the glittering red eyes beneath the blindfold staring back. The image was very disturbing to him as he pressed it in place.

+++++

Days passed and when Simon entered The Tattoo Shop on the twentieth for his noon appointment, he saw Mark munching hungrily on a greasy egg roll and laughing wildly with a corpulent, heavily tattooed man behind the counter. The man looked up briefly at Simon as he entered and then looked away disinterested. Simon approached the red leather sofa and sat down. The heavy man who had looked up, continued to speak and uttered something guttural as uninhibited, raucous laughter erupted.

Mark almost gagged on his lunch, waving his free hand in a gesture of feigned protest for the man to stop speaking altogether. When he was able to swallow his food, Mark looked at the tattooed man through tears, and said "Dude, you are some sick fuck!" They both roared with laughter again.

After Mark had wiped his mouth and hands with several loose napkins, he called out to Simon across the room, "Come on back, Simon." Simon sighed deeply as he got up and followed Mark through the two swing doors and down the brightly lit hallway. Mark had set up his work station as before and motioned for Simon to sit on the cushioned leather table.

Mark glanced at Simon and the latter felt that the tattooer had something he wanted to say. Simon asked Mark, "Is there something you need to say to me?"

Mark held the sketch of the tattoo he was about to create in his hand and looked carefully at it for several seconds. Finally, he said, "You haven't asked me to show you what I sketched. I'm not aware of all the particulars but I'm more than aware that this tattoo represents some very bad shit for you, stuff that's fucked up and dark. But, I mean, this is going to be on your flesh forever, man. Don't you want to see it? Aren't you curious?"

Simon simply replied, "No, Mark. Not this one. I trust what you've drawn from the sketch I gave you. I don't want to lay eyes on it until it's imbedded in my flesh forever. If I had a real choice here, I would never request to have this with me for the rest of my life. But I need to voice it through this image and face it. That's very clear to me."

Mark locked eyes with Simon for the slightest, most minute part of a second and then looked away. Simon couldn't read his thoughts but was grateful Mark didn't pursue it further. He simply asked Simon, "Ok. Where are we putting this tattoo, buddy?"

Simon gestured toward his right upper thigh, just a bit closer to his backside. "I want it here. Far from my view."

Mark said nothing and moved in closer as he adjusted his purple colored work gloves and then tore at the sections of paper towels in his customary fashion. Then, in a matter-of-fact way, he said, "You'll need to take your jeans off, buddy." With a crooked smile, he added, "Yeah, get naked for me dude, ha, ha, ha. Just kidding. Keep your underwear on. You are wearing underwear, right?" The question momentarily surprised Simon and when he looked up, Mark smiled and said, "I'm just messing with you, buddy. I want you to relax. You're good here." He winked at Simon as he said this and added, "But seriously, you are wearing underwear dude, right?" They both laughed as Simon removed his shoes and shed his jeans.

Standing in his underwear briefs, Simon once again was aware of how erotic he felt in the curious setting of a tattoo shop. It is a place where one man touches another man's flesh in order to drive a long, sharp needle deep into him. The willing receiver is held tight in the giver's grip as searing, almost unbearable pain is driven into him. The receiver might very well have his qualms but he is there voluntarily and freely. It was all undeniably erotic to

Simon for another, more significant reason too. He had come to learn that there is an intimate exchange of words and stories involved with getting a tattoo and more so if the tattoos are numerous. While one is being touched and perforated, the two men alone in a room, in close proximity, become confidants of each other's lives. Certainly they are not lovers and never will be. It all belongs to another, very different realm. But the two men will exchange hidden experiences of their lives with each other as lovers often do when they become involved and trust deepens without limits. Both men will hand over delicate, secret details in confidence to the other without question or fear of ridicule. This kind of timeless fraternal bond between two men and the intimacy involved, seemed highly erotic to Simon as he lay back in his underwear ready to reveal himself emotionally to the other man. The spiritual aspect of this exchange far outweighed the physical and Simon was keenly aware of his growing excitement rather than his dread of the oncoming pain.

But today there was also another element that was fundamental to Simon in his process of cleansing himself as God had commanded. He had asked Mark not to show him his finished sketch beforehand, as he had done with the Heart of Mary. For Simon, it wasn't ever a question of admiring this image, but of the necessity to rid himself of the monstrous experience and finally come to terms with the deep wound it caused in him. He needed to be done with it, like an exorcist that necessarily needs to confront and cast out the demon in question.

Once everything was in place, and Simon had been shaved, the tattooer took the purple copy of the tattoo and positioned it meticulously on Simon's upper thigh toward his backside. Then he announced as he had done before, "Ok, Simon, here we go." The needle gun whined into life and Mark began his work. Simon said nothing for the first several minutes as the tattooer was bent over the tattoo gun working silently. He moved back to draw more black ink for his outlining when he gently said into the room, "Okay, so you told me about the good priests and your faith in them. But were they the only good priests? Where did they go?"

Simon closed his eyes and saw the faces of Father Cornelius, Father Francis and the towering Father Michael. "Well, it's like I told you, a lot of stuff changed drastically in the Church all of a sudden. It was like a whole new religion was invented and forced upon us overnight. The old priests died and the new priests that came were middle aged or younger and it seemed they were all in favor of the changes suddenly being imposed."

"Didn't people say, like, hey, we don't like this new shit! What's going on?"

"There was, of course, some of that but Catholics were well taught to obey and shut up. We had been taught that priests knew better. Hell, we were taught not to question anything that the priest said or did. Many Catholics didn't necessarily like the changes but simply accepted the new stuff because the priest said so. No real questions were asked and the changes flowed in like a fast running river, raging and uncontrolled. Every Sunday something else was changed and people squirmed and complained mostly silently but finally just accepted it."

"When a priest arrives anywhere in the Catholic world he is met with unquestioned, instant credibility and respect. This was true before the changes and at the very beginning of the outward changes. A lot has happened since then."

Mark smiled to himself but said nothing in this regard. When he did speak, it was to say, "I get all that blind respect mentality. Society at large has usually thought that way about anyone in authority. Shit, that's how people looked at government. But tell me, dude, what happened? Sounds to me like all these great holy old guys disappeared and everything changed from day to night. Well, at least for you it did, am I right?"

Simon thought about Mark's assessment. It wasn't quite so black and white but he said, "Let me put it this way: I was just a kid of twelve or thirteen when everything changed like crazy. But even as a know-nothing kid I knew that something huge had shifted. For sure, the priests who now came to our church didn't seem to me to be like the older ones had been."

"How was it so different that a snot-nosed little shit like you could tell?" Mark chuckled to himself.

"The mystical part was greatly missing in the newer priests. The whole setting in church became different for me. It seemed like it had all been turned upside down." Simon had closed his eyes and was lost in thought thinking about all of that as Mark continued to outline the tattoo. The needle hurt his flesh, to be sure, but somehow his upper thigh and backside hurt less than his arm had hurt the last time. The tattooer wiped Simon's thigh of excess ink and the blood that beaded up occasionally.

The two men remained enveloped in their solitude until Mark finally asked in a gentle tone, "So, you wanna tell me about the bad guys, dude? The ones that hurt you?"

Simon thought about Mark's question and had to admit to himself that he was surprised at how calm he felt at that moment. Without opening his eyes, he said, "One of the new, middle-aged priests that came was Father Norman. He was put in charge of us, the altar boys." Although he wasn't like the old priests I had admired, he was still a wonderful priest all the same. He always had time to talk especially if I had any questions about the faith or Mass. He was always present at church functions especially at carnivals and fundraisers. Everyone in the parish loved Father Norman. He had wavy hair with the beginning of gray, a beer belly and was a chain smoker. He never wore his cassock but he did wear black trousers and a clerical shirt and priestly collar. He could speak to anyone about anything and his smile seemed genuine and was contagious. He transmitted tranquility and goodness and once I remember him saying, "When I go to bed at night, once my head hits the pillow, I'm fast asleep. My conscience is clean."

"For these reasons I was honestly confused when, one day, he asked me a question I really didn't expect from him. Although the question bewildered me, it didn't really frighten me because, after all, he was a priest. I could trust him."

Mark suddenly looked up. "What did he ask you, dude?"

Out of the blue that day when we were outside the rectory, he said to me as if in passing, "Larry, I was wondering, do you have a long dong?" At first I wasn't sure I had heard correctly and asked with embarrassment, "What do you mean, Father?" He didn't miss a beat but casually asked again, after taking a drag from his cigarette, "Do you have a big, long dong? You're a skinny guy and skinny guys usually have long dongs." I felt hugely uncomfortable at that point but didn't want to show it for fear of somehow embarrassing him or angering him for not answering correctly. Somewhere in the back of my head I had said to myself that because he was a priest he had every right to ask me such things. I reasoned, telling myself that I was feeling uncomfortable because there must be something wrong with me, not him.

In any case, I said, "I think it's a normal size, Father."

But then, he repeated the question in another way, "Well, is it big, is it long and hairy? Sometimes skinny guys have long hairy dongs." He used that word 'dong'. It would have been stupid if I or one of my friends had used that word in our adolescent bantering. It was an outdated expression that we would have never used. But the fact that a priest had used it made the word sound very creepy to me. I asked myself at that point why he was talking that way? I knew he shouldn't be asking me about the size of my cock but gee, he was a priest after all. I reasoned with myself that he must have had a justifiable reason for the question. Still, it sounded out of place to me, a twelve-year-old because we weren't in the confessional. Not that it would have been less creepy in that milieu. But gee, I mean, the priest was right out wanting to know the size of my dick! I couldn't understand why he would want to know that.

Mark concentrated on his work but did interject, "Well, dude, that's fucking messed up, even if he was a priest, the mailman or the butcher."

"Well, I said as best I could that I thought my dick size was normal. At that point he just dropped it. He was looking away, like out into the distance as he took another drag from his cigarette and smiled to himself. He never asked me anything else concerning sex and he never tried anything weird with me. In fact, he remained the same jolly priest we all loved and respected. On the day of my First Solemn Mass, he drove many miles from northern Florida to our town and was there to congratulate me and ask for my priestly blessing. I only ever saw him as a good priest and dismissed his strange questions as not important. Of course I never told anyone that he had asked me about the size of my dick when I was a boy. Years later I heard that he had been charged and arrested for child abuse and that he did time in prison."

Mark drew more black ink as Simon finished telling him about Father Norman. "Damn, Simon, I believe that priest was what you gay folks would term a 'size queen'. If somebody would've asked me about the size of my dick when I was a kid I would have thought that was pretty strange without trying to make excuses for the perv."

"Yeah, but you have to understand it in the context of being a Catholic back then and even now in some corners. Now it seems all fucked up but back then the priest could get away with it. He was untouchable."

"Ah, an untouchable bastard who likes to touch kids. I'm not so sure it's about context, dude. I think even back then a pervert was a pervert and anybody with two brain cells to rub together could understand that. I think maybe you Catholic folks were in a fog about the priests. Shit, c'mon, admit it, maybe you were willing to let it all pass as 'weird but no big deal' because a part of you needed to. I think your understanding of good and bad was all fucked up when it came to your priests. Am I right? The older guys were good, no doubt, and even holy as you tell me, but this other guy was a sick bastard. Yet, even now, you are willing to look the other way. You seem bent on calling them all good or at least not labeling any one of them bad."

Mark's words stung Simon ears and he countered. "It's not like that, Mark, it's just that—"

"It's clear as spring water, dude. The guy was after your rocks. You just couldn't possibly gauge how close he came to doing shit to you because you were only twelve. It could have gone down really bad. You just got lucky for some unknown reason. He was a pervert." Simon felt that Mark's assessment sounded cruel and hurt him somehow, although he couldn't have said why. He wondered why he, Simon, refused to consider Father Norman as anything other than a good priest. He had learned very well everything the nuns and priests had taught him. He lay there feeling deceived and sad but said nothing. Mark continued his intricate tattooing and Simon was relieved he had finished with his harsh commentaries, until Mark said, "This tattoo is creeping me out, man, but the fact that you basically sketched this tattoo and asked for it is proof that what I'm saying to you is true, whether you wanna admit it or not." Simon said nothing, so Mark inched further, saying, "Can I ask you something?"

"Sure, Mark, fire away." There was anger in his voice and he didn't feel bad about it.

"Was this dong hungry dude the only one who was blatantly inappropriate? I mean, were there any others who struck you as queer? Pardon the pun." Simon did not offer to tell Mark that Father Norman's questions were really only the beginning of what he ultimately experienced. It got much worse. Simon was puzzled by his own concern to remove obvious guilt. Maybe Mark was right. "Were there any other creeps that put the move on you or any of the other altar boys?"

Simon hesitated and hated to admit it but Father Austin naturally came immediately to mind. "I didn't know it then, Mark, but there was another priest assigned to our church who was flamboyant and witty. Still, he was received by everyone in the way we received all our priests."

Mark turned off the tattooing gun and stood up to stretch. "Gotta take a leak, man. How are you doing?"

"I'm good." Simon lied.

"Okay, I'll be right back." He left the room and could be heard walking down the long hall. Simon heard the bathroom door slam and thought about Billy. As he lay there he was tempted to look over at his thigh and see the progression of Mark's work, but something completely aligned with the tattoo gnawed savagely in the back of his mind. In the tattered cobwebs of memories buried long ago, Simon could see the face of Father Austin.

This priest was completely bald and was boisterous and funny. He had just told Mark he was flamboyant but there he was making excuses again. Simon remembered how his father had said angrily that Father Austin acted like "una mujercita", a little woman. Even now, Simon struggled with mixed emotions as if his father were uttering the hateful words all over again toward a consecrated priest.

Still, Simon recalled how Father Austin's wit and sense of humor had a way of getting into all his sermons and this helped to make him popular in the parish. The people responded positively to that new kind of preaching. The sermons from before, from the older priests had been solemn and grave. Father Austin made people laugh as they sat in the pews. They were more like jovial conversations than stern lessons about God's anger being tempered by his mercy. After Mass, parishioners could be heard saying how much they enjoyed his words. He said outrageous things sometimes that we had never heard before coming from the lofty, intricately carved pulpit. And while not everyone was so accommodating, once again the great majority of faithful Catholics accepted Father Austin as he was, flamboyant or acting like *una mujercita*, a little woman.

Father Norman was eventually replaced by Father Austin as the priest in charge of the altar boys and this therefore, put some of us boys in much closer contact with Father Austin than before. As soon as he had arrived, he had solicited help from some of the boys to aid him in works of the parish. Most boys didn't come forward, but Simon remembered how eager he had been to impress the priest and work side by side with him, because after all, he was God's ambassador. Simon volunteered for phone duty in the rectory during non-office hours at Father's request. Simon also helped him in teaching languages to adults in the evenings in the church office. He and another boy were chosen to learn French from Father Austin as a recompense for their generosity but the other boy mysteriously stopped attending midway through the course. Father Austin always surrounded himself with young people and had all the time in the world for them.

Simon thought back and could see the priest's round face and shiny bald head perfectly in his memory. Everyone loved him. Simon corrected himself. Almost everyone loved him.

Mark burst into the work room saying, "Okay, Simon! I am back and we are ready to move on. You sure you ain't gotta take a leak? You can sneak down the hall in your underwear. There's hardly anybody here and nobody out front. It's lunch hour."

"Naw, I'm good, Mark." Simon was momentarily disoriented by Mark's sudden reappearance. Dark memories were gathering in his head like the menacing clouds that begin to gather before a violent downpour.

"Okay, just checking." He put on fresh purple gloves and repositioned the needle. "Okay, buddy." Simon closed his eyes and thought about Father Austin as Mark picked up where he had left off and Simon waded into very dark, murky waters.

In a far away corner of his memory Simon recalled the time he had invited Father Austin to come for supper at home. He recalled that the funny priest had actually invited himself and brought another young man with him uninvited. Simon's dad was working late at the bank that evening and Mom was all busy making sure the lasagna was perfect and the table properly set. The lasagna had actually been too salty but Father Austin had said cheerfully, "Oh, it's no problem really, Mrs. Zayas! We have a legitimate excuse now to drink more wine!" Mom, Simon, his brother and the extra guest had laughed at Father's joke and by the time the priest and his guest had left, it was quite late. When his father arrived everyone was in bed and the dinner was long over. Simon remembered how his mother had told his father the next day about Father Austin's visit and his joke about the wine. Even Simon's father had to laugh at the priest's wit.

One day not long after the salty lasagna, to Simon's surprise, Father Austin offered him a gift for his upcoming fifteenth birthday. He remembered it perfectly now as he lay with his eyes closed. Mark interrupted his train of thought, asking, "So what are you thinking about, Simon? You seem pretty lost in your thoughts."

Again, having been immersed in his memories Simon couldn't shake the feeling that he had been caught in the act of some wrongdoing. "I'm thinking about Father Austin, another one of the newer priests that came to our church when I was an adolescent."

"Was he a pervert too, like the size queen? Tell me about him." As Mark said this, Simon felt the sharp needle continue to tear into his thigh. Mark wiped away the excess ink and the blood and concentrating, cocked his head to one side, looking closely at the tattoo he was working on.

Simon recalled, "When I was about to turn fifteen, this priest, Father Austin, invited me to fly with him on a plane from Tampa to New Orleans. I was beside myself with joy. I had never been on a plane nor traveled very far from home before. Plus for me and my family it was such a singular honor for me to be in the company of one of our priests."

"Was that a common thing for the priests to do, I mean, invite a teenager to take a plane trip with him?"

"I know what you're getting at. No, it wasn't common but it wasn't construed as something sinister either. Rather, it was seen as a huge gesture of generosity on the priest's part. I mean, he paid for my ticket and all." Simon thought back on the event. "The plan was to go to New Orleans where his fellow priests have a university and then travel on to a place called Grand Coteau in the swamplands where they have their novitiate."

"What the fuck is a novitiate?" Mark asked this without much inflection in his voice as he worked on the tattoo.

"It's one of the levels of training a young man receives when he is preparing for religious life or priesthood. Anyhow, he knew I wanted to be a priest and since he was going to Louisiana for a few days, he said it was a perfect opportunity for me to go with him and live a couple weeks with their guys in training. Plus, as he pointed out, it wouldn't cost me or my folks a dime."

Mark looked up briefly with a sarcastic expression that Simon did not see because he spoke with his eyes closed. Mark lowered his eyes and kept working as he asked, "So it wasn't considered out of the ordinary for a priest to invite a teenager on a plane trip to New Orleans? Your mom and dad were cool with the trip?"

"Oh yeah, they gave me permission and the priest and I flew on a direct flight one evening. We arrived in New Orleans and stayed at one of Father Austin's former student's home that first night. The wealthy family was very gracious to me and Father Austin introduced me as a future seminarian of theirs. They had a maid that served me fresh squeezed orange juice the next morning at breakfast! I was so impressed. Hell, at home we drank the 'frozen from concentrate' orange juice but never fresh squeezed. That evening Father Austin took me to dine at Brennan's in the French Quarter. The owner was another former student. It was definitely a taste of the finer things in life that Father Austin seemed to be familiar with."

"The next day one of the priests from the university drove us to Grand Coteau. The old buildings there were nestled among the moss-covered trees near the swampy areas and throughout the day I could hear the different buzzing sounds of insects. It was all very old Louisiana, elegant, laidback, tranquil."

Mark asked, "How long were you there for?"

"We were there for about twelve days. Father Austin was there for a 'retreat' as he put it but I think it was more of a get-together with his fellow priest friends. He was real loud and jovial in the dining room during meals. He introduced me to all the priests and novices there, both young and old. We even went to the infirmary where all the old and sick priests were. It was such a head trip for me to be with all of them and eat in their dining room. They treated me as an equal."

"During the day, Father Austin would see me first for a walk in late morning and then in the afternoons I would meet him in his room for a talk, a kind of spiritual retreat with a meditation. The rest of the time was mine to wander and mingle with the younger men in formation although I really only saw them mostly at meals. I read in my room and went to the chapel a lot."

"Everything the first few days went smoothly but then one afternoon, everything seemed to change. It was like the third or fourth day there. Something really weird happened that would have consequences for me later on. I had gone to Father's room for one of our meditations. It was a lazy, southern summer afternoon."

Simon trailed off and Mark looked up from what he was doing. The tattooer waited for Simon to say more but he was far away in his thoughts. Mark waited a few more seconds and then said, "Dude, c'mon, you're killing me. What the fuck happened that afternoon in that guy's room?"

Simon spoke slowly, remembering that room now, as if he were a fly on the wall. "You know, now that I think about it, there was nothing physical but it was probably the first real incidence of sexual abuse I experienced, I mean, it fucked me up in my head for some time." Mark listened as he worked and said nothing. "I had knocked on his door and a voice from within told me to enter. Father Austin was sitting behind a large wooden desk that sat squarely in the middle of the shadowy, humid room. The only sounds were the ceiling fan and the buzzing insects outside his opened window. He wore black trousers and was in his white undershirt. I entered and said, 'Wow, Father, it sure is sticky today, isn't it?'"

"Oh yes, it's important to keep the electric lights off as long as we have natural light from outside. Otherwise it gets warmer in here. Keep the fan on overhead and don't move around too much or you'll melt. How is your day coming along so far, my boy?"

"Really great, Father. This place is beautiful and everyone is so friendly. Thanks so much for taking me to New Orleans and for bringing me here. I'm so grateful. It's the best birthday gift ever!"

"Oh yes, that's right! Your birthday is tomorrow, isn't it? I'm so happy you agreed to come along with me. It's a perfect chance for you to see what goes on in the training process to become a priest. Plus you are meeting the young men you will come to know as your brothers if you join our fraternity."

"Yes, I met the novices yesterday after supper and some of us stayed up talking for a good, long while. I also walked over to the place where Saint John Berchmans appeared. You know, over at the nun's convent."

"Father Austin smiled, and sat back. 'Oh yes, I know that place very well. I used to go there when I was a little older than you. My how the years pass!' As he said this he wiped the top of his bald head with one palm and dried off the perspiration on the side of his undershirt. I could see how the dome that was his head gleamed with the afternoon light outside. Then I remembered something and suddenly changed the subject, 'Something awful happened to me this morning after breakfast while I was walking near the nun's convent.'"

"Really? Do tell, my boy, do tell."

"I almost ran face-first into a huge spider web that had been spun right across one of the stone walkways. I was looking down as I walked the narrow path through the trees. Luckily, I looked up for some reason for an instant and froze in my tracks! Right there, not more than two inches in front of my face, smack in the center was a large, colorful spider all stretched out on her web! It really freaked me out to think I could have run right into it."

"'Oh? Ha! ha! ha!' Father Austin laughed exaggeratedly into the room, throwing back his head in a silly theatrical way as he clapped both his hands together. 'Yes, little buddy, you need to be real careful when you walk these twisted, narrow paths. There are a lot of poisonous insects and things that would love to bite you out here in this swampy, sleepy place.' He laughed again strangely and then appeared really nervous to me. His calm demeanor suddenly vanished and something else took its place. I waited for the priest to finish. Secretly, I enjoyed the fact that I had made the witty priest laugh but there was something that seemed artificial and staged about how long it was taking him to continue speaking. The room went strangely silent for several seconds and only the humming fan and buzzing insects filled the void."

"I stood there in front of the desk and waited for him to say something. He gestured with his hand for me to sit on the top corner of the desk. It was all cleared off except for a book he had been reading. Then out of nowhere, looking up at me as I sat there, he asked, 'Do you masturbate a lot, little buddy, when you're alone? I mean, do you enjoy taking your penis into your hand and touching yourself so that it gets hard? Do you enjoy masturbating?'"

Simon felt Mark bolt upright in his swivel chair, tattoo gun in hand, as he cried out, "No shit!" What the hell happened next, dude? Tell me. Mark had turned off the tattoo gun and stared at Simon.

"The questions took me by surprise. I felt cornered to be asked such a weird personal question. No one had ever asked me that. At fifteen years of age, I would not have admitted to anyone that I jerked off except in the anonymity of a darkened confessional while a Sacrament was going on. Yet, because he was a priest, I had no choice but to answer him honestly. 'Yes,' I said quietly into the cavernous, shadowy space of the darkening room as afternoon was giving way to the inevitable twilight to come. I couldn't look at him. I was sitting on the desk, in his room. I felt trapped in his turf."

"He seemed nervous at first, but then his tone changed and he asked sternly, 'Yes, what?'"

"'Yes, Father, I masturbate often when I'm alone.' I could feel my shame rising. 'And do you enjoy it? Do you enjoy holding yourself when you're rock-hard?'"

Opening his eyes, Simon turned toward Mark and said, "I wanted to fucking run out of that place, Mark! I wanted to jump off the desk and run home to a safe place. He repeated the questions, though, and there was nothing for me to do than to give in to his obscene interrogation. Father Austin persisted, 'Do you enjoy it? Do you?'"

"'Yes, Father,' I managed to say softly, wounded in my disgrace, found out and ashamed. I looked down at my hands not wanting to face him. 'I enjoy it.'"

"'Ah,' he said slowly, savoring every word he uttered next. 'Now I see very clearly. If you admit to masturbating because you do enjoy giving pleasure to yourself, let me ask you this, my boy. How many times a day do you do it?' I was momentarily without words and didn't answer anything, so he pressed on, enunciating each word slowly in a tone that was pure, fucking diabolical mockery. It was awful. 'How... many... times... a... day... do... you... do... it?'"

"I felt that he was making fun of me by the deliberate way he asked me the questions. He wasn't put off when I didn't answer, but asked, 'So what do you think about when you jack off? Do you think about anyone in particular or do you make up scenes? Tell me, go ahead.'" Mark's face had a sad look and Simon thought that Mark seemed almost wounded himself as he listened to the sordid tale.

Simon laid back on his side and continued but had closed his eyes again. "It all seemed terribly wrong to me that the priest was asking me all this shit and I remembered Father Norman wanting to know about the size of my 'dong'. I felt very diminished and vulnerable in front of the bald man who now made me feel cheap, filthy and perverse. As I said, in the Sacrament of Confession the priest could ask me anything he wanted to ask. But there was a huge difference here, Mark. I wasn't in Confession. I was sitting on the edge of a wooden desk, in my jeans, t-shirt and black Converse. I was just a normal, fifteen-year-old that didn't know shit about life. The priest wasn't in his sacred robes but in his undershirt. We were supposedly having an afternoon meditation talk because as he had promised me, the days at Grand Coteau were going to be like a little spiritual retreat."

Simon heard Mark say, "That's all messed up, man."

"I know that now, Mark, but at that moment, I was lost. Finally, I blurted out, 'I dunno, Father, I don't think about anyone in particular.'"

"Well, where do you usually masturbate? Do you jack off in your bed at night, under the covers? Do you do it at school in the locker room after the other boys have showered and left and you can still smell their sweaty jockstraps?"

"Not at school, Father, but sometimes in my bed at night. Sometimes in the bathroom at home before I shower." I was humiliated beyond words to be admitting to the things I had done in secret. I was staring at my hands which I held tightly together in my lap. I was incapable of looking the priest in the eyes. 'Oh, I see, finally some truth. And you feel pleasure, don't you, Larry, when you masturbate? When you touch yourself in a sinful manner?'

"I sat there almost unable to breathe and managed to answer weakly," 'Yes, Father.'

"'Yes, Father, what?' he growled sternly. 'Yes, Father, I feel pleasure.' I wondered when the embarrassing interrogation was going to end. Then he sat up in his desk chair and asked authoritatively, 'When you spill the seed, do you think it's a sin? Have you ever stopped to think about that?' He used that terminology, *spill the seed*."

"I had never heard it expressed that way. I looked at him then, 'What do you mean, Father? What do you mean by *spill the seed*?'"

"'I mean when you jack off, when you touch yourself sinfully,' he raised his voice now and bellowed, 'when you masturbate and you shoot your seed from your hardened penis.' He was irritated now and sounded impatient. 'My question is, do you realize that doing that to yourself is a very grave sin?' His tone was definitely arrogant and judgemental and his anger was not lost on me."

"I kept looking at him and heard myself say, 'No, Father, I don't think it's a sin. I've never felt dirty or sinful after doing it. I only feel relief. I never thought about it being sinful.'"

"'Really?' He asked sarcastically and smiled to himself briefly. 'Really?' he dramatically repeated again as if possessed by great disbelief. Then I saw that his smile had nothing to do with kindness nor humor. It was something far more evil that I was incapable of understanding then. The smile completely evaporated and he looked at me unforgivingly, like a harsh judge handing out a cruel sentence to an unrepentant criminal. I sat there on the edge of the desk staring at the man I had held in such high esteem. I feared what he would say next to me. I mostly feared his rejection and condemnation."

"I tried to give an answer to his questions but began to stutter, 'I-I…don't…' Before I had a chance to finish responding, he unleashed the fury of his contempt for me, 'Well, let me tell you something, little boy, you will need to know full well from this moment on that masturbation and touching yourself to the point of spilling your seed is a horrible, filthy sin. You must cease doing that immediately. You should feel very disgusted about touching yourself that way. It's a dirty, sinful act and makes a man unworthy of approaching the priesthood.'"

Mark said softly, "Damn, Simon, I'm so sorry."

"I was stunned beyond words, Mark, mostly because he now knew this personal, horrific secret I had kept from everyone else." In that humid room of shadows, I answered, 'Yes, Father.' I felt crushed and lost to think that he now saw me as a filthy pervert unworthy of priesthood. From that day on I always felt guilty, dirty and sinful when I masturbated. I made weekly visits to confessionals in different churches on Saturday afternoons during my high school days so that I could worthily receive the Body and Blood of Jesus on Sunday. I felt just awful about myself and tried my best not to masturbate. Sometimes I was victorious in my battle with lust but usually I gave in and felt miserable afterward until I could find a priest to hear my confession.

"Father Austin had told me it was sinful and I believed him because he was a priest. During all my years of religious formation and for many years of my priesthood, I confessed this 'terrible, horrible, filthy sin' and often felt great disgust over my weakness. The 'dirty, sinful act' of masturbation weighed heavily upon me and I often became discouraged and wondered if God would strike me down in His just wrath."

During this monologue, Simon was aware that the tattooer had stopped working and listened in rapt attention. "You were just a horny kid, Simon." Mark sighed. "Gee, you were just a normal guy."

Simon continued, "The afternoon light was waning in the humid room by the time the tirade was over. Father Austin had nothing further to say to me. When he did finally speak, the pace and tone of his words had returned to their normal cadence and he didn't ask me any more questions. I felt deflated and of course I felt completely exposed. Father Austin got up from his chair then, and walked toward the door. He switched on the pale ceiling light and casually said, 'It's beginning to get quite dark, you know. It will soon be time for prayers and supper.' There was no judgement in his tone now. 'Best get to your room and wash up before then. See you in chapel.' I left his room in silence, feeling as if I had been badly beaten up. But I also felt very grateful."

Mark asked, "Grateful? You felt fucking grateful, dude? For what?"

"I felt grateful because the priest had dismissed me without any apparent rejection. I mean, he told me to go wash as if I were still a good, decent person and I was grateful that he had not cast me away altogether."

"Dude, that conclusion about gratitude sounds fucked up to me."

"I felt grateful, Mark, because he hadn't said something like, 'You're a pervert and I never want to be seen with you.' I felt grateful as I walked alone down the endless, sterile corridor of that religious house, even though I was confused and very wounded."

"He sure as fuck called you a pervert." Mark sounded angry.

"Not long after we returned to Tampa, Father Austin called me and said that he was going to northern Florida to preside at the wedding of a niece. He wanted to know if I would like to accompany him. I was overjoyed that he had asked me. It only proved to me that he didn't think I was a complete sinner and pervert. I felt so vindicated in the priest's eyes. His invitation meant to me that he still considered me worthy to have a vocation to the priesthood. I felt relieved because Father Austin didn't think any less of me because I had admitted to him that I masturbated often. My gratitude toward the priest only increased. I begged my parents to let me go for the weekend with Father Austin and they said 'yes'." Simon raised his head and looked at Mark.

Mark's brow was furrowed as he stared at Simon and said, "Look, I get it that you were all giddy because you were only a kid of fifteen. You were grateful. But you're telling me that your folks said yes?"

"Why not, Mark? Why would my parents have said no? After all, he had taken me to Grand Coteau for the retreat and paid for everything. I had raved about the trip and the plane ride. I hadn't said a word about the interrogation. How could I? You think a fifteen-year-old kid is going to talk to his folks about jerking off? You think that same kid would have exposed the priest because he asked him all those weird questions? I think not. Anyway, nothing seemed out of order. Remember, I wanted to be a priest and as far as I was concerned, Father Austin was only helping me to gain a better understanding of priesthood and to prepare for it."

Mark chuckled sarcastically. "Oh, yeah, I'll bet that fucker was preparing you."

"C'mon, Mark, I'll admit it was strange but…"

"Ever hear the term 'grooming', man? Damn, Simon, sounds like you're always making up excuses and covering for the priests."

"No, I haven't heard that term but you don't even know the priest I'm talking about and you already stereotyped and judged him."

"I'll be honest with you, Simon. What you're telling me is some creepy stuff and it sounds to me you've still got your head up your ass about who some of these fuckers really are. You really didn't tell your folks or brother or somebody about the weird shit he said to you in that swamp-place you were at?"

"No, I didn't." Simon felt embarrassed.

"Well, there you go, man. You fucking had that priest on a pedestal." Mark's low opinion of the priests somehow hurt Simon and he was irrationally offended. In his mind, Simon reasoned that Mark couldn't possibly understand about the priests because he hadn't grown up as a Catholic, especially in the old days when the Catholic Church was different.

As he lay there, Simon felt that maybe he had said too much to Mark. Maybe all he was doing was giving Mark an edge to criticize priests. He felt he needed to be protective of his faith and was on the defensive until Mark suddenly blurted out, "Dude, I meant no disrespect and the stuff you're telling me sounds awful but I have to challenge you. I really think you're full of shit and the proof will be in your honest answer to my original question. Did you ever get fucked by a priest when you were a kid?"

The question hung in the air between the two men. Simon asked meekly, "What does being 'groomed' mean, Mark?"

"Answer my question first, Simon. Tell me what happened on that trip to the wedding up in northern Florida with that priest. Don't make up excuses just admit what the fuck happened to you? You did go with him, didn't you? I'm sure you did." Simon was speechless. His first reaction was to strike back at Mark, ask him who the fuck he thought he was. "Answer my question, dude, by telling me what happened to you. I don't think you really want to admit what happened. Shit, you might not even be aware of what really happened, are you?"

Simon started to say, "It's just that—"

Mark cut him off rudely, without much grace. "Just tell me what happened, Simon." Mark had held the tattoo gun in his hand even though he had turned it off. He now switched it on and said, "I'm almost done here. Just about another forty minutes. I'm all ears." As he said this, he wet a paper towel and wiped off the excess ink and the blood once more.

Simon felt the bite of the needle again and it reawakened in him the hideous memory that Mark demanded to know. "My folks weren't well-off financially," he slowly began as he closed his eyes and remembered his family and their home. "My father worked as a banker by day in two separate banks. At night he worked as a janitor cleaning various office spaces and warehouses. Sometimes my grandmother and my brother and I would help him by emptying trash cans, cleaning toilets and sweeping hallways in order to help make ends meet. My mother worked for a large insurance company. By the time I was fifteen years old, we were a family of four plus my grandmother who lived with us."

"When Father Austin invited me to accompany him to the wedding in northern Florida, he offered to cover all my expenses as he had done on the trip to Louisiana. I was anxious to impress him on the upcoming trip. As the days drew near I fretted over what to do about the few things I needed to bring with me on the weekend trip because I had no luggage. This had been a problem before my previous trip to Louisiana but I had improvised then and took care of it. The truth was that we really didn't have any suitcases. Our family trips were limited to the nearby beach and when we did go there we simply took our clothes and things in a variety of baskets and woven handbags. I remember saying to my mom, before my first trip with Father Austin, 'Mama, I can't take this trip with Father Austin using a brown paper bag from the supermarket as a suitcase!'"

"So now, once again, I improvised. I used the same empty, hard black carrying case that once held a Smith-Corona typewriter. I simply turned it into a weekend suitcase and convinced myself that no one could tell otherwise. I told myself it looked like the Samsonite cases I had seen downtown in the windows of the expensive department stores. I secured a sticker right where it read Smith-Corona on the handle with my name and address to hide the evidence. No one would know."

"I packed my little 'suitcase' and tried to act cool and collected as Father Austin and I left Tampa on the long drive early one morning. As we left Tampa, news came to us that a tropical storm had been brewing in the Atlantic and was aiming for the coast of Florida. It was threatening to be a dangerous storm but it was still far away and didn't seem at all real. I was fifteen and very naïve.

Father Austin drove and I sat in the passenger seat next to him. We listened to the radio and between programs, storm alerts warned of the approaching menace on the horizon."

"Father Austin was his comical self throughout the long journey. He made jokes and sang funny songs. He told me about the priesthood and its demands and answered all my questions. I relaxed and immersed myself in the knowledge that I had been chosen by the priest to accompany him on this trip. We stopped for hamburgers and cokes along the way. Angry clouds were well in place on the horizon as we reached our destination. Huge rain drops began to fall as we climbed the front porch where many relatives had already gathered for the wedding the next day. It might sound strange to you, Mark, but it was the first time that it actually dawned on me that priests also came from regular families like mine."

Mark didn't look up as he said, "You thought they dropped out of the damned sky, huh?"

Simon ignored the remark. "We hurried to the church for the rehearsal that late afternoon, everyone scurrying about, trying not to get wet by the downpour that had gripped the small community on the eastern side of Florida. After the rehearsal, we all went back to the family house for supper. The adults had drinks. I was the only teenager there and Father Austin once again introduced me as a future candidate for the priesthood. It made me feel like an adult myself. Although there was some concern about the worsening weather conditions, the evening passed quickly mostly because Father Austin entertained everyone with funny family stories that made them howl and squirm with laughter. Everyone was giddy as the booze flowed and he held sway over them."

"When it got to be late, someone suggested that it might be bedtime given that the next day would be full of activity and celebration. Father Austin explained to me what the sleeping arrangements would be as he whispered, 'There are too many relatives staying here at the house already. There won't be any privacy here for you or me. My older sister already reserved a motel room for us nearby.' Then he added, 'None of us had counted on this awful weather, but it seems that the storm is just going to be a nasty inconvenience. It's nothing to be concerned about and should pass quickly, soon to be forgotten. It's just some crazy, Florida heavy rainfall. No sense in making a big deal about it. No worries.'"

"He got up and began saying goodnight and before I knew it, we were running to the car again, trying to dodge the sheets of heavy rain that enveloped everything. The storm continued pelting everything in its path as we made our way to the motel. It was night and the violent storm was well in place. The priest had said that the motel was not far and sure enough, it was only a short distance from the house and we arrived at the tiny office there in a matter of minutes. Father Austin jumped out of the car and said to me, 'You wait here, I'll register and get the key.' Then he added, 'No sense in both of us getting swept up by this storm.'"

Mark stopped working and stared at Simon, but did not interrupt him. Simon's hands were rolled up into tight fists as he spoke and his eyes were tightly shut now, not merely closed. Simon had quickened the pace of his words as he said, "I don't know why but I felt very homesick as I had felt in the humid room in Grand Coteau. I felt terribly uneasy and frightened and wanted to jump out of the car and run home, to be in my room with my brother and hear my grandmother's television down the hall blaring the evening news in Spanish. I longed with every fiber to be close to my parents as they argued in the kitchen and hold my dog close to me as he licked my arms. Something was very wrong and I knew it was wrong but I didn't know what it was. I knew it would be time to go to bed soon and that meant Father Austin and I had to undress and get into bed in the same room in front of each other. The thought made me shudder."

"He finally came out of the office and ran to the car. His bald head was beaded with water and he wiped his face with both hands. He drove us around to the other side of the gravel parking lot and stopped in front of number five. When we got out of the car in silence, I could feel and see that the gale had gained incredible momentum since we had left the house. I gripped the handle of my 'suitcase' and quickly jumped out. The gravel was inundated with water and I realized that this was no mere heavy rainfall. I was walking into a terrible storm."

"Father had only a small leather suitcase which he took with him to the room. Under the narrow, slanted roof that served as an awning over the long corridor outside the doors of the motel rooms, black bugs flew crazily around a bare, orange colored light bulb as Father inserted the key and entered the room, switching on a bulb that hung in the center of the ceiling. I followed him in and immediately recognized the strong aroma of pine oil cleanser. A brown colored, threadbare rug covered the entire floor of the tiny motel room and I could make out at least three or four distinct stains on it that reminded me of the great clouds I often saw in the sky on summer afternoons. Two narrow, sagging beds were side by side and a bedside table was between them. It was chipped and scratched and topped by a tall lamp with a dented, oversized shade. Father Austin lit it and a yellowish light exposed the flatness of the pillows perched up against the wall. There were no headboards and I could see that the wall was splattered here and there with dried yellow drippings that ran down and disappeared beyond view."

"I stood by the door staring at a crooked curtain rod when I heard Father Austin saying merrily, 'Well, what are you staring at, my dear boy? It's not a Waldorf Astoria but it's only for one night. Plus, once you close that door, you'll forget all about that storm. Trust me.' I had no idea what he was talking about because I didn't know what a Waldorf Astoria was. I only knew that I felt terribly out of place. He chuckled as he said, 'Close the door behind you, why don't you, before you let all the light out into the night, there's barely enough inside for us as it is.' I pushed the door shut and felt trapped. I approached one of the beds and put my 'suitcase' down on it when I heard Father say, 'I'm going to take a shower', and with that he disappeared into the bathroom, closing the door behind him."

Mark sat still as he listened. Simon's throat went dry as he said this last and remembered that night. The memory of the noise he had heard next made him wince. It was the sound of running water, pouring out profusely from the shower head in the bathroom. This was the ghastly noise that thundered in the nightmares that visited him so often and left him soaked and full of shame.

"I heard the loud sound of water pouring out of the shower head through the cheap, thin walls of the bathroom. I could hear Father Austin clearing his throat and spitting in the sh-sh-sh-shower. Everything star-star... ted... started... started... to move too quickly then, and I-I-I sat on the edge of one of the beds."

Simon paused and Mark slowly said, "Dude..."

+ + + + +

But Simon didn't hear him. He was lost in the fiendish memory and continued speaking, "The bedsprings creaked and protested as I sat down. The sound of running water filled the tiny motel room as I saw in my mind the frail, bent figure of Father Cornelius in his worn-out, shiny cassock getting ready for Holy Mass. A single thought came to me and it was that Father Cornelius would certainly never bring me to a motel room where he and I would sleep together. Father Cornelius would never go in to take a shower while I waited in the next room. I was a naïve fifteen-year-old kid but I wasn't stupid. It was crystal-clear to me that being in that shabby and grungy motel room was terribly out of place and that things were moving too fast."

"Father Austin finally came out of the bathroom with a towel wrapped around his generous waist. To me he seemed to be an old man, ancient even, but I knew he was only middle aged. He looked different wrapped in the towel. He had a big belly and skinny legs. His jowls looked drooping and he needed a shave. His flabby chest and abdomen were covered in matted gray hair and as he dried his bald head with a smaller towel, he said excitedly, 'Oh boy, that was a great shower! Lots of pressure. You need to get in there, lad! Into the shower you go. Wash up before bed.'"

"But I protested loudly, 'No, no, I don't think I'll take a shower right now. Tomorrow morning is way better. My hair will be all wet if I shower now and I hate putting my wet hair on the pillow like that. I think I'll take a shower tomorrow morning before we leave for the wedding.'"

"'No, Larry.' Father's voice was steady. 'There won't be enough time tomorrow in the morning. I have to be at the church early and you need to come with me then. Go on and get in the shower now.' I hesitated but knew I could not win. Still, I insisted, 'I'd prefer to shower—'"

"'Didn't you hear me, boy? Wash that wax out of your ears while you're in there,' he joked. 'Get in there and wash up now! Don't make me say it again!'"

"I took my pajamas and underwear out of my 'suitcase' and laid them nervously on the bed and then put them back in the case. I walked toward the bathroom to take a shower as I had been told to do. As I neared the brightly lit bathroom I realized that the strong scent of pine oil came from this space. The red linoleum floor was cracked but clean. I noticed that several pieces of the beige tile along the walls had been replaced by tiles of another color and still others were missing. I locked the door and saw my expression of fear reflected in the mirror that faced me behind the door. I could hear the storm beating wildly against the small window panes in the bathroom as if it were intent on breaking in. Lightning and thunder intensified."

"I began to undress as I had been told to do by the priest and stripped down completely. I tried not to think about how uneasy I felt. I turned the hot water on in the shower and waited. In the mirror, I saw my reflection again. It struck me as odd and out of place that I was actually in this eerie space completely naked now and that in the other room beyond, a stranger was waiting for me. He was probably naked too. I wanted to cry. How had this happened?"

"As I stood there and glanced in the mirror, I felt lost and abandoned. Even though I was well into puberty, becoming a man physically, still, inside, I was just a kid, and now a very frightened one. I felt deep down in my gut that something awful was going to happen to me. I knew without fully knowing that something horrific was lying in wait for me on the other side of the thin wall. Whatever it was that was there, I knew it wanted me and that I was powerless to stop what was coming."

"As I dried off, I thought about Father Austin in the room and I hoped that he would be fast asleep by the time I came out and got into my own bed. I was sure that I would fall asleep quickly. It had been a long day and by tomorrow morning everything would be okay and by nightfall I would be home."

"I wrapped the towel tightly around my waist and made a knot which I tucked in carefully just over my waist. I opened the door and saw that the room was dimly lit in the sickly yellow light of the lamp between the two beds. I thought that Father must be asleep and that he left the light on for me to find my way to my bed. As I exited the bathroom, I saw that my worst fears had become reality."

"The priest had removed the bedspread and was lying on top of his narrow bed, completely naked with his skinny legs spread wide apart. His penis was fully erect and he was stroking it as he displayed it for me to see. Even more disturbing to me than that was when I saw he was wearing a black knitted ski mask over his head. It covered his face and went down over his chin. Only his eyes, nose and mouth were exposed and it made him look monstrous. He was staring directly at me. As he played with himself, he seductively said to me across the room, 'Come over here now, Larry, and climb up on top of me. I have something for you. Don't be scared now.'"

"I stood in the middle of the room incredulous of the spectacle before me. Of course, I didn't want to go to him but he was the priest. In those few seconds, I tried to reason with myself that something must be wrong with me, not him. He wouldn't hurt me, would he? He repeated to me that I was to lie on top of him and barked with growing impatience, 'Come over here right now!' My mind was a blank and my feet wouldn't move. I was frozen in place until I heard him again and saw that he had raised himself up on one of his elbows while he continued his stroking slowly with his other hand, 'I said get here now! Am I going to have to get up and drag you here, boy?'"

"I began walking as if in a dream toward his bed and from that moment on I remember things as being in slow motion. In the blur that ensued and enveloped me, I walked like a dead man and as I neared him on the bed, he sprang up suddenly and grabbed the towel around my waist, roughly pulling me to himself as he muttered, 'Dammit, get moving! You've made me wait!'"

"He tried to lift one of my legs over him but the towel was on too tight around me and heaving, he undid the knot I had made and yanked the towel away coarsely, tossing it carelessly onto the floor between the two beds. I was totally naked in front of him as he looked me up and down. He said nothing but I could hear his labored breathing. Then with both hands he lifted me making sure that one of my legs went over him so that I would be straddling him. Water trickled down my back as he lifted his knees up, making sure that I was in place on top of him. He pulled me down by my wet hair and I could feel his flabby, bloated belly rubbing against my chest as if he were made of jelly. I instinctively moved up and away as my flesh touched his but it was far too late for that. I could not get away now as he wrapped his arms around me and began to roughly massage the small of my back. I was pinned against the course hair on his chest."

"I struggled to get away but he was stronger than me. With one strong arm, he held me to himself and with his other hand he took his time to feel my ribs and groan to himself. Then his hands moved down my thighs as he held me and applied pressure. He massaged me as he moved and rubbed deliberately and slowly, reaching as far around as he could. He brought a hand up and over my bottom and taking his time, massaged me there. Then he moved his fingers knowingly into my crevice and pressed in deeply."

"I let out a gasp as he invaded me and heard him whisper to himself, 'Yes, my boy, that's the sweet place.' He continued to prod and felt as much of me as he desired, reaching as deep as he could inside of me. He sighed over and over again and heaved out loud. His groans sounded much deeper as I became a ragdoll in his arms. When in this way he had violated me from behind, he put his hands under my armpits and pushed me up further onto himself so that my face was now on his. Roughly, he tugged on my penis and I felt him jab his hardness between my legs, pushing under my testicles repeatedly like a piston. There was no fight left in me at that point because his voracious hunger and insistence had overwhelmed me."

"I moved my head down to one side of his face trying to avoid his gaping mouth and felt the lump of his damp ear brushing against my nose. Forcefully, he took me by the ears and straightened out my face on his, pushing me down on himself. His mouth devoured mine as he kissed me violently. The edge of his ski mask was heavy with his saliva and went slightly into my mouth as he slid his tongue onto mine. A wave of shock and revulsion swept through me like nothing I had ever experienced as he raped my mouth with his tongue."

"He overpowered me physically and emotionally. He invaded me as long and as much as he desired. My skin broke out in gooseflesh as he held my mouth on his. I could feel the hardness of his erection brushing against my inner thigh. I tried in vain to slip away from his tight grip and managed to turn my head away from his mouth as his teeth clashed with mine. I was panting from fear like a hunted animal caught by one more powerful and it was then that I finally succumbed to my fate. I had no fight left in me and I succumbed to the beast who held me captive to do whatever he wanted with me. I had once admired and considered him to be holy and good but now I only grew numb and cold in his self-absorbed, ravenous embrace."

"I remained on top of him, impaled, sprawled and straddling for what seemed to me to be an eternity as he violated me. He moved me around as he pleased and I heard his moaning and his sighs as he pleasured himself at my expense. I went to a distant, faraway, place within myself, a dimension where the horror of what was being done to me would seem harmless and ethereal. I went deep into nothingness. I felt like an object and not a person and I was so frightened that I hardly breathed hoping only that it would soon be over and I would be freed."

"Outwardly, I must have appeared passive because I had stopped thrashing and fighting to be free. But inwardly, there was only thrashing and chaos in the deepest recesses of my soul. Within me I silently screamed wildly and as loudly as I could, to God, to anyone who might hear and save me. But there was no one. No one came to help me. I was on my own, utterly abandoned. My mind raced and spun on itself as I spiraled way down, into boundless nothingness, into my only hiding place. I have no idea how long it lasted or what else he did to me, but at some point he shoved me off callously with both hands and I fell to one side, away from him, almost onto the floor between the two beds. I could see my damp towel there, in a tangled heap."

"He said nothing to me as he got up off the sagging mattress with effort and headed toward the bathroom. He was done with me and although he had not uttered a word, I sensed his rage in the room. I was afraid to move and did not change the position I was in for a very long time. Even when I heard him return and crawl into the other bed, the one reserved for me, I did not stir but kept my eyes tightly shut as if I were asleep. I heard the mattress screech as he moved and turned off the lamp not far from my head. The tiny room was swallowed up in total darkness. I have no idea when he removed the ski mask from his face and I did not see it anywhere in the morning. All I could do was simply lie there, too bruised and broken to move."

"A monstrous, wretched thought crept into the corners of my mind then. In the gloom of that night, I wondered to myself if he would return for me once more. I wondered with horror if he would again do to me what he had already done. In those endless hours of unspeakable loneliness and abandonment I even dared to wonder if the beast snoring loudly in the other bed might be roused from sleep and come to kill me in his rage. I felt like I was somehow the cause of the rage he bore. In the utmost solitude I have ever experienced in my life, I lay in that unknown, foul place alone. On the sagging bed that was not my own, with my hair and ears still wet, I dared to wonder what would happen to me."

"The hours passed and I remained in the same position. The water in my ears eventually dried somewhat as did the trickle of bright red blood that had run lazily down my inner thighs. I was aware that the place under me on the mattress seemed less damp than before. I had no pillow and no bedspread to cover myself in my nakedness. I was cold and felt empty, violated in body and soul. My limbs ached for days afterward because of the rigid position I was in and because of the stress and misery I had endured. At some point, I dozed off into shallow sleep. The violent storm had passed."

"After the wedding the next day, Father Austin and I began the return trip. He was witty throughout the ride and no one could have guessed what he had done to me the night before. Even I had to remind myself that all was not well and that the man sitting next to me was not who he appeared to be. The soreness in my limbs and the heavy shame I wore were my constant reminders of the unspeakable things that had been done to me."

+++++

Mark sat motionless on his swivel stool. The tattoo gun had been turned off. He stammered as he said, "Simon, I'm so sorry."

When Simon opened his eyes and focused on the bright lights overhead in Mark's workroom, he didn't look at the tattooer but softly said, "That is the answer to your question, Mark." Then he turned his face toward him.

Mark sat dumbfounded by what Simon had told him. His eyes were not focused on anything in particular. Unable to say another word, he took the tattoo gun and switched it on. He finished the tattoo of Simon's abuse in a jarring, perplexing silence that neither men knew how to undo.

Chapter Four
Trusting

What loneliness is more lonely than distrust?
Sir Arthur Conan Doyle

Only one thought seemed to be coherent in Simon's mind and it dominated him entirely as he lay on the tattooer's worktable in his underwear. In that frigid space the only thought that gripped him was simply to get the fuck out of there. He felt he would start screaming like a lunatic if he didn't get out of there soon. In his mind, bits and pieces of agonizing memories and shame flew around and fused with each other causing him this unbearable desire to flee. What had he just told the other man about himself? Simon wondered almost aloud to himself if he had gone completely mad? How could he have revealed such horrible and personal experiences to someone who was practically a stranger off the street? What was he thinking? How could he completely trust someone he had only just met a short time ago?

Simon looked up at Mark who was quietly cleaning up his workspace. What had driven him to reveal so much of his dark, frightening past to this man? He hadn't told a soul in the entire world about the things Father Norman and Father Austin had asked him and he sure as hell never told anyone about what Father Austin had done to him in the motel. Why had he let it out now? It seemed to Simon that it was like that involuntary reaction that takes place when you eat and drink too much. It had been like vomiting violently once he had gotten started, without being able to control it. As he looked at Mark, Simon had no doubt about why there was such a stark silence between them now. Mark now knew some bad shit about him. At the very least he must certainly think he was a pervert. A dull fear overtook Simon's heart that suggested to him that Mark would not ever want to see him again, let alone touch his flesh and tell all that remained to be told. Why had he given himself away so completely? Why? He was so angry with himself. He had to get the hell out of the shop and he had to do it as fast as possible.

Simon sat up stiffly. He felt ridiculously exposed as he looked at his bare legs. He could feel the back of his t-shirt damp with his own perspiration. It stuck disgustingly to his skin. How long had he been there spewing the sordid details of his past?

Mark's voice interrupted his anguished musings, "Okay, buddy, take a look. We are done here. For whatever its worth, your tattoo's complete." Simon remained rigid and silent, looking fixedly, at no particular object. He did not know what to say. Mark was facing away from Simon when he had spoken and now as he turned toward him on the table he looked at the work he had just completed and gravely said, "I've never tattooed anyone with anything close to this." Then he added, "Just a sec, let me wipe off some of the gunk and blood before you get up." Gently, he cleansed the area of tender skin on Simon's upper thigh that now bore the appalling tattoo. "There you go, dude, take a look."

Simon barely heard the tattooer's words as he moved close to the edge of the table and dangled his feet. His mind was racing and he could only think of his shame. He had pushed so many terrible memories far down into himself that he really never thought about most of it anymore. Until now, that was. He could not bear to look at the new tattoo that everyone would see. Worse than that, they would want to know what it all meant and of course, they would judge him. He had no doubt about that. What had possessed him to do such a thing? All that terrible shit should have remained buried inside of him forever.

A flood of emotion was building in him like a pressure cooker and he knew he had to get out right now. The unspeakable pain and shame that had once beaten and ruined him so intensely now pierced his heart like a finely sharpened sword all over again. Bits and pieces of the recurring nightmare that visited him so often now ran amok through his mind, competing with each other for primacy in his frazzled mind. Beads of fresh blood ran down his thigh and reminded him that this new impression stamped into his flesh would never go away. All that had happened so many years ago could not ever be removed or washed clean. It was a hideous, diabolical stigmata he would never want to contemplate. For so many years he had managed to fetter the loathsome truth of what had been done to him against his will. But now it was out. He had let it out freely and could barely believe he had not considered the consequences.

He himself was the irresponsible jailer of his carefully kept secrets. He had stupidly let out the disgraceful truth of his terrible shame. No one had ever known except he himself and the one who had done it to him. Not even another priest because he had never confessed it to anyone. Now Mark knew and everyone else in time would know of his iniquity. Simon felt himself slipping away into an ocean of despair and he looked up at Mark without saying a word, not knowing what to say.

Mark tilted his head crookedly to one side and asked, "You okay, man? You seem distant and on edge. Your face is all fucked up." Simon looked at his feet and did not move. Mark was unaware of the unchecked fury building within Simon. Simon simply sat there and an uncomfortable silence filled the room. Then Mark asked unwittingly, "So, tell me Simon, you've told me all about the good, holy priests and about the really bad ones. What about you, Simon? Are you a good priest or a bad priest?"

As Simon heard this question, it struck a terribly fragile, bruised chord in him. The questions had begun as he had suspected they would. The judgements would follow. He felt himself being pulled away and losing control. He was caught somewhere between sorrow and anger and thrown up between profound disappointment and shame.

He looked up at Mark with a blank expression on his face and managed to say in an exhausted tone, "Depends on who you talk to…it depends on so many fucking things…so many fucking, rotten things." The tattooer waited for him to say more but Simon unexpectedly jumped off the table and grabbed his jeans, intent on dressing himself. He was ready to flee.

Mark suddenly asked in disbelief, "Hey wait, dude, aren't you gonna look at your tattoo? I thought—"

"No!" The word sprang out between them like some wild beast springing forth unexpectedly, suddenly free from its confined cage.

"What? I don't get—"

"I said, fucking 'no', dammit! I don't fucking wanna look, okay?" Simon had his jeans on and was searching the room for his shoes.

"Dude, wait, what are you doing? I'm at a loss here. At least let me put some antibacterial on that tattoo and wrap you in plastic. You're still bleeding a little and that's gonna hurt like hell by the time you get home if it dries on your jeans. Hang on, man." Mark found the tube of antibacterial gel and approached Simon who was bent over, struggling clumsily with one of his shoes. He finally got the shoe into place without bothering to tie the laces. Mark barely put his hand on Simon's shoulder when he said, "C'mon, sit a sec and let me wrap that thigh." He was taken aback when Simon retracted wildly and pushed his hand away.

He growled at Mark, "Don't you touch me!"

Mark looked wounded for an instant and then said in angry disbelief, "Huh? What the fuck is wrong with you, man?" Simon didn't bother to respond as he worked on getting his foot into his other shoe, grunting impatiently. Mark was clearly upset as he threw the tube of ointment violently on his worktable. "Dude, it was just a fucking question, I mean, we were talking about all your shit with wanting to be a priest and all. Don't freak out on me, man. Sorry if I crossed a fucking line somewhere. You told me some crazy shit is all. Damn, I was just making conversation when I asked if you were a good or bad priest. Truthfully, I really couldn't give a shit either way."

Simon straightened up now and stared at Mark. In a low voice that was barely audible, he managed to say, "Yeah, I know you couldn't give a shit, but you wanna know, don't you? Well, it just depends, Mark. It depends on so many things… I mean, I didn't become a priest overnight. It took all kinds of shit and years to become a priest. But I will tell you this…" Simon breathed out impatiently and finally said, "I've always wanted…I've always only just wanted…" His voice betrayed him and he could not continue, realizing he would lose control over his emotions if he kept speaking. His eyes filled and stung. Several large, burning tears ran down his face as he looked down at the floor. When he was able to compose himself, he looked up at Mark in his blurry vision and wiping away his sorrow whispered, "I've always…only…just wanted…to be a good priest. I just wanted to be a holy priest, the very best priest ever. But things happened. Bad shit. Life got in the fucking way, man. Why did it all have to be so fucking rotten sometimes along the way?" He looked down and tried to control his emotions.

"I get that. But you were the one who wanted to tell me all about it. Now you're in my shop acting like a fucking crazy man. You won't even look at your tattoo. What the fuck are you doing here, man?"

"Honestly? I don't know what I'm doing here but I'm outta this place right now! I'm done here. I have no idea what possessed me to even come in here."

"That's fucked, Simon! Grow up and grow a pair, why don't you. You think you have a monopoly on pain? Everybody has skeletons, everybody hurts."

"Fuck you, Mark! I don't owe you any explanation. Fuck you!" Simon's voice was high-pitched now and he was pointing a finger at him.

Mark warned him, pointing right back, "Lower your voice, dude. Nobody comes into my shop and screams at me like a fucking nut job. You get the fuck out now!"

"I'm outta here, asshole!"

Mark stood in the center of his workroom and glared at Simon. "You little pussy. You come in to me and talk all this shit and want me to listen and you feed me all your fucking Catholic crybaby stories and now you tell me that you don't owe me any explanations? Dude, you're the one with all the tales of nuns and shit. You're the one so damn eager to talk about priests wanting to suck your cock and fuck your little boy ass!"

"Fuck you, motherfucker!" Simon screamed and glared incredulously at Mark. "Fuck you!" Simon turned and walked hurriedly out the doorway and down the hall toward the reception area.

He saw that Billy had entered the corridor and was standing there by the swinging saloon-like doors with a look of disbelief on his face. As he passed him, he heard him ask meekly, "Is everything okay back there?"

Mark was right behind Simon and roared angrily, "No, everything is not okay here!" Simon pushed Billy aside and entered the reception area of the tattoo shop. He was momentarily surprised to see that the small reception area normally vacant was now quite crowded with clients.

The room was in complete silence and all eyes were on him. As he tried to push through toward the front door of the shop, all eyes went from Simon to Mark as the tattooer emerged and bellowed at Simon, "Dude, get your ass over here, we need to talk!"

Simon kept moving blindly and did not turn around but simply answered, "Fuck you! I owe you nothing!"

"Get over here, dude!"

"I'm done talking!" Simon knew he had to get out of the place because he was losing it with every second he remained there.

"Don't be such a pussy. You're the one who was going to face all his demons and have them right there every day to look at! It was all bullshit, wasn't it, you pathetic priest shit. You're such a fake. Now you're backing out!"

Simon froze in his tracks and turned around slowly, barely able to contain his wrath, "Who the fuck do you think you are? I may be pathetic but I sure as fuck don't owe you any explanations." Simon began to walk toward Mark and several people standing in the room moved away and huddled together as everyone witnessed the unbridled display of outrage and insults. When he had reached Mark, Simon stared up at the taller man and finally asked slowly, enunciating each word carefully, "Who…the fuck…do you think you are…to call me a pathetic priest shit?"

He got in his face and continued, "You think you're so fucking cool? Who told you that you have your shit completely together? You think you're a fucking god in this tiny corner of the universe putting out your little ink cups and driving your needle into people's skin. You think its hot shit to talk about pain in here. There's all kinds of pain, dude, and you haven't got a fucking clue about my life and my pain. You have no idea what I'm talking about. You couldn't possibly understand my pain."

"Hey, you're the one who wanted to come in here and tell me all the fucking details. I didn't seek you out, you stupid fuck! You came to me, remember? Fucking crazy stories about religion and altars, about God appearing and disappearing. Old baldheaded priests fucking you in cheap motel rooms."

"Don't go there you bastard. Leave it alone." Simon glared at Mark.

"You're the one who wanted to talk about all the shit they put into your head about jerking off in your bed or in the locker room. You're the one who told me how much guilt and pie-in-the-sky bullshit they fed you as a kid in that all powerful Catholic Church. And now you have the balls to come in here and call me a motherfucker? You're the sick motherfucker if there ever was one, Father! You need to pull your head outta your ass and live in the real world instead of that LaLa-land fantasy you refuse to let go of and your precious suffering, grief and pain." Mark looked around the reception room carefully. Nervous coughs could be heard but no one moved.

Simon took a step back and said weakly, "Shut the fuck up, bitch!"

"No, you shut the fuck up, bitch. You're in my house now. You came here to disrupt my place of business."

Simon was drained and had crossed his arms tightly against his trembling chest. "I came searching for someone to help me look at myself. Someone I could trust again. I thought it was you!"

Suddenly, an uncomfortable silence between the two men hung in the air. Mark softened his tone, "Hey, buddy, you're the one who fucking freaked out in my workroom just a few minutes ago. You're the one who's acting like a fucking Doctor Jekyll and Mister Hyde. What happened back there, Simon? Tell me 'cause I don't have a clue. What the fuck happened back there a few minutes ago? One minute you're one person and the next you're some fucking asshole."

Simon looked at Mark but was unable to hold the other man's stare. He looked away saying, "You can't possibly understand. You can't even get close to knowing what I'm talking about. All you want to know are the gory details of priests and nuns. All you're interested in is knowing if priests really fuck altar boys and how they do it." Simon looked angrily at everyone gathered in the room and said, "That's all everybody wants to know. You don't stop to think for one second that I'm just a man, a regular guy trying to make sense of a whole lot of bad shit that derailed my dreams."

"I thought that was what we were doing. You came to me and we were getting to know each other. You were the one talking your ass off to me, dude."

"I talked my ass off because I trusted you. For some fucked-up reason, I trusted you. I needed to trust you." Simon paused and then added bitterly, "I thought I could trust you. But then you were the bastard asking me all the fucking questions. You don't really give a shit. Nobody does. The truth is I am alone and what I most loved has disappeared and what I wanted to be is gone. It slipped away through my fingers way before I realized it was long gone. I wanted to tell you, Mark, I wanted to confess and purge myself but it hurts so damn much. It fucking hurts me so much." As he said this last, he was hugging himself very tightly and could not control his tears. He looked up at Mark and then turned around again at the crowd that was gathered in the tattoo shop. He now saw that there were all kinds of people there bearing their own tattooed stories. Some had brown or black hair and there were blondes. But he now noticed those with orange and purple hair. Some had embraced the emo look while others had shaved heads and bleached beards. Ears, noses and lips were pierced with rings, barbells and labrets. There were overweight men and women, some terribly so but also muscular, handsome men. Most were young but there were a few middle aged people and in the small crowd there was also an old man with a long flowing white beard. Every inch of his body appeared to be tattooed. Simon looked at each of their faces and saw that some looked shocked while others appeared to be simply baffled by the show he had just put on with Mark. Through stinging tears, he said to them as a crowd, "I only always wanted to be a good priest. I only wanted to be God's best. My one desire was to stand every day at the altar, wearing the sacred vestments and bow there in that sacred place for hours. To offer God the Sacrifice for myself and others. I've only ever wanted to be a bridge between God and the open wounds we all have." Simon paused and not caring, sucked up the mucous that was threatening to drip out his nose. He wiped his eyes and dried his hands on his jeans, adding, "But things got complicated and I got lost. I got so fucking lost."

From behind him, Simon heard Mark's familiar voice, gentle and calm, "How did it get complicated, Simon?"

"You couldn't possibly understand, none of you could."

"Well, try me." Simon took a deep breath and exhaled. He closed his eyes and tried to gather his frayed thoughts. He finally said, "I…I realized I was gay and I didn't know how to manage my hedonism. I still desired to be holy but I wanted to fuck and explore. And then there were certain priests when I was a kid and in Rome…" Simon trailed off. "God pulled a fast one on me. He gave me the desire to be a good priest and he made me a gay man with a hedonistic appetite to be reckoned with. He created in me an adventurous and mischievous spirit. I tried my best, I tried for years to do both things, to live in two worlds." Simon turned directly toward Mark and said, "I admit that I was wrong to create this scene here, man. I'm sorry. It all got tangled up inside of me and I lost control. I don't know how to unravel it. I need someone to help me unravel it, but no one seems to understand. But I don't know. I thought that by talking about it, getting it out of me…"

Mark moved in closer to Simon and said "Dude, keep talking to me, tell me."

"You can't understand how horrible I am. I dream sometimes that if I wasn't gay and so lecherous everything would have worked out. I could have been that good priest I dreamed about becoming. I wonder what my life would be like if I were a good priest. I wonder how things would have turned out if the Church hadn't changed almost completely and disappeared for me. It seems to me like it's almost gone. If I had never broken my vows I could be worthy of God. But I fucked it all up. Yet I know that if I hadn't accepted being gay and if I hadn't come out mostly to myself, I'd be all screwed up like so many are because the truth is that God is the one who made me a priest and a gay man. I couldn't change that. I can't change that now. Like I say, there was a point in my life when I ran from the truth of who I am and I lived in two worlds. It was awful and I turned my back on love when it did come and threw it away as if real love is something cheap and easy to find, as if it was worthless. I hurt people because of my hunger for power and opulence. I created huge wounds because of my lust, but most of all…most of all I hurt myself badly. I betrayed myself over and over again. I covered for some fellow priests and kept my mouth shut for the good of the Church. In some cases they were powerful people but some of those guys fucked me over later on and threw me to the lions. No one can possibly understand all this." The crowd in the shop remained in place and no one moved. Muffled coughs and clearing of throats could be heard.

When Simon had finished, Mark said softly to him, "Well, tell me then. Tell me so that I can understand." He cleared his throat and whispered to Simon, "And just for the record, bitch, you can trust me."

Simon's eyes filled with tears at hearing Mark's words and admitted, "I need to unravel my past. There's too much there that wears me down. I'll always be a priest and I'll always be gay. I'll always be me. I'm still trying to reconcile the two."

Simon could feel the rawness on his skin as the dried blood on his tattoo tore here and there when he moved. He turned and saw that some of those who had been standing had left and others were now sitting on the large red sofa in the center of the room. There were two or three people talking to Billy and pointing to the jewelry cabinet on the wall.

Mark reached out and held Simon by his shoulder. "I hear ya. I do." He looked at him but said nothing more and then let go and went back down the hall to his workroom. Simon was spent and he turned around and exited the tattoo shop without looking at anyone. He walked out into the stifling afternoon heat.

+ + + + +

Several days passed before he had the courage to return to the tattoo shop. He hadn't paid Mark for his last tattoo. Billy told him that Mark was with another customer but that he had written down what he owed and Simon then settled his account. With some trepidation he asked Billy, "You think I can I go back just for a sec? I need to ask Mark something about my next tattoo?"

Billy smirked and murmured, "Shit, it's no skin off my ass, dude. You know where he is."

Simon walked down the corridor and as he approached Mark's workroom he could hear the whining of the tattoo gun. To have said he felt uncomfortable would have been a massive understatement. He didn't know how to approach Mark since that awful scene he created in the shop. Simon reasoned with himself that it would be brief and this helped him to enter Mark's space. With trepidation, he knocked on the doorframe. "Hey Mark, sorry to bother you, man, but I forgot to pay you the other day on my way out."

Mark looked up from the young man he was tattooing and drew more ink onto the needle in his hand. "Yeah, you fucking little cheat! Trying to get away without paying! I know your kind." He laughed to himself, although Simon thought that his voice was more guarded than playful.

"I paid Billy what you said I owed." Simon felt terribly insecure and his nerves were frayed as he stood in the familiar place.

"Cool." He was concentrating on his work now and didn't look up when he asked, "So what's your plan, your strategy? When am I gonna see you next?"

"I know what I want next. It's very similar to the heart tattoo you already gave me." Simon extended his arm and gestured to the tattoo of the Immaculate Heart of Mary.

Mark glanced up and then returned to his work. "Okay, cool. Tell you what, gimme a call later today and we can set up an appointment. I'm busy here now and can't really stop to get to my book. You say it's pretty similar to that tattoo?"

"Yeah. It's called the Sacred Heart of Jesus. Some of the details are different but it's basically the same size and the same amount of work."

"Okay, gimme a call later and we'll set it up. You can drop off the sketch whenever, before we meet, okay?"

"Actually, I have it here." Simon walked in and set it down on a stool near Mark. You can look at it later when you have a chance. "Thanks. I'll call you later then."

"You bet." Just before Simon turned around, he was surprised to hear Mark ask, "You doin' okay, Simon?"

"Yeah, man, I'm good."

Mark hadn't looked up from his work, but said, "Cool."

As he walked out of Mark's shop that day Simon realized he needed to shake off his doubts about trusting Mark. He had to vow to himself as he drove home that afternoon that he would not bullshit the man. If he truly desired to come clean and heal, then he had to do so honestly like he had always done in the sacramental confessional. He never lost control confessing to a priest and he certainly would not do so confessing to Mark. God had been clear on the point of coming clean. He would need to remember that often.

+ + + + +

Simon returned to the tattoo shop some days later. He stared at the bright lights on the ceiling while lying on the tattooer's cushioned work table. He had asked Mark to place the tattoo of the Heart of Jesus on his left arm in the same position as the heart of the Mother of God. Mark had teased him, "And let me guess…you want it upside down so only you can see it right side up? Correct?" They had both laughed.

Simon was thankful that things were good again between them. "Yeah, I want to see it."

"So why do you want this strange-looking heart?"

Simon hesitated, trying to find the right words. He certainly didn't want Mark to think he was going to start going down the same, twisted path. He wanted to be honest and so he said, "It reminds me of my wanting to be a priest, when I began my first steps in that direction, when I finally left home to do so."

Mark was starting to fill the small plastic cups as he said over his shoulder, "Okay. Keep going, I'm listening."

"This heart is all about God calling out to me. It's about God searching for me."

Mark turned on the tattooing gun and looked at the purple sketch he had already transferred onto Simon's arm. As he dipped the needle into black ink he asked, "How so? Tell me about it, dude. What does it all symbolize?"

Simon gestured toward his right arm. "Well, remember this other heart?" Mark nodded. "Well, this represents the human heart that searches for God through good stuff in life but also through bad times."

"Oh yeah, the sword and the roses, right?"

"Yeah, exactly. Well, the heart you're working on now it's called the Sacred Heart of Jesus. It represents God's heart, which is both divine and human, since Jesus was both God and man."

"You lost me, buddy."

"Let me put it this way. This heart is the symbol of God yearning to be always with us, in the stuff of our lives. It's a symbol for the compassion God feels for us because God knows we get lost a lot."

Mark was listening as he drew more ink and said, "To be honest, Simon, I've seen it represented in tattoos all the time but I had no idea what it all means. It's a common symbol for tattoos."

"This heart is surrounded by a crown of thorns. It means that God shares in our suffering so we know that He knows how painful it is to be human. God is constantly in the middle of our sufferings rather than just on a lofty throne looking down at us from a faraway Heaven."

Mark stopped working and asked, "Okay let me see if I got this right. This heart is about God suffering as a man just like us? It means that he knows our shit just like us? Do you really believe that? I'd never thought of God as being right here in the middle of our mess. God usually seems so absent in our fucked-up world."

"Mark, that's the whole symbolism here. The heart of God is wracked by pain as our lives often are, but at the very top of the heart there are flames that burn wildly."

"Yeah but where the fuck is He most of the time?" Mark drew more ink and then asked, "What do the flames mean, anyway?"

"It means that God understand us and he burns with the desire to be with us. God is always aware of our whereabouts even when we think we are lost. God is always present in our fucked-up world even if we don't feel like He is."

"What do you mean by 'when we think we are lost'? We are either lost or not."

"Sometimes we feel we are lost but God is actually right there with us. We're never really lost in that sense. I guess it's more accurate to say 'when we wander'. God is never absent, though. Even if we think so. There's a reason for why we stray. There's a plan for everything. If we never got lost we'd never know what it really feels like to be found and home again."

"So you believe God lets us get in trouble?"

"Well, I can't read God's mind but I do believe He lets us be free. We're allowed to choose what we want and go where we wanna go. Sometimes we choose good and sometimes we choose stuff that ends up hurting us. But in any case, God never loses sight of us. He's always very close by, ready to help us pick up the pieces and start again."

"Pretty heavy stuff, dude. I'm not sure I understand it and I don't think I believe it. I am curious to hear you say this stuff today, though." Mark looked at Simon and continued speaking slowly as he worked, "It's just a different tune you're singing today from the one you belted out last time. Don't get pissed, but you sounded like you were lost to the hilt last time you were here and had no fucking idea where to go." Mark turned off the tattoo gun and looked at Simon. "I mean no disrespect, dude, but today you sound really calm and clear with all your neat and calculated explanations about God being close always and so on. I'm smelling a massive pile of bullshit. You didn't sound so convinced last time. Am I wrong or did I miss something?" There was silence in the room but it was quickly dispelled when Mark turned on the tattoo gun again. "I dunno."

Simon felt his face reddening as he realized the truth that Mark had just served him. He had had a meltdown when he was faced with the reality of the abuse and all its ramifications. "I was all wild and fucked-up last time. I'm really sorry for that."

"That's ancient history, buddy."

"But there's a reason I freaked and that reason is I never told anyone about that. I kept it buried like I keep so many other things buried and that is what fucks me up. I know now that God wants me to tell the whole story." He paused, then continued, "I know now it's the only way for me to heal. If I hide my shit, I'll stay in a very bad place. Still, it's not easy for me." Simon wanted to be clear with Mark and added, "I really need someone I can trust in order to do this."

"I understand." Mark said nothing more and Simon was embarrassed to say what he needed to say.

Finally, Simon blurted out, "I need to trust you, man. I need that right now more than anything if I'm going to heal." Simon felt that his face was on fire and hoped Mark wouldn't notice. But more than this, he hoped Mark wouldn't reject him.

"I'm just a guy here, I'm not perfect but you can trust me." For what seemed like a long time of silence to Simon, Mark said nothing more. He concentrated on his work and Simon didn't know what else to say. He certainly didn't want Mark to think he was weird. He let it rest there. Finally, Mark asked, "So all the religious preaching and explanations aside, did choosing this heart have anything to do with you becoming a priest?"

"Absolutely, Mark. I left home to answer a call. Remember you asked me if I was a good priest or a bad priest?"

"Do I ever! The question made you panic and freak." Mark's remark embarrassed Simon and he recalled the scene in the reception area. Simon thought Mark had every reason to be alarmed.

"Yeah, again I'm sorry about that. I have to admit that you are right. I mean, I was crazy with panic because the question is so huge for me. It can't be answered so easily with just a simple 'yes' or 'no'. Not if I'm really honest, it can't."

"Well, answer it a piece at a time. Tell me about how you began. Where did you go, to some training academy or workshop and then simply apply for a priest job at a Catholic church?" Simon thought back and remembered the long ago journey.

"Naw, naw, Mark, it's not like that at all. It's really a way of life that you begin to live from the time you arrive. They call it being 'formed'. It takes about ten years to be formed and receive the studies to become a priest. After all that formation, a bishop passes on the priesthood in an ancient ceremony by imposing his hands on your head. Being a good priest or a bad priest depends on all kinds of stuff but I guess it's fair to say that all of us who feel called and answer the call begin at the very same place. In my case and the guys I lived with, it meant traveling to Pennsylvania to an incredibly beautiful abbey that lies in one of the most peaceful places I know on this earth."

"Ten years, huh? And imposing hands on your head, dude? Gee, help me out here."

"Yeah."

"That's a long time to prepare. Did you know it would take that long to become a priest?"

"I did but I had no idea what the ten years entailed. I only knew that I wanted to be a priest and that desire is what helped me get the courage to leave home. I'm from Florida. The hike to Pennsylvania was scary in many ways."

"How old were you, dude?"

"I was seventeen."

"Damn, that young? How could you be so sure you were doing the right thing?"

"I just knew it was the right thing. I only desired to be a priest since I was a kid, like I told you."

Marked smiled. "Oh yeah, since you were sneaking under the house, huh?"

Simon smiled as well. "Yeah, since then. But after the shit went down in the motel room with that priest, I had a period of time in my life when I still wanted to be a priest but I didn't talk to anybody about it. It was about a two year period, give or take."

"Why not?"

"I'm not really sure why. I guess that really fucked-up, scary experience shook me and a part of me was reluctant to even think about it too much. But a huge part of me still wanted to be a priest because God was doing the calling. This was the main reason I wanted to be a priest. It's still the only reason I desire to be a priest today. It's because God personally called me. He chose me, not the other way around. It wasn't simply a career choice for me."

"I never thought about it that way but I think I'm starting to get the picture. Don't you think that God is a smart enough guy to know who He was calling when He called you? I mean, don't you think He was aware of your weaknesses and that you're a horny gay fucker?"

"Seriously? No, I never thought about it that way. I only thought that I had to be perfect and that I get myself involved in my sins. That's how I've always seen it." Mark shot him a disbelieving sideways look.

"Not too realistic, huh, dude? You really think it was your sin in that motel room? C'mon, you were just a scared kid trapped in a nightmare squarely in the path of a fucking pervert."

"No, I suppose I'm not too realistic sometimes and I know now it wasn't my sin. But it took me a long time to wade through all that shit. Anyway, I didn't talk about wanting to be a priest after that went down. Before that motel shit happened, it was all I could talk about. Everybody knew. But after the motel thing, I kept my vocation to myself. Then in my senior year in high school I befriended a nun who had always been at the school and now was one of my teachers. Sister Mary Agnes, the young, beautiful nun. She taught us a class in creative writing. After school, I'd stop by to help her with anything she might need and we would eventually end up talking about all kinds of things. She was traditional-minded like me and was sorry to see the changes in the Church as well. One day I confided in her that I wanted to be a priest. She was very cool and encouraged me to pursue it. I remember that she reminded me that the call did not come from within myself but directly from God. I trusted her."

"Did you tell her about the motel?"

"Fuck no, I didn't! I never told anyone about that until the other day when I told you."

Mark dipped the needle to retrieve more ink. Then he said, "Really? No one? I guess you really did trust me the other day. Why didn't you trust that nun? You didn't trust her with that kind of info?"

"I don't think it was about trust then, as much as it was about my shame. I couldn't talk about it because I felt it was my fault, my sin."

"That sounds so fucked up to me but I understand how it could make sense to you. But you did trust this nun with letting her know you wanted to become a priest? So there was a level of trust."

"Yeah, I knew that she would understand. I wrote a piece at that time which really marked the new period when I once again spoke openly about wanting to be a priest."

"What's it about?"

"It's entitled, 'A World Altogether Different'." It describes going into a lofty, beautiful temple and discovering God inside.

"I'd be interested in reading it if you have a copy."

"Actually, I do somewhere. I'd have to search but it's one of the few things I've ever kept from those days in high school. Sister Agnes thought it was very well written."

Mark smiled broadly to himself, and said "You and your nuns. Sorry, dude, but I gotta say it. You almost cream outta your huge boner when you talk about your nuns. Ha ha ha."

Simon had to smile at Mark's grotesque expression but was getting to understand the tattooer better each time they met. "Yeah. I loved the nuns. They were always there for me. Anyway, it was my senior year and we were always being pressured about the career we wanted to pursue. Once I told Sister Agnes, I was encouraged to tell one of the guidance counselors at school, and not long after that I told a classmate or two at school and my closest friends at work after school."

"Where did you work after school?"

"It was a hamburger joint. All my closest friends worked there. They weren't Catholic and went to public school but knew I wanted to be a priest once I graduated. The guys were all cool about it and rarely made any comments but there were three or four girls there on our night shift that kidded me all the time."

"Oh yeah? What would they say?"

"Well, most of them said it was such a waste to go lock myself up in a monastery but this one girl promised me that she was going to make sure that I lost my virginity with her before I left at the end of summer."

Mark bolted up and excitedly asked, "Whoa! That chick said she was gonna fuck you, dude? Damn!"

"Yeah, that's what she said."

"Oh, fuck, but wait, hold on! You're gay. What happened? Fuck!" Mark held the tattooing gun slightly up in the air as he waited for an answer. It whined and whined in his hand as if it were angry for the sudden interruption in work.

"Well, I actually had the hots for a guy my age that worked there. His name was Bill. He and I used to hang out a lot after work with another guy I was also attracted to named Dave. They didn't have a clue I was queer for them. Now, just for the record, Mark, I really didn't have any clear understanding that I was gay. I mean, at that time I felt attracted to these guys but didn't think about it too much. In fact, I would have denied it. I was seventeen and really didn't know I was gay. I talked and acted like I was straight and gave the appearance of being so."

"Yeah, buddy, you had me fooled. Cost me a beer with that bastard, Billy."

"I believed that I belonged to God and that it was important for me to answer the call. I didn't fuck around with anyone then. I had never experienced sex with anyone in my life except for that abuse in the motel room."

"Dude! Was the chick hot?"

"Huh?"

"That chick that promised to fuck you. Was she hot?"

"She was blond with perfect teeth and big tits. I remember she would sometimes follow me when it was my turn to take all the trash to the dumpster out back on the property. She would sneak up behind me and try to make out with me."

"Dude! You're killing me! What would you do?"

"She would follow me and she would try and make out. I wasn't interested. Nothing happened. Nada. I was a seventeen-year-old kid who was gay but didn't know it yet. Plus, I had plans with God."

"That sounds fucked up. Sorry, just kidding."

"It's cool. It was easy to get rid of most of the girls who made a move because by the summer everyone at work knew I was leaving in August for the abbey to begin to study for priesthood. Most everyone said they didn't believe I would actually stick with it except for my two best friends. They totally understood me. We were a group of about ten who always worked the night shift on Fridays and Saturdays and afterward we'd all drive down to a nearby beach. We'd go swimming and drink beer and sometimes smoked weed. Some of the guys did pair off with a girl and make out and fuck behind the dunes but most of us were just friends. Like I said, I was attracted to Bill and Dave but at that point in my life was ill-equipped to do anything about it. I was really just a kid. The only one who explicitly offered to fuck with me was that girl I mentioned."

Mark was applying color to the Heart of Jesus and immersed in his work, but managed to inquire, with raised eyebrows, "The chick with the big tits?"

"Yeah, her, but it never materialized as I knew it never would. Months earlier I had already written to the abbot in Pennsylvania about entering at the end of the summer. Several weeks later I received a letter from him confirming my acceptance at the end of August. It was all set."

Mark stood up and stretched. The intricate design of the divine/human heart was completely outlined. Red ink had been applied to the image. "Simon, I think I'll do the fire around the heart in tones of yellow and orange. It'll contrast really well with the red. I need to stretch and make a couple calls. Need anything to drink, you know where the fridge is, okay?"

"Thanks man, I'll get to the restroom if that's okay."

"Sure. Let's break for a few minutes."

Returning from the restroom, Simon could hear Mark's muffled voice from the reception area of the shop. He went back into the workroom and stood in front of the large mirror admiring the tattoo of the Sacred Heart of Jesus. He held out both arms in front of him and examined the hearts of Mother and Son. He sat on the work table and laid back. His thoughts broke free and he was back in time. He thought about his own mother. He saw himself in one of the wooden nooks of the public library where his mother would take him and his brother Bobby when they were boys. It was a hobby they all shared in a place they loved which smelled of old books and waxed wooden floors. The silence there permitted each of them to escape into their favorite world.

Since Simon could remember, he had always been fascinated by anything Russian, especially history, and Tsar Nicholas II, the last Tsar of All the Russias. It was a tragic piece of history that both enthralled and deeply saddened him. When the revolution finally broke in Russia during the First World War, glory, grace and opulence in Russia had been replaced by stupidity, cruelty and ugliness. The loving family had been mercilessly butchered by much lesser men and literally chopped into pieces like cattle before being thrown into an abandoned mine shaft. During the course of one night, the devil had been busy about his work and a dynasty spanning over three centuries was wiped out, just like that, gone as if it had never existed. As a child, Simon was deeply moved by those historic events and when his mother would take him to the library she always knew where to find one of her little boys. The other one, Bobby, was always in the sports section. Simon remembered going up to the checkout desk to a severe-looking librarian glaring down at him and saying, "These books are for older children and adults. I don't think these are for you." Then turning to his mother and the stern woman would ask, "Is he going to be able to understand these books?"

Simon's mother assured her, "Oh, yes, he's quite capable, trust me. It's right up his alley."

One by one he had read the books in the Russian history section, especially those about the Romanov family, the powerful and ancient Russian Orthodox Church, the Ballets Russes and Russian art. He loved the tragedies, especially Petrushka and the puppets. He had savored the things he read about Russian villages and the spirit of the Russian people. Tsars like Ivan the Terrible, Peter the Great and Michael the first of the Romanovs, fascinated him but the one he most identified with was Nicholas, the very last Tsar. It was this Tsar's faith in God and love of family that moved him most and Simon understood why the people recognized him as the true "Little Father", that is, God the Father's earthly representative. To Simon, everything in that magical world of palaces, power and beauty had been as it should be. Then terrible things had begun to take place in a series of horrid events that ultimately spun out of control and spiraled into an unspeakable nightmare. It had all changed almost overnight.

As he remembered this period of Russian history that so captivated him, Simon heard footsteps coming up the hall and heard Mark's words before the man himself entered the workroom, "Hey buddy, you doin' okay?"

"Yeah, everything is great. I'm loving your work, man."

Mark smiled. "Thanks. I'm glad you're happy with it. I'm embarrassed to say so but I need to step out for just a bit. I normally wouldn't do this but it's a personal thing I need to address like right now. We can either book you for another appointment this week or if you're cool with it you can wait for me here. I shouldn't be that long but I do need to take care of this. It's really urgent. Sorry."

"No problem, Mark. I can wait here."

"Cool. I shouldn't be more than an hour or so, okay? Sorry, for this interruption, man. Make yourself at home here."

"No problem, I'm good."

"Okay buddy, thanks for your patience." Simon heard Mark go out through the saloon-like doors and faintly heard the cowbell clang. Then the shop was silent once again except for the sound of a radio playing in another workroom and a distant whining sound. He saw his reflection in the mirror and stood up. He tried to imagine his life's journey recorded all over his body. He turned away and stretched out on the work table. He stared at the white ceiling above him and thought about a Russian prince he had once read about. It was because of that prince and how he had lived his life, that Simon had decided to write to the abbey in Pennsylvania and request admission there.

Prince Demetrius had been born in Saint Petersburg, Russia, toward the end of the eighteenth century to devout Orthodox parents belonging to the court of the Tsar. When the prince was a teenager he had been profoundly moved by a book he had read on the life of a Roman Catholic martyr. This prompted him to read more about the life of that saint. It was not long before he held in his heart an earnest desire to convert to the Roman Catholic faith.

His parents were so opposed and embarrassed by their son's behavior that they threatened to disown him and take away his inheritance.

Simon had been moved to his core as an adolescent when he had read of Prince Demetrius' resolve not only to convert but also to become a Roman Catholic priest despite strong opposition. The prince followed the call from God and was summarily discarded by his family. For months his life had actually been in danger and he had fled his beloved Russia for Paris where he prepared for the priesthood. After years of preparation and study, he had been ordained a priest and traveled alone across the Atlantic. After months of an arduous journey he arrived in the small, wilderness village of Leicester, Pennsylvania. The Archbishop of New York had happily appointed him pastor of souls in the tiny, rural, forgotten village. The people there were mostly German settlers and life was stark. The young Russian prince-turned-priest worked hard for many years in his priestly ministry to the people and he was rewarded by the Church for his abilities and his dedication. Prince Demetrius was eventually consecrated Bishop of Leicester and under his authority the Catholic community grew by leaps and bounds.

Not long afterward, Bishop Demetrius requested the aid of German monks who came to work with him from Europe. These men were hard working, devout Roman Catholics who brought with them knowledge and skill. A few were university professors of theology, philosophy and anthropology. There was a painter or two among them and several who were organ builders and musicians. Others had been farmers, bakers, skilled carpenters and architects. Many of them had brewed beer and ale in Germany their entire lives and brought their craft to America. The monks, both priests and lay brothers, were thus highly respected by the people of the region for their solid personal character as well as their skills and soon their numbers swelled as many young men came to Leicester expressing a desire to live as they did. These devout men assisted the prince-bishop in the pastoral needs of the growing numbers of German immigrants in western Pennsylvania. The brother monks did the manual labor and in this way sustained their daily needs while the priests received jurisdiction to administer the Sacraments to the people and prepare future priests. By the middle of the nineteenth century it was obvious to all that more space was needed to house the monks. Bishop Demetrius himself planned on taking up residence there and the cornerstone of the massive foundation was laid for the great abbey in Leicester in 1856. It would house the bishop and the community of German monks who worked alongside him. At that time the community numbered ninety eight professed members, as well as provide a much needed, adequate seminary and houses of formation for the training of future priests and religious.

The abbey was an impressive stone and brick structure representative of the architecture of its day and would be self-sufficient, primarily through the brewery and the dairy farm run by the monks. The production of their beer and ales were well known all the way to Pittsburgh in the west and Philadelphia in the east. Thus it was, that in the span of a few short years, the abbey filled with many young men and there were plenty of strong hands and sharp minds among them to run the brewery, the dairy farm and the seminary that was attached. Bishop Demetrius' abbey was a model to follow in its day and continued to be so for many years into the future.

Simon could have joined a seminary close to home in Florida if he had chosen to do so but it was this connection with Russia and the prince that drew Simon to the abbey in Leicester. It was the personal story and determination of the prince that had inspired him to follow God no matter the cost. As per his wishes, Prince Demetrius was buried in the crypt under the main altar of the immense Gothic church there.

Simon closed his eyes and remembered the night before he had left home for the abbey at Leicester. His suitcase had been packed between his mother and grandmother. They had embroidered his name on his shirts and his underwear according to the instructions of the abbey because laundry was done there in common by the brothers. He was to take one black sweater, two white shirts, two black trousers, one black tie, underwear, black socks, and pair of black shoes. He could bring a pair of jeans or casual trousers for work days. He was to present himself in a black suit, white shirt and black tie. Room and board would be taken care of by the abbey. The letter he had received indicated that very little clothing should be brought since in one month's time, he would receive his first religious habit which he would wear daily. No need to bring a coat since two woolen capes would be supplied, a light one for fall and another heavier one for winter.

Packing the small suitcase had been bittersweet for them that night prior to leaving the next day. The three of them had gotten giddy with laughter as a way of dealing with the impending departure the next day. A dream was finally unfolding but the beloved boy of seventeen was leaving home forever and this fact was difficult to deal with. Friends had come by the house to say farewell and he had sat with them for hours on the porch drinking beer and wondering when they would see each other again. The guys were jovial but again there was sadness in the air. He was letting go of everything he knew and everyone he loved.

When his friends had finally left, it was far past midnight. The train was slated to leave in about nine hours. He entered the large living room, carefully shutting the screen door behind him and making sure the latch was in its place. It was late August and the heat was stifling. As he crossed the length of the darkened room he heard the sound of muffled crying coming from the sofa on the far side. He approached and recognized the small, unmistakable form of his mother lying in her dress there. Tightly, she held a handkerchief in one hand and rested the other across her eyes. As he knelt next to her on the floor he felt as if his heart had been torn out from within him. A great weight of sorrow pressed heavily upon him as he saw his mother weeping in the shadows.

They had always been close and they had grown closer still since the death of his father some years before. Even though he had never been close to his father, Simon still loved him. They had never told each other, but on one exceptional occasion, father and son had told each other as much. It was a secret that Simon never forgot and held on to.

As a boy, Simon relished the fact that his father was a banker and worked in a large bank that was air conditioned and had very high walls covered in marble slabs. Sometimes Simon's mother would take him and his brother to see his father work at the bank in his dark suit, white shirt, and tie looking very handsome and dapper. He remembered his father now as he knelt in the darkness. Bobby, his brother had always been closer to their father, sharing a mutual interest in sports, especially baseball. They had a relationship Simon never knew. Still, even though Simon never had that with his dad he remembered what had bonded them together. It was their love of dogs. Simon loved listening to his father often talk to him about Nellie, his own childhood dog in Cuba when he was growing up. There was even an old, crumpled black and white glossy photograph that Simon kept and often studied privately. It was their intimate narrative.

There had been one particular dog, Becky. She had been special to them. His father had shown him how to carefully remove the fat ticks that had gorged themselves on Becky's blood and then step on them and hear the crunch. It was important not to pull on the parasites but to light a match and quickly apply heat on the tick. Even now, in the darkness, Simon still remembered and smiled to himself. And there was the matter of food and water and how important it was to remember to feed Becky. Simon had loved Becky so much that he would sleep with her in her dog house and drink water with her from her bowl. His father had taught them about the importance of giving money to homeless and needy people, doing homework every day and taking a bath. Although they had not been exceptionally close, his father had been there for him in his own way. And then one morning, he had suddenly left them all, without warning. It had all been very tragic and surreal when his father had suffered a fatal heart attack. That horrific event had changed everything at home. His brother had become the man of the house, but then not long after, Bobby had left home to get married and the responsibility fell to Simon. Every week on payday he had given his mother his entire salary and she in turn would give him half.

Now there was only his grandmother, his mother and himself at home. In nine hours he too would be gone. He knelt there not knowing what to say and only held his mother's hand in his own. They both wept in the darkness understanding what a bittersweet moment this was. It was a wonderful moment because he was beginning his life's journey. He was finally able to respond to God's call and would one day stand at the altar as a consecrated priest to offer the Sacrifice. But it was also a terribly sad moment because he was going very far away.

In the stillness of the darkened living room, he heard his mother ask hoarsely, "How will I get along without you, mijito? I don't know how I can possibly bear it."

Through tears of his own he had tried to remain lighthearted but he was losing ground, and only managed to say, "I'll be back at Christmas time. The abbot said in his letter that for just this first Christmas we are allowed back home. So we'll be together this Christmas. It's just a few months till then, Mama."

"Your father has already left home and so has Bobby. Now you. Your grandmother and I will be all alone. I realize that you must go and begin your own life. I'm happy for you because I know that this is what you want and what you must do, but it's very hard for me. What will I do without you? How will I get along?"

In the stillness all around them, they wept together and held onto each other. Sighing, his mother had repeated in Spanish, "Despedirse es morir un poco." Sobbing in the clenched embrace of his mother's arms, they remained this way for a very long time, not wanting to let go, knowing only too well, that "to say goodbye is to die a little". There was so much he wanted to say, but didn't yet know how, managing only to tell his mother, "I love you, Mama. I love you so much."

Early the next day, he woke up and knelt down by his bed to say his prayers. Without thinking, he made his bed as he always did and then headed for the kitchen to make the coffee. His grandmother and mother had beaten him there, and were already busily preparing breakfast. His grandmother admonished him, "You have to eat a big breakfast before you get on that train, mijito. Only God knows when you'll eat next before you get to where you're going."

"I'm going to Leicester."

"Looster, Lista, Looca, I don't care what it's called. It sounds very far away to me. Come on, eat up." As she said this she placed a plate in front of him piled high with eggs, chorizo and potatoes. On the side were large slices of warm Cuban bread with plenty of butter. "Here's your café con leche, dark with lots of sugar the way you like it."

"Stop doting on him," his mother had chastised. "You're making him nervous."

His grandmother retorted, "He needs to eat or he's going to faint along the way."

Simon sighed deeply. "I'm plenty nervous already, Mom. When is Tio and Tia picking us up to go to the train station?"

"In about an hour but I'm sure they'll be here any minute." Then she said softly to herself, "Everyone is so nervous today."

On that very clear, hot, sunny day in Tampa, Florida, they all gathered at the old Union train station on Nebraska Avenue. It was a sturdy brick edifice built in 1912 and had seen many departures and arrivals, some happy and others sad. Inside, large bronze plaques adorned the walls recalling the names of those who had left the place and made the ultimate sacrifice to die in the Great War in 1917 and in World War II in 1943. Now, on this morning, tall, heavy doors had opened up to them and the small, huddled group had entered the cavernous space. The only furniture were long, wooden benches, now mostly filled.

"Let's go outside where the train's waiting to leave," his mother said. "I need some fresh air."

They all exited to the where the numerous train tracks were and waited patiently for him to board the train north to Philadelphia. A breeze barely blew over the small cluster of family that had gathered to say goodbye. Everyone spoke Spanish rapidly and at the same time, trying to appear calm and happy as they gestured excitedly. The older aunts and uncles spoke in hushed tones but the young cousins were boisterous and pushed him around in circles, messing up his hair. In this way everyone dealt with the inevitable farewell as best they could. No one wanted to say goodbye and then suddenly, the train blew it's deafening, high-pitched whistle and a conductor in uniform cried out, "All aboard! All aboard for Philadelphia! Last call in two minutes!"

Everyone froze and then suddenly showered kisses, hugs and tears on him, reminding him that Christmas was just around the corner and they'd all be together again. The old aunts unwittingly pinched his cheeks with their cropped whiskers and as they hugged him tightly, his uncles smelled of cigars and Cuban coffee. Everyone, men and women gave him one last hug and kiss. It was now time to go.

Simon climbed the narrow steps onto the train with his suitcase in front of him and the conductor took it. He turned for one brief moment and wished that he had not. Better for him had he just looked ahead rather than look back. His mother seemed to him at that moment as if she had shrunk in size and her face was awash in tears. He read her eyes perfectly and knew that they said he was leaving her behind. Everyone was waving now as the grinding sounds of the train's wheels and engines screeched and shrilled on the tracks. The train began to move slowly out of the station. They waved and shouted as they all walked together alongside the tracks on the open corridor. No one was smiling now and through his tears he cried out to them, "No lloren! No lloren! Don't cry!" He had no idea that letting go of those he most loved would be so awful. He had many lessons yet to learn.

He took his seat by a large window and as the train rocked to and fro on the tracks covered in overgrown weeds, he realized that in an instant his life had changed direction. Distance was now firmly in place between his former life and his new life that was unfolding. When the train finally took a great turn out of the station, he glanced back and could no longer see them. His young life up to that moment was now his past and he was moving at great speed toward his unknown future. He sat back in the ample, tweed covered seat and wiped away the hot tears that continued to flow.

The young man from Tampa gazed out the window without really focusing on the ugly abandoned houses that lined the train tracks in this part of the city. He was focused elsewhere, in a fog within himself and without any effort heard himself whisper, "It's really happening. I'm really beginning my first steps to priesthood. My dream is coming true. Thank You, God." He thought of the pictures he had seen in the pamphlets that had been sent to him from the abbey and tried to picture himself there, among those massive walls and towering firs and evergreens.

He thought of himself wearing his habit and a wave of excitement washed over him. The time for crying was over. A wonderful feeling about what he was doing filled him. He wasn't afraid of the unknown that lay ahead. He reminded himself that the blood that pulsed through his veins was the same blood that had pulsed through the veins of his great-grandmother Maria Andrea Marichelar.

He thought about her now. She had lived in the house when he was a very young boy. He and Bobby had called her "Lela" since they first began to speak because "abuela", grandmother in Spanish, had just been too difficult for them to pronounce. He slightly remembered her sitting on the front porch in a comfortable, expansive armchair. She always wore black, tightly laced, no-nonsense high shoes that barely looked out from under her spotless, long dress. A large woman, to be sure, with white hair pulled back neatly into a bun. Her kind face bearing a broad, large nose and bushy, dark Spanish eyebrows over bright, sparkling, knowing eyes behind spectacles. Her lovely skin, creamy and fair. Sitting gracefully on that front porch, she now reminded him of an image of God the Father sitting on His majestic throne.

She was only a young girl of fifteen years or so when she had left her entire family in the Basque Country from the medieval seaport of Bilbao in northern Spain. It was the end of the nineteenth century and completely alone, she had boarded a ship which would take her to America, far away from everyone and everything she knew. "Why had she left?" he and Bobby would ask, and their mother would explain in great detail.

Her father had insisted that she marry a wealthy, much older man whom she abhorred. He would shower her with gifts that she ignored and wouldn't even open. Wedding plans were well underway regardless of what she wanted. And so, late one night, her mother and her eldest brother had helped her escape with some folks from a neighboring village going to the New World. Her mother and brother accompanied her on the path that led out from their small hamlet and then said their goodbyes there. She walked further on, alone in the night and met up with her traveling companions. It was all well planned and her absence would only be for a while until her father's wedding plans for her could be set aside. They would tell her father that she had gone to visit family nearby.

Sickness broke out on the ship's long journey between Spain and America and it was forced to dock in the port of New Orleans. From there she wrote her father begging for forgiveness and acceptance of her own plans. As could be imagined, her father was furious and remained firm. If she returned to marry according to his plans, he said, all would be well. Otherwise, she should consider her family dead. Ultimately, her father disowned her when she wouldn't return for the nuptials. Her mother and brothers were forbidden to write to her and she never heard from any of them again. She had been true to self but at a terrible cost. She had lost her family and was alone. It was an important lesson to learn.

Simon's mother had awaken in him a deep understanding that his great-grandmother's blood, courage and single mindedness also flowed through him. It was the blood of Maria Andrea, "Lela", flowing through him now that gave him courage. Nothing was beyond his reach. Only one thing was required and it was to know what God wanted of him. He trusted God completely. God had been calling him for years and he was now answering that call. If he had had the opportunity to share notes with Maria Andrea, "Lela", she would have told him to pursue all his dreams without hesitation. But she would also have cautioned him to be aware that in life there is always a cost involved in doing so. All our actions produce a price tag. But at that moment, sitting on the train bound for Philadelphia, Simon was very much like her on that ship sailing for America. The price tag was yet unknown. He was caught up in his dreams, inexperienced but very brave and determined.

The next day, his train arrived in Philadelphia and he was all eyes as he glanced out the window and took in the enormity of the train station. It made the one in Tampa look like a gas station. People raced back and forth and train tracks covered every inch of land like so many spider's webs here and there.

The letter he had received from the abbey informed him that one of the monks would be waiting for him outside his train in the station in Philadelphia. He wondered how he would be recognized if he had never seen him. No photographs had been exchanged and suddenly he worried what would happen if he didn't meet up with his ride to Leicester. Dressed in his black suit, white shirt, black tie and black dress shoes, Simon was unaware that he was the only seventeen-year-old dressed that way exiting the train. He took his suitcase and stepped off the train.

"Are you Larry, the boy from Tampa?" A jovial, voice spoke up from behind him. He almost jumped out of his shoes at the unexpected question and turned awkwardly toward the confident, male voice. Standing there was a stout man in his very late twenties or early thirties. He was completely bald on the top of his large head and straight black hair covered the back and sides of his expansive scalp. The hair which fell just above his ears was neatly trimmed. He wore a bushy, small moustache that reminded him somewhat of Hercule Poirot, Agatha Christie's fastidious Belgian detective. He was dressed in the black, flowing habit of the Order which was impeccably ironed and when he stretched out his right hand to greet him, he noticed that the monk wore a thin, elegant gold wristwatch. He saw that the man was wearing black leather loafers shined to a perfect gloss, with thin soles and a leather tassel on top. He appeared to be wearing black silk socks. He also noticed that the monk was wearing a familiar silver bracelet and thought it odd that he should be wearing jewelry. "I'm Brother Shawn."

The lack of austerity confused Simon and before he could catch himself he blurted out, "Hey, I used to wear a bracelet just like that, you know, for the P.O.W.'s. The name on mine belongs to a Major who's still out there. I just took it off a couple days ago before entering the abbey."

"Yeah, exactly! This one has the name of a Private, First Class lost somewhere in Vietnam. Why, did you take the bracelet off, little one?"

"Well, because I'm entering the abbey and I'm leaving everything behind." The monk smiled but said nothing. Then Simon added, "I thought any kind of jewelry was forbidden, you know, because of the vow of poverty."

"Well, it's still on the books I guess and so technically it is against the vow, but you should have brought it anyway. No biggie. Nobody would have said anything at the abbey. It's 1974, I mean, we all need to open up and relax a bit. No need to get all crazy about ancient rules that don't mean that much anymore." Larry wanted to ask what he meant but decided against it. He thought he knew what he meant and didn't agree. Then he realized he hadn't introduced himself, "I'm so sorry, I forgot to introduce myself! Yes, yes I am, Father! I'm Larry Zayas from Tampa."

"Wonderful! I'm so very happy to finally meet you!" "I'm not a priest yet. I'm still studying and preparing. It doesn't seem like my formation is ever going to end but someday I'll get there. I was a lay brother for many years when I entered about your same age. Then I asked to become a priest and was accepted. My name as I said, is Brother Shawn. I help Father Chris in the office with the first year men just coming in to the abbey. I've been seeing your name on the rosters and paperwork for months now. It's nice to finally put a face to the name." He hesitated and then joked, patting him on the back gently, "You're a Postulant now, little one!" The monk took him into his arms and squeezed him tightly. "Welcome to the family, Larry!" The boy from Tampa was taken aback by the embrace from this rotund, excessively cheerful man he had never seen before. He thought he smelled cologne on him and wondered to himself if the priests and brothers also used cologne at the abbey. He had to admit that he smelled good. Simon awkwardly returned the embrace and then let his arms fall to his side, saying meekly, "Nice to meet you, Brother…" He trailed off not remembering the curious name he had only just heard.

"Shawn. Brother Shawn. Nice to meet you too, Larry." The monk gazed at him and chuckled to himself. "It was the religious name I was given when I entered the novitiate at the abbey."

"You say it's the name you were given at the abbey? What do you mean?"

"In all the ancient religious Orders of the Church, like ours, religious names are assigned when you enter the novitiate. That's the second year of formation, after postulancy. You receive the religious habit of the Order and your religious name which will be yours until the day you die."

"Oh, I see." He wasn't sure how he felt about this.

"Yeah, so now you are Larry but in nine months, if you are accepted by the abbot and his council, you will need a new name. Start thinking about one. Time flies."

"He hadn't known about the name change and supposed there was a lot he didn't know about the new life he was embracing."

"Yep, I was John in the world, but have been Shawn now for several years. You can call me Shawn, please. You can drop the 'Brother' with me. We'll be brothers at the abbey." Then he added, "The older priests and brothers will expect you to address them with their title, just so you know." Then he chuckled to himself again as he said, "Not all of them but some would freak if you called them by their first name. But you don't need to use the title of 'Brother' with me. It used to be that a postulant or a novice couldn't even talk to a professed monk unless he had permission. Glad all that's gone." He put his hands on his ample hips and said, "You're probably dying from hunger. Am I right? I know I am! Let's grab a burger and a soda just outside the station where I left the truck. We have a long drive to Leicester and I'd like us to get there before the sun sets."

"Sounds great to me. I am starving now that you mention it."

Without any further ceremony, Brother Shawn took the small suitcase out of Simon's hand and led the way. As they walked through the crowd no one seemed to notice Brother Shawn in his flowing, black habit. Then Larry noticed nuns in various religious habits walking hurriedly and scurrying about and a priest in a purple toned cassock waving to a group of students in uniform. He thought to himself how different the north was to the south. He never saw any of this in public there. As he walked outside the station he was happy to be getting closer to his destination and this gave him a sense of security. He was unsure, however, how he felt personally about Brother Shawn. He had to admit that he was very friendly and well-mannered but there was something too forward about the man that he didn't like.

As they drove out of the hustle and bustle of Philadelphia, Brother Shawn filled him in on all the details. "All the guys belonging to your class already arrived. There's twenty one at the abbey already and you are number twenty two."

"Wow, I didn't realize we were going to be such a large group. Are they from around the country?"

"Sort of. I believe there are a couple guys from New York State and one from the Washington, D.C. area. There's a chance we might have an arrival later this month from Puerto Rico, but that's not really confirmed. Another guy, Silas, is from Tennessee and Kyle is from outside Chicago. Everyone else is from Pennsylvania, from all over the state."

"I see."

"Yeah. Well, and then there's you! From faraway Florida! I'd love to get down there someday. The beaches have to be incredible!"

"Yes, they are. I practically grew up on the beach." Simon thought it odd that this monk sitting next to him wanted to be on the beach. He couldn't exactly picture him sitting there on a beach towel in full, flowing black habit, with seagulls flying overhead.

The drive was picturesque beyond anything he could have imagined. Rolling hills and great forests gave way to sprawling farms that seems to be everywhere along the way. Barns, brightly painted red and others abandoned, dotted the countryside. A black horse-drawn carriage appeared up ahead on the highway and Brother Shawn slowed down.

On the carriage's backside was a fluorescent triangle. He was intrigued. "What's that?" As they passed the carriage, he saw a long-bearded young man wearing a broad-brimmed hat and vest over a plain faded blue shirt. He held the reins loosely and looked straight ahead. Next to him sat a young woman carrying a child. Her head was covered and she wore a very long dress. The little boy was dressed identically like the young man, probably his father.

"Oh, those are Amish folks." Brother Shawn waved to the young couple in the carriage. No one returned the gesture.

"Amish?"

"You're not in Kansas anymore, little one." Then he added laughing to himself, "It's like Dorothy said in 'The Wizard of Oz', remember?"

Shadows of night were rapidly approaching as the distance closed in between them and the hamlet of Leicester. Up and up they climbed into the Allegheny Mountains toward the abbey that would soon be home. Simon thought about how far he was from home and wondered what his mother was doing. He thought about Prince Demetrius making this trek on horseback so long ago and couldn't believe he was almost there.

"Tomorrow there will be an orientation in the morning after breakfast. Father Chris will explain everything to you guys. Your rank of seniority in the Order is determined by the time and date you pass those front gates up ahead. Since you're the last man to arrive, that puts you at number twenty two in your class. That's the order in which you will profess your vows someday and also when you're ordained a priest, considered for offices, etcetera." Simon wasn't bothered by being 'last' on any roster. The fact that his last name began with a "Z" had usually placed him last on almost every list.

He was excited beyond words. Everything he had dreamed was now becoming reality. It had seemed like such a long time to wait since he was a little boy wanting to become a priest. Now everything seemed to be happening so fast. They drove down a country road lined with massive evergreens and canopied by thick forest trees and climbed one last hill before Brother Shawn took a quick turn to the left off the main road. Simon heard the gravel rumble under the truck's tires and saw the sign up ahead that told him he had arrived. It was a massive steel marker that bore a huge Gothic cross at its top. It's letters were gold on black and read, ABBEY OF THE MOST SACRED HEART OF JESUS. Below this, in smaller letters, FOUNDED 1856, LEICESTER, PENNSYLVANIA.

Up ahead, they drove under the impressive stone arch of the main steel gates of the abbey. Two stone pillars stood like sentries on either side, ready to receive the dark of night. Atop, each one held an imposing metal and glass lantern that glowed brightly among the gathering shadows. Simon felt deeply moved as he realized he had finally arrived. This was the place where he would begin his preparation for the priesthood.

They drove ahead a short distance and he caught his first glimpse of the gargantuan edifice. He had seen it in photographs but what he saw now was far more impressive, and grander than anything the photographs suggested or he could possibly have imagined. It was like going back in time, into the opulence and finery of the Roman Catholic Church in the nineteenth century. What he saw represented the power, authority and confidence of a Church that was solid and unchanging in its truths.

Tall, majestic chimneys rose like graceful columns of brick and stone toward the night sky. Endless squares of dark slate covered the high-pitched roofs and numerous gables jutting from the rooftops that now shone clearly by the bright light of the late August moon. Simon saw turrets and towers that reached high above the old firs and pines, sentinels keeping watch over the exquisite fortress.

"Once you get settled in and classes start, you will see the abbey, well, most of it anyway. It's a crazy maze of endless hallways, cloisters, gardens and buildings all wrapped up into one. There are some parts that are cloistered or off limits to those in formation until you profess your solemn or final vows. What's really impressive is the abbey church where…"

"Where the Prince Demetrius is buried!" He could barely conceal his excitement as Simon said this.

"Yes, exactly, as well as the past abbots and monks. Someday you will rest there too, in the crypt, with them. How do you know about Prince Demetrius? Outside of Leicester, he's not really a celebrity."

"I've read about him."

"I see." Brother Shawn gestured toward the left and said, "Well, anyway, that's the abbey church. It's really the main entrance to the abbey where visitors are allowed on the grounds. The brother porter is there and there are a couple of visiting rooms and two halls where lay people are allowed to enter and gather on certain occasions when visiting the monks is allowed. Everything else is cloistered and prohibited to the public. No one from the outside is allowed in unless it's an emergency and the abbot gives permission."

"I'm excited about seeing the abbey church. It looks unreal in the photographs I saw in some of the pamphlets I received."

"Oh, it's a singular place, no doubt. Once you're professed you'll pray several times a day there in the great choir. Until then, you guys, the postulants, have your own separate, small chapel in the postulancy. That's where we're going now. It's on the east side of the abbey complex. When you become a novice, you'll move to the novitiate on the other side and be invited into the abbey church on feast days, otherwise, the novices also have their own chapel apart. Then when you're professed, you will pray the breviary and attend Mass in the upper abbey church with the abbot and professed monks."

"Upper church?"

"Yeah. The abbey church has three levels: the great upper church above, the lower or secondary church which is less ornate and finally the crypt. There's an altar down there too among the tombs." Simon was captivated by all the information and couldn't wait to seeing it all soon. Brother Shawn playfully punched Simon's shoulder as the truck turned right and he said, "Maybe once you get settled I can show you around most of it."

Enthusiastically, he answered too loudly, "I'd love that!"

"But for tonight, you still have to meet your Postulant Master, Father Chris, as well as your classmates. I'm sure you're tired but you'll be up half the night talking. That's what I did when I arrived here."

The gravel road was dimly lit by lamp posts. Simon could see the outer wall of the abbey running in the distance to his far right, and behind it, beyond the wall, there appeared to be a forest. They passed a small gravel circle and entered it. In the middle of the circle was a marble statue of the Mother of God atop a small, bubbling fountain. Everything about this place spoke to him of tranquility and the fact that he was certainly off the beaten path. He wondered if this is what it meant to "leave the world". He had read that often in the lives of those who had left their former life and had retired to a monastery.

"Okay, Postulant Brother number twenty two. You're home!" The truck came to a stop and Brother Shawn turned off the engine. He turned toward Simon and extended his hand. "Again, very nice meeting you, Larry. I'll probably disappear once I get you and your suitcase inside. It's going to be noisy and a blur for you tonight but this is your new family, so just relax and be at home. I'm not sure if I'll be around tomorrow but I want you to feel at home here, okay? If you need anything I'm usually not too far away." As he said this last, he tightened his grip on Simon's hand and shook it firmly.

"Thank you, Brother, I mean, Shawn."

"Come this way." The portly monk took Simon's suitcase and they both walked on the gravel path toward the entrance of the postulancy. A moss-covered stone arch, supported by two granite columns greeted them ahead. Massive, leaded glass windows aglow with interior lights, gave no indication that this was the entrance to the first phase of the long preparation to the priesthood. Once he entered this fortress, his life would be set firm on the path he had so much dreamed about. Two worn, wooden doors met them as they approached. Brother Shawn rang a buzzer that was barely visible to one side. They waited in semi-darkness. On either side of them were iron sconces casting a dim glow. The sounds of crickets could be heard all around them and in the distance, a great bell rang solemnly in its tower announcing that it was ten in the evening. The monk extended his hand and rang again and from within they could hear a heavy latch being turned. Large metal hinges screeched loudly in protest as the heavy doors were pulled open from within.

Simon stood still at that moment and gasped with eyes wide open.

Chapter Five
Learning the Ropes

Tell me and I forget,
teach me and I may remember,
involve me and I learn.
Benjamin Franklin

A tall, spidery man, dressed in baggy trousers and a short-sleeved shirt greeted them. He wore a large watch on his wrist held in place by a thick leather band. His shoes were scuffed and he wore no socks. His thinning hair was uncombed and his skin was significantly tanned. The scrawny man's head looked like a prehistoric bird's and this was probably because his pronounced nose was boney and looked like a beak. He wore glasses and his eyes bore proof to the fact that he was a man of books and studies.

Brother Shawn pushed into him playfully as if to move him out of the way, "Chris! You're getting old, daddy! It took you forever to open that door! I thought you were using a walker." The older man's smile was crooked and in it a trace of sarcasm and cynicism was evident to Simon. Despite the obvious kidding between him and Brother Shawn, this man was a figure of unquestioned authority, a man who did not suffer fools easily. It seemed to Simon that the older man barely put up with the younger man's sarcasm.

He replied dryly, "It's Reverend Father Christoferos to you, urchin! Don't forget that! You're not ordained yet and you will be voted upon." Then he turned to Simon, his gaze penetrating the younger man's eyes and as he extended his slender arm and large, skeletal hand, he said, "That's Christopher in Greek, my name that is." Then he asked with sincere interest, "And who's this latecomer you bring us at this hour, Shawn?"

Simon took the priest's hand in his own. Father Christoferos tightened his hold and continued to gaze into his eyes. Simon managed to say, "I'm Larry, Father. Larry Zayas."

"Ah yes, the man from Tampa, Florida! Welcome to Leicester! You must be exhausted. I'm Father Chris, the Master of Postulants. Come on in!" Then in a mocking gesture, he cupped his hand around his mouth as if keeping a secret from Brother Shawn and said in a stage whisper, "Watch out for this Shawn-guy, whatever his name is! He's nothing but trouble."

Brother Shawn pushed his way between the two men and said, "Nay, I'd say watch out for this Christoferos-guy. He's a big wig here at the abbey. Not only Master of Postulants but Professor of Theology to the clerics in the major seminary. They say he studied theology with the best minds in a famous university in Belgium but, hey, who has ever really checked that out?" Brother Shawn nervously combed out his neat moustache with his index finger, first to the left and then to the right. He snickered loudly to himself as he ran ahead with suitcase in hand.

The older priest reached out to grab Brother Shawn but he managed to skip away. "I'll deal with you later, wise guy!"

Simon observed that the interior of the postulancy was sparse to the point of being ascetical, yet the great rooms that now opened up before him reflected the elegance and importance to detail of the nineteenth century. The walls were pale white plaster and the ceiling of the corridor was arched and domed with bricks carefully placed there in a herringbone pattern. The intricate Victorian metal fixtures hanging from above along the way were originally gas lamps now turned into electric ones. The floors were all highly polished oak parquet displaying intricate geometric patterns in light and darkish woods. Simon had never seen any place like this before.

There were large statues of angels and saints placed on high pedestals here and there and stately, religious paintings hung on the walls, encased in ornate, golden frames. As he drew closer to the main room, the din of laugher and loud voices could be heard. Simon walked down the long corridor and saw a beautifully carved wooden staircase to his right. It had a landing on it, and placed in front of a huge bay window there was a bigger than life crucifix of Jesus in His last agony. To the left was a massive stone fireplace which dominated the main room. Several sofas that had seen better days were scattered about and all along the walls from floor to ceiling were sturdy bookshelves of carved mahogany filled with books of every conceivable size and hue. The tall leaded glass windows were dark now but Simon thought to himself that this room must be a wonderful place to read in.

He turned just as Brother Shawn was announcing, "Okay gents, listen up." Simon was immediately struck by the friendly, handsome faces of the young men gathered there that night.

The loud chatter in the room ceased immediately and then the Master of Postulants entered and said, "Gentlemen, may I introduce to you your brother, Larry." Father Chris stood next to him and pressed his boney hand into his shoulder as he added sarcastically, "A little late but we welcome him anyway!" Everyone cheered and from some of them there were whistles and raucous laughter. It was the kind of reception you would expect from young men of college age. Then he added, "Your postulant class numbers twenty two guys from various parts of the country! That's a pretty numerous bunch."

A hearty applause broke out spontaneously and then every one of them came up to Simon and extended their hands, introducing themselves. It was impossible for him to get all their names, although two or three of them from the crowd, struck him in a particular way he couldn't explain. It was brief and subtle, but something about those men had impressed him. He did remember a taller boy saying he was from Philadelphia and another boy saying his name was Silas. Fueled by the Master of Postulants, a joke began to emerge about the latecomer and Simon had to admit that he enjoyed being at the center of attention. Brother Shawn was moving about the room catching bits and pieces of conversation.

"Okay, brothers, listen up." It was the voice of the Master of Postulants again, Father Chris. He didn't need to raise his voice as he continued. "You can stay up as long as you want tonight. I emphasize, 'tonight'. As of tomorrow, the 'Grand Silence' will go into effect for the rest of your religious lives from ten in the evening until breakfast begins the next day. No talking will be tolerated. But for tonight, and tonight alone, I suggest you enjoy but don't stay up too late for your own good. Tomorrow morning at five-thirty you will hear a large hand bell ringing in the hallways of each of the three floors of the postulancy. For tomorrow, Brother Shawn will do the honors of clanging the hand bell. One of you will have that charge after then. You will get up at promptly five-thirty. Listen to me!"

He looked sternly around the room, "You will get up immediately upon hearing the bell. If you find it's too much for you, I will make sure you go home to Mommie and you can sleep as much as you want there. Understood? It's a heroic moment when you hear that bell. Nothing to contemplate. It's mechanical. You just get up and wash your face, get dressed and we'll meet down here at six o'clock to begin your first day in the abbey. From here we will go to chapel for Mass, then breakfast. We will meet here in the main room at nine o'clock and get everyone oriented. Our Most Reverend Abbot, Father Edmund, will stop by and greet you then. If you have any doubts about our schedule for tomorrow, check the bulletin board on that far wall. Anything you will need to know will always be posted there so make sure you check the bulletin board every day, morning, afternoon and night." He gestured to a spot under the beautifully carved grand staircase.

He then quickly ended his discourse and added as he turned and walked away, "Goodnight, men." Most everyone was in awe but as the priest left the room conversation started again. Some of the young men left as well, saying they were still unpacking and really tired.

There was a sensual electricity in the air that Simon could not deny and had never experienced before. He enjoyed the new sensation it produced in him. He looked around and heard the familiar voice from within a circle of laughter. Sure enough it was Brother Shawn moving through the crowd. He looked up and winked at Simon and approached him saying softly into his ear, "I've got your suitcase by the bulletin board, little one. Let me show you where your room is. You lucky guy, you show up last and still managed to get the best room here. There are three floors in the postulancy. It's on the third floor, known as the 'tower room'. It's cavernous up there and you'll have plenty of space to yourself even though three of your brothers will share it with you. It was where I first went when I arrived. C'mon, I'll show you."

Simon followed him as they climbed the ornate staircase under the ghastly gaze of Jesus crucified and together they walked on to the second floor. They turned left, down a crooked hallway and climbed another set of steps that creaked and protested loudly. At the top they turned left and went down another short corridor. Brother Shawn failed to knock and simply threw open the creaking oak door there.

It was cavernous just as he had said and Simon understood why it was called the tower room. He said more to himself than to anyone, "Wow, what a room." It was obviously one of the great round towers standing up high from the abbey walls, its ceiling soaring above them and suspended there by great planks of roughly hewed wood that resembled great branches of trees spreading here and there and interlocking together. On all sides of the immense form of the tower walls, slender windows stood in place. The windows were innumerable triangles of beveled glass held together by lead and even now in the semi-darkness of evening, they held prisms of light cast from the bedside table lamps.

The spacious room held four beds, four desks, four chest of drawers and four kneelers for prayers, above which was a crucifix at each. On one wall was a common clothes rack in lieu of a personal closet. Brother Shawn put Larry's suitcase down. "Here you go, little one. Welcome to the abbey. Not exactly the Hilton but pretty cozy, I'd say. Your room mates are Silas, Robert and Robby."

Simon looked around and said, "Thank you, Brother Shawn, I mean, Shawn. Thank you."

Two young men were there. Simon immediately recognized the one who was reading barefoot in bed. He had said downstairs that his name was Silas. The other was unpacking a box on his bed. The young man reading in bed made no move to get up. Simon felt drawn to him again as he had in the main room earlier that evening. Silas now looked up briefly over his glasses. He was older than Simon by two or three years, handsome and slim, with jet black, longish hair, sideburns and a moustache. He had not shaved in a day or two and his heavy beard was evident. His bright coal-black eyes studied the newcomer and all he managed to say was "Hi, man. I saw you downstairs. I'm Silas." Then he went back to his reading. Simon wondered where he was from since he had a very particular way of speaking. Simon wondered about the other boy, the one from Philadelphia. Could he be Robby, the other roommate in the tower?

Simon had no opportunity to respond to Silas because the other boy in the room suddenly drew close and took his hand into his own in a friendly, casual way. He was heavy set, with Slavic features and no trace of facial hair. He was pale and had light brownish hair cut in the same short fashion as Simon. He smiled the most sincere, kindest smile Simon had ever encountered and it seemed to him at the moment that he knew him somehow from before, but of course, that was not possible. He said, "I'm Robert from Johnstown, not too far away down the mountain." Simon was struck by another particular way of speaking. Robert's accent was different from Silas'. It was more a kind of sing-song when he spoke. He wondered if it was a local accent of sorts. "What's your name, again? From Florida, right?"

"I'm Larry. Yes, from Tampa." He didn't know what else to say and blurted out nervously, "I just got here. I'm the last guy."

"Yeah, I heard. Well, hell, you're coming from so far away. Welcome to the wee hamlet of Leicester."

"Thank you, Robert." Looking around the room, Simon saw only one bed that was still made up and untouched. He went over to it and throwing his suitcase on it said with a sigh, "Well, I guess this one's mine."

"Yes sir," Robert said. "Robby is over in that bed. He's still downstairs, I guess."

Simon asked, "Is Robby that tall guy from Philadelphia with the beard and longish hair?"

"Ha ha ha," Robert laughed with abandonment. "Naw, you must mean Michael. He's from Philly. Tall, good-looking, suave, smartass. Robby is…well kinda skinny and timid and he's older than us. He's kinda odd…loose in his shoes as they say. Well, don't mind me, you'll meet him downstairs or tomorrow and come to your own conclusions. Nothing like that Philadelphia guy, though, you'll see." Simon wondered why Robert found his question funny and had laughed out loud to himself.

With a sudden thud on the floor, Robert absentmindedly threw the box he had been unpacking and pushed it out of sight under the bed with one, swift kick. He walked over to Simon and said whispering, "You already met Silas over there in the tower proper. He's from Tennessee, I think or one of the Carolinas. He's not a real talker and gives me the impression of being guarded and distant. Seems like a loner to me. But there's something about him that's attractive." Simon and Robert looked up just in time to see Brother Shawn sitting on the edge of Silas' bed, saying something and then pulling hard on one of his big toes. Silas let out an exaggerated moan of pain followed by laughter. Robert looked at Simon and rolled his eyes, saying under his breath, "Oh, geez."

Brother Shawn suddenly got up and said into the big room, "Okay, so tell me, what did you guys think of 'The Beak'?" The three young men looked at each other confused. Brother Shawn let out a conspiratorial, giddy squeak and said, "Your Master of Postulants. We all call him that on the other side of the abbey."

Robert asked, "Why 'The Beak'?"

"Are you blind? It's because of his nose and his scrawny body. He looks like a vulture." Then added, "And sometimes acts like one." Brother Shawn paused and said in a conspiratorial tone, "Disregard that last remark." Then he asked, "What's your take on him?" None of the three had any comment and Brother Shawn sighed. "Well, you can tell me in the weeks to come. Guess I ought to get my bones to bed as well." He walked away gingerly and as he opened the creaking door and stepped out into the corridor, he looked back in and said. "You boys behave and see ya tomorrow." He caught Simon's gaze and winked as he walked away and closed the door. It made the boy from Florida feel special to be singled out.

Robert, however, said gravely, "Lord, there's a piece of work if there ever was one." Silas was reading and Simon felt awkward to hear Robert's criticism of the monk. He said nothing and opened his suitcase to begin unpacking. Robert asked, "Are you guys gonna head down stairs?"

Simon answered, "Yeah, sure, Robert. I just need to throw these things into this drawer here and hang my suit. Wait up for me?"

"Yeah." Robert looked over at Silas and asked, "Hey, Silas, you gonna head down with us?"

"Sure, why not?" was his response. The three newly found "brothers" headed down the maze of corridors and stairwells.

Downstairs, all twenty two men sat on the various sofas and chairs in the spacious room. Some were in more or less awkward conversation but most were quickly getting to make first acquaintances. Everyone was aware that the dreaded morning bell would sound at five-thirty but the room was alive with emotion. Most of the young men were seventeen or eighteen but three or four seemed far older to Simon and his companions and Simon thought that they must have been twenty six or twenty seven years old. One of them looked funny to him. He was skinny and balding. When he spoke, he moved too much and his wrists looked like they needed tightening. Simon thought that his father would have labeled him *'una mujercita'*.

Robert, who was sitting next to him, laughed and said softly, "That's Robby. You might as well call him 'Body Splint'." Then he gestured across the room to a young man leaning on a pillar that looked like a model from GQ magazine, adding, "And that's Michael from Philadelphia." Simon now understood Robert's earlier laugh and remarks in the tower room.

Simon was excited and nervous but was also filled with anticipation of his new life. These first hours told him that this was the place where he needed to be and he had no doubt that God was behind it. He felt at home now and this helped him relax. Tomorrow he would meet the Abbot and sometime soon get the tour of this grand abbey. In his letter the Abbot had explained that his first years would be lived only in specific areas of the abbey. First in the postulancy, then if approved, to the novitiate and from there if he professed his first vows he would move to another section of the complex for those still in philosophy. Someday, he would move to the major seminary section of the abbey and study theology. And if he was further approved, he would then profess his Solemn Vows for life and move to the central part of the abbey where the Abbot himself lived and prayed with the other monks. Finally, the day of his priestly ordination would come if he was found worthy by his superiors.

He found it comforting to think that after passing all the stages of formation in various parts of the abbey he would profess his vows, be ordained a priest and be buried in the same abbey church. For now, this three tiered zone known as the postulancy would be his home and these young men sitting around him would be his brothers. He looked at their faces and felt exhilarated to be among them.

The great room where Simon sat was ablaze with sensuality and testosterone. He could feel some kind of energy building within himself on that very warm August night. He was seventeen and beginning to pursue his life as he had desired for so many years. He felt that a promising future lay at his feet. He had known that he would be joined by other young men his age in pursuit of the priesthood and closer union with God but he had never thought about himself as a budding young man, with physical needs and appetites. He had only centered his thoughts on the spiritual and he realized now that here in the abbey he would be confronted with the physical. He thought of Bill and Dave and the curious attraction he had felt for them. Some of those feelings were present now but he pushed them away.

Here, in this sacred place, he reasoned, he would be formed to be the best monk and priest. It impressed him that he felt this way even though he had just arrived a few hours ago and had not seen much of the place nor those who lived there. Yet in his heart, he knew he had been blessed with clarity and that he had chosen well. He had no doubts about belonging to this place. God's plan for him was now unfolding and he was pleased to be where he now was.

He laughed and returned the playful punches he received from his new found fellow brothers as he sat in that room on that night taking everything in. He joined in their conversations and searched the room for the boy named Silas. He didn't really understand all the ramifications of what he was feeling that night because he was unequipped to do so. He was seventeen but knew very little of himself and far less about the world because of his inexperience. The passions that now raced unfettered within him felt wonderful even though he was unaware that it was all rooted in his sexuality. He confused what he felt in his sexual core as merely comradery and good fun.

That night as he sat with the others, he had no idea that God had brought him to that splendid place for many reasons. Reasons he couldn't possibly have known. Priesthood was only a part of it. He was sure that he would stand at God's altar someday and that he would be one of the ones to make it through the long years of formation and study. Yet, he could not have grasped the enormity of God's complex plan for him on that night. No simple human being like himself could have. Any thinking adolescent would have been incapable of grasping it. If it somehow had occurred to him that what was blossoming within him belonged to the sphere of the flesh and desire, he would have likely confused the sublimity he was now experiencing for something sinful, even filthy and undignified of God's calling to the priesthood. Had he been aware of it he would have wrongly labeled it temptation and the devil messing with him. He would not have guessed it was God's hand in the matter.

But none of it occurred to him that night because it was impossible for him to know it. The divine plan for him on that night was an intricate one in which Simon could not have understood nor appreciated it in its totality. As he sat on that couch, he only considered one dimension of where he had been led. It was the lofty spiritual sphere to which God had called him.

That night, however, for the very first time and in a very faint kind of way, he began to grasp his sexual self without really knowing what it was or being capable of labeling it. It was taking place deep inside of him and it was inaugurating the complete plan God had forged for him out of love. He was aware of a growing desire in his flesh that hitherto he had not considered for himself. This door to self-knowledge was opening up within him in the most subtle, gentle way.

Simon realized that he was surrounded by young men like himself who wanted to serve God at the altar. But now there was something new that he was unprepared to receive. He was also aware that some of those young men sitting next to him, knocking knees with him, and laughing with him, had awakened a very primal desire in him. It wasn't spiritual, it was sexual and he had not ever felt it so keenly before as that night.

He looked up several times and caught glimpses of Silas sitting by himself looking at a magazine. Then later, he had again searched the room for Silas. When he located him, he couldn't easily take his eyes away from him. Without warning, Silas looked up across the room, matching Simon's insistent gaze with his twinkling black eyes and a seductive smile spread across his handsome face. He lifted his eyebrows comically and saluted him. Simon looked away as if caught in his game but completely satisfied that he had been noticed by him.

It grew late and finally everyone retired, talking excitedly about the next day as they found their rooms on the second and third floors. Father Chris' office was next door to the priest's bedroom and Simon noticed under the door that the light was still on in there. That night, Simon lay in bed unable to sleep. He heard Robert's muffled coughs in the night and was grateful that Robby made no noises at all in his sleep. He could hear Silas turning in his bed, which creaked loudly. He thought about Bill and Dave again. All of that seemed so very far away now as he lay in the darkness of the tower room in Leicester, hearing the great bell of the abbey sound the passing hours of night. As Simon lay in bed that night he realized that he felt something much more powerful and defined. What he felt now was keener than what he had felt for Bill and Dave back home at work. He lay for a very long time realizing that he could not voice what it was exactly that he felt. He only knew that he felt a real hunger inside himself. It came from within and it was part of him. He thought about Silas lying in his bed just a few feet away. He had noticed that Silas had stripped down to his briefs before climbing into bed. Robert had worn baggy, flannel pajamas and he really hadn't noticed what Robby wore. Simon wore his t-shirt and briefs as he had always done at home.

He wondered what Silas was dreaming and if he was thinking thoughts like his own. He hoped to become his friend even though he had to admit that he was a loner and not very friendly. Robert had certainly hit the nail on the head in regards to that. He thought about Robert and hoped to grow close to him as well. But it was different than the closeness he desired with Silas. Michael was another story, very different from Silas. Michael was so outgoing and friendly and Silas so reserved. Sailing through dreams that night, he thought about his long journey from home and how faraway it seemed. He wondered how his mother and grandmother were doing and then allowed himself to be led away in slumber.

Brother Shawn clanged the large hand bell with gusto at precisely five-thirty the next morning. The golden silence which had permitted blissful sleep was shattered by the hand held bell. This in turn gave rise to groans and not a few four-letter expletives from some of the newly minted postulants. Simon rose immediately and instinctively got to his knees next to his bed as he did at home. He made the sign of the Cross upon himself and uttered his prayers. He rose and was embarrassed by his erection. He quickly got his trousers on and headed barefoot to the common bathrooms down the hall which were already filling with his sleepy companions.

Once there, in the crowded lavatory, he grabbed one of the towels and was washing his face when he heard one of the older guys laughing at a skinny kid who had just walked in, wearing only his underwear and disoriented with sleep. He was saying, "Hey, everybody, we got a boner here!"

Another brother chimed in, roaring, "Woody just got here!"

Then another, "Check it out! That thing is bigger than he is! What the fuck! It looks like a damn pickle!" He called out, "Hey, Pickles, that meat is bigger than you are!" The nickname would catch on and last for years until Pickles left the abbey.

Everybody piled in and the small bathroom with rows of sinks on one side and open toilets on the other, got more crowded. Pickles got lost in the small crowd and Simon didn't even look up from the sink, grateful that his own swelling was diminished by the cold water he was splashing on his face.

Everyone scurried about when a second bell, accompanied by the announcement, was uttered, "Fifteen minutes till meeting in the main room downstairs! Everybody get moving. You don't want to make Father wait!" By six o'clock, all twenty two postulants were gathered in front of the fireplace.

Father Chris entered, cloaked in his black habit and simply said, "Follow me." He led them down a darkened hallway and then up a small number of steps that led into a charming, beautifully decorated, Gothic chapel. This was the chapel for the postulants. Everyone filed in and Simon made it a point to sit next to Silas who gave him a wink and barely whispered, "Good morning, sleepy."

Brother Shawn assisted Father Chris at the altar. After Mass, as is the custom, the priest made his thanksgiving prayer and as he rose, Brother Shawn quietly said to everyone, "Okay, little ones, follow me." He sped down the short aisle and all followed him into a small dining room with several round tables. Silas signaled to Simon that he had saved a place next to him and Simon joined him. Prayer was said and all were invited to sit. Most of the postulants were still half asleep when an older, short monk with a long gray beard, wearing a white coarse apron came in through a small door. He was pushing a steel cart loaded with covered dishes. He placed everything on a side table and simply said, with the hint of a German accent, "Breakfast is here, brothers. Come and get it." He rolled the cart away and disappeared. After breakfast, the dishes were gathered in piles and left on the tables.

Father Chris said, "Today being the first day, one of the professed brothers brought in breakfast for us and will do the same for lunch and supper today. They will take care of cleaning up as well. But only for today. Assignments will be given this morning and some of you will begin kitchen duty tomorrow for all three meals, including washing our plates." Groans could be heard and Father Chris held his hand in the air as he said, "Don't worry, its rotating so everybody gets a chance. Same thing for some of the other duties. I'll explain everything when we meet at nine in the main room." He looked at his immense watch sliding to one side on his boney wrist and, straitening it, said, "It's a quarter to eight o'clock. You have one hour and fifteen minutes to get to the bathroom…I don't need to get into details, do I?" Scattered snickers and grunts were heard and he continued, "It will give you time to get in order, make your beds, etcetera. Be punctual." He stood up and began the thanksgiving prayer and left in silence. The postulants walked out alone or in two's and three's. Simon and Silas walked out with Michael.

Simon asked Michael, "Where did they assign you your room? We're up in the tower, third floor."

"You lucky buggers. I hear that's a great room. I got stuck in the back in a small room with two other guys. It looks like it was a cedar closet or something at one time. Anyway, we have a single bed and two bunk beds and a long table we all use as our common desk. It's tight. Come see. We have time."

Simon and Silas followed the handsome, easygoing Michael, and Silas said, "That's a bummer, Mike." Brother Shawn could be heard coming up the main flight of stairs issuing orders to everyone in general to get moving as time was not at a standstill. Both Simon and Silas were in Michael's room when they heard the voice coming their way. They both stepped out of the room just as Brother Shawn was ready to climb the stairs up to the third floor. He looked harried and impatient as he stopped dead in his tracks and turned to face them. He raised his voice in order to make a public point and asked, "Aren't you two in the tower room?"

Simon answered, "Yes, Shawn, but Michael asked…"

Brother Shawn moved in closer and got into Simon's face. "It is forbidden to be in anyone else's room other than the one assigned to you!" He snapped as he said this and then growled, "You two are lucky 'The Beak' didn't see you. He'd tear you both a new asshole if he did. He's got that point very clear in his ugly head and as a matter of fact will address it this morning. Get moving upstairs, ladies, and I don't want to see either of you down here again."

"Yes, Brother," they both said. They followed the angry monk upstairs. Brother Shawn moved further down the hall as they went into the tower room shaken and embarrassed, closing the door behind them.

Robert was making his bed and shot a bird toward the closed bedroom door in Brother Shawn's direction. He looked at Simon and Silas and said, "He's full of his own shit. In fact, he's so full of shit his hair could grow strawberries!" Robert laughed at his own joke, then added, "But you guys need to be careful of him."

Much to Simon's surprise, Silas put an arm around Simon, saying, "Let's not get freaked. It's all a big show to scare us into submission. He never should have screamed at us like that. He's not the damn Master of Postulants." He ruffled Simon's hair. "Cheer up, it's all a bullshit show. It'll pass." Robby was listening from his corner in the ample room and just nodded agreement but said nothing.

Suddenly, the tower room door flew open and Brother Shawn burst forth, unannounced. He came over to where Silas had his arm on Simon's shoulder and said, "Well, well, well, isn't this cozy? What are you guys discussing? I can see it's earth shattering by the look on your faces."

Silas looked disgusted and turned around and said nothing as he began to make his bed.

Robert piped in, "Oh, we were just talking about the assignments and how all that's going to be set up. Plus, we were wondering what all Father Chris is going to talk to us about. Is it true somebody always gets named the barber and actually cuts our hair this year?"

Brother Shawn didn't bother to answer but kept looking at Silas. Finally, he turned to Robert and said, "Get ready, boys, because 'The Beak' is gonna deliver his world famous 'first sex talk to the postulants' at nine o'clock right after the Abbot makes his stunning appearance to you guys."

Robert tried to be nonchalant but his tone gave him away, "Sex talk?"

"Yeppers, my little ones. He gives the oratory every year. It's 'The Beak's' yearly trademark introduction to Postulancy 101 and it can get creepy just so you know."

"Creepy?" Robert was hooked. "How so?"

Brother Shawn gave Simon his best smile and said, gesturing to him, "Come here and stop that weepy face thing. I was hard on you out there only because 'The Beak' would go bananas if he saw you in somebody else's room." He looked over at Silas and said, "Come here, handsome, you need to hear this." Silas stared at Brother Shawn and dragged his feet but eventually schlepped over to where the three were gathered. No one noticed it at the time but Brother Shawn had made it a point to exclude Robby from this intimate gathering. Simon looked over at Robby and saw that he was now sitting up in bed with his knees held up to his chin. His eyes were closed. Simon was going to say something when Shawn whispered, "Shhh, just leave that poor little sick bird to die. He's not gonna last."

Brother Shawn looked around at the door as if to make sure it was completely shut and said, "You guys are gonna think I'm bullshitting but I'm telling you this for your own good so you are prepared when we get down there and 'The Beak' starts his carnival show. He's gonna be all sweetness while the Abbot is there but once the Abbot leaves, listen well to what he says and don't even think about challenging him on any of his rules. He will send you home so fast you won't even know you were here. You guys understand? I'm telling this because I like you." Simon and Robert were all ears. Silas listened but his eyes told that he didn't want to play Brother Shawn's game.

Robert asked cautiously, "What's he going to tell us?"

"He's going to warn everybody against any possible homo-shit activity. He will lay it out in glowing details and smack his lips. If it wasn't so damn pathetic it would be funny." He turned to Simon and said, "You guys understand why I told you what I did downstairs, right? Once 'The Beak' gets an impression about someone, you are dust and you disappear. Stay out of everybody else's rooms." Simon nodded but said nothing although the clarification made him feel much better and he forgave Brother Shawn for embarrassing him in front of the others. Silas was looking at Robby. Brother Shawn cleared his throat and this got Silas' attention. He looked around at the three of them and in a hushed tone continued, "But the real kick in the ass is that he loves to wrestle with the cute ones."

Robert, Simon and Silas looked at him in disbelief and finally Silas asked, "What do you mean, he loves to wrestle with the cute ones? Where does he wrestle and who are the cute ones?"

Brother Shawn went on, not missing a beat, "All you guys are gonna catch on real quick as the first few weeks pass. Everybody always does. Hell, it was the same thing a few years ago when I was a Postulant. It works like this: everybody in the house is basically put into two groups by 'The Beak'. I mean, it's not a public thing. No list goes up, and there's no formal proclamation, but everyone knows to which group he belongs."

Simon furrowed his brow and asked, "How will we know?"

"Oh, honey, you'll know. You'll know real quick by the way he treats you, by the remarks he makes, by the attention or disinterest he places in you. The two groups are 'wrestlers' and 'dumps'. Life is much more secure and enjoyable here if you are privileged with a beautiful face and a slender body. If you have green toe nails, are overweight and have wiry hair growing out of your ears, 'The Beak' will not be interested." Brother Shawn moved in closer, "Michael will be a wrestler and you, Silas, for sure," He looked at Simon and said, "You will be a wrestler for sure."

Brother Shawn looked at Robert and was about to say something just before Robert said, "Yeah, I can guess what group I'm in. I'm bulging in all the wrong places."

"I'm just telling you guys so you get a head start. Nothing personal here." He put his hand on Robert's shoulder and said, "Stay out of his way, Robert, and he won't mess with you." Brother Shawn nodded toward Silas and Simon. "I'm just saying these guys have an edge."

Silas spoke up, "Well, how does this wrestling thing work? It sounds creepy as shit."

Simon looked from Silas to Shawn, shaking his head in agreement. "Yeah, it's creeping me out. I don't even know how to wrestle and I sure as hell don't want to wrestle with 'The Beak' anyhow." As Simon used Brother Shawn's nickname for the Master of Postulants everyone laughed.

When the laughter subsided, Brother Shawn continued, "The wrestling is creepy. There's a weird and deadly connection between his public tirades of homophobia, his use of homophobic language and the way he will bait you into slithering and writhing with him on the floor when he's in heat. It will all start with a silly provocation to one of the cute guys. Then he'll jump on you and begin to squirm with you while you 'wrestle' each other on that ratty rug outside his office on the second floor landing. It's always there, in plain view of the huge crucifix and it's always public. He wants everybody to see." Robert, Simon and Silas were speechless.

The hand bell began to sound on the second floor and someone called out, "Meeting with the Master of Postulants in ten minutes. Everybody down in the main room now! Father Chris' orders. Don't be late. The Abbot is on his way!"

Brother Shawn wasn't finished, however and went on, disregarding the announcement, "You guys be aware. It's all I'm saying. I'm trusting you here and going out on a limb. The drill is always the same. 'The Beak' will single you out in front of whoever happens to be there by putting himself directly in your path. He'll make believe you've been defiant and playfully push you around. It will gather a couple of guys and then a whole crowd. They will take sides and it will all appear to be in good fun. There will be whistling, jeers and screaming. He will dare you and call you 'scrawny'. Imagine that shit! Him calling you guys scrawny! He called me scrawny too. And he looks like the damn Grim Reaper! Anyway, it's time for the show. See you guys downstairs." Robby remained on his bed. As he turned to leave, Brother Shawn patted Simon gently on his abdomen and said in his ear, "I'm watching out for you. Be careful. You can call me if you need anything, anytime."

"Thank you, Shawn." Simon gestured toward Robby and whispered, "What about him?"

"It's something Father Chris is already aware of. He spoke to me about it after breakfast." Then he got real close to Simon and again, barely whispered in his ear, "Robby will be on his way home before Father Chris' talk is over. It's all arranged."

"But, how…" Brother Shawn put his hand on Simon's mouth and massaged it gently, saying, "You gotta learn not to ask so many questions, little one. Just go with the flow even if all kinds of crazy shit is going down around you. It's up to the superiors to worry about all that and they take care of it. It's not for us to question." Then he added, smiling, "If and when you become an authority someday, you will understand." Brother Shawn turned and left without saying anything more.

Silas followed Brother Shawn downstairs and as Simon began to move toward the door, Robert called out to him, "Hey, Larry, hang on a minute."

Simon turned and said, "Yeah, what is it, Robert?"

The chubby young man, years ahead of his age in common sense and wisdom, said in a matter-of-fact way, "Listen, we just met last night, right? I'm not trying to be an idiot here or anything but be careful of Shawn. I've been coming up here to the abbey for years with my folks and I know who he is. He's not trustworthy, Larry, and I can see he's working on you."

"What do you mean?" Simon was innocent in comparison to Robert. "I find him to be a nice guy."

"Oh, he's a charmer alright. Just remember what I'm telling you: be careful." Then he seemed to be hesitant to continue but pushed ahead anyway. "There's something else. Don't take this weird, okay? Promise me?"

"Sure, man, what is it?" Simon was puzzled.

Robert appeared unsure as to how to say what he needed to say. "Let me put it this way. I'm a dump, okay. I'm a butterball and I'm not a looker. You are. You're cute like our Brother Shawn just pointed out. And so is Silas, very much so. You strike me as a good guy and I hope we get to be friends for life and this is why I gotta tell you. Silas is experienced in life from what I can tell and that's why I think he's a loner and not a very likeable personality. He has Brother Shawn's number, though." Simon felt that he must have looked embarrassed. Then Robert blurted out, "I think you could easily fall for him. Be careful is all I'm saying. Lots of sharks here in this pool." Simon just stood there not exactly understanding everything Robert had just said but it made him feel exposed and terribly uncomfortable. He did feel that his friendly roommate was sincere and he liked Robert very much. The bell rang one more time from downstairs.

It drew Simon out of his thoughts. "Oh, shit, we better run or we'll be late."

By the time Robert and Simon descended the main staircase and scurried past the massive crucifix, almost all the postulants were gathered. Simon saw that Silas sat near the fireplace and had one hand slightly hidden out of view down between his knees and he motioned for Simon to sit with him. He had saved him a spot. Brother Shawn saw this and took hold of Simon by the shoulders as he passed by, intending to keep him away from the fireplace, but just as he was steering Simon away from Silas, the Master of Postulants tapped Brother Shawn on the shoulder.

Quite brusquely, he said to him angrily, in a low voice, "Get your ass outside and meet the Abbot. Where were you, dammit? I've been looking for you all over the place. He's going to be here any second."

Brother Shawn let go of Simon and said calmly, "I was upstairs trying to console that Robby kid. He's pretty much devastated."

"Well, he should have thought of that before he engaged in that display of homo eroticism late last night."

"Did he really even do anything? Wasn't it more gossip than anything else mixed in with a bit of hysteria?"

"He created scandal and left things open for misinterpretation. That's enough in my book. This postulant class is only hours old and I'm not going to have this postulancy crawling with fags and then approve them for the novitiate and so on. Not on my watch." Brother Shawn had heard the tirades too often to argue.

"I understand. Nobody ever said your job was easy." He hurried toward the main doors of the postulancy, but not before shooting a glance in the direction of the fireplace. Simon and Silas were tightly fitted against each other on the crowded fireplace hearth and talking animatedly. On either side of them the other postulants squeezed in as well, seated as they were on the same tiny space at the foot of the fireplace. Brother Shawn made a mental note to take care of that ASAP, before it got out of hand. He exited and saw that the Abbot indeed was already walking on the gravel circle near the fountain of the Mother of God. The Abbot's personal secretary accompanied him.

Father Edmund, Abbot of the Abbey of the Most Sacred Heart of Jesus was a man in his late sixties. He was a short man with little hair on his head and therefore kept his head completely shaved. He was of medium build and he wore a pectoral cross over his habit. Anyone meeting him for the first time who did not know him, would think that he had a dark sense of humor and an angry disposition. His facial expression could be mistaken as belonging to a severe, unbending man. Yet, nothing could be further from the truth. It was true that he had the reputation of being an honest man and therefore keen on upholding the rules of the abbey. But in his many years of service to the abbey as Abbot, he had won the respect and love of his fellow monks. He was known for having an open mind and a great heart capable of being compassionate. It was a custom in the abbey that the first full day of postulancy began with the visit of the Abbot.

When he entered the main room, everyone stood and the Master of Postulants introduced His Grace to the newly arrived postulants. For his part, the Abbot noted, as he did each year, that someday any one of them could conceivably be called upon to be Abbot of the grand abbey at Leicester. Father Edmund put everyone at ease and reminded the young men to pray and be obedient to the Master of Postulants. He explained to them that Father Chris was his representative and therefore, represented the Will of God in whatever he commanded them to do for their own good. Simon looked at the boney Master of Postulants and wondered if the Abbot knew that 'The Beak' commanded the cute boys to wrestle with him in public. At the conclusion of the visit, all knelt and the Abbot imparted his paternal blessing and best wishes to the postulants in the coming months. The large ring he wore on his right hand, glittered in the morning sun streaming through the tall windows of the salon. Once the Abbot had been escorted by his secretary back to the other side of the abbey, Father Chris assumed an authoritative manner.

In middle of the main room, a table was set with four chairs. An immaculate white tablecloth had been meticulously spread out. On top of this were the silver, plates, cloth napkins, goblets and a bread basket containing fresh rolls. The Master of Postulants took great care in explaining how a table should be set and a detailed lesson was then given to all present as to proper table etiquette, including how to pass things and how not to.

After this, prayer books were distributed and everyone was commanded to write the words "Ad Usum" inside the cover, followed by his own name. This was a lesson in poverty and humility because the words in Latin simply stated that the breviary in question was 'for the use of' so-and-so, not the property of so-and-so. When everyone was handed a pen to write these words above their name, Simon was impressed to see the long list of previous postulants who had had 'the use of' the prayer book.

House chores and assignments were explained and given out. Simon was given the assignment of sacristan and that meant he was in charge of keeping the chapel clean, setting up for Mass and Benediction of the Blessed Sacrament, decorating for the great Liturgical Seasons, making sure the candle before the tabernacle was always lit and that there were sufficient candles for use at Mass. He would be responsible for triple washing the altar linens and starching and ironing everything from altar cloths, to priest's albs, to purificators, corporals, finger towels and anything else related to the chapel. He was overjoyed with this particular assignment even though it was a heavy responsibility. Silas was given the task of barber and that meant that all in the postulancy who wanted their hair cut would go to him. In the basement there was a barber chair and a small cubicle set up like a barbershop. Robert was now archivist and librarian. All kinds of chores were distributed and on top of these were the weekly duties of bringing in breakfast, lunch and supper to the postulant dining room, from the great kitchen at the center of the abbey. It was there that all meals were prepared for the three hundred plus residents of the abbey. Large metal carts on wheels were used to take sustenance to the various refectories: the postulancy, the novitiate, the seminary and the professed wing as well as to the individual monk's cells in the infirmary. Those assigned to this weekly chore were also responsible for cleaning up and transporting dirty and clean dishes and silver back and forth. The Master of Postulants explained how laundry was taken care of at the abbey and what could and could not be expected.

Then he said he had three points of great importance that he would now address. First, he explained that in one month's time, everyone would receive the postulant habit of the Order and that this would be everyone's regular form of dress unless you were doing manual labor, participating in sports or gathering for recreation time each evening. Investiture of the simple tunic and belt, with a short cape was a private ceremony in the postulancy chapel. Father Chris, the Master of Postulants would preside.

Next, he spoke about the end of the period of postulancy, which would take place in nine months-time. If one were accepted to continue forward and enter the novitiate it was necessary to receive a religious name in place of your given name. Each postulant would approach the Abbot privately for this purpose. When receiving the habit of the Order from the Abbot himself in the novitiate chapel, the new names would take effect. "Start thinking of three names you would want to submit to the Abbot for his approval of one. It will be your name for the rest of your life. And give reasons for your choice because he will ask." He explained that names normally are not repeated unless a monk is dying in the infirmary and it is deemed that shortly, he will no longer need his religious name on this earth. In those cases and other rare cases, exceptions can be made but only by the Abbot.

Finally, when it seemed that all topics had been exhausted, Father Chris became very serious. The tone of his voice shifted dramatically as he hissed, "Now we must discuss a very serious and sadly, often prevalent evil, namely, the subject of sexual passions. I'm talking about self-abuse for pleasure, that is, the sin of masturbation. And most importantly, I'm talking about avoiding the dangers that can exist in an all-male environment such as ours. The Church is conscious that not all men can restrain themselves even if they believe they have a sincere vocation to the priesthood and religious life. Holy Mother Church is committed to weeding out the perverts and I can assure you that I take this very seriously and will not hesitate to throw out of this religious house anyone who is even suspect of being depraved. Does everyone understand this first point?"

A nodding of heads gave assent and barely a murmuring could be heard from the young men assembled. Everyone had become very serious by this point and Simon and Silas looked at Robert who sat across the crowded room. They were aware that the famous discourse was now unfolding as Shawn had said it would. The Master of Postulants continued, "Take note then of what I am saying. It is your duty to come to me if you suspect anyone of being a 'homo'. It is your obligation to tell me if anyone touches you in an impure manner or suggests that you touch each other. It all begins so easily and so innocently…" The Master of Postulants stared at everyone, face by face, as the tirade continued. "It begins with, 'I'll show you mine if you show me yours'." He said this with a bizarre smile.

Some in the room laughed out loud more out of nervousness than mirth. Still, it provided some comic relief and the priest went on to relate a funny tale of a postulant who had once confided in him that God had called him to be "a flower of the Old and New Testaments." Everyone now burst out laughing again and when it subsided, Father Chris said in a fatherly manner, "Oh, no, sons, we don't want any 'flowers' here, I can assure you of that! Men, honest and pure is what we seek." He went on to explain specific homo erotic behavior to look out for, especially "particular friends" or "P.F.'s" as they are referred to. "Particular friendships will not be tolerated since this is usually the beginning of the end. Two guys becoming close and always together until they end up lusting after each other and acting upon it sexually." Although explicit sexual situations were not described, it was clear to everyone in the room, even the virgins, that if you engaged in flirtatious situations, touching or sex, and were discovered, you would be cast out immediately. No exceptions, no second chances, no excuses. "It is important that I remind you to begin the discipline of yourselves over your own bodies as of this first full day of postulancy. Master your passions and be on guard. If you discipline yourself and stay clear of the sin of self-abuse you will be victorious over this selfish, disgusting habitual sin. Remember that you cannot profess vows nor enter the sacred priesthood if you masturbate." With this last warning, you could have heard a pin drop in the massive room.

"Having said all of this, and understanding it, let's get to work now on our chores. The lunch bell will call you soon enough in the refectory. Today, as you know, is Saturday. Chores are done in the mornings on Saturdays. Sometimes in the afternoon, there's an event to participate in. After that, everyone is free to study, rest, write letters, etcetera until the supper bell rings. Sundays are reserved for Holy Mass and the entire afternoon and evening are free. Once classes begin, and they will soon enough, you will need Saturday afternoons and Sundays to study and prepare. Good day, gentlemen."

The meeting was over and those assigned to kitchen duty were dispatched as well as everyone else to their designated areas. There was no conversation as now twenty one postulants scurried off to their chores and think about what had just been said. No one spoke to the other about what Father Chris had said, at least this was Simon's impression. The discourse had rattled his own cage because of the feelings that he was aware of. He was determined to put himself in order, impose discipline upon himself and master his passions.

One by one, they all left the main room and headed upstairs before beginning their chores. When Simon got to the tower room, Robert and Silas were already there. He looked in disbelief at the empty bed in the corner. The bed had been stripped and the mattress was rolled up and held down in place by the pillow. Robby was no longer among them, having been escorted away from the abbey during the discourse of the Master of Postulants. It was as if he had never arrived and the message left by the rolled up mattress was a warning to all.

Simon went directly to the chapel and upon entering, walked all the way to the altar, genuflected and knelt before the tabernacle there. The wick inside the red globe burned and danced, signaling the Real Presence of God in the tabernacle. It was truly an unexpected blessing that he had been assigned to the chapel. He needed to open his heart to God. The tall, elaborate tabernacle sitting on the altar was what most consoled him at that moment. He stared at the two angels depicted on either side of the silver door that bore the inscription: HIC CHRISTUS EST. He had no doubt that Christ Himself was in the tabernacle and was at that very moment looking down at him as he knelt there trying to unravel his knotted emotions and myriad expectations for himself.

Simon looked down at the floor and prayed softly, "Lord Jesus, have mercy on me. I don't understand so many things inside of me right now. I want with all my soul to serve you and be pure and holy. But dear God, what are all these feelings inside of me? I know I have desires that come out of nowhere." He stopped and looked up at the tabernacle. "You know everything and you know that some of the stuff Father Chris mentioned is what I feel." He stopped himself and suddenly turned around, making sure that there was no one else but God in the tiny chapel. He closed his eyes and thought of Silas. He knew that as the hours had passed since arriving in Leicester, he wanted to be with him but he didn't understand why.

Father Chris had basically said it was all a slippery slope in an all-male environment. "But it's not like that with him. I want to be his best friend, yes, and be with him but I don't want it to be depraved like Father said." Simon had understood what the Master of Postulants was getting at but he knew in his heart that he was not a pervert or some kind of a "homo". He only wanted to be special to Silas and be accepted by him. He wanted to love him like a real brother, the way he loved Bobby back home. He asked for grace and strength in being faithful to God's call to him. He had it very clear in his mind that God's call to the priesthood came first, above all other plans and desires. He had to be careful that nothing should ever impede that.

He got up and got busy. The rest of the morning he did his chores and after lunch there was talk of a volleyball game out in the field behind the abbey. Simon approached the bulletin board beneath the grand staircase and sure enough, there it was all typed out and signed by Father Chris himself: NOTICE TO ALL: VOLLEYBALL GAME THIS AFTERNOON AT 1:00 PM. TEAMS WILL BE SELECTED AT THE FIELD AND DIVIDED INTO SHIRTS AND SKINS. I WILL BE THE COACH. SEE YOU THERE.

Simon hated sports as a kid and he still hated them now. He also felt embarrassed if he was to be on the shirtless team because he felt he was too skinny and not muscular like some of the other guys in the house. He thought of Silas and Michael and how toned their bodies were, like a swimmer's, unlike his own. Simon could not envision himself at the volleyball game. He wasn't coordinated and athletically inclined. He panicked just to think that the ball might come his way. He would look totally ridiculous in front of the other guys. Absorbed in his angst, he was unaware that someone had come up behind him until he felt the unmistakable sensation of breathing on the nape of his neck.

"Hey there, brother, getting all psyched for the volleyball game?" Simon turned around. It was Brother Shawn.

"Oh God. I hate volleyball games. This note seems to imply its mandatory."

Brother Shawn let out a cynical laugh that was more a sneer. "Honey, it's not implying anything. It's outright commanding you. 'The Beak' doesn't imply or suggest anything. He commands and intimidates. That's how he controls."

"Damn. I hate sports and feel really, really awkward. I don't wanna go."

Brother Shawn stood in closer to him and whispered, "So why not just stay behind?"

"Huh?" Simon was baffled by the suggestion.

"Why go? I'm thinking maybe I can cover for you if we make up an excuse after the fact. It's a whole lot easier to get forgiveness for not showing up at the game than getting permission from 'The Beak' not to have to be there." Brother Shawn was looking at Simon who tried to process what the monk was saying to him. Then he added, "Just sayin'. Your call."

"I don't want to get into trouble or get thrown out."

"Oh, I can assure you 'The Beak' ain't gonna throw you out for not going to that silly ass game, especially if I take part of the blame."

"I dunno, but I sure don't want to go to the game."

Brother Shawn hesitated until Simon looked up at him and then said, "So don't go. Hey, I have an idea. Why don't I show you the abbey, take you around. We can see the dairy and brewery and the large refectory. I can't take you into the cloister, though, because you're not professed yet."

"Can you take me to the abbey church?"

"Oh, absolutely!"

"And the crypt?" Simon was almost pleading now.

"To maybe see the prince's tomb down there in the shadows?" Brother Shawn knew perfectly well what button to punch.

Simon's face lit up. "Yes!"

Brother Shawn looked at his watch. "Date! Wait until a little after one o'clock when everyone, especially you know who, will be on their way to the athletic field for their volleyball event. I'll pick you up in the chapel and we can slip away in the opposite direction."

"Thank you so much, Shawn!"

"Hey, I told you I'm here for you, little one." Then he lowered his voice and said, "Plus, I need to talk to you about something serious that I think you need to hear and are unaware of."

Simon's heart sank, "What about? Am I in trouble?"

Brother Shawn smiled and pushed him away. "Naw, you worry wart. Just something I need to tell you. Be in chapel by one o'clock." He looked at his watch again. "That's in about twenty minutes." He walked away and Simon slipped into the chapel. Within minutes he could hear familiar voices, especially Father Chris'. He was obviously joking with some of the guys. Simon could hear Michael's voice. Father Chris was calling him a weakling and Michael was hitting him back, "Me a weakling? Ha! I can take you on any day, grandpa." Michael was laughing loudly as he said this.

"Oh, really, tough man?" Father Chris was goading him as Brother Shawn had said he would.

"Yeah!" Their voices got muffled as they ran past the chapel and toward the main room. Then he heard the scuffle down the hall past the chapel door and imagined that Father Chris was wrestling with Michael. Simon could hear the shouts of laughter and glee from the other boys gathered at the scene. Some whistled and called out to either Father Chris or Michael. It didn't last very long and he heard the small crowd go out the front doors of the postulancy.

Next, Simon heard Robert and Silas talking. Robert was asking Silas, "Hey, Silas, have you seen Larry?"

"No, I haven't, Robert."

Simon couldn't wait for everyone to go outside. He was nervous about missing the volleyball match and a part of him told him it was a bad idea to absent himself from the activity. But then he was thinking about the crypt in the abbey and the prince and the personal tour he was about to experience. A thought, however, gnawed at him. He wondered what Brother Shawn had to say to him with such urgency.

All of a sudden, the postulancy went silent and Simon knew everyone had left for the game. Everyone except him. He told himself that Brother Shawn would protect him and cover for him. He wanted to believe that Brother Shawn enjoyed great clout in the abbey. He didn't want to think that he had simply disregarded and therefore disobeyed Father Chris's mandatory note. He preferred to believe that he would be forgiven as Brother Shawn had said. The door to the chapel opened and Simon jumped in his seat. It was Brother Shawn. He came to him, genuflected to the tabernacle and sat next to him. He was not wearing his habit but a pair of faded jeans and an old t-shirt.

He turned to Simon and taking his right hand into his left, said, "Before we go on our world wind tour through the abbey of Leicester, I need to talk to you, Larry." Simon's heart sank in his chest as he felt Brother Shawn's hand tighten slightly on his. Brother Shawn faced him and Simon looked up as the monk said, "I want you to know something. Since I saw you at the train station I've felt a kind of connection to you and now that you're here and I'm getting to know you I want you to be happy here. I want you to stay here with us and never leave. I guess I want you to see me as your real brother but I especially want you to know that I'm your friend." Simon was grateful for the monk's words and a much needed sigh escaped him as he realized Brother Shawn wanted to be his friend and not the bearer of bad news. He had thought Brother Shawn was going to reprimand him or warn him of something he was doing wrong.

"Thank you, Shawn. I want to be your friend as well. I feel like I've always known you. I think that's the connection you're talking about." As Simon said this, Brother Shawn smiled at the naïve young Postulant.

Then he said, "Not exactly, but someday I'll get to that. What I need to tell you now is something for you to keep under your hat, between you and me, okay?"

"Sure." Simon was very nervous now and waited for Brother Shawn to continue.

"You'll agree with me that everything I told you about 'The Beak's' famous discourse was true, correct?" Simon nodded and listened. "I'm sure you understood all the homophobic things he said exactly in the way he wanted you to understand it, right?" Simon nodded again, looking away from the monk's face. "Well, everything he said about weeding out anybody and everybody is true and you need to be crystal-clear about that. You're a sweet kid and I can see you love God and are serious about your vocation. But there's something that maybe you're not completely aware of yet, something you're beginning to learn about yourself and I want to protect you." Simon exhaled loudly now and waited for Brother Shawn to continue. "I can see you are attracted to Silas."

Simon felt a shock of freezing cold run up his spine. He glared at Brother Shawn and defended himself, "I'm not attracted to Silas." He spoke too loudly. "What are you saying?" He was agitated now. "I'm not in love or anything weird like that! Gee, I just really want to be his friend, his brother. He seems very cool. That's it."

"Right, right, that's what I meant. Of course I didn't mean anything else." Brother Shawn paused and then said, "But others may not understand and not see it that way, especially 'The Beak'. You heard how he put out a call for spies. Robby is already gone. There's the first casualty among your classmates. He was accused of sucking one of his roommate's toes last night. Somebody turned him in." Simon stared in complete disbelief at the monk and Brother Shawn continued speaking slowly and gently, "I noticed that last night, you and Silas were exchanging glances in the main room. I see you guys sat together at breakfast. Then I saw you both in Michael's room."

Simon protested, "Michael just wanted to show us the crowded conditions in there. The door was open."

Brother Shawn spoke in soothing acknowledgement of those facts, "Yes, yes, of course. I know that. You and I know those are the facts. But how do you think it might look? Not only are you always together but you were visiting in another room as a couple? Then I saw Silas saving you a space next to him in front of the fireplace just before the Abbot arrived. You guys were getting really close there, no?"

Simon looked at the monk in disbelief. "Everybody was sitting closely together near the fireplace! It was crowded there!"

"I get that but Silas had saved you a place next to him and gestured for you to go to him. I saw it."

Simon felt exposed and caught red-handed in the act of wrong doing. Meekly, he asked the monk, "You saw him wave to me?"

"I did, between his knees." Brother Shawn moved a little closer. "I'm telling you all this so that you can be aware of it. I'm not telling you it's a bad thing to want to be friends with him but I'm telling you that you are in no position to be accused of being somebody's 'P.F.' You heard 'The Beak' this morning."

"P.F.?" Simon repeated it slowly. "P.F."

"Particular Friendship. 'The Beak' was very clear about it this morning. Any suggestion, any accusation from anyone in your group accusing you guys, saying that you and Silas are 'P.F.'s' and 'The Beak' will label it 'homo shit' and your ass will be thrown out. Understand?" Simon was understanding now and he was grateful to Brother Shawn for his vigilance. He looked at the altar and thanked God for sending the monk to him to be his friend and protector.

"I understand." Simon was filled with shame because he knew he had been stupid and giving himself away. He remembered what Robert had already seen between him and Silas.

"You need to cool it with Silas and mingle with all the other guys, okay?" Brother Shawn let go of Simon's hand and slapped his hands on his faded jeans in feigned excitement, "Well, what the heck are we doing here wasting time! Let's go visit Prince Demetrius!"

"Yes!" Simon was glad to get up and end the conversation.

The two men walked the length and breadth of the abbey property. Brother Shawn took Simon in to the brother porter's little room and introduced him to the keeper of the doors, "This here is Brother Gabriel. Porter of the abbey for many years and more years to come!" The timid old monk shook Simon's hand not knowing what to say and Brother Shawn ushered Simon inside. He was surprised beyond words when he saw the great abbey church at the very top of the tier. Stained glass windows permitted the bright afternoon sun to fill the sacred place with multicolored light. The white marble main altar and the side altars were awash in this splendor. Great oak carved choir stalls lined the length of the church and Simon noticed how high the Gothic ceiling was above them. Gold-leafed stars covered the dark blue vaulted ceiling and life-sized statues of saints served as columns all along the nave. Simon thought he could not possibly take it all in at once.

From this church, they disappeared through a small doorway and down winding stone steps into the lower church and after visiting the beauty that was there, they descended into the damp coolness of the crypt. In this place, all along the walls were the tombs of monks. Everything in the shadows seemed gray to Simon until Brother Shawn led him to the front of the crypt chapel. There, everything was bathed in deep tones of purple and blue light.

"Everything is so marvelous here." Simon had never seen such splendor in a sacred place.

"The stained glass windows here were specially designed to create this purplish glow. It was meant to recall Gethsemane where Jesus endured His Agony and also Golgotha, the 'Place of the Skull', where he endured His passion and death." Simon was speechless. The colored light seemed to transport him to all the holy pictures he had seen when he was a boy. The nuns had explained the last hours that Jesus had endured because of humanity's sins. Simon could feel that now and see it in the crypt, a place of dust and bones. "Come over here, I want to show you something."

Brother Shawn led him to the main stone altar. As they walked down the endless aisle, Simon could see the marble sarcophagus that awaited them. Placed squarely in the middle of the sanctuary was the tomb of the Prince-Bishop Demetrius. It was covered with several coat-of-arms chiseled into it, bearing various designs. There were crowns and miters, crosiers and swords. It was no more than four feet high and seven feet long and lying atop the length of it was the image of the prince-bishop reposing in death. The master who had carved it had been careful to represent it as lifelike as possible and Simon could not help but extend his hand and touch the effigy of the great man on his forehead, kissing his own hand at once. The depiction of the prince-bishop's head appeared to be real and Simon saw that it rested comfortably on a pillow of marble with many tassels of stone. The double-headed eagle of Byzantium and the Tsars sat protectively at the head of the pillow, guarding as it were, this member of the once powerful Romanov dynasty. He was truly overcome by what he saw and experienced there. He was in awe of the four bronze angels that knelt at each corner of the tomb, each one cradling his bowed head in a gesture of sorrow and reverence. The pale marble everywhere was bathed in purple light as was the magnificent stone altar set above the tomb. It was accessible by climbing the winding marble steps on either side of the sarcophagus.

Simon asked aloud, "Is the religious name 'Demetrius' already taken?"

"Actually, yes, a kind monk, the Prior of the abbey, bears that name. The Abbot probably won't allow anyone else to ask for that name until Father Demetrius gets buried down here. He's not sick or anything but who knows, you might get lucky."

It was late afternoon when Brother Shawn and Simon left the dairy and the brewery. Much of the abbey remained a mystery to Simon since he had not yet professed religious vows and therefore, it was cloistered and out of reach for him. Brother Shawn had been the perfect host and tour guide, pointing out the exterior walls of the abbey complex where the novitiate and seminary buildings were located. The great bell tower located almost in the middle of the complex between two cloistered gardens was visible from every angle.

On their way back to the postulancy, Simon spoke up, "Thank you so much, Shawn. That visit is something I will never forget."

"So you did enjoy your first encounter with the abbey? You liked my tour?"

"Wow, did I ever! Thank you so much for showing me everything."

"I'm happy to be at your service." As they walked the perimeter of the massive walls toward the postulancy, it occurred to Simon that the volleyball game must have ended. He now worried about facing Father Chris. "What's going on in that head of yours, Florida boy? All worried about facing 'The Beak' back home?" Brother Shawn pushed him playfully away.

Simon smiled and laughed nervously, realizing that Brother Shawn had read his thoughts perfectly. "Yeah, I'm afraid I'm gonna be in some deep, bad shit."

"Well, that may well be true but it's not the end of the world. I think 'The Beak' will want to scare you because intimidating others is what he does best but you'll be okay. I'll be right there to make sure of it." Simon shot Brother Shawn a grateful glance and walked on in silence. They were still a few minutes away from the postulancy when Brother Shawn said, "Just remember what I told you in chapel today. Be careful about getting accused of anything that will get you bounced. Look at what happened to Robby." Simon cringed and Brother Shawn continued, "The guy was stupid. He was utterly stupid. It was his first night and he was already getting down on somebody in another room he wasn't even assigned to! C'mon! That's just plain stupid!"

"How did he get found out?" Simon was feeling the freezing cold again at the base of his spine.

"Well, 'The Beak' told me that one of the guys woke up in the room, on the lower bunk and in the dark thought he saw somebody bending over the only single bed in there, holding that other guy's foot in his mouth. The way I heard it is that the informer was willing to let it go because he wasn't even sure what he was seeing in the dark and just rolled over trying to get back to sleep. Then he heard a wet, sucking sound coming from across the room and when he got the lights on, he saw everything. There was Robby sucking the other guy's rigid root."

Simon was shocked. "Why didn't the other guy get thrown out?" Brother Shawn was apparently unwilling to reveal too much and was certainly not going to tell him that it was Michael on the receiving end. It wasn't yet time for Simon to know everything.

Brother Shawn simply said, "Well, the spy who turned Robby in, said that the other brother was asleep and when the lights came on, he was awaken and jumped out of bed shaking and frightened. Since he was supposedly not a participant in the depravity, 'The Beak' excused him."

Simon barely managed to say, "Oh."

Brother Shawn walked alongside the young postulant who was now lost in thought and said, "You know, Larry, it's okay to have sexual feelings toward others." Then he added, "Even other men. Nobody makes up those feelings if God hadn't put them there when he created us. Sexuality is a gift from the Creator. It's okay to be attracted to others, but I'll tell you what isn't okay. It isn't okay to be careless and stupid about what you do so that other people can turn you in and accuse you and the result is you get sent home." Simon was staring at Brother Shawn now, somewhere between complete disbelief and gratitude. He wanted so much to make sense of his feelings and to be able to trust someone who would understand him rather than judge him.

Simon took a chance and asked, "It's okay to feel attracted to another guy? Is that what you're saying?"

"Look, I just want to say this to you. If you're attracted to Silas, I'm certainly not going to condemn you. He is a very handsome guy and it totally makes sense. But what you can't do is be reckless about your feelings for him. This is why I spoke to you earlier. You can't be seen together all the time, every day." Then he put forth the question he needed Simon to answer for him, "Are you attracted to Silas? Do you feel sexually attracted to him?"

Simon stood still and faced Brother Shawn. He knew that he was at a crossroads and that this moment in his life was pivotal. He had never admitted this kind of thing to anyone. Father Norman and Father Austin came to mind and he pushed them away, far, far away within himself. What he had begun to feel here since yesterday was different. The feelings he had now, in this place, felt wonderful and pure, not dirty and weird. Now that Father Chris had given his talk, he also realized he could get into big trouble. It could put his call to priesthood in serious jeopardy. He struggled with the question he had never been asked before and wondered how he could answer Brother Shawn without sounding like a "homo" and a pervert.

He was unsure what "being attracted to" even meant in his case. He finally answered the question with a question of his own. "Can I be real honest with you, Shawn?"

"Of course, Larry, that's why I'm here for you." Brother Shawn said no more.

"I have never, ever said this before but I will now to you because I'm beginning to get flooded inside myself with all kinds of feelings and emotions I don't quite understand." He trailed off and then confessed, looking up at Brother Shawn, "Yes, I guess I am attracted to Silas. I haven't touched him or anything because I know it's a serious sin but I think about it more and more. When I look at him I can't seem to look away and when he notices me, I just sort of melt in my heart. But I know it's wrong and I need to stop those feelings and those thoughts."

Brother Shawn smiled at hearing the answer and simply said, "You know you can trust me. Thank you for being honest with me. We can talk about it some more another day." Then he added, as he touched Simon's elbow, "Your secret is safe with me."

Simon, unlike Brother Shawn, was incapable of understanding that at that moment, something had been sealed between them, something intimate had been forged. They arrived at the postulancy and when they entered, the hall and main room were in shadows and completely empty. From upstairs came the sounds of footsteps and conversation. Simon was frightened beyond words to even think about facing Father Chris. Brother Shawn said, "Go upstairs. I'll accompany you part of the way. If you don't see 'The Beak' just go to the tower room and stay upstairs till the bell rings for supper at five-thirty. You can shower and rest before then."

"Okay." Simon was more than grateful for some direction.

The two men climbed the grand staircase and Larry looked up at Jesus in His agony. The steps creaked and groaned as they climbed and when they arrived at the landing, Simon saw to his right that Father Chris' office door was wide open and the man himself was sitting at his big, wooden desk working on papers set out in front of him by the light of a lamp. The Master of Postulants looked up at them and then looked away, concentrating once again on his papers. Brother Shawn pushed Simon to the left, toward the back staircase leading to the third floor and mouthed the word, "Go!" As Simon walked quickly down that other hallway, he heard Brother Shawn greeting Father Chris and then he heard him shutting the door of the office behind him.

Once he got to the safety of the tower room, Simon saw that Silas was sprawled out on his bed fast asleep and that Robert was snoring in his own bed. The bed Robby had used stood barren, with the rolled up mattress continuing to serve as a warning. Simon saw that it was close to five and decided to take a quick shower and dress for supper. When he was done, he went down to the chapel and sat there with too many loose ends dangling crazily on his mind.

At long last, the supper bell rang and Simon joined everyone else in the refectory for supper. He sat alongside some of the brothers he had not really met yet and dared not look up to see if Silas was searching for him. It was a lively supper and Simon heard the Master of Postulants laughing at something someone had said. Simon thought that this was a good omen and that maybe Father Chris had already forgiven him for opting out of the volleyball game. He had almost convinced himself of this tale when he looked over and locked eyes with Brother Shawn, whose facial expression seemed to tell quite another story. Brother Shawn appeared quite forlorn and looked away. Simon felt miserable and insecure for the rest of the meal. He wasn't receiving good signals from anyone.

When at long last everyone left the refectory, Simon joined some of his companions for recreation in the main room. Some were reading magazines and others were searching for books on the shelves. Robert was going through a pile of acetate records whose cardboard covers looked pretty much beaten up. He held one up and said to Simon, "Hey look at this one! The Mormon Tabernacle Choir. We have this same album at home and it's a great selection of Christmas carols." He turned it over and read the back side out loud to Simon. "Check it out, 'Hark the Herald Angels Sing'. When I was in sixth grade, me and some friends would drive Trout crazy with our own rendition."

"Trout?" Simon was confused.

"It was the nun we had in sixth grade. We used to call her Trout, well, not to her face, obviously. Her mouth and lips looked like a fish's mouth so we'd call her Trout."

"Nice," was all Simon could muster. He was worried about having skipped the volleyball game. Brother Shawn's facial expression had told him all he needed to know.

"Yeah, so anyway, when we'd have rehearsals for the school Christmas show, we'd sing these words a bit differently." He chuckled to himself as he put the record away and kept sifting through the pile. Simon heard Robert singing softly to himself as he did so, "Hark the Hairy Angel's Thing…"

Some of the rowdier guys in the great room were having heated conversations and in one corner someone had put a 45 acetate record of the Rolling Stones on the player. Simon noticed Silas sitting by himself in a far corner, reading a book.

From the second floor landing, the familiar voice of the Master of Postulants called down, "Is Brother Larry down there, please?"

Simon put his best, cheerful voice, and called out, "Yes, Father, it's me, I'm down here."

"Come up to my office now, please." His response was stern and to the point. Simon's heart sank and all conversation ceased in the main room. All eyes followed him up the grand staircase. When he had knocked on the door, Father Chris, who was sitting at his desk did not look up, but simply said, "Close the door behind you and sit down." Simon saw that Brother Shawn was sitting in one of the two chairs opposite the priest's desk. Simon did as he was told and sat in the other chair. At long last Father Chris looked up and folding his hands on the desk asked in a flat tone, "Where were you today? Brother Shawn tells me he took you on a tour." Father Chris looked in Brother Shawn's direction but did not initiate any conversation with him. "He was wrong to keep you from the group. You were instructed to be present at the volleyball game. It is unacceptable that you decided on your own not to participate. It's not your call, understood?" He was stern and matter-of-fact about it but Simon also sensed gentleness in his voice.

Simon spoke up in his defense, "I'm sorry, Father, I know I should have been there. I just hate sports and couldn't bear the thought of being all awkward at the volleyball game. I'm not athletic."

"I can understand what you say but I repeat, it's not your call. Whenever you are told to do something you must submit and obey. Got it? It's fundamental in religious life to obey the will of the superior."

"Yes, Father."

"And that includes anything that goes up on the bulletin board from me. Understand? I realize you guys just got here but this can't happen again, it's unacceptable and I won't put up with it. Got it?" Then he turned toward Brother Shawn and said sarcastically, "Our Brother Shawn has completely forgotten these things, it seems. And worse still, he has driven a younger brother astray." Brother Shawn kept his head in a bent down position.

Simon was unsure what to say and repeated his apology, "Yes, Father, I'm sorry. It won't happen again." Simon was amazed to see that the priest had been stern but was not overly angry with him as he had feared. His anger seemed directed elsewhere.

Without looking at Brother Shawn, Father Chris said without much emotion, "You may go now, Brother Shawn. You will do well to keep in mind the things I told you earlier." Brother Shawn rose in silence and as he neared the door, Father Chris said, "Leave the door open when you leave."

A curious silence permeated the room for several seconds as Father Chris eyed Simon closely. The Master of Postulants then changed gears and engaged Simon in light conversation, asking how things were going and how he felt at the abbey. "We have every expectation that you will be happy here. I have read all your letters to the Abbot during your high school senior year. I agree full-heartedly with Father Edmund that you belong here with us." They chatted and laughed and Simon was put at ease. Things had actually gone smoothly and Father Chris seemed to have forgotten the volleyball affair. It was their first real conversation alone.

A knock came to the door. It was one of the brothers asking if it was possible to order pizza from somewhere in the village below the abbey. The

Master of Postulants simply said, "I don't think so, brother. Pizza is for feast days. Tonight is not a feast. There are some snacks in the cupboards down in the main room. Be sure to remember others get hungry too." He smiled at Simon and winked saying, "You guys will learn, you'll learn." The boy left to relay the news to his hungry friends. Simon sat in the chair completely relaxed now and looked about the sparsely furnished room. It was filled with books and papers everywhere and was in semi-darkness now that it was night. Brother Shawn had said that Father Chris was a professor of theology at the seminary on the other side of the abbey complex.

Simon wanted to impress the priest sitting in front of him. He had the greatest admiration and respect for the few monks he had met since he arrived. He wanted to prove to Father Chris that he too had the capacity to reach their lofty position as they had done before God. It gave him pleasure to be noticed by the Master of Postulants and was grateful that he had not scolded him too severely for his transgression but had in fact expressed approval of him. Simon thought that it hadn't gone so well for Brother Shawn. He understood somewhere within himself that he had indeed been forgiven and this motivated him to do anything that might be required of him by those in authority.

It was a total surprise, therefore, when Father Chris got up from his desk and ushered him to the door and suddenly locked his head within the grip of his arm saying, "So you decided to take a tour of the abbey instead of obey your superior, huh?" He said this laughing. Two young men who were crossing the landing outside the office stopped and were amused to see the Master of Postulants in a playful mood with one of their own who was struggling to break free. One of them, a lanky kid from Upstate New York chimed in, "Punish him, Father! He deserves it! Make him pay!"

The other boy was Michael who was quick to say, "Yeah, pin him down and make him beg for mercy!" Then Michael said in Simon's direction, "The old man can't hold you for too long!" At this, many of the brothers who were down in the main room, climbed the stairs two at a time trying to create some fun in an otherwise dreary and boring Saturday night. Simon squirmed and Father Chris lost his grip. He ran ahead of the priest but the guys standing in the semicircle that had formed, pushed him back.

One of them shouted, "Pay for your disobedience, brother!" It was all good fun and the adrenaline was building.

The Master of Postulants, breathing heavy, combed back his thinning hair with his hand and put himself in the center of the room unable to suppress his laughter. The crowd was shouting now. Some dared Father Chris to take action against the disobedient postulant and some urged Simon to pin the old man down and become the new Master of Postulants. Simon was walking along the semicircle facing the priest in front of him who playfully mimicked a surprise attack. Then Father Chris dared him, to the delight of the noisy gathering, "Who do you think you are, you scrawny, skinny boy from Florida?"

Simon forgot himself in the excitement and retorted, amazed that he would ever address a priest this way, "At least I'm a lifetime younger than you and can surely whip your butt." The crowd went wild.

"Oh, really?" The Master of Postulants was laughing and it was clear that he was enjoying himself as much as everyone else. Round and round they slowly walked and threatened each other.

"Yeah. What are you looking at, grandpa?" At this, Father Chris lunged forward and took Simon by surprise. He pinned him to the floor and the serious wrestling commenced. Arms and legs entwined as guttural insults of a good nature were exchanged. The Master of Postulants certainly had his technique well practiced over the years and when Simon could not move and the crowd counted to ten, he gave in. Father Chris pushed his face into the rug that was now all piled up against a wall and commanded, "Ask for forgiveness, you disobedient postulant!"

"Forgive me!" Simon cried out in earnest.

Father Chris taunted him, "What? Huh? I can't really hear you."

"I'm sorry all powerful wizard Master of Postulants! I am your servant! Forgive me! Have mercy!" With one last push of the face into the rug, Father Chris arose to the triumphant cheers of his fans. His hair was a mess atop his reddened, sweaty face. His shirt tails were all pulled up and he had lost a shoe in the process, exposing a boney foot of considerable length. Simon stood up and attempted to fix himself as well. Some of the guys patted him on the back and one of them pushed him in the direction of the priest. Simon managed to escape the grasp of the man who reached for him and stood there in the middle of his peers, catching his breath and laughing, sweaty and disheveled, but happy to have been the centerpiece of tonight's show.

The days passed and summer seemed to end abruptly. Before he had time to realize it, the trees began to change the color of their leaves and the mountain air around him became truly enticing to breathe. Classes had begun and study time became one of the priorities in the house. Simon felt comfortable rising early, attending Mass, saying his prayers, attending classes with his classmates, doing his chores, going to the library to do his homework, more prayers and finally easily falling asleep by ten o'clock every night when the Grand Silence was imposed upon everyone. It was strictly forbidden then to say one word until after prayers in common, before breakfast.

Simon continued to seek out Silas when he was free and the two of them enjoyed each other's company although Simon had made a conscious effort to control his desires in order to safeguard his priestly vocation. He also made it a point to mingle with everyone else. A few weeks before Christmas, Simon expressed outrage one afternoon in the library of the postulancy over an advertisement he had seen in the small Catholic College's newspaper in Leicester. It was an open invitation by a group of gay students to get together to pray and socialize before the holidays. Simon had become enraged. He said it was offensive that such an ad should be printed in a Catholic College newspaper. Some of his brothers disagreed vehemently and Robert in particular, challenged him.

Silently, Simon could not deny his sexual attraction to Silas but had somehow managed to separate it from his spiritual life. He was guarded in how he showed his fondness for his handsome friend. Silas for his part was not an easy nut to crack and demanded little to no emotion from him. He was often evasive whenever Simon shared bits and pieces of his personal and home life and asked Silas about his. The boy from Tennessee was often alone reading and was not given to idle conversation. He seemed sad and aloof and this melancholy made him even more attractive to Simon.

It was obvious that Brother Shawn's wings had been clipped and he was no longer permitted to be in such close contact with the postulants. In fact, during the course of the following months, Simon only saw him on rare occasions and he never saw him upstairs for the rest of that postulant term. Even on those occasions when Brother Shawn was present, he didn't interact with Simon as he had done before. Simon concluded that the monk had obviously been severely reprimanded for what he had done. He realized Brother Shawn had overstepped. For the moment, distance was required. But Simon hoped that there would be other opportunities up the road to pick up where he had left off with Brother Shawn.

The months passed, and several of the postulants left on their own and abandoned the monastery. Among them was Michael who returned to Philadelphia and eventually married a girl there. Simon was saddened by this and he and Father Chris agreed that it was a significant loss to the group and the abbey. Other young men were found out and dismissed for sexual inappropriateness. One boy had been found going down to the town of Leicester to have sex with a woman there twice his age. Jesse, the boy in question, was not a handsome guy but was built like a brick shit house. He admitted to Father Chris that he could never be celibate. Another companion, from New Jersey, Kyle, had been turned in to Father Chris for inappropriate behavior in the shower room. This kid had the habit of offering unannounced and unsolicited favors behind shower curtains while some of the brothers showered. Two other postulants returned home for health reasons and another was required at home to care for his sick parents. Four more left the postulancy weeks before it was to conclude simply stating that it was not the life for them and that they had no desire to commit to entering the novitiate year. This left eleven brothers to be voted on by the arrival of spring.

As the weeks passed, the time for entering the novitiate neared. Simon was looking forward to entering the novitiate year and canonically become a part of the Order. They would receive their religious names and the professed habit of the Order even though profession of vows would still be a year and a day away. To be accepted into the novitiate was an important step for Simon because it meant that he had been found worthy and capable of moving forward on the path to priesthood. All eleven brothers were accepted by the Abbot and his council, through votation, to enter the novitiate and the Abbot himself came personally one afternoon to announce the glad tidings. Simon felt that everything was complete. He had been found worthy and Silas and Robert were also going with him on his journey toward the priesthood.

Several days later, the eleven postulants were called to the great abbey church to meet with Father Edmund personally. The Abbot was ready to determine religious names. It was an informal ceremony but one steeped in tradition. One by one, each Postulant approached the Abbot who awaited him on a kind of throne to one side of the choir stalls. They knelt, one by one, at the Abbot's feet and asked him to consider three names. The Abbot would take the three names as suggestions but was free to reject them and determine another name as equally suitable.

Simon, being the last in seniority in his class, approached and ascended the throne and knelt down. Father Edmund was kind and gracious and asked him what names he wanted to suggest.

Simon said in a hushed, nervous tone, "My first choice is Demetrius, in honor of the prince-bishop."

Father Edmund smiled and responded, "I am sorry, Brother, but that name is already taken. It is the name of our Prior. Your second choice?"

Simon had known it was a long shot but had tried anyway. Then he proceeded, a bit more confident now, saying, "I would like to request the name Simon in honor of Saint Simon the Zealot, one of Our Lord's Apostles."

"What a curious choice." The Abbot had been leaning forward in his throne and now sat back to consider the request. "Why not Simon Peter in honor of Saint Peter, the Prince of the Apostles? That name has not been taken yet."

"It came to me in prayer, Father." Simon responded. "I thought about Saint Simon's nickname, I mean, he being referred to as 'the Zealot'. It moved me because he had such great zeal in following Our Lord, even to the point of shedding his blood in a terrible martyrdom."

"I see. What other reasons motivated you to request this Hebrew name?" The Abbot played with the immense ring he wore on his right hand.

"Well, I read that it means 'he has heard' or even 'the listener'. 'I want to listen to God and respond to His call faithfully my entire life.' Simon hoped he had convinced the Abbot."

"Yes, I believe that those are very good motivations. It's a very good choice. We had a Brother Simon many years ago when I first came to the abbey. He was a good, German soul. He's buried in the crypt below us. You might visit his tomb now that you share something with him." The Abbot patted Simon affectionately on his head and said, "The name 'Simon' it is, dear boy, in honor of Saint Simon the Zealot, companion martyr of Saint Thaddeus. Go in peace." Simon was happy that his second choice was accepted because he did not have a third choice. He got up and returned to the little group of his brothers who were waiting curiously to hear what name he had received. The Abbot got up, genuflected toward the gilt tabernacle on the altar and said farewell but not before saying, "Brothers, pray for me. I will pray for you."

Silas was sitting alone in one of the wooden pews near the main altar, admiring the architectural magnificence of the place. Simon walked over to him and sat next to him. Silas asked, "What name did you receive, Larry?"

"Simon. And you?"

"I didn't want to change my name." Silas was staring at the star studded ceiling of the nave of the church.

"Why not?" Simon was intrigued.

"Well, I was told once that Silas is a Latin name and probably refers to Silvanus. He accompanied Saint Paul all over the place. He did God's work in a hidden kind of way. I mean, all the light fell on Paul but Silas was there all along the way. That's how I want to serve God. I thought my Silas name was perfect in this sense but then I heard we had to change our names. It was a bummer for me. I asked the Abbot if I could keep Silas but he said no."

Simon was wondering what name Silas had ended up with.

Silas continued, "Silas was the name of the Roman god of the forests. It has to do with nature all around us and the powerful forces there that we barely ever think about much less see and feel. But they are there." He looked at Simon now, and repeated, "The powerful forces are there, man." Simon wasn't sure he understood. Silas went on, "Silas literally means, 'man of the forest'."

Simon asked, "So what name did you receive?"

Silas smiled and said, "The abbot gave me the name. It's Tobias. The Abbot said it's a Hebrew name and said that Tobias in the Old Testament restored his father's sight. I like that image, I mean, of being God's instrument to restore other people's sight." Then he nudged his elbow into Simon's side and said, "I think I'll go by Toby. I like the sound of that." They were both happy beyond words and in a rare gesture of affection, Silas reached out and squeezed Simon's hand.

Robert came over to where Silas and Simon were sitting and asked in a hushed tone, "Hey, fellow tower mates! What names did you get?" They both answered and Robert said laughing, "I wanted to ask for Thaddeus but I was afraid you guys would all call me 'Fatty-ass'." The three young men laughed quietly well aware of where they were. Robert continued, "I asked the abbot for the name Seth and he said yes. The name means 'placed or appointed'. I'd like to believe I'm here because God intends it."

The following days were spent cleaning and painting the postulancy for the incoming class of new postulants in August. During the day they were called and allowed to enter the cloister on the other side of the abbey in order to be measured for their new habits by the monks assigned as tailors. Simon was fascinated to see the endless hallways and the beautiful cloistered gardens with arches and columns in perfect symmetry. The German brothers who served as tailors were friendly and jovial. They had been sewing at the abbey for their entire adult lives.

The atmosphere in the postulancy was festive and Father Chris seemed more like a grandfather now that his brood were on the eve of leaving. They were going to live on the other side of the abbey, in a complex of buildings near the dairy and two sets of barns but completely separated from it. A massive stone wall set the novitiate apart and included fields planted with corn and hay for the cattle. There was a forest there, as well, that was deep and permitted plenty of space for silence and solitude for the year of training and prayer.

Their names were approved and their habits sewn, both would be given tomorrow evening in a solemn ritual of entrance into the novitiate. Many of the monks of the abbey would crowd the small chapel there to welcome their new brothers in a private ceremony. Afterward, a grand supper would be offered in the professed monk's refectory and then before midnight, eleven young men would be enclosed for a year and a day without leaving the walls of the novitiate.

+ + + + +

Mark suddenly broke into the small workroom, like a bull in a china shop, "Hey, Simon, buddy, you still there?" Simon opened his eyes and the bright fluorescent lights from above momentarily blinded him. As he got his bearings he had the feeling that a great part of his life now seemed like a faraway dream, in a faraway place, in a faraway time. He realized that Mark had been away for quite a while and he had fallen into a kind of memory dream.

"Safe and sound, man." Simon tried to clear the cobwebs from his mind.

Part of him was still back in Leicester when Mark turned on the tattoo gun and began to work, saying, "Okay, here we go, almost done. Sorry for this delay." Simon felt the first cruel bites of the needle on his flesh but as Mark worked he was still in the process of letting go of Leicester and the abbey. Forty minutes later, Mark finished. "Okay, my man, we are done. Take a look!"

Simon awkwardly slid off the work table. He had been lying there quite a while. He studied the colorful tattoo of the Heart of Jesus and for one brief second was transported again to that night so many years ago when he saw the sign that read: ABBEY OF THE MOST SACRED HEART OF JESUS. He said, "It's beautiful, man. Thank you so much."

Mark was cleaning up his workspace as he turned around and asked Simon, "So I might really be opening a fucking Pandora's box here, dude, but I gotta ask you 'cause you never answered me the last time."

"I think I know your question, but go ahead." Mark had paused and Simon asked, "Well, what's the question?"

"I asked you if you were a good priest or a bad priest? You never answered. You said it was a long story and not just a 'yes' or 'no' answer. So, I ask you again, do you think you're a good priest or a bad one?"

Simon was silent and when he shook hands with Mark to leave he said, "I won't answer you yet because you need to know more but I do have a photograph for my next tattoo."

"He, he, he. Okay, evading my question AGAIN!" Mark was shaking his head in disbelief. "Cool, let's see the drawing." Simon unfolded a sheet of paper he had in his wallet. Mark smiled as he examined the photograph and exclaimed, "Ah, yes, the Green Man! Excellent image by the way. Let's do the colors in greens and pale reds. Can I keep this and do the drawing from this?"

"Yeah, sure, that's why I brought it. Can we meet in two weeks from today?" Mark took out his appointment book. "That depends, let's see…" He studied his calendar. "That would be a Friday. Wanna aim for four o'clock?"

"Yeah, excellent. Friday the 28th at four o'clock." Mark smiled broadly, so much so that Simon asked, "What? What are you smiling at?"

"Don't worry about paying me this week, we can just tack it on to the tab when you come next time. Billy is out and I'm done for today. It's been crazy."

Simon was the one smiling now and asked the tattooer, "You're smiling that shit-eating grin and knowing smile to tell me that I can pay you next time. What is it?"

Mark smiled again and finally said, "Naw, I'm just busting your balls." Then after a moment, he added, "You didn't answer my question. When are you gonna answer it, dude? Are you a good priest or a bad one?"

Simon was silent. He wanted to answer but there was still so much he had to reveal in order to answer honestly. Finally, he said, "I think you'll get a better picture when I tell you about the forest next time."

"Ah, the Green Man, yes." Mark paused and then asked, "Am I gonna hear some horny shit next time?"

Simon laughed. "We are all intimately tied to nature if that's what you mean by horny shit. My answer lies in the Green Man."

Chapter Six
Sexual Awakening

Chastity. The most unnatural of the sexual perversions.
Aldous Huxley

"I have to tell you, dude, seriously, you don't look gay. You remind me of Benny, another one of my clients. I just completed a full back tattoo on this dude." Mark was sitting in his swivel chair getting things ready for Simon's new tattoo.

Simon was curious. "Why do I remind you of Benny?"

"He's Latin and gay like you. I'd swear you're both straight but from what you guys tell me about yourselves I know that's not true at all."

"You got that right! I'm about as gay as they come."

"You sure as fuck don't look it."

"Yeah, well, looks don't always mean shit when it comes to sexuality." Mark nodded understanding. Simon removed his t-shirt over his head so that the tattooer could begin to apply the purple stencil to his skin. It wasn't necessary to shave Simon on his upper bicep, almost near the beginning of his right armpit.

Mark was talking more to himself than to Simon when he said, "Honestly, I always thought I could pick out the gay guys easily but I guess my radar is all fucked up."

"Gaydar, Mark, not radar."

Mark turned around suddenly to face Simon. "Sorry, what's that you just said?"

"You said your radar is fucked up. When you want to pick up on gay vibes you need to have your gaydar up, not your radar. Radar is for straight folks."

Mark smiled and laughed softly. "Oh, right. You gay guys are all alike. Maybe that's why you and Benny got under the wire from me. I'm intrigued, though, I gotta tell you."

"Intrigued about what?"

"I can't say I've ever had any gay friends I actually knew about." He stopped what he was doing and added, "Hell, I sure as fuck never had any Catholic priest friends! I wanna know more about all that from you. Tell me, 'cause I'm not clear on how all that worked out. How did you get from living in the real world to checking yourself into that monastic prison?" Simon remembered the nine months he had spent in postulancy and all that happened to him since he had left home and gone to Leicester. It was a lot to take in and Simon wondered if Mark would be interested in all of those details. Postulancy and meeting Shawn had certainly played an important part in the introduction to the abbey. He couldn't deny that his first impressions of Toby and Seth had also been foundational but Simon felt that what Mark was asking lay elsewhere. Mark had put forward a question to him and Simon now recalled the night he and ten other young men entered the high walls of the novitiate on the far, west side of the abbey and figured that this might be a better place to begin to answer Mark's question.

He said, "It was no prison, man. It was in a massive, magnificent abbey, in a section called the novitiate, not so much a place, really, as much as an experience lasting exactly a year and a day. It began with an ancient ritual late at night. That's really what drew me to that place. The organization and the traditional things there."

"I'm all ears, dude. Hey, by the way, don't mean to interrupt you, but here's the sketch I came up with for your Green Man tattoo today." Simon glimpsed at the purple stencil Mark held out to him. The green, leafy face in the drawing smiled back at him and Simon remembered the forest at the novitiate in Leicester and those moments of clarity he had experienced there. He heard the tattoo gun whine into life and began to tell Mark about that long ago night at the abbey when he officially entered the Order.

Simon thought and then said, "It was evening and the chapel at the novitiate was crowded with monks. There were no outsiders since it was a private ceremony only for the community of religious men. The eleven of us who were to receive our names and be clothed in the black habit of the Order were giddy with excitement but also filled with anticipation. This was now the moment to take another significant step toward the dream." Simon closed his eyes and could see himself dressed in his slim, black suit, wearing his white shirt and black tie. He barely heard himself speaking to Mark, as he slipped deeply into his memory.

+ + + + +

A Solemn Sacrifice of the Mass was begun and Simon did his best to stay focused, although his nerves made most of it a blur. When the moment in the Mass arrived, the ritual of Investiture began. Simon and his ten companions laid face down on the cold stone floor of the novitiate chapel before the main altar. The Abbot was dressed in heavy gold vestments and wore a tall miter on his head. He knelt and faced the tabernacle that sat on the altar. Simon looked up briefly and noticed a thin black line lying across the bottom step of the altar sanctuary, behind the kneeling Abbot. After the Litany of the Saints had been sung by the chanting choir of monks in the loft, two monks approached the black line from either side of the sanctuary. They took it and lifted it up. It was clearly a black cloth that had been neatly folded on the floor in front of the young men, which was now stretched out over them, covering their heads, backs and feet completely. The thin black cloth bore skull and crossbones representing death. The action that had just taken place was nothing less than spreading a pall over a catafalque during a Requiem ritual.

A monk intoned the first words of Psalm 129 and as the "De Profundis" began in plain chant, the other monks joined in: "Out of the depths I cry to you, O Lord, hear my voice; Let your ears be attentive to my voice in supplication." It was definitely a ritual of death. Death to the world, death to a former way of life, death to sin. The "De Profundis" is a penitential psalm that commemorates the dead and expresses sorrow for sins committed. It was being chanted for Simon and his ten young companions prostrate on the stone floor. Clouds of heavily perfumed incense wafted solemnly throughout the chapel in thick gray layers and slowly moved upward like the prayers of supplication being chanted to God in Heaven. The incense also curled up into itself as it reached the narrow Gothic crevices of the vaulted ceiling above and descended, wrapping itself around those gathered in the sacred place reminding them that God had heard their cries and was responding.

When the chanting of the psalm was ended, a sense of melancholy permeated the small chapel. In silence, the Abbot stood up and turned around. A high-backed throne was brought out and carried up the three steps into the altar. The Abbot sat down. One by one, each of the folded black habits were brought to him and he blessed them with holy water in silence. Then the black funeral pall was quickly removed off the young men. One of the monks knelt next to Robert and whispered to him to stand up and approach the Abbot, which he did. He knelt before him and two other monks helped him remove his suit jacket. The Abbot took the long, black tunic and placed it over Robert's head, assisted by the two monks who helped him get his arms into the ample sleeves.

"Receive this tunic in remembrance of Our Lord Jesus Christ's terrible Cross, Passion and Death. May you never forget what God has done for you in His Sacrifice." Then he placed the belt around his waist saying, "May you discipline your passions and guard your loins and keep from sin." And finally the capuche, saying, "May this holy cape and hood protect you from the wiles of the devil as you labor steadfastly in the Eternal Father's vineyard without worldly distraction." Once invested with the habit of the Order, the Abbot took the young man's hands into his own and said, "In the world you were known as Robert. The old man has now died and the new man rises to life in you. You have left the world with all its lies and vices. From this day forward you will be known as Seth."

The Abbot embraced him and Seth returned to his place and knelt among his prostrated companions. The next brother stood up as commanded and approached the Abbot. All ten did so and when the tenth had returned and knelt, Larry got up and approached the throne. He was the last of his class and his heart swelled with gratitude and joy when he finally felt himself clothed in the religious habit and heard the words, "From this day forward you will be known as Simon."

After the Solemn Sacrifice was concluded, Simon and his companions, now canonically recognized monks, joined the abbot and their professed brother monks for a grand supper in the main refectory of the abbey. Simon had never been in the colossal dining room, with its arched high ceilings covered in frescos. They depicted the history of the abbey in Leicester, the Prince-Bishop Demetrius and the arrival of the German monks into that locality. It was a veritable feast and Simon and his companions were beside themselves when they were led to sit at the head table on either side of the

Abbot. Over three hundred monks were in attendance as was the custom on this night.

At precisely midnight, the Abbot and many monks accompanied the eleven new novices to the front door of the novitiate. The Abbot knocked three times with his golden crosier and the door opened from within. Father Bartholomew, the Master of Novices, greeted the Abbot and the monks. They stepped back when he called the novices by name to enter the enclosure. Once inside, the novices did not look back and the door was locked behind them. The novitiate year and a day had begun.

This was a significant change from the postulancy when they had merely been candidates. Simon and his brothers, because they were now monks of the Order, each had their own, private bedroom or "cell" as it was called. There was a sink in the small cell, a mirror above it, and just enough space for a cot and small writing desk with a free standing crucifix on it. A narrow closet would easily accommodate the few clothes each novice possessed since the religious habit would now be worn daily for chapel, classes and all meals. It was not required for chores inside nor farm work. It would also be required for recreation time in the evening and final prayers before bedtime, after which the Grand Silence commenced. Shower stalls and toilets were still in common down one of the long halls. During this year they would all prepare for their profession of the vows of poverty, chastity and obedience if they were approved. Every day was carefully planned and structured for them. It was a spiritual year, with ample time for reflection, study and preparation.

The novitiate buildings themselves were built as a kind of square, enclosing two small cloistered gardens each with a fountain at its center. One was dedicated to the Sorrowful Mother and the other to the Guardian Angels. The chapel here was larger than the one in the postulancy and was also Gothic in style. Its narrow nave was bathed by the mesmerizing glow of light that streamed in through the stained glass windows. The old altar remained in place and was facing east toward Jerusalem, but a smaller modern altar had been placed before it according to the recent liturgical reforms and faced west. Simon longed for the old liturgical forms and this chapel filled a void in him and made him feel at home in the sacred space still preserved there.

Fields, thick with corn and hay lay within the novitiate stone walls and livestock on the property was kept in two large wooden barns. The novices cared for and fed the animals as well as harvested corn, vegetables and hay according to the seasons. Hay had to be baled by hand and then carried into the barn, stacked and salted. The previous year's novices had done this same work but the newly arrived men would soon need to replenish the supply in the barn and prepare for the harsh winter to come. There was also a plush forest to the north of the novitiate property. On his first full day there, Simon looked out the small window of his cell and noticed the forest. It was deep with pines, firs and evergreens. He was drawn to it immediately and promised himself to visit it soon.

Several weeks passed and Simon became much more aware of himself in a way he hadn't before. He was drawn gently to face himself as he began to awaken sexually. He still desired with his whole heart to serve God and was very happy in religious life but little by little he became more aware of his body and his new sexual feelings. He was now eighteen years old and was quickly becoming a man. He had never really cared much for dating girls when he was in high school but now, all of a sudden, his thoughts often times involved his fellow brothers in a way that was unsettling for him. He struggled with the fact that he longed to be with some of them in a sexual way. These desires began to disconcert Simon more and more. He decided at some point that he needed to mention this inclination in the confessional to the priest confessor. Yet he hesitated, fearing a severe reprimand for having contemplated these thoughts. He had been taught that those things were depraved.

He would sit in chapel in his habit on those terribly warm afternoons. There, in his assigned choir stall during meditation, his mind would wander during the readings of sacred texts. As passages from the inspired writings of Saint Leo the Great, Saint Augustine and the Church Fathers were being read aloud in the chapel, Simon wondered to himself if the brother doing the reading had a hairy chest like his own. He let himself be carried away by images of slender thighs and abdomens. His thoughts would lure him to images of slender, hairy legs hidden from view under the folds of the religious habit. His thoughts made him ask himself if the brothers across the chapel from him in choir, also masturbated themselves during the hot, stifling afternoon siestas, on their cots as he did. Simon let his musings take him where he had never gone before. He often wondered what it would be like to strip down and get naked with one or two of his fellow novices. These musings intensified when, as prayers concluded, some of them often smiled at him when everyone stood to sing the closing hymn.

Sometimes Simon felt powerless before these insistent fantasies. What would it be like to lie down with one of them and give them pleasure in the same exact way that he gave himself pleasure? He knew that these thoughts and feelings were prohibited and that he had to keep them hidden within himself. Otherwise, he would be severely reproached and certainly dismissed if he acted on them. He knew these thoughts and actions belonged to the realm of grave and serious sin. Why did these thoughts fill him with such intense desire? Where did they come from?

The only place he could discuss these things without fear of being found out publicly, was in the confessional. In the secrecy of that Sacrament, the priest was bound to keep everything he heard to himself and take it all to the tomb with him when he died. Still, Simon knew enough to know that he had to be very careful about what he said and how he said it. He had an urgent need to speak about it with someone and who better than the monk priests assigned to hear their confessions on a weekly basis. It was vastly important to Simon to confess his sins as a way of reigning them in and taming them. It would lessen the guilt that would build up within him. He would prepare himself carefully for the moment of the Sacrament, believing in his heart what he had been taught by the nuns, namely, that going to Confession and telling the priest your sins was nothing less than a personal encounter with Jesus Christ Himself. The priest was only there "a persona Christi", in Christ's person, and therefore, it was Jesus Himself who sat there and listened. It was Jesus who gave you counsel and it was Jesus Himself who forgave you your sins through Sacramental Absolution if you were truly sorry. The penance given and satisfied, was a way of sealing the deal and then, peacefully, you could get on with your life. But Simon worried about the priest's response to his confessed transgressions and the reprimand he would receive. He knew that his musings were unacceptable if he was truly serious about the priesthood.

Nevertheless, Simon went to confession one afternoon after having decided not to hold back anything, any longer.

He entered the small confines of the confessional box and heard the priest say, "In the name of the Father, and of the Son, and of the Holy Ghost."

Simon closed his eyes and responded, "Amen."

The priest asked, "What are your sins, brother?"

"Bless me, Father, for I have sinned. It has been a week since my last confession. These are my sins." Simon hesitated, and finally said, "For many weeks now since I began my novitiate year, I get these certain thoughts and they don't leave me alone."

"What kind of thoughts?" The priest asked flatly without expressing too much interest.

"Bad thoughts, Father. I try and push them away but they only come back stronger."

The priest shifted in the dark on his bench and asked, "What do you mean by bad thoughts, brother? Do you wish ill to others?"

"Oh, no, Father, nothing like that. It's more about me and certain desires."

"What kind of bad thoughts visit you? Can you explain it better?"

Simon had to finally say it plainly and get it out, so he said, "Sexual thoughts, Father."

The priest suddenly bolted upright in the shadows of his side of the confessional box with renewed interest. "What kind of sexual thoughts?" Simon could see that the priest had moved closer to the screen that separated them. He pressed his ear to it and his tone darkened, "What kind of sexual thoughts are you entertaining? Be specific."

"I think about some of my fellow novices in a way I know I shouldn't. The bad thoughts just come out of nowhere."

"And what way is that, brother? How do you think of your brothers?"

"I think often about some of them being naked and the things that I would like to do with them."

The priest moved away from the screen, and exhaled loudly. Simon could see that he was shaking his head from side to side. His hands appeared to be tightened into fists, tapping on the armrests of the bench he sat on. "No! No! No! This is the devil's work, plain and simple. What have you been giving in to? You say you think about this often?"

"Yes, Father." Simon knew where this was going. He had the urge to run out of there as fast as he could but he knew that it wasn't an option. He was talking to God.

"How often? How many times?"

"Very often, Father. Lately, it happens very often. I think about it when I am in chapel and in my cell. Sometimes when I am in the refectory. I think about it at night when I am in my bed."

The priest looked right at Simon through the screen separating them. He growled, "You listen to me, boy, you listen good. There is no place for that kind of perversion here! And if you insist on slithering into that muck, then there is no place for you here! Do you understand? God Himself is calling you to be a sacred vessel, not a whore from Sodom and Gomorrah!"

For what seemed like an eternity to Simon, the priest remained silent. Simon felt like he would suffocate in the tiny, dark space. His knees ached as he waited. Simon finally broke the silence, "I'm sorry for these thoughts. I truly am, Father."

"You should be! God gives strength to those who seek it in order to fight the greatest evils, but we must beg Him for that Grace." The priest exhaled again and then, lowering his voice, asked Simon, "Have you asked God to defend you from this foulness? Have you begged Him to help you?"

"Yes, Father, I have but the thoughts and desires persist. They are stronger than I am."

The priest erupted in anger as he gesticulated in the shadows, "You wretched sinner! Are they stronger than God? Is that what you're saying? Are these thoughts and desires stronger than God's power and strength? You haven't trusted God! Instead you have given in and enjoyed thinking these thoughts. Isn't that really what's going on here?"

Simon sighed, defeated and worn. "Yes, Father, I guess it's what I have done."

The priest erupted again, "You guess! You guess, do you?"

"I'm sorry, Father. I meant to say, I know it's what I have done. I am truly sorry."

"Do you think for one fleeting moment that you can defend yourself alone, without the help of Almighty God? You are slipping down a path of certain destruction and you GUESS and you are barely aware of the serious danger you are in. If you keep entertaining what the devil is feeding you, you will lose your vocation and ultimately your very soul!" He moved close to the screen again and asked gravely, "Have you acted on any of those thoughts? Tell me and God truthfully, have you acted out any of these perverted fantasies with anyone here?" Simon did not answer and the priest repeated his question. Then he added, "The fall into the eternal fires of Hell is an easy one, boy. Have you acted out any of these sinful thoughts and desires?"

Simon found his voice and answered, "No, Father, I haven't touched anyone else. I promise. But I have touched myself in an impure manner several times because of the thoughts and desires."

The priest tapped hard on the screen now and Simon looked up and saw that he was pointing his index finger at him. "It is a grave sin, it is a filthy habit. You know it is!" Then he added, "At least you have confessed it. I cannot give you absolution unless you are sincerely sorry for your sins."

Simon felt completely broken and beaten up. He could say nothing and bowed his head so low in the darkness that his neck ached badly. The priest repeated his remark and asked him if he was truly sorry for his sins. Defeated, Simon answered, "Yes, Father, I am very sorry for my sins and ask God for strength to help me avoid the near occasion of sin. I beg you for absolution."

"For your penance, you will pray five rosaries and ask God to give you the Grace to resist these filthy temptations. Now make an Act of Contrition."

"Oh my God, I am heartily sorry for having offended Thee…" Simon finished the prayer, relieved that his confession was over.

Then the priest added, "And you will refrain from accepting dessert for one week. Think well on what you have done."

"Yes, Father." It was finally over.

Even though he experienced deep humiliation when he confessed to a priest and was scolded, he continued to approach the confessional often because it gave him inner peace. He also believed he was the only one in the abbey that had such sinful inclinations. He couldn't compare notes with anyone because he wouldn't dare give himself away. Sometimes he wouldn't get into much detail even when the priest pressed him for such. Some fear began to take hold of him when he considered that the sexual feelings and thoughts were becoming just as powerful within him as God's call for him to become a priest. Simon could not believe that these sinful, lower instincts that were awakening within him, had anything to do with God's sacred plans for him. He had no way of knowing what God had in store for him.

He was told continually that he must not masturbate nor indulge in sexual feelings or fantasies. He had been told that these were beneath the dignity of a religious and a priest. It had been made clear to him that the things of the world and the flesh must never be coupled with the things of Heaven and God. He had begged God for strength and tried to stop the feelings and thoughts but had not been very successful. He was moved to read Saint Augustine's admission in the saint's writings, found in the ancient text entitled *Confessions*. Augustine had been tempted like him and repented. He had been capable of avoiding his sins, saying to God, "Why do I always say, tomorrow, tomorrow? Why not say 'yes' today?" Augustine had asked for strength and received it. Simon didn't understand why he put off conversion and holiness. He had tried to say "yes" to God but more and more he still fantasized. He felt weak in this regard.

Life on the farm during the novitiate year was different than the previous year had been when they all simply went to college classes. Now, after a full day of haying and being out in the sun, he felt charged as any young man of eighteen years would. The common shower room became an erotic environment for him and the smell of soap and sweaty bodies that permeated it, became almost overwhelming for him at times. These aromas awoke in him great passions. Even though everyone showered separately behind shower curtains, his thoughts took him to new heights of fantasy. He didn't know how to deal with everything he felt and therefore, he took it to prayer and to the confessional. It wasn't a permanent fix for him but it served as a source, in order for him to have inner peace. Yet, the process made him feel battered and his soul felt bruised. He would confess, be severely reprimanded and begin again.

Then slowly and without any kind of planning or much thought given, Simon began to deal with his duality in another way, as best he could. He made another kind of peace within himself by dealing with the two opposing forces on his own terms. He realized he didn't have the necessary will to fight within himself, and he gave in to his weaknesses. He decided to entertain both and simply keep them apart. It wasn't a perfect plan by any means and sometimes it didn't work so well. But ultimately, not knowing what else to do with the opposing realities in his life, he began to create distance between his sexual self and his spiritual self. He didn't know how to stamp out his sexual feelings and thoughts, while at the same time, pursue God's lofty call. So he built a kind of fortified wall between them, within himself. In this way, not fully realizing it, he began to take his first steps toward living in two worlds at the same time. It would become a taxing affair, but it seemed to him that it was the easiest and most practical way out of his complex dilemma.

On one particularly warm, summer afternoon, when they were given free time by Father Bartholomew, whom they called affectionately, Father Bart, Simon and some of his companions were in the recreation room chatting and listening to records. The door to the room suddenly flew open and a familiar face entered the room triumphantly.

Seth murmured under his breath, "Oh, shit, look what the cat dragged in."

Simon was happy to see his old friend, and said, "Hey, Shawn! How are you, my man? What a surprise! How did you get in?"

Brother Shawn smiled and spoke directly to Simon, ignoring the others, "It just got to be too much living here without seeing you!" Then he turned to the other brothers assembled and said, "Hey boys, is everybody getting all holy and such?" Some of the brothers laughed at Brother Shawn's remark and got up to hug him. Brother Shawn hugged and tugged and pushed them around playfully. Simon joined them. At long last, Brother Shawn said, "I want to introduce you to one of your fellow monks, Brother Arnold. He's one of our lay monks, although, who knows, maybe someday he'll change his mind and study for the priesthood. He teaches at the Catholic school we staff down in the town of Leicester." Brother Arnold at first seemed easy to get to know and friendly. Physically, he was a little on the stocky side and walked with a pronounced limp as if his legs were of different lengths. He wore his straight blond hair covering his ears and forehead. Simon studied this middle aged man and his impression shifted, thinking that his smile and laughter were too sweet and exaggerated to be genuine. He thought that his friendly manner wasn't authentic at all.

Brother Arnold shook everyone's hands with eagerness and when he came to Simon, he took one of his hands into his own and squeezed. "Oh, yes, very good! So you're Brother Simon from Florida! Brother Shawn has told me all about you." He smiled knowingly as he glanced over to Brother Shawn and they both giggled, obviously sharing a private joke. Simon looked at Brother Shawn who was busy messing up Toby's carefully combed hair. The two visiting monks sat down and spent a good hour with the novices. Brother Shawn had moved around the room and planted himself next to Toby, trying to make light conversation.

Toby asked, "I thought no one was allowed in to the novitiate unless they had something to do with us? Does Father Bart know you guys are here? How did you get through the locked doors?"

Brother Shawn smiled smugly. "It's all on the up and up, Officer Tobias. Honestly, we haven't broken in! And thank you for your warm, kind reception, Brother! As a matter of fact, I've been assigned by the Abbot to help Father

Bart with you guys in your classes. It wasn't easy, but I managed to convince old Daddy Ed."

Toby was on the defensive, "And your sidekick?" Toby motioned over to Brother Arnold who was busy straightening his hair with his fingers as he spoke to some of the brothers around him.

Brother Shawn acted as if he was offended, saying, "C'mon now, that's not very nice. Brother Arnold is a lot of fun once you get to know him. Maybe one night we can come over and liven up your recreation." Then he said, "I was given a key to the novitiate by the Abbot himself so I can let myself in when I come to help Father Bart. Anyone who comes with me is allowed in under my discretion." Toby said nothing but stared at Brother Arnold who was limping around the room making some of the brothers laugh and roll over in the sofas.

Toby overheard Brother Arnold saying in a high-pitched female voice, "Okay, I'm now one of the Sisters of Mercy in Philadelphia and this is how they used to walk in the classroom, up and down the aisles." He had thrown back his capuche over his head to resemble a nun's veil. Brother Arnold had one hand under his chin and supported it at the elbow with his other hand in a mock nun-like gesture. Then he began walking around the room as if he were in a real classroom, playfully hitting the novices with the belt of his religious habit. Brother Shawn caught Toby's disapproving stare and blew in his ear, making Toby move away.

He moved in closer and said softly, "Oh, come on, rugged, tough man. He's harmless, just a buffoon that makes us laugh." Toby continued to stare unblinking, at the middle aged man imitating the nuns. He said nothing.

Simon had gotten up laughing and changed the record on the player, asking, "Can I put on Godspell?"

Brother Shawn took advantage of the opportunity and once the record was in place went over to where Simon was and said, "Hey, stranger, wanna take a walk outside? I've missed you."

Simon was pleased to be singled out by the monk and asked him, "Is it true what I heard, that some of you will be considered soon for ordination to the diaconate?"

"Well, it's in the works, but things move slow around here if you haven't already noticed. Let's go outside, I'll tell you all about it." Then he added, putting his arm around Simon and gently ushering him away, "Let's take a walk and get some fresh air."

"Okay." Simon was swept away and led out a side door, into one of the cloistered gardens. It was the garden dedicated to the Sorrowful Mother. It was Simon's favorite of the two gardens within the walls of the novitiate. There was a statue there of the Blessed Mother enveloped in sorrow and hunched over, overcome by the passion of Her Son Jesus. The two men began to walk around the cloister garden, under the vaulted, stone ceiling above them.

Brother Shawn kept the pace slow, sensing that Simon was tense and somewhat apprehensive. "What's wrong, little one? You don't seem at ease." Brother Shawn rubbed Simon's back in short, deliberate circles.

"Nothing. I just didn't think I'd be seeing you this afternoon. Plus, won't Brother Arnold be looking for you?"

"I brought that fool precisely to entertain the others with all his mindless nun shit. He's such a closeted queen but for some reason, a real hit with the older monks. They believe all the bullshit he tells them because he knows what those old farts wanna hear. He's got the wool pulled over their eyes, that bullshitter! Arnold thinks he's out because he's so outrageous in the abbey but you ought to see him down at the school in front of teachers and parents. He's a big fake. Anyway, I brought him so that you and I could spend a little time together away from everyone else. It's literally been ages since I've seen you or we've spoken. You say that nothing is wrong with you. Is that true?"

Simon protested vehemently, "Yeah, of course, it's true, Shawn. I just thought the powers at be would keep you away from us in formation since you suddenly disappeared from Postulancy when…"

"Oh, that fucking fiasco! That shit was awful. 'The Beak' was just an asshole with all that and stirred up trouble for me. He's so homophobic and the kick is he's such a closeted old queen himself!" Brother Shawn walked a little faster now fueled by his anger. "He tore me a new asshole because I kept you from that friggin' volleyball bullshit game. He said I was getting too close to you and some of the others. He was all crazy that others in the abbey would take notice and start talking and create a scandal."

Simon looked at Brother Shawn with wide eyes and asked, "Really? Did you get in big trouble?"

"Well, that fucker sure tried but I have my connections. Eddie covered for me."

"Who's Eddie?" Simon was sincerely baffled.

"Daddy Ed." Brother Shawn smiled as he said this then added, "Father Edmund, the Abbot."

"Oh, sorry, I didn't understand."

"Well, yeah, 'The Beak' tried to get me in trouble, saying I was a bad influence and bad example. As I said, he suggested some people might even think it was 'homo shit'. Eddie was real cool, though, and agreed that it was just best that I keep distance from the postulants. I told him it was prudent that I keep distance from 'The Beak' and we both had a good laugh over that. I was able to swing it to help Father Bart here and also be close to you. I don't want you getting lost in the shuffle here." Having said this last, Brother Shawn slowed his pace again and then stopped walking altogether. Simon joined him and Brother Shawn put out his hand and placed it on Simon's shoulder. "Yeah, I worry about you because I know you need someone to talk to." He looked at Simon with a compassionate expression. He finally said, "Father Bart was happy for my help and besides, Eddie knows we're far away from the clutches of that boney assed bastard in the postulancy. The Abbot knows only too well how homophobic he can get. He knows that monks often get close to each other and that it's not always a bad thing." Brother Shawn now put his free hand on Simon's other shoulder and moved in closer to him, pushing him gently backward, toward the stone wall. When Simon's back was flatly resting against it, he admitted, "I'm glad it worked out, little one."

"Me too, Shawn." Simon hesitated and spoke carefully, afraid that his emotions would betray him and that he'd start crying. "I have been…dealing with difficult feelings."

"Go ahead, I'm listening."

Simon looked away and when he looked back up and into Brother Shawn's eyes, great tears welled up in his large, dark Latin eyes. All he could manage to say was, "It's been real crazy for me lately. I have so many thoughts crashing into me and flying around in my head. I don't know how to stop it. I go to confession but the priests don't help any. They mean well, but they beat me up pretty bad. I've found that I can't be completely honest with them." Simon hesitated and then added, "Like I can be with you."

Brother Shawn was standing very close to Simon when he said, "I'm happy to hear you know you can trust me."

Simon rubbed his eyes and wiped away the moisture gathering at his nostrils. He cleared his throat and continued, "Yeah, remember what we talked about on that day you gave me the tour?"

"Refresh my memory, little one."

Simon was nervous now because he was moving into unchartered waters but pushed ahead anyway, "You asked me stuff about Silas, I mean, Toby. That's his name now. Well, Tobias but he prefers Toby."

"Yes, I know he's Toby. What did we talk about?"

"You told me in the crypt that you were afraid I was getting too close to him or that he and I were getting too close to each other. You said there was nothing wrong with that but that there was a danger other guys would be jealous and say we were 'P.F.'s'. Then the shit would hit the fan and I could get thrown out because 'The Beak' was all homophobic."

"I was helping you because you are special to me, Simon. Did you understand that then? I told you those things because I care for you, even though I knew they would scare you and be hard to accept."

"Yes, I know that. I remember you said you felt a special connection."

"Yes, that's right." Brother Shawn was massaging Simon's shoulders as he spoke.

"So I listened to you and did my best to control what I was feeling for Silas."

"Silas. You mean Toby."

"Yeah, Toby. Sorry." This made Simon smile.

"Go on."

"I distanced myself from him because like you said to me, I shouldn't be stupid with my feelings."

Brother Shawn moved his head slightly in agreement and pressed down on Simon's shoulders. "Go on, what else?"

"In confession, the priests all said that masturbation is a serious sin but that men being attracted to men is far, far worse." He looked up pathetically at Brother Shawn for an answer and asked, "That's not true, is it? I mean, you said it's okay to have sexual feelings toward other guys. You told me that God put those feelings in some of us. And I told you that I was attracted to Silas, I mean, Toby. I'm sorry, I still can't get used to our new names."

Brother Shawn glanced into Simon's teary eyes and asked, "Do you think I was lying to you, Simon, when I told you that? Do you think I was misleading you on purpose? I was honest with you and you were honest with me." He looked away dramatically then and let his words sink in. Finally, he looked back into Simon's eyes and said, "Men who desire other men and share intimacy together is something that has always existed. It's not something dirty and sick and it sure as hell is not sinful in my book. In fact, how can we ever help people as priests unless we too have allowed ourselves to touch other people's lives and have the experience of giving ourselves to another and being taken by them? You just have to know how to keep it to yourself. If nobody knows, there's no problem."

"But the priests are all telling me the opposite thing. That I need to avoid it and be strong. They're clear in that anything sexual is sinful if I act upon it. We are called to be celibate and chaste once we take our vows."

"Look, they are repeating the shit they learned from a million years ago. But grow up. The guys that tell you that shit in the confessional box are hot for somebody, or were hot for somebody at some point in their life. I can guarantee you that. Most of them are closeted, decrepit, old farts, incapable of getting a hard-on anymore, let alone be honest with themselves about their sexual appetites." Simon said nothing, not sure he agreed with Brother Shawn. He honestly wondered where Brother Shawn got his information about the older priests. How could Brother Shawn be so sure? Plus, it all sounded terribly irreverent and against what he had been taught were God's unchanging laws. Brother Shawn continued, "You just need to know one thing. It's perfectly okay to have sexual fantasies about men. Sometimes, in some situations, it's even okay to act upon them. But let me repeat, just don't be stupid and careless. If it gives you joy, where's the fucking harm? It's nobody's business what you do behind closed doors. It's your life."

Simon looked at Brother Shawn and wanted to believe him with his whole heart. "I'm having so many feelings and thoughts about sex all the time and I don't know what to do about it anymore. I jerk myself off a hundred times a day it seems and I know that's a sin too."

"Oh, Simon, c'mon. That's another bullshit line they've fed you and you obviously still believe. Jerking off because you get horny and stroking one out is way overrated. Grow up. You're just blowing off steam."

Simon looked at Brother Shawn in disbelief and asked, "It's really normal and healthy to have sexual feelings toward other men?"

"Yes, it is, little one. It's a gift from God. Sex is meant to happen for every human person. That's why you have that junk between your legs and sometimes it even stands up and begs for attention. It's not just for pissing."

Simon was struggling. "But is that true for us? Those of us called by God to become monks and priests? It's prohibited for us if we take vows."

"Look, that's how they've set it up for centuries but it's hardly a perfect arrangement. Hell, I'd even go so far as to say it's hypocritical. We're only still, just men, made of flesh and blood. Sex is fundamental to humans. Just don't fuck it up by being careless in this environment and giving yourself away. Sadly, there are so many ways you can do that."

Simon wanted to say something but didn't know how to phrase it. He struggled with the secrets he was keeping so carefully. He only managed to say, "I…just…"

Brother Shawn moved in even closer, his face almost brushing up against Simon's, saying, "Let it out, little one, tell me what you need to let go of. Don't live in fear, all tied up in knots within yourself. Let it out. You know you can trust me."

Simon looked deep into the other man's eyes, wanting so much to believe everything he had just been told and said, "Well, in the last few weeks, a lot of times I think about the guys. Not just Toby but other guys too. It comes to me in chapel and in class. Sometimes in the shower room after working outside or at night when I can't sleep. I think about some of the brothers being naked and I wonder what it would be like to touch them. I jerk myself off in my room thinking about it and in the shower I hear their voices and it drives me crazy. I feel like a great pressure builds up in me and I can't release it even when I masturbate. There's nobody to talk to."

Brother Shawn whispered, "I'm here for you. You can always talk to me like you're doing now."

"Yes, there's you. I can trust you, Shawn. I don't know what I'd do if you weren't here in this abbey." Simon was totally unprepared for what happened next and it would be a very long time before he would be able to forgive himself for what happened. Without warning, Brother Shawn had eased one hand around Simon's back and firmly planted his other hand on the back of Simon's neck. Then he had moved in and kissed Simon firmly on his lips. The feeling of newfound pleasure that spread through Simon was so intense that he instinctively opened his mouth without resistance. He had never experienced anything like that before.

Laughter was heard abruptly as a set of double doors squeaked open not far away. Brother Arnold could be heard approaching them. Simon and Brother Shawn jumped back quickly, away from each other. Brother Arnold announced in the high-pitched voice of an imaginary nun that perhaps it was time to go, lest, "Reverend Mother Edmunda will become angry with us for bothering the novices and decide on tightening our veils as a punishment!" Brother Arnold burst out in silly laughter. When the visitors had left, Simon returned to his cell but was too tense and nervous. He made his way to the chapel and sat before the tabernacle, knowing that God would listen. Simon had an awful lot to think about.

A week or two passed before Father Bart announced that the novices would be free the following afternoon. He had a meeting to attend in the abbey and could not schedule their usual time for class. The Master of Novices did give them an assignment of meditation, however, and as the priest spoke, Simon already knew how he would spend the afternoon. He would go into the forest on a hike and meditate on all that God would show him there. He also decided that it would be important to go alone and tell no one where he was going. The next day after lunch, the novices dispersed. Some went to chapel and others set themselves up in one of the cloister gardens to meditate that afternoon. Some went out into the corn fields and one found refuge in a high loft in one of the barns, lying down comfortably on a bed of sweet hay. Simon set out by himself toward the forest he had so much desired to visit. He searched for an overgrown entrance to the forest and entered it there.

After walking some distance he discovered a bubbling creek of fresh, clear water that sparkled in the sunlight. It ran at the far end of the abbey property. Simon saw on that day that beyond the creek stood the continuation of the great stone wall that enclosed the Novitiate property. He continued walking along the banks of the creek in a secluded area of woods and pine trees where many fallen trees made excellent places to sit or lie back. The nearby sound of the rushing water of the creek made it refreshing there. He was drawn to that place from the moment he discovered it. There was a clearing of a few firs and evergreens and Simon knew he had found his haunt. Pine needles and small decaying branches thickly covered this one particular spot like a comfortable carpet underfoot. He sat on the bed of needles completely relaxed. Sunlight poured through the tall trees above like shards of glass and penetrated this particularly cool, dense area of the forest, lighting up everything that was in its path. He noticed that beyond, the forest seemed to be in greater darkness. He could literally feel the coolness coming from there and it lulled him to sleep. Simon stayed there for a very long time that afternoon. He had found it easy to pray and meditate. When he woke, Simon took his journal out and began to write. His thoughts flowed out of him easily and he recorded the assignment of meditation that Father Bart had given them that day. He hiked slowly back to the novitiate knowing that he would visit that place again.

Whenever Simon had several hours of freedom to himself, he would slip away to his special place in the forest. Often he would fall asleep there, in the dense shade and wonderful smells that enveloped him. It was his favorite, secret place. Everything there spoke to him of God's presence. Moss and ferns grew out of the various fallen trees that were scattered about. Even though the forest was heavily shaded, the brightness that always shone through, here and there, made him feel secure and safe. Simon grew in understanding that everything there was fully alive instead of decaying. He sensed that the examples of decay lying all around him was only a decoy to confuse those intruders who did not belong there. He came to understand that he was a part of the same life that was well rooted there.

The forest permitted Simon a haven in which to think about what he felt rising within him. While he was inside the novitiate itself, he often felt ill at ease by his growing sexual awareness. As these desires blossomed in him, he sought solace in the forest. He felt completely free there. It was easy for him to pray when he visited and whenever he could, he'd escape to the forest because he felt the burden he carried, being lifted away from him. He could have his sexual thoughts in that place and deeply immerse himself in them without feeling guilty. Once there, he could actually unleash the passions that were building in him. There, in that unique place, he belonged not only to what he could perceive but also to something much bigger.

This is why, on a Saturday afternoon, when the novices were free, Simon hastened to the forest making sure no one followed him. As he entered the shaded sanctuary on that particular afternoon, he experienced an energy and hunger within himself that he had never before felt so keenly. He let the forest lead him to the secret place and once he arrived he suddenly got the idea to strip down completely naked. At first, Simon hesitated but the desire in him was too overpowering and without much thought, he gave in.

In the back of his mind he figured that if an intruder suddenly showed up unannounced, the forest would let him know. He would certainly hear the intruder stepping on branches and twigs well before they could see him in his nakedness. Without holding back, he removed his sweaty clothes but kept his shoes and socks on. He looked down at himself and saw that every fiber of his body was exhilarated and on fire with desire. The sounds of birds and insects all around him made him aware of God's presence. The hairs on his neck, arms and legs stood out from his gooseflesh and he felt God grazing his skin delicately and lovingly in the light breeze that caressed him as it blew by.

Simon believed that God was there, watching him, enthralled with the world of His own creation. He believed that God was deriving pleasure at that moment as He contemplated him. He lost himself so entirely in the divine presence that he was unaware of someone else, other than God, who was also contemplating him and his every movement that day in the forest. The intruder had been clever enough not to step on twigs and branches.

Simon was filled with many emotions at that heightened moment and slowly began to walk around. First, he went to the bubbling creek where he knelt down and cupped his hands in the moving stream. He drank and reveled in the cold water that spilled on his chest and ran down into his aching loins. He hiked up and down familiar paths and then returned to the carpet of pine needles that awaited him. It was then at the peak of his passion that Simon felt the hand of God upon him. He experience in an instant, the loving embrace of God and realized that God was not simply outside of him but that the Creator, the Almighty who sat on the altars, was bursting forth from a fountain within him.

Something significant took place that afternoon, in that hallowed sanctuary where he had been led by God. In his total nakedness he had surrendered and moved forward to where he had not dared go before. Simon reached down and took hold of himself. He embraced the thought that he was not just a spiritual person but also a sexual one, made of flesh, bones and blood. His God given nature allowed him to love in a different way. He now began to understand what he had read in high school about two different kinds of love. It was in a book in the school library on English literature which contained a curious poem. He couldn't understand it's meaning then, but now, in the womb of the forest, it came together for him.

It was penned by Lord Alfred Douglas in a lengthy poem entitled "Two Loves". He had wanted to ask Sister Mary Agnes about a certain passage but had hesitated. There was something about it that disquieted him. Now, the passage that had caught his eye on that day, opened up for him, and he grasped its hidden meaning.

Sweet youth,
Tell me why, sad and sighing, thou dost rove
These pleasant realms? I pray thee speak me sooth
"What is thy name?" He said, "My name is Love."
Then straight the first did turn himself to me
And cried, "He lieth, for his name is Shame,
But I am Love, and I was wont to be
Alone in this fair garden, till he came
Unasked by night; I am true Love, I fill
The hearts of boy and girl with mutual flame."
Then sighing said the other, "Have thy will,
I am the Love that dare not speak its name."

On that day, Simon understood that he was not an abomination before God. Rather, it was quite the opposite. He was struck by how much God loved him. As he held himself in the heart of the forest, he recalled playing under his grandfather's house and sensing that love. It was the same love that held him now. Standing there completely nude, something else occurred to him which was more specific. It was that the same and only Creator expressed His love to him through another man in a way that was natural to him. Simon thought of Toby.

As perspiration rolled off him, he sat down on the edge of a great, fallen pine tree that was returning to the earth. Another delicate breeze from the forest passed over his moist skin and he felt God, his beloved, caress him once again.

The pungent smells of the forest invaded his sense of smell and taste as never before. The damp warmth all around him continued to make his flesh shiny and slick with sweat. It had rained the night before and everything there was ripe and bursting with musky aromas. He was very aware of his nakedness, of his exposed skin and the pressure of his hardness jutting out from him. He felt that he belonged to everything that was exposed around him.

His sexual hunger became so intense that his mouth watered as it often does when one is famished and about to take part in a rich, succulent feast. In response to his growing sexual appetite, he lifted one leg over the great fallen tree and straddled it, feeling the rough texture of the bark against the slippery surface of his inner thigh. Once again, it seemed to him in one sweeping glance, that the living, all powerful God was everywhere and not hidden from him. The One who had created everything, and so often seemed obscure, was now right there before him, in every fiber and sound of the forest.

Simon was euphoric as he remained enthralled by the rich, earthy smells, and saw the sunlight breaking through the coolness of the shade. He heard the bubbling creek below and felt fresh drops of sweat roll off his body and onto the forest floor. Spellbound, he mostly felt the heart of God in his own beating heart, which produced in him a boundless hunger he had never known before. In response, he began to stroke himself slowly and then he quickened his pace as he approached a realm of intense pleasure he had hitherto never known.

When it came time to orgasm, he surrendered himself to the One who created him and he erupted on the bark of the great decaying tree. His intense orgasm astounded him because of how entirely it had devoured him. He felt that the passions that overtook him had been breathed into him and then exhaled out of him by his Creator. He was keenly aware that God still continued to fix His gaze upon him.

At that moment, Simon realized that God took pleasure in his pleasure and that his response to God on that afternoon was his offering, albeit his fragile gift to the Almighty. He remained straddling the decaying tree, fully spent but completely satisfied. His mind was refreshed as never before and in repose, he recalled a passage from the Song of Songs, written by King Solomon. It came to him imperceptibly, as subtle as a brittle, stray leaf falling from a tree. In that singular instance, Simon received the words as coming from the lips of his Creator, saying to him, "I am for my beloved and my beloved is for me." He knew as he had never known before, at that moment, what God was revealing to him, namely, His own deep yearning for him. He could sense God's hungry desire and love for him and this caused Simon to smile broadly to himself, realizing his own, very deep desire and love for God. He was overcome with emotion as he understood that God loved Him unconditionally, precisely in the way He had created him. He wondered to himself how he could have ever doubted God's infinite love for him. He now chastised himself for the times he felt frightened, filthy and despised and had therefore, run away and hid from the One who loved him.

God had contemplated him masturbating. For years, Simon had believed that the act of self-pleasure was dirty and sinful as he had been told in that awful room by Father Austin. Now, it seemed different. It felt like a natural response to the gift of life that flowed within him. He believed in that moment that it was why the forest had drawn him in. It was meant to open his eyes and heart. On that day in the forest, every tissue in his body, every cell, every pore, felt healthy and good. For a long time he remained straddling the huge fallen tree. He was captivated by the way his semen glistened unobstructed, in the crevices of the tree's bark. It was exposed there, for all to see, nothing to do with shame nor sin. His issue, from deep within him, was a marker, translucent in the waning shadows of late afternoon. It was a totem of his response to God's sublime love for him. Simon laid back on the old tree and fell into a dreamless, restful sleep.

Brother Shawn had removed his shoes carefully before reaching Simon's secret place in the forest. He had sneakily hidden himself behind the foliage that was everywhere and Simon had not known that the other man had seen him in his most naked moment. Seeing that Simon had fallen blissfully asleep, Brother Shawn slithered away as carefully as he had crept into the forest that day and made his way back to the abbey. He moved slowly and was careful not to wake the sleeping young man with whom he was obsessed. What Brother Shawn had witnessed that afternoon in the forest aroused him tremendously. To him, Simon was unlike the rest and he had difficulty accepting how easily Simon attracted others without any apparent effort. Jealousy and something very dark and ancient, filled his heart and went beyond the simple act of lust in witnessing how a young man came to orgasm by himself. It was far more sinister than a simple twisted desire and had to do more with possessing another selfishly for one's own plans.

When Simon awoke, he got off the tree and brushed away great pieces of bark that clung to his back side. He dressed himself, unconcerned with the wetness that had gathered between his legs, looking forward to a warm shower as soon as he returned. He hiked through the forest and finally came out through the overgrown entrance he was so familiar with. He was filled with a new kind of joy and recognized that it stemmed from the realization that God really did love him as he was. He was surprised that he felt no guilt for having given himself pleasure in the forest. It had been different there for him today. He would never forget the blissful series of shudders and spasms he had experienced. He could only describe it as the closest thing he had ever known to union with God. In his room that night, feeling content and close to God, he took out his journal and wrote the words from Godspell he knew so well.

Day by Day,
Day by Day,
Oh Dear Lord,
Three things I pray:
To see Thee more clearly,
Love Thee more dearly,
Follow Thee more nearly,
Day by Day.

Not long after that day in the forest, Simon was assigned for a week to kitchen duty with one of his fellow brother novices. His heart jumped excitedly in his chest when he saw his name written next to Brother Tobias'. Simon no longer wished to play the game with himself in which he denied his sexual attraction to Toby. He admitted to himself that he wasn't attracted to him emotionally and really didn't like him as a person. He couldn't understand why Toby was so aloof and cynical at times nor why he sounded so bitter and negative about almost everything. Simon only knew that it was his physical appearance that mesmerized him and filled him with desire.

Toby's physical looks took center stage in Simon's fantasies. Lying in his bed, Simon would think about how he would kiss and cuddle Toby's unshaven face. Fully awake, he dreamed about how he would caress the hair on Toby's chest, and massage his arms and legs. Standing now in front of the bulletin board, a swarm of butterflies took hold of his stomach. Father Bart's list of weekly duties meant that he would be paired off with Toby for an entire week, away from all the others. He would have Toby's attention all to himself.

Kitchen duty was not a simple chore and consisted in setting the tables for all three meals that week, plus planning and cooking the meals themselves. Afterward, it involved putting away the leftovers and pots and pans each day.

Rising earlier than the others, they would be excused from Lauds, or morning prayers, in the chapel in order to prepare breakfast for their brother novices. This assignment meant that they would spend many hours together in the kitchen and that it could not be construed as inappropriate nor the budding romance of a 'particular friendship' because the religious superior had assigned them together for a week's worth of kitchen duty.

In the course of that week, the two young men grew closer as they talked and spent hours working. The second afternoon of their assignment, Simon went to the kitchen before Toby met him there to begin preparing the evening meal. He had a surprise for his kitchen companion. He had drawn up a sign and taped it above the great stove. His art work depicted a huge cooking spoon filled with nasty chunks of mystery food, dripping with grease. Green and purple fumes emanated from the spoon. Under the spoon, bold letters proclaimed: "T and S Greasy Spoon".

In his white apron, Simon waited for Toby in the kitchen and when at last he arrived, Toby smiled when he saw Simon sitting at the small table in the corner. He knew Simon was up to some kind of mischief and asked, "What are you smiling about?"

Simon gave him his best smile. "Oh, I'm just admiring the sign of this fine cooking establishment."

"Huh?" Toby was at a loss.

Simon stood up and announced, "This cooking establishment has a name, you dummy." Simon pointed to the sign taped firmly to the exhaust fan above the large black stove.

He was thrilled to see the delight register on Toby's face as he turned in that direction and read out loud, "T and S Greasy Spoon." He turned and stared at Simon. For an instant the two men stood looking at each other that way and Simon thought he saw Toby's eyes mist over with what could very soon become tears.

Toby awkwardly moved close to Simon and hugged him. He said softly into his ear, "That's so clever. You and I, Simon and Toby, we really are 'T and S'." Then he added, "Can I tell you something?"

Simon felt his own heart pounding loudly in his ears, as he felt the other man's hot breath on his ear. "Sure, what is it?"

Toby hesitated. He looked at Simon briefly but then looked away. Then he pulled back. "Nothing important, really, just that that is a very sharp sign, brother." Then in an exaggerated gesture, he extended his hand and added, "I guess we're kitchen partners in crime! Here's to a great week working with you!" Simon extended his hand and they exchanged a handshake that was charged with unexpressed emotions. Simon wanted to say something but was unsure how to phrase his feelings. For him, the sign over the stove was far more than simply a funny caricature of a greasy spoon. It was a fragile message from deep within his heart. It was a delicate emotion that had broken free and frantically fought to reach the surface before it could be suffocated by fear. It was his way of telling Toby what he could not yet say out loud to him. It was his only way of publicly saying, "This here is my friend Toby and I want him and myself to be one." In his heart Simon felt a burning, growing desire to be with Toby in an intimate way, even though he was unsure about how to proceed. He only knew that as every hour passed in that kitchen, the desire to be with him was building and intensifying.

Simon was unsure how Toby felt because the man was so difficult to read. He was like a closed book, tightly shut and terribly cautious about showing any emotions. Simon couldn't know therefore, if Toby desired to be with him but after he put that sign up he noticed that Toby's attitude changed. The first day had been friendly but Simon had felt no real connection. Now, on this second day, as they waited for the others to come to supper, they sat at the small kitchen table. A tension had been building between them all afternoon like an approaching electrical storm and Toby had become playful and relaxed with him. He would push Simon out of his way or throw a wet kitchen towel at him when he wasn't looking. Simon would return the gestures. As that afternoon passed and shadows grew on the wall, they sat in silence at the small table covered in oil cloth. Simon was writing down the next day's menu while Toby drew invisible, imaginary shapes on the table with the bottom of a salt shaker.

Suddenly, Toby spoke without looking at Simon, "You know I feel like I need to tell you something that has been building in me these past couple days of working in the kitchen."

Startled, Simon looked up from his writing and asked, "What would that be?" They sat in the shadows silently. Simon waited patiently for his friend to speak but in his heart he hoped that he already knew what the other man was going to say.

At long last, Toby looked up and across the table. Great tears welled up in his eyes and his voice quivered as he said quietly, "I really don't know how to say this and I hope you don't take it wrong, Simon, but…" He looked behind himself toward the kitchen door that led to the refectory and then turned around and said, "I have to tell you that I can't stop thinking about you. I mean, I feel really attracted to you." With that admission, he stood up and leaned forward and kissed Simon gently on his lips. Then he sat down and again stared at the salt shaker on the table.

Simon's mind was beyond racing and he was speechless. He only managed to reach over and take Toby's hand in his. Then he whispered, "I feel exactly the same way." Simon's eyes spilled over with tears as he admitted, "I have felt this way since I first saw you the night I arrived and met you in the tower room." He wanted to say more but had no idea how to continue. He only knew that the most important thing had been said and he was on fire with desire because the man sitting across from him had said something magical. Toby had chosen him, Simon, from all the others. Toby desired him and wanted to be with him. He felt almost dizzy realizing that he was the object of this man's desire.

It was the very first time this had ever happened to him. Simon stared at Toby. He was unconfused about his physical lust for Toby but now he felt something new. It was a new emotion he had never experienced. Suddenly, he wanted to know Toby as a person. He asked himself who the handsome man really was. He wanted desperately to know if Toby was only beautiful on the outside or equally so inside. He wanted to know the person that was carefully shielded away inside himself.

The great bell of the abbey sounded and it was suppertime. Within seconds footsteps could be heard coming down the hall from the chapel as the brothers filed into the refectory. Brother Shawn appeared out of nowhere as he flew into the kitchen accompanied by two brothers assigned as waiters. He didn't hide his anger in finding the kitchen in shadows and Simon and Toby sitting quietly in the corner at the small table.

Brother Shawn hissed at them, "Are you guys asleep in this darkness! Are you both in some kind of trance? Is the chow ready? Get moving, it's supper time in case you didn't hear the great bell." He glared at Toby who missed it because he was looking down at his hands.

Simon however caught Brother Shawn's agitated glare straight on and met it with his own. Empowered, he defiantly answered, "Everything at the 'T and S Greasy Spoon' is under perfect control!"

It was enough to break the spell that had enveloped them and Simon and Toby quickly rose to their feet as Brother Shawn turned the lights on. He was short with them and didn't bother hiding it. "Let's get moving in here! Touchy, feely time is over, boys. Folks are hungry in that refectory out there. Snap outta your fog!" He stormed out without another word. Simon was beginning to understand that Brother Shawn was jealous of his attachment to Toby. It was the reason for the little scene that had just transpired. He brushed away his thoughts and moved quickly around the kitchen.

Supper was on the metal carts and ready to be taken out into the refectory and served by the brothers who were waiters that week. Both Simon and Toby went out to join in the prayers before sitting down at table. That night Simon was unable to sleep thinking about Toby and his admission. He was unable to put to rest what the other man had confessed to him. Their feelings of attraction were mutual. He knew that now and Simon had never felt so utterly happy and complete in his life. He finally slipped away into sleep and dreamed odd, disconnected dreams that night. When he awoke the next morning at the sound of the alarm clock, his first thought was of Toby. He felt connected to him like he had never felt connected to anyone in is life. He got to his knees and prayed.

During the course of the next few days they both expressed a desire to know everything about the other. Simon spoke about his family and his vocation at length and provided Toby with all kinds of details regarding his personal life and vocation. He mentioned his brother Bobby and how close they had always been growing up. Simon surprised himself because he spoke about his father and his death. He rarely did this with anyone.

Toby for his part, however, was very guarded, not sharing any details nor information about his past. Whenever Simon asked about something he answered with another question about Simon's own past rather than divulge details about his own. Simon was both frustrated and intrigued by Toby's reluctance to open up and one afternoon while they were working in the kitchen, he said, "Toby, can I be honest with you?" Without waiting for a response, he continued, "Why do you run away from my questions when I ask you about your past life? You never want to tell me anything significant about your childhood or your family. Whenever I ask you something you ask me more about my life."

Toby protested, "I'm not hiding anything in particular, Simon, it's just that it's hard for me to talk about it. You're the first person I feel I can trust but I'm scared to talk about it. I'm scared you'll run from me if I tell you about myself. My experience has been that most people judge unfairly without really listening."

"What?" That's crazy! I won't run from you! "And I certainly won't judge you!" Then Simon lowered his voice and said, "I want to get close to you, Toby. Please don't push me away."

"I don't want to push you away, trust me. I want to get close to you too. Really close." He brushed his shoe against Simon's ankle and winked.

"Then tell me about yourself. You haven't told me anything, really." They were both sitting, peeling potatoes and there was a bucket near them full of green beans that needed to be cleaned and cut.

Toby kicked Simon gently again and said nervously, "Well, there's plenty of stuff to peel and cut." He looked away. Simon sat quietly, and waited for his friend to speak. Toby had gathered several large potatoes and was busy arranging them in a line according to size. He hesitated and at long last managed to say clumsily, "Just promise me you'll give me room, I mean, don't rush me or ask me questions all at once, okay? It's a real bitch to tell you about my shitty, horrible life, okay? Just let me get through it without interruption because I've never really told anyone about it."

Simon shook his head in acceptance of the terms wondering what he was about to hear, then said, "Go ahead."

"Simon, I wasn't born into a loving family environment like you. Hell, there was really no family environment to speak of in my case. I was born in Tennessee, in rural Tennessee. I'm one of nine kids, several of us from different fathers. My father left when I was little and my mom had to distribute us among aunts and uncles and cousins because she sure as hell wasn't capable of raising us. She had a close, loving relationship with booze and strange, wandering men. I was shipped out several times and returned several times. We were so poor that there was no heat in the shack we called home. Up to the time I was in high school, our toilet was a box." Toby looked up at Simon who listened wide-eyed. "Yeah, you heard right, our toilet was a fucking box. Any box. Sometimes it was a shoe box, sometimes it was an empty milk carton, sometimes it was a box that had held soda bottles. We'd piss outside, in the back and we'd shit in the box anywhere we could find some privacy. There was no real toilet paper so we'd use any kind of paper we could find to wipe our asses. Sometimes newspapers or catalogues and magazines. Then one of us would walk down the road and throw our 'boxes' away in the dumpster behind a fast food place near the gas station down the road. We had to do it at night because they were on to us throwing our boxes into their dumpster. It was humiliating. I would be so nervous that somebody, anybody, would know what I was throwing away. It was a ritual I performed about every other night full of shame and embarrassment. Sometimes I'd wait till there were several boxes. It wasn't so bad in winter but in summer the smell, well, you get the picture."

Simon heard himself say, "Damn."

"Yeah, it was real bad. Little by little I sort of shut down socially and became a loner. I had no friends in school and the school bus rides were hell for me. Some of the kids called me names and I began to think they were right. There was no affection for me in any of the houses I was sent to. Aunts and uncles bitched and complained and they always tried sending me back to my mother just as soon as they could but she didn't want me either. That's when I was sent to my cousin Robby's house. He was around thirty or so and lived by himself in an old trailer. At first I was treated like a fucking pariah, like a moocher by him. I felt miserable. I had really bad acne by then and it was a mess because I needed to shave and it was painful, cutting myself trying to avoid the zits. The kids who were cruel on the bus loved calling me 'pizza face'. Then there was another thing that held up its ugly head in my pathetic life." Toby paused.

Simon wanted to hug his friend and say a million things but he had promised not to interrupt. So he stayed there and waited. Uncomfortable seconds sprang up and Simon finally broke the spell by saying, "Go ahead, man, I'm listening. Take your time."

By high school I already knew I was attracted to men and not women. I had to face the fact that I was queer. My cousin Robby sometimes left the trailer for days on end. I'd lie on the sofa at night and jerk off to porn magazines he had lying around in his smelly bedroom. There was barely anything to eat in the trailer. There was no toilet at his place either. Then one night he came back to the trailer all drunk and crazy. I was already asleep on the little sofa in the living room. He dragged himself down the hall, bumping into the walls as he went. Then he called me to him, "Hey, Silas. You hear me?" I was so scared I didn't answer but he screamed louder the second time, saying, "I'm not going to call you a third time you fucking little bitch! Get over here!" So I went to him.

Toby stopped speaking now and closed his eyes. He had put his hand over his eyes. He stayed that way for the longest time. Simon looked at him but said nothing. Then, without removing his hand from his eyes, he said, "I've never told anybody this before but the time I spent with Robby that night and afterward, were the best months I ever lived in my entire life. He wasn't gentle or understanding but held me tight on many nights like I was his lover and he fucked me whenever he wanted to. The thing was, he figured I was queer and he never asked permission to have sex with me. On the other hand, I never said no. I wanted so much to belong to somebody, to be held and loved. At least he noticed me and held me and kissed me just before he'd blow his wad. Most times he would say he loved me while he was building up to his orgasm. And sometimes he was so drunk he'd put his dick into me and after a few clumsy thrusts he'd just pass out."

Toby opened his eyes now and looked at Simon. "He had the biggest cock I've ever seen. It was huge and he loved showing it off. He'd get me to go down on him and when he was ready he'd roll me over and have his way with me. When he was done, he'd let me sleep with him on those nights. It was a treat for me because it was a lot warmer in his bed with him, than alone on the little sofa over in the freezing living room. There was no heat in the trailer." Toby stopped again and frowned, concentrating on the memories that now filled him. "Robby wasn't handsome but he was young and slender. He was the only one who told me I was handsome. He'd say, 'Do something about those fucking zits, would you? Get rid of that shit on your face and you'll have all the ass and cock you'll ever want. You'd be a looker, a real good one.'"

"It was really horrible, then, when I came home from school in my senior year one afternoon and near the trailer was a police car with my mother in the back seat. It was my mother who told me Robby had died that morning while I was in school in a terrible car accident down the road. It appeared he had been drunk. My world caved in on me. I moved back in with my mother for about a year but it wasn't a good place to be." He looked at Simon. "Pretty bad shit, huh? Most of the time people think I'm an asshole, an arrogant bastard and I suppose I usually am anti-social. I just felt so ugly then. I thought I had found a place with Robby but then he died and that was gone. I had no idea what I would do after high school. There was nothing at home with my mom. It was a shit-hole, plain and simple. Toward the end of my senior year I got a job in a nearby diner taking out the trash and wiping down tables and all that. One day this church lady came in and starting talking to me about God. I had heard about Jesus but had absolutely no real understanding about who He was supposed to be. And I didn't care. This lady seemed really nice though and said she belonged to a movement in the Catholic Church that was new. None of us in those parts of Tennessee were Catholic. There was a Baptist church nearby but we never went. Anyway, this lady told me about a spiritual renewal in the Catholic Church that was Charismatic. She told me that people prayed spontaneously and raised their hands up to God and that they got 'filled with God's Spirit'. She told me about speaking in tongues and people getting healed. She asked me if I was baptized in the Holy Spirit and I had no idea what that meant. She knew it too. She asked me, 'Do you have a copy of the New Testament?' 'No, I don't. I've never read that book.' The lady was very sweet and took a copy of the New Testament out of her purse and gave it to me. 'Read this first and then you'll understand what I'm talking about'." Toby looked at Simon, and said, "I swear to you, Simon, I couldn't put it down. I'd read it when I was in school and when I got home and when I went to work. And then the lady took me one night to a Charismatic prayer meeting at a Catholic church that was miles and miles away. While I was there in that prayer meeting, it all hit me at once. I took instruction and became a Catholic and a year later I wrote to the abbey saying I wanted to become a priest and serve God. They didn't take me at first because I hadn't really been a Catholic that long but after a year I applied again and I was accepted and entered the abbey in Leicester on the same night as you did. And that's my story, Simon. Wonder why I never talk about my past? It hurts less to be a loner."

Simon didn't know what to say. For the first time since he had laid eyes on Toby, he now saw him differently. He saw him as a fragile person just like himself, full of past hurts and fears. Everything he had just revealed to him explained his aloofness and his negativity. Talk about a shitty life! Simon wanted to take Toby into his arms right then and there, kiss him and tell him that he was falling in love with him. He continued to look at the man sitting across from him in the kitchen but didn't know what to say. He then looked down and continued peeling potatoes. Toby remained silent.

In the next few days of that week, they did their chores engrossed in each other's tales. Both of them wanted to know more about the other and they hung on to every word. A bond had been established and neither Simon nor Toby felt hesitant about telling the other all about their past and their future dreams. But they weren't the only ones affected by the cooking assignment that week. The monks who ate their three meals were pleased with the assignment because all during that week the quality and diversity of the cooking was definitely a step up from what usually came out of the kitchen. The connection between the two cooks that week didn't make kitchen duty seem like work at all. They were beginning to fall in love with each other and this changed everything for them. Every detail they created was something unique only they shared together. They consulted cookbooks and created meals and desserts that were not ordinary. During the rest of that week there were rarely any leftovers.

This activity in the kitchen was not lost on Father Bart who had been alerted by Brother Shawn concerning Simon and Toby. Brother Shawn, who was consumed with jealousy, went to the Master of Novices and feigned great concern over the relationship that was unfolding between the two novices. He understood perfectly the connection that had taken place between Simon and Toby and he was determined to put an end to it.

What Brother Shawn did not know, however, was that Father Chris in the postulancy had spoken with Father Bart advising him to be careful about Brother Shawn's unhealthy presence among the novices. Father Chris had warned Father Bart about Brother Shawn's jealous manipulations among the young monks in formation and had alluded to his penchant for some of the younger, more attractive young men.

However, what Father Chris was unaware of was that Father Bart had no stomach for dealing with cases of "Particular Friendships" and budding homosexual relationships. Unlike Father Chris' deep-seated homophobia, Father Bart had decided that Brother Shawn's jealousies would be very useful indeed to deal with those matters in his stead. No one was aware that it was Father Bart himself who had approached the Abbot after being advised by Father Chris and had personally requested "the young and talented" Brother Shawn to help him with the novices. It was on the second to the last day of their kitchen duty that Father Bart asked Brother Shawn to take a walk with him in the cloister of the Mother of Sorrows.

Once the Master of Novices had checked to see that no one was around, he spoke plainly, "Thank you for coming to see me. There's something I need to speak to you about and it's a very delicate matter involving the two novices you spoke to me about in the kitchen this week." Brother Shawn listened very closely and wore a grave expression on his face. He was flattered to be consulted regarding so delicate a matter. The Master of Novices continued his discourse, carefully choosing his words. "It's something that seems to be trending in the direction of a 'particular friendship' and we are all aware of the dangers of 'P.F.'s' in an all-male environment. It can so easily lead to homosexual activity and that's something completely unacceptable for the consecrated life."

Brother Shawn nodded his head in agreement and said, "Of course, of course, Father."

Father Bart continued, "I believe that their friendship and brotherhood has deepened this week as a result of their enthusiasm in the kitchen together. Having said that, I also truly believe that nothing serious is developing yet. However, I trust your judgement and would like to consult with you. I have been thinking about the things you alerted me to. What is your take on this situation?"

Brother Shawn cleared his throat and spoke authoritatively, "Thank you for considering that my opinion counts in this matter. As I told you, I think it's a very serious matter that is quickly deteriorating and is already well on the road to being a 'particular friendship'. I agree that it has not yet become physically homosexual but that could easily happen. Brother Simon shows great potential for his future life as monk but he is young and still very innocent. However, I worry about Brother Tobias and believe he could be a bad influence on Simon. His background is spotty and he's worldly. It's obvious he's been around the block a few times. I don't think he's a good fit here in the abbey."

The Master of Novices arched his eyebrows. "Really? You think he's that bad of an influence?"

Brother Shawn continued, "He doesn't come from a stable, Catholic family environment, at least that's what I remember Father Chris saying to me when he first applied to the abbey and was rejected. He only recently became a

Catholic convert and it was due to that liberal, arm waving Charismatic charade."

Father Bart interrupted, pointing his finger into the air, "It's approved by the Holy Father, the Pope, so it's not a charade, just for the record. It's one of many fruits of the Holy Ghost in the Church today."

Brother Shawn sounded sidetracked and corrected himself, "Yes, uh, well, I meant to say that it was a new movement just beginning and not traditional. Anyhow, I think Brother Tobias knows perfectly well how to mislead Simon and take him down the path of moral perdition. I really believe they are getting too close for comfort."

As Brother Shawn said all of this, neither he nor Father Bart were aware that Brother Seth had approached quietly behind them and was waiting for Brother Shawn to finish. That was when he cleared his throat loudly and spoke up and said, "Excuse me, Father and Brother. Father Bart, you have a phone call from the Abbot's secretary in your office, which is urgent. I was told to relay the message. Sorry for the interruption." Brother Shawn slanted his eyes and pierced Seth's gaze trying to read the novice's face. How much had the novice heard him say? He could not know for sure. Seth smiled and turned away, walking quickly down the cloister. His smile widened along the way.

Father Bart continued, "Well, I need to take that phone call. In any case, I ask you, Brother Shawn, to please keep an eye out for those two young men. We don't want an unfortunate situation to worsen, especially when it can easily be corrected from the beginning. I entrust you with that, okay? If you see anything out of place please report back to me."

Brother Shawn nodded agreement and said nothing as the Master of Novices walked quickly away. Under his breath Brother Shawn barely heard himself whisper, "Oh, yes, I'll be on top of it before it worsens, you old, cowardly fart."

Just before Compline, or the last prayers of the day were prayed in the chapel, Seth hurried to find Simon. He had to warn him about what he had overheard Brother Shawn saying to the Master of Novices. However, he could not find him anywhere. It was almost time for the last hour of prayers from the breviary. Once they concluded those prayers, the Grand Silence would begin until after breakfast the next day. Seth was concerned by what he had heard Brother Shawn say to the Master of Novices. Seth tried his cell again but Simon was not there. He went to both cloisters but again, did not find him. Finally, he tried the kitchen but was unlucky. He had almost given up when he saw Simon coming down the hall, unrolling the sleeves of his habit.

Seth ran up to him and whispered breathlessly, "Dammit, Simon! Where in the hell have you been? I've been searching in every nook and cranny of this damned place for you. Compline is about to begin and I need to warn you about something I overheard. You need to be careful."

It had been a long, last day in the kitchen and Simon was worn out. He asked more out of politeness than of any real interest, "I was throwing out the trash from the kitchen and putting away the last of the pots and pans with Toby. We are finally done with our kitchen assignment. It was fun but brutal work. What did you overhear that's so earth shattering?"

Seth was almost out of breath as he blurted, "You might be in deep shit, brother, and listen good to what I'm gonna say before that damn bell rings and we go to chapel. I overheard that fucker Brother Shawn tell the Master of Novices all kinds of stuff about you and Toby."

Simon felt his heart drop. He cautiously asked, "What kind of stuff? What are you talking about?"

"I told you to be careful months ago because I've been watching that manipulating, motherfucker, Brother Shawn ever since I met him. He's a huge shit and is nothing but trouble. He's had his eye on you since you came."

Simon protested, "Oh, come on, stop saying things like that."

"You need to wise up and get your head outta your ass. Listen to me and listen good. I went to look for Father Bart this afternoon because he had an urgent phone call and he was walking with Brother Shawn in one of the cloisters. I walked right up behind them but they didn't seem to notice so I stood there and that's when I heard every word Brother Shawn said."

"And what did he say that's got your kitty in an uproar?" Simon tried to sound calm but he was nervous now.

"Among other things, wise guy, he told Father Bart that you and Toby are definitely 'P.F.'s' and getting way too close. He implied that it could easily turn physical, you know, homosexual." Simon's blood ran cold at the thought of being found out. "You know what comes with that kind of an accusation."

Simon stared at Seth and then asked, quite deflated, "What else did he say to Father Bart?"

"Brother Shawn said you show great potential here at the abbey and that you are probably innocent, not really knowing how dangerous your 'particular friendship' is. But he made it very clear to Father Bart that Toby is quite another matter. He obviously wants Toby far from you and said he was nothing but trouble. He went on and on about how he will mislead you."

Hearing these words made Simon want to cry because now he could not envision his life without Toby. Simon wanted to share everything with him and had already thought more than once about taking Toby to his secret place in the forest. The news he was hearing from Seth devastated him and threatened to destroy everything that was beautiful and important in his life. He asked Seth, "What else did you hear?"

"That's about it. You need to be real careful, buddy. Brother Shawn is obviously mad with jealousy and won't stop at anything if he means to get Toby thrown out. If it was only a matter of Brother Shawn's interference I wouldn't be so worried for you but Father Bart is now fully aware about your intimacy with Toby."

"Stop calling it that!" Simon barked. He felt guilty and threatened. What he was sharing with Toby was sacred and nobody's damn business. He felt Seth was overstepping and might have a hidden agenda.

"I'm just saying, Simon, don't ignore what I just told you. Things have escalated since I warned you in postulancy. You might not see it but it's obvious you and Toby are…into each other."

Simon snapped back defensively, "What the fuck is THAT supposed to mean?"

"Hey, I'm just telling you for your own good."

"Oh yeah? For my own good? Why are you so damned interested in my relationship with Toby? It seems to me you've been watching me since I got here."

"I just don't want you to get thrown out is all. I think you don't understand how serious this can be." Seth looked at Simon who stood in the darkened hallway. Suddenly the great bell of the abbey announced it was ten o'clock and time to gather for Compline.

Simon was relieved the bell had sounded and said, "It's time for prayers. I guess we need to go."

"I was thinking…" Seth put his hand on Simon's shoulder. "I know it's time to go but I was thinking that if you want I can look out for you."

Simon was confused at the suggestion. "What do you mean, I don't understand."

"Well, I was thinking…if you want I can make sure that you and Toby don't get any closer. I can warn you when I see you guys getting too close. You can even come tell me when you feel tempted to be with him and I can make sure you avoid him."

Simon was incredulous and brushed Seth's hand off his shoulder as if it were something disgusting. "What? Are you kidding? I can take care of myself and my friendship with Toby. I don't need a damn bodyguard around me!"

"I'm just trying to help." Simon saw that Seth's face had reddened.

"I don't think so, Seth. I'm beginning to think that there's more to it with you. I think you have other motives. I think you're jealous of my friendship with Toby. I think you'd like to be in his place. I think you'd want to be that special friend in my life. Hell, is there any real difference between your jealousy and Shawn's?" With this last, Seth got quiet. "I even wonder if that whole conversation you 'overheard' was as dramatic as you say. Just for the record, I can take care of myself. You don't need to monitor me." Simon went around Seth and left him standing in the darkened hallway.

It was customary to have a full free day after serving kitchen duty. The two novices who had cooked for the monks were expected the next morning to be present for Lauds and the Sacrifice of the Mass that followed with the others but after breakfast they had the entire day to themselves until Vespers, or evening prayers. They were free to read, write letters, take a walk or nap if they desired to do so. Simon and Toby had already planned during the last day of kitchen duty to take a hike through the northern part of the abbey property that was strictly speaking, within the confines of the novitiate. They were not allowed to go any further during the novitiate year. They knew enough, however, to know that the property they could explore was vast. They had planned a hike from the barns out into the cornfields and to the overgrown fields that lay beyond. One of the brothers had said there were creeks and that in one of the clearings out that way there was even a log cabin that Prince Demetrius had once used during one of his first winters here.

After breakfast, Simon and Toby began their trek. They got into thorns and out of them and wandered into heavily treed areas. They had taken a bagged lunch with them and shared sandwiches in a clearing not far from the log cabin they came across. Simon felt butterflies in swarms again inside his stomach which made him feel thrilled and sick at the same time. They kidded each other and laughed easily together. The sun was bright and warm high above them. It was late summer and along the way they took their shirts off, hiking in just their cut-off shorts, shoes and socks. Everything was splendid and in place and there was still plenty of time before getting back for evening prayers.

"I hope I didn't sound weird the other day when I told you about myself in the kitchen." Toby looked over at Simon. "I mean, I shared some really personal stuff with you I've not told anyone here about. I hope it wasn't too much." Simon stopped hiking and looked at his handsome friend. Toby was taller than Simon and just a couple years older. To Simon he was impossibly handsome. His toned chest and abdomen were shiny with sweat and Simon couldn't take his eyes off the trail of hair that went from Toby's chest, down over his toned abdomen and disappeared deep into his shorts. He was completely smitten with his beautiful companion.

Simon finally managed to say, "Not at all. I'm really impressed that you trusted me enough to share those details. You shouldn't be embarrassed at all. None of us is responsible for where we're born or if we're born into poverty. My family isn't well-off financially either."

Toby smiled to himself. "Still, extreme poverty is hard to talk about. But I meant more the sexual stuff I told you about. About knowing myself to be gay and about my cousin Robby. I worried after I told you that you might think I'm some kind of a pervert or whore." Simon felt an emotion he was unfamiliar with. It wasn't exactly love nor admiration but had more to do with hunger. He wanted to reach over and touch Toby, to smell him and taste his sweat. He even wanted to bite him gently.

He dared not move, afraid of his new found sensations and only managed to say softly, "I don't think you're a pervert nor a whore, Toby. Relax. I think you're beautiful." Then he added, "I think you're beautiful inside and out." They stood looking into each other's eyes as they stood in a clearing. The sun felt prickly on their bare torsos and their shoulders were beginning to burn slightly. Simon was keenly aware of his desire but unsure about moving closer to Toby who stood so close to him that Simon could smell the ripeness of his friend's arm pits. It was intoxicating and increased his growing appetite.

"When Robby died a whole part of me went with him. He was the only person with whom I could be completely me. He made me feel…beautiful, like you just said. He was the one who showed me all about sex and made it something loving and intimate." Toby was lost in thought now, perhaps grasping a phantom memory from those lost days of his painful adolescence. Finally, he said smiling, "He used to kid me and call me 'needle-dink'."

"Needle-dink?"

"Yeah." Toby held up one of his pinky fingers suggesting the size of a tiny penis. "*Needle-dink*, it was one of his favorite expressions for just about everybody. Hell, I already told you he had the biggest damn cock I've ever seen between a guy's legs." Simon instinctively gazed at the front of Toby's tight denim shorts and the bulge he saw there told him that Toby was no "needle-dink".

Simon swallowed dryly and looked up at his friend. "That's funny. I've never heard that expression."

"I knew that it was a playful thing for him to call me that. It wasn't a put down or anything like that. Instead, he made me feel that he really desired me when we got intimate." Simon was unsure how he felt hearing Toby speak so openly about sex. He wanted to say something that was up to par. Images and memories threatened to invade his thoughts and he pushed these hurriedly away. The awful memories were stubborn and insistent. Disfigured thoughts of Father Austin now loomed unabashedly before his mind's eye. These memories were also about erections and penetrations. He wanted to share his own sex stories with Toby but the experiences he had had with sex did not make him feel beautiful. He only knew he had to bury them far away and deep where no one would ever know and where they could not hurt him. He could never share those stories with Toby. "You okay?" Simon felt Toby touch him with the palm of his hand on his own sweaty chest.

Simon looked into his friend's eyes and put his own hand over his friend's chest and pressed slightly into Toby's beating heart. Then he grasped his friend's hand and said, "I want to take you somewhere now. A secret place of mine."

Toby let his hand slip out from Simon's. He put both his hands on either side of his small, fit waist and rocked playfully back and forth on his shoes as he looked all around. "Out here? You have a secret place out here? A secret place on the abbey grounds? On the abbey grounds, you say?"

"It's not exactly here, I mean, we need to hike there but yeah, I have a secret place. It's mine." Simon realized that his tone was too serious but he couldn't help it. He hesitated and then said, "No one knows about it but me. It's in the forest."

Toby stopped rocking on his feet and said, "Take me there."

Simon led the way and took Toby's hand firmly into his own as they crossed the creek over a fallen tree and walked on hand in hand. He could barely hear the birdsong all around him as his heart pounded in his chest and echoed rhythmic heartbeats in his ears. He was aware of the heat emanating from his face. His body felt as if he were on fire. They were both slick with sweat as they trekked onward. Simon never let go of Toby's hand and felt his friend tighten his grip on his own. As they drew closer to the secret place, they both felt the coolness of the forest. It was the same caress that had enveloped Simon there. "Wow," they both said at the same time and laughed together. They both had felt the refreshing touch upon their damp bodies at the same time. It breathed out to them from within the hidden, shady sanctuary of the forest.

"It's just a little further this way."

"I've never been here. How did you find this?"

Simon stopped and turned toward Toby. "I was drawn here since we first arrived in the novitiate. I've never brought anyone here. Now it belongs to us." Simon pulled gently on Toby's hand and they entered.

As Simon said this last, Toby remarked, fascinated, on the bubbling sound coming from the creek. He was beside himself as he contemplated the magnificence of the place. "This place is an oasis. Thanks for bringing me."

"Come this way. We need to climb just a little." Toby followed Simon up the steep climb and all at once the two young men, standing next to each other, were enveloped in the natural magic of the forest where the great fallen pine tree lay and greeted them. They were breathing heavy because of the climb but also because of their excitement. Simon turned to Toby and they looked into each other's longing eyes. Simon was at the peak of his passions and sensed that Toby was not far behind. Simon could barely speak, but said, "Here we are."

No further words were spoken. They naturally moved toward each other, taking each other by both hands. They stared silently and intently studied each other for several seconds, trying to catch their breath. Unfettered desire swept over them and they moved close into each other's arms. As they held each other awkwardly, they began to kiss instinctively and roughly pressed into each other. Nothing else existed for them at that moment except to hold and taste each other's salty flesh. They were lost in their lustful appetites and were aware only of the guttural moans of pleasure they each emitted. They held on to each other and surrendered to the instinct that was overtaking them completely.

It was impossible for them, therefore, to have noticed the obscure figure kneeling not three yards away from them and completely hidden from view. The man had been lying there for several hours, miserable and filled with hate. He had fondled himself grotesquely but dared not masturbate. He did not feel sexually aroused in the least. His hunger lay elsewhere. He knew they would come today and he had patiently waited for them. Now he peered out from his hiding place behind the massive pine trees. His testicles felt heavy and ached from his continual fondling. He watched the young lovers as they kissed passionately not far from him.

Simon and Toby stood sweating and squirming, entangled in each other's embrace. Mosquitos and flies buzzed crazily around their heads as they breathed heavily and ground themselves into each other. In that blessed sanctuary, surrounded by infinite vestiges of the Creator, aware of the mighty energy building up between them, Simon took Toby's hand and guided him to the great fallen pine tree which lay awaiting them. In their slippery embrace, they took in the strong perfume of their sweat drenched bodies. It was unlike any embrace Simon had ever experienced in his life. His heart seemed to him to be lodged in his throat. Simon had led Toby to the spot, and without saying a word, they began to kick off their shoes and socks and then they removed each other's shorts and underwear.

Completely naked, they once again clung to each other and held on tightly in the endless shadows of the forest. Toby unexpectedly knelt down in front of Simon and took him into his warm mouth. He caressed him with his tongue and then stood up before him, his eyes bright and alive. Simon had never experienced anything like the pleasure Toby had just given him and taking his example, he nervously knelt down before his first love. Simon awkwardly took Toby into his own, hungry mouth and pushed himself forward, reveling in the scent of his lover. This newfound intimacy made Simon dizzy with desire and he sucked hungrily on his friend.

Rising, they gathered their clothes and spread them out on top of the pine needles that were spewed about and together they laid down in their unquenchable appetite and craving. They never took their eyes off each other but gazed into each other's eyes in awe. They smiled as they caressed each other's bodies and embracing, their bodies entered into a timeless rhythm, fondling and stroking each other deliberately. They moved as one body and completely surrendered to each other and to the overpowering sexual energy and force that had been building in them for months. Their passion swept them away together and when they were both at the peak of their pleasure, they erupted in orgasm at the same time, bathing each other entirely as they laughed with abandon. When they had emptied themselves, they lay back panting uncontrollably as they continued to hold on to each other. The aromas of their lovemaking mingled with the primeval aromas of the forest. On that warm afternoon, in the forest, locked arm in arm and facing each other, they easily slipped away into sleep.

Brother Shawn wasn't aroused by the powerful display of love between the two young men, but rather was consumed with rage at the realization that the place he had imagined for himself had been taken by another. The deadly sin that took hold of him in the forest was not lust but anger. One thought only possessed him now and he was resolved to give himself to it entirely. On that afternoon, kneeling and watching, he had decided that Toby had to go. He determined to get rid of him. Things had gone exactly as he had feared. He was not surprised they had. After all, he had seen it all too clearly on that first night of postulancy and the following day. Brother Shawn believed that Simon belonged to him alone and he would remove Toby and anyone else who came to take Simon away from him. He quietly zipped his trousers and carefully retreated from the forest.

When they awoke, Simon and Toby kissed each other slowly and deliberately as only lovers know how to do. They hugged each other tightly for the longest time. Both of them looked at each other without saying a word, searching for a response to an event where words were useless. They helped each other up and approached the creek. There they washed each other in silence and still wet, dressed themselves.

As they hiked back to the novitiate, Simon was filled again with that wonderful sense of completeness he had experienced not long ago in the forest with his Creator. Before getting too close to the abbey, the two men sat amid the multi colored wild flowers in a vast field, sharing the majesty of the late afternoon sun that was beginning to set. They held hands and then they reached out. Simon and Toby could not stop touching each other and caressing their faces and hair. It was impossible for them to keep from kissing each other on that blessed afternoon.

When they reached the novitiate, Simon and Toby went to their separate cells in order to undress and then shower and get ready for supper and Vespers. After he showered, Simon dressed in his habit and went to the chapel for a few minutes of prayer before supper. He was exceedingly happy and content with the events of his day and the strong connection he had now established with Toby. They had shared more than just intimate stories now and Simon was filled with an array of emotions. He wanted to thank God for this exceedingly generous gift.

He entered the small chapel of the novices and genuflected toward God in the tabernacle. He took his seat in the choir stalls and he had barely sat down when suddenly the awful memory of Father Austin sprang up before him. Simon was remembering the stifling room in another novitiate far away from this one. It was in Louisiana, nestled among the swamps and venerable old trees covered in Spanish moss.

Father Austin, sitting in his undershirt was telling him why he should feel guilty and dirty. It all rushed unexpectedly over him like a violent, merciless flood of waters, destroying everything of beauty and order in its wake. A terrible thought came to him now and would not go away. He recalled the horrible night in the motel room with Father Austin and all that had taken place there. What was in his mind now was a scenario like an old movie playing crazily in his head and it made him shudder. Simon could almost hear Father Austin screaming at him in mockery and in judgement, saying, "What did you do with that young man in the forest today? You should feel dirty and guilty! I certainly do, my boy! That's why I wear a ski mask when I abuse children!" Caught up in the painful memory and coupled with human inexperience, it never dawned on Simon that what that priest had done to him in the motel room was totally different to what he had experienced with Toby in the forest. The powerful events of the day with Toby suddenly began to fade for Simon and he allowed himself to be immersed in guilt and self-loathing.

He hated the feelings that rushed into him at that moment and held him captive. He was powerless to escape them. Guilt, anxiety, and fear weighed heavily upon him as he sat in the silence of the chapel. How could he deal with the confusion that now reigned in him? There was no one with which to discuss it. Who could he possibly run to for clarification. Where were the arms to receive and console him and put things back into proper perspective? Who was there that could ease his mind and deliver him back to the splendor of knowing he was loved by Toby? The wall he had been building within himself was not quite as fortified as he had thought and it began to crumble within him. His sexual desires and fantasies began to collide violently with his desire to be faithful to God's laws. Shame won out and swept him away. The wall had not kept him safe.

Simon cringed as he realized that there was only one option open to him. The only way to clear his mind and conscience was with the priest who would be coming the next day for Confession. He dreaded to go.

In his confusion he concluded that the person he needed to avoid was Toby. Now that he recalled Father Austin, he allowed the experience in the forest to be transformed into something un-Godly and grotesque. In that state of mind, Simon got up from his place and went to supper which on that day, was in community silence. Later in the evening he returned to the chapel for Vespers and finally prayed Compline with his brothers. Afterward, the Grand Silence began until after Lauds the next morning at breakfast.

The despicable memories of what Father Austin had done to him were center in his mind and he began to contemplate, once again, how much of what had taken place that night in the motel, was actually his fault. It was in this distraught frame of mind that he went to bed, completely pushing away any thoughts of Toby and the forest and the presence that dwelled there. He felt terribly lost and confused.

The next day, even before he got out of bed, he resolved to go to Confession as soon as possible. He desperately needed to confess the sins he had committed with Toby in the forest. He desperately needed to be chaste. Simon avoided Toby throughout the day and felt terrible about what they had done together. When the jovial priest finally arrived in late afternoon for Confession, Simon waited in the chapel to be the last penitent. He did not want to rush his confession.

Simon waited for the last of his brothers to finish their confessions and then walked into the small, shadowy space and knelt by the screen. The priest began, "In the name of the Father, and of the Son and of the Holy Ghost."

"Amen."

"Yes, brother, what are your sins?"

"Bless me Father for I have sinned. It has been one week since my last confession and these are my sins." Simon hesitated and then opened his mouth again to speak but nothing came out. He literally had no idea where to begin his confession so he finally just blurted out what was agonizing him, "I ask forgiveness for all the sins I have committed…and…and especially…"

The priest's demeanor was kind. "Yes, brother, go ahead. God is merciful and forgiving. You have no need to be afraid. What are your sins?"

"I am especially sorry for…having gotten naked with a fellow novice. We touched each other in an impure manner and masturbated." A deafening silence filled the tiny confessional box and through the screen that separated them, Simon could see that the priest had closed his eyes shut. Simon waited but the priest said nothing.

Then he opened his eyes and the kind jovial priest was no more. Instead, he became outraged and indignant. "You did what?" He was seething in his barely controlled whisper. "Repeat it for me!"

Simon mechanically repeated his sins, realizing that it was not going to go well for him. "I got naked with a fellow novice in the forest and we touched each other in an impure manner and…we masturbated each other."

The priest suddenly bellowed out, "Oh, dear God in Heaven!" He was looking straight ahead and not at Simon on the other side of the screen as he usually did. "You have committed a terrible, disgusting sin. You should never have put yourself in that situation! It is a serious, deadly sin you have committed. How has this happened? How have you gotten yourself into this filth during your novitiate year as you prepare for your profession of vows? Answer me! How have you gotten yourself into this filth?"

Simon answered pathetically, in a barely audible voice, "I don't know, Father. It happened so fast."

"Fast! Fast, you say? It happened so fast? It happened fast, did it? Did you not have time to plan it and contemplate it before it took place? Answer me!"

"Yes, Father, I did think about it beforehand. Lots of times."

"Ah, so you see, it didn't happen so fast did it? You planned on doing it, didn't you?" The priest stopped and let out a long, exasperated sigh. He regained his composure and then continued in a low voice, "Don't tempt the mercy of God with your lies and your blatant arrogance, mister!" Simon closed his eyes and bowed his head. He felt miserable and knew he was guilty of a terrible, filthy crime. How had he let himself fall into such a trap? "What other disgraceful sins have you committed?"

Simon considered telling the priest that he and Toby had sucked each other's cocks briefly but decided against it. He had already said they had gotten naked and touched each other. He didn't specify how they had touched each other. It was best to leave it at that, without mentioning hands and mouths. He knew it was a flimsy justification but he had been beaten up enough for the moment. That should cover it for now. "No other sins for now, Father. For these and all my sins I am sorry. I beg you for absolution and a penance."

The priest was not deterred so easily, however, and hissed, "Not yet! Not so fast. The sin you have just confessed is something you must never, ever commit again. It must not ever happen again, do you understand?"

"Yes, Father."

"You must avoid the brother who committed these serious sins with you. You must avoid him and never speak to him about the sins you committed. Do you understand?"

"Yes, Father."

"Yes, Father, what?" It seemed to Simon as if the ski-masked Father Austin was sitting in front of him wearing a hateful, judgmental scowl on his face. He could almost hear him say: "You should feel dirty and guilty because that is what you are! You are a pervert and a whore!" Simon held his head bowed. He was filled with deep remorse and self-loathing.

He answered weakly, "Yes, Father, I understand the seriousness of my terrible sins and I am very sorry."

The priest remained silent again. Simon could see that he had closed his eyes again and was rubbing the temples of his forehead slowly. He finally said, "Make an Act of Contrition now, as I give you absolution."

Simon prayed the prayer of contrition as the priest began the sacred prayer of absolution through which Simon would be forgiven the terrible sins he had committed with Toby in the forest. As Simon heard the solemn words he did not think about stripping naked and kissing Toby and neither did he think about the pleasure they had shared. Nothing of the powerful experience in the forest with Toby appeared in his mind now. He forgot the colors of the wild flowers and their kisses there. The majesty of the setting sun that afternoon, faded.

Instead, an image came to him as the priest continued uttering the words of God's forgiveness. It was an old print that now came to mind. Sister Mary Thomasine had had it in her sixth grade classroom when he was a boy. It depicted a magnificent and glorious scene of all of God's elect in Heaven and on earth. Sister had said it was the Church Triumphant and the Church Militant. It depicted all the souls faithful to God's Will. This image now came to him as he bowed his head in the darkness, filled as he was, with shame and regret for what he had done with Toby. Yet there he was getting another chance to get back on the right path in order to become God's best priest someday.

Now, even more clearly than the scene of Heaven, Simon remembered the bottom part of the print in Sister's class. It was less glorious and terribly frightening. It showed the dreaded depths of Hell and Hell fire. Sister had said that Hell fire burned the souls painfully and continually but did not consume them and that it was for eternity. Hell fire was different from earthly fire. Sinners had to pay for their sins. It depicted the souls who had turned their backs on God and lived as they pleased.

As the priest concluded the words of absolution and made the sign of the Cross over him, Simon accepted that very often he must certainly be an abomination to God for what he had done and for the things he thought about and desired to do. He also accepted that he was weak to refrain from it. He wondered at the core of his being, however, if everything was his own doing or had he been created that way?

Simon raised his head at the exact moment that the priest uttered the merciful words of forgiveness and made the sign of the Cross on him, "And I absolve you of all of you sins, in the name of the Father, and of the Son, and of the Holy Ghost."

"Amen." Simon sighed quietly, relieved that it was over.

"Go in peace, God has forgiven you all of your sins."

"Thank you, Father." Then the priest said something very odd to him. It was something he had never heard before.

"I want you to do something for the good of your soul which is in grave danger. Instead of giving you a penance myself I want you to exercise the virtue of humility. You need a good dose of humility. I want you to think some more about the terrible sins you have committed and make sure that you are truly sorry. Go to Father Bartholomew, your Master of Novices and ask him for a penance. Of course he will never have any knowledge of your confession here nor of your sins but it will be beneficial to your soul for you to ask him for a penance. If he asks you why, you are simply to say to him that you lack humility because you are a sinner in need of God's mercy."

"Yes, Father." Simon dreaded what the priest had just commanded. He wanted the whole thing to end right here and be done with it but now he would need to speak with Father Bart. In any case, Simon figured he got off easy because of the terrible sins he had engaged in with Toby. As he was getting up off his knees, he remembered the souls burning eternally in Hell in Sister's framed print hanging on the wall. "Thank you, Father." The normally friendly priest did not answer him.

As he left the chapel, he glanced down the hall to the right and saw the soft light coming from Father Bart's office. The Master of Novices would be there until it was time for supper. He made his way to Father Bart's office. A large lamp was the only source of light in the room. The middle aged monk was sitting at the large wooden desk wearing a pair of horn rimmed glasses. He had an open file in front of him. The glasses gave him a wise, bookish appearance that he normally did not possess. Father Bartholomew was of average build and his hair was thinning on the top of his head. The office was sparsely furnished and decorated. There was a large crucifix on the wall behind him which depicted Jesus still alive but suffering His terrible agony on the Cross for the sins of men.

Simon remembered the forest as he knocked gently on the door and softly said, "Father Bart, may I speak with you for a moment?" The Master of Novices looked up startled and removed his glasses.

He seemed to squint as if he were adjusting his eyesight in the poor light and then immediately a warm smile appeared on his face. "Ah, yes, Brother Simon, so glad you came by. Please, come in, sit down." He gestured to a chair on one side of his desk. "What a pleasant surprise. I'm so glad you stopped by."

"I saw the light in the hallway."

"Yes, of course. How may I help you? Is everything okay?" Simon liked Father Bart and took him to be a gentle, honest soul. He only had Father Chris to compare him to and he much rather liked this monk over the other. Yet as he sat in his office he felt nervous and quite frankly wanted to get his business over with as soon as possible and get out.

"Everything is fine, Father. In prayer and during meditation time I have been thinking a lot about the theme of conversion. Last week you told us about the Greek word 'metanoia' and its meaning. Well, it certainly struck a chord in me, I mean, I have been thinking a lot about straying from God because of sin."

"Yes, it's a reality for all of us."

"Well, I guess what really impressed me was the image you used, I mean, you said 'metanoia' is about when we're hiking down a road and realize it's the wrong road and that it's taking us far from where we need to go. It's the part about stopping dead in our tracks, turning around and returning in order to begin the hike again that really got me thinking."

"I'm glad to hear that I could offer you something of value for the good of your soul."

"I've been thinking about the many ways I often take the wrong road, especially, in the little things. I'd like to ask you a favor, Father."

The Master of Novices sat back in his chair and listened to the young man sitting in front of him. When Simon had finished speaking, he said, "You show great potential as a monk and someday as a priest. You should know that we have high expectations for you. Don't lose sight of the high road, brother." He cleared his throat and asked, "So, what can I do for you?"

"I come to ask you for a penance. I realize I'm a sinner who often gets lost and takes the wrong path." Simon got up and knelt before the priest. "Please, Father, may I have a penance?"

Father Bart took the novice's hands in his own and said, "For your penance it will be good for you to do something kind for a brother you least like right now. Take him for a walk and listen to him or offer to do one of his chores. Just be sure to spend some time with a brother you normally would ignore." He pulled on Simon's hands indicating he should stand. "Then he said, 'Ubi caritas est vera, Deus ibi est'. Remember that 'Where love is genuine, God will be found there'."

Simon felt his eyes brim over with tears. His thoughts raced crazily between images of the cool, damp forest and the print in the nun's classroom. Somewhere deep inside him, the wall began to be repaired and strengthen once again. Simon thought about Father Bart's words and knew that his love for Toby was genuine and therefore, God was present there. However, something seemed terribly out of place with his conclusion. It was not sorted deep within himself.

Simon made his way toward the refectory to join the others for supper. The bell would ring any minute now. Tomorrow he would do his penance. Maybe he would do something kind for Seth. He hadn't been too charitable with him lately. As Simon walked along the corridor he looked up, aware that someone was coming toward him in the opposite direction. It was Brother Shawn.

He was all smiles as he stopped in front of Simon and playfully pushed him against the wall, with his hands planted firmly on either side. "How are you, little one? Don't you look all cute and holy in your little monk outfit! What's going on with you?"

Simon broke free and slipped away under one of his arms. "I'm great, just getting ready for supper." He scurried off.

Brother Shawn called out to Simon as he hurried away, saying "Save some for me, kiddo." He turned around and walked in the direction of the office of the Master of Novices. Father Bart was exiting just as Brother Shawn approached and the priest said, "Let's walk over to the refectory. It's almost time. I'm famished." The two monks neared the chapel doors when the priest said, "Let's go this way," indicating the cloister garden dedicated to the Guardian Angels, "I want to pass something by you."

Brother Shawn was all ears. "Sure, what is it?"

"I have been thinking a lot about our little conversation the other day regarding Simon and Toby and their possible 'particular friendship'."

Brother Shawn barely smiled. "Oh, it's not just a 'possible', trust me."

Father Bart continued, "Well, in any case, I've been giving it a lot of thought and I really think it would be wise to continue to watch them but also to let things run their course because—"

Brother Shawn interrupted him, "I'm not so sure that's the best strategy."

"Would you let me finish!" It was a command more than a request. "Like I was saying, I think it's prudent to watch them, like all the other novices, but I really think we shouldn't jump to conclusions. It's best, I think, to let things run their course. Give the boys some room and benefit of the doubt. Simon is a smart lad and I really believe that if he and Toby were getting too close, well, I believe he is more than capable of steering away from a dangerous relationship that could become, well, you know…" The priest didn't finish his sentence. Then he added, "I think in time he himself will approach the other brothers and eventually mingle with them more and establish healthy relationships with everyone, not just with Toby. They've all only really just met a few months ago."

Brother Shawn said nothing as the priest spoke. He had all but suggested that Father Bart's assessment and hopes for the future regarding Simon and Toby were pure bullshit. He knew what he had seen in the forest. The two monks walked ahead and just before they reached the refectory, Father Bart turned to Brother Shawn and said, "So let's just drop this angst about Simon and Toby. I really believe there's nothing to be concerned about there. If Simon is on a wrong road, I know that he's capable of changing course." A bell sounded in the refectory and the priest said, "Ah, first call, it's finally suppertime."

Brother Shawn simply said, "You're the boss."

To which the Master of Novices responded, "Yes, I am."

Simon was walking down the corridor and actually turned twice to look behind him and make sure Brother Shawn wasn't closing in on him. As he neared the refectory he thought again about his confession and about what Father Bart had said about love. He was lost in thought when all of a sudden a bell rang up ahead announcing first call for supper. The bell distracted him and as he moved up the corridor an outstretched arm, clothed in the black habit of the Order reached out and grabbed him. Simon was pulled into a small room and out of the corridor.

It was completely dark in the tiny room and he could hear the voices of the monks gathering for supper just a few yards away. Simon stared into the face of his captor and smelled as well as felt the now familiar warmth of his breath when the stranger spoke, saying seductively, "Hello, my beautiful man." Toby wrapped his arms around Simon's waist and pulled him close.

Simon whispered softly, "Toby!"

Without hesitation, they kissed hungrily, reveling in the pleasure of their encounter. Simon instinctively held on to Toby. Thoughts of the forest came to him. God had been in the forest and was now in the handsome man who held him tightly in his arms. Then other thoughts came to disrupt these, but Simon pushed them hastily away. Urgently, he had begun to fortify the wall within himself again. It would need to be reinforced, more than it had been. Without being able to voice it nor wrap his brain completely around it, he definitely needed to rebuild the wall. His sexual and spiritual sides needed to be kept completely and safely apart. It would be the only way for him to stay sane and keep his head above water.

Days passed quickly into weeks for Simon and weeks into months as the contemplative year of novitiate ran its course. His new found sexual feelings never subsided but rather took root in fertile ground. In the same way, his resolve to serve God through the vows of poverty, chastity and obedience never diminished. Simon's heart was firmly set on becoming God's best priest.

Simon continued, therefore, to build and fortify the wall within himself. He built the wall out of need. He now fully understood that the two powerful forces in him had to be kept apart if he was to answer the call and reach the altar as God's priest. For a time, Simon believed that he was the only one caught in this dilemma of sexual energy and desire on the one hand and authentic, sincere priestly vocation on the other. But it would not be long before he discovered that many of his brothers at the abbey struggled with the same thing.

On a lovely spring morning, Simon and his ten companions, duly approved by the abbot and his council, professed their first religious vows of poverty, chastity and obedience before God. The Abbot of Leicester received their consecration in God's name. Simon moved another notch closer in his path to the priesthood. He reflected and concluded that it was God's Will that he should profess his vows even in his duality. Thus it was that the day of religious profession was a festive one and he and Toby hugged each other not only because of the intimacy they continued to share but because they had been found worthy to proceed in God's service.

The eleven newly professed monks left the confinement of the novitiate and moved into what was known as the seminary. It was a massive network of cells, corridors, classrooms, gardens and huge meeting rooms all assembled on three floors on the western side of the abbey. It was the middle seventies and the world was changing drastically outside the Abbey of the Most Sacred Heart of Jesus. In time, many of those changes would make their way inside.

+ + + + +

The whining of the tattoo gun ceased and Simon realized that Mark was finished.

"Damn, Simon, that's quite a slice from your life!" To Simon, Mark sounded impressed. "I gotta say I'm jealous. Those are some awesome moments."

"It was a long time ago. I haven't thought about all of that in ages. It was my period of sexual awakening."

"Sexual awakening! Jesus, dude, it was a sexual explosion! Fucking in a forest? Damn, that shit even got me hot." They both laughed. "Okay, buddy,"

Mark said. The tattooer had completed his work. "Take a look. There's your tattoo of the 'Green Man'."

Simon got up off the work table and looked at his reflection in the mirror. The smiling face stamped forever into his flesh peered back at him. He was thrilled with the image and said, "Damn, Mark! I love it!"

Mark came up behind Simon and said, "There's the Green Man, keeper of your erotic forest."

"Yes, exactly! He was the gatekeeper of the breezes, God's caresses, the fallen tree, the bubbling creek, the bed of pine needles, the evergreens, the shards of light…" Simon thought about those long ago afternoons in the forest. He thought about Toby.

"Yeah, the Green Man saw you and your bud blow your loads."

"I suppose he did."

"So I guess the same old question comes up. Were you a good priest or a bad one?"

"Toby loved me. He really did." Mark did not respond. "It was young, early love but it was still love. And I loved him. Many will say that a vow of chastity implies, well, a life of celibacy."

"Celibacy?"

"Yeah, celibacy. You know, no sexual activity at all."

Mark said, "But dude, you guys weren't celibate."

"But I understood chastity by then, as being pure in my heart. I was engaged in sexual activity, yes, of course, but what were my intentions? I loved Toby and I single-mindedly wanted to serve God as His priest. On that day of profession of vows, I felt chaste even in my duality because my love for God and Toby were pure."

"You felt chaste even in your duality, even though you were sexually active?"

"Yes, I would say so. I felt chaste then and there, but doubted of course that those in authority in the Church would consider me so. Of one thing I had no doubt, though."

Mark listened and asked, "What was that, Simon?"

"I had no doubt that God was still calling me, sex or no sex. It was a constant call and it was clear to me. It still is. I just had to say 'yes' to God and I did on that day, in my profession of vows. When I finished professing, it seemed to me that nothing of God's promise had moved and nothing had changed. I looked around and the world was the same. I took it to mean that God had accepted my consecration wholeheartedly." Simon paused and then added pensively, "And once God consecrates, He doesn't take it back."

Chapter Seven
The Seminary

Some people go to priests.
Others to poetry.
I to my friends.
Virginia Woolf

Since he had last seen Mark at the shop several weeks earlier, Simon felt uneasy with the memories he had awaken within himself. He felt he was digging up too much of his past and there were moments when he wished he could put a lid on his emotions. Once again he was feeling "a little crazy inside" like Seth used to say and today had been a particularly difficult day for him. He had not left his house. He was terribly depressed but didn't exactly know why, although he suspected that it had everything to do with raking up his past. God had been very clear when he commanded him to face himself and not run anymore. He was being obedient to that command but it was costing him. It was costing him big time. There was so much to face and so much to own up to.

There were so many memories to sift through. He hadn't thought about many of those things in more than thirty or forty years and now it seemed like he was bringing everything to light every other week. Some of the memories were good and gave him comfort but other ones were too dark and too sinister to remember, let alone to voice. So many things had changed including himself, and so many people he had known then and that made up his world were now dead.

He sat barefoot and bare-chested in his briefs for most of the afternoon, alone, in his darkened bedroom. There in an overstuffed chair in front of the large, stone fireplace, he had poured himself several generous tumblers of Jack Daniel's and thought long and hard about his life, especially his past. He gazed down at the two heart tattoos that he now bore in his skin and lifted up his right arm. In the semi-darkness he could see the Green Man tattoo smiling at him. He dared not look at his upper thigh and the image that was imprinted there. What was tattooed on his flesh there was hideous and unspeakable. Was he really going to recall everything about his past? There seemed to be so much that he had felt necessary to run from. There were so many things he had done that he buried deep within, with the intention of never addressing again. Until God had commanded him to face his reality, that is. Simon chuckled to himself thinking that in his trunk of secrets, now there was something new: tattoos! Could he bear to be reminded every day about so many things that had turned out so differently than he had planned?

+ + + + +

On a cool, rainy morning in November, when autumn had begun to make itself felt in Dallas, Simon drove his truck to the tattoo shop. He had given a drawing to Mark the week before which had caused the tattooer to laugh uncontrollably.

Mark had held out the sketch in front of him and exclaimed, "What the fuck is this, you dirty bastard!"

Simon defended himself laughing, he said, "I'll explain it to you when I come in to get the tattoo." With that, Simon had left. Now he was slouched on the red leather sofa waiting for Mark to call him into his workroom to begin. He glanced at his reflection in the two glass cabinets that held jewelry for body piercings. He had never imagined himself visiting a tattoo shop on a regular basis. Life never ceased to amaze him.

"Hey, Simon, buddy, great to see you, man. Come on in." Mark had walked up behind him and shaken his hand. Then he led the way as he walked in front of Simon down the corridor. The other workrooms were all occupied and the sounds of tattoo guns whining like a clowder of cats, poured out into the corridor. It was a bit unnerving.

"Damn, Mark, you have a full house today, huh?"

"Yes sir. Business is great. You know we just got voted best Tattoo Shop in Dallas?" Mark was smiling broadly as he set up his ink and needle gun.

"Really? Damn, congratulations." Mark opened a manila envelope and out slid the purple stencil of a large gecko with a curled up tail. The gecko was sporting a huge pair of testicles and a good sized, erect penis.

Mark held up the stencil ceremoniously in Simon's face. "Okay, dude. Explain! Tell me what the fuck this is all about." He could not control his laughter. "You are such a fucking pervert!" He looked at the gecko and turned it this way and that and finally setting it down, he prepared Simon's abdomen for the tattoo. "I'll tattoo you with this, but I gotta say, you are some sick fuck."

Simon joined in Mark's laughter and then said "And I want his two low hanging balls to be bright red."

Again, Mark laughed as he shaved Simon's abdomen. "Not blue?"

"Hell no! Are you crazy? Blue balls? Not for my worst enemy! Ouch!" Simon cringing, cupped his genitals exaggeratedly and they both laughed.

"Red balls it is! Consider it done, you crazy motherfucker." When he was finished shaving him, he wiped the area clean and asked seriously, "Now where exactly do you want this critter placed?"

"I'd like it to go right over my ribs and down into my shorts, like the gecko is…"

"Wait, dude, let me guess! Like the fucking gecko is feeding on your one-eyed trouser rat! Is that about right?" He could barely contain his amusement.

"Yeah, that's my idea."

"Well, that's where we'll put him. It's feeding time, ladies and gentlemen! Let's release the kraken, or the gecko or whatever." He hesitated, then laughing, said, "I'll do the tattoo but I gotta say you are fucking pervy, dude!" Both men laughed as Mark carefully applied the purple stencil. As he concentrated, he asked, "Now what are you gonna tell me about today? Why not start with the meaning of this green little bugger on your abs?"

Simon got very serious and changed his tone, saying somberly, "It's about sex without love, Mark. The gecko represents that empty part of my life when I betrayed love."

"Explain, dude." Mark was now immersed in his work. He had turned on the tattoo gun and began to outline the gecko in black ink.

Simon closed his eyes and said "I think you'll agree with me that our eternal question is, 'good or bad priest?'"

"Oh fuck, yeah, I won't forget that, but I gotta say you haven't answered it yet."

"I will, I will, it's just that the answer is complex and needs to be explained through stories. I can't just say good or bad. I want to tell you first about how I learned to betray real love when it came to me."

Mark looked up suddenly. "What do you mean by betray?"

"By the time I professed my vows and moved up into the seminary section of the abbey I could clearly distinguish within myself the two opposing forces that had been battling within me for my full attention. On the one hand, I wanted to be myself, a young gay man, and love Toby. It felt so natural to love him and to be loved by one special person. I was totally smitten by him. But this powerful force in me was constantly at war with the Church's demand that we stay away from any and every kind of sexual expression, especially a homosexual one."

Mark didn't look up but said, "You obviously wanted both things. You wanted to fuck the person you loved but you also wanted to be a part of an institution that made it clear that that was never going to be tolerated because according to its rules, it was considered perverse. Unless, of course, it was not done openly. Right?"

"Exactly. But I still insisted on making both things work at the same time."

"You mean you were fucking obstinate and obtuse." Simon felt wounded by Mark's assessment.

The truth hurt but he still defended himself, "I took what I was told by Brother Shawn to mean that I could make both of these things work."

Mark kept working but smiled crookedly. "Can I be honest with you, dude? Can I tell you what I think?" He didn't wait for a response. "I think you're full of shit. You took his word to mean that because it's what you wanted to hear. It's what you wanted to believe. It's what you fucking wanted to do, come hell or high water. Don't tell me you didn't understand the rules of the game. Hell, from what you tell me you were always hiding what you thought and did anyway." Mark kept working.

Simon dismissed Mark's accusations. "Shawn had said it was okay to be gay. He had told me clearly that it was okay for me to be gay but that I shouldn't fuck it up by giving myself away. I guess he meant by making it all messy, by falling in love. It's difficult to hide that when you're in the thick of it." Simon's mind was racing into the past now. "When I fell in love I guess it became obvious."

"But you weren't real successful at hiding that nor of not falling in love with the guy, were you, bud? I mean, you did fall in love, didn't you?" Simon didn't answer Mark. The tattooer then added, "I'd bet my left nut that the problem in your case wasn't the fact that you were gay and fell in love with that guy, Toby. I'd say your problem was that in the process it got too be too much for you. You couldn't handle it because you were trying to balance within you two worlds at once. It got to be too messy for you and you threw some people under the bus as a result. Better them than you, huh?" Mark straightened up and drew more ink. As he did this, he said, "You wanted to enjoy all the warm, fuzzy shit about being in love and you wanted to fuck as a natural response but then you had to face reality. Your problem was you didn't want to choose. It seems to me that you were perfectly okay with living in two worlds even if it meant sacrificing those people who you drew into your web."

Simon jerked his head up and to one side. "That's not fair!"

"No? I'd say it's a very fair evaluation. I'd say you needed an honesty check back then, let alone a reality check. Seems to me you weren't confused, dude. I'd say you knew what you were doing. You wanted your cake and you wanted to eat it too." It embarrassed Simon to be confronted so aggressively but he had to admit that he was guilty. He hadn't simply had sex with Toby. It was more than sex as time had passed. He had to admit that he had fallen deeply in love with him and he didn't know what to do with that. Simon also knew he had betrayed Toby when it dawned on him that he could not love Toby openly and honestly and at the same time, serve the Church as a priest. And he knew what God's call meant to him. Simon was ready to accept that Toby had been sacrificed in order for him to move ahead in the Church. Simon thought at that moment that God had been justified in holding up his cowardice in his face. He desperately needed to come clean with himself. It wasn't difficult for him to be on the same page with God on this.

Mark interrupted his thoughts. "So this boned lizard is supposed to represent sex without love? Is that what you said?" Simon had closed his eyes and was licking his wounds quietly. A part of him hated Mark for what felt like quick judgments. He felt that his painful struggles couldn't be so easily summed up as Mark had done. Or could they?

"Yes, sex without love," he repeated flatly. Then he said, "It represents what I was first taught by Brother Shawn." Simon corrected himself, admitting,

"I mean, it's what Shawn had said to me and what I totally wanted to believe for my own gain."

Mark mumbled, "Yeah, what you were taught by that scheming Shawn dude? I'd say it totally represents what you gladly embraced because you wanted to. I think it represents what you thought was gonna work for you because you weren't willing to give up the sex. Don't get me wrong, I'm with you on the sex drive thing but it seems to me that the priest who scolded you in confession was clearly telling you something else, something you really didn't want to hear."

This angered Simon but he recognized the truth in what Mark said. "I was young."

Mark drew more ink. "Yeah, you were young. I was young once too and had my head up my ass as well." Simon remained silent accepting the rebuke. "The Church was clearly saying to you, 'no sex'. You were the one who accepted what Shawn was feeding you about sex because it was an easy fit. And then you took the whole thing to another level when you actually sought sex without love. It's like that old show on television, Door Number One: NO SEX, Door Number Two: SEX WITHOUT LOVE and Door Number Three: SEX WITH LOVE. Admit it, dude, of the three options I just pointed out, you settled for door number two, sex without love."

Mark stopped working and looked at Simon. "I'm sorry if you think I'm busting your balls but you need to hear this. You betrayed love because it would have meant you would have had to leave the abbey and give up all your priestly dreams and well laid plans. It was the price tag for sex with love with Toby and you knew it."

Simon opened his eyes and stared at Mark. "Damn Mark, you have my balls in a vise. They're beyond busted at this point."

Mark said gently, "Listen, Simon, I really think you need to hear this. I guess what Shawn was trying to tell you after all, Simon, was some kind of common sense. I'd guess some of you guys locked up in the abbey weren't going to stop fucking each other as your hormones exploded. But you needed to play by some set of visible church rules if you were going to survive there. It's a much tidier scenario if you have hidden sex without love. Hell, I'd say that kinda shit is alive and well today." For all his anger, Simon had to admit that Mark was right. Simon also knew how easily he could fall in love when he wanted to. It would never be accepted openly in the Church. Shawn had been right. "Get what I'm saying?"

Mark listened as Simon said, "I guess he was trying to help us survive but there was more to his teachings than that."

Mark looked up. "How so? Why do you say that?"

Simon looked at the ceiling, trying to get his thoughts in order and said, "Oh, I'll get to that in a bit. Let me just say that Shawn had lots of hidden agendas." Mark didn't respond and the two men kept to themselves. Finally, Simon said quietly, "Silas, well, I mean Toby and I had fallen in love and our attraction was getting stronger and stronger. But it was dangerous because we wouldn't be allowed to love each other openly in the Church. It was the middle seventies and the sexual revolution was all over the place except within the abbey."

"So why didn't you have a plan B?"

"A plan B?"

"Yeah, you could have left together. You guys could have made a life together somewhere far from the abbey."

Simon glared at Mark. "It wasn't an option for me! I was called by God to be a priest! Toby was called to the same thing by God. How could I just abandon that call?"

Mark worked on Simon's skin. "It was an option for sure, only you decided against it. You shouldn't blame God because He called you to the priesthood. You could have chosen Toby over your plans to become a priest but you didn't. It was your choice, not God's." Simon closed his eyes again. "You couldn't do both, Simon, so you betrayed love instead of betraying your plans."

"Instead of betraying God. His plans!" Simon corrected. He was getting uncomfortable.

"Yeah, well, whatever. I would guess you did the same thing every time you got close to somebody and you felt you were falling in love." Mark hesitated and then said, "Tell me about it. What happened to you and Toby? Did you really betray his love for you?"

Simon felt grossly exposed now but answered anyway. He was in too deep with Mark. "I betrayed his love. That's exactly what I did. It was my only way to stay afloat in my conviction that I was called by God to be a priest. I did the best I could, dammit. I tried to keep both worlds going at the same time but things caught up with me." The tattooer did not answer and Simon decided that perhaps Mark realized he had trashed him enough.

After some time, Mark said, in a lighter tone, "Well, tell me about when you moved into that other section of the abbey, after you guys professed your vows."

"I thought you wanted to hear about my betrayal of love?"

"I do, but let's take it a step at a time. Tell me about your life in the new section. You said it was called the seminary? How was it different from the novitiate?" Mark waited but Simon didn't speak. "Then tell me about what was going on between you and Toby."

Simon didn't hear Mark change his questions but in his mind he slowly began to unravel his past. He was once again easily wrapped up in his memories as he began to speak. "Back then, in the early 1970s, like now, driving through the narrow road from Crescent to Leicester was a real nature experience."

"How so?"

"Everywhere in that part of Pennsylvania, there are tall pine trees and massive firs on either side of the winding roads that make you feel like you're taking a ride through an unspoiled forest. As you drive and go up and down hills and winding roads, the evergreens enshroud you and the cool shadiness of the drive in that part of the state gives you an undeniable sense of tranquility, order and inner peace. Then, all of a sudden, above the trees, you see the turrets of the massive stone structure of the abbey against the sky."

"Driving from the cozy hamlet of Crescent into Leicester, the structure is built high upon a hill and far back from that country road. There are several ways to approach the abbey but it is this particular road that offers the most impressive view as you approach. Dominating the entire complex of buildings is the great bell tower attached to the two abbey churches and crypt like a giant backbone. It's topped by a soaring pointed cone-like roof, with a huge, ornate cross on the very top that can be seen for miles. This bell tower filters purplish light down onto the tomb of the Prince-Bishop Demetrius directly at its base in the crypt. The tower stands as a kind of marker for his legacy and impressive tomb and people can see it from far away. No one can deny that the abbey is a remarkable set of buildings architecturally but what is equally impressive is what lies within its walls."

Simon was lulled by the sound of the tattoo guns all around him and as he closed his eyes he immersed himself in the memories of that separate world he came to know and love as home for so many years. He spoke more to himself now than to Mark as he recalled that part of his life.

+ + + + +

One of the main corridors of the seminary wing of the abbey was used exclusively for the student monks preparing for priesthood. It was where all the classrooms were located as well as the impressive, semicircular lecture hall. In these rooms generations of men had been formed as candidates for the priesthood and now Simon joined their ranks together with his other ten newly arrived brothers. The seminary housed all the "clerics" or professed students in individual cells. Those who entered as "lay bothers" or "non-clerics", that is, who were not studying for the priesthood, received their training outside the seminary wing, in the brewery, kitchens, barns, libraries, laundry rooms, garages and other general areas of the abbey. These brothers served the abbey through manual labor whereas the clerics prepared for the demands of the ministerial priesthood someday in parishes, hospitals, universities and foreign missions.

Several days after settling into the seminary, Simon wandered off alone through the abbey. As a professed monk, he was now allowed to enter every section of the abbey except one: the wing that housed the solemnly professed monks. These brothers had made their final profession of vows or vows "for the whole of their lives". As he walked around the abbey, he quickly realized that it would be impossible for him to see the entire abbey in one afternoon.

His first stop was the great bell tower. He felt drawn to the structure. Simon could see with amazement that the bell tower had its base on the ground itself, but was attached to the back of the apse of each level. He peered down, into the tower and saw once again, that the white marble altar sat elevated above the tomb of the prince-bishop, enveloped in the mysterious purple and blue light Simon had first witnessed as a postulant. Soaring purple and blue stained glass windows adorned the rounded walls all the way to the top of the Gothic vaulted ceiling of the bell tower. It was the light that filtered through this glass and all the way down, into the cylinder of the tower, that was responsible for the surreal light surrounding Prince Demetrius' tomb way below.

Simon knew that there had to be a door up into the tower from the level of the upper chapel. He wanted to see the massive bells up close. He found a door with words carved upon it that read: "Angel's Roost". He opened it and he peered inside. He could see a winding staircase hugging the tower walls and disappearing above. Simon climbed the winding steps without looking down, fearful that he could lose his balance. He could hear a constant whistle coming from an opening above, through a small metal door. He tried the latch and it swung open. Cool fresh air blew upon him and as he stretched his head up, he was rewarded with a breathtaking view of the mountains, valleys and surrounding fields. Four great bells hung above him, each bearing inscriptions in Latin. He could make out the names of the Archangels on each bell: Michael, Gabriel, Rafael, Uriel. He sat down and remained there a very long time. There was something about this place that reminded him of the forest. Possibly it was because it was a place of solitude where it was easy to feel God's powerful presence, especially in the strong gusts of wind that blew unexpectedly through the tall metal grates all around him. Simon instinctively breathed in this presence. Conversation and interaction with God could be uninterrupted in this place as it had been in the forest. Perhaps it was because there he was high up, into the sky, away from everyone and everything below. He had been secluded in the forest by the bubbling creek in a similar way. He thought of Toby and promised himself to bring him to the Angel's Roost just as soon as he could. They would share that lofty space alone, together.

 Simon descended and continued his trek through the endless nooks and crannies of the abbey. He passed a few monks here and there but in general he was alone. He entered the Chapter Hall whose arched stone ceiling was as high as a cathedral's. He passed a huge carved door that had the words "Hall of the Secret Archives" carved on its front in large, imposing letters. Simon tried the door knob but it was securely locked. From there he went on to spend time in three different cloister gardens admiring the flowers and landscaping he saw there. One garden was completely filled with spice plants and a kindly old monk explained to him the various varieties that grew there. He walked to the front doors of the abbey and greeted Brother Gabriel who did not seem to recall him. Simon walked to the great kitchen of the abbey. There he poured himself a glass of cold milk from the dairy and greeted the monks who were busily working in the kitchen that served up meals for more than three hundred men a day.

At long last, seeing that he still had time for a nap before prayers, he was almost ready to return to his cell when by pure chance he came across a fascinating discovery. At the end of a small corridor not far from the refectory was a room whose walls were covered with three great pieces of furniture resembling postal boxes. At the base of each box was a monk's name. He searched for his and sure enough, there it was. These were the cloth napkin boxes and was the last stop daily before one entered the refectory for all three meals. Near the far wall of this "napkin room" Simon saw a wooden half door that appeared to be locked. It was carved with the image of a strange-looking, horned griffin and the word "Purgatory" written under it. He didn't think it would unlocked, but he tried it anyway and was surprised to find that it swung open quite easily. Steps descended into dark coolness and a musty smell tickled his nostrils momentarily. A thin chain hung from above and he tugged at it. Immediately, a weak, yellowish light filled the space below and he saw that it was a kind of entrance below the level of the floor on which he stood.

He went down into what appeared at first to be a cellar and began to walk cautiously. It was about seven feet high by six feet wide. The walls were made of solid stones cemented one over the other and interlocking every ten feet or so. No one was there but him. Soon enough he realized it was not a cellar but rather it appeared to be a hidden, underground tunnel. As he walked cautiously he figured that it must run the length and width of the abbey buildings like a maze of some kind. Exposed on its low ceilings were multicolored pipes and electrical wires. Simon thought that this space was probably meant to make water and electrical repairs easier.

Another thought came to him. Perhaps it could also provide safe passage for going unnoticed between one end of the abbey to the other if one had clandestine business to tend to. One twisted walkway led to a dirt path which opened up into an underground cellar of sorts. This space smelled earthy and very damp and had a dirt floor. It was filled with wooden shelves and crates were stacked neatly here and there. Simon had heard about root cellars in Pennsylvania and figured this could be such a place although he had no idea for what purpose. He had never seen anything like it in Florida. It seemed to have a wide trap door toward the back and Simon could see tiny slivers of sunlight breaking in from the outside into the deep darkness. Next to it, through a narrow walkway, Simon saw another smaller room and drew closer, but it appeared to be empty and there were no shelves nor crates there. It also appeared to have a dirt floor but he was unable to determine its use either since it was enveloped in blackness.

He returned to the walkway that was paved up ahead and continued his tour. Throughout this network were intermittent, short ladders or steps leading up onto the floor above. He climbed one and then another and saw that they led into trap doors or were semi-hidden in broom closets or were more accessible and visible in the open corridors themselves. Simon figured that this tunnel was rarely used now and it intrigued him because it appeared to be an important part of a bygone era of the abbey structure, albeit a hidden one. It must have served a purpose if it was there. There was something fascinating about it that was imperceivable from the floor above and this intrigued him a great deal. How many other secrets did the abbey keep to itself? Simon made a mental note to ask Brother Shawn about it. He definitely had to bring Toby down into the tunnel as well.

He returned to his cell that late afternoon and decided he would take a nap. Classes would begin soon and the newly arrived had been given time to settle in and prepare for the fall semester. They had been assigned to their small cells. In each was a narrow cot with a crucifix hanging on the cinderblock wall, a desk, a bookshelf, a sink built into the wall and a tiny closet without a door. Three tall windows of leaded glass panes stood between him and the outside world. Simon had a wonderful view as he peered out. Endless rolling hills and evergreens spread out below him and on the horizon were the Allegheny Mountains, sometimes appearing blue and sometimes blue and gray.

He had already hung his black suit, shirts and only pair of jeans on hangers. Hanging there were also the two woolen capes he had been issued. Above this was a shelf where he had organized his underwear and socks. He now removed his black habit and hung it in the closet as well. Standing in his underwear he saw that his closet was full to capacity. He took off his shoes and socks and climbed into his bed covering himself. He crossed his arms behind his head and stared at the ceiling.

When he and his brothers had arrived in the seminary wing, Simon was very pleased that Toby had been given the cell right next to his, to his right. Seth was assigned to the cell on his left. Having Toby next door made it extremely easy to see him frequently and interact with him daily without raising any eyebrows. Simon and Toby had developed a way of communicating through the rough cinderblock walls of the cells. They would tap out a short code on the wall between them just to let each other know that the other was in his room. On either side of that wall they each had their cots. Simon and Toby continued to explore with each other sexually as well as deepen their friendship. Their sexual lives had been limited to what they had shared in the forest during their novitiate. Therefore, Simon was unprepared when his curiosity took him further in his sexual yearning with Toby. Part of that had to do with Simon's own questions and doubts about himself. It became apparent to Simon, during those first few months, that Toby was quite experienced sexually and knew what to do when they were together, away from everyone else. On those occasions when it was safe to do so, when Simon would visit Toby in his room or vice versa, they would touch, kiss and hold each other. They spent long periods of time lying down together in one of their cots just staring into each other's eyes telling each other their secrets and how much they loved each other. It was forbidden, of course, for them to be in anyone else's cell other than their own. There were no locks on the doors to the cells as this was also forbidden. Being discovered in each other's cells would have been a very serious deal. Being caught lying together in bed or enjoying intimacy of any kind would have gotten them instantly thrown out of the abbey. This is why on some occasions when their sex was still limited to fondling each other, they would do so standing by the window, fully dressed, with their trousers barely down around their thighs, ready to pull them up if any voices were heard in the corridor beyond the door.

The fall semester finally began in the seminary and Simon, like everyone else in the abbey, followed a very strict schedule of prayers, meals, classes, study times and chores. There were periods of free time but very quickly everyone learned to discipline himself regarding the use of that time. Simon would rise earlier than most of the others in order to gain access to the toilets and showers before the long lines would form in front of each. As the weeks and months passed, Simon and his ten classmates joined the larger group of young men who were already there to continue their studies for the priesthood and new friendships were forged among them.

In the corridor where Simon was assigned his cell, there were close to forty other young men in formation preparing for the priesthood. On the other two floors of the seminary there numbered another eighty or so in different stages of study. On one floor alone, twenty eight young men were preparing for ordination to the diaconate at the end of the spring semester. Brother Shawn lived there and was among those being considered for ordination as a deacon which was the last step before priesthood.

Everyone was expected to wear his religious habit for prayers, meals and classes. Wearing his religious clothing made Simon feel safe against the sexual urges and temptations he often felt toward some of his fellow clerics. Simon felt that his habit was like a suit of armor because it had been blessed by the Abbot and it served to remind him what it was he was trying to be and what he was trying to achieve. There were many distractions for him on a daily basis and Simon couldn't deny the occasions of temptation that existed all around him. Aside from what he shared secretly with Toby, no one spoke openly nor publicly of sex nor of sexual things since that kind of behavior would have singled you out immediately as some kind of deviant or sexual pervert.

Yet, when three or four of them gathered in the recreation room in the evenings or outside after supper before evening meals began, there was often indirect conversations about sex or sexual themes. Raunchy jokes often made their way into their conversations in the shower rooms in the mornings or even at one of the endless number of tables of eight monks in the refectory during meals. Simon and many of his companions were still naïve about many aspects of sex but little by little they matured and understood more, thanks to those in their company who were older and had been more experienced in the world before entering the abbey.

Simon was drawn to several of his new brothers who were two or three years older than him and many of them responded by becoming his friends. There was a young monk named Lorenzo who was Latin like himself. His family, like Simon's, was originally from Spain and Cuba but he also had Italian blood. He possessed the toned body of the ballet dancer he had been before arriving at the abbey. Simon was greatly taken up by him for his prowess in ballet and would often sit in his company as Lorenzo practiced his dance in the locker room out by the barns that was usually empty, enthralled by his tales of New York and his previous life experiences.

Then there was Anthony or Tony as Simon called him who was short in stature and kept his wavy, black hair, long. He wore an impressive thick handlebar moustache on his chiseled face. Tony was from an East Coast Italian family and had a terrific personality. The two became instant close friends. Simon helped Tony harbor a stray dog once in the seminary until they were found out and reprimanded by the Master of Clerics. On another day, they went to the clay beds about a mile away and brought back clay in various containers. They had planned to sculpt with it but ended up having a clay fight in which they rubbed clay into each other's hair and face. This strong connection between the two of them was undeniably sexual although Simon was incapable of identifying it as such at the time. Tony even kissed Simon once when they were practically alone in the recreation room and he enjoyed the attention he received from him. They never got sexually involved beyond that flirtatious kiss but Simon was well taken up by his sexy, Italian friend.

Another close friend was Noah who wore thick wire-rimmed glasses, longish hair and was brilliant in his studies. He spoke softly and didn't waste his words but mostly listened. Noah, or Noey as he was called by his inner circle, was tall and walked with an air of confidence that Simon admired. He was extremely liberal in his ideas and even though Simon was on the traditional end of the spectrum, he admired Noey for his honesty when he expressed himself. Simon couldn't keep from admiring the pronounced bulge in the front of Noey's jeans when they were at recreation. It was difficult not to stare at the very faded area of denim which stood out so pronounced due to that which lay comfortably nestled beneath it. He was lanky and very easy on the eyes and this made Simon nervous in a good way when he hugged him. He would do everything possible to sit at Noah's table during meals and be noticed by him. Sometimes when Noah listened to music after Vespers in his cell, he left the door open and Simon made it a point to stop and say, "Wow, what kind of music is that?" Simon had very little interest in the pseudo jazz music he heard, but it was an excuse to be invited into Noey's cell. Sitting on the floor with Noah, on a padded rug he would later inherit from him, Noey would explain the genre of music playing softly and Simon could not have thought of a better place to be. Simon was simply thrilled to be with Noey, close to him in his cell, intoxicated by Noey's smell and interesting conversation.

There was Shane who was from out west somewhere in rural America, from a farming family. He was a year younger than Simon and probably as naïve. Something sexual always hung between them when he and Simon took walks or worked together. Shane was always smiling and had a beautiful face and brownish blond hair. Like Simon he was slender. Shane and Simon often shared spiritual conversations and enjoyed being in each other's company. A definite bond was established between them at some point and Simon considered him trustworthy.

Finally, there was Joshua. He had long blond hair and had perfect white teeth. Simon thought he looked like the "Ken" doll opposite "Barbie". Simon had heard that Joshua was sexually involved with someone in the abbey that Simon only knew superficially. However, he had to admit that he was attracted to the good-looking, cheerful young man and struck up a conversation with him any chance he got. Simon wanted to get to know him more and suspected the feeling was mutual. Like he often did with Noey, Simon did his best to sit at Joshua's table for breakfast or supper as often as he could.

Although Simon continued to spend most of his time with Toby, these five brothers befriended him during that first year. Yet, of the five, Simon was especially close to Anthony and Noah in a way that was different from his relationship with Toby. As time passed, when he was not with Toby, Simon enjoyed being with them as often as he could. There was a sensual vibe between them that Simon could not deny and had he not been so involved with Toby he would have probably pursued his sexual inclinations with them. He considered these five brothers and Toby, to be his circle of close friends. In a short time, together with Toby, they became Simon's trustworthy companions.

Those who were in charge of priestly formation in the seminary were all monk priests of the Order and almost all the professors there were priests with the exception of three or four who were laymen. It was a varied collection of personalities and soon, Simon and some of his fellow students had nicknames for most of them. There were also many professed monks who were indirectly involved with the seminary wing and interacted daily with the clerics preparing for the priesthood.

Simon met one of the older monks toward the end of that first summer in the seminary before classes started. He was a lay brother and had worked for many years in the abbey brewery. This German monk had come alone to America and had no family here. He was proud to be from a place called Bitburger where beer had been brewed for centuries. Brother Anton was completely bald. He was a tall, large man beginning to curve noticeably because of his advanced age. Still, Brother Anton was strong and he enjoyed repeating the story often that he had worked in New York City excavating the subway tunnels when he had first come to America as an adolescent. He had entered the abbey just before he turned twenty one. This elderly brother was lighthearted and loved to tell corny jokes. He was seriously traditional in his Catholicism and possessed a no-nonsense kind of faith easily described as fire and brimstone. When he became angry or emotionally excited, it was almost impossible to understand him because of his pronounced German accent. That first summer in the seminary wing, Simon and Brother Anton became good friends and the elder monk took him under his wing.

The property around the abbey was vast and Simon had signed up to drive one of the old tractors that summer which was equipped with a wide lawn mower underneath. He would mow a different field every day of the week on those waning, lazy days of summer. He enjoyed getting outdoors and sitting high atop the slow moving tractor shirtless. He only wore a pair of cut-off shorts, socks and a pair of work boots he had found in the abbey commissary where it was possible to find second hand habits and clothing, shoes and even table lamps. Simon felt virile and masculine as he switched gears on the tractor and took in the beautiful landscape all around him.

One day, as the afternoon was giving way to twilight, Brother Anton sat on a bench that overlooked the western side of the abbey, not far from the high wall surrounding the novitiate building. He had a small box next to him. He wore a great, white straw hat to protect his bald head from the sun and he waved animatedly to Simon each time he drew near with the tractor as he mowed. When at last Simon returned to the abbey garage before the sun set, sitting high above in the tractor seat, Brother Anton opened the box next to him, took something out and stood waving it at Simon. He had uncapped a cold bottle of beer from the abbey and held it out. Simon was grateful for the gesture and drank greedily. Anton repeated the scenario every afternoon for the remainder of summer.

The aging, German monk from Bitburger also requested a favor one evening after Vespers. He waited for Simon to emerge from the abbey church and approached him. "May I speak with you, brother?" The word "brother" came out as "bruder".

"Yes, of course! What is it, Brother Anton?"

"I'm old and not getting any younger, as you can see. Every evening I need to have a massage because my circulation is not good in my arms and legs. One of the clerics has been helping me in this for several years, but he is getting ready to be ordained a deacon and therefore I cannot ask him to continue in this service to me if he is soon to be consecrated for service at the altar of God. Would you be able to help me with the massages?"

Simon didn't expect to be asked such a favor but because he had grown fond of the old monk he dismissed any initial doubts and prejudices. "Would it be every evening, Brother Anton?"

"Yes, brother, every evening. Preferably at ten."

"Sure, Brother Anton. Where?"

"You know that now Compline is prayed privately instead of in choir. It is unfortunate but the Grand Silence has also been suppressed, so there is no need to keep quiet. These changes signal too much laxity, brother. But anyway, could you come to my cell this evening at ten, please. I will be most grateful. My name is on my cell door."

"Yeah, sure. I'll be there." The Master of Clerics was away and Simon was unsure who was next in the line of command. He felt that he had to ask permission to enter the solemnly professed cloister and Brother Anton's cell. Since it was summer, things at the seminary were relaxed until classes began in the fall. Therefore, that night at ten o'clock Simon entered the forbidden cloister without permission from the Master of Clerics and knocked gently on Brother Anton's door before entering.

"Yes, come in." Simon heard the familiar, thick German accent from within.

"It's just me, Simon, Brother Anton. I'm here for the massage." Brother Anton was lying in his cot, face down, obviously waiting for Simon. He wore a pair of huge white boxer shorts and a t-shirt. A radio was blaring the fundamentalist, Protestant program that aired every night in Leicester and which Brother Anton faithfully listened to. Brother Anton's cell was filled with old Catholic prints and statues of the Mother of God and the Saints. There were worn-out prayer books stacked high by an overstuffed chair next to his cot. The rooms of the solemnly professed monks were much larger than the cells of the students. The room was strongly impregnated with the fragrance of "Ben-Gay" cream.

Brother Anton looked up and said merrily, "Oh, Brother Simon, how wonderful to see you. Yes, I'm ready for my massage. I have poor circulation in my arms and legs." Then he sat up and removed his t-shirt. Simon saw that the large German monk had a massive beer belly. His chest was covered in thick, white hair. Then he said angrily, "Now listen to the nonsense on the radio, Brother Simon. Oh, the Protestants! Why don't they just get the truth and be done with it!" The host on the radio show was in the midst of a tirade against the "papists and all others of their same ilk, surely condemned to perish in the everlasting fires of Hell."

Simon didn't quite know how to respond and only managed to say, "It's some pretty strong stuff."

Brother Anton rolled onto his back with a huff and a puff and kept his shorts on. With impatience, he muttered, "Such nonsense! Lies and lies because of no truth!" Then he said to Simon, "Please can you begin with my arms and then my legs. The bottle of Keri lotion is here on the small night table with the tube of Ben-Gay."

Simon saw the bottle and tube and moved forward. He uncapped it and first poured some lotion into his palms and began the massage on the old monk's arms. Then he moved to his legs. Nervously, Simon blurted out, "I hope I'm doing it right."

Brother Anton disregarded the question and asked matter-of-factly, "And could you please rub my feet as well? They are sore."

"Yes, Brother, of course."

When Simon was done, Brother Anton rolled his massive frame to one side. The cot creaked and complained under him and seemed to threaten collapse as the large man moved with difficulty. When he was face down again, he instructed Simon, "Brother, would you rub my neck and my back as well, after you rub my arms a bit more with the Ben-Gay?" It was more a gentle command than a request.

"Sure, brother, no problem." There was a part of Simon that was uncomfortable for an instant but he quickly dispelled any doubts within himself. Simon told himself that it was not inappropriate and that he shouldn't read more into the old man's request. When he was almost done, Brother Anton spoke into his pillow and his words came out muffled and unclear. Simon didn't understand and said, "I'm sorry, brother, I didn't get that. Could you say it again?"

The monk lifted his head off the pillow momentarily and said matter-of-factly, "Brother Simon, could you rub my buttocks, please?" The old man began to pull his boxers down as he said, "Could you help me with these?" Simon said nothing as he pulled them down and saw the two fleshy, white mounds of German flesh. He rubbed as he had been told by the old monk.

Simon cared for Brother Anton in this way for the next eight years until he was ready to be considered for the deaconate. Shane followed him in service.

In addition to the rubbing, Simon clipped Brother Anton's toe nails regularly, kept tract of his medicines and helped him when the old monk was bed ridden. His close friends all kidded him about the "butt rubbing" and Simon realized it was an open secret in the abbey. Those in the know had given Anton, the old German brother, the nickname of "Nancy Anne" which eventually morphed into "Annie", for "Little Orphan Annie".

One of them had said to Simon, "It's because she has no family here in America, and since her name is Anton, we call her 'Annie'." It was the first time Simon had heard a woman's name and pronoun applied to a man. He was unsure about how he felt using alternative pronouns to refer to the old monk since he really was fond of Brother Anton. Yet he had to admit that he did feel grateful to be included in the joke and began to use the common jargon of his small, close circle of friends.

When Father Wade, the Master of Clerics, returned several weeks later, he laughed out loud when Simon approached him. "Father, I'm here to ask your permission to assist Brother Anton with his massage in the evenings. May I please enter the cloister and Brother Anton's cell for this purpose?"

"Oh, so you're the new masseuse! Congratulations! You are officially assigned, twenty four seven, three hundred sixty five days for the next eight years!" Then he added, "How in the hell did you ever get saddled with that yoke around your neck?"

Simon smiled meekly and said, "It's no yoke. I'm happy to help with Brother Anton."

"Well, good for you. Somebody's gotta do it."

+ + + + +

Mark suddenly spoke up and startled Simon out of his reminiscing. "You mean to tell me that that old guy had you rub his ass every night and everybody thought it was cool?"

"Well, it did seem strange to me at first but I didn't think it was inappropriate at the time."

"Are you fucking serious, dude?"

"Look, Mark, I'll admit that I thought it was odd but everybody around me sort of took it in stride, like it was more of a harmless joke than anything else. Like calling him Annie for Little Orphan Annie and all."

"Damn, that is all some weird shit, dude. How in the hell did that old guy get away with having a young guy come in every night to rub his ass and nobody raised any eyebrows?"

"I did wonder about that myself. Certain boundaries were somewhat blurred, I guess. I'll admit that. But I saw him as a kindly old monk without any malice or bad intentions." Then Simon said as an afterthought, "You know, I never thought it was weird in a sexual way until right now that you mentioned it. I guess we were all on the same page in that environment and it didn't feel especially out of place but normal somehow." Mark looked at Simon as he drew more ink and just rolled his eyes in mock exasperation. Simon added, "Honestly, I only had great respect for Brother Anton. He was very fond of me."

"Yeah, I'll bet."

"He was, genuinely. All the way till he died."

+ + + + +

Simon closed his eyes again and remembered out loud. Faces and names came to him in rapid succession. It had been years since he had recalled the individuals who served in positions of authority at the seminary. The Master of Clerics was a trained musician before he had become a monk. He was lanky, high strung in temperament and had salt and pepper, unruly, long hair, like you might imagine on Merlin the Magician on a bad hair day. He was also terribly homophobic and had a reputation for dismissing anyone suspected of homosexual behavior. He, Father Wade, had been Master of Clerics for many years. He wore thick glasses and bore the unmistakable accent of a Boston born native. He could be the most charming man in the abbey on a good day and the most menacing on a bad day.

He had his favorites among the clerics and Simon readily recognized the Master of Cleric's fondness for one of the clerics in particular who would soon be ordained a deacon.

The young monk in question was impossibly handsome and possessed the physique of a professional athlete. He rarely wore his habit and wore faded jeans, tight fitted t-shirts and sandals from India where the little leather strap hugged the big toe. He wore his golden blond hair long and sometimes he wore a close trimmed beard. He too was a musician and was often in Father Wade's suite of rooms, lying about on a couch that the priest kept there. Laughter and animated conversation could always be heard coming from those rooms when Brother Ethan was with Father Wade. The Master of Clerics was careful to keep his door open but Simon noticed that often times they were hidden from view in the second room, in Father Wade's bedroom. Tony and Noey referred to the Master of Clerics as "Wanda", but Simon had no idea why and he was embarrassed to ask. He only knew that when they spoke about "Wanda", they were speaking about Father Wade. Most feared him rather than respected him, and Simon was certainly in that first group.

There was a sixty-something-year-old monk whose name was Father Theobald. He too was of German ancestry but born in Pennsylvania. The brothers named him "Aunt Tess" or "Aunt Tessie". He was a gentle, effeminate gentleman and aside from his administrative duties in the seminary, he was also a painter and gourmet chef. He had a studio in one of the many nondescript rooms not far from one of the small doors that led into the underground tunnel under the abbey. Approaching that place, the visitor was immediately struck by the strong smell of oil paints and solvents associated with a paint studio. His suite of rooms where he lived, were in one of the oldest sections of the abbey and had originally been some sort of library. It was rumored that Father Theobald often had extravagant clandestine suppers late at night for a chosen few in his apartments, where the booze flowed and Wagner recordings played deep into the night. Simon recalled the conversation he first had when this monk was pointed out to him in the huge refectory.

Lorenzo had said, "Look there, Simon, have you met Aunt Tessie yet?"

Simon had turned around but did not see any woman in the refectory. "Whose aunt is she?" Simon asked innocently. "How can a woman be in here if this is cloistered?"

There had been snickers and chuckles. "Oh, trust me," the young monk had said, smiling to himself. "She's a real German lady from the old country and has lots of cute nieces."

Simon was momentarily thrown off but then understood. "Are you pointing out a monk to me?" Simon had caught on.

"Yes, of course, silly. As you say, we are in the cloister. But there she is over at that head table of priests by the crucifix." Then Lorenzo added playfully, "She's sitting right next to 'Marcia' and 'Proud Mary'. 'Fruit Fly' is sitting across from her."

Simon shook his head as he laughed nervously. "Now you lost me." He had turned to look at the impressive, heavy wooden table topped with a thick slab of marble. It was a long table with thick, carved legs in the form of powerful lion's haunches and limbs. It dominated the refectory at the far, main wall. Under a life-sized crucifix, sat the Abbot surrounded by the priest professors and those in charge of running the abbey. Lorenzo's dark, seductive eyes slanted as he said, "Aunt Tessie is the one with that damned sweater over her shoulders."

Simon saw the priest in question. "Oh, you mean Father Theobald." Then he asked, "Who are 'Marcia', 'Proud Mary', and 'Fruit Fly'?"

"Never mind for now. You'll know soon enough, I'm sure. They are Tessie's intimate sidekicks." The young monk remained looking at them and whispered to Simon, "Yep, that's Aunt Tessie. Be careful around her. She likes pretty boys like you, young and slender." Simon felt a pang of embarrassment for Father Theobald who was gesticulating wildly at his place at table completely unaware that they were making fun of him.

"Why do you call her...I mean, him that?" Simon was curious.

Lorenzo looked away from the head table and said to Simon, "I'm not really sure of the genesis of that name but you see that sweater over her shoulders?"

Simon looked up again at the priest. "Yeah, I do."

"Well, they say that when she's wearing that sweater over only one shoulder, it means she's on the prowl. She's looking for fresh, sweet meat. Young meat."

Something deep inside Simon rebelled against this name calling. It seemed terribly disrespectful to him to be referring to the priest monks using women's names and female pronouns. Still, he wanted to belong to his circle of friends and felt he was a part of some funny, sordid secret name code. He really enjoyed the company of his clever friends whom he admired greatly.

A few weeks later, Simon heard a short but insistent knock on his cell door as he studied for an upcoming exam. Simon was surprised to see it was Aunt Tessie at his door. The priest seemed fidgety and his words came out in a nervous avalanche, "Oh, Brother Simon, I hope I'm not disturbing you at this late hour."

"Not at all, Father." Simon could not take his eyes off the priest's sweater, which he now wore over one shoulder.

"I was just passing by on my way to the paint studio I have here in the abbey. It's a small place but cozy and great for concentrating on my models when I paint. I am always on the lookout for live models, you know." Uninvited, Father Theobald walked into Simon's cell and in a breathless display of admiration, suddenly lowered his voice and said, "I have noticed that you have a very narrow torso. It's not muscular but perfectly slender for a painting I'm doing of the Prophet Jeremiah. I wanted to stop by to ask you if you would pose for me. I want to paint your clavicles." He stretched out his hand as if he were going to touch Simon but only gestured to the spot, taking away his hand quickly as if he had been stung, saying "Oh my, yes, it's perfect for the prophet."

Simon managed to ask, "What are clavicles, Father?" Beyond that, he remained speechless.

"Why, they're your collarbones, my boy." Father Theobald looked Simon up and down. "I can totally use you for another painting I have in mind, but I need your collarbones for the prophet." Then he added, speaking more to himself than to Simon, "You are certainly well put together."

Simon just stood there. It was true, then, what Lorenzo had said. He was on the prowl. It was all very bizarre but at the same time Simon felt noticed and he liked the attention. "Oh, I see," was all Simon could muster.

"Yes, well, if you could come down to my studio whenever you are free this Saturday afternoon, I'd be very pleased." The priest looked quickly around Simon's cell.

"Yes, Father, of course. If it's a help to you."

Aunt Tessie turned to leave but then seemed to remember something. "Oh, by the way, you can come in your jeans and t-shirt. Dress comfortably. Once we begin, I'll only need you to remove your t-shirt so that you are bare-chested and your clavicles, your collarbones, are exposed." Then in haste, he turned around as if needing to run. Simon saw that the sweater fanned out wildly behind him like a matador's cape during an afternoon faena, leading to the kill by the matador. Aunt Tessie caught the sweater before it slipped off and replaced it on both shoulders. As Father Theobald walked hurriedly away Simon got up to close his door and wondered when he would meet Marcia, Proud Mary and Fruit Fly.

In the abbey, there were many prestigious assignments that ranged from the Abbot to the Porter, this last being the monk who locked and unlocked the great abbey doors on a daily basis. These positions were often times held for almost an entire lifetime. One of the more important assignments fell to the monk who had been named Prior of the abbey. The Prior was the monk delegated by the Abbot to act in his name concerning almost every aspect of the governance of the abbey and the activity of the professed monks in his absence.

Father Demetrius, the Prior of the Abbey of the Most Sacred Heart of Jesus, was in his early forties. He was very short of stature, slender and possessed a very deep voice that did not seem to go with the rest of him. Father Demetrius wore his honey colored hair somewhat long and his fine, narrow nose and angular jaw gave him a graceful, elegant aura that unquestioningly commanded respect. He acted like a much younger man and this youthful demeanor made him instantly likeable to Simon. It was easy to fall under the seductive spell of his charming personality. He had been born in England, in the northwestern part of the country, near the Irish Sea and loved to talk about his youth to anyone who was genuinely interested in listening. Father Demetrius would inform you that he had been a promising child star on radio and the stage. Sometimes an English accent could be noted in his diction when he was passionate about something and wanted to stress a point. It was also quite pronounced when he consumed large amounts of Scottish, single malt whiskey.

The Prior was effeminate in an elegant, refined aristocratic way that yet, could be construed as theatrical by some. Simon had heard the rumors that Father Demetrius was gay and gay friendly, although no one would have dared openly, to suggest either. It was rumored that a young, recently ordained priest in a nearby town was his lover but no one ever spoke of proof. He was great fun to be around, especially with the younger monks in formation because he was always full of mischief and open to adventures and pranks. Simon enjoyed being in his presence from the moment he met him and felt that the Prior of the abbey was fond of him as well. Simon thought of him as belonging to his circle of close friends, although in a different way, since Father Demetrius was not his peer. As far as Simon was aware, this monk had no nickname.

One night Tony and Simon returned late from Pittsburgh after enjoying a day away. They had driven one of the priests to the airport there which was then the closest airport to the abbey. They decided to take their time returning to the abbey and were giddy with laughter with a plan they had devised. At a restaurant on their return, they spoke with heavy accents and acted as if they had just arrived from Italy. The young, local waitress who served them believed every word of it which only encouraged them in their caper.

When they got to the seminary most of the lights were out and they giggled like two fools on their way down the long, shadowy corridor toward their cells. Father Demetrius' voice suddenly boomed out of the darkness. He invited the two young men into his suite of rooms for a drink and of course, they accepted. Neither of them had ever entered the Prior's suite before. The living room where they sat was in complete disarray. Used clothes, shoes, books, boxes as well as class notes for teaching, were haphazardly strewn about everywhere. But the thing that caught Simon's eye were the empty whiskey bottles and filled ashtrays everywhere displaying small piles of cigarette butts like well-constructed pyramids. The Prior had smoked those cigarettes and had stacked the filters carefully into the organized pyramids, all over the suite, layered in this way: ten across the bottom, nine carefully placed on top, followed by eight and so on until one capped the entire edifice. They seemed to be everywhere and at one point when Simon went into the bathroom to pee, he noticed several of these around the edges of the tub, neatly stacked in the same way.

The three of them drank that night and Tony and Simon told Father Demetrius all about their Italian adventure. The Prior clapped his hands like a merry child and laughed with delight as he heard the tale of deception and thought it was superb. He confided in them similar capers of his own making and the three monks lost track of time. By the time they excused themselves, Father Demetrius was quite drunk. Simon and Tony had sipped their strong drink slowly whereas the Prior had generously refilled his tumbler many times.

Talk in the abbey was that Father Demetrius drank every night by himself and it was no surprise for Simon to see him that way now. Being with Tony made it seem fun and he didn't think much about it until a few nights later when the Prior phoned Simon's corridor and asked to speak to him. Simon was concerned at first and wondered if someone had noticed him coming out of Toby's cell. When he reached the phone and answered, it was actually something far removed from what he had anticipated.

"Yes, hello, this is Brother Simon."

In a strange voice that sounded garbled and slurred, he heard, "May I prevail upon you to come to my rooms, brother. This is the Prior speaking."

"Yes, Father Demetrius. Is everything okay?"

"Of course it is, my boy, why wouldn't it be so? Splendid, I'd say. Things have never been better. Come now and have a drink with me like you did the other night."

"Tony, I mean, Brother Anthony isn't with me right now, Father, so I…"

"Dear child, I'm asking you to come. Alone."

Simon felt dread in the pit of his stomach but had to accept because the priest had summoned him. "Yes, Father I'll be right over." As he walked down the corridor he began to feel panicked. A familiar, uneasy hunch took hold of him, as it had in the cheap motel room when he was fifteen years old. Simon suddenly felt alarmed and unprotected like he had when he had emerged, dripping wet from that shower long ago, totally vulnerable to what awaited him beyond his control.

When he arrived at the Prior's door he knocked and Father Demetrius answered, "Yes, come!" and Simon opened the door. Father Demetrius' hair was disheveled and he had a cigarette in one hand and a scotch in the other. He sat slouched among the clothes, books, bottles, papers and pyramids and handed Simon a scotch he had already poured for him. He must have sensed Simon's fear because he smiled sadly and said in his deep, theatrical voice: "Now don't be frightened of me. I'm not the big bad wolf. I'm not going to do anything bad to you, like eat you up. Just sit with me and have a drink. Can you do that for a lonely old man?"

Yet, it was as if the big bad wolf was in fact speaking to Goldie Locks except that this wolf was quite drunk. The same fear Simon had felt with Father Austin in the motel room in northern Florida so many years before now surged uncontrollably through him. He was frightened beyond words but remained outwardly calm. He was able to do this because he told himself that the man in front of him came after the Abbot in the chain of command. In Simon's inexperienced mind, that mattered significantly.

The scotch quickly performed its magic on Simon as it raced and burned through his veins, finally mellowing him out of his fears and anxieties. The sophisticated, older man sitting in front of him was very drunk but held his own even as he gesticulated exaggeratingly and didn't always finish his sentences. His appearance was confusing to Simon because he looked old and haggard, sad and beaten one minute, then suddenly youthful and handsome, laughing and carefree the next. But as they spoke, the Prior opened up his soul and it was disturbingly apparent to Simon that Father Demetrius was terribly bruised and broken inside, filled with loneliness and shame. The painful, pointless life of Father Demetrius was on full display to Simon that night.

"You rather remind me of myself, you know. There was once so much promise in me." Father Demetrius paused, barely pressing against his chest, the yellowed tips of the graceful fingers of his boney hand which held the cigarette loosely. As he gestured this way, almost in slow motion, Simon couldn't help but notice the long, fragile ash that hung precariously from the end of the nearly consumed cigarette and threatened to break loose. "Hopes and dreams…I had plans once. Did you know I studied in Rome?"

"No, Father, I didn't." Simon listened.

"Of course you didn't know that. Why would you? Here we sit in this shithole of a town so far from any place of real value." He took a long swig from his glass, swallowed and then a drag from his cigarette as if thinking back, blowing the smoke out slowly as he looked faraway. "Yes, I was in Rome and I had plans."

"Rome." Simon's eyes lit up. "That must have been fascinating. Tell me more, Father."

"Don't patronize me, boy!" He looked at Simon without blinking. "You need to be careful. You see, you are just like me. I've been watching you since you came to the seminary wing. If you don't watch yourself, you'll end up just like me."

Simon asked, "Watch myself? What do you mean?"

"I mean that you need to choose the Church and give yourself completely to her demands or you need to leave it. The Church has certain demands you may not be aware of quite yet although in time…" Father Demetrius emptied his glass and refilled it. "Shit or get off the pot! This game you play, I played it too. Living in two worlds never ends well. I could have been a great man out there but instead…" The man looked worn out to Simon, as he extended his arm toward the large window and pointed to everything that lay outside. Simon heard him say, "But instead… I'm here in this dump, never to leave its confines…not now, in any case." The Prior suddenly stood unevenly and said, "Let me pour you another drink."

Without waiting for a response, the Prior filled Simon's glass. Simon tried to protest saying, "I think I've had enough."

The man waved him away, saying with somewhat slurred speech, "Don't be silly and obey for once." Father Demetrius continued, "You think you know everything, as I thought I knew everything when I was your age. But you don't. You don't know a damned thing. There's an awful lot you still need to learn." Then he added bitterly, "Don't give me that look of pity." He stared at Simon and said, "A lot of times we look at others and feel sorry for them when all the while, the others, ironically, are looking at us and feeling sorry for our pathetic situation."

When late into the night Simon left the drunken man, Simon wondered if the walls he kept fortified within himself would eventually destroy him as well. Simon wondered about all the things he hid from others and the many secrets he kept about himself. The things that Father Demetrius had said to him, resonated somewhere within but he pushed it far away where it wouldn't disturb him. As Simon fell asleep in his bed that night, he felt sorry for Father Demetrius, because there was no one with whom the Prior could share his pain except his booze. Simon was comforted by the thought that he had Toby and his other close friends.

+ + + + +

Simon was aware that Mark had stopped tattooing and had gotten up. Simon opened his eyes and saw the tattooer standing at the cabinet over his work space searching for something. "Ah, there you are," Mark said to a bottle of ink. Simon realized that Mark was talking to himself. When he turned around he held a small plastic bottle of lime colored ink in his hand. Mark saw Simon looking up at him and smiling said, "This is going to be your gecko's skin color as he munches his way down your abs to your junk."

"That's a great looking color, man. I love it."

Mark sat down again and prepared the ink cup for the new color. Simon observed him and neither of them said a word. Finally, when Mark had cleansed the needle and drew fresh ink, he turned toward Simon, and said, "Those are some interesting, colorful characters. Damn, church folks are rarely presented being that way. You sound to me like you really trusted your close circle of friends and relished in their zany behavior. That Demetrius dude reminds me of that song on the old Beatles' Revolver album, 'Eleanor Rigby'. That's some sad shit."

"He was a tragic figure. I got to know him better that fall when classes began. Father Demetrius was a Biblical scholar and had studied at the Biblicum in Rome. That's one of the Pope's best schools, I mean, like one of the best for studying the Bible in the world. Father Demetrius taught us Scripture in the seminary and was brilliant. He never came to class drunk although sometimes his class was canceled at the last minute and we had study hall."

Mark listened as he applied the bright green color on the gecko. "So did you ever tell him about any of your shit?"

The question caught Simon off guard. "What do you mean?"

"Did you tell him about the worlds you were living in, I mean, did you come clean with him as he had with you? I'm talking about the fact that you and Toby were hot for each other and messing around together."

"No, of course not! Are you crazy? I would have gotten thrown out, or at least I was fearful of it. We all lived scared of that kind of shit, I mean, of the possibility of saying too much about our real selves."

"How did you figure that? Maybe that guy would have understood you. Maybe he would have helped you to face all the stuff you were hiding within yourself. Maybe you didn't even need to tell him much 'cause it sounds to me like he already had your number." Mark looked at the tattoo he was creating. "Shit, maybe you could have helped him out. Seems to me he probably lived it himself when he was young, only later, pretty much destroyed, he had no one to share it with either."

Simon thought about the irony of that if it had been true. "You know, Mark, it was a strange world we lived in at the abbey. Lots of stuff was out there but nobody talked about it directly. It wasn't addressed openly."

"How so? What do you mean?"

"I mean that most of us had struggled with the same shit but we all kept secrets and those secrets fucked us up inside. Nobody dared share anything about being gay when we first got to the seminary that first summer. And a lot of those older guys would never confront their own sexual lives openly. It just wasn't done."

"Keep talking," Mark said.

"But that would all change soon enough in the abbey. The changes from outside were coming to our world. The sign that it was imminent, I think, was that we were already using language that reflected the change. Code names and change of pronouns were ushering in a real revolution. It was the seventies and a sexual revolution was already boiling over and exploding all over the place in America. The Stonewall riots just a few years before, had opened a door that could never be closed again. It was just a matter of time before that revolution hit the Church, the seminaries, the monasteries and convents. But for that first summer and fall, it still hadn't hit head-on. It was coming and angry clouds were forming on the horizon but all of us were still hiding all kinds of shit from each other and playing word games."

"Well, you said you got to know that Demetrius dude better that fall. Did you finally tell him as time went on? I mean, if you guys got closer and shared things, couldn't you have told him by spring or by summer?"

Simon closed his eyes as he remembered a sad, rainy night in January when the winding country roads around Leicester were slick with rain turned to ice. "On a really freezing night in January, Father Demetrius was driving back to the abbey in Leicester. He was drunk it seems and on a lonely road, one of his tires got a flat. He tried to get control of the car but it was swerving because the rain was turning to ice. He finally was able to stop the car on a curve in the road by sliding a little into a ditch." Mark had stopped working. "In a drunken stupor, he had wandered from his car out into the dark, slippery road. An unsuspecting driver didn't see him on the curve of the road in the darkness until it was too late. The driver hit him and killed Father Demetrius instantly."

Simon paused. Then he said, "He had been a young man full of promises once but then, along the way, was anguished and tormented by so many demons. The little I got to know him I realized how many walls he had built within himself." Simon suddenly paused, mostly out of need. When he regained his composure, he continued even though his voice seemed ready to crack. His eyes had misted and he turned away momentarily, afraid of the onslaught of unwanted tears. "Demetrius had accepted, at some point in his life, to live fragmented, disconnected and shattered inside. It was a fucked-up way to live."

"Damn, Simon, that's a fucking, tragic story."

Simon faced Mark. "Sad thing is, Mark, it's not 'a story', I mean, it all happened for real. It happened in a real life. Lots of people decide to live in two or more worlds with disastrous results. I decided to live that way for a long time." Simon looked down at the gecko tattoo taking shape. "Walls are bad. Hiding is bad. But for a long time it's all I knew how to do. I wanted to tear the walls down but in time I only built them stronger and higher. It gave me a sense of security even though it was seriously fucking me up."

"Whew! That's some heavy shit, Simon." Mark turned off his tattoo gun. "Let's break for a few minutes and stretch. Take a leak if you need to. There's still a lot of small detail I need to put in. Just relax. We have time."

"Yeah, I think I do need to piss." As Simon moved to get up he felt the sting on his abs. He looked at the full mirror across from him and saw that the gecko tattoo was emerging.

"See you here in five, ten minutes. I need to make a phone call. When we get back I want you to explain something to me that I didn't quite get from the things you told me earlier, okay?"

"Deal." Simon dreaded what Mark would ask him.

Not quite ten minutes passed when Mark came into his workspace and saw Simon lying on his worktable. He asked, "Ready to continue?"

"Yes sir, I am!"

"Cool." Mark looked at the tattoo he was working on and said, "It's really looking good. I'm gonna get to all the details now that will make it look awesome. It's worth the time and effort." As the tattooer drew ink again and continued working on Simon, he asked, "Okay, so I need some clarification. How does this sex without love theme come in with the betrayal of love? I'm confused. I mean, it seems to me that you were clear about playing around with Toby behind closed doors, right? How did all of that get complicated for you to the point of you betraying him if you kept it compartmentalized?"

Simon felt exhausted but pushed ahead, "It's a tangled mess but hang on and I'll explain. It was way more complex than that."

Suddenly, Billy appeared at the door, out of breath, saying, "Mark! Sorry to interrupt but you need to come out front. There's a phone call you need to take."

Mark sighed impatiently and said, "Gimme a sec, I'm in the middle of some delicate work here."

Billy insisted, "Yeah that's cool but you need to get this call now."

"I said gimme a sec. I'll be right there." Billy ran down the hall dramatically to stay by the phone. Mark sighed again and said, "I'm sorry, dude, but this phone call business is fucking me up. Family shit I need to tend to. I don't want to hurry doing the details on this gecko because the details are the most important part of it and honestly, it's turning out fantastic." He turned the tattoo gun off and looked at Simon, "I'm really sorry but can we finish this later, like in a few days? I hate to ask you this, but would that be cool?" He rubbed his eyes as if he was in discomfort and added, "This call is gonna take some time." Mark reached for his appointment book.

Simon sat up and said, "Actually, I'm really tired here and I'd welcome a respite. Talking about all this stuff is getting to me."

Mark showed Simon his appointment book. "Since I'll be working on the same tattoo and your skin's looking a bit angry at this point, it's better to wait and let it heal before I continue."

"I'm cool with that. No worries." Simon was more than ready to go home.

"How about in ten days or so? It's really all detailed work but I'd rather let your skin rest a little. Does Wednesday the twenty third sound good?"

"Yeah, that's perfect."

Mark made an annotation and slammed the book shut, tossing it aside. "Let me clean up that gook and put some antibacterial on it before I wrap it up."

Simon felt drained to his core and was more than eager to get home. He desperately needed some generously poured bourbon.

Chapter Eight
Toby

Pleasure of love lasts but a moment.
Pain of love lasts a lifetime.
Bette Davis

That afternoon, when Mark excused himself and took his phone call, Simon had returned home. He showered and dried off, then he put more antibacterial on his new tattoo and poured himself a hefty amount of Jack Daniel's. He had been drinking for several hours since he had returned home. At some point, as the sun began to set outside, he mindlessly crawled into bed in a thick fog of bourbon. In his anguish, he begged for sleep to come free him from the insistent phantasms that continually plagued him.

When sleep finally came, Simon surrendered. He descended easily into deep repose, and he allowed himself to be led into that realm where imagination and mental imagery are wedded and held together so perfectly that those who are dreaming would swear it was all really happening. On this night, as he slept, he was ushered into a dream that was at first all sweetness and bliss.

+ + + + +

Simon is naked in his dream but he does not feel exposed nor vulnerable. He is confident and understands that he is a strong, young man, full of life. He is unaccompanied in an unknown place, yet, he does not feel lost nor frightened. He is strolling through a lovely meadow. The sun is out in full force and beats down deliciously on his bare skin. This gives him pleasure and as he moves along, he runs his hands face down through endless patches of wild flowers of every conceivable color that are in full bloom. He is uninhibited and unashamed of his nakedness, boldly allowing himself to be aroused in the open field, as the fragile flowers brush against his masculinity arousing him as he strolls.

In the distance Simon hears water running endlessly like it would through a shower head and fear automatically grips every corner of his heart. He is momentarily paralyzed by the unnerving sound which gets closer and closer. Suddenly, he falls to his knees, his body drenched in sweat and he realizes that he is now by the side of a bubbling creek that is flowing merrily in front of him. This is no shower head and there is no threat of imminent danger in this place. Instead, this oasis is familiar to him and gives him comfort. A cool damp breeze sweeps over him and the exquisite sensation of it makes his sweaty frame shiver with delight.

He looks around him and takes in the immensity that is enveloping him. He is stunned by the sublime beauty and majesty that surrounds him. He is now in the very heart of a heavily shaded forest. Simon stands up slowly and stares all around him. He is stunned by what he feels, sees and hears. It is other worldly but at the same time it is strangely familiar to him. A twig snaps loudly behind him and he knows he is not alone. Simon attempts to turn around but can't. His legs refuse to obey him and his arms do not cooperate. He can only listen and smell and it is then that he hears the exquisite masculine voice, deep, confident and sensual. He inhales deeply and smells his friend, his lover. Simon remembers him clearly and his eyes fill with stinging tears, wondering if it can be true. Is it really him?

He wants to turn around but he is paralyzed momentarily in his tracks. His longing to turn around and face that man becomes almost unbearable. Then he hears him as he says, "Hello, my beautiful man." Simon recognizes the voice instantly even though it has been so many years. There is no doubt who is speaking to him. He feels the gentle, familiar touch on his skin, first on the back of his neck, then sliding down slowly over the boney bumps of his damp back and finally, gently, over his buttocks in a gentle caress. Simon knows perfectly well who it is but he can't remember his friend's name. The voice asks, "Are you really here? Is it really you?"

Simon can barely speak, "Yes, it's me but…"

"Why did you die and leave me? Why?"

"I didn't die. I'm alive. I'm right here." Simon struggles to free himself as he says this but is well shackled in place.

"You died to me, Simon, when you left me. When you abandoned me, you died. And when you died, I began to die. It was just a matter of time." Simon continues to struggle in order to turn and clarify things, face to face. But he can't turn around, no matter how much he tries. His limbs burn and ache.

Suddenly, he hears the words that once, long ago, pierced his heart to the core and wounded him like no other words he had ever known, "I thought you could handle it." In that instant, Simon breaks free and turns around completely to meet his friend and lover.

The handsome young man is naked as well and they smile at each other knowingly, touching and caressing each other, completely familiar with the other. His friend's eyes are terribly sad and no longer bright and alive as Simon remembers them. He feels the young man's dampened skin press forcefully and desperately up against his own as he moves into his arms. They kiss hungrily in the dream. Simon revels in the intense pleasure of their reencounter. He is in a kind of sleepy fog now. With his eyes half closed, he surrenders completely to the passions of lust raging within him.

The incubus that is the master of nightmares and comes uninvited to lie with those who sleep, now seizes Simon violently as he dreams. His lust increases, and he grinds himself into the squirming body of his lover. They are in a kind of dance as they pleasure each other but Simon is shaken all at once in his dream by a brilliant white light. It pierces his eyes from above.

He instinctively opens his eyes just in time to hear his young lover once again. However this time, his lamentation sounds raspy and ominous and Simon hears the awful accusation once again, "I thought you could handle it." And then he hears the chilling accusation, "Why did you push me away like I was disgusting to you? Why did you leave me all alone?"

Simon is aware that the brilliant white light above comes from fluorescents and that he is in some kind of hospital ward. The person who now stands in front of him wearing a hospital gown is barely the shadow of what once had been a healthy, strapping young man. Simon recoils in horror and almost trips over his own feet as he jumps back from the sickly mass of rotting human flesh in front of him. He screams in panic, with all his might as he stares incredulously and yet he does not hear his own mournful, tortured cry.

Simon screams a second time and realizes that no sound is coming from him and that no one will hear him. He feels responsible for the young man's decaying, horrifying wounds and guilty because he suspects he has had a hand in giving him so much pain. Simon believes that he deserves not to be rescued. He is staring at the ghost of the man standing in front of him who was once so beautiful and cannot believe what he has become. His face now resembles a shriveled old skull set with deeply sunken eyes, heavily lidded, feverish and despairing. His waxen, ravaged flesh covers his frame loosely and he notices many open wounds on his once well-proportioned and toned body.

Simon meets his lover's penetrating, accusatory stare and doesn't know what to say. He wants to run but although he is no longer paralyzed, his legs are sluggish. The hospital gown that his accuser wears, reeks of stale urine and is stained with damp, runny feces. He is drenched in foul perspiration. He reaches for him slowly and Simon notices a thin strand of cloudy mucous barely hanging from one reddened nostril swing toward him. Simon screams again and wants to run. A thought flashes through his mind and he believes he will go mad because he fears that he is responsible for what his lover has become. He is delirious with guilt thinking that he caused this ruination and putrefaction.

Suddenly, and without warning, Simon knows in his heart that he must run to the safety of the fortified abbey wall. The massive bell in the great tower of the abbey begins to toll dolefully and in the nightmare, Simon snaps out of his lethargy. He runs with all his might out of the forest which has now become a cavernous, long dark corridor. He runs without looking back and as he does so, a wail of guilt bursts forth from him. "I'm so sorry! I'm so fucking sorry!" He screams again as he runs, sobbing through the darkness. He is unable to control his appalling grief.

It was his spine-chilling, anguished screams that awoke him in bed. Simon's first thought was that he sounded like a wild animal caught in a deadly trap. His cries poured forth from the very deaths of his anguished soul. As his profound sobbing subsided, he began to pant and shiver. He was soaked in his own urine and an overwhelming sense of shame and guilt clutched him. In the darkness of his bedroom, he endured, like never before, a devastating sorrow that ran deep in him. Once again, he felt as if his guts had been yanked and ripped violently out of him. In his crushed condition, he accepted, perhaps for the first time in his life, that he had genuinely betrayed someone who had loved him. He realized that he had never taken responsibility for what he had done to his first love. Lying in his bed, reduced to the pathetic truth of his past actions, he grasped for the very first time that he had betrayed extravagant love when it had come to him. He had arrogantly pushed away someone fragile and beautiful who had dared to love him very much. Simon however, had been very much afraid to love back.

+ + + + +

He returned to the tattoo shop on the date and time he had agreed with Mark. He was looking forward to seeing his gecko tattoo finished but was anxious about the things Mark had asked him last time.

When he was lying down and everything was ready, Mark said, "Ok, man, sorry about that interruption last time. It won't happen again. Lately it's just been one thing after another at home."

Simon answered, "It's cool."

Mark began tattooing the details of the bright colored gecko. He said, "Wanna pick up where we left off last time? I asked you about the connection between sex without love and betrayal of love."

Simon closed his eyes dreading the onslaught of Mark's interrogation. Nonetheless, he tried his best to concentrate. "Like I said, it's a tangled mess."

"I'm all ears." Mark was immersed in his work.

Simon explained in detail how things had gone down. The weeks passed and Simon found his niche within the walls of the abbey. He continued to pursue various friendships. Foremost was his sexual relationship with Toby which was center in the lives of both young monks and which they enjoyed every day as lovers do. He also continued to seek out his other friends, especially Anthony and Noah and of late, Joshua. Yet among all his acquaintances there was a figure he had continued to trust.

Brother Shawn remained an important presence in Simon's life as a true confidant. Simon could tell him anything and usually did. Brother Shawn made it a point to engage Simon to some degree almost every day. Sometimes it was just a simple gesture like winking at him in acknowledgement while Simon was in the company of other monks. At other times, Shawn would ask Simon to take a walk with him or invite him into the crypt for a fraternal chat. They would sit in the front pews facing the elaborate tomb of the prince-bishop. On those occasions Simon felt especially at ease to share his secrets with Brother Shawn, even though the latter shared very little about himself. He usually only listened carefully and gently offered his observations.

On one such occasion in the crypt, Simon revealed to Brother Shawn that he had discovered the tunnel and the bell tower, saying, "I've taken Toby to both places."

"Really?" Brother Shawn smiled and asked, "What did you guys do there?"

Simon had looked up and giggled nervously. "We made out and got all hot for each other. Sometimes I feel like I'm going to explode when I'm with him. He gets me so damned excited."

"Well, anyone can understand that, but…" Brother Shawn didn't continue.

"But what?"

"You need to be careful, little one. The walls here have eyes and ears. Trust me. This place is crawling with closet queens who hate themselves and are ready to pounce on those that they envy."

"We are always real careful about not appearing to be together in public. We mostly mess around in his room or mine always careful about who may linger in the corridor."

"Don't ever think you are being real careful as you say. Instead, be VERY careful. You think you might be fooling everyone but it's tricky here within these hallowed walls." Brother Shawn's smile had faded and when Simon spoke, it disappeared completely and was replaced by a barely visible, bitter scowl.

Simon was lost in his emotions as he shared his recent experiences with Toby. "Our love for each other is really becoming more intense. When we kiss each other I want to literally taste him and explore other parts of him. When we were novices, we once messed around in the forest and fell asleep together, but lately I have this hunger for him. I love him and have gotten to know him better even though he's not an open book. He's told me some very personal things about his life. But lately I want to share more of myself with him."

Brother Shawn sat next to Simon and simply asked, "How far have you two gone? How far do you want to take it?"

Simon felt uncertain about answering too quickly. Yet he felt he could trust Brother Shawn and finally admitted, "Well, I took Toby up to the great bell tower and we took our shirts off and held each other for a long time that way. We kissed and it really set us on fire. We touched each other but never removed our jeans. I thought I was going to burst but then he'd stop at the last second. Talk about blue balls!"

Brother Shawn nodded his head. "You said you went down into the tunnel, the one under the abbey. Did you guys discover the root cellars there?"

Simon piped up, "Yes, we did. I didn't know what that place was, I mean, all dirt floors, damp and enveloped in darkness."

"It was a root cellar. The monks used to use it in the old days for a kind of refrigeration in summer and for keeping potatoes and turnips and such during the long winter months when everything outside is like a frozen tundra. There are several rooms down there that form the whole root cellar."

"Oh, I get it now. It makes sense now that you explain it." Simon looked up at Brother Shawn. "And now it's not used for anything?"

Brother Shawn looked behind him, the length of the darkened crypt and in a conspiratorial way, whispered, "Well, not for a root cellar, in any case." Then he added, "What did you guys do down there?"

"Nothing much because it was so dark. Toby held my hand as he walked in front of me but we could barely focus down there." Then he said, "I could have sworn I saw old blankets piled up down there in one of the smaller rooms, toward the back and I told Toby. He and I walked slowly into that space and sure enough, there were blankets piled up in there. Ratty and pretty musty."

"Oh, yeah, I'm sure there were blankets. Did you guys stay in there long?"

"No. Well, maybe just a little. Toby wanted us to take our clothes off and I wanted to but I got nervous. He said it was the perfect place for us to be completely ourselves."

Brother Shawn took Simon's hand and said, "I gotta be honest with you, little one. When I was first professed, a group of us would meet down there every now and then."

"Really? So you know the place?"

"Oh, yes, I know it. I know it well." He whispered to Simon, "Some of us used to meet down there and plan all kinds of stuff. Mostly, we'd take our shirts off and make out. The darkness made it crazy erotic because you really couldn't tell who you were kissing or feeling up until you were both into each other. Then one night, it happened."

Simon was all ears. "What happened?" Brother Shawn hesitated and Simon moved in closer to him on the wooden pew. "What happened? Tell me!"

"It happened spontaneously, I mean, no body planned it. We were maybe six guys." Simon's eyes were huge now and his heart beat wildly in his chest.

"All of a sudden, we started taking our clothes off and before we knew it we were having an orgy."

Simon had no words to express his amazement. He only sat there imagining the place and the small group of men huddled together having sex. All he managed to say was, "Wow, I would never have guessed…"

"Yeah, well, that's what went on in there. It didn't last long. I think we met as a group down there two or three more times. Somebody got wind of it somehow. I mean, not all the details but enough so that two of the guys cracked under the interrogations and were weeded out and sent home immediately. The powers that be never knew where exactly we had had our orgies but they knew something was going on down in the tunnels. The two guys that were thrown out didn't rat on the rest of us."

Simon said sadly, "Sometimes I worry that Toby and I will be found out. I worry too about what God thinks of me, I mean, we're blatantly breaking our vows of chastity before God who sees everything." Simon's gaze wandered briefly and he said softly, "God…He knows everything…"

"Oh, come on, Simon, don't beat yourself up." Then Brother Shawn asked, "You're still a virgin, right? I mean, Toby hasn't taken your virginity, has he?"

It didn't take Simon long to answer although he wore his shame like a heavy yoke on his shoulders. "I'm afraid I have lost my virginity with Toby."

"What? When did that happen? You didn't tell me he robbed you of your innocence!"

"I lost my virginity with Toby in the forest one day when we were novices. I took him there. We got naked and sucked each other a little bit. Finally, we jerked each other off—"

Brother Shawn interrupted him. "Well, hell, Simon, you sure didn't lose your virginity then! You're still a virgin, dear boy, if Toby didn't actually fuck you. He didn't fuck you, did he? As in penetration?"

Simon looked up through tears that welled up in his eyes. He felt his face was on fire with shame. "Well, no, but we sucked each other and then masturbated. We came all over each other."

"Let me fill you in on a little secret. You're still a virgin." Brother Shawn smiled as he said this to him. Simon was looking at the floor and his eyes had finally spilled out his tears. His shoulders were drooped. Brother Shawn put his hand under Simon's chin and lifted his face. Gently, he said, "Don't you worry about all that. You're still intact before God. You are still a virgin.

You're still what you want to be before God." Then he added, "It's a big deal for you now and that's okay."

Simon looked up suddenly. He smiled and asked, "Are you sure?"

"Of course I'm sure. Toby hasn't robbed you of anything."

"I want to be worthy to stand before God, it's just that when I'm with Toby I lose control and lately it's gotten more intense."

"Yeah, I'm getting that loud and clear, little one."

It was deep winter in Leicester now, and when the wind blew on those winter days and nights, it howled and whistled through the abbey. Temperatures dipped very low and their cell windows often frosted on the inside, creating beautiful geometric shapes on the triangular, beveled-shaped glass held together by lead. These frosty shapes, all different, came alive when the sun penetrated them and only sometimes melted away. Simon and Toby could no longer visit the great bell tower nor descend into the darkness of the root cellar because it just got too cold. Instead they schemed and found time to be with each other as best they could. They usually met in one of their cells although once, wanting to throw caution to the wind, they managed to find a seldom used janitor closet but it was too filthy and crowded to get aroused and enjoy themselves.

Then, something happened on a cold, wintry, Saturday afternoon when most were taking a nap, studying alone or had left the abbey for several hours because it was a free afternoon. Toby came to visit Simon in his cell while he was at his desk studying. He bent over Simon and kissed him on the top of his head, saying dreamily, "How's my beautiful man?" He sat on the edge of Simon's cot and looked at him. They looked into each other's eyes, each one searching for something deep within themselves. Finally, Toby broke the spell. "Can I ask you something I've been struggling with for some time now?" Simon nodded and Toby abruptly asked, "Are you happy here, Simon?"

Simon smiled. "I'm very happy here, like this, when you're next to me, lover boy." He blew him a kiss.

"I didn't mean are you happy being together with me and messing around together and making each other feel good. I'm very happy being with you too and deepening what we share with each other. One of the best things in my life has been meeting you and getting to know each other. It blows my mind how our paths crossed, I mean, you being from Florida and me from Tennessee. Yet, there it is. It happened. For God, there are no coincidences." He looked into Simon's eyes. "I meant, are you really happy here in the abbey, pursuing priesthood?" Simon looked up confused and Toby repeated his question another way. "I mean, are you fulfilled here in this place? Sometimes I wonder if this is the right place for me." Then he quickly added, "I wonder a lot if it's the right place for us? If it's the best place for us as a couple."

Simon wasn't expecting him to say such a thing and alarmed, asked, "What do you mean? Aren't you sure about becoming a priest?"

"Well, that's the thing, I've been thinking about it a lot lately. I wonder if all of this is really for us. I've been asking myself a lot of questions and I believe you and I together, away from here…we can totally serve God in any number of ways. But mostly, I want to be in a place where we can be openly loving with each other. A place where we don't have to be afraid of who we are." Then he added, "Never again be afraid of openly being who God created us to be."

"Toby, please, don't say that! God has called us to be His priests someday and for now, to prepare for that. He doesn't just call anyone. He's called us. How can you just want to throw that away just like that, as if we were preparing for something far less lofty?"

"It's not that I want to throw it away. I just think that maybe you and I could leave and make a life together. Like I say, serve God in another way. Something that's more normal. Here, trying to be ourselves is like continuing to struggle in a terribly uphill climb."

"What?" Simon was lost now.

"This whole environment is unhealthy. I mean, we're always hiding and afraid of getting caught because of who we are. We can't even lock the door when we get intimate. I imagine us living openly, unafraid and free. You do realize that there are places where that's a reality. Take San Francisco or New York City as examples. There are whole neighborhoods where you can live openly and love the man in your life. You can go down the street holding hands and kissing and it's no big deal." Toby ran his hands through his longish, thick hair and sighed. Simon looked at Toby in his anguished discourse and his heart melted for the young man he loved. Toby continued, "I have been wondering lately if all this priesthood stuff is for me, well, I mean, for us." He looked at Simon sitting at his desk and asked, "Don't you love me enough to leave this place with me and be together? Every day that passes I love you more and want to express that love to you openly. But here it's forbidden." Toby pleaded with his eyes as he said this to Simon. "Why don't we leave and begin a real life together, just you and me?" Toby sighed, "Wouldn't you want to build a life together, I mean, a real life together with me?"

Simon was examining his own trembling hands now, and not knowing how to respond, he placed his hands under his thighs. He loved Toby and desired to be with him, in his arms and in his bed. He had no doubts that his best friend, sitting inches away from him on his bed, loved him. Slowly he asked, "Toby, man, what about God?"

"What about God?"

"We're called to be priests, to offer the Sacrifice. He's called us from among men. What about that call from God? Our vocations?"

Toby's eyes filled as he and Simon looked at each other. It was snowing outside and everything was covered in white. The only sounds that could be heard was the wailing and whistling of the insistent wind through the nooks and crannies of the old abbey like a faraway train blowing it's mournful whistle as it said goodbye and passed on. At long last, Toby got up and went to Simon. He knelt beside the chair Simon was sitting in and hugged him tightly, nestling his head in Simon's shoulder. Simon lifted his hands and caressed Toby's hair, smelling the man he truly loved and whose scent had become so familiar to him. Simon moved sideways in his chair and Toby looked up. Their lips met. They kissed slowly and then Toby straightened up and returned to the edge of Simon's cot. "We're just men, Simon. Flesh and blood, created out of dust made into clay with very fragile feet. I think God gets that." As Simon said nothing, Toby said softly, "I love you so much. I love you like I've never loved anyone."

Simon was beyond nervous at this point. What Toby was suggesting seriously rattled his cage and he said, "We are just men, simple people but with a vocation that comes directly from God. It's greater than just our flesh and blood and our needs and wants." Then he added, "We are just dust and clay but God wants to fill us who are fragile vessels of clay, with his mysterious gift of having the power of transforming bread and wine into His Body and Blood, Soul and Divinity. That isn't just any old profession."

Toby sounded tired when he answered, "I just want to share my life with you instead of living in this abnormal, empty place."

"But don't you see, Toby? We CAN share everything here. We can make it work if we want." Simon was unsure how to proceed because he didn't want to anger nor distance Toby. He chose his words carefully. "We can make it work for us here in the abbey and be together plus continue to follow our calling from God."

"I'm just thinking about you and me, 'Us'…Simon and Toby, Silas and Larry and our dreams and plans. Our dreams and plans…the ones we choose and map out for ourselves together with no interference nor accusations. It's no coincidence that we found each other. We love each other but here…damn, here everybody watches and waits, ready to devour. Everybody wears a mask or different masks, in order to survive and hide their true self."

Simon said softly, "Don't take this wrong, Toby but I think maybe part of the problem is that we keep too much to ourselves. There are other guys here like us, men who see things as we do. We could open up together to them and have a support group in order to get by and get through this. We're not the only ones who feel the way we do sexually."

"Get by?" Simon detected anger and frustration in Toby's voice. "I don't just wanna get by in my life, dammit!" Silence hung between the two young lovers for what seemed like an eternity. Simon didn't know what else to say. Finally, Toby said, "I don't want to impose anything on you, I'm just saying that this place and its games are getting to me. The only one that matters to me here is you. The only thing that matters to me in this place is my life with you." Toby pleaded, "Let's leave together, Simon. Let's just leave and love each other in the way that is natural for us."

Simon felt trapped and confused and didn't know what to say to Toby. A part of him understood what Toby was saying but another part of him rejected the idea of leaving and abandoning the dream of priesthood. Pathetically, he answered, "I really think that we need to open up to other guys in the abbey who are our age and of our thinking. We can have the necessary support you're talking about in order to deal with the dark side of this place in order to get through and come out the other side of the tunnel as priests someday." Halfheartedly, he added, "We don't need to leave, we just need to open up a bit and be a bit more flexible."

Toby stared at Simon and asked quietly, "Open up to other guys here? Are you serious?"

"Yes, of course I'm serious. I think you'd really like them if you opened up to them." Toby made a sarcastic face but Simon chose to disregard it. "Tony and Noey, especially, are a lot of fun and I'm getting to know them more. Even in the refectory, I usually try and sit at their table."

"Yeah, I've noticed. You sure do perk up when they're around, especially with Noey. It's like you get into a trance." Toby had stretched back then put his hands on his knees and looked around the room in a gesture that seemed to imply to Simon that Toby was ready to end the conversation and leave. "Ugh, I don't know." Toby looked sadly at Simon and said, "Maybe you'd prefer to be with them than with me. Maybe staying here with them works better for you than leaving with me."

"You know that that's not what I'm saying." Simon was beginning to feel angry but also very frightened by Toby's insinuation. "Don't get crazy on me, ok? You know I love you but sometimes you're such a loner. This is a real family, Toby. Community life in a monastery is what makes this situation here tick."

"No, it's not. That's bullshit. It's a fucking make believe world full of drunks and homophobic men just waiting to pounce. Guys acting like nuns and mean fuckers. Pretty boys who get all the attention and the free ticket forward. It's a place where, if you belong to a click, everybody is referred to as 'her' and 'she' and men are given women's names. It's so fucked up mostly because I can see now it's how people really cope here." He paused. "People here cope, they don't live normal lives and grow. They say they're out of the closet because they're out to each other but it's always hidden within the click, within the inner circle you happen to belong to. No one here is really out of the closet. They only tell themselves that story because the absolute worst thing here is realizing that in order to survive in this place you have to hide. I guess my problem is that I just don't want to hide anymore. I want to live openly with you and let the whole world know that I truly love another man." His eyes teared up and his voice cracked as he said, "I want the whole world to know that I love Simon because I do, Simon. With all my heart."

Simon finally got up and sat next to Toby on the cot. Simon kissed him on the side of his face and loved the way Toby's unshaven skin felt on his lips. He truly loved Toby but wanted this discourse to end. It was just too much for him to process. At last Simon whispered, "Toby, please, let's give this place a chance. We can do it. Think about what I said: there are other guys here like us who feel—"

Toby stood and cut him off, "Never mind, Simon. Just forget I ever mentioned it." Simon didn't want to hear anything more about leaving the abbey. For him, it simply wasn't an option.

When Toby left his cell, Simon felt drained and treading dangerously on the brink of depression. He remained sitting on his cot, hearing Toby's footsteps echo on the wooden floor as he walked down the long corridor and disappeared somewhere beyond in the shadows of that endless, wintry Saturday afternoon. Simon remained sitting there for a very long time, stunned by what Toby had just revealed to him. His thoughts were in shambles as he realized what Toby was actually saying. He didn't think about Toby's declaration of love as much as he thought about his proposal to leave the abbey and take him away with him, away from the priesthood and so many boyhood dreams. Simon cradled his head in his hands and felt confused and frightened by what lay ahead. He felt very much alone and lost and didn't know what to do.

Within himself, Simon had no doubts that he too loved Toby and wanted to be with him forever. In fact, what was now tearing cruelly at his heart was the realization that he could not live without him if Toby left. He knew he would be miserable to spend even one day without Toby. He loved him and had gotten to know his wounds. He also desired him physically. He wanted to be Toby's lover and best friend in the most intimate way. Yet Toby had said some scary things that afternoon. Simon felt at that moment that his carefully created world was tottering and threatening to fall apart. He thought of Brother Shawn and going to him but lately there was something odd between them that Simon couldn't pin point. Lately Simon felt that Shawn was always watching him, always keeping him within his reach and this was beginning to feel suffocating to him. Maybe Toby was right in what he had said about so many people watching them constantly and this thought tried to break in further but Simon pushed it away. Shawn was complicated, to say the least but he was also someone he could talk to. For right now, however, it didn't feel right telling him any of this.

Simon thought of his classmate, Seth. Since they had left the novitiate and come to the seminary after professing their vows, their relationship had cooled considerably. Simon liked Seth when he remembered how clearly Seth could assess situations and people in those situations. He certainly had Shawn figured out and had pegged that hypocrite Brother Arnold with incredible accuracy.

Maybe Seth could help him sort things out now. After all, Seth was well aware of how close he had gotten to Toby and hadn't bothered him about it. Simon knew it was a gamble to talk to Seth or anyone about him and Toby, but he was desperate for some clarity, some direction.

Simon got up from the narrow metal cot and washed his face with cold water in the tiny sink in his cell. His head felt like it was full of cobwebs that needed to be cleared away if he was to figure things out. As he dried himself he decided to take a walk in the snow and get some fresh air in his head. It would be very cold outside, so he put his winter woolen cape on and reached for the door knob. As he stepped out into the darkened corridor, Tony and Noey were coming in his direction out of the shadows. They were boisterous as they usually were, pushing into each other and laughing with abandon. Noey was pulling Tony by his long curly locks as Tony squirmed and tried to break free. They were carrying towels over their shoulders and both of them wore the same heavy woolen cape that Simon had been given in the abbey.

"Hey, Flatty Patty!" Tony was looking Simon up and down and gestured toward his own chest and traced out the size of his well-defined pecs. "You need to grow real tits, honey! Like these babies! Fur covered and hard." He traced the space on Simon's chest and whined sadly, "You're flat as a pancake!" Then he slapped Simon's face playfully and said, "You look bored out of your mind! You okay? What's with the long face?" He didn't wait for Simon to answer but instead added, "Wanna come with us, we're going…"

Simon needed to get outside by himself in order clear his head. "No, sorry, I can't. I've got a paper to write for tomorrow."

Noey emerged out of the darkness behind Tony and blatantly pinched Tony's ass. A high-pitched squeal of exaggerated indignation and pain escaped from the brawny young man as he squirmed with obvious bliss. In retaliation, Tony grabbed Noey by the crotch saying, "If you grab my ass again, I swear, I'll choke that Italian anaconda, that python monster-thing you keep in your pants once and for all!" The two younger monks laughed wildly in the corridor as they turned their attention on Simon.

Noey looked closely at Simon and said to Tony, "This boy looks terribly lost to me. Doesn't he look lost to you, honey?"

"Oh, my yes. He looks so sad. Reminds me of a song." The two looked at each other and then moved in closer to Simon and laid their heads gently on Simon's shoulders. Imitating Freddy Mercury, they sang in perfect unison.

"I'm just a poor boy and nobody loves me…" Noey put his arm around Simon's waist and pulled him close. "Come with us, Simon, we're going to the sauna on this cold, wintry afternoon!" Then he added, "Even though it's dark outside already, it's way too early to stay in your cell to study or go to bed."

Simon stepped back and away but Noey grabbed him in a tight embrace from behind. He kissed Simon lightly on the back of his neck and asked with genuine concern, "Why the sad face?"

"No sad face and no bedtime." Simon laughed easily as he struggled to break free. "I really do need to study. Papers are due."

"Hmm, no wonder you look so sad. All you think about is studying and being obedient. It's really rather boring, Brother Simon." Noey turned to Tony and asked, "Isn't it rather boring, Brother Anthony?"

Tony smiled broadly, "Oh, yes, Brother Noah. It's quite boring and exceedingly sad. I am completely distraught over the matter!"

Noey squeezed Simon tighter and looked at Tony. "I believe we need to take this overly serious boy with us to the sauna right now, don't you think? Maybe loosen him up a bit in the heat of the sauna."

Tony nodded approval as he looked at Simon closely, "No, dear Brother Simon, it's not a request nor an option but a command."

Simon was feeling better just being around the two crazy friends. "Okay, okay, you guys win! Let me get my towel."

"Wonderful." Tony clapped his hands cheerfully.

The three monks left the corridor through a side door wrapped in their capes and nearly fell on the slippery slope of ice that had formed there. They caught each other and laughing, walked carefully toward the nondescript, beige brick building that sat just behind the brewery of the abbey. It was an indoor Olympic-sized swimming pool which had ample locker rooms, showers and two saunas, one wet and one dry. It was for the sole use of the professed monks of the abbey. It was seldom used, a relic of a past benefactor's enthusiasm.

Great drifts of snow piled high against the building and a north wind blew mercilessly upon the three huddled young men. Their capes flapped uncontrollably in their faces as they pulled them down and hurried to safety within the pool building. They pulled each other up the snow covered steps and yanked open the glass doors that were at the entrance. As usual in winter, once they entered the main lobby, they were enveloped in silence. The strong scent of chlorine tickled Simon's nose as it always did. The pool house was empty as they expected on a freezing late Saturday afternoon. This excited Simon because the three of them could be completely free to be themselves without anyone else listening and watching.

Noey, Tony and Simon hung their capes on pegs that lined the walls of the locker room and stripped down completely naked as they made their way to the common showers. Even though the building was heated, they crossed their arms tightly across their chests and ran, partly due to the cold they had experienced outside and partly because of their nakedness. They pushed and bumped into each other along the way, screaming silly things as they did so. Simon enjoyed their lighthearted banter immensely.

Noey had run in front of them and was turning on the cold water on several showers. Simon looked carefully at him and could not look away. To Simon, Noey was the perfect male specimen. Now that he was naked, Simon realized even more how handsome and lean Noey actually was. His dark hair, long and flowing, now fell seductively on the curves of his shoulders. Noey moved gracefully. His abdomen showed the faintest signs of a six-pack and Simon lost himself in fantasy. He noticed that Noey had very little body hair, unlike himself, except for his genitals and the crevice just above his ass. But what most made him gawk was something that was difficult to ignore. Between Noey's well-formed, slender legs, hung the longest and thickest penis Simon had ever seen or imagined. Suddenly he caught himself staring and looked away.

Tony caught Simon in the act and cried out, "Don't even think about getting near that thing, honey! That monster snake will burst you open like a ripe watermelon, girl!"

Simon laughed nervously and felt himself blush at Tony's warning, and then he heard Noey announce, "Okay, everybody! The cold water is on! Everyone get over here now!"

Tony and Simon cried out together, "Cold water?"

"Yes!" Noey was adamant. "Get under the cold water, we need to open our pores before getting into the moist heat of the wet sauna."

"But…doesn't cold water actually close our pores?" Simon asked nervously.

"Oh, whatever, Simon, don't be a pussy. C'mon!" Noey grabbed Simon by the beard on his chin and Tony by his waist and pulled them both with him into the cold spray shooting relentlessly from the shower heads above. The three screamed in unison, their laughter and screeching echoing throughout the empty pool building. The cold water, however, actually did energize them, and Simon could feel his sexual energy rising. The closeness he felt with his two friends was exhilarating. He felt exhilarated with Toby, of course, but this was different.

Noey turned off the water and the three of them scurried off toward the door of the wet sauna and pulling it open, jumped inside in unison. Reddish orange light from three huge bulbs hanging overhead, bathed the large wooden room and it's mist, in a surreal otherworldly-kind of fog. The three young men took their seats on one of the three tiers of creaking teak wood benches that lined three of the walls. The scent of years of stale masculine sweat mingled with eucalyptus was intoxicating as well as highly sensual. That musky scent left by generations of male pores intoxicated Simon in a way that pleased him. He inhaled deeply.

No one said a word for the first few minutes as they adjusted to the sudden, drastic change of temperature, air quality and surroundings. Very soon, the three of them were shiny and dripping with sweat. The wet heat was working its magic on their bodies as if an invisible, wizard masseuse was gently kneading their bodies and souls.

Simon broke the silence by saying meekly, "I wish Toby was here enjoying all this with us."

Tony piped up immediately and challenged Simon for what he had said. "Why do you say that, honey? Why do you even hang out with him? He's a strange bird, that one. He's cute, hot even. I'll give you that, but definitely strange. I hear he comes from a real shit-hole place in Tennessee or something like that. Sounds to me like he's from a banjo thumping, hick town right out of a scene from the movie Deliverance."

"Hey, c'mon! That's not fair." Simon felt he needed to protect Toby in his absence and protested as he stood up from his place on the bench. "You just don't know him, Tony, like I do."

Tony snickered from his place near Noey, "I bet."

"Toby's life has never been easy. He just doesn't trust a lot of people." Simon heard himself and thought that he sounded halfhearted and unconvincing.

"I definitely have to agree with Tony." Noey had stood up on the third tier above Simon and yawned loudly as he stretched, cracking his knuckles above his head as he did so. Then he carefully wiped away the copious drops of sweat that now ran continuously down his entire body. He sat back on the bench, dangling his legs lazily. Simon wanted to reach out and massage his large narrow feet just inches away from his face. The pale skin on the top of his feet made the network of raised blue veins there so visible. "You deserve much better, Simon. Toby is far beneath you." Then, without warning, Noey stuck out one of his slick, slender feet and pushed gently on Simon's head. He said seductively, "You ought to be my lover. I'd take care of you and I wouldn't let you out of my sight for a second."

Simon spoke too loudly when he said in response, "Toby isn't my lover, guys. We're close brothers, yes, but…"

"Mmm hmm. That's right. Of course he's not your lover, but I could easily fill that capacity." Noey pushed again against Simon's head only this time it was with greater force.

"You bitch! Did you just propose to Simon?" Tony had gotten up and strutted in the middle of the sweltering sauna, hands firmly set in place on his muscular hips, shaking his great mane, feigning profound concern over what Noey had just said and done. He stuck his furry pectorals out exaggeratedly as he strutted about like a proud, jealous cockerel in a hen house.

"Shut up, nosey." Noey was grinning from ear to ear watching Tony's show. "What do you care what I say to Simon?" He shifted on the wooden bench, reached down absentmindedly and pulled his cock out from between his legs. Then he sat back on his hands, leaning his head against the wall, closing his eyes in thought.

"Fuck you, Noey!" Tony was pointing at Noey as he said this.

Opening his eyes, Noey responded, "Gladly, you nosey fucker. Just bend over for me so I can plow you." Noey shot Simon a wickedly lustful look as he pronounced the last four words. Without taking his eyes away from Simon's gaze, he said, "I'm game…I'll fuck you." Noey thrashed his hands through his sweaty, damp hair and shook his head from side to side. A spray of salty wetness rained on Simon and Tony below. He arched his back, exposing his hardness. "I'm getting a little dizzy from lack of blood to the head. I think it's time to let Mother Nature cool us down."

"I hate it when you show off like that, but I agree. Let's get cooled down!" Tony was headed toward the door of the sauna.

Simon chimed in, "Yeah, I agree, I'm getting light headed myself." Simon tried not to look at Noey but lost the battle within himself as he sneaked a sideways view. Noey had stood up, unabashed by his arousal. Simon wasn't exactly sure what came next.

"That's it, then! Let's go!" Noey jumped down gracefully from his lofty position on the top tier of the teak benches and Simon couldn't help but stare and enjoy the view of Noey's hardened penis bobbing up and down. Noey winked at Simon as he put an arm around Simon's equally slick shoulders. Noey and Simon caught up with Tony outside the sauna and put their arms around him as well. The three of them walked down the long corridor of cinderblock walls toward a small metal door at the rear of the pool house. Just before throwing the latch that was there, Noey screamed out, "Okay bitches, here we go. Hang on!"

Simon suddenly stopped. "We're going outside?"

"Of course!" Noey didn't pause to hear a response nor to give an answer. He simply threw the heavy latch to one side with a thud. A burst of freezing, utterly unbearable wind mixed with snow engulfed the three sweaty, naked bodies and blew into the hallway where they stood. They squealed and laughed at the encounter, pushing themselves out toward the raw, icy blast that hugged them without mercy. Holding each other tightly by the waist, they stepped out barefoot onto the snow covered metal steps, taking the final steps two by two. Hand in hand, they threw themselves head first into the closest drift of snow they encountered, rolling around madly in every direction. They couldn't stop laughing and throwing themselves into the snow. Simon had never experienced such freedom and joy, even though his skin burned as it erupted in great red splotches the color of summer beets.

Noey, the ring leader cried out the command seconds later, "Back inside! Back inside you crazy bitches!" He could barely speak because of his laughter. The three young monks, lost in the fun and intimacy of their friendship, climbed the snow covered metal steps and returned to the blessed warmth of the pool house, coughing and hugging each other. Noey turned on several showers but this time, great clouds of vapor filled the space as steaming hot water welcomed them. They gathered in a cluster, under the delicious, scalding torrent until little by little they defrosted together.

Two nights later, after Vespers that night, during study time, Simon sneaked out of his room and knocked gently on Seth's door. Seth got up and opened the door. He smiled broadly at the welcomed, unexpected visit. He gestured for Simon to come in and neither of them spoke because it was forbidden to do so during study time.

Once they were safe behind the closed door, Seth said in a low voice, "Hey, it's so great to see you. What a surprise, Simon. Seems like we never see each other much anymore in this big place. Is everything okay? You look odd." Then he said, "Sit here on the edge of my bed."

Simon sat and said, "Yeah everything is okay...but..." Simon's voice became weak and he thought he was going to break down and cry. He swallowed and looking at Seth, he said, "I'm really confused, Seth. I mean, I don't know what to do." He stared at the chubby monk, searching his face for an answer. His classmate got up from his desk chair and sat down next to him but said nothing. Simon found it difficult to get his words out coherently.

Seth waited for him to speak. When Simon said nothing he said, "Go ahead tell me what it is. Nothing is ever that bad. You can tell me."

Simon looked at him and confessed, "Toby just told me today that he's thinking of leaving. He said that this place is unhealthy." Simon sucked in his runny nose and wiped his eyes. He continued, "He also said he wants me to leave with him. I don't want him to leave without me but I can't abandon God's call and the priesthood. I don't know what to do." Then Simon whispered, "Please don't tell a soul about this. Please!"

Seth sat up, alarmed by what Simon had just said. He was gentle but very stern when he said, "Are you crazy? You can't leave! You clearly have a vocation to the priesthood. I know you understand what that means! Look how many years you've worked to get to where we are now."

"Of course I understand it. But Toby...I can't live without him." Simon looked at Seth through tears, "I love him."

"Yeah, well, love is all fine and good and all that but get a grip. Look, I don't know anything about that but dammit, Simon, don't throw God's call away. Don't throw away the priesthood!" Seth didn't stop there. He warned him. "I told you a long time ago to be careful of your attraction to Toby. It's one thing to be hot for somebody and it's quite another thing to throw your whole life away because you let the head on your cock think for you instead of the head on your shoulders." Simon looked at Seth and said nothing. "I saw it coming and that's why I warned you. I hate to say it but Toby probably doesn't even belong here. I mean, he's not been a Catholic that long. He's a convert.

Does he really even understand what priesthood signifies like we do? He may tell you he loves you and you might think you love him but I'll bet it's more like the two of you are in lust with each other. You belong here, not out there living a sordid life. It won't last. I'm sure it won't. And when your relationship with Toby ends where will you be then? You won't be able to come back here. No sir! They'll never take you back knowing the reasons why you left. They eventually know everything about us here."

Simon was stunned by what Seth was saying and it stung. He knew that there was truth in it but Seth wasn't in love with Toby. Nobody but he, Simon, could know what it was to be in love. Bitterly, he answered, saying, "You make it sound so simple, like it's a no brainer decision."

"It is a no brainer decision. You say Toby tells you he loves you but what happens when he gets tired of you? When happens when he changes his mind about what he wants in his life the way he's changing his mind now? Where will you be then?" Seth didn't expect an answer and said, "You know, Simon, I'm telling you all this because I love you. I really do love you. But you don't seem to notice anyone or anything since you laid eyes on Toby that first night. It's just Toby for you, all the time."

"That's not for you to judge, Seth. My love for Toby and his love for me is personal. Don't presume to know the depth of it."

"I'm just saying that you're on a very bad path, one that is only going to bring you heartache and destruction. I can see it."

"Oh, don't be so dramatic." Simon was sorry he had come to Seth. He should have known Seth wasn't going to help him but rather, confuse him more.

"Don't you be so stubborn. I'm the only one who ever really cared for you but you never gave me a chance. You've never given me any indication that you even know I'm alive!"

"What? I'm not sure I'm getting…"

"I never see you. We never talk. You're so damned wrapped up in that P.F. with Toby. It's so obvious you guys are queer for each other. I don't know how you've gotten away with it this long. I sure as hell am aware of it and if I am then…" Simon glared at Seth who stopped short of saying what he wanted. Simon stood up to leave. Seth stood up as well and went to take Simon's hand but Simon pulled away and stood back. "You can keep your head up your ass as long as you want," Seth hesitated, then said, "Or keep it up Toby's ass, I don't really give a rat's ass, but mark my words, you are working your way into a dangerous corner way too fast. I can see it. I tried to keep you from it once and you pushed me away."

"I gotta go. It was a mistake to come here." Simon wanted to run from the small cell and the man standing in front of him.

"You think it's a mistake because you want everything your way. You want all this, priesthood and Toby, a heightened spirituality and acting out your queer fantasies at the same time and you refuse to admit to yourself that you're going to have to choose at some point. You can't have it both ways, pretty boy." Simon pushed Seth out of the way as he stormed out of his room, not caring if anyone saw him coming out of another monk's room. He walked down the dimly lit corridor not knowing where he was going.

That night after recreation, before retiring, Seth made his way toward the refectory. If he was stopped by anyone in authority he would say he needed a glass of milk to ease the discomfort he felt in his belly brought on by the grease at supper. He passed in front of the refectory and paused to look behind him. No one was in sight. He walked a little further and entered the room where all the napkin boxes hung from the walls. He searched in the near darkness and located the section that began with the letter "S", saying to himself under his breath, "Father Samuel… Father Sebastian…Brother Sergius." Seth stopped and looked closely to make sure he had the right box. He narrowed his eyes, "Let's see…Brother Shawn, is that really you here? There you are you arrogant fucker." Seth took out a small sealed envelope he had brought with him in the folds of his habit. On the envelope he had written; FOR BROTHER SHAWN and under this, to one side he had written PRIVATE-MATTER OF CONFESSION. He placed the envelope just under the napkin. Brother Shawn would see it immediately tomorrow morning. Inside the envelope, Seth had written a brief note: "Brother Shawn, Something to tell you about your beloved Simon you need to know. IT'S URGENT. Time is of the essence. After supper tonight I will approach you outside for a brief walk and a chat before we go in for Vespers." Seth didn't sign the note in case it was intercepted. Then as an afterthought, he touched the edge of the envelope and kissed it, saying the customary prayer, "Saint Anthony guide."

Brother Shawn tried not to show his anger the next morning at breakfast. He looked around the refectory at all the monks as they ate and talked. Seth eyed Brother Shawn from a table not far away and secretly enjoyed the benign torture he was inflicting on his arrogant brother. Later that evening, as they left the refectory, Seth made it a point to walk with some of the monks and engage in conversation. He saw Brother Shawn exit the great wooden doors of the abbey surrounded by other monks going out for a stroll before the prayers of Vespers in the choir as was the custom. Brother Shawn, however, walked off by himself but remained close enough to be seen by the mysterious person who had left him the note.

Seth walked in Brother Shawn's general direction, but not toward him. Finally, he approached Brother Shawn and said, "Beautiful evening, Brother Shawn, don't you think?" Brother Shawn ignored the younger monk and started walking away in the opposite direction when Seth drew closer and said, "Mind if I join you for a stroll?"

Brother Shawn exhaled loudly and answered, "Look, I don't mean to be rude, brother, but I'm expecting someone and I'm not free right now for endless, idle chatter. Why don't you run off and join your classmates over there?" He gestured to a little group huddled and walking together.

Seth wasn't put off in the least and said, "I wrote you that note, you proud peacock. You know, one of these days when you're not looking, somebody's gonna pull all your haughty feathers right outta your ass and it's gonna hurt you like hell. You aren't even gonna see it coming."

"Oh?" Shawn slanted his eyes and gazed at the chubby monk standing in front of him. He finally asked, "You were the one who wrote it?"

"Yes sir." Seth gave him his best smile.

Brother Shawn locked eyes with him, "Well, aren't you a bold little bitch. I would never have suspected you had the balls to talk to me like that. Or anybody else, really." Then he said, "Well, what bit of nonsensical gossip do you think you have that might interest me? See, I've got a shit load of things I should be doing, like studying for one, and I can't just piss away my time the way you do talking about something you overheard in the bathroom."

Seth smiled. "I understand, brother. Maybe we can just forget it. You're right. You're very busy and I'm just some shit head loser with time to throw away. Best for you to go study in your cell. It wasn't anything important. Just something that has to do with Simon thinking about leaving the abbey." He said these last words smiling as he turned away to leave.

"What the fuck did you say?" Brother Shawn grabbed Seth's sleeve.

"You heard me." He faced Brother Shawn. "Oh, suddenly interested in my bathroom gossip?"

"Okay, I'm sorry I beat you up. Let's talk. Tell me what you got. It sounds serious."

Seth filled Brother Shawn in on all that Simon had said to him the evening before, saying at last, "I know he's making a huge mistake. He's just hot for Toby. I'm sure you're aware of that fact."

The older monk disregarded Seth's remark and said, "Simon is way too innocent for that low life from Chattanooga or Memphis or wherever the fuck he's from in Tennessee. I've seen it all along how he's worked on Simon and gotten him into his web. Simon is a good kid, full of enthusiasm and he has a solid vocation to the priesthood. He's just blind when it comes to Toby." Brother Shawn got so close to Seth that the chubby monk from Johnstown had to step back as he said in a slow, hissing whisper, "Now let me tell you one thing, kiddo, and you better get this straight in your twisted mind right now. You are not to tell anyone about this. You understand me? No one. If you do, and it gets back to me, I'll make sure you're the one who goes back home. I have ways of making bad shit happen. You got that?"

Seth protested, "Yes, I understand but..."

"Listen here you stupid, arrogant little prick, it's not complicated. You keep your fucking mouth shut about this. If it comes out and I hear about it, you're fucked." Then he added, "You're a nosey little shit for bringing it up to me. I'm sure Simon told you to keep it to yourself. Am I wrong?" Seth nodded his head and felt his face redden considerably. "You can go play with your little friends now. Not a word to anyone! Go!" Brother Shawn turned around without saying anything more. He walked aimlessly around the abbey property that evening and never made it to Vespers. When asked by Father Wade, a.k.a. "Wanda", why he was absent from prayers, he made up an excuse that he knew would be accepted. The Master of Clerics believed him and he was off the hook.

The next morning after breakfast, Brother Shawn approached Simon, saying "Hey, little one, I need to talk to you about something important. When can you give me a couple of minutes?"

"Is everything okay?" Simon was worried.

"Yeah, yeah, worry wart. When is good?" Brother Shawn asked, in a jovial, upbeat manner.

"How about after lunch. Father Demetrius canceled his class again." Simon and Shawn both knew the probable cause for that. "How about we meet in the crypt?" Simon tried to read Brother Shawn's eyes but had no clue.

The older monk smiled, "Ah, great minds think alike. I was just going to suggest the crypt. See you there at one o'clock next to the prince?"

"Yes." Simon then inquired again, asking, "Is everything okay?"

"Oh, yeah, no worries. I just want to pass something by you. No biggie."

That afternoon, bathed in the bluish purple light of the crypt, Brother Shawn met with Simon. He was already there in the shadows when Simon walked into the cool dampness. He genuflected before the presence of God in the tabernacle and sat next to Brother Shawn. For his part, he didn't look up, neither did he turn to face Simon. He was looking down at his hands and this somber attitude alarmed Simon from the get-go.

Simon sensed that Brother Shawn had something unpleasant for him to consider and therefore decided to cut to the chase. "There's a serious problem involving me, huh?"

To Simon, it seemed that Brother Shawn looked gloomy as he turned to face him, saying gravely, "Yeah, Simon, there's a problem. It's potentially a big problem but it doesn't have to be. I think there's still time to save you."

"What is it? Tell me." A part of Simon dreaded the news.

"It's about you and Toby."

Simon's heart sank as he considered himself being at the center of a scandal that could get him thrown out of the abbey. "Me and Toby?"

"Yes."

"What's the problem?" Simon could hear his heart beating in his ears.

"There are a lot of people talking. In fact, I'd say there are already too many people talking. They're concerned that you and Toby are P.F.'s. There are serious insinuations that could damn well get you both thrown out of here ASAP."

Simon listened in disbelief. "How? What's being said? Who's saying these things?" He thought about Seth but doubted that he would have the nerve to approach Shawn. "What insinuations are you referring to?"

Brother Shawn took Simon's hands into his own and moved in closer to the younger man. "I've heard you guys might be getting sexual with each other in a way that is cause for alarm." Simon felt a chill run down his spine and his stomach wretch at the intimidating news. "That's very bad shit around here, little one. Wouldn't you agree?"

"I just don't understand who could say such things. They can't have any proof. I mean, there are no photographs to substantiate such gossip, there's no tape recording, no eye witnesses. I've been very careful when I go see Toby and when he comes to my cell." Brother Shawn listened but said nothing. He had heard this before. "They have no proof."

"They don't need proof, and by 'they' I mean the Abbot and his council. If they suspect homosexual activity, you guys are outta here just like that. Proof or no proof." Brother Shawn snapped his fingers and the sound echoed in that place of bones, dust and shadows. "You don't deny that you guys have been hot for each other, right? I mean, from what you last shared with me I would guess you guys are messing around with each other, more and more. Am I right?"

Simon looked at Shawn and then looked away in shame. "Yeah, we have been. I love him so much. He told me yesterday he's thinking about leaving and wants me to go with him. To San Francisco or New York City or wherever, to live together openly."

To Simon, Brother Shawn appeared to be shocked by this news. "He said that? He actually said he wants to leave and take you with him? Oh, no! Please, pray God he didn't say those things to you." The scheming monk put an arm around Simon's neck and with his other hand he rubbed Simon's knee deliberately. He said, "I can only imagine your confusion." Then without warning, he moved his hand further up.

Simon jumped back and almost cried out in shock, "What are you doing? Why are you doing that to me?" Brother Shawn sat back up and dropped his arms, barely moving in the purplish shadows. "I don't know who's been talking about me but they have no proof. It's just jealousy and bullshit." Simon felt like he was spiraling downward into an endless tunnel. The news Shawn had brought him was only adding to his angst. He also didn't feel comfortable with the other man's touching. It felt out of place and threatening to him.

Brother Shawn didn't miss a beat and agreed, "They might not have proof but they don't need it. We're not in a democracy here, little one, in case you haven't noticed. This is a fucking dictatorial situation, another interpretation of the Fascist state. Justice has no place here. It's all about control, envy, fear and as you said, jealousy. It's just enough that people talk. That alone can get you canned and fast." He went to put his hand on Simon again, but Simon moved away on the pew.

Simon asked him, "Do you really care for me? Do you really worry about what will happen to me? Or are you out to get something for yourself?"

"What? I have no idea what you mean. Of course I care for you, I just…"

"I just told you that I love Toby and that he might leave and wants me to join him. That's something very high on the list in my book!" Simon hesitated then added, "It means we have something together. Something real."

Brother Shawn stood up. "I guess I'm done here. I just wanted to warn you. You obviously don't think I care that much about you. It almost sounds like you're accusing me of putting the move on you! Like I have some hidden agenda."

Simon was embarrassed now and immediately backed off and apologized, "No, no, it's not that, it's just that…I don't know. I'm just confused, Shawn. I'm so damned confused." Brother Shawn turned and walked away slowly. Simon felt badly about how he had treated him. After all, Shawn was taking the time to alert him to danger. Simon called out, breaking the silence of the crypt. "Shawn, I'm sorry I misjudged you. I'm sorry. I didn't mean to accuse you of anything."

With a smirk, Shawn turned around and simply said, "No offense taken, little one. All I know is you've got lots to think about." With that he slipped away past the tombs and walked far from Simon.

Simon remained near the tomb of the prince-bishop for a long time that afternoon. He gazed up at the pale white marble altar with its matching reredos and mournful-looking statues of angels bowed before the gilt tabernacle. In a flood of emotions, Simon opened his heart to God. "Most powerful God, you know and see everything. Help me!" He was overcome with fear and grief at the prospect of being found out and cast away from the abbey. The idea of being at the center of a sexual scandal filled him with dread. He tried to imagine a scene where he and Toby would be found out, surprised as they lay in each other's arms on one of their cots. He felt the sting of possible shame and disgrace fill his heart and he said, "Help me, dear God. Help me because I'm beyond being afraid. I love Toby but I know it's wrong and against your plans for me. I know it's against your Will and your Law. I know we are committing serious and grave sin." Then his tears began to flow as he continued. "Sometimes I'm so tempted when I'm with him. Sometimes I feel so weak. Help me, dear Lord. Give me strength to break it off." Simon peered at the red lamp full of oil burning before the tabernacle. He knew without doubt that God was present on the altar and that He had heard every word he had said. He had no doubts that God knew his heart. But he also realized that God was silent. God was terribly silent and he took this to mean that it was up to him to do something. Shawn had warned him that people were talking. Important, authoritative people were taking notice but he knew in his heart how he felt when he was around Toby.

Simon felt something at that very moment, a great void being torn wide open within him. He felt that something very fragile and irreplaceable was being violently yanked from him and taken away forever. He looked straight at the tabernacle and simply said, "I will end it. I will end it now." He got up, genuflected and walked out of the crypt.

Simon returned to his cell and without removing his shoes, lay on top of his bed. He put an arm over his eyes and tried to think about what he would do. It was getting dark outside and he knew that snow was coming. He heard the wind wail and shriek as it made its way through the weathered windows of his cell and down the long, winding corridor outside his door. Light was beginning to give way to early dusk brought on by the coming snowfall and his thoughts were racing. Sorrow filled him at the prospect of losing Toby.

He heard Toby enter the cell next to his and close the door. Simon could hear him moving around in his own tiny room and Toby's image filled his mind. He heard him pull his chair back and sit at his desk. He heard him get up and turn on the water in his sink. Then Simon heard the familiar rapping on the cinderblock wall that separated them. Simon heard the rapping and did not move. Toby did not hesitate and rapped again. Simon could not restrain himself and rapped back.

It was the sound that had become their secret communication. Toby was rapping for him and it overwhelmed and electrified Simon beyond his strength. His heart was pounding madly in his ears as he listened carefully to determine if a single, second rap followed. That was their secret code. It was how they communicated through the wall. One set of raps by the arriving lover meant, "Hey are you home?" Responding in the same way confirmed it, "Yes I am!" A single rap after these by either of them meant, "Come on over, I'm here." The wind shrieked louder now and as Simon sat up in his cot he saw the first flurries outside his window descending on Leicester that late afternoon. Simon dared not rap another time and yet he desired with his whole heart that it would come. Then Toby rapped once, "Come on over, I'm here."

Without another thought, he rose from his cot and opened his door carefully. With great care he stuck his head out into the corridor and saw that no one was in sight. Simon moved quickly toward Toby's door and opening it, slipped stealthily inside, shutting it behind him gently. When he turned around he saw through the leaded windows of the room how dark it was getting outside and how profusely it was snowing. Toby's room was cloaked in semi-darkness, yet Simon clearly saw that Toby was in his bed under the covers. Moreover, he knew that Toby was naked because he was bare-chested and caressed himself lazily with one hand. He had one arm behind his head which accentuated the muscles on his bicep. Simon was captivated by the purity of his masculinity. He sat on the cot and tried to appear relaxed but within himself he was quivering, rattled by his lover's attention.

In his ruffled state of emotions, Simon briefly considered how similar this moment was to that other moment they had shared in the forest. The thought of being naked and in a state of complete surrender to Toby overtook him and he automatically extended his hand. Simon desired to touch him. His hand rested on his lover's unshaven chest, and when he touched him he felt Toby's intense heat press against his coldness. Their hunger and their need burst into flame, like two firestones colliding perfectly.

Toby tugged playfully but with insistence at Simon's shirt tail indicating that he should remove it, which Simon did. In what seemed to be one rapid movement, Simon kicked off his shoes and removed his socks. He slid off his pants and underwear together as Toby pulled back the covers. Simon was ushered in and welcomed under the warm, flannel sheets of his lover's bed. The immediate feel of Toby's warm, furry skin against his own, consumed him completely and Simon let go of the last vestiges of hesitation that held him back. He only wanted to be held and loved. He gave himself to Toby and surrendered his soul and his body.

Simon was aware that Toby knew where and how to take him where he wanted to go. Simon was now in unchartered waters, well over his head. He remembered the tall waves that had engulfed him when he was a little boy on that fateful day immersed in so much danger. But this was different, even though now, as he was then, Simon was incapable of stopping what was coming. He completely trusted his lover. Instinctively, Simon realized where

Toby was going and he responded generously to Toby's lead. Amidst kisses and passionate fondling, their hearts were on fire and Simon knew it was time. He kissed Toby and rolled over, facing away from Toby, slightly impaling himself onto him when he felt his lover ready. Simon gasped in ecstasy when Toby first entered him from behind. Their bodies merged into one as Toby went deeper into him. They rocked and cradled each other in the tiny, creaking cot on that snowy, sublime afternoon. They no longer heard the frigid, howling wind racing under the eaves outside nor the insistent whistling that continued to find its way through the tall windows. They were only aware of their pleasure as pressure built within their bodies to the point of bursting. Toby reached around and held Simon tightly and when it was time, they both released together and shuddered, holding onto each other, lost in their love. Toby pressed with all his might against Simon's back and Simon reciprocated, pushing himself against Toby. They remained bounded and joined as they drifted into sleep, like two spoons held tightly together, listening to the persistent winter gale outside that never ceased.

When Simon woke, he knew that his relationship with Toby had crossed a line. He couldn't fully understand the range of emotions within himself. He was fully awake now and could feel Toby's warm breath on his shoulders. He pressed down on his lover's arms encircling him and Toby pressed back. Simon rolled over and faced him. Toby smiled at him from one end of the singular pillow and Simon smiled back. Neither of them felt the urge to speak. He kissed Simon gently. Simon returned the kiss but deep in his heart he knew that something had definitely shifted. Things had been escalating between them necessarily taking them to the intimacy they had just shared. He had allowed himself to be caught up in his passion and he had been incapable of withstanding the force that welled up within him. He had told God he would end this relationship but instead things had slipped away from him, events had boiled over and he had been incapable of doing what he knew he must.

Toby held him close and Simon closed his eyes. Simon felt different, shaken somehow but unable to pin point his feelings. He felt that he had been one person when he had entered this room and that now, when he would leave, he was quite another. Toby cuddled him and pressed against him even as Simon began to allow a monstrous thought to dominate him. He felt shattered in his soul. He felt that he had been robbed of the gift he had promised God. His innocence and his virginity were gone and would never return. He panicked to think that God would not love him nor find him worthy anymore. Chaos ripped into his tender, unprotected heart, wounding him irreparably. What had he done? Would God abandon him?

Simon sat up in the cot and his feet touched the cold floor. Toby caressed his back and ran his fingers over him playfully, saying softly, "My beautiful man." Simon said nothing but began to dress, untangling his clothes from the pile near the bed. When he replaced his shoes, he stood up and turned awkwardly toward Toby who had been looking at him from his pillow. Toby lifted himself on one elbow and asked with genuine alarm, "Are you okay, Simon? What's wrong?"

Simon looked out the window and with tears filling his eyes, concentrated on the snow that was being tossed around outside. "I just need to get to my room. I...I...need to go. To shower. Get my habit on." Then he faced Toby and said, "I need to get to confession. I have to go see Father William, my confessor. You and I both need to confess. What we've done is wrong, Toby. I mean, we just professed vows a few months ago and we're preparing to be priests, to offer Sacrifice."

"What? Are you serious? I thought..."

"I want to be your friend but having sex has to stop. It's gotta end. It's wrong. What we did...I don't know."

Toby's face became distorted and he sat up in bed with his back on the cold, cinderblock wall. A tense, uncomfortable silence hung between them for what seemed a long time. Simon shifted on his feet and was ready to leave when Toby blurted, "I thought you could handle it." It sounded cruel and hateful to Simon. "I thought we understood each other. I really believed we could have a life together. A real life, something healthy that makes sense. Two men who are honest with themselves and with each other. Two men who aren't afraid to embrace their nature." Then he added, "Their God given nature. Two men who love each other and are willing to take care of each other for the rest of their lives."

Simon felt that Toby was talking down to him. An image of Father Austin flashed through his mind and Simon pushed it away. "Don't make it sound like that, okay? I'm able to understand how special we are to each other. It's just that you moved too fast for me."

"What? I moved too fast? What are you saying? You don't understand shit, you big baby. Don't tell me you didn't enjoy what we just did, don't deny you wanted it as much as I did. Don't act like it's all my fault, like it's all my doing. You're making it look like I'm the one who led you into this. We were both on the same page when you came in here. Hell, this has been waiting to happen since we first got naked in the forest." Then he said angrily into the tiny room, "Since we BOTH got naked in the forest."

Simon felt that he had disappointed Toby. "I'm sorry, but I just can't..." Toby looked at him and got up off the bed. He made to embrace Simon but Simon moved back. "I can't. I have to go. It's wrong, Toby. It's got to stop." Simon walked toward the door.

"I thought you could handle it." Toby turned away from Simon and let him go. "Leave, then. Just go." Toby was hugging himself tightly as he stood in the center of his cell completely naked. Trembling, he said, "Just go."

Simon showered that afternoon and dressed in his habit. With trepidation but filled with remorse, he made his confession. He was rebuked without mercy in the confessional box, but felt that he deserved the insults he received because of what he had done. Then he was absolved because he was sorry and he walked away from the priest resolved never to sin that way again.

When he returned to his cell he could hear Toby in his room but could not bring himself to rap on the wall. An indescribable sadness overtook him. Simon felt depressed and confused and in the confusion that swirled in his heart, he hoped that Toby would rap on the wall and bring him to his arms, tightly holding him without ever letting go. Toby never called him.

The carefully fortified wall was not serving him well. God's jealous demands were clear to him. The plates he had been twirling atop the billiard sticks, were beginning to wobble and threatened complete collapse. Simon had never known such anguish and it caused his soul to ache like never before. He avoided Toby the next couple of days and Simon thought he saw him smiling sadly at him across the refectory several times during meals. Yet he knew that if he was going to be faithful to God, he would need to be unfaithful to his friend whom he loved. He realized that it would be necessary to betray his love for Toby if he was to honor his promise to God. He resolved to avoid Toby at all costs, regardless of the excruciating pain it caused in his soul.

A day arrived, therefore, when Simon closed his heart to his friend, whom he loved. Toby made several attempts to engage Simon in simple conversation but Simon was guarded and distant. Toward the end of that week Toby asked to move down the corridor, to a cell away from Simon and was granted permission. It hurt Simon to see how things were going with Toby but he was afraid to let his guard down. He would not admit to himself that he still loved him and that what he most desired was to share his bed with him. Neither did he allow himself to remember the pleasure they had shared together. Instead he reminded himself that he had been called by God and that maybe, there might still be a chance to appease God's wrath because of what he had done. He tried to console himself by a passage he found in the Book of Leviticus that reads, "I will set my mouth to the dust; there may yet be hope." He had to push Toby completely away if there were still a chance to please God.

The complete rift between Toby and Simon was not lost on Brother Shawn although he couldn't figure out what had been the cause. Shawn made it a point to find out. One afternoon, Brother Shawn strolled down Simon's corridor intent on finding him. Just before knocking on his door, he saw that the door to the cell that had been Toby's, was ajar. He peered in and saw that the room was empty. "That's strange," he murmured to himself.

He knocked gently on Simon's door and Simon responded, "Yes, come in."

Brother Shawn stepped into Simon's cell and said, "Hey, little one, I have a gift for you."

"Oh? What's the occasion?"

"No occasion, I was just thinking about you and decided to give you this." He held out a narrow rectangular box, gift wrapped, about five inches high and three inches wide. Simon was captivated. "Go ahead and open it."

Simon took the gift carefully in his hands. "What is it? Thank you."

As he unwrapped it, careful not to tear the wrapping paper, the older monk said, "Is everything alright with you? You seem down in the dumps lately."

Simon ignored Brother Shawn's inquiry and when he had unwrapped the gift he said laughing, "Oh, wow!" He read the label on the small, elegant bottle he held in his hand, "It's Royal Copenhagen cologne!"

"It is! It's the only thing I use. Especially when I'm invited to supper somewhere."

"So that's what it's called. It smells wonderful on you. I always wondered what it was. I'll bet it's terribly expensive."

"Just enjoy it. Don't even ask how much it costs. You'd never be able to afford it. Think of me when you wear it. I only share it with my special, little ones." He winked at Simon as he said this. Simon was touched that Shawn had given him such an expensive gift. He wasn't embarrassed at all. Shawn then sat on Simon's cot and pressed him for an answer, "You haven't answered my question. You ignored me. That's not very nice. Is everything okay with you?"

Simon sat on his desk chair and carefully spread out the gift wrapping paper with his hands as if ironing it. He didn't want to get into it with Shawn and said, "No, nothing is wrong. Everything is good. I guess there's a lot of studying now that exams are getting close and maybe I'm getting something of a cold. It's wearing me out a little."

Brother Shawn sighed and said, "Look at me." Simon looked up and then looked away. "I said, look at me and tell me that everything is okay." Simon remained silent. He tried to concentrate on the gift wrapping paper. He began to iron it out again but said nothing. Shawn got up and put his hands on Simon's shoulders. "I know something is up. Look at me and tell me what it is."

Simon held back but finally fell apart. He began to cry and said, "Something terrible happened. Something really awful. I feel like I want to die." Shawn waited for him to say more but Simon put his head down on his arms on top of the desk. He sobbed without restraint.

"What happened?" Shawn gently lifted Simon's head and took one of his arms. "Come here." He led him to the edge of the cot and together they sat down. "Nothing can be that bad. Tell me what happened. You can trust me. You know that."

"I already went to confession and spilled my guts there. It's too awful to repeat. Please understand."

Simon looked at him with a pleading expression but Shawn refused to accept his excuse. "That's so fucking lame. You look like shit and you walk around like a zombie. And what's with the empty room next door? Where did Toby go?"

At the mention of Toby's name, Simon opened his mouth and the only thing that came out in a raspy voice was, "Toby." Then he felt the terrible grief that was growing in him. An agonizing groan rushed up his throat and he began to tremble and shake as he cried without solace. Shawn put an arm around him and waited for the sobbing to subside. He waited patiently. When Simon had calmed he told him everything he wanted to know and answered all his questions. "It all happened so fast on an afternoon last week." Simon described what took place in great detail and confided in him that he had lost his virginity with Toby.

"That son of a bitch!" Brother Shawn cried out. "That fucking, no-good bastard took advantage of you. He took your innocence." Simon remained silent. He was cradled in Shawn's arms and stayed that way until he no longer wailed and convulsed, finally catching his breath. When he had calmed, the older man led him to the sink. "Wash you face, baby, it's gonna be okay. Don't you worry about a thing."

"It all happened so fast," Simon lamented. "Why did it have to end like this?"

"Things will happen while they can, little one. Life is a bitch and sometimes bad things come to bite you. You have to be smart now. Remember what I told you a few days ago about what people were saying. You need to stay completely away from that fucker, do you understand me?" Simon nodded that he did understand. "And another very important thing. Do not, I repeat, do not tell anyone about what happened, okay? Promise me!"

"I promise." Simon said it weakly and Brother Shawn hugged him. "You must think I'm awful."

"I don't think that at all. You just need an older brother to help you out with this mess. That's why I'm here." He winked at Simon and said, "That's what I told you the first day I saw you. If you need anything, I'm here to help you. Don't worry about any of this. I'll handle it."

Usually in the afternoons and at night, Simon struggled with all that had happened between him and Toby. He would stare at the wall of cinderblock and remember his friend. He knew he had to forget Toby and he understood that he could never again do what they had done. He understood all of this with perfect clarity in his head but his heart would not relent so easily. With his index finger Simon would slowly and deliberately trace the crevices of cement between the blocks that made up the wall next to his cot and wonder where his friend was and what Toby was doing. He felt a terrible void. He recognized that he was incomplete and sad without him.

Talk on the corridor and at meals was that Toby had changed. Even on the evening stroll after supper and before Vespers, Simon's classmates voiced their opinions openly, saying, "Toby's so arrogant. I mean, the guy acts like he doesn't need to be nice to anybody. He acts like he doesn't need to talk to anybody. He ignores everyone and is in his own little world."

And another student piped in, "I tried to make conversation the other day and it was like talking to a brick wall. He just sits in the sewing room, working on vestments for Mass, oblivious to everybody around him. What's his problem?"

Then somebody suggested, "Maybe he's gonna leave? He's got that look. I've seen it before."

One afternoon, several weeks later, Simon was returning to his cell when he saw Toby coming up the corridor in the opposite direction. He stopped and said, "Hey, Toby." It felt awkward and he didn't know what else to say. It felt like so very little, after all that they had shared together.

"Hi, Simon. How are things? We hardly ever see each other anymore."

"I know."

Toby looked straight into Simon's eyes and simply said, "I think about you every day even though I'm down the hall. I miss you."

Simon was lost in a whirlwind of emotions. He just stood there and stared back at Toby. Finally, he said, "I wish that things would have worked out differently and that—"

Toby wasn't listening to him and interrupted, "I still love you very much. I can't just forget about you so easily." His eyes misted. "I still dream in my fantasies that one of these days…" Then he cleared his throat and whispered, "We can still leave this place together."

"It can't happen, Toby. It can't happen if we want to serve God as priests someday. I mean…"

Toby looked into Simon's eyes and repeated, "I still love you very much, Simon." Without warning he stepped up to Simon and kissed him gently on his lips. Simon froze, fearful that someone would see them. "You're still right here," Toby gestured to his heart. "I can't ever get you out."

"Don't carry a torch for me, Toby. It's over. I just can't."

Toby smiled sadly and said, "I'll always carry a torch for you, Simon. You crept into my heart and I won't let you go." Simon hurriedly opened his door and slipped into his room. His heart was pounding wildly in his chest as he closed the door and heard Toby say softly, "Don't keep me out of your heart, man, don't push me away."

Simon was terribly frightened to betray God again and so stayed away from Toby. The decision to betray one of them was imperative because he had come to the fork in the road. The days passed and turned into weeks and then into months. The two lovers drifted apart and grew completely distant from each other. Simon put away the remarkable memories he had shared with Toby since they were postulants. He especially erased from his mind the day in the forest and the afternoon in Toby's cell on that wintry day filled with passion.

Toby withdrew more and more from the others and isolated himself in the sewing room whenever he wasn't in class, meals or prayers. He would be there designing and creating splendid priestly vestments for use at Mass and everyone was in agreement that he was quite the tailor. Simon often wanted to go into the sewing room late at night and be with Toby as he worked but he told himself that he would be playing with fire if he did so. Brother Shawn was pleased that Simon was so resolved and praised him for his strength. It would serve Brother Shawn in his ultimate plan to remove Toby from the abbey.

Brother Shawn had already put his plans into action. One day he requested to see the Abbot together with his council when they met to discuss matters pertinent to the abbey. He waited patiently outside the meeting room until finally a heavy wooden door creaked open. The Abbot's secretary summoned him to enter. He took a seat at the far end of a long, broad wooden table surrounded by tall backed chairs. In those chairs sat the Abbot and his council. The Master of Postulants was there, as well as the Master of Novices and the Master of Clerics. The Abbot sat in the center, the Father Prior to his left and the secretary of the Abbot to his right. Eight other monks made up the council together with these. Brother Shawn felt dwarfed by the stone columns that rose along the walls and supported the wooden beamed ceiling far above their heads. An imposing, stone fireplace sat against a far wall and on its mantelpiece, a metal, ornate clock ticked loudly, echoing the passage of time. There were few windows in this room which made it more of a vault than a cozy, meeting place, albeit, very formal. Framed historical artifacts lined the walls and locked cabinets held the forgotten secrets of many souls whose lives had been affected by the abbey. The portraits of former abbots looked down sternly upon them. This room was known as the Hall of the Secret Archives.

"Yes, Brother Shawn," the Abbot said, as he entered the cavernous chamber. "The council and I will receive you now." Then he held up a sheet of paper as Brother Shawn took his place and he said to the members of the council, "Brother Shawn has called our attention to a very serious matter here in the abbey, one that concerns me greatly." The members of the council stirred in their chairs, their interest piqued by the Abbot's comment. The secretary began to take notes.

"Let's see…" The Abbot looked carefully at Shawn's letter and then looked at him. "You say that one of the brothers in formation has been having an overt homosexual relationship with another brother in formation. Is this correct?"

Shawn sat up, "Yes, Father, that is correct."

"If it was overt why has it not come up before now?"

"From my understanding it was a kind of open secret." Brother Shawn spoke slowly. "I didn't feel it was up to me to move on this."

The Abbot looked away and studied the letter in front of him. "Your accusations are very serious, Brother Shawn. You say that you had your suspicions since they were both postulants?"

At this, Father Chris spoke up, "What are these brother's names? I would have noticed immediately. Nothing of the sort could have taken place under my nose without me being aware. I always weed out the perverts."

"They are Brother Tobias, who was formerly Silas and Brother Simon, who was formerly Larry."

"I never saw anything out of line between them," Father Chris retorted. He shot a menacing glance at Shawn, who looked away. Then he said, "Brother Shawn, isn't Larry the boy from Florida you kept all to yourself from a volleyball game once, am I correct?" Brother Shawn didn't lift his eyes and didn't answer.

The Abbot continued, "You say in your declaration that you spied on them engaged in sexual activity behind the novitiate when they were novices. Is that correct?"

"Yes, Father, in the pine forest. Remember that I had your permission to enter the novitiate and help Father Bart with the novices. I suspected something was up and followed them out there one afternoon. Toby took Simon to the forest under some pretense I could not hear. I saw Brother Toby push himself on Brother Simon and manipulate him sexually. Simon tried to get away but he was stronger and had his way with him. In any case, I saw him masturbate Simon until he spilled his seed."

At this Father Bart took his head into his hands and a stifled moan escaped him, as he said, "Oh, dear God, no, it can't be true."

Father Chris, "the Beak", aggressively admonished Father Bart, saying "Oh, stop that pompous, religious bullshit, Bart. Don't be so damned quick to refuse to see the perversity that can exist in an all-male environment. Homos need to be weeded out and I say the faster, the better. Why wasn't this resolved last year when they were novices?"

Father Bart looked up, "Why wasn't this resolved in the postulancy?"

Then, ignoring Father Bart, the Master of Postulants turned to the Abbot and asked, "What more does that letter say? I want to know."

The Abbot continued, "Brother Shawn testifies that he was fearful of saying anything at the time because he wasn't sure if it was the right thing to do." The Abbot looked at Brother Shawn and then the letter. "He says he took it to prayer."

"Prayer? Ha!" Father Chris turned to Shawn. "What's the real reason?"

Brother Shawn looked tense and hunted now that the Master of Postulants was confronting him. In his own defense, he murmured, "I wanted to be sure it was the right thing to speak up. I know it's a serious accusation."

"I'll bet you wanted to be sure." Father Chris didn't take his eyes off Shawn but said flatly, still looking at him, "So let me get this straight, Abbot Edmund. Brother Shawn testifies that Toby put the move on Simon and practically forced him to spill his seed in the forest? Is that correct?"

The Abbot said nothing. Nervous, muffled coughs were heard as some of the monks shifted uncomfortably in their seats. When "The Beak" said no more, the Abbot proceeded, "Brother Shawn tells me in his letter that many brothers in the student corridor are now saying that Toby and Simon are engaged in a particular friendship. He says here, and I quote, 'several of the students have come to me with notes expressing concern for Brother Simon because Brother Tobias has control of him in an unhealthy relationship which is deadly to our life in religion'." The Abbot looked up and around the room. Then he cleared his throat and said, "There is one final point and it is very serious." He stopped and looked at Brother Shawn. "Are you sure and do you swear before God that what you have written here is true?"

Shawn looked directly at the Abbot and said unflinchingly, "Yes Father, it is all true in as much as I can remember and what I saw. I swear it before God."

The room was deathly quiet as the Abbot peered down the letter and found his place. He read aloud the accusation Brother Shawn was putting forth. "Brother Simon came to me several times, expressing doubts about his relationship with Brother Tobias. He said on several occasions that he wanted to end the particular friendship but that he was threatened by him. Brother Tobias said he would tell others openly about Simon's complicity in the sexual affair because he, Tobias, himself was planning to leave the abbey shortly and had nothing to lose. He no longer felt a call to priesthood." The Abbot looked at him. "Brother Shawn, Brother Tobias told Brother Simon he wanted to leave the abbey? Are you sure?"

"Yes, Father. Brother Simon confided in me that Toby said that he no longer desired to study for the priesthood, let alone become one and that he no longer desired to live our life. He said to Simon, I mean, to Brother Simon, that they could leave together and go live as openly gay men either in New York City or in San Francisco."

The Abbot twisted his face in anguish and groans and sighs of disbelief and disgust were heard around the table. The Abbot continued to read the letter he had been given. "Brother Simon told me that Toby was pressuring him daily and that he was getting confused. Finally, his sway over Brother Simon became so great that on an afternoon not long ago, he called him to his cell and attempted to have sexual intercourse with him. He forced him to engage in sex and almost penetrated him anally."

Several members of the council let out a surprised gasp. Father Chris looked at Shawn and asked sharply, "You say he almost did what?"

Shawn faced him sternly now and answered evenly, "Brother Tobias almost penetrated Brother Simon anally." Then he added quickly, "Brother Simon broke away and saved himself." The Abbot was speechless and looked up and around the table. Finally, he set his eyes on Shawn. He removed his glasses and rubbed his eyes and said, "Brother, do you stand behind these terrible accusations against Brother Tobias as truthful before God? Do you swear they are true?"

"Yes, I do, Abbot Edmund. I swear...I swear that every word is true. I come today because I feel that I am the only voice Brother Simon has to defend himself. He has confided in me. He is young and impressionable and is basically a boy with no experience of the world. All of us who know Brother Simon will agree that he is the kind of vocation we are looking for and that his vocation is solid. Toby, Brother Tobias, on the other hand, has led a very different kind of life. He's from a broken home that was built on his mother's loose morals, alcohol and drug use. He's a convert and a very odd, introverted person. He's…"

"That's enough, Brother Shawn." The Abbot appeared to be shaken. Thank you for your concern. We will deliberate and take this into consideration. You will cease speaking about these things to anyone. "Do you understand?" The Abbot looked at him without blinking.

"Yes, Father. But I do have one last thing to say before I am excused."

The Abbot sighed and then nodded, "Yes, go ahead."

"Brother Simon has been greatly affected by all of this, as you might imagine. He is fragile and I fear that Tobias still controls him to the point of possibly convincing him to leave the abbey with him whenever he decides to go." Shawn saw that many members of the council were listening closely to him. "I would like to humbly suggest that Brother Tobias be expelled for homosexual activity immediately and that Brother Simon be spared as much embarrassment in this matter as is possible. I believe that he is the victim here and that there is still time to save him. Lack of experience put him in the path of destruction but if he is assigned a good Spiritual Director and Confessor, he will, in time, put all of this behind him. It would be a great loss to the abbey if we let him go. I believe the Church would suffer a great loss."

Brother Shawn was excused and left the Hall of the Secret Archives, confident that Toby was a dead man. The council remained behind locked doors for quite a long time after he had left. That day, after a lengthy deliberation they had cast their votes and voted unanimously to expel Toby from the abbey. It was agreed that it should be carried out swiftly that very evening and Father Wade was dispatched to do the deed and carry it out smoothly. Toby was not at supper that evening. Simon had been spared.

At supper that night, a rumor spread quickly that Toby was gone. Most students opted out of the evening stroll before Vespers and headed to their corridor to verify if the rumor was true. Simon went into his cell not wanting to follow the small crowd that headed to the other end of the corridor. Then he heard the shouts that drifted back, "Toby's gone! His cell is empty!" Other doors opened now and everyone hurried down to where Toby's room was. Simon joined them. When he peered in through the crowd he saw that Toby's mattress was rolled up on his bed and that all of his things were gone.

Simon felt his heart sink as he realized that Toby was gone forever. He knew that he had had a part in this although a little voice convinced him that there had been no other way and that Toby would have left in time, with or without him. As everyone left the tiny, empty cell, Simon went in and looked out the window. From this side of the abbey he could see the barns and the novitiate buildings rising above the tall, stone walls that encased it. His eyes misted when they fell on the forest beyond and he remembered Toby on that long ago afternoon they shared there. He wondered to himself how it had all come down to this. Sorrow welled up in him and he was filled with aching remorse.

Suddenly he felt a hand on his shoulder and the familiar voice that said, "I told you I would handle it, little one." It was Shawn.

"Why did he leave so suddenly. I mean, why didn't he come tell me before he left?" Simon let his tears flow freely now, not caring who saw nor who heard.

"There, there," Brother Shawn soothed him. "Put it behind you and let it go. It's for the best."

"He told me he wanted to go to San Francisco or New York City. He said he wanted me to go with him." Simon looked at Shawn, almost pleading, "But how was I going to leave the abbey? My life is here."

Shawn smiled and then gently turned Simon around. "That's totally correct, baby. Your life is here, with us. Now get to your room and wash your face. It's almost time for Vespers."

Simon looked back out the window and toward the forest. Shawn moved up behind him and said in his ear, "You'll eventually learn, as we all must. The sex you shared with Toby wasn't the problem at all. You guys were always queer for each other, that much is understandable. That stuff happens. Toby just had more experience and knew exactly how to take your innocence and enjoy himself at your expense." He paused then added, "Listen to me. I repeat, the sex wasn't the problem at all here. The problem was the love that blossomed. It screwed everything up and should never have gotten to that. It was coming between you and the very reason why you are here. He had to be removed because it wouldn't ever be tolerated here." Shawn pulled Simon away from his contemplation of the forest and led him by his shoulders in the opposite direction, back down the long corridor of the abbey.

That evening after Vespers, the Master of Clerics rose in his place at choir to face the monks and without emotion simply stated, "Brother Tobias has left the abbey and has requested the dispensation from his vows. Let us remember to pray for him." Simon never heard from Toby nor ever saw him again.

+ + + + +

A cold paper towel against his irritated skin, almost dripping with a cleansing solution, is what pulled Simon out of his recollections. He focused first on the bright fluorescent lights on the ceiling and then heard Mark's voice telling him he was done. The tattooer chuckled to himself as he said, "You can check out your horny gecko tattoo now. We're all done." Simon sat up on the worktable and dropped his legs over the edge. He felt lightheaded and an old familiar sorrow tugged at a terribly frayed side of his heart. Melancholy once again pierced his soul for the love he had betrayed. He remembered Shawn's words, namely, that the sex had not been the problem but rather the love had been the problem. Simon understood now that it wasn't love that was the problem but rather, the betrayal of love. The betrayal of real love is what screwed everything up. That is what had been the unforgivable problem. His heart ached terribly as he thought of Toby.

He saw his reflection in the mirror and could see the curled up tail of the gecko. "I think I'll call him Baby Logan."

"Why is that?"

"Damn, Mark, I'm not going to tell you all my secrets. I have my reasons."

"Fair enough, dude. I'd say you spilled enough of your guts here for one day." After he had put antibacterial on Simon's abs and had wrapped him in plastic he sat on his stool as he dried his freshly washed hands and asked, "Do you think you did the right thing, Simon? I mean, by staying and all in the abbey? Was it the right thing to have let Toby leave without you?"

Simon was pulling his t-shirt carefully over his head trying to manage the stinging pain he now felt across his abdomen and naval, down near his crotch. When he succeeded, he sat momentarily on the edge of the worktable to catch his breath. He faced Mark and said, "In the months that followed after Toby disappeared, I heard that he had gone to live an openly gay life in San Francisco. My heart ached when I heard the details because he had been true to his word when he said I was in his heart. I knew it was true because he had taken a part of me with him and had left a part of his heart with me. For many years after he was gone, I was assigned to the sacristy again and daily I set out certain priestly vestments in the early mornings that were used for the Sacrifice of the Mass. There were hundreds of vestments I could set out for the priests to wear but I always chose the ones that Toby had sewn. I did it to honor him in my own, pathetic way because he himself would never wear the magnificent priestly vestments he had so meticulously created."

Simon's voice cracked and he stopped. He closed his eyes. "Then one cold, gray winter afternoon, when the wind howled and shrieked through the abbey, Shawn came to tell me that Toby had written to him confiding that he had contracted HIV and was diagnosed positive. In those days, it was a death sentence. A few months after that, Shawn came to me one afternoon and suggested we take a walk. It was almost a perfect, beautiful, crisp spring day with just enough chill in the air. As we walked, Shawn gave me the terrible news that pierced my heart. He said, 'One of Toby's friends wrote from San Francisco and I received a letter today. He said he was writing to everyone in Toby's address book, just like Toby had asked him to do.'"

"I looked up at Shawn, frightened, but asked, 'Did Toby die?' Shawn said, 'Yes, he did, Simon. Toby died of AIDS last week.'"

Mark exhaled audibly as he said, "Fuck me! That's awful."

Simon did not speak. Toby had loved him and Simon had betrayed that love in the worst way. Simon didn't care to wipe away the stinging tears that now flowed freely from his reddened eyes. He felt beaten and worn out by so many things from the past that he forgot Mark was even there, watching him closely.

At that very moment, Simon remembered when he had stood at the altar in his tiny chapel and had first gotten the idea of tattoos as the way of coming clean. It had seemed then to be a completely ridiculous, even frivolous idea that had crept into his mind from only God knew where. God, however, had remained completely silent. Simon recalled now how he had taken that silence to mean "consent" and so he had believed that through tattoos he would face the truth within himself and tell the whole world his sins. It had baffled him then because he had never had any inclination to get tattoos. Now, suddenly, he realized with perfect clarity that tattoos really didn't matter, did they? It was only one of a million ways to come clean and heal. He realized that others would look at his tattooed body and only see the tattoos and nothing else. It would be impossible for them to know the meaning of each tattoo unless Simon himself explained it to them. No, the tattoos in and of themselves really weren't going to proclaim anything to the entire world.

Simon now understood what God had done. God had lead Simon to a tattoo shop and to a tattooer. It could have been any other scenario except that God had lead him in this direction and he, Simon, had accepted. The tattoos only mattered because Simon would recall, out loud and in great detail, his entire life in the presence of another. God had wanted Simon to listen carefully to the details of his life and what he had done. By telling Mark about the tattoos, and Mark asking Simon questions and even challenging him without mercy sometimes, Simon had had to come clean and face himself and admit his lies. The tattoos, of course, served a purpose. In order not to ever forget, God had seen to it that Simon would bear in his skin, as a reminder, the symbols that spoke that truth about himself. He would see his acceptance to God's plan of coming clean, every day.

At that moment, Simon had his "Ah ha" moment in this regard. There were still so many tattoos for him to get, so much still to voice to Mark. The world would only see tattoos but Simon was beginning to see himself as he really was without excuses. This had been God's plan from the beginning. The tattoos and the tattooer, as well as the tattoo shop, all just happened to be the vehicle, the prop for Simon to face himself.

He remembered his dream about being with Toby in the forest and then in the hospital ward. Toby's words had been, "Why did you die to me?" He met Mark's eyes and said, "You asked me if I thought I did the right thing?" Mark waited for an answer. Simon didn't know how to voice his remorse and his repentance and only managed to say weakly, "I don't know, Mark. I honestly don't know."

Chapter Nine
The Sexual Revolution

I have no doubt we shall win, but the road is long and red with monstrous martyrdoms.
Oscar Wilde

There were no clients in the tattoo shop when Simon arrived for his appointment early that winter afternoon. He walked briskly and as he approached from the sidewalk, he felt drawn to the shop by the glow of lights that emanated from inside. The illumination made the reception area look cozy and warm compared to the frigid conditions outside. As he walked, a chill wind was picking up and Simon noticed that the sky was thickly padded with the threat of freezing rain. He thought to himself that he might just see the first flurries of the new season before he got home.

He had barely entered the shop when Billy looked up and from across the room said cheerfully, "Mark's waiting for ya, bud, back there. You know the way." Simon immediately became aware of the difference in Billy's tone. Having said this, Billy did not look away but followed Simon's approach toward the two saloon-like doors that led to the corridor and workrooms beyond.

"Yeah, thanks, man." As he walked across the reception area, Simon thought it curious that Billy had not looked away but had continued to follow him with a steady gaze.

Simon passed Billy and suddenly he piped up, saying behind him, "No more baggy shorts, huh, Simon? Gettin' too damn frosty for that."

Simon stopped and turned toward Billy, surprised again by this noticeable change in his demeanor. "How's that, man?"

"You look good in jeans is all. You look even better in shorts, though. I'd say much better in baggy shorts." He gave Simon his best smile. "Just sayin'."

Simon pushed through the swinging doors amused by Billy's first attempt ever to be somewhat engaging. It was the first time Billy ever called him by name. Simon no longer felt out of place here as he had for so long.

As he walked down the hall, he called back, over his shoulder, "Thanks, Billy." The tattooer was sitting in his workroom on his swivel stool preparing his cups of ink as Simon entered.

Mark looked up and with a smirk asked, "What you thanking your good 'ole buddy, Billy, for?"

"He's not my good 'ole buddy." Simon smiled with embarrassment.

"Hmm, sure sounded like he's your good 'ole buddy." Then Mark asked, "Hey Simon, you do know what the definition of a good 'ole buddy is, don't you?"

"Not exactly but I guess I'm about to know."

"A good 'ole buddy is a guy that goes downtown and gets two blowjobs then comes home and gives you one of them."

Simon tried his best not to burst out laughing and said, "Damn, that's really classy, Mark!"

Mark appeared pleased with himself and managed to say, "This is a classy shop, dude. Only expect the finest." Then he asked again, "So what were you thanking your good 'ole buddy, Billy, for?"

Simon was embarrassed to mention the reason but answered Mark honestly. "Billy was like real nice to me when I got here. He even called me by name! Hell, he's never done that." Mark said nothing as he continued smiling to himself, filling the small plastic cups with different colored ink. Simon continued, "And as I passed him in the reception area he said something weird about my jeans."

Mark looked up now, incapable of hiding his laughter. "Oh yeah? What did Billy say?"

"He said he had never seen me in long pants and that he thought I looked much better in baggy shorts."

"Fucking looney queen!" Mark shook his head back and forth as if he couldn't believe the information he had just received.

"How's that?" Simon was confused.

"All the guys that work here in the shop have this in-house joke that Billy gets really frisky when the weather gets cold outside. He's the walking, living, bone thermometer. Guess he's getting horny for ya, Simon!" Mark laughed without restraint as he finished setting up his work area.

Simon couldn't help but join him and could only muster a, "Shit, well that's weird!"

"Yeah," Mark said, as he gestured for him to sit down on the work table. "He's been acting weird all day, jumpy and nervous kinda like a bitch in heat." Simon had an instant flashback of Aunt Tessie acting nervous. He remembered the old guy wearing the sweater on one shoulder and speaking breathlessly. The thought made him smile and Mark asked, "A penny for your thoughts, you dirty fucker."

"I was just remembering someone from long ago who used to act that way from time to time." He added, "You know, frisky and looney."

Mark said suddenly, "Hell, I know who! Let me guess! You told me about it. That Aunt Flossie queen! Flossie, Bessie? What was HER name?" Mark shot Simon a quick glance and winked with one eye when he emphasized the pronoun. "You said that dude used to get all queer for some of you pretty boys in the abbey and charge at you like some wild ram in heat wearing a sweater on one shoulder!"

"Oh, fuck! Yes!" Simon saw the image clearly in his mind. "You mean Aunt Tessie!"

"Flossie, Tessie, whatever! Yeah, dude. What did you guys call it when he did that?"

Simon felt a definite kind of connection with Mark like he had never felt before this moment. He realized for the first time that Mark knew and remembered personal details from his past and they were sharing that common knowledge. Simon said almost absentmindedly, "We used to say he was on the prowl when he did that."

"Yeah, that's it! On the prowl!" Mark stretched back and reached for a small envelope, saying to himself, "Yeah, that's it. It must be getting cold outside and 'ole Billy Boy is on the prowl at the tattoo shop…" Simon sat down on the edge of the work table and looked at Mark as he took out the small sketch and purple stencil from the envelope. "Ok, you left me this sketch a few days ago. Let's see what we got here. I'm looking at one almost three inch by three inch triangle, in the color pink." He brought the drawing closer to his eyes and asked, "What are these crooked, broken lines all along the inner edge?"

"I drew them to look like thread that's been hand stitched along the way. The pink triangle is supposed to be like a cloth triangle stitched to my skin." Mark studied the drawing and said, "Tell me about it, Simon."

"In the death camps, during World War II, the Nazis made some people wear colored, cloth triangles on their prisoner uniforms." Mark looked at Simon who pointed to a spot under his left pectoral and then his right thigh. They had cloth triangles sewed onto their uniform jackets and pants to indicate the purported reason the individual was in the concentration camp. Each triangle was of a different color and in the case of Hebrew people, they had to wear two yellow triangles. Some had to wear a yellow triangle for their first "crime" of being Jewish. Some Jews were forced to wear a second colored one for other 'crimes'. "These two triangles were sewed one over the other to form a six pointed star like the Star of David. There were several colors to indicate all the prisoner's 'crimes' and if you weren't Jewish you only wore one triangle pointed this way." Simon turned the drawing around and put it in Mark's hand, with the bottom point of the triangle going down.

Mark was fascinated by the explanation. "What colored triangles were there?"

"There was, like I said, yellow for Jews. Then there was brown for gypsies and green for habitual criminals. There was red for political prisoners and black triangles for asocial individuals."

"Asocial individuals?"

"Yeah, folks like prostitutes, vagrants, known murderers, thieves, lesbians, sometimes gypsies and those who had engaged in sex with Jewish people." Marked looked questioningly at him. Simon continued, "It was a crime in Nazi Germany to do that. And there were blue triangles and also purple ones for others. Some had letters on them to indicate their nationality and above these, their prisoner numbers to identify them."

"Damn, buddy, I had seen the triangles in movies but never paid much attention. You colored this triangle for your tattoo the color pink. Why?"

Simon looked at the drawing and remembered all he had read about those who had been forced to wear the pink triangle. "Homosexual men were forced to wear the pink triangle. Sometimes men who were not homosexuals were forced to wear them to degrade them even more in the eyes of the Nazis and fellow prisoners. Remember, there wasn't a whole lot of gay pride back then."

"Why do you want this tattoo, Simon?"

"Different groups who perished in the death camps are often remembered, like Jews, Catholics, Lutherans, but gay people are usually forgotten. Millions of people, Mark, suffered unimaginable shit in the camps. Thousands of them were homosexual men and women who are mostly forgotten. They too suffered the most hideous persecutions in the camps. But that wasn't the end of it, man. Many of them went to another prison after the liberation of the camps because homosexuality was still a crime on the books in many places until just a few years ago."

"Really? You mean they went to other prisons after the war?"

Simon repeated what he had said, "Yeah, after the Second World War, a lot of gay people went straight to other prisons for the crime of homosexuality after they had suffered all kinds of shit and had been humiliated at the hands of the Nazis."

"Dude, that's crazy."

"It's true. The pink triangle represents one of the greatest persecutions suffered by thousands. And they are often forgotten today. I want to remember. I want the tattoo of the pink triangles to represent their persecution and the persecution I myself suffered in the Church because of my homosexuality. It was real as well and often forgotten. It's still very real to me." Simon hesitated and then said, "I'm still told by the Church to forget about it. I've been told: 'Why do you keep bringing that up? It was so many years ago. Forget about it. All you're going to do is make the Church suffer if you bring it up. Bury it once and for all!' It's such a hypocrisy on the part of the Church. It makes me so fucking angry!"

Mark said nothing and picked up a narrow, separate strip of paper and asked one last question, "And what about this number? What prisoner did that number belong to? I would guess he was gay."

Simon admitted, "Yes. That number belongs to me. It goes above my pink triangle on my chest and on my thigh: 1281956." He thought about how he had conceived of it as his prisoner number, and added, "It's when I was born and entered this world as a gay man, on the twelfth day of August in the year one thousand nine hundred fifty six. Persecution would follow soon enough in my childhood and throughout my adulthood."

"I'm impressed. That's powerful stuff. Go ahead and remove your sweatshirt and tee. You can just lie back." Mark got to work silently, first shaving him where one triangle tattoo would go and then applying the purple stencil of the first pink triangle under Simon's left pectoral. "I'll put the number above the triangle, correct?"

Simon pointed just above his rib cage. "Yeah, just above it, right here."

"Okay. I'll leave space for that right there." He put the strip of paper down and got to work.

As he worked meticulously, he said, "We only have time today for this triangle tattoo. I'll put the other one on your right thigh the next time you come in, okay?"

"Sure, that's cool."

After he had turned the tattoo gun on and had begun the outlining, he said, "Simon, that's some creepy shit about the colored triangles. I can't get it out of my head. Labeling people like that! Fuck!"

"Yeah, the pink triangle was once used to humiliate and crush people but it's a powerful symbol today used among gay people to represent us. The pink triangle appears in a lot of places to represent persecution but also pride and resistance to persecution."

Mark nodded as he worked silently. After some time he said, "Can I ask you something?" He kept his eyes steady on his work.

"Sure, go ahead."

"Well, now that we're getting into this gay symbol I'm thinking that you never really answered my question the last time you were here. I mean, it was all about Toby and you. You never answered my question. Well, you sort of did but it was with an 'I really don't know', as an answer. What do you really think about your response to Toby, I mean, how you finally treated the guy?"

Simon had kept his arms folded behind his head but now waved them excitedly. "Geez, Mark, I appreciate your interest but I gotta say, you don't give up, man!" Simon realized it had come out defensively. Neither man spoke and the only sound in the room was the vibrating needle. Repositioning his arms where they had been he said calmly, "Talking about all that stuff makes my head spin for days on end. Sometimes I can't even get to sleep at night or I have bad dreams." Mark said nothing and listened. "Most of the time, when I leave here and go home, it depresses the fuck out of me." Simon thought about how often he drank alone in his bedroom these days. "I do have to admit, though, that I realize I need to talk about it even though it's very painful for me afterward. It's the remembering that's the hardest part now. Remembering and taking responsibility. Taking responsibility is the real bitch. That's why

I'm here, though. The stuff with Toby and how it went down hurt me and I ran from it, not wanting any responsibility. I was inexperienced and he was my first love but that's a lazy ass excuse. I did betray his love and that was awful on my part. I can see that now. I couldn't see it then." Simon closed his eyes and remembered his friend, his first love. "Let me tell you what happened after that and it will explain why you are giving me the pink triangle tattoo of persecution for prisoner 1281956."

+ + + + +

Simon remembered perfectly well how it had unfolded. On the night Toby had been expelled, he and Shawn were the last ones in Toby's cell. Simon was trying to take in the fact that his friend was gone forever. Something changed in him on that night. He turned inward and stopped all sexual behavior. The radical shift had been so complete in him that he even ceased masturbating himself, something that he had unsuccessfully struggled with since he entered puberty. Time passed and Simon dedicated himself to study and prayer. The daily grind of classes continued in the seminary and every night Simon could be seen entering the crypt quietly and praying before the tabernacle that sat on the altar, high above the ornate sarcophagus of the Prince-Bishop Demetrius. In his prayers, Simon begged God to be merciful and hear him and to accept his repentance. He petitioned Mary, the Mother of God to intercede for him before Her Son, Jesus, begging for God's acceptance. He sought the help of the saints and asked the prince-bishop to help him as well. He needed to be considered worthy of the priesthood again. This thought dominated most of his waking hours. He would pray mentally throughout the day, while he was in class and in studies, walking down a corridor or while he waited to fall asleep at night and upon waking, he'd say out loud, "Please All Powerful God, make me worthy of the priesthood of Jesus Christ once again."

Celibacy would be the way to gain God's complete acceptance and so he distanced himself from any physical, sexual activity. Yet, all around him, many of the other young men who were his peers continued to express themselves sexually, albeit in a hidden fashion. But for Simon it had stopped. It all completely ceased for him and remained so for a very long time. He continued to have friends but his demeanor was reserved. Inwardly, he imposed discipline upon himself when his thoughts drifted and became sexual in nature.

This new behavior did not go unnoticed by the Abbot and some of the others on the council who observed him carefully during this period without him realizing it. After two years, Simon was considered a success story by them.

Brother Shawn, however, had his own thoughts on the matter. He had observed Simon's new behavior and the same things that the others had seen except that he knew perfectly well how Simon ticked inside. The others did not. He had understood that Simon was a curious blend of the sacred and the profane, of being authentically drawn to holiness and at the same time, profoundly attracted to lusty, worldly things. He was deeply spiritual yet struggled constantly in his search for God. He was also very drawn to physical pleasures and to exploring his sexual nature. Shawn knew that Simon was being strict with himself but that he wrestled with his sexual desires. He knew Simon had created a house of cards for himself in this regard and it wouldn't take much to bring it tumbling down.

As students, Simon and his companions were all aware of the constant battle between the sacred and seeking holiness and the profane, that is, one's sinful nature, because it was taught in the seminary classroom as part of their formation. The professors had been clear in their lectures, and Simon had taken much to heart, a particular lecture that seemed prepared for him. He wrote the points down and read them often during this period in his life. The professor had said, "Saint Augustine, one of the great pillars of the Christian Church was largely responsible for identifying the profane with evil and evil inclinations in the fifth century. After all, he had struggled in the same way we all struggle at times and even the great and wise Augustine knew the temptations very well. He had strayed and had given himself to the pleasures of the flesh. The Catholic Church took this Augustinian understanding of the sacred and profane to mean, basically, that spiritual things were good and worldly things led to evil." But the professor had warned them, saying, "This would later lead to heresies and a warped understanding of the two." This lecture was fundamental in the minds of the student monks preparing for priesthood and Simon, like many of his companions, took it to heart.

In Simon, there continued to be a growing, ravenous hunger for God and for the things of the world at the same time. Brother Shawn was perhaps the only one who truly understood this. He grasped that as Simon matured into manhood, he would be unable to stifle this hunger for mundane things in himself. He had seen how Simon's deep spirituality was interlocked with his innate hedonistic self. This is why Shawn took it upon himself to confront Simon about his new behavior and strict observance of celibacy. He would be the judge of how authentic and enduring Simon's newfound conversion really was. He had been drawn to Simon since the first day he met him at the train station. This fascination obsessed him and he considered it his mission to mentor Simon and be by his side, protecting him from others who might want to do the same.

One afternoon, Simon was returning from classes and headed to his cell. His course, black habit made a ruffling noise in the otherwise stillness of the endless corridor. He was exhausted from the lectures in philosophy and theology and did not see Brother Shawn walking toward him from the opposite direction. The corridor was usually dark even on a sunny day and Brother Shawn's habit served as a kind of camouflage in the shadows. He was looking for Simon and was amused by the serious young man's rapt attention in himself. He waited until he was almost in front of him and then took Simon by the shoulders and pushed him aggressively against the wall. He laid a heavy arm on each side of him and said to him, "Oh, little one, you're ever so serious these days! You're beginning to look like some of the boring, dreadful old German diehards around here. Lighten up."

Simon snapped out of his somnolence and literally blinked at Brother Shawn several times, trying to focus on the man who held him captive against the wall. He felt like a prisoner in his arms and tried to squirm away but the man held him firmly in place. Simon finally blurted out, "I can see you're up to no good as usual."

Shawn's face was inches away from Simon's as he whispered, "That's what makes me fun."

"You better be more careful and less fun if you expect to be accepted for ordination to the deaconate soon."

"Oh, honey, that's a done deal. I have my connections in high places, plus I know how to watch my own back. Speaking of connections, I have an invitation to relay to you."

Simon was suddenly intrigued and opened the door to his cell and entered. Shawn followed him in. Simon asked, "What kind of an invitation is it?" Life in the abbey could get monotonous very quickly and an invitation to anything was definitely not common. "Huh? C'mon tell me. What kind of invitation? Who…who is inviting me to what?"

"Inviting us, little one. Get it right. It's an invitation for the two of us. It's not all about you." Brother Shawn snickered to himself as he stepped back and adjusted the belt around his imposing waistline. "Speaking of you and the tiny, air tight world you seem to live in lately, how have you been?"

Simon was exasperated with Shawn's endless, little games. This was the game of entrapment. "Just relay the invitation. I'm really tired from classes and need to take a nap."

"Oh, poor little one." He raised his right hand and dramatically caressed Simon's hair. "You poor, tired baby." Shawn inhaled deeply and tilted his head to one side as he stared into Simon's eyes and exhaled seductively. He looked at Simon without saying a word and Simon could continue to feel the man's breath on his face. It made his skin crawl to realize how close Shawn's lips were to his own and he didn't doubt what the man's intentions were.

Simon stared back defiantly and said, "I've been keeping my nose clean."

Shawn walked around Simon's cell and picked up the bottle of Royal Copenhagen he had given him some time ago. "Have you used this yet, little one?" He didn't give Simon an opportunity to answer and asked, "Are you going to wear it tomorrow night?"

Simon was curious, "What's going on tomorrow night?" Shawn was waving the bottle of cologne. "What's the occasion?"

"I'm trying to tell you but you're so damn somber and serious. I told you I have an invitation to relay. The Royal Copenhagen is for you to wear, silly, not just keep hidden away in this cell. Nothing but the best for my boys." He put the bottle in Simon's hands and said, "Anyway, I've been observing you for quite a while now."

"Oh, am I a specimen in a laboratory to be observed by you?"

"You'd be surprised to know how close to the truth that is in this place!" He moved in closer again. "Not a specimen, little one, but definitely someone I'm interested in watching." Then he said with an edge, "I'm so happy you reformed your ways and that low life Toby is gone."

Simon shot him a hateful look and said, "Don't you talk about him that way. What I shared with him was personal and my business." Then he added sadly, "Plus, he's in Heaven now."

"He's certainly dead. I'm not so sure he's in Heaven but let's not get into that."

Simon hated Shawn in that moment more than he could have expressed and exhaled impatiently. "Look, I need to rest."

"I guess I said it all wrong. I didn't mean to hurt your feelings. I'm sorry." Shawn softened his tone and said, "What I meant to say was that I'm glad you embraced your celibacy and have shown the Abbot and the others on his council that you're serious about your life here in the abbey. It has certainly made an impression on them. It was very smart of you to cool your rocks even though there's all kinds of activity in the abbey at all levels." Simon wanted to say something about the temptations but remained silent. Shawn continued, "I've been very happy about all that but I gotta say that you seem really sad and isolated." He looked at himself in the mirror above the sink and as he adjusted the hair on the sides of his head, he said, "Any way, this invitation came up and I really believe it'll be good for you to relax and unwind." Shawn put his right index finger gently on Simon's lower lip. He dragged it down over his chin and down over his Adam's apple and across his chest, asking sarcastically, "May I now relay the invitation?"

"Yes, please."

"The cologne is for you to wear tomorrow night to an intimate supper in Aunt Tessie's apartments at 7:00 pm sharp. We must be super punctual because she gets all catty about guests arriving late. It's a German thing. An invitation to Aunt Tessie's rooms is not something just anyone receives. She explicitly said to me that she was having a little supper tomorrow night and would I please extend the invitation to you."

Simon was curious. "Why didn't he invite me himself?"

"Oh, she's very timid and would never invite you personally until she gets to know you better." Then he added, "Tessie is very well connected here in the abbey and has the Abbot's ear as well as the older monks." Then correcting himself, "Well, most of the older monks. Some of them think she's a ridiculous, silly old queen. Some of those old German guys are real he-men, macho, strong silent types in love with their long beards, making beer and drinking it day and night." Simon thought Shawn's assessment of the older monks was disrespectful but said nothing in their defense. "Anyway, it's a small gathering and we're invited."

"Who's going to be there? What do I wear? Where is it going to be?"

"Questions, questions. Martha, Martha, you are worried and upset about many things, only one thing is important and that is for you to get your ass ready and over there at seven tomorrow night. I'll come by around twenty to seven. Aunt Tessie's rooms are situated in one of the oldest parts of the abbey, way above the high ceiling of the abbey church. It's a twisted, winding climb, up rickety, creaking wooden steps but a very cozy and neat place. It's all low, pointed ceilings and narrow, leaded windows. There are two fireplaces and three rooms in all, each one leading into the other. Her bedroom is way at the end." Shawn smiled to himself. "Pray God you never have to go in there!"

Simon interrupted, "But where's the dinner going to be? In a local restaurant?"

"Oh, dear boy, you have so much to learn and I have so much to teach you and there's so little time!" Then he put his hands on his hips and said, "Aunt Tessie's suppers are over-the-top gourmet affairs. She cooks everything up there, in her rooms."

"She, I mean, he has a kitchen up there?" Simon couldn't wrap his brain around the information he was receiving.

"Don' be silly. Of course not! She has hot plates, a portable oven and a fridge. And she puts out fine, Limoges dinner plates that belonged to her grandmother and Baccarat crystal for all the drinks. There's also no stainless steel at her table. Only old, polished silver is set on the immaculately starched and pressed white damask tablecloths."

Simon was at a complete loss with all the information Shawn was giving him and unprepared to understand most of it. He couldn't imagine such a place existed within the walls of the abbey. "Where's the dinner served?"

"She has a table for four or six, depending on the invitations and the intimacy that night. Tomorrow night two others are invited that you need to impress. They are both old queens but wield great influence. The dinner will be served in the second room. It's a kind of library. The first room is a sitting area. We'll take before and after dinner drinks there." Shawn was pleased to see Simon's eyes widen and sparkle at the mention of drinks.

"Before and after dinner drinks?" His face had changed.

"Yeah. The booze flows at Aunt Tessie's 'hauschen' to be sure."

"Haus...what?"

"Hauschen. It's German. She'll throw German words and phrases around in conversation tomorrow night. You'll see. Hauschen is what she calls her rooms. It's her 'cottage', her 'manor house'. Hell, it's her damn bunker. You'll see how German it all is tomorrow night at Aunt Tessie's place."

Simon was perplexed by it all and asked, "So who all is going to be there? I know Aunt Tessie and you and I, but who are the other two? You said they are influential."

"Well, the Prior usually stops by if she catches wind of a supper there. She doesn't need an invite because, well, she's the Prior of this abbey and ranks after the Abbot. But she may not show, who knows? As you well know, she's given to missing her classes." Then he said, "Father Reinhart and Brother Heinrich are the other two. Reinhart is a proud old queen who has lived most of her life in Europe. She went as a newly ordained priest right after the war to study at the University of Fribourg in Switzerland. She also served at the General Headquarters, the Mother House of the Order in Rome. Her nickname is 'Proud Mary'. You can figure out why after tomorrow night's supper. Brother Heinrich is another story altogether. She was brilliant as a young monk but had a problem early on with booze and was not allowed to pursue studies for the priesthood. Poor old queen had to settle for being a lay brother. However, that didn't mean she was going to wait on priests or scrub floors. She demanded to study accounting and proved to be a financial wizard. Her nick name is 'Fruit Fly' because she's very short and small and flitters about like a tiny fly, gesticulating and talking non-stop, especially when she drinks, which is always. And, she's not exactly butch."

Simon was speechless. He tried to imagine himself at a fancy dinner with booze flowing, French porcelain and crystal on the table and Aunt Tessie, Proud Mary and Fruit Fly. He remembered something and suddenly asked Shawn, "What do I wear? I mean, what are we wearing? Our habits?"

"Oh, God, no! Of course not! In any case, those old queens wanna take a good look at you. We can wear jeans and a dress shirt."

"I only have my white dress shirt. The one I brought when I entered the abbey as a postulant. It's kinda worn."

"That's perfect. It'll look great with your jeans. You know, the stressed look." Then he added, "And wear your Royal Copenhagen, that's why I gave it to you. The old ones like boys to smell nice." Shawn winked at Simon and said, "Plus, you're my date and I want to show you off. Keep that in mind."

"Well, okay, yes, I guess I accept the invitation. I have to admit it sounds strange but…"

"Wonderful! It's a date, then. I'll pick you up twenty minutes before seven. Be ready and on time! It's in your best interest to make connections. It's also important for you to snap out of your boring, little life." Simon said nothing and resented Shawn's comment. Celibacy was what they had vowed to live and Simon struggled to be faithful to the vow. He was relieved when Shawn finally backed away from him and walked down the corridor in the direction he had come from. Sometimes Simon felt that Shawn was suffocating him and invading his space. As he removed his habit and lay in bed in his t-shirt and underwear, he thought about the comments Shawn had made about his boring, little life.

He had been struggling for so long with sexual temptations and had put anything remotely sexual completely out of his life. He was exhausted with the fight. He knew that some of his companions were sexually active with each other and they didn't appear particularly debilitated to him. Quite the contrary, he envied some of them because they seemed to be at peace with themselves and happy. Now Shawn was inviting him to a bizarre supper that had all the makings of decadence, at the very least. Still, Simon had to admit that he was thrilled at being noticed among those who held clout in the abbey, even if the evening would be peculiar. He was also very nervous about going with Shawn. He wondered what Shawn had told them. He had called him his date and the implications were clear. Simon had been avoiding him for a very long time because he knew that he was lax in morals and didn't bother hiding his gay connections. Simon still felt very guilty about all he had experienced sexually with Toby and yet all the old feelings were still there, front and center. Even though he had made a heroic effort to be celibate, an overwhelming part of him ached to be held and touched once again as Toby had done.

The following evening, true to his word, Shawn came to Simon's cell door at precisely twenty minutes to seven. He didn't knock nor did he wait for Simon to invite him in but instead burst into the tiny space without closing the door completely behind him. The smell of Royal Copenhagen filled the tiny cell. Simon was combing his hair and looked up with comb in hand. Shawn examined him up and down and said, "Well, don't you look cute and good enough to eat."

"I don't like the white shirt." Simon pressed it down with his hands, saying, "It looks ratty."

"Why not? It goes great with the faded jeans. Plus, I hadn't even noticed the white shirt...truth be told, your jeans caught my eye. They look great on you."

"I found them at the bottom of a box piled high with old, smelly habits in that room labeled 'The Commissary' down the hall, just before the stairwell. I was so happy when I realized they were my size!"

"Ah, yes, the finery that one can come across at 'The Commissary'." He turned Simon around one way and then another, saying to himself out loud, "Oh yeah, just tight enough." Then he asked, "Don't you have another pair of shoes? Those tattered black ones go great with drab religious clothes but not tight hot jeans."

"It's all I've got. Well, except for the work boots I found in 'The Commissary'. I use them when I work outside and sit on the tractor."

"Oh, yeah, you look all butch and tasty in those boots for outside work but not to go to Aunt Tessie's for supper." He added, "There's not enough time now for me to go back upstairs but I've got a pair of black leather boots that you would look stunning in. I bought them in an antique mall in Pittsburgh about a year ago. I saw them there and they caught my eye big time. They're Carabinieri boots. Authentic Carabinieri. Just knowing that, I had to have them."

"What's Carabi…?"

"Carabinieri. Men who belong to the Italian national police force. Buff, built men. 'Body by Fisher', if you get my meaning. They wear these incredibly perfect ceremonial uniforms on special occasions with sleek, black boots shined up to hell and back. I swear to you, the photographs I've seen of those guys are breathtaking. They're all hunky with five o'clock shadows at ten in the morning and seven feet tall, wearing capes and broad, impressive hats. I saw the boots in the shop in Pittsburgh and asked the lady if they were authentic Carabinieri boots. She said they were and that they had just arrived. She said they were used, of course and I didn't bother to tell her that that's precisely what got me all hot about them." He made like he was wiping his forehead and said, "Whew! To think that one of those tall, dark, furry Italian beasts had his feet in those boots gets me all hard and hot." Simon smiled not knowing what to say. He grabbed Simon by the waist and said. "Stand here. Put your foot out." Simon obeyed and Shawn put his foot right next to Simon's. "Yep, I think those boots would fit you. Next time we have something to go to, you can try them on and if they fit you can wear them."

Simon was hooked. "Really? Are you serious? I'd love to wear a pair of boots like those!"

"I'll bet you would, you little perv." He pushed him toward the sink playfully. "Finish combing that mop of hair and let's get going. We don't want to be late and get old Aunt Tessie's kitty in an uproar."

Simon combed his hair and turned around smiling awkwardly, "Okay, I'm ready, I think. Gee, I feel like I'm going to some kind of state dinner."

"Believe me, you are, honey. Her Highness, Tess, the Dowager Empress of Queerdom is receiving you for the first time in her private apartments. Her ladies-in-waiting are literally waiting for you to arrive tonight."

Simon smiled nervously. "Ok. I'm done."

"I don't think so, little one."

"What? Why? What do you mean?"

"Aren't you forgetting something?"

Simon patted his pockets and looked in the mirror. "No, I'm all set."

Shawn raised one eyebrow and gestured negatively with an index finger. At long last, he blew out air in a dramatic, exaggerated way and said, "Where's your essence? Where's your soul?"

"Huh?"

"The Royal Copenhagen, silly! The cologne! I'm not smelling it."

"Oh, but I already put some on!" Simon opened the small cabinet above his sink and took out the bottle of the cologne. "Do you think I need more?"

"Not wearing enough of it. It can do wonders around the right people to smell nice, you know." Simon put some more cologne on himself and returned the small bottle to its place and shut the cabinet door.

Shawn completely opened the door to the corridor and ushered Simon out first. Then he led the way and Simon followed obediently. It was indeed a winding path to Aunt Tessie's 'cottage'. They went down corridors Simon had never seen and up wooden, narrow flights of stairs that creaked and threatened to give way under their combined weight. As he climbed, Simon looked out small windows and saw how high they had climbed. Below them was the garden of spices and the fountain at its center looked ridiculously diminished from where he stood staring down. At long last, they arrived on a landing of hand hewn planks of knotty wood. He saw that it was dark outside through the only window in the narrow, serpentine corridor that wound its way to a single door at the end. Simon heard raucous laughter up ahead and was suddenly apprehensive and nervous about meeting the older monks.

Shawn turned and whispered, "The show is about to begin. Brace yourself and hang on for the wild ride ahead tonight."

They approached and Simon saw Father Reinhart's massive frame at the open door. Aunt Tessie was just inside. Father Reinhart's impressive voice boomed in the tiny corridor, as he asked his host politely, "Entschuldigen Sie bitte, konnen Sie mir sagen, ob Satan hier wohnt?"

Simon was at a loss and looked up at Shawn who rolled his eyes and whispered, "It's a queer little game they play from when they were students in Fribourg, in Switzerland, a million years ago." Then added, "I'll explain later."

Aunt Tessie was all aglow and bowing gracefully, in almost a kind of curtsy, said to Father Reinhart, "Ja, mein schatzchen." Both men laughed uncontrollably, holding their sides. Father Reinhart entered but had to stoop down in order to get in through the door frame. Once inside he straightened up again and his powerful voice could be heard greeting the other guest who had already arrived.

Puzzled, Simon looked again at Shawn, who said, "Later, baby." The two men approached the door and Simon stood nervously at Shawn's side. Aunt Tessie was radiant with pleasure and a small gasp escaped from his lips as he eyed them both. "How lovely that you youngsters accepted my poor invitation."

"Guten abend," Shawn returned the greeting, as he said politely, "Good evening to you as well. I wouldn't miss it for the world, Tess." Simon was shocked that Shawn had called the priest by his nickname and that he had not even flinched. Then the host turned and looked at Simon. He kept his eyes on him while he said to Shawn, "I'm so pleased that you brought this fine, young buck." He smiled and put a hand on Simon's shoulder and kneaded him there, as if to convince himself that his guest were real, saying to Shawn, "I remember his collar bones so well when he sat for me. The Prophet Jeremiah would be pleased indeed." He removed his hand, saying "I hope you enjoy yourself at our little party tonight. Nothing fancy, just a little gathering of friends. Please come inside my little cottage, Simon." As Simon entered, he heard Aunt Tessie saying to Shawn, "I'm so very pleased you brought him tonight. He looks so vigorous and cute." Then he added, "And he smells divine!"

"Indeed," was all Shawn could muster.

Simon was mesmerized upon entering Aunt Tessie's "cottage". The room was, as the expression goes, a veritable plethora of old German hodge-podge.

What first struck him were the dim lights glowing from lamps fitted with burgundy colored, silk lampshades. A massive stone fireplace dominated the room. It was out of proportion to the size of the wall but Simon figured it had been built in an age when central heating was nonexistent. Hanging above the mantelpiece was a gold framed portrait of a stern-looking man with long sideburns. A bronze plaque on the frame identified him as Richard Wagner. A green velvet runner trimmed with tassels covered the mantelpiece from one end to the other. Two white marble busts sat on opposite ends and between them were sepia colored photographs in ornate, metal frames. "Those magnificent busts are of Gustav Mahler and Anton Bruckner, both Austrians. I come from a German family but our ties to Austria are very close. And why shouldn't they be? The German people themselves peacefully requested that Austria should be annexed to Germany. The 'Anschluss' was greatly desired. It was a natural connection."

Father Reinhart spoke up. "Your love of the Fatherland makes your understanding of German history at that time a bit…prejudiced I think."

Aunt Tessie disregarded the remark and the interruption. Simon didn't understand a word of what he had just heard. Then Aunt Tessie gestured to the photographs and said, "These are my parents, grandparents and great grandfather. And this is the family home in Bavaria." Aunt Tessie gestured gracefully from one photograph to the next, with fingers upheld, like the tall blond ladies Simon remembered as a boy on game shows when a brand new, sparkling refrigerator was about to be given away if the contestant knew the correct answer.

In the back ground, a phonograph was on and exquisite music played. Aunt Tessie saw that Simon was aware of the music and said, "That's the music of Richard Wagner." Once again, he gestured gracefully to the oil painting like one of the blond ladies on television. Simon was enthralled by the incredibly depressing, dark and melancholy music he was hearing. Aunt Tessie put his arm around Simon's waist and asked, "Do you enjoy Wagner? This is the funeral march from Wagner's 'Siegfried'. It's very moving."

Simon had never heard such music before and had no idea who Siegfried was and when he had died. "I love it. I've never heard anything like it before!" Aunt Tessie applauded, pleased with Simon's sensibilities and said, "I'm so pleased that you came tonight." One of the other guests chuckled sarcastically at the remark but the host ignored him.

Father Reinhart was sitting in a great backed, leather chair in front of the fireplace and said to Simon, "Oh, child, you will be hearing that kind of music all night in this lair!"

Brother Heinrich was sitting on a small settee and held a tumbler filled with a honey colored liquid. He held the glass up to Reinhart and the ice cubes clinked merrily as he said, "Oh, Mary, touché! That was good. Very good." He took a long swig of his drink and sat back.

Aunt Tessie waved them away with his right hand, "Oh, don't listen to them. They're savages, up to no good."

No one paid heed to Brother Shawn who pulled Simon gently away from their host and said, "Tessie, may I show Simon your suite of rooms?"

"Yes, of course, mein schatzi."

As they walked away, Simon whispered quietly to Shawn, "What does that mean?"

"What? Mein schatzi?"

"Yeah, Father Theobald just said that to you."

"It literally means 'my treasure' but implies, 'baby'." He winked at Simon, "Remember, it's Aunt Tessie in here."

"Oh, right."

The sitting room they were standing in was heavily draped along the walls with tapestries depicting hunting scenes, great forests and castles. Shawn said, "Aunt Tessie defends this décor by saying it keeps the cold drafts out in winter."

Simon said, "I love it! It's like a womb in here. Beyond cozy!"

"I figured you would like it. Check out the old rugs and two hutches over there." He gestured to two, heavily carved wooden cabinets. Everything was old world and antique. There were numerous porcelain and crystal pieces on the shelves behind beveled glass doors and intricately decorated beer steins were lined up according to size. In the room were two leather overstuffed chairs with lace doilies which sat next to the settee and another tall backed leather chair was next to the one Father Reinhart occupied. In the middle of all this furniture was a short, marble-topped table. The four small leaded windows were draped in heavy laced curtains. Large platters of old porcelain hung on the walls between them, displaying castles and fortresses atop snowcapped mountains.

The second room was a library. The walls in this room were lined with books neatly set on thick, wooden shelves. Each bookcase was fitted with glass doors that reflected the soft glow coming from the crystal chandelier in the center of the low beamed ceiling. Simon approached one of the bookshelves and saw that all the books were in German. A sturdy rectangular table in the center of the room was prepared for that evening's supper. Shawn turned to Simon and whispered, "There's the Limoges porcelain, baccarat crystal, Italian silver and Belgian lace I told you about. Did you think such things existed in our abbey, little one?" Simon gawked at the splendor spread out before them. He had never seen so many eating utensils set out in such order nor so many different kinds of glasses and goblets assembled for a single meal.

They approached a doorframe at the back of the room. Shawn said to Simon, "This is her nest." There was no door to this final room. Rather, a heavily embroidered velvet curtain served as a door. Shawn was ready to push it open when he heard, "Not there, Liebchen! Not there!" It was Aunt Tessie waving his arms. "I have the kitchen set up in my bedroom. It's a mess. Please, come to the salon and formally introduce Simon to the others. Let's have some drinks."

They returned to the first room. Candles had been lit as well as the fireplace. Simon sat next to Father Reinhart in one of the chairs in front of the fireplace. Shawn stood and said, "Father Reinhart, Brother Heinrich, may I present Brother Simon."

Both older monks gazed longingly on Simon and Father Reinhart said amused, "My, how very formal we are this evening, dear Sheila."

Shawn shot them a glance and said to Simon in an awkward tone, "That's my nickname. Sheila." He exaggeratedly curtseyed before the older men.

Both raised their glasses to Simon and Father Reinhart said, "Welcome, dear boy, to our little rendezvous." Then he added, "You smell good enough to eat. I know the fragrance but can't remember its name."

"Royal Copenhagen, Father." Simon responded too eagerly.

"Yes, yes, of course." He took a drink from his glass and asked loudly, "Sheila wouldn't be responsible for that, would she?"

Shawn didn't miss a beat and with eyes downcast and a hand over his chest, said "Guilty as charged, Mary."

"Ah, you have such fine taste. Maybe you'll become Abbot someday." Brother Heinrich was busy ogling Simon and Aunt Tessie had gone into the bedroom, apparently to check on what was in the oven there.

Shawn startled Simon when he asked him, "What would you like to drink?" Simon was at a loss. He had never had much alcohol except beer on the beach with his friends. "I dunno, what do you suggest?"

Shawn put ice into a glass and poured generously from a square shaped bottle with a black label. "Here, drink this. I'm sure you'll like it."

Simon took the tumbler and sipped Jack Daniel's for the first time in his life. Without thinking, smacking his lips, he blurted out, "Oh, damn, that's good!"

Brother Heinrich said, "It is good, isn't it? That's my poison as well, Simon."

Aunt Tessie stepped into the intimate mood of the sitting room and asked, "Is everyone served? Are we having a good time? Is everyone happy to be here?" Without waiting for a response to any of his questions, he said, "Sheila, dear, could you pour me a double Manhattan? The bitters are right there with the vermouth." He took his place on the settee next to Brother Heinrich and patted him on the knee. "I'm so happy you are all here. Let's relax and have our libations, away from all the noise and undesirables." Shawn handed him his drink and Aunt Tessie tasted it, saying under his breath, "Heavenly!"

Shawn sat in one of the overstuffed chairs with the doilies and held his glass up high, "Prost!" Everyone held their glasses up, including Simon. Shawn toasted, "To our wonderful host, Aunt Tessie!"

Brother Heinrich said, "Yes, cheers!" Father Reinhart said nothing as he drank from his glass.

Simon felt nervous about saying anything and kept quiet. He felt he was out of his league with those present. Idle conversation ensued and various monks and topics regarding the abbey were discussed. A second round of drinks was served and then a third. Conversation was lively and Simon felt a definite buzz taking hold of him.

Aunt Tessie had brought an assortment of hot hors d'oeuvres and had placed them on the marble-topped table. Everyone was eating and drinking amicably when Father Reinhart said, "I had a ghastly experience yesterday in the refectory. They served that filthy garbage they call tuna fish casserole. Its putrid cat food, not fit for an alley cat."

Brother Heinrich said, "Well, I don't mind it." His speech was slightly slurred.

"Yeah, well, that's probably why you have psoriasis."

Brother Heinrich sounded wounded and protested loudly, "I don't have psoriasis, I have dry skin due to the fact that my skin is fair and delicate."

"It's almost certainly that damn tuna fish casserole you like so much. Sometimes you have scales like a fish on your elbows. I've seen you, Fruit Fly." Father Reinhart said this last trying to keep from smiling.

"Don't be a bitch, Mary. It's not true. I have dry skin is all." Fruit Fly was rubbing his elbows as he said this. "The tuna fish casserole is actually tasty when they serve it hot."

"In my estimation, it's pure shit, pardon my French." There was indignation in Father Reinhart's tone. "Can you imagine serving ME that excrement?" He took a long swig and emptied his glass. He exhaled. "Can you imagine putting that, that…"He was at a loss for what he wanted to say and finally spat out the words with a slur, "…that dung in front of me!" He reached for his empty glass and seeing that it was empty, raised and shook it for Shawn to see. Small, diminished ice cubes clinked weakly as he did so. "I am indignant that they should serve that feculence to me. To ME! IMAGINE! I who have dined in the capitals of Europe!" Shawn handed him a glass generously filled with scotch whiskey. The old priest took it and winked at him. Shawn reached for Simon's glass and whispered softly to him, "There's a perfect example why we call her 'Proud Mary'." Simon stifled a ripple of laughter that threatened to rise up his throat. He struggled with it until Shawn returned with another Jack Daniel's and he sat back drinking thirstily, afraid that he would not be able to control the unruly laughter building within himself.

Aunt Tessie had gotten up and changed the large, shiny acetate record on the phonograph. When the needle was in place, he wound his way back to the settee and sat down with a thump. Simon saw that he had a fresh Manhattan in his hand as well and thought to himself that it most certainly must be a double. As the music began, Aunt Tessie interrupted the conversation and announced solemnly, "Let's listen to Wagner's 'Tannhauser'." Shawn looked at Simon with a mischievous smile and raised his eyebrows seductively and then blew him a kiss. Simon moved his eyebrows in the same way but looked away nervously around himself, worried that one of the others had seen Shawn's kiss.

Only the crackling sounds coming from the blazing logs in the fireplace could be heard as the overture began. Then the first somber notes filled the room and Aunt Tessie walked over to Simon and stood next to him. He bent down and whispered in his ear, "Listen closely to this divine music, my dear boy. It's based on two German legends and it's like nothing you've ever heard. It's the story of a great struggle. A struggle between sacred and profane love." He straightened up and closed his eyes as he concentrated on the music flowing through the room. Then he bent down low and again whispered into Simon's ear, "It's about being redeemed through love. There is nothing more sublime. This is the best of Wagner." Simon closed his eyes and thought about his own struggle with temptation. He thought about his soul and his body. He thought about Toby and that magical afternoon long ago in the forest.

When the overture was over, something like reverence hung above the sitting room. It held the three Germans completely captive. Once again Simon heard only the crackling fire behind him. Little by little, as the opera continued playing, conversation sprang up again among them. There was apparently no rush to begin supper and by the time drinks were replenished for the fifth time, Simon felt he was quite drunk. His nervousness had abated and he now joined in the conversation freely, without inhibitions. Shawn took his glass to refill it and Simon said, "I think I'm a little drunk."

"How can you tell?" It was Father Reinhart and his voice was deep and sensual. "Oscar Wilde noted that when he drank alcohol in large quantities, he acquired all the effects of drunkenness." Everyone laughed. "And of course there's that absolutely wonderful thing Frank Sinatra said about feeling sorry for people who don't drink. He said when they wake up in the morning, that's as good as they're going to feel all day!"

Brother Heinrich tried to get up but his legs betrayed him. He raised his glass saying with a pronounced slur, "Oh, Proud Mary, you're so clever in your haughty wisdom!"

Father Reinhart looked at him with one arched eyebrow and raised his glass back, saying, "Why thank you, Fruit Fly. And you are so fucking drunk! What is our young and handsome guest going to think about us carrying on like this?" Everyone joined in on the laughter.

Fruit Fly sat back pouting and sipped his drink quietly. Then he said, "Well, I have no idea what he thinks about us old queens, but I know how young people think. I was young once…" He trailed off and everyone waited for him to continue.

Proud Mary laughed quietly and said into his glass before he took another swig, "Oh my, hang on everyone, here we go."

Fruit Fly heard him and stuck his tongue out at Proud Mary and made a face. He sipped his drink slowly, trying to pronounce his words carefully which were coming out garbled and somewhat mumbled. "When I was young long ago and secretary to Abbot Dietrich, I didn't think much about the older monks. The Abbot was fond of me. He gave me responsibilities and I was in charge of all his personal finances. I was young and pretty and he gave me the title of Secretary to the Most Reverend Lord Abbot." He took a huge drink from his glass and swallowed, grimacing. He belched and then continued, "But then the Abbot died suddenly one night and the one that came after him…that bitch took away my crown and my checkbook. She thought she didn't need me. I was cast aside like something useless and she found herself a new secretary. A young, handsome one. The new secretary was all blond and meaty and had her golden hair cut real short in a flat top so she looked like an athletic stud from the Hitlerjugend, a regular poster boy for the Hitler Youth. She had the Abbot wrapped around her little finger."

Aunt Tessie giggled and asked, "Are you sure it was his little finger the Abbot was wrapped around? Or was it his swollen blutwurst?" Aunt Tessie said to Simon, "His blood sausage." Snorts and raucous laughter went off in the cozy room.

When it finally subsided, Fruit Fly continued, "She was a young lay brother but thought she was ordained. Blondie never made it, though. Off she went to the gay bars in Pittsburgh and never came back. She always acted straight around the old farts but was soooo campy around the young ones. A big phony, that trite little slut."

Simon spoke up boldly, "Like that Brother Arnold! What a fake. She's such a pathetic joke!" Simon surprised himself that he had referred to the monk as "she".

Fruit Fly nodded agreement and said, "Oh, that clubbed foot bitch with her bleached Dutch boy haircut. She'd throw anybody under the bus to move ahead in the abbey. I hear she wants to study to become a priest. She kisses the asses of all those old monks. Probably wants to be Abbot someday."

Simon sat up excitedly, fueled by the bourbon and repeated, "Definitely a joke and a real fake. Talk about thinking she's ordained! She's such a bullshitter too! I've seen it so often in the refectory and recreation room." Shawn smiled stupidly as he looked at Simon who was obviously on a roll now, looking pleased as he saw how well he fit in with those gathered in the room. "You know what I'd call her? 'Club Foot Heidi'. That's what I'd call that Teutonic bitch." The room burst into applause and laughter. Simon felt good about himself. He now felt like an insider sitting in that special place. He felt accepted and part of an elite, small group. Then he added facetiously, "No offense to the Germans in this room, of course."

All three elderly gentlemen said in unison, "Oh, no offense taken! You said it all so well."

Fruit Fly proclaimed, "Scheisskopf. That's all she is."

Simon looked up, "What does that mean?"

Proud Mary answered, "Shithead."

"Shithead." Simon repeated the word in an effort to have it sink in. He was in a bit of a fog. "You know who's another shithead, a 'scheisskopf' if ever there was one?" Everyone looked at him, intrigued. "Father Wade, the Master of Clerics."

Shawn whistled loudly and everyone turned to look at him. "You think Wade's a *scheisskopf*? Now where would you get that idea?" They all laughed hysterically. "That's Wanda you're talking about! Wanda the Wicked Warden. She runs the Cleric Wing like it's a fucking prison and it's hotter than Hell there!"

Simon asked, "Why did you name her Wanda?"

"We saw an advertisement once in the Leicester newspaper for a porn movie called, 'Wanda the Wicked Warden'. In the advertisement it showed a tall lanky woman with long, wild hair, in high leather boots, sporting a long whip in one hand and a drink in the other. Underneath that, it said, 'Her prison is hotter than Hell!' Those of us who have been under her whip in the seminary think it's a very accurate assessment. Bony-assed, lanky Wade is Wanda the Wicked Warden! Wouldn't you agree, Simon?"

"Absolutely! Yes!" He shook his head sideways and then back and forth. "I guess I do! I'm not really familiar with all the nicknames, I mean, I only just learned you're 'Sheila'." He hesitated and added, "I'm only just beginning to understand about your names." He glanced around the room but did not dare say, "Aunt Tessie", "Proud Mary" and "Fruit Fly."

Shawn spoke up, "Well, explaining all the other names…that's for another gathering. I think you'd all agree!" Everyone smiled and nodded in agreement.

"Well, speaking of things I know but don't understand…" Simon was unsure if what he just said made any sense but he plowed on anyway. "When Sheila and I got here tonight," he looked at Proud Mary, "you said something in German to…to… Aunt Tessie that I totally didn't understand."

The two older men looked at each other and burst out laughing. Aunt Tessie said, "Oh, that's just an old game we still play from the days at our beloved Universitat Freiburg. Remember those days, Mary?"

"How can I forget, mein Schatz?" Proud Mary had a hand to his lips and sent a kiss across the room.

Simon insisted, "Well, what does it mean?"

Proud Mary piped up, "Whenever either of us would visit the other's rooms, and mind you it was strictly forbidden to do so, we'd knock and ask, 'Entschuldigen Sie bitte, konnen Sie mir sagen, ob Satan hier wohnt?' It means, 'Excuse me, can you tell me if Satan lives here?' Then the other one would say, 'Ja, mein schatzi!', which means, 'yes, sweetie'!" The two men looked affectionately at each other, sharing their ancient secret.

Aunt Tessie stood up suddenly. "I'm going to serve the supper so please, everyone, get up and let's gather at the supper table. Please drink up and leave those glasses here. Everything is perfectly set in the next room, with fresh crystal and more to drink and enjoy. It's the season of Advent and so it's festive in Auntie Tessie's cottage. In a few weeks it'll be Christmas so I have prepared a festive, simple meal like we used to eat as children. There's creamy sauerkraut with chives, and roasted goose with pate stuffing complete with red currants and peaches." Fruit Fly applauded like an excited, little boy when he heard this last and looked excitedly around the room at the others. "There are also potato dumplings, my famous rye bread and there's plenty of butter. Dessert is a surprise, so don't…even…ask!" Everyone applauded and made their way into the cozy library. Candles had already been lit. The French crystal sparkled in the semi-darkened room and everyone sat down eagerly to enjoy the feast.

While they waited for Aunt Tessie to bring the cream of sauerkraut, Shawn carefully opened a bottle of wine. His fingers weren't quite as nimble as when he had first arrived. Proud Mary and Fruit Fly were eyeing Simon who sat somewhat glassy eyed, sporting what might be construed as a shit-eating grin.

Proud Mary asked, "Simon, dear boy, your velvety dark hair and gorgeous eye lashes look Moorish. Where is your family descended from? Zanzibar?"

"They originally came from northern Spain, from a small village which today is a national monument. I mean, the whole village is a national monument." The two older men listened, captivated by Simon's every word. "It's near Santander, a village called Santillana del Mar."

Proud Mary interrupted him. "That's where the famous prehistoric caves are, correct? I visited there once."

"Yes, in Altamira. Very impressive."

"I was there centuries ago! Well, go on, tell us more."

Aunt Tessie appeared with a gaudy silver tray carrying five small, white bowls. As he offered the tray to each guest, he said, "Yes, Simon, do tell us about your origins. We have been wondering and speculating among ourselves earlier." He looked at the two older men, "We are curious about him, aren't we? We want to know where this strapping, young buck with the luxurious black hair and seductive eye lashes is from."

"My mom's side of the family is from Santander and the Basque country. I was always told that the Basques most probably originated from the Vikings who traveled from what is Scotland today, all the way across Europe to the Pyrenees Mountains. My origins are also from the Rioja region in Spain. My dad's side goes way back to Madrid and the Rioja region as well. He was born in Cuba."

Fruit Fly blurted out breathlessly, "Oh, how exotic is that?" He put his hand on Proud Mary's wrist and gushed, "Imagine being from an island in the Caribbean!"

"Yes, my father was born in Havana, right near the bay there. As I say, that side of my family were originally from Spain as well."

"And the Moorish features?" Proud Mary held his hands clasped under his chin as if he were caught in the act of praying in some sacred sanctuary. "I'm seeing those beautiful dark features right now by the glow of this precious light."

Simon blushed at the attention he was receiving and said, "Well, coming from Spain as we do, my features could be mistaken as being from the Moors but I'd say my features are actually more Sephardic, I mean, originating from the Jews of Spain than they are Moorish. I was taught as a boy, that our last name originates from the Hebrew word Zayit before it was Latinized into Zayas. In Hebrew it can mean 'olive' or 'olive branch'." Simon paused and saw that his small audience held on to his words with rapt attention. He continued saying, "In the Book of Genesis, Noah sends the dove out over the flood waters and the dove returns, literally, with a 'zayit in the beak of her', or 'an olive branch in her beak'. It's in the Hebrew text." Simon added proudly, "My father and I did some research when I was a boy and we found some interesting leads about this. For example, we discovered that our last name is already listed in books kept by the Spanish Inquisition in the late 15th century and that some members of the Zayas family fled to the colony in Cuba to escape persecution in Spain."

"Fascinating," was all Proud Mary could manage to whisper hoarsely. He had not blinked throughout Simon's explanation. Then he cleared his throat and said thoughtfully, "Yes, I'm definitely seeing the middle-eastern features of the Jewish people now in the glow of these candles. Those long lashes, oh my. Exquisite." Fruit Fly was busy tasting the cream of sauerkraut. The priest continued, "Yes, it totally explains the dark looks of this robust, virile lad." The three older men agreed as Shawn poured wine and they all toasted Aunt Tessie for the wonderful evening that was still far from over. After they had tasted the wine and the white bowls had been removed, Proud Mary looked at Simon and matter-of-factly said, "I would guess you receive many offers."

Simon looked at him blankly and asked, "Offers?"

"I said I'm sure you receive many offers from your fellow students to have sex." The conversation at table suddenly ceased and Fruit Fly filled his wine glass nervously. Shawn wanted to say something but didn't know what it was and Proud Mary finally said, "Oh come on, girls, let's cut to the chase. This boy is hot and juicy." He looked at Simon and said, "I mean that as a compliment. I'm sure you get plenty of offers to jump in bed, am I right?" Simon was shocked out of his drunkenness by the sheer brashness of Father Reinhart's words. He had not expected such a question. No one at table had either. Simon opened his mouth but didn't know quite how to answer. He sat stunned, looking at the dinner guests, half embarrassed and half pleased to be noticed in such a way.

Aunt Tessie got up and said, "I'll be right back with the goose. Speak up so I can hear from over there. I don't want to miss a word of this conversation."

"You shouldn't be so direct, Mary!" was Fruit Fly's reprimand to Proud Mary. "You're scaring the poor boy."

Proud Mary was sipping slyly from his wine goblet, looking pleased with himself. "Oh, come now, I only voiced what each of you are thinking." When he finished swallowing and wiped his mouth with the damask napkin on his lap, he said in a thunderous, melodramatic voice, looking at the others, "I AM THE VOICE OF YOUR CONSCIENCE! All of you admit to me that you want to know about the sex going on in the student wings of this august abbey."

Fruit Fly spoke up. "Well, I think it's a given that some of those boys are blowing each other. Others are circle jerking to be sure. Some might even be fucking with each other. I mean, it's just been going on since the beginning of time. Get a bunch of boys together and they're gonna have sex. It's nature. Boys are always horny." All of this came out more or less understandable. It was clear to all in attendance that Fruit Fly was quite drunk by now.

"That's my point." Proud Mary appeared lucid for an instant, but of course that was impossible. "Tell us, dear Simon, how you boys play with each other. It's been years since we were in that wing. It was such a happy time." Simon looked nervously at Shawn.

Shawn suddenly spoke up, "Gentlemen…did you guys ever visit the root cellar for anything other than bringing fruit and vegetables in there?"

Aunt Tessie appeared with two porcelain dishes piled high with steaming, dark, tender goose meat. On the side was the stuffing and dumplings "Oh my, I thought nobody knew about the root cellar that way?" He placed a dish in front of Simon and another one in front of Shawn.

"So, it was true, then, for you guys back in your day?" Shawn asked. "Did you guys ever go down there to have sex when you were clerics?"

"It wasn't like that, I mean, not everyone knew about it. Only a few of us, maybe five or so." Aunt Tessie had left the room again and was on the way for two more dishes.

"We would agree to meet down there sometimes," Fruit Fly said. "It was the perfect place. No one ever found out." Proud Mary nodded in agreement, obviously lost in his memories of the root cellar.

Shawn piped up and said, "Well, some of us have gone down there to see the place. It's still a kind of legendary place among a few. I think, however, that it must exist because Wanda is suspicious. Rumor says that she makes the rounds on some late nights down near there, trying to surprise any horny monks with the idea of playing." Then Shawn added sarcastically, "Or maybe on those late nights she's looking for some horny strays." He cleared his throat loudly.

"I see." Proud Mary was looking at Simon.

Shawn persisted, "Rumor also has it that Wanda believes there's more to the root cellar than the average eye beholds. I mean, that it's still an active place for a chosen few." He looked straight at Proud Mary and asked, "Do you believe that?"

"Rumors, rumors, rumors…the old legend of the trap door persists." Proud Mary smiled pensively as he drank greedily from his wine goblet.

Simon suddenly spoke up, "I think it's the perfect place." Proud Mary smiled as he put his thoughts to one side and lowered his goblet. Simon continued confidently, "I think the danger of getting caught down there adds to the adventure and makes it more erotic." Proud Mary raised an eyebrow and looked at Shawn smiling.

Looking from Simon to Proud Mary, Shawn said, "Adventurous lad."

"Indeed!" Proud Mary moved back as Aunt Tessie placed a dish in front of him and the other in front of Fruit Fly.

"It's very hot, so don't touch the dish." Aunt Tessie said as he turned and headed back to the bedroom.

"We managed to play sometimes down there with each other even though things weren't then as they are now." Proud Mary was eating the stuffing of pate, red currants and peaches. "You had to be real careful back then. Today, it's a sexual revolution that's taking place in the world and there's no stopping it. The sexual revolution is growing in America and it's eventually going to embrace the monasteries and convents. You mark my words, there's no withstanding it. I think it's already here in some ways although when it does come fully, there will be a lot of shit to suffer because of the closeted ones among us. They'll fight it tooth and nail and heads will roll. Trust me, HEADS WILL ROLL."

Aunt Tessie had returned and reminded them, "Now don't touch the dish, it's very hot."

Proud Mary disregarded the warning and continued, "A scheisskopf like Wanda and all the other closeted queens will wave the banner of morals, chastity and vows in our faces ad nauseam. Hypocrites like that Master of Postulants who wrestles with the pretty boys and is ready to instigate a witch hunt at the drop of a hat will lead the crusade. Bastards, they are! All of them!

Closeted hypocrites! A lot of talented, beautiful men will be destroyed because of their homophobia and cowardice."

Shawn and Simon stared at Proud Mary. Simon was impressed with the older man's honest assessment. Simon asked him, "Do you really think monks in formation will be dismissed from the abbey because of sex? I mean, if what you're saying is true about the sexual revolution, won't the superiors at the top eventually realize that there's no stopping it as you just said? I would think that it would open people up and the Church might even reconsider the celibacy question."

"Ha!" Proud Mary shouted. "You are very naïve dear boy. You are very cute but very naïve. It will never happen, not for us homosexuals. The Church will never admit to our presence even though I suspect we gays are in the majority and our numbers always have been. Much less will there be an open acceptance of sex among us. The hypocrisy is too great. There's too much arrogance in the Church to be honest about such a fundamental thing as sexual orientation and sexual expression. Hubris blinds the really mean queens who make the rules and dish out cruel punishments. It's always been that way and it will always be. Centuries of stupid fear and prejudice have sealed it."

Simon persisted, asking, "Don't you believe that things could change?" Simon looked at Shawn who lifted his wine goblet and drank. "Don't you believe that?"

"No, I don't. Not now, anyway." He quieted and added sadly, "Maybe a few years ago I believed things could change. I wanted them to change so badly, but then…" Proud Mary went silent. Finally, he managed to say, "A few years ago, not many, we had a case here in the abbey that proves my point perfectly."

"Brother Cas." Fruit Fly said sadly. "Our brother, Casimir."

"It was a hideous event here, under our roof, that was hushed up by the Abbot and his council but finally blew wide open when it hit the papers." Aunt Tessie said, finishing up the last of the dumplings, red currants and peaches on his plate. He sounded angry as he mumbled with a mouth full of food, eager to say, "Talk about hubris! It never should have happened." Proud Mary took a drink of his wine and set his goblet down gently, lost in his thoughts. Aunt Tessie continued, "Casimir, or Cas as we called him, was such a beautiful, gentle man. He was built like a brick shit house and had to have been seven feet tall. He was large, of good German stock."

"More like a lumberjack, with his thick, black beard." Fruit Fly touched his own chin lightly as if he wore such a beard. "He was so good. It never should have happened but it does prove what you're saying, Mary."

Simon asked, "What happened? Who was Brother Casimir?"

"Casimir," Proud Mary said, "was from a small town near Leicester. His parents were staunch German Catholics, exceedingly proud of him because he was preparing for the priesthood here in the abbey. Every Sunday they came to visit him in a beat up, old station wagon and brought all nine siblings. Then something awful happened…" Proud Mary's eyes misted and his voice quivered. There was momentarily no strength nor haughtiness left in his voice, as he trailed off. Simon stared at him, wondering what had happened to Brother Casimir that had had this effect on the usually boisterous monk. When he composed himself, Proud Mary continued. "One day he was denied further studies for the priesthood because of his alleged homosexuality. The powers at be made it a point to say that he was being demoted to the status of 'lay brother' because of what he had done. They only gave him this option because he was in Solemn Vows. The only other option was to leave the abbey altogether. Back in those days you didn't get the option of being sent to 'Bad Girl's School' like they do now, with all those shrinks and counselors. In any case, it crushed him terribly and I remember him saying to me that he didn't know what he would say to his family. For the moment, it was all hushed up and swept under the rug. I guess they hoped it would go away."

Simon interrupted, "How was he found out to be gay?"

"Casimir was the kind of person who fell in love easily. He had met a man in town who was married to a woman who was a judge, a very prominent Catholic judge in this county, I might add. The man was closeted but that didn't keep him from having an affair with Casimir. Then, the wife began to suspect something. She thought it was another woman. It was all very classic like a fucking novel."

Fruit Fly said, "Oh, yes, she dug around and had private detectives on the lookout who finally unraveled the mystery for her. 'Not another woman', they said to the judge, 'but a man, a monk no less'."

Proud Mary continued, "The wife confronted her husband who of course, denied the entire thing but it was too late. The detectives had done their job and the Abbot was called. Everything pointed to the fact that Casimir was guilty and he would have to take the fall. It was never considered that the judge's husband should appear guilty because it would ruin his wife's political career. Their lawyer was very keen on pointing out to the Abbot and his council how the judge could affect the abbey's future both positively and negatively, depending on the outcome of the scandalous situation. The Abbot asked the detective and the judge to keep a lid on it and for a few days it was handled quietly. But then it leaked. It was believed that it must have been a detective getting greedy and trying to sell the story to one of the tabloids. It blew wide open. It got very messy."

Fruit Fly sat on the edge of his seat and gesticulated nervously as he relived the events. "When it leaked that it was a homosexual scandal involving a monk and a married man, people came out of the woodwork to falsely say that Cas had molested them as adolescents when he taught at the school in town. He was no pedophile, I know that for a fact because we were very close. He wasn't a predator, never had been and never would be. He was just a healthy, sane man who fell in love with another man. He would have been a gentle, understanding priest if they had given him the chance. But instead, it was all about money and retribution, greedy bastards. Everything changed then. It wasn't just the scandal involving the judge's husband now but something much bigger. It turned real ugly when all those people started crying about their supposed 'molestations'. Isn't that true, Mary?"

"Yes, it got out of hand and the Abbot didn't know what to do. Lawyers were called and he waited several days, hoping that it would die down or somehow be worked out quietly. Then the accusations hit the papers in Leicester and surrounding towns of the county. Finally, the story went national. It was in many papers and on the evening news. The supposed victims of child molestation and their lawyers were suing the abbey for millions of dollars."

Aunt Tessie got up and started to clear the table and said, "I told Edmund and Demetrius to watch Casimir and to never leave him alone. The fact that he had been demoted and not allowed to pursue studies for the priesthood had hurt him terribly. He wasn't the same after that. You'd see a strong, big man when you looked at him, but inside he was a soul filled with shame and self-loathing. He was shattered inside. The look in his eyes was nothing but pure sadness, fear and shame. He looked like a poor animal caught in a wretched trap. When the scandal hit I was afraid for him. I was afraid for his safety."

Proud Mary said, "I spoke to the Abbot myself and told Edmund to get him help. I also told Demetrius who had just been appointed Prior of the abbey not to leave him alone." Proud Mary closed his eyes and paused. Then he said, "I told them that I was afraid he would hurt himself and do something stupid. The tension here inside the abbey was awful even though the Abbot and his council tried to keep it under control. Reporters came and the story kept getting bigger. The council was concerned about the millions of dollars in damages they would be expected to pay. The Abbot worried if the abbey would ultimately be reduced to shutting down because of it. He had every reason to be concerned. Those people and their lawyers acted like ravenous sharks." Proud Mary looked up, "Casimir was under terrible pressure. During that time, I continued to warn Edmund and Demetrius and other monks again and again, but no one did anything. They were all so fucking concerned about what would happen to their precious abbey that they didn't stop to think about what was going on inside Casimir." He simply stopped speaking and the small room went silent. The only sounds were the clinking of silver and plates as Aunt Tessie cleared the table. Shawn went into the other room and returned with a bottle of Spanish brandy. He filled snifters with the dark brown liquid and then sat down. The fire had stopped crackling in the sitting room. Everything had become deathly silent and there was a chill in the room. No one got up to replenish the firewood nor light a new fire.

Simon drank the brandy and felt it burn in his throat as he swallowed. It warmed him and gave him comfort as he listened to the awful tale. Proud Mary looked at his own hands spread out in front of him on the table. Aunt Tessie returned and sat down. He took a small sip of his brandy and swallowed slowly, then, Aunt Tessie said, "It was all so terrible and needless. It was so cruel and unfair. Just because he was queer like us. That was his crime."

"Yes, that's the long and short of it." Proud Mary was speaking now. "Casimir suddenly disappeared from the abbey. No one knew where he had gone. The Abbot went to Casimir's family home but he wasn't there. Others thought he had run away with the judge's husband but that proved to be false as well. As the first days passed, the tension grew and no one had a clue as to his whereabouts. The police were alerted and a search began. Several more days came and went. And then they found him…"

The three older monks drank their brandy in silence and Shawn glanced over at Simon who glanced back but said nothing. Aunt Tessie got up and disappeared into the bedroom without saying a word.

Proud Mary said gravely, "A monk had gone down into the crypt. It was the morning of the monthly Mass for the Dead of the abbey. Very early that morning he had climbed the steps above the prince-bishop's tomb to dress the altar and get it ready for the Requiem. It was early but the sun was already streaming in through the blue and purple glass windows of the bell tower. When the monk reached the altar, that's when he saw the mess." Proud Mary stopped and took a drink. He swallowed and finally sighed softly, saying, "The top of the altar was splattered and dripping with urine, feces and muck. Some of it had already dried. It apparently had been there for several days. They say the stench was horrific. The monk stared at the appalling mess on the altar and then instinctively looked up. And there was Cas, way up in the tower, hanging lifeless and bloated, with a thick rope tightly bound around his neck. Before killing himself, he had stripped naked and dressed himself only in red priestly vestments, the color of martyrs in the liturgy. It would be the only time he would vest completely like a priest ready to offer the Sacrifice, with chasuble, stole and maniple. When they took him down they said that rigor mortis was so prominent that they had to break his fingers to remove the crimpled, linen, maniturgium he still held on to. On his ordination day, he would have given it to his mother after his consecration." Proud Mary shook his head slowly and wistfully admitted, "They fucked him over. They all did. Poor Cas. They drove him to that rope in the tower. And his crime was that he loved a man."

Fruit Fly nodded his head in agreement and put his hand on Proud Mary's shoulder. "Hypocrites. They did drive him to it. You both warned them about how fragile he was."

Proud Mary agreed. "They didn't give one fuck about him, damn hypocrites. It was just like what they did to Oscar Wilde almost a century before. They fucked them over and they were dead men way too young to die in such shame." He wiped his eyes and said, "Wilde said it best in his letter to George Ives when Wilde got out of prison for his crime of 'indecency'. He wrote, 'I have no doubt we shall win, but the road is long and red with monstrous martyrdoms.' Poor Casimir died a monstrous martyrdom on that very road."

"Yes, he did." Simon whispered faintly to himself. He was beginning to know only too well the same fear and dread that Casimir had experienced. After all, Simon realized he was one of them. He felt that he was coming to understand all about that long and red road and it felt devastating.

Chapter Ten
Coming of Age

"Where should I go?"-Alice
"That depends on where you want to end up."-The Cheshire Cat
Lewis Carroll

When very late into the night, they finally left Aunt Tessie's rooms and the door had been shut, Shawn and Simon schlepped down the narrow, winding corridor in a zigzag kind of way, each supporting the weight of the other. Shawn put his arm on Simon's shoulder and asked, "Did you have a good time, little one?"

"Oh, yeah. I never could have imagined that experience here, at the abbey. It was incredible!" Then Simon added, "It was very sad, though, what Proud Mary and the others recalled about Brother Casimir. I don't think I'll ever forget that when I visit the crypt in the future." Shawn didn't say anything. Simon continued to ramble, "I think I ate too much. Did you notice that no one said much when we had dessert? I felt bad for Aunt Tessie after all the trouble she went through making all that fancy stuff for dessert."

Shawn held Simon up as they walked slowly down the corridor and said, "Yeah, the party atmosphere went to shit there at the end. Still, it was a great night."

"Oh, yeah, yeah. It really was." Simon felt his legs giving out on him as he leaned more on Shawn, saying, "I drank way too much but I sure do love that Jack Daniel's. I'm gonna sleep like a rock." They walked down toward Simon's wing and stopped at the stairway that lead to that floor. Simon turned and said, "Well, I'll see you tomorrow. Goodnight. I need to get to bed. My legs are ready to fold like a cheap card table."

Shawn didn't let go of Simon's arm and said, "Proud Mary really set her eyes on you tonight. Hell, the three of them did."

"Oh, stop!"

"You know it's true." Then Shawn tugged on Simon's arm and put it around his own neck, as he began to walk ahead. "Walk with me a little further." Simon didn't say anything as he leaned more into Shawn who supported him as they walked in the shadows. He was beyond tipsy and swayed as he walked. Shawn continued, "You know damn well, Simon, that Proud Mary got all wet for you tonight. So did Fruit Fly and Tessie." Then he got closer to Simon and added, "You do look nice tonight. Like you heard a couple of times, you look good enough to eat, except for those hideous shoes. Come with me a sec, I want to show you something."

Simon stopped and protested, "It's late. I think I need to get to bed. Plus, I'm very drunk. How am I gonna get up tomorrow for Mass?"

Shawn got him walking again, whispering, "It'll only take a sec. C'mon, you'll love what I'm gonna show you."

"No, really, I need to crash."

"I think the Carabinieri boots will fit you perfectly. Wanna try them on right now?"

Simon was dying to try those boots on ever since Shawn had told him about them. "Where are the boots?"

"In my room."

"I'm not allowed on that wing. You know that."

"It's one in the morning. Nobody's gonna be wandering around. And if they are they sure as hell don't want to be seen either, so there's no danger."

Simon thought about that as best he could and said, "Okay. I really wanna try those boots on." Shawn smiled.

They walked to the corridor of the student monks preparing for the diaconate. Simon had no idea which one of the endless doors was the entrance to Shawn's room. Shawn almost carried him now as they walked in silence and finally opened a door at the far end of the corridor. He stepped back and whispered to Simon, "Welcome to my castle and my keep." Simon entered, again walking zigzag and Shawn followed him in. He turned on the lights and shut the door gently behind them.

Simon saw that Shawn's cell was bigger than his own but furnished with exactly the same furniture except for a wide armoire that sat next to his desk. The desk was piled high with text books and papers. To one side was an electric typewriter. Shawn had few personal possessions on the walls. He sat Simon on the edge of his bed and opened the wardrobe closet. To one side were interior shelves and to the other Simon saw the man's collection of clothes hanging neatly. Shawn took out a bottle of dark colored liquid from one of the shelves of the closet.

He poured some into two glasses that were nearby and handed one to Simon who didn't protest but took a drink and after he swallowed, smiled and said sleepily, "Damn, I recognize this!"

"Yep! It's Jack Daniel's. See how I'm teaching you, little one, and broadening your world! Before tonight, you were incapable of identifying it. Now you know. You're gaining experience." Then he added, "Stick with me, baby, and you'll go places." He clinked his glass with Simon's and said, "Cheers!" Simon, with heavy lidded eyes, held his glass up and took another swig. Shawn also took a drink and then turned around and pulled two, sleek black leather boots out of the closet. Simon's eyes grew wide when he saw them. "Here they are, just as I promised. I like to keep them shined to a high gloss."

Simon was enthralled and said, "Wow! They're over-the-top incredible!"

"Well, don't just stand there. Try them on, silly."

Simon put his glass down on the small bedside table and took the boots in his hands. The leather was supple to the touch. "Damn, they're so soft." He sat on the edge of the bed and removed his battered black shoes. He angled his foot into the first boot but wasn't able to coordinate himself too well.

Shawn knelt in front of him and said, "These boots fit well below the knees of the Carabinieri but from the photographs I've seen of those guys, they're really tall. They'll still fit guys like you and me, though, but they'll reach up a bit closer to our knees."

Simon tried in vain to slip his left foot into the slender boot. "I think my jeans are getting stuck. What kind of pants do those guys wear?"

"Not sure but I know they don't wear jeans. The denim is too thick. Your leg won't go in and your foot gets stuck midway." Shawn pulled the boot away and looked at Simon and said, "You're going to have to take your jeans off if you want to try on the boots. Here, I'll help you."

He reached for Simon's belt buckle to undo it but Simon pushed his eager hand away rudely. "What are you doing?"

"I'm helping you. I can see the Jack Daniel's is making you clumsy."

"I'm good. I can undo my own belt." Simon struggled with the buckle and finally got it unhooked. He undid the top metal button of his jeans and the next four buttons on the fly. Shawn saw that Simon was wearing white underwear briefs. Without saying a word, he took the boot in Simon's hand and set it aside. He pushed Simon back on the bed and he fell easily on his back, protesting, "Hey!"

"Oh, don't belly ache so damn much!" Shawn then took the edges of Simon's pants legs and pulled them off easily in one, short tug. His socks had come off as well. "There you go, mister boney feet and hairy legs, try the boots on now. I'll betcha your feet and legs will slide in easily."

Simon sat up and took the boot Shawn handed him. His foot slid in all the way to just below his knee. Simon suddenly felt erotically charged and feeling the impeccable boot grazing on his skin electrified him. He took the other boot and slid it on. He looked down at himself and felt that wearing the boots had made something click in him. Instead of just being magical he felt it was something else that had suddenly and powerfully taken hold of him. His feet felt comfortably snug against the leather interiors and he wondered for a brief second about the towering Italian officer who had worn them. He was aware that the boots had aroused him and that he was easily on the way to getting erect. He looked at Shawn who was kneeling on one knee in front of him and asked, "What do you think? Is it me?"

"Are you kidding me, little one? You were born to wear these. You can have them. They're yours."

Simon looked up like a little boy on Christmas morning near the base of the tree. "What! Are you serious? Tell me you're serious!"

"Okay, I'm serious. The boots are yours!"

Shawn stood up and Simon sprang off the bed. He extended his arms and hugged Shawn tightly. "Thank you! Wow, I can't believe you just gave me these boots. You're crazy. Tomorrow you're going to want them back but it'll be too late!" Simon was walking exaggeratedly in place, barely able to contain his glee.

Shawn smiled, well pleased with himself, mirroring the effect his gift had on Simon. "Stand up and walk around. Let me see you from behind. I wanna see how you walk in the boots."

Simon was in his element now, enjoying the adulation that the other man was all too happy to shower on him. He strutted jokingly away from him and across the ample room in his underwear, then returned with his hands firmly planted on his hips, swinging slightly from side to side, as he said roughly, "Hey, carissimo, what're you looking at? I'm the man here! I'm the officer with the Italian boots on!"

"You sure are! Turn around for me." As soon as Simon did so, Shawn pressed himself against Simon's back, wanting him to feel his own arousal. He wrapped his arms around Simon at his chest and whispered in his ear, "You make me so happy when you're like this. You're incredible when your heart is soaring and you're your real self." Then he reached down quickly and cupped the front of Simon's briefs, massaging him there.

Simon pushed Shawn's hand away just as quickly, mumbling, "No, please stop. You shouldn't do that." A wave of guilt came over him. "C'mon, please stop." Simon's shame grew because he couldn't keep his body from responding to the man's insistent touch.

Shawn lifted his hand for an instant and then slid it into Simon's underwear. He moved his hand at will. He could feel Simon's heart beating wildly in what he now held in the palm of his hand. "Don't fight it, baby, just let go."

"It's wrong. We're breaking the vow of chastity!"

Shawn tightened his grip on Simon and barked angrily, "Oh, stop it, Simon. Stop the bullshit. Grow up! What makes you think you're so damned special and elite? You're just like anybody else!"

Simon thrashed against his captor and cried back, "It's wrong, dammit! I've been strong all this time. Stop! We're not supposed to do this."

"This is what we do, little boy. Get over yourself and your fantasy! I hate to burst your bubble, but we're just men. I have needs and so do you." He began to knead Simon, saying, "You know you want this." He moved his hand expertly within Simon's briefs and felt Simon give in completely to him. Then he pulled on Simon's underwear and they slid and fell easily, resting on the rigid edges of the shiny black boots.

Shawn again reached for Simon and caressed him as before, only now he increased his stimulation. It wasn't long before Simon shuddered and a barely audible splattering was heard on the worn, wooden floor. He was breathing heavily as Shawn kissed him on the side of his neck and asked, "There you go, beautiful boy. Don't tell me that it didn't feel good. Did you enjoy that as much as I did?"

Simon caught his breath as he wiped away what was dribbling onto the shiny boots below. He reached for his underwear and awkwardly pulled them up, covering himself. He felt vulnerable in his nakedness and because he was completely spent, he felt weakened. He shook his head in defeat and managed to say, "Dammit Shawn, I swear…"

"C'mon, Simon, don't you remember what I told you long ago and why I was so keen on protecting you from Toby?" Simon tensed in his arms but said nothing. Shawn turned him around and faced him, putting his hands on his shoulders. Simon stared, listening to him. "It isn't the sex that's the problem, little one." He reached down and tugged playfully on the spot where Simon's underwear had become significantly damp. "Love. You won't have to worry about that with me. It won't ever happen."

+ + + + +

Mark had finished working on the first tattoo of the pink triangles. He wheeled his stool away from the worktable as he removed his gloves and said, "That Shawn character never ceases to amaze me. What a cynical motherfucker." Then he added, "All done here, Simon, go ahead and take a look."

Simon got up off the table and walked to the mirror. The bright pink triangle imprinted on his chest looked as if it were actually a piece of cloth sewn on him. "Damn, Mark, that looks terrific."

"I'm glad you like it. It was a great idea you had to add those small stitch-like markings to the edge. I like the way it turned out."

Simon suddenly said, "Hey wait! Something's missing."

Mark, still sitting on the stool, wheeled himself over to the mirror and examined Simon's chest closely. "What's missing? It looks finished to me."

"My prisoner number, man! My number! 1281956."

"Oh, fuck, you're right!" Mark got up and picked up the strip of paper, reading the inch-long numbers printed there, "1281956. Damn, buddy, I forgot about the numbers. Get your ass over on this table again and let's knock it out. It won't take too long." He sat on his stool and prepared the tattoo gun. "Black ink, correct?"

"Yeah, I'd think so. Or what?"

"Yeah, yeah, black ink."

"Okay. You're the expert."

Mark winked at Simon. "So tell me what happened after that night in Aunt Flossie's lair."

"Aunt Tessie."

"Yeah, whatever. I guess I'm curious. You held back for so long and kept your pecker in your pants but then that Shawn guy jumped you. After all that happened, did you retreat within yourself again?"

Simon thought about Mark's question. "Several things happened after that night that affected me in the path I took."

Mark was applying the purple stencil with the numbers on it. "Tell me about it."

"The late 1970s brought what Father Reinhart had said it would. The sexual revolution that had swept through every corner of America in the late sixties and seventies came rushing in like a determined wave at high tide, unstoppable. It crashed upon the abbey, making its way everywhere. It filtered into every nook and cranny of the old abbey and in particular, it found fertile ground in the seminary wing and in us that lived there." Simon thought about what he had said and added, "The Stonewall Riots in 1969 began as a rebellion against sex laws in the City of New York but certainly became much more than that in a very short time. The gay rebellion that sparked in New York City on that particular night was repeated over and over again in various forms throughout America. At the abbey we rebelled as well in our own way."

Mark worked as he said, "Sounds like you boys were becoming men and taking control of yourselves."

"Yes, that's exactly what happened except that we were enclosed in an abbey where there were strict rules to follow. It would have been naïve to think that somehow those who lived behind the fortified walls of the abbey would be exempt and unaffected by the sexual revolution of the time. Yet, that is exactly what some of the monks in authority wished to believe. Their denial of reality proved disastrous and painful for many of us in their care. What made it awful was that many of those men who persecuted us with a vengeance were closeted gay men. It was a vicious attack and heads did indeed roll."

Mark looked up. "You gay guys got bashed by dudes that were queer as well?" It was more a statement than a question. Mark shook his head slowly from side to side, expressing disbelief.

"Yeah, it was pretty bad. But that happened after a whole lot of stuff. First came the rebellion and sexual liberation. We were crazy and got pretty wild as the sexual revolution made its way among us who were fully awakening to the fact that we were gay. The straight guys didn't make any noise as I recall."

"There were straight guys in that place?" Mark asked sarcastically.

Simon returned Mark's sarcasm with a bit of his own, "Hell, I guess so, maybe one or two or possibly three!" They both chuckled. "I didn't really think about the straight guys. The sexual revolution had many facets but the one I experienced was the gay revolution. It brought us liberation but also defiance. We got very bold and in our struggle to break free we did outrageous stuff that would change the course of our lives forever."

After a pause, Simon continued, "I already told you that I had had a sexual awakening in the forest. It's what led me to have a sexual relationship with Toby. When I decided to stop being sexually active, I still kept maturing as a man." Simon stopped and thought, then said, "I guess what I mean is that I was still waking sexually. The stuff I did sexually with Toby scared me, especially after I lost my virginity with him. It threw me into a spiral of confusion that made me hide within myself. I can see clearly now how naïve it was of me to think that I could just cancel my sexual nature as a man. Little by little, as the sexual revolution grew in the seminary, I began to search for myself with a newfound brashness I had not been aware of before. I could see that this was happening to other guys around me. The fear we experienced before gave way to a very real shameless boldness. Anyway, that's what happened to me. It's the best way I can explain it." Simon remembered that time in his life with great clarity. "Therefore, it didn't take me long to know that I wasn't alone. I quickly learned that many of my companions were struggling with their sexuality just like me." Then he said, "I began to see Brother Anton's need for rub-downs every evening, for what it was, without making excuses." He paused and added, "I suppose that now, looking back, I can understand better what Shawn was trying to teach me, even though I realize he had his own, personal agenda."

Mark was concentrating on his work but asked, "Dude, c'mon, you didn't always know that old guy Anton was getting his rocks off by having a younger dude touch him every night?"

"I swear, man, it hadn't occurred to me. Or let me put it this way, I guess I hadn't wanted to see it. But as time moved on, it became clearer to me."

"So how did it happen?"

"Well, nobody said the word 'gay' or 'queer'. It wasn't really that anyone approached the subject openly at first. A kind of homoerotic undertow was silently unleashed. A kind of current among us began to stir. When did it start? Who started it? No one will ever know. It just sort of did and took off and it was so damn liberating." Simon remembered one of his companions, Thomas. "One guy, Tommy, cut out two or three small photographs from magazines of these really hunky, hot guys. One was in shorts and the others in bathing suits. It wasn't pornographic or anything but the guys in the pictures were shirtless and grinning suggestively. He had framed the photographs and boldly hung them on the wall in his cell."

"The Master of Clerics came into his cell one day and demanded to know who it was in the photographs."

"They're my brother and cousins," Tommy had said boldly.

The priest examined the photographs and said sternly, "They don't look like you nor like one another. I'm not seeing a family resemblance." Tommy had told me the story laughing to himself. He said he had enjoyed looking Wanda in the eyes and repeating, "Yeah, those are all 'Family'."

"Things like those happened more and more. Another guy had a life-sized poster of Andy Gibb on the back of his cell door. He enjoyed showing it off and said he loved seeing the youngest brother of the Bee Gee's looking directly at him when he woke up in the morning every day. He'd say, 'That hairy chest with the gold chains gets me so hard.' It was kinda like the famous Farrah Fawcett poster for straight guys." Mark looked up and winked at Simon but said nothing. "Comments like that became natural among some of us and the shame that had previously clouded our sexuality was gone and rebellion took its place. It was the birth of a new 'normal' for many of us."

"When we weren't obliged to wear our habits during study time, recreation or meals in hot weather, many of us wore torn up, faded cut-offs and t-shirts. It was not uncommon for many of the monks to wear trousers and shirts to the refectory during the warm summer months at that time. A lot of the observances from before had been relaxed, but many of us wore cut-offs and tees instead of trousers and shirts."

Mark said, "So what's the big deal with you guys wearing shorts? Everybody wears shorts."

"The cut-offs we wore were ridiculously short and worn out. So short that a lot of times our balls slipped out." Simon smiled to himself, remembering. "I guess that's why we wore them that way."

"Oh?"

"It's like I said, the homoerotic undertow just got stronger and stronger. We started using feminine pronouns openly, in our daily conversations. It got to be commonplace to hear guys talking about fellow monks that way. 'What did SHE say?' or 'Look at HER now!' Before it had been guarded and whispered. Now it was in the open. And then there was the routine of dressing up like nuns."

"Nuns?" Mark's tone registered amusement as he worked.

"Yeah, nuns. Two in particular put on a private show for a few of us as a kind of entertainment whenever there were clandestine parties going on in some parts of the abbey."

Mark raised an inquisitive eyebrow and asked again, "Nuns?"

"Yeah, I know it sounds fucked up."

Mark laughed softly and said, "Did you say, 'fucked up'? Gee, that word hadn't crossed my mind!" Then he added, "Yeah, dude, that sounds totally fucked up!"

"Well, it sounds totally fucked up because it was. I was invited several times with Tony and Noey. Tony would come get us and say, 'There's drinks in Arnold's rooms, plus she's putting on a show with Shawn'."

Marked looked up, "Hang on, wasn't that Arnold dude the one you couldn't stomach in the novitiate and the one you trashed in Aunt Flossie's hideaway?"

Simon smiled, "It's Aunt Tessie, man, not Flossie."

"Whatever, you knew who I meant. So now you were amused by Arnold?"

"I still thought he was a fake and a real manipulator but the guy was offering free drinks. We rarely got drinks in the abbey. Hell, after a few of those, I'd see him in a different light. He was still a buffoon, but the drinks took the edge off, know what I mean?"

"Gotcha." Mark was busy working again. "Go ahead."

"Well, we'd get over there and Arnold would put drinks in our hands and say, 'Sit down.' Then he would disappear and finally reappear out of his bedroom dressed as a nun in full traditional habit and say, 'Lock…the door.' He had this way of moving his right index finger as he said it, imitating a nun.

He'd move his finger in a circle, clockwise, as he slowly began the celebrated phrase and said the word, 'Lock…' Then he'd move his finger back in a circle, but counter-clockwise, simulating a mechanism, finishing the phrase, '…the door'. It would get us giggling which I suppose was his intention. He'd strut around the room in his pronounced limp, with his dopey blond head held stiffly beneath a veil and starched linen, announcing in a high-pitched voice, 'Franciscan Sisters from Peeksville', and then he'd return in another habit and still others, saying, 'Sisters of Saint Joseph from Philadelphia' and 'Dominican Sisters from Adrian' or 'Sisters of Mercy from…' etc. He had a whole trunk full of nun's habits. Shawn would also use this same dialogue and mannerisms, dressing up in other nun's habits, replenishing our drinks constantly."

Mark arched his eyebrow. "Fuck me."

"The three of us would sit there, drinking and laughing our asses off. It all became the way we lived. Without establishing a committee to study it, nor agreeing as a body to discuss it, a sizeable number of us began to confide in each other that we were gay. In a short span of time a lot of us had come out this way to each other. I came out to Shane first. Remember I told you he was from a rural, small town and that I had come to think of him as being trustworthy. Anyway, I asked to meet him in a tiny chapel. I was deathly frightened about what I had to say to him but I still managed to confide my secret in him. To my delight, he felt his own burden lifted from him in having the same opportunity to confide his own same secret. We cried like babies and hugged each other in that tiny place, in front of a tiny altar that had an image of the Sacred Heart of Jesus over it. A great weight of guilt and sorrow was lifted from each of us in our confession. I can still remember it with so much clarity. Anyway, these scenes were repeated among us and took place in the greatest secrecy. A strong bond was established between those of us who were willing to participate and a new brotherhood emerged within the existing religious brotherhood of the abbey."

"It wasn't per se a completely public coming out, but enough so that we lived openly with each other. A closely bonded group emerged. Fear and self-loathing were greatly replaced with confidence and we became, as I've said, very bold. Looking back now I'd say that sometimes we were bold to the point of being stupid. But I'll explain that later. We were young and inexperienced and the freedom we breathed was like nothing we had ever experienced before. This is how we participated personally in the sexual revolution within the abbey and why it took root so strongly. We were twenty or so." Simon closed his eyes and remembered it all so clearly as he stopped speaking to the tattooer. He remembered the night it was taken to a different level. On that night an elite group was established within the new brotherhood.

+ + + + +

Shawn had walked up to him in the cavernous library as Simon read and wrote behind a pile of open books. He barely saw him when he heard him say, "My, my, so serious. You look so studious, little one." Then he whispered, "Tonight, in the root cellar. Be there!"

There was no need to ask where it was or why he was being invited. Simon nonetheless asked him, "What?"

"Midnight. In the secret chamber. You know what it is." Then he added, "It was briefly mentioned that night at Aunt Tessie's."

Simon asked, "The secret chamber?"

Shawn whispered, "Yeah, it's the small, backroom, beyond the root cellar. Very few know it's even there. There's the first, big room and then a smaller one off to the side. Remember, you told me you had seen it once. Go in there. There's a place in the far, back wall that actually has a small trap door that's well hidden. Wait in there against the wall until you're told what to do next. Let your eyes adjust to the darkness and you'll see what I mean. Once you see the signal, crawl in through the trap door near the floor. We'll be back there. It's a safe place. Wanda doesn't know where it is exactly."

A little past midnight, Simon quietly left his cell for the root cellar as per Shawn's instructions. He nervously entered the darkness of the main root cellar and proceeded into the yet darker second, smaller room. He was aware of others standing against the walls because he heard muted sniffles and nervous coughs. Then someone cleared his throat softly. Simon said nothing and waited in the darkness for his eyes to adjust as he had been told. When his eyes finally adjusted, he saw two others standing not far from him. He was edgy beyond words and his heart was pounding loudly in his ears. He was jittery thinking about what was going to happen and his arousal was overwhelming.

The trap door Shawn had mentioned opened up. It was very small and barely made a creaking sound as it moved on rusty hinges. It was near the dirt floor. Beyond it's opening, Simon could see a dim light inside. Now he understood about the secret chamber.

"Okay, gentlemen…" Simon recognized Shawn's whisper in the darkness. "Get your horny asses in here." Simon recognized Noah in the shadows, as he moved in through the opening and crawled into the space beyond the trap door. Someone else followed him. Simon was the last one to crawl through. The trap door was securely latched behind him and Shawn was careful to hang a heavy piece of carpet in front of it.

He saw Simon observing him and he said, "That way we are sure no light leaks out." Shawn was completely naked.

Simon looked around him. The space was actually not very small and was a kind of box made of heavy, rough planks of wood. It smelled very musky in there but wasn't unpleasant. The floor was packed earth and the walls went up about four feet. Blankets were spread out so that no one touched the dirt and the only light source in the chamber was a single burning candle. Joshua was there but still dressed and there were two other students that Simon recognized but didn't really know.

Shawn spoke up, "Welcome, little ones." Some of them looked nervously at each other and then at Shawn. Some murmured a word or two in response. "We're down here to have a good time. Feel free to do whatever feels good. The idea is to have a good time. I've picked each of you out because I think I know you enough to know that you can handle this." He looked at each of them and added, "In fact, I know you can. That's why you're here." Then he said, "Some of you have been down here before so you know the drill. Don't be nervous but if you are, I have some libations here and you're welcomed to have as much as you want." He gestured to an opened crate containing several bottles of alcohol. "Okay, guys, have some drinks, introduce yourselves if you don't know each other and get naked. We don't have all night. Remember to keep your voices down. Other than that, we are safe." He smiled at each of them and then said, "Tonight we are seven. Let the games begin!"

The first few minutes were awkward at the very least. Shawn opened a couple of bottles. There were no glasses so the bottles were simply passed around. Everyone took a drink and in little time everyone got naked.

Shawn paired off with one of the guys Simon didn't know very well. Two guys joined Noah. From the moment he had entered the secret chamber, Simon was sitting next to Joshua. For many months, Simon had noticed Joshua among the newer students. He found him attractive but had never really gotten to know him. Now he was sitting completely naked next to him.

Joshua reached over to Simon and put his hand on Simon's thigh. He moved in closer to him and said, "I've had my eye on you for a long time." To say that a billion butterflies took flight within Simon's stomach would have been a gross understatement. Simon and Joshua crossed paths that night and momentarily forgot everyone else around them. Both of them were smitten with each other. They moved in closer together and lost themselves in each other's gaze.

Everyone lost track of time and the orgy lasted as long as the candle in the secret chamber burned. The seven men had mixed well as a group. Shawn passed a bottle around and said, "Okay, guys, I can see we all had a great time together. Unfortunately, it's time to go so get dressed. I'll let you know when we meet again. It won't be soon because we need to be careful but it will happen again. Remember that this is an elite group tonight. Do not discuss this with anyone." With that, everyone dressed and left the root cellar.

The next day, Shawn met Simon after supper. "Let's take a little walk before Vespers." It was almost spring and the snow was melting everywhere. Winter was finally over and the air was sweet and fresh with the promise of beautiful days ahead. When they were at a safe distance from the others, Shawn asked, "So how did you like our little gathering last night?"

"I don't think I can sum it up easily. I had no idea the root cellar thing actually existed. I thought Proud Mary had made it up and the others were teasing us. I've never done anything like that before."

"No, I wouldn't think so."

"But I loved it!" As soon as Simon said it he realized how free he felt. He was aware that he didn't feel guilty in his newfound freedom. "Thank you for inviting me."

"I'm happy to see you enjoyed yourself. Did you get to play with everyone?"

"Most everyone, yes. I didn't really know Aaron and Kurt." Then he added, "Nor Joshua."

"But you do now." Shawn was looking at Simon.

"Oh, I sure do now! Thanks to you." Simon looked at Shawn and asked, "What are you thinking?"

"What do you mean, little one?"

"You're looking at me funny. What are you thinking?"

"I'm thinking that I hope you now understand and believe what I've always said to you. I've always promised that I'll be there for you and take care of things for you." They walked on. A couple of monks passed them and they waved, appearing to want to get closer and say something but Shawn quickened his pace and they continued on. "I want you to know those things. I don't want you to get confused anymore."

Simon looked at Shawn and said, "I'm not a baby, you know. I'm not some stupid adolescent."

"I know that. I'm not saying that, I just want you to know that I'm always here for you." Then he said, "You're not a stupid anything. You're smart and you show great promise, but let's admit it, you lack experience. That's all I'm saying and it's an easy fix." Simon looked down as they walked and said nothing. Shawn continued, "All I'm saying is that sometimes you get muddled…" He hesitated and said, "You're a romantic soul, Simon. I think it's a safe assessment to say that you fall in love too easily."

Simon stopped and said, "Now what's that supposed to mean? It makes me feel…"

"Baby, baby, please. Why the temper? Oh that Spanish hot blood that runs through your veins! What am I gonna do with you?" Then he shook his head playfully and hugged Simon with one arm saying, "Calma, calma muchacho."

Simon laughed at Shawn's silly attempt to speak Spanish. "Listen to you!"

"Si, muchacho, bueno, bueno!" They walked on a little further and Shawn said, "I'm happy to see that you can enjoy yourself sexually without falling in love. I've explained it to you before. Leave the love out of it and life is good. I saw how well you did in the secret chamber."

Simon opened his mouth to say something and Shawn waited. At last Simon admitted, "Yes, it was painful for me with Toby."

"I know it was but I think you learned that you can be a great priest and have a private sexual life at the same time as long as you don't fall for anyone and don't get careless. You gotta be careful." Simon nodded. "Things have opened up so much here at the abbey. The sexual revolution that's taken America by the balls is finally here too. I don't see it quite as dark as Proud Mary does. I think you're right in saying that if we're careful no one will make waves." Simon looked at Shawn, interested in what he was saying. "I really believe, Simon, that we can have a sexual life as long as we keep it secret and are prudent. The secret chamber last night was a perfect example of that. We can answer our call to God and be effective priests. That's a given. That doesn't mean God expects us to stop being men. Just because we fuck doesn't take away anything from being faithful to God."

Simon spoke up, "I think I still struggle with that. A lot."

"I know you do. You worry me sometimes, little one." Shawn put a hand on his shoulder and said, "Why do you struggle with that? One thing shouldn't have anything to do with the other. Think about last night. We can't go down to the root cellar all the time. It's too risky. But we can have really strong bonds between us who have come out to each other. We can mature as sexual beings with each other and enjoy being with each other as long as we don't mess it up." He looked at Simon in the eyes, "You gotta learn that and be convinced." Simon stared back, wounded. "Don't give me that sad, little look. You know it's true. As long as you feel shameful and dirty about sex you're going to believe you have to stay away from it. And what happens to you next? We've seen it already." Shawn waited but Simon didn't say anything further. "I'll tell you what comes next. You start acting weird and you stop having sex altogether because you think it's 'either/or'. You come to some warped conclusion that either you protect your inner spiritual persona or you contaminate it when you have sex." Simon said nothing. "And then comes the worst part, baby. Don't get angry with me but you know it's true. You stop having sex and you become miserable. Then when you start having sex you fall in love. Somehow in that pretty head of yours you think that you have to fall in love in order to make it okay to have sex and that's where you fuck the whole thing up. Keep love out of it. You'll be a great priest and serve God as long as you don't fall in love." Simon exhaled and felt suffocated. Shawn looked at him and finally said, "If no one ever finds out you're fucking somebody else, then you have nothing to worry about. No love. Remember that."

"Okay, okay! I got it! I got it!" Simon said impatiently and spoke too loudly.

"Keep it down, you don't have to announce it."

Simon quieted and said, "I understand already, okay. I have no intentions of falling in love again. I got what you're saying the first hundred times you said it." He looked Shawn in the eyes and said, "Do you really think I want to go through all that again? You think I want to repeat how I felt when I fell for Toby?"

"I don't know why you would! God wants your total, personal love. Don't give it to anyone else. Don't give your personal love to anyone else. Then you'll be a great priest." Simon's eyes misted as he looked at Shawn and heard his words. He repeated to Simon, "Our intimate love belongs only to God. He's a very jealous lover. I'm not talking about generally loving others. You know what I'm talking about. Having sex is purely physical. God gets that we need that. He put that appetite in us. If you learn this and live by it, you belong to an elite group in the Church. Trust me, it's time tested and really works at all levels." Shawn looked at his handsome young friend hoping that it would eventually sink in. The bell in the tower began calling them to pray the hour of Vespers. "Guess it's time to get to chapel." As they walked toward the abbey Shawn said, "You'll hear your professors like Father Dennis tell you the story when you get further along in theology, but it's a tale he's repeated a million times over the years to students." Simon was listening. "It expresses what I've just been saying to you. Denny tells all young priests that if a woman comes to your office and sits in front of your desk crying, do not get up and go over to her side to embrace and comfort her even though everything inside you tells you to do so. Even if your heart is begging you to do so. And do you know why you should stay on your side of the desk?" Simon nodded negatively. "Because if you sit behind your desk you can be sure that your dick isn't long enough to reach where she's sitting! And neither are your arms and hands." Simon smiled as they walked and Shawn finally said, "That's my point, baby, well, with a few obvious twists to the story. When you allow your personal feelings and love into the picture, it's finished for you in the priesthood. It's been taught for ages in the Church." Simon listened to Shawn carefully that evening, not completely sure it was all so simple. They entered the chapel and prayed.

Months before, when Joshua arrived in the seminary wing, he had been given Toby's old room. Not the one at the far end of the long, dark corridor but the cell right next to Simon's. Joshua was two classes behind Simon in seniority. For the better part of the first year after his novitiate, Joshua kept mostly to himself. Simon noticed that he was close to one of his classmates and jealousy stirred within him even though he never would have admitted it.

For the better part of that first year, Joshua and Simon barely spoke to each other.

It wasn't difficult to go in and out of each other's cells as it had been before. The rules had never been officially relaxed but no one seemed to pay much attention to it anymore. Seth put it well one day when he said, "On any given night, this hallway looks like Grand Central Station during rush hour on a Friday afternoon." It was a fair assessment. A good number of students were bedding each other on a nightly basis and not making any great effort to hide it. Some engaged in casual, one night stands, but after that night when Shawn had invited them and the others into the secret chamber, Simon and Joshua became inseparable.

The next day after the root cellar, when classes were over, they searched for each other. Joshua had gone to his cell after lunch in the refectory, hoping to catch Simon there but Simon had skipped lunch. Joshua would have found him in the library had he looked there. Later that afternoon, Joshua heard Simon in his cell and quickly went over and knocked on his door.

Simon called out, "Yeah, come in."

"Hey, it's just me." Joshua walked in timidly and closed the door behind him. "What are you doing? I've been looking for you all over the place. Where were you?"

Joshua's presence in his tiny cell suddenly reminded him of Toby. The memories came crashing in unexpectedly and he found it difficult to speak. His mind went blank. Finally, he managed to say, "I was…in the library, trying to get caught up. I have a paper due this Friday." Then there was silence again but not because they didn't know what to say to each other. There was silence because of what they wanted to say. They stood there motionless, aware of each other's subtle signs. Joshua moved toward Simon and barely pressed himself against him.

Simon pressed back and boldly said, "I love you. I want you."

They undressed, sliding under the cool sheets of Simon's narrow cot. There, Simon and Joshua once again expressed their love for each other. Afterward, they fell asleep together.

When they woke, Joshua said softly, "I love you, dark stranger." It was a term he would use for Simon.

"I love you back, golden boy." Simon hugged Joshua as he sat on the edge of the cot putting his shoes on.

Simon was now, no longer celibate. He desired his relationship with Joshua and cultivated it. Joshua was blond, fair skinned and had blue, pale eyes. Simon's hair was jet black, he was olive-skinned and his almond shaped eyes were black as coals. The two of them became inseparable as a couple and were received as such by their closest friends in the abbey. It wouldn't be long before Simon took Joshua to the top of the great bell tower. It would become a favorite haunt of theirs. Sitting up against one of the pillars beneath the great bells of the abbey, Simon would cradle Joshua, holding his arms around his waist, as Joshua pressed his back against Simon's chest. For hours the two of them alone, high above the abbey, would discuss future plans and share dreams.

Simon was careful to keep his fondness for Joshua away from Shawn's radar. He was also careful to keep under control the two colossal desires that raged within him. He immersed himself in the pleasures of the flesh and at the same time, in the secrecy of the crypt, he continued to seek God and prepare for the priesthood. Still, the two forces battled within him for his heart and complete attention and sometimes they gave rise to untold fears and insecurities. Quite often, Simon felt that he couldn't face God. None the less, he would make his way to the altar and kneel before the tabernacle, his head bent low. He would whisper to the One who had called him, "I know you can hear me. I know you're there." Simon would stare at the tabernacle, remembering what a searching soul had once said long ago in the Church's past, "I sit there looking at Him and He looks at me." Simon didn't know what else to say or do in God's presence.

Shawn knew enough to know that a close relationship between Simon and Joshua had been blossoming for some time. He was aware that they had first paired off in the root cellar that night long ago when he had invited them. And as time elapsed, Shawn became convinced that what was going on between them was more than something that was simply sexual. He had lectured Simon very often about the dangers in such a relationship, but Simon didn't seem to listen. Shawn saw the same disastrous patterns he had seen before when Toby got involved with Simon. He determined to gauge how bad the situation had gotten. Then he could do something about it when the time was right.

One evening after Vespers, during study time, Shawn decided to check up on Simon and Joshua. He figured the two would be together. He had prepared a large bowl of popcorn and made his way down the familiar corridor. He listened carefully outside Simon's cell door and heard nothing. He stepped quietly to the next door and listened. He could hear whispered voices and he made his move. Without waiting to be invited in, he pushed himself on the door and threw it wide open. Laughing, as if he were tripping inside by accident, he said loudly, "Oh, no! I'm falling!" With that he let the bowl fly and it hit the bed, spreading popcorn everywhere. As he starting picking it up and eating it, he straightened himself up and said, "Hello, little ones." Then added, "Shouldn't you two be studying separately, I mean, alone, by yourselves, each in his own cell?"

Simon and Joshua were sitting on Joshua's cot with their backs resting on the wall. They looked up, just as the bowl of popcorn was flying and stopped in mid-conversation, surprised by the intrusion. Joshua laughed and said, "Hey, Bro, what're you up to?" He picked up the popcorn and put it in his mouth. "This is good!" He mumbled, "Really good!"

Simon was angered by the rude intrusion. He sat there eyeing Shawn carefully and asked, "Didn't they teach you how to knock and wait to be invited in? Did you grow up in a barn?"

"My, my, such a Latin temper, this little brother of mine." Shawn sat on the cot and with a mouthful of popcorn took Simon's foot in his hand intent on massaging. Simon pulled it away quickly and jumped off the cot. Joshua had left the cot and was on his knees picking up popcorn off the floor.

Joshua stood as Simon passed him and said, "I'll catch you later at recreation." As he passed Shawn he murmured in Joshua's direction, "After study hall is over we can get together again privately." Simon went out the open door and disappeared down the hall.

It was very late and particularly warm one Saturday night not long afterward. Shawn had looked for Simon in the recreation room but had not found him. He next searched the television room but was unlucky there as well. He decided to check the pool and the sauna. There was a crowd in both but Simon and Joshua were not there. He thought about the root cellar but then remembered Simon telling him about the bell tower. He decided to try his luck there first.

Shawn made his way to the tower and as he did so, the night bell announced that it was eleven o'clock. He saw that the trap door was shut but not latched from the outside. He opened it slowly and it creaked loudly in his hand. He stuck his head out and listened. It was quiet. He made his way up into the tower and closed the door again. It creaked on its rusty hinges and then he heard the ruffled sounds coming from the other side of the bells. It was dark and his view was obstructed by the great bell in honor of Saint Michael.

Gusts of wind blew in and out of the space and it was then that Shawn heard Simon's voice coming from the other side, whispering in the darkness, "Somebody's there." There was silence and Shawn heard it again, "Somebody's there, dammit. I heard footsteps." Shawn stood still, hoping to hear more but only the wind spoke. He removed his shoes and walked in the opposite direction, near a great metal box that contained the cogs and wheels that moved the bells at their appointed times. He knelt down on one knee and waited but heard nothing. Then he heard the ruffling sound again and something that sounded like stifled laughter. He rose slowly and made his way carefully around the metal box. He stretched his neck out in the direction of the sounds and that's when he actually smelled them before he saw them.

The pungent, unmistakable scent of smoked weed reached Shawn's nostrils as his eyes finally focused in the darkness of the bell tower. In the far corner were Simon and Joshua. Simon was sitting up against a pillar with his legs around Joshua, who had his back against Simon's chest. They were passing a joint back and forth between them. They each took another drag and exhaled.

Shawn slipped out of the bell tower and made his way to his room. He walked quickly, his hands balled into fists. He murmured to himself as he made his way through the darkened corridors, "That little, motherfucking whore. That stupid little fucker hasn't heard a word I've said." He went into his cell and opened the armoire. He took the square bottle out and poured himself a generous glass of Jack Daniel's. He stood in the middle of the room and drank, staring out into nothingness as he concentrated. As he drank he said, "You haven't learned a fucking thing, have you? But I'm going to teach you a lesson that's going to sink in. You bet your sweet ass I am."

In the days that followed, Shawn took pains to be especially gracious toward Simon and Joshua and made every effort to engage them in friendly conversation. He was careful to give them space and respect their privacy. The semester was coming to an end and soon exams would take place. All the students, including Simon and Joshua were immersed in their final preparations before the exams began. Once exams were over, the abbey prepared itself for the annual spiritual retreat. All the monks of the abbey were expected to be present for the annual retreat which lasted the entire week. At the end of the retreat, the abbey would go into summer mode. This meant that some were off to summer studies in various universities, others to their sabbaticals, and some others to help in parishes for the summer months in cities and villages across the country. Most in the seminary went away but some remained behind to help with the fields and the production of beer in the brewery. Simon and Joshua had made their plans to remain at the abbey for the summer months and spend it together.

On the last day of exams, at the conclusion of Vespers that night, the Abbot stood up from his throne and made several announcements. At the end he said, "I congratulate our clerics tonight on the conclusion of their exams. We expect everyone did well and those grades will be posted soon." Then he said, "Tomorrow we begin our annual retreat before the summer begins. We will commence precisely at six o'clock in the morning with the celebration of Mass. Unless you have been excused by me personally, you will be in attendance for the week of retreat. This is a time of grace for all of us here in the abbey and to the degree that you allow God into your soul," he paused and looked up and down the great choir of monks, "to that same degree you will allow God into this abbey." The Abbot paused and then said with great ceremony, "The Retreat Master this year is Father Pancratius. He is a monk from our sister abbey of the Reparation." The Abbot gestured toward a gaunt, severe-looking monk dressed in the same black habit as their own. "Father Pancratius will be with us for the week of grace. He has brought with him several student monks who are clerics of the Abbey of the Reparation. They will be with us for the retreat during this week. Please make them feel welcomed here in the abbey and assist them with whatever they might need." The Abbot stepped down the three tiered dais and walked out followed by the majority of the monks.

Shawn sat back down and observed the Retreat Master and his little band of students. He had seen them when they first arrived that early afternoon from Upstate New York. Brother Gabriel had let them inside the cloister and helped them with their suitcases. Shawn had been there and had introduced himself to the Retreat Master. He had also met the little group of student monks. One was downright handsome. He had impressed Shawn with his looks, and he had introduced himself to them, saying, "Welcome to the Abbey of the Most Sacred Heart of Jesus. I'm Brother Shawn." He had gone around the group shaking hands.

He locked eyes with the handsome young monk, who was lean and looked Mediterranean to him. He had a full head of black hair that curled naturally like the kind you'd find on the head of a Roman or Greek god. The monk's large, dark eyes never left Shawn's as he said, "I'm Brother Joseph. You can call me Joey."

Shawn squeezed his hand and said, "Brother Joseph, welcome." He continued to stare at him and finally winked. The young man winked back and smiled. Now, sitting in his choir stall, Shawn looked at the little group of visiting monks. He studied Father Pancratius and said under his breath, "Typical, arrogant old fart." Then he looked at the students. One was looking around nervously and Shawn hissed, "Hideous shit-for-brains."

Others were being greeted by some of the monks of the abbey. Shawn then looked at two others and barely whispered, "Silly queens." For another three he said to himself, "Damn cute twinks." Brother Joseph who had introduced himself to Shawn as Joey, was looking up at the impressive vaulted ceiling of the chapel. Shawn studied him carefully, whispering, "Joey," and followed his gaze. Under his breath, he said, "Yambo, Mamma Luke." Shawn smiled broadly to himself. That was a revered expression he and his closest friends in the abbey had come up with years ago. They used it among themselves as a code word to mean a guy was exceedingly hot and sexy. The etymology of this expression would be considered quite twisted and lost in the outside world but in the abbey it expressed the sentiment perfectly.

They had created it from a scene taken from the movie, "The Nun's Story", starring Audrey Hepburn as Sister Luke. Brother Arnold knew the entire movie dialogue by heart. As Shawn was lost in thought, the young monk named Joseph looked in his direction. They locked eyes again except that this time it was not brief. Shawn flirted without shame and winked at him again. Joey flirted back by raising his eyebrows playfully and winking back. Then he gave Shawn a slow, seductive smile. Father Pancratius said something to them and they all turned around and followed him out.

Joey turned around once more, for an instant and caught Shawn's gaze before he left. As Shawn saw Joey leaving the chapel, he sat back in the hard, wooden seat of his choir stall. He chanted softly and jokingly to himself, in the made-up Gregorian Chant he and his friends likewise used whenever they gazed upon a man they thought exceptionally sexy, "Ecce…ecce quam bonum et quam iucundum est…" They were the first words from Psalm 133, again, applied with a twist, "See how good and how pleasant it (he) is..." Joey was looking very good to him for many reasons. Shawn smiled with great satisfaction deciding that Joey would serve him well. He had not counted so soon on his plan that what was now unfolding neatly. He thought of Simon and Joshua.

At breakfast the next morning, Shawn made it a point to find Joey and sit with him at table. He also needed to find Joshua. Joey needed to sit facing or next to Joshua at breakfast if his plan was going to succeed. Shawn had already checked the list of student waiters for breakfast on that first day of retreat. Simon was first on the list for breakfast and supper so as far as Shawn was concerned, Simon was out of the picture because waiters sat at a specified table near the kitchen, away from the others.

As fate would have it, Joey came into the refectory alone and Shawn went up to him. Putting an arm around his shoulders, he said smiling, "Brother Joseph! Good morning. I pray your dreams were real sweet."

The visiting monk whispered back, "Sweet and juicy."

"Just like you!" Shawn flirted with Joey a few moments until he saw Joshua coming in to the refectory. He took Joey by the elbow and walking up to Joshua said, "Brother Joshua. Help me be hospitable to shy, Brother Joey, who's not from here." Shawn winked at Joshua who was only too happy to oblige. They approached the closest table as the refectory was noisily filling with hungry monks. Shawn put Joey at one end of the table set for six. He said to Joshua, "Sit there, baby, next to Joey," gesturing to Joey's right. "I'll sit here, near Joey's left hand." They stood at their places patiently, waiting for the Abbot to intone the prayers at table. When they made the sign of the Cross, a rumbling, screeching sound filled the dining hall as chairs were dragged away from tables and the monks sat themselves at table. Shawn looked at Joey and said, "I'm so happy you came to visit us at the abbey."

Joey smiled and said, "Thank you, Brother Shawn. I'm really happy to be here. I can't believe we're all the way down here in Pennsylvania." Joshua gawked at Joey and hung on every word the handsome young monk uttered. Joey looked at Joshua and asked, "Good morning, brother. I'm Joey. I don't think we've formally met yet."

Joshua was at a loss for words yet managed to say weakly, "I'm Joshua." Then he said, "You're really handsome."

Shawn smiled at Joey, content that things were going the way he had hoped and said, "I think Joshua likes you."

Joey looked at Joshua and said, "Aw, you looked so cute when you said that. I'm gonna ditto that back at you, blondie." Joshua was on a cloud for the rest of breakfast.

Shawn saw Simon looking at Joshua as he wheeled one of the stainless steel food carts that held the enormous platters of eggs, bacon and potatoes to the monks. He was busy refilling platters of buttered toast but managed to glare at Shawn once as he passed their table. Joshua was oblivious to everything and everyone around him except Joey. Then as Simon brought fresh coffee around, he put a pot in front of Joshua and said too loudly, "Good morning, Joshua!"

Joshua looked up and came out of his trance. He said, "Hey, Simon, good morning." Then he looked at Joey and said, without looking back up, "This here is Brother Joseph, but we can call him Joey." Joey smiled at Simon who didn't smile back. Joshua didn't introduce Simon.

"I'm Simon. I guess Joshua forgot that." Simon looked at Joshua and said this with an edge, more to Joshua than to Joey. Before Joey could respond Simon was gone, having been called from another table demanding more food.

Shawn said smiling to Joey, "Don't mind Simon's lack of manners. He's Spanish and they just get nervous that way sometimes." He looked at Joshua and back at Joey saying, "You guys make a really cute pair of monks sitting together like this."

Joey was already looking at Joshua when Shawn said this and chuckled, "Oh, you're a trouble maker, honey. You're gonna get Josh in trouble."

Joshua appeared confused and took turns looking at Joey and Shawn questioningly, "Why am I gonna be in trouble? I don't get it."

Shawn and Joey both laughed and each took one of Joshua's hands in their own. Shawn said, "Never mind, it was a silly joke that Joey made." He kicked Joey gently under the table.

Breakfast didn't last very long and when the Abbot rose from table, he said the concluding prayers and gave the blessing. Then he added, "Everyone is expected in choir for the first meditation that Father Pancratius has prepared for us at exactly ten o'clock." As the Abbot said this, he gestured toward the tall, grave-looking monk who was seated near him. Father Pancratius bowed slightly, without emotion, solemnly acknowledging the Abbot's words.

Shawn muttered under his breath, "Gee, where did they dig up this pompous-assed, old scheisskopf?"

Father Pancratius' meditation lasted one hour and forty five minutes and when it was over Shawn said, "I need a drink." Instead, he went outside to get a breath of fresh air. He had walked a distance from the abbey, trying to clear his head when he became aware of someone approaching him from behind on the gravel road. He looked up. It was Joey. Shawn studied him as he approached and waved to him. When he was within hearing, Shawn asked, "What're you doing out here? I thought you'd be inside, mingling with everyone."

Joey smiled, "I could be if I wanted to. I never have any trouble arousing interest." He smiled seductively.

"So why are you out here?"

"I wanted to be with you." Then he added, "You arouse my interest."

"Really?" Shawn feigned shock. "I'm so impressed that you'd want to be with an old timer like me. I'd think you'd prefer to be with the likes of Joshua."

"Oh, Joshua. Yeah, he's a cutie, alright."

"A bit of an air-head, a space cadet, but cute, yes, I agree."

"I'd say he's taken, though. I wouldn't want to get on the bad side of his dark, Latin lover. Simon looks intense to me and very territorial. He probably charges his enemies like an angry bull when threatened."

Shawn chuckled at the image, but said nothing. They walked on a little and he said, "Simon is very intense, yes. He's just put together that way. But Joshua…"

"What about Joshua?" Joey was intrigued. "He seems like a flirt to me."

"Oh? Is that your assessment? A little tease like you, perhaps."

Joey was amused and said, "I like you, Shawn, you're wicked."

Shawn laughed, "I'll take that as a compliment."

Joey moved closer to Shawn. He looked at him and said, "I know you like me." He smiled and whispered, "I know you want me."

"What makes you think that?"

"Oh, I know enough to know that. I could tell from the minute I met you."

Shawn stretched back, yawning as he did. He looked in the direction of the abbey. Monks were streaming out of the abbey's main doors, apparently seeking fresh air as well. He looked at Joey and said, "You're very bold. It only heightens your sex appeal." He smiled, "I can only guess what you look like naked."

"I've never gotten any complaints."

"No, I wouldn't think so, but what about after you strip down? Can you seduce or are you just a little prick teaser interested in giving unsuspecting guys a bad case of blue balls?"

"Wow, you don't mess around, do you? You cut to the chase." Joey stepped back, pressing down the front of his black habit. "Does this look like it could work?"

"It's not the size of the stick, baby, but the magic of the wand. You talk the talk but, I don't know. You might disappoint me. You might be all talk and no walk."

"Come to my room and find out."

Shawn made his move. "Not so fast. Not so fast. Before I get involved, I need some proof." He looked at Joey. "Actually, I have a proposal that would be fun for me to watch and you'd enjoy."

"A proposal?"

"Yeah. Something tells me that you like to talk but that there might not be anything behind it. Prove to me that you're capable of seducing someone."

"Seduce?" Joey pondered this. "How do you propose I seduce you?"

Shawn held his hands up, "Not me, silly, you don't understand. Show me that you're capable of seducing someone else completely, and then I'll think about you and me."

Joey didn't flinch. "Who you got in mind?"

"Joshua."

"Joshua is cute. But Joshua's taken."

"That's why he's perfect. If you're the real lover you say you are, seduce Joshua." Shawn saw he was getting to Joey. "Bed Joshua and I'll know you're not just a tease, not just a talker." Then Shawn went in for the kill. "Personally, I don't think you can seduce Joshua."

Joey smiled to himself. "I can seduce anyone I put my mind to seducing," he said smugly. "Guys never turn me away. I'll seduce Joshua easily. Piece of cake. He's a flirt and I can tell he's a horny slut."

"Oh, he's both those things and more. But the proof of your seduction is to get Simon to see it. If you drive him insane with jealousy, then I'll know you're who you say you are."

Joey looked into Shawn's piercing eyes. He smiled and licked his lips slowly. His eyes were shiny and bright, sparkling. "Deal," he said and held out his hand. "I'll seduce Joshua completely. Simon will have no doubt about that."

Shawn shook his hand, "Deal."

"Then before I leave at the end of this week, you'll bow down for me and grab your ankles. I'm going to give you a pounding like you've never experienced."

"I doubt that, but you're on."

"I'll have Joshua for breakfast and you for supper." Joey turned to leave and then stopped, as if he remembered something. "I gotta question."

"Go ahead."

"Why Joshua? Why not somebody else?"

"I think Joshua is all wrong for Simon. Simon could do far better. He's emotionally blinded and wrapped up in a relationship with Joshua that's only going to bring him grief. I want Simon to be free of it. If you can drive a wedge between Joshua and Simon then you and I have a deal."

Joey smiled. "I get it." He turned around. As he walked away from Shawn he said, "I'll drive a wedge between them and then I'll drive something else into you."

The great bell in honor of Saint Michael the Archangel began to sound, and throughout the abbey, the Angelus was prayed. Lunch would follow and then the afternoon meditation by Father Pancratius would take place. Shawn was well pleased with himself as he walked back. Joey had taken the bait and now it was simply a question of waiting.

Brother Joseph, a student monk from the Abbey of the Reparation in Upstate New York put the move on Joshua that very evening during supper. Simon was on duty as a waiter again and Joey made it a point to sit with Joshua. He had flirted with Joshua throughout the meal and had massaged Joshua's legs with his foot under the table. Joshua looked at Joey with open desire and when supper was over he invited Joey to walk with him outside before Vespers and the evening meditation in chapel. Simon had seen them walk out of the refectory together. Joey was whispering something in Joshua's ear as they walked. Simon heard Joshua shriek loudly with laughter. He had wanted to run up to them and confront Joshua but he was stuck in kitchen duty along with nineteen other waiters that night.

Joshua took Joey down the eastern side of the abbey and they walked past the postulancy in the direction of the volleyball court and the ball field. As they walked, Joey suggested they get together that evening after the meditation. "I have a bottle of gin I brought, if you wanna come over to my room or we can meet out here. Do a few drinks."

"Yeah, that's sounds perfect." Joshua had cautioned, "I think it's better out here somewhere. Some bad shit would go down if we got caught together in your cell with gin!"

Joey chuckled, "Yeah, really!" Then he suggested walking off the gravel path and into the growth of trees beyond. "How far does the property go down this way?" He asked as he walked ahead making sure that Joshua followed.

"Uh, the property here goes down a ways until the road that comes from Crescent and takes you into Leicester." Joshua had joined Joey and the two walked side by side. They agreed to meet behind the pool building that night and have their gin picnic not far from there. Joshua had said, "There's a little spot back there in the woods where some of the guys go smoke sometimes. There's logs set up like benches and it's rarely used. We can sit there."

Joey was curious, "Guys go to smoke back there? Smoke as in...?"

"Smoke as in weed. Seth and a few others have joined Simon and I on occasion for a smoke there." Joshua thought about it and added, "Its way better to smoke up in the bell tower. That's where Simon and I usually go to smoke and..." He stopped what he was saying when he felt Joey's hand massaging his neck quietly. Joey moved in front of Joshua and kissed him on the mouth. Joshua returned the kiss equally as passionate. Joey made sure to keep both his hands on Joshua's shoulders, as he ground himself into Joshua.

The second of the great bells, the one in honor of Saint Gabriel the Archangel, began to peal loudly now from its lofty position and the two men knew it was time to return to the chapel. They groped each other one last time before they came out of the woods straightening out their habits. Carefully and looking to see if anyone else was around, they stepped onto the gravel path and quickly walked in the direction of the chapel. They agreed to meet behind the pool building at ten o'clock that night. Joey would bring the gin and Joshua promised to bring some weed that he and Simon kept together if there was any left.

Simon was distraught to think that Joey had walked off with Joshua. He searched Joshua's cell once he was done in the kitchen but did not find him.

He looked for him outside, in front of the abbey but Joshua was nowhere to be found. When he heard the bell calling them to chapel, he reluctantly postponed his search and made his way among the gathering monks. He felt a sickening, sinking feeling within himself. It was something like dread and rejection, humiliation and fear all mixed together. He felt nauseous to think about what Joshua might be doing with that creep from Upstate New York. He felt he was being robbed.

He saw them coming into the chapel together and sit next to each other. The Abbot stood and everyone got to their feet. The organ burst into life and the chanting of the Psalms for Vespers began. Simon felt lost and on edge as he saw Joey and Joshua looking at each other and smiling. No one seemed to notice them except Simon in his anguish and tears welled up easily in his dark eyes and ran down his face.

However, this wasn't true. Someone else was closely watching Joey and Joshua. In the highest tier of the choir stalls, sat Shawn, looking content that his plan was now underway. He could see Simon's grimace as he sat in choir barely singing the Psalms in praise of God's Divine Will. As soon as the Abbot gave the blessing, everyone sat for the evening meditation. Father Pancratius spoke for two hours on this evening and when he was done speaking everyone filed out of the chapel so that a bottleneck was formed at the main chapel exit.

Shawn moved down the steps of the choir stalls quickly and reached Simon before he could find Joshua. "Where are you off to, little one?" Simon was tense and offered Shawn little explanation. He pressed on in a mocking tone, "Where's your other half? Where's Joshua tonight? I'm not seeing him." Simon looked at Shawn with disdain realizing that he was making fun of his suffering. He said nothing. Shawn then said, "Oh, I think I see him way over there with Joey, the young monk from the Reparation." Simon saw that Shawn was smiling sarcastically as he said this and then continued, "I think they've become good friends."

Simon was unable to find Joshua in the crowd when it finally dispersed. He searched Joshua's cell and the recreation room but was unsuccessful in finding him. He walked to the refectory and went to the pool and sauna but Joshua wasn't there. Simon returned to his cell and paced in the tiny room. He felt he would go mad with anger and jealousy. Mostly, he didn't know how to handle his feelings of utter loss. How could Joshua do this to him? Hadn't

Joshua told him that he loved him? Why did this Joey guy have to come and ruin everything?

Simon was overcome with grief and he felt sick in his soul. When Joshua finally slipped into his own cell at nearly four o'clock in the morning, Simon heard nothing, unaware as he was, immersed in dark, troubled patches of light sleep. He had vomited in his sink several times that night and his stomach hurt him badly the last time, when only yellow bile hung from his mouth in a single strand.

The next morning, Simon rose and after he had showered and dressed in his habit knocked on Joshua's cell door. No answer came. He knocked again and opened. Joshua wasn't there. At breakfast he had no appetite as he looked for Joshua and saw that he was sitting at a far table with Joey and three of the other young monks who were visiting. Their table was rowdy with laughter and good cheer and Simon again felt miserable and sad. He was nauseated by the smell of fried eggs, pork sausages and hash browns. He tried to be pleasant at table but found it difficult to carry a conversation with any of his fellow monks.

Shawn looked at him from another table and when breakfast was over, he walked up to Simon and said, "Little one, you look pale." Then he asked merrily, "Have you found Joshua? I think I see him over there." Simon walked away without saying a word. At lunch, Simon ate nothing and specifically sat at a table with elderly monks who ate and spoke little. During the afternoon he lay in his cot, getting up regularly to go relieve himself of the watery diarrhea that plagued him, having taken the place of his tortured vomiting. He had no idea where Joshua was but was sure he was with Joey somewhere.

That evening at supper, Simon sat once again with the older monks and managed to eat some bread. Shawn came up behind him and whispered, "Are you doing okay, little one? You look absolutely awful." Simon turned and faced him and responded in a raspy voice, "How do you think I'm doing? I'm shitting yellow water and throwing up bile. I haven't heard a word from Joshua in three days nor seen him." Then he turned around toward his plate and said quietly, "I guess it will end when that fucker leaves and gets back to New York." Shawn said nothing.

Joshua and Joey had indeed been together the entire time. They had shared gin behind the pool before going deep into the woods and stripping down together. The next day they had gone with some of the other brothers to swim in the lake that was near the hamlet of Leicester and that night they had slept together in Joey's bed. Joshua had taken Joey up into the bell tower and they had also visited the root cellar although Joshua couldn't find the trap door into the secret chamber. At long last, the spiritual retreat ended and Father Pancratius and the student monks from the Abbey of the Reparation in Upstate New York prepared for their imminent departure.

Before he had left, Joey confided in Shawn that the seduction had been easy as he had suspected but that he himself had been seduced in the process. "Joshua and I have actually become friends in and out of the sack. I'm hoping to see him this summer in Philadelphia. My parents have a place at the shore." Then he added, smiling, "He could suck the chrome off a fender."

The next day, a great number of monks left the abbey for summer assignments. Simon had some coffee and toast for breakfast and approached Joshua as he was walking out of the refectory, "Hey, Joshua. Can we talk later today?"

Joshua was aloof and asked, "Talk about what?"

"Please, I just need to clarify a few things. Can we meet later, say after lunch? Around one-thirty?"

Joshua sounded evasive and disinterested to Simon, but finally said, "Yeah, I think I can make it."

At quarter to two, Simon had not heard from Joshua and knocked on his cell door. "Come in." It was Joshua.

Simon entered and saw Joshua lying on his cot. He sat to the edge of the cot and faced his friend. "Joshua, we need to talk because I don't understand what happened."

Joshua was on the defensive, "What are you talking about? What happened about what? What are you referring to?"

"You know what I'm referring to. I'm talking about that fucker that you got tangled up with the last five days. That motherfucker you've been blowing and fucking."

Joshua sat up and pointed at Simon, "You know I don't like that 'f' word, Simon. Stop using it." Then he leaned back on the wall and closed his eyes, saying, "And don't call Joey that either. He's my friend."

"You're friend? What am I? I thought you and I loved each other? Is it over, is that what you're telling me? Just like that? No warning, no nothing?" Simon stared at Joshua who looked away and said nothing. "Answer me.

You've disappeared these last few days. I've looked for you every fucking place imaginable."

"Don't use that word. And I'm not your property, you know. If I want to have friends and meet other people, you're not going to stop me."

"You weren't meeting other people. You were fucking that slut queen from New York."

"Honestly, Simon..." Joshua trailed off, exhaling in disgust. "There's no talking to you. All I did was spend time with him and some of the other students that came with him. Listen to yourself accuse me." Joshua saw that Simon had looked down. "I mean, really, you come in here, accusing me of all kinds of stuff you have absolutely no proof of."

"I looked for you and couldn't find you! What was I supposed to think?"

"I have no idea what you thought. But I'm telling you that nothing went on between us. Joey is just a nice guy and so are his fellow monks. You should have joined us instead of getting all crazy the way you did."

Simon looked at his friend and had a very difficult time believing him. He was exhausted from the events of the week. He was still physically weak from not eating and sleeping badly. He looked at Joshua and loved him even though his friend had hurt and disappointed him badly. "Can we get back to where we were? I mean, do you still love me?"

The door to Joshua's cell burst open and Shawn came prancing in, waving his hands up in the air, saying, "Little ones, my oh my, it's grim and silent in here."

"Can't you see we're having a fucking private conversation! Leave us alone, dammit! And knock! Can you learn to fucking knock on the door and wait to be invited in? What is it with you?" Simon was in a rage as he bellowed at Shawn. "Just get out and let us have some privacy!" Shawn's face went red the color of crimson and he turned around quietly and walked out, shutting the door gently as he left.

"Simon!" It was Joshua protesting. "What is wrong with you? You can't just..."

"Hey! Can we just talk about us? Can you just forget about him and listen to what I'm saying?" The room was quiet now and Joshua said nothing. "I haven't seen you in four or five days. You haven't come by or looked for me." He paused. "And when I have seen you, it's with him. You've been with him all this time, haven't you?"

Joshua didn't look at Simon but said, "I already told you. I was with him and some of his friends. I don't like what you're implying."

Simon didn't believe Joshua but was too exhausted and wounded at that point. He also figured that Joshua wouldn't change his story. He knew what a flirt Joshua was. Simon wasn't stupid and knew that that Joey guy was a looker and a flirt as well. In any case, he was gone now. Possibly he and Joshua could figure this thing out. "I really have missed you these last few days. I haven't eaten or slept."

"Simon, why did you do that?" Joshua had awkwardly kicked Simon on his thigh playfully. "You blew the whole thing sky high in your jealous head."

"I missed you because I love you." Simon moved up and sat next to Joshua, laying his head in Joshua's lap. Joshua caressed Simon's hair and he stared straight ahead. Simon was aware that Joshua was far away and not really listening to him. Nonetheless, he continued, "We should go up to the bell tower tonight, have some gin or smoke." Simon looked up at Joshua and moved his head up.

"I don't think we have any smokes left. I checked some days ago." Joshua hesitated and added nervously, "I checked and there wasn't any."

"You were going to smoke our weed with him? With that guy?" Simon sat up, indignant.

"C'mon, Simon, stop it. I was checking to see if there was any for us, for you and me. Let's just put all these fears of yours behind us and move on."

Again, Simon didn't believe him and he didn't feel that everything was due to his fears as Joshua was suggesting. They sat there in Joshua's cot like that until shadows grew on the wall. Joshua had drifted away in sleep with his head to one side and Simon could hear him breathing easily. Simon, however, couldn't sleep. He was troubled and felt that something fragile and beautiful between them had shattered and could not be the way it was before the events of this week. Still, he would try and pick up the pieces and put them where they had been. He desperately wanted his friend to love him as before.

A great number of monks were gone for the summer and the few that were there shared an informal comradery especially at meals. Even the older monks spoke up at table. Shawn had not said a word to Simon since the afternoon that Simon had demanded him to leave Joshua's cell. He had been furious with Simon when that had happened although it had not surprised him. One evening after supper, just before Simon was to leave for vacation, Shawn approached

Simon as he was walking alone out of the refectory. "Hello, little stranger. Are you still not speaking to me?"

Simon felt embarrassed and said, "Look, Shawn, it was a very bad moment in my life. Everything seemed to be falling apart for me during those days of retreat." He paused and looked at him, "I'm very sorry for how I spoke to you. I just needed space with Joshua to try and figure things out."

Shawn said, "Let's get some fresh air outside together, like we used to." They walked down a narrow hallway near the napkin room and out a small door that led to a gravel path on the east side of the abbey. Shawn spoke slowly as he said, "I hope you clarified things in your head by now."

"What do you mean?"

"I'm not going to lie to you, Simon. I saw what that snake, Joey, was up to when he was here at the time of retreat. In fact, he told me that he wanted to get into Joshua's pants even though he knew you guys were close." Simon said nothing and listened carefully. "I was shocked. He didn't seem to care how he came off to me."

"And how was that, Shawn? How did he come off to you?"

"Like the flirting little whore that he is. In any case, I could see how much it hurt you that Joshua betrayed you."

"It hurt me real bad."

"I could see that. I wanted you to see what Joshua was doing to you by going off with that guy. That's why I asked you where your friend Joshua was. I wanted you to see what was going on. I have no doubts that Joshua took him to the bell tower, or to the root cellar or that they got together in the room that that guy was assigned to."

Simon didn't want to go through all these details again and said, "Joshua denies that they got intimate. He insists that they're just friends."

"What?" Shawn stopped walking. He turned to Simon and asked, "Do you really believe him? C'mon Simon, you know what you felt because of what you saw. It was in your face."

"I don't know what to believe anymore."

"Well, you believe me when I tell you that they weren't holding hands for five days. That Joey guy only thinks about himself. And I know he got what he wanted." Shawn put a hand on Simon's shoulder and Simon looked up at him. Simon wore a grimace that revealed the anguish that now rose freely from deep within him. Shawn said gently, "Why didn't you listen to me?"

"About what?"

"About keeping love out of everything. Why didn't you and Joshua just enjoy each other's bodies. You wouldn't have suffered so much when that Joey, that snake came slithering into this abbey. You would have seen Joshua for what he is and dumped him and gotten on with your life." Simon looked lost and didn't respond. Shawn began walking again and Simon followed him. "Well, at least you've come to your senses about Joshua. I mean, you just said you don't believe what he said to you which means you dumped that traitor. Well done, I say! I felicitate your courage."

Simon stopped walking. "I said I didn't know what to believe." Then he added, "It all hurt me real bad but he and I have talked and we're making a new beginning of things, albeit a rocky one." Simon hated to admit to Shawn that he believed Joshua had betrayed him and lied to him even now.

"What?" Shawn rolled his fists into tight balls as they stood there. "You still believe what Joshua told you?"

"I love him, Shawn. I know you don't get that."

He said nothing and Simon understood that he was not pleased with him. "Are you angry with me, Shawn?"

"You have a lot to learn, little one. An awful lot to fucking learn." They walked the rest of the way in silence until they came upon Father Chris, the Master of Postulants who was walking out of the postulancy. They said hello and walked with him back to the main doors of the abbey. A few minutes later, the bell in the tower called them to prayer and the three monks disappeared inside for Vespers.

The summer months passed slowly as they always did in Leicester. Simon visited his family in Tampa for two weeks. He felt insecure as he said goodbye to Joshua before leaving the abbey. "I really hate to leave you behind. Why not come with me to Florida? There's plenty of room at home and we can get to the beach everyday if you like. It's not a long hike from our place."

Joshua was noncommittal. "I can't, Simon. I really need to get home to Philadelphia. Two weeks isn't really that long anyway." Then he added, "I still might get to the shore near Jersey, though." He said nothing more.

Simon wondered if Joshua was telling him the truth or not. Part of the sinking feeling that held his stomach in a vise told him that he would run into the arms of that guy from Upstate New York. Simon felt nauseated to think what Joshua would be doing behind his back while he was in Florida.

It was late afternoon when Shawn cleared some of the papers on his desk to make room for the letter he needed to write. This time he would make sure that things were set right. It was to be the first draft of several and would be given personally to the Abbot. He poured himself a glass of bourbon and concentrated. Then he wrote an outline. He tore it up and wrote another. By the fourth outline, his thoughts were getting scattered and he felt he needed some direction. Several days passed and Shawn approached one of the older priests for Confession on a Saturday afternoon in the crypt. There were several monks in line there, waiting to make their own confession. He hoped the visit would give him the direction he needed.

He had entered the small space of the confessional box and said, "Bless me Father, for I have sinned."

"Yes, my child, tell me. Are you a student monk?"

"Yes, Father. I'm preparing for ordination to the deaconate."

"Wonderful. May God guide you and fill you with wisdom and grace as you approach the altar." Then he asked, "What are your sins, brother?"

"Actually, Father, I've already confessed my sins to another priest. I'm here because I need direction with a very serious problem." He said the next few words slowly but dramatically. "It's something very serious that could tear the abbey apart and destroy many vocations."

The elder priest sat up in his seat and cleared his throat. "Dear child, what can be so grave?"

Shawn chose his words carefully. "I have decided that I must approach the Abbot on a very serious matter but I'm not sure when to do it. That's why I'm here with you, Father. I want to make sure that I inform our Abbot when it's right to do so. Right now, most of the students in question are away and the Abbot couldn't really address it."

"So it's a matter involving our student monks?"

"Yes, Father, involving some of them."

"I see. And what is this serious matter you speak about?" The priest moved in closer toward the screen separating them in the darkened confessional box.

Shawn made sure to hesitate before he finally said, "It's about the vow of chastity, Father. I have proof that a good number of the students in the seminary are breaking their vow of chastity and have been doing so for some time now. Some have even paired off like lovers. Some run to Pittsburgh often and openly go to gay bars there. I can give the Abbot names."

The old priest gasped loudly and moved uncomfortably on his side of the confessional box and asked, "What? Are you certain of this? And if everything you're saying is true are you willing to swear to it before God?"

"Oh my yes, Father. I will swear before God that what I'm saying is taking place and is true."

The priest breathed heavily and Shawn waited. Then the white haired cleric asked, "Have you written things down, I mean, names, dates and places? And the acts themselves, can you prove they're true?"

"I haven't written it that way, Father. I have written an outline stating what I've seen and who I know to be guilty. The only way I can prove the acts themselves is to testify to what I've seen and to supply written testimony from a couple of other witnesses."

"I see." The priest drummed his fingers on the armrest of the wooden chair he sat on. "Well, you need to write everything you know down on paper in specifics, brother. It's the only way that the Abbot and his council can take it seriously. Otherwise, it can fall back into your own face and just be considered shameful accusations with no proof, just a bunch of hateful gossip." Shawn smiled in the darkness. The old monk sitting across from him was right. This was the direction he needed. "Begin to make a careful inventory of names, dates, places and specific acts. Put the dates down as close as you can to when things happened and get reliable witnesses to write confidential testimonies to which they must affix their signatures. Then and only then will you be prepared to launch such a deadly accusation." Then he added quickly, "You must be very sure it's all true, before you proceed, brother. Your intentions must be transparent before God." Shawn waited and said nothing. "I'm worried by what you're saying, my son. I'm worried about it all and if it's completely true. Might you not be imagining some of it? Certainly the Abbot and the Master of Clerics would be aware of serious wrong doing of this nature if it were going on right under their noses."

"Oh, sadly, it's true, Father. It's been festering for a long time now. Things have gotten too far and it's time to address it."

"Oh dear, oh dear. Pray God help you." The priest sounded terribly nervous and agitated as he said, "A person's conscience is supreme. Your conscience will tell you if you are to proceed with this or not. Pray about it and if you still believe you should do it then prepare it well. Wait until you have gotten it all clearly documented on paper. Don't rush into it even if you have to wait several months. Then take it to the Lord Abbot."

"Yes, Father. Thank you."

"I hope that I've been God's instrument and have helped you in this grave and serious matter. I'll pray for you, my child."

"Oh yes, Father. I needed direction and you've given it to me." Shawn almost chuckled out loud. "I know exactly how to proceed now. Thank you." Then he asked, "May I have your blessing now, Father?"

+ + + + +

Mark had finished working on tattooing the numbers above Simon's first pink triangle tattoo and had sat back in his swivel stool listening as Simon spoke. When Simon finished, Mark asked, "I don't get it, Simon. What's the persecution angle here? You said this tattoo is about persecution. Educate me, because I ain't getting the meaning."

"Oh, you will, Mark, you will. In his anger, Shawn was putting the finishing touches for a scheme that we later called 'The Night of the Long Knives'. It was devastating and heads rolled."

"Long knives. Fuck, man that sounds ominous."

Simon drove home in a distracted fog of emotions after he left the shop that day. Mostly, he felt drained and terribly sad.

When he finally got to his house, he parked and turned off the engine of his truck. Simon sat there for a very long time, looking out the window at nothing in particular. Bits and pieces from the past flew in and out of his troubled thoughts. At long last, he stepped out of his truck without thinking too much more about anything. For the moment he only had a very simple plan. He didn't hesitate to go directly to Jack Daniel's once he got inside his safe place at home.

Chapter Eleven
The Heart

The heart has reasons that reason does not know.
Blaise Pascal

Simon showered the next morning and studied his reflection in the full body mirror that hung on the wall just beyond the glass doors of where he stood. He contemplated the bright pink tattoo that was now just under his left pectoral. Slowly, he ran the tips of his fingers over the seven prisoner numbers and thought of those who had suffered and perished in the Nazi death camps. He allowed his thoughts to flow easily while he reveled in the stream of hot water gushing over his skin. He looked down at his thigh and touched the place where later today he'd receive his second pink triangle and prisoner numbers from Mark.

In his mind he hung on to a tattered black and white photograph that he had seen some time ago in the local Holocaust Museum. Faces of exhausted, persecuted, tortured souls in the death camps of Europe stared back at him in his thoughts. He considered their suffering and knew he could never fully grasp what they had suffered. No one could unless you had been there, in the thick of it. Simon always remembered what an elderly Jesuit priest had once told him in a confessional when he was a boy. "It's the foot that is stepped on that hurts; not the foot that does the stepping." Simon recognized this to be a simple truth and he often went back to it. Suffering and persecution certainly had its differences in human history but every person's suffering was sacred and valid. Simon knew what it felt like to have his "foot stepped on."

"Shoah," he said softly. The Hebrew word expresses so well what took place in the death camps. It underlines the malevolent desire and intent to actually annihilate, it captures so completely the desire to inflict and cause utter catastrophe, complete destruction and not just "a sacrifice" be it by "fire" or some other means. What took place in the death camps was not simply a "Holocaust", a "burned offering". "Shoah" goes much deeper as a term to fully understand the horror of what took place. It is far more sinister. The death camps were not simply places to sacrifice but to completely wipe out and obliterate on many levels, in the most diabolical of ways. Persecution and suffering comes in many forms and degrees to different souls. But it must be said that annihilation, catastrophe and utter destruction always has the same effect on souls regardless of the scale to which it is carried out.

It was beyond Simon's capacity to grasp the kind of suffering that existed in the death camps, those kinds of unimaginable wounds. Yet, he too had been persecuted and had suffered simply because of "how" he had been born. To be hated and punished because one is born gay or Jewish or black or Asian is something that can hardly be justified. Simon accepted that his suffering had certainly not been the same ghastly, inhuman monstrosity that those in the death camps had endured. He knew that on one level it didn't and couldn't ever even come close. Still, the "foot" that had stepped on him had hurt him deeply and the persecution he had endured was no illusion. Those experiences had left him with open wounds and ugly scars. It was what Truman Capote so aptly expressed. "Happiness leaves such slender records; it is the dark days that are so voluminously documented." He remembered his dark days all too well.

Simon turned off the shower and wiped away the excess water on his skin. Then in quick, jerking movements, he thrashed his fingers haphazardly through his hair and beard, shaking out the remaining water that was still trapped there. He stepped out of the shower and dried himself and as he did so he had to admit that he still felt drowsy in spite of the shower. It hadn't invigorated him as it usually did because once again, he hadn't slept well the night before. He recalled only too well how much he had tossed and turned and felt cold one moment and hot the next. It had been a long night during which he would drift off to sleep only to awaken suddenly, frightened and insecure. Too many bad recollections had kept him from sleep. He had wrestled with the reality of being born gay. On the one hand, he believed it was God's Will. He had no doubt about this. It had been specifically and intentionally woven into him by the Creator of the Universe as an integral part of who he was. On the other hand, Simon hadn't had any say in the matter. Could he be held responsible for being gay?

Yet, there was something else that gnawed at his conscience in the dark of night. It was the acceptance of the truth that much of his suffering might well have been the fruit of his own actions and this was a bitter pill to swallow. He wondered to what degree he was guilty of this? Assuming responsibility for it wasn't easy, to say the least. Too many demons often come to rouse one from slumber because we can't go back and erase the wrong we've done, the bad shit we've inflicted on others and even on ourselves. We must face the consequences when it all comes back to bite us in the ass. Geoffrey Chaucer used the image so well in The Parson's Tale. It had remained in Simon's memory since the day he first read it as a student in the abbey library:

And ofte tyme swich
cursynge wrongfully
retorneth agayn to hym
that curseth, as a bryd that
retorneth agayn to his
owene nest.

The awful memories that had invaded his fitful sleep had been like an unruly crowd gaining momentum during an angry protest. The troubling images flashing in and out of his troubled dreams had come and gone as the minutes ticked away slowly into hours and the empty feeling of despair enveloped him. He felt nauseated as he finished drying off and chastised himself silently for having consumed so much Jack Daniel's the night before. It was a way for him to take the edge off the awful memories, but the truth was that the present hangover griping him like a vise, was killing him.

He opened a chilled liter bottle of San Pelegrino and pouring, added lemon juice to his glass. His mouth was dry and he remembered that line from W.C. Fields recalling a bad hangover the actor and comedian had endured: "My tongue feels like the entire Russian Army marched across it…in their stockinged feet." Simon smiled to himself, remembering how he and his brother Bobby as kids, had admired Field's dry wit and knew many of his lines by heart. Simon drank greedily as he sought to diminish his thirst. Then he poured himself another glass of the refreshing Italian mineral water and lemon, but this time added two aspirins for the headache that was quickly blossoming deep between his eye sockets. Just for good measure, Simon added a third aspirin to the mix. "Happiness and dark days…" he whispered to himself as he walked to his library searching for Capote's "Other Voices Other Rooms". There was something there that he needed to read aloud in order to reassure himself.

He found the worn book with the blue hardcover he knew almost by heart and, naked, sat in his overstuffed chair in the bedroom. The writings of Truman Capote had always been sacred for him since he had first encountered them in high school. It was as if Capote's words and thoughts had been carefully garnered from Simon's own heart in much the same way as one deliberately chooses and carefully gathers delicate flowers from an untended garden.

He turned to Chapter Eight and read the passage that was underlined there: "The brain may take advice, but not the heart, and love, having no geography, knows no boundaries: weight and sink it deep, no matter, it will rise and find the surface: and why not? Any love is natural and beautiful that lies within a person's nature; only hypocrites would hold a man responsible for what he loves, emotional illiterates and those of righteous envy, who, in their agitated concern, mistake so frequently the arrow pointing to Heaven for the one that leads to hell." Simon closed the book and laid his head back. He thought about how true these words had become in his life. His brain and his heart had had their own set of rules but Simon admitted to himself now that his heart, by far, had always won him over. He would have liked to be that image of himself that proclaimed the opposite, that is, that he had always been cautious and tempered in his life. He remembered one of his father's favorite sayings: "un hombre precavido vale por dos," and closing his eyes, he repeated softly to himself saying "a cautious man is worth two". Yet, he had not been cautious in his life. Far from it. The truth he faced now was that he had given full reign to his heart long ago. It was his heart that told him what to do without restraint and he had obeyed willingly.

+ + + + +

Simon arrived at the tattoo shop a little early and looked through the glass door. He was relieved to see that only one other person was there, slouched on the red leather sofa, apparently asleep. Simon entered and Billy smiled and waved at him as he spoke in hushed tones into his cell phone. He hung up almost immediately and came around to greet Simon, "Hey, Simon, buddy!" He extended his tattooed scrawny hand and Simon took it.

"How's it going, Billy?" Simon wanted to slouch on the red leather sofa and close his eyes.

He turned to sit when he heard Billy say almost with something like concern, "Damn, dude, you look like shit."

"Top of the world to you too." Simon heard the sharp anger in his voice and added, "I'll just sit over here and wait for Mark."

"Late night, huh?" Billy was unfazed. "I've been there way too often, baby." He stood there looking at Simon nervously and added, "You do realize you're early for your one o'clock, right?"

"Yes and yes," Simon answered without much inflection as he reached the red sofa. "I'll just lay back here till it's time. No hurry." Billy remained standing, looking at Simon as if he wanted to say something more. He wore a stupid grin on his face. Simon wondered if sunny days also made Billy as horny as cold, gray days did. Carefully, he sat down on the sofa and sighed. His head threatened to give way any minute to a colossal headache and Simon braced himself for the onslaught. He leaned back cautiously and gently rested his throbbing head on the low backside of the sofa. He was grateful that it was blessedly cushioned and was happy that he had a few minutes of repose before seeing Mark and dealing with the needle. He thought to himself that he should have had a beer or two before getting to the shop. It was a perfect, time tested, old Mexican remedy he had learned years ago for curing a hangover.

Simon closed his eyes, away from the bright ceiling lights and tried not to think about how nauseated he felt. His bowels gurgled and growled deep within his gut and he reminded himself that the bathroom was down the corridor, past Mark's workroom in case he had to run there. Without much effort, Simon let himself drift in and out of a light slumber that was quickly taking hold of him. As he drifted he was aware of the other person on the sofa, not far from him. Simon had only briefly looked at him before sitting down and they had made eye contact, nodding politely to one another. He supposed that the young man was in his early twenties. He was pierced in both ears and wore a red, sleeveless undershirt. An expansive, impressive tattoo of the kraken overtaking a ship covered one of his shoulders. Some of the sea monster's tattooed tentacles wrapped themselves onto the vessel while some tentacles spread down his arm and others across his chest. He had noticed that there were other tentacles that hugged his neck all the way around and went under his jaw line, disappearing behind one ear. The young man on the sofa was slender yet toned without really being muscular. His head was completely shaved and Simon thought about the term skin head as he considered the man's highly polished, heavy black boots. He thought about the kraken tattoo and the deep, dark waters of the ocean as he allowed himself to slip away and doze without much of an effort.

A phone suddenly began ringing loudly in the shop and Simon jumped in his seat, almost saying, "Dammit, my head is about to burst! Somebody please shut that damned thing off!" But then the ringing stopped just as abruptly as it had begun and he allowed himself to slip back into blessed nothingness. Then the phone rang again. It seemed to be even louder than before and his head throbbed painfully. He hesitated to open his eyes, knowing it would hurt his head to do so. The phone rang and rang and Simon couldn't understand why Billy didn't answer it. He was about to lift his head and search for Billy when he felt the young man sitting next to him, shift and squirm, struggling to pull the cell phone out of his tight jean's pocket.

Simon heard the unmistakable click and the ringing stopped as his sofa companion said groggily into his phone, "Yeah, what's up?" There was silence and then he coarsely answered, "You want to talk to who? Who the fuck is that?" Silence returned and then Simon heard a gentle voice near his ear, "Dude? Hey, dude, the guy on the phone says it's for you." Simon barely opened his eyes into slits as he turned to face the young man who now held his silver cell phone out to him. He shrugged apologetically and said, "It's for you. The guy says he needs to talk to you."

Simon was barely able to say, "Huh?"

"It's for you, dude. The phone call is for you. You're Simon, right?"

Simon opened his eyes now and sat up slowly. He tried to focus on what the stranger beside him was saying. It didn't seem to make much sense. "Yeah, I'm Simon but why would…"

"Dude, I have no fucking idea. It's for you. The guy on the other end says it's urgent." He practically put the phone in Simon's lap, "Here you go, buddy."

Simon took the phone out of his hand warily and spoke into it, not fully understanding what he was doing, "Hello, hello, this is Simon. Can you hear me?" He could hear static and the interference of voices coming from other phones trying to break in. It was almost impossible to decipher anything. "Who is this? I don't understand who this is. What do you want with me…?"

Like an unexpected bolt of lightning, static crackled loudly in his ear and Simon instinctively pulled the phone away as if it had wanted to bite off a piece of him. The crackling continued and when it finally seemed to have subsided, Simon once again put the phone to his ear. He was astonished and speechless when he heard the familiar voice speaking to him. He knew it couldn't be possible, yet, he tried to identify the male voice.

"Hey, little one. Where have you been? I've been trying to get you like forever. Where have you been hiding from me?" It was the young, frivolous voice Simon recalled so well and his caller laughed freely. "I can see you've tried to forget me." He sounded far away even though the connection was perfect. "Well, isn't that some kind of shitty gratitude for all I've done for you?"

"What?" Simon was confused and his inability to understand fully frustrated him. Simon was sitting on the edge of the sofa now and the young man next to him was staring at him with a knowing smile.

The voice on the other end of the phone continued. "Ha, ha, ha! Don't make me shit myself with that kind of an attitude, lover boy. I'd say we damn well know each other. We've lived so many things together over the years. Good stuff and bad shit. You know perfectly well who this is. Don't give me that pathetic 'I-don't-know-who-this-is' routine."

Simon wasn't so much confused now as he was terrified. He tried to concentrate but his head ached far too much for any kind of real concentration. A chill ran up his spine and all the memories of a lifetime made his skin crawl. He managed to say weakly, "But none of this makes any sense. How could you be calling me here? How could you possibly know where…? This is total lunacy, this isn't even my phone, dammit!"

"Oh, this might not be your phone, baby, but it's you on one end and me on the other. Don't pay too much attention to the crazy shit details in life. None of it makes much sense anyway." Simon felt, rather than heard, the sarcasm in the caller's voice. "Life is often a bitch that way. Anyhow, I've got you covered like I always have. I promised you that and here I am just to remind you again that I'm always true to my word." There was a pause and complete silence followed. Finally, the voice said, "There is something I called to tell you. Watch your ass, okay? Watch that nice, little furry ass of yours real good because some bad shit is coming down and you don't know how bad it's gonna be. Watch your ass real good because it's gonna get bad. You don't know how bad BAD shit can get. You don't have a fucking clue, little one."

"But how did you know where to call me? I mean, how could you possibly know where…?"

Simon heard laughter on the other end. "Watch that nice ass, watch it real good."

Simon felt as if his head were splitting open but when he looked next to him, his heart froze. The young man was laughing too and the kraken on his shoulder appeared to be three dimensional and moving. With one hand the man sensually caressed a strand of the kraken's tentacles. Simon could see how the tentacles adhered momentarily to his skin and then let go and slid lazily between his fingers. Simon instinctively feared that the sea monster would jump out at him. He felt the young man's other hand on his own shoulder pressing and then shaking Simon gently. His voice was changing now, becoming confident and breaking in to Simon's dark, sinister dream.

"Simon, dude, are you okay? Wake up, buddy. It's me. Time for your one o'clock appointment. I've got everything set up." Simon gasped for breath as if he were breaking the surface of a turbulent, menacing sea. He felt himself coming up and out of confusion and fear toward light and clarity. He tried to focus his eyes and rubbed them roughly as if trying to remove the stubborn scales that had formed there and had veiled his vision. He realized he didn't have a cell phone in his hand and then recognized Mark immediately. The tattooer was smiling at him and Simon was embarrassed if he had created some kind of scene. The dream, nay, the nightmare had seemed so real to him. Mark asked, "Long night, huh?"

"Shit, I must have fallen asleep on the sofa."

He looked around him and then stared at the young man with the tattooed kraken and shaved head sitting next to him. He was smiling cautiously and said, "Mister, you was trippin' away in shit-land far, far away. Some bad dream or nightmare, it looked like to me. Or some fucked-up, funky ride on whatever you're doing." He turned to Mark and frowned, saying, "Creeped me the fuck out when he turned to me with his eyes wide open and starting reaching for something."

"You were calling out to somebody by the time I got here, Simon." There was a trace of concern in Mark's voice along with something else, possibly curiosity. "Looks like somebody gave you a bad time in that dream. You okay now?"

Simon could still feel his heart thumping wildly in his chest and ears, kind of like when a plane has left behind violent, turbulent skies and is trying to steady itself to land onto firm ground. "Yeah, yeah, I'm good now. I can't believe I fell asleep so soundly. It all seemed so real." He got to his feet and swayed a little. Mark helped him. "I didn't sleep so well last night and Jack Daniel's has put a hurtin' on me." He felt cold sweat breaking on his forehead and run down his back. He combed his hair nervously with his fingers and dried his sweaty hands on his t-shirt, saying, "Too many demons in my bed."

"Come on back and let's get started."

Simon followed Mark on unsteady feet and consciously made a wide berth around the young man with the kraken tattoo. He was still preoccupied and shaken by the dream that had been way too clear to dismiss so easily. Brother Shawn's voice had been unmistakable and ominous. Simon shuddered as he remembered the dreadful warning he had issued in the dream: "watch your ass real good because some bad shit is coming". He knew perfectly well what the bad shit was all about.

A phone rang loudly behind him and Simon just about jumped completely off the floor. He continued down the corridor behind Mark and heard Billy say, "Yeah! Tattoo Shop. What do you need?"

The small plastic, thimble-sized cups filled with different colored ink and set in place with Vaseline, stood near the worktable. Mark unwrapped a razor and poured soapy solution into a paper towel. Simon had removed his shoes and jeans and stood in his underwear briefs anticipating what would come next.

"You can go ahead and lay down up here for me, man." Mark gestured for Simon to climb up onto the cushioned table. "I need for you to tell me exactly where we're putting this other pink triangle, so I can shave the area on your thigh."

"Right here, Mark." Simon pointed to the right side of his upper thigh. Mark applied the soapy solution and shaved the area with the razor. When he was done, Simon saw how odd it looked now that a space on the skin of his thigh was completely smooth.

Mark cleared away the soap and hair and rinsed the area with another wet towel. "You're a fucking ape, dude. Honestly." Mark laughed as he finished applying the purple stencil and then took the needle gun in his right hand. The high-pitched sound of the needle signaled it was time to start. "Okay, Simon, here we go. Same exact tattoo as the one on your chest, correct?"

"Yeah, exactly the same."

Mark traced the form of the triangle on Simon's thigh and as he did he asked, "So when you came in last time you were telling me about a weird night when heads rolled and everything changed. What was that all about?"

"It was something that had been building and building like the pent up force inside a pressure cooker that's way past where it should be. Suddenly, it erupted without warning and when it did, it took a lot of folks with it, even though I was spared somehow. Not many of those who stood accused survived it."

"Accused? Damn, now I'm really curious about that night, dude, but not only that. You said it has to do with these two triangles and the numbers. Sounds twisted. How's it all connected?"

"Like I was trying to say last time, the triangles are all about persecution and being hunted down and labeled. Some really bad stuff rained down on the abbey one night and affected those of us who were gay for the rest of our lives. The ripple effect from that night was devastating. It was so awful we referred to it as the 'Night of the Long Knives'." Insecurity gripped his heart as he remembered the ominous warning Shawn had uttered over the phone in his dream just a short time ago: 'watch your ass'.

"The Night of the Long Knives," Mark repeated. "Damn, that sounds creepy. What the hell was that all about?"

Simon tried to remember how it had all begun. "I don't really know who of us said it first but it stuck. Whenever we remembered that night, that's what we called it."

"Why the long knives?"

"The historical 'Night of the Long Knives', I came to find out, was actually a term used for a murderous event that took place in Germany when the Nazis were in power and rising. I think it was the summer, early in the 1930s. We even memorized the German term for it: 'Nacht der langen Messer'. We used to whisper it in German among ourselves. It had to be whispered because all around us were some of the older monks who would be able to understand." Simon remembered only too well and added, "The event, in its beginning had actually been referred to as 'Unternehmen Kolibri'."

"What was it? What does that mean?"

"'Unternehmen Kolibri' means 'Operation Hummingbird', but that sounded too innocent to us and what we suffered. We chose the more sinister term that was used by Hitler, Goring and Himmler for it. 'The Night of the Long Knives' was basically when the Nazis cleaned house overnight. A shitload of bloody executions took place without too many questions. It was like what Pancho Villa used to say in Mexico during the revolution there, 'Shoot first and ask questions later.' The Nazis at the very top already knew who they wanted to eliminate. There were no trials. It was another way Hitler could be sure that no rivals existed who could threaten his complete power. It was a blood bath."

"Fuck me, dude."

"Yeah, the message was clear to those who survived: 'Don't fuck with us because we are in charge. You fuck up, you die.' Our own 'Night of the Long Knives' in the abbey was really bad and like those swept up into the original one, we didn't see it coming either. In Germany more than a hundred were murdered and a shitload more were arrested and disappeared. In Leicester, in our 'Night of the Long Knives' at the abbey, about thirty some of us were rounded up and cross-examined. We were accused by the Abbot and two or three others from his council without much real proof at all. They had letters from so-called witnesses. In a matter of hours, lots of guys I had lived with and knew, disappeared. I remember walking down the corridor afterward and noticing how much brighter the corridor was because so many doors were now wide open. In those many rooms, door after door, the mattresses were rolled up on top of the metal cots and remained that way as a clear warning to everyone else."

Mark listened as he worked and said softly, "I get the persecution thing now."

"They came at us one night like ravenous wolves without warning. We were ill prepared, of course, to handle any of it because we were young and stupid. We didn't see it coming. After it was all over, I found out that it had been in the planning stages for months and that Shawn was the one who had instigated and orchestrated the entire thing. That fucker had fanned the flames that early summer night."

"The whole thing sounds like the Inquisition to me, dude. What a sick bunch of shit. How did it all come down? Damn, I think your term about the 'long knives' fits in perfectly, even though I don't even know how it went down." He was tattooing the small, thread-like marks on one side of the pink triangle when he added, "I'm intrigued. Tell me more."

"Before the purge of the original 'Night of the Long Knives', everything was as it had always been." Simon corrected himself, "Well, that's not entirely true. Things 'seemed' to be as they had always been. The fact was that without our knowing it, a storm was festering and brewing as it had been for those guys who caught the bad shit in Nazi Germany. The festive atmosphere we had created was about to implode. The sexual revolution was about to receive a death blow in the abbey. We couldn't have known it but Shawn was taking inventory. He had drawn into his confidence several guys who were not a part of our inner group but lived on our corridor. They were aware of our charades because by this time we didn't hide very much. Shawn saw that they were closeted and more than willing to expose us before anything reached them."

"I'm not following you, dude." Mark had stopped working momentarily and was looking at Simon. "Those guys were gay too?"

"I don't have any way to prove they were or not but my gaydar told me and my friends that they were just as gay as us only closeted. I guess they felt left out and that might have contributed to their double crossing us. They felt left out but were unwilling or unable because of their fear, to come out as we had done to each other. Still, I suspect those 'witnesses' were driven by the fear Shawn was capable of using against them."

"A fear thing, then?"

"Yeah, Shawn probably told them a witch hunt was about to come down and those guys didn't want to be swallowed up by it. God only knows what he must have told them to get them to be 'witnesses' against us and spill their guts before the authorities. In any case, that's what they did. I have to admit we were a bunch of naïve, albeit, horny fuckers. Did we see ourselves like that? Not really, I mean, as far as we were concerned, we were all there answering God's call to the priesthood. Our faith in God had not lessened. We went to Confession every week and never missed prayers every day."

Mark nodded, saying, "I can see what you're saying but I don't get how you guys still moved along without wondering if you belonged there or somewhere else, like the Castro in San Francisco or the Village in New York City. I mean, c'mon Simon, admit it, you make it sound like you guys were living a gay lifestyle in the very place that forbid it while at the same time, you were training for something holy." He added, "Training for something holy and fucking your brains out." He looked closely at the tattoo he was working on and added, "That's like oil and vinegar, dude."

Simon was unsure how to answer Mark. He was in agreement with his assessment but he felt that Mark didn't quite understand the whole thing. "We were living a gay lifestyle, yes, but it wasn't really 'open' like regular guys out in San Francisco or New York City. I mean, we didn't hold hands nor kiss in public and this, in our minds, somehow made it different. It could never be in the open if we remained in the abbey."

Mark looked up and shot Simon a penetrating gaze, asking him, "Different? How the fuck so? I'm not getting it."

"Yeah, okay, it was against all the rules but as we came to terms with our sexuality, it seemed acceptable and normal for us to carry on the way we did. In our minds, it wasn't obvious but a well-kept secret among an elite few. I know it sounds flawed, but I'm being completely honest here." Simon paused and then continued, "But more than that, Mark, we still wanted to be priests. We advanced in our studies of Scripture, philosophy and theology day after day. It was at night when we got wild. I mean, we were all twenty-something-year-olds and our libidos were overloaded to Hell and back. We were totally willing to have sex and forge relationships that were sexual even though it was prohibited. Ridiculous as it may sound, we didn't see a disconnect. It just came natural to many of us to act the way we did. Maybe it was our network of trust among friends that sustained the whole thing. I remember years later, talking to guys from other religious Orders who had been in the same situations and their experience was pretty much a carbon copy of ours. The sexual revolution that swept through America exempted no one who was willing to recognize it and jump on the wagon, as it were."

Mark looked at his work while saying, "No one who was willing to recognize it? That sounds lame to me, Simon. I'm sure there were guys who were faithful to their vows too. You can't expect me to believe that everybody was fucking everybody just because of unruly hormones and libidos gone crazy. I have to believe that some guys had the strength and conviction, to keep their peckers in their own pants."

"No, not everyone broke their vows but a very large number of guys in my age group did. The Church may want to deny it but I can tell you from personal experience that it was true. I was there. And I can tell you it was true in other religious houses too. We got swept up into it without really realizing where it was taking us. It was like a tsunami."

"So how did it go down? How did the shit finally hit the proverbial fan when the bubble burst? How did the long knives come out?"

"Ah, you wanna know the steamy details, huh? Who's the perv now?"

Mark chuckled to himself as he drew more ink and continued working. "I'm just asking you to tell me what happened so I can understand. Your take on it doesn't really convince me." Then he added, "I'm thinking the important thing going on here is for you to say it, to come clean and be honest with yourself." He paused and drew more ink, "And just for the record, yeah, I'm a horny perv too, but I think you got me won." He chuckled to himself.

Simon remembered clearly how it had happened. "After Joshua and I had our fight over that Joey bitch…"

"Joey bitch! Wow, it must have messed you up."

"Oh, it hurt me real bad and something died in me in regards to Joshua. I never fully trusted him again. I understood perfectly what betrayal of love feels like when you're on the receiving end. Anyway, when Joey went back to wherever the fuck he was from, Joshua and I stayed together but it wasn't the same as it had been before. Like I said, something fragile had died. At least, it wasn't the same for me."

The sound of the needle lulled him away from the stinging pain on his skin and he allowed the profound current of memories to pull him away.

Those faraway days at the abbey came into focus now as he spoke. "The days all seemed to flow into each other. We would get up at five-thirty in the morning, shower and throw our habits on. We marched to prayers and meals and classes all day. On early mornings or late afternoons we were at Mass daily and then supper, followed by more prayers, evening study and recreation together. Night prayers were no longer obligatory and the Grand Silence wasn't observed either but that didn't mean that there weren't still rules and schedules to follow. It wasn't as strict as it had been before, though, that much is true. The loosening of discipline was part of the changes that came about on their own from the modernization of the Church known as Vatican Council II. There really wasn't much variety and sometimes it was downright boring for some of us. I wonder if that didn't contribute to our getting wild at night."

"Sounds like it to me, dude, but I gotta say, nobody held a gun to your head, forcing you to live that kind of boring, regimental life."

"That's my point, Mark!" Simon said this excitedly. "We wanted to be there and be men of prayer but we were also lulled by our sexual appetite and the freedom that loomed among us because of it. During the day we appeared and tried to be pious young men preparing for the priesthood and at night we let loose. We became libertines, unfettered and bold. There was some drinking but it wasn't so often. We weren't allowed to have any personal money and couldn't get booze as a result."

"Tell me again how you guys got crazy." Mark turned off the tattoo gun and changed the needle. Simon thought back and remembered how it was. He hoped that Mark would be able to understand how it had all happened without judging. Sometimes he felt Mark judged without really knowing how that life had been. He remembered a particular afternoon…

+ + + + +

There had been a picnic organized by the guys from the inner group late that summer. They had left the abbey early one Saturday morning, in the big, yellow seminary bus, and had headed for a state park with a large lake a couple of hours away.

All of them had snuck away into the bus well before the sun was up. Prayers on Saturday morning were done individually. It was another innovation that usually meant most guys skipped it altogether. The night before, when no one was around, they had raided the abbey kitchen for food to take on the picnic.

"Hey, Lorenzo, do you think this can is too big?" Simon held up a large, gallon-sized can of pitted black olives.

His sleek, handsome friend from New York had given him a broad smile and said, "Oh yeah, Simon, bring those! Black olives are aphrodisiacs, you know."

"Huh?" Simon wasn't sure he had understood.

"Ha, ha, ha. You innocent little boy! Those olives will get you really hard and horny and keep you that way where you need it…right here." Lorenzo had playfully touched Simon's crotch unexpectedly with an index finger. Simon jumped back understanding what he meant.

"Oh, okay, okay, I see," he said embarrassed by his lack of knowledge. He put the large tin of olives in a cardboard box that was already overflowing with stolen supplies. Blocks of cheese, a thick roll of genoa salami, slices of ham and loaves of bread baked in the abbey kitchen had been selected. Before getting on the bus, Kurt and Aaron had somehow gotten into the walk-in refrigerators and grabbed two cases of beer from the brewery. They took their goodies to the bus and left quietly. Other guys were going from the large kitchen to the bus and back again. Simon had made sure not to tell Shawn about the picnic.

They found a secluded place far from the picnic tables and charred, steel barbeque grills used by families on Saturday afternoons. Kurt knew of a hidden spot that was well secluded from weekend visitors. Once at the park, they swam in the lake and sunned themselves. Joshua and two of the others had disappeared into the woods saying they were going on a hike. Simon remained with the others, lying next to Anthony and Noah. The three of them lay shirtless together in their bathing suits and shared a tattered blanket at the water's edge.

Simon smiled to himself now as he remembered the closeness he felt with those men. They had enjoyed a bond that made him feel protected and accepted in a way he had never really felt before. Kurt was especially responsible for this. He was perhaps the oldest member among them. Simon could still remember being in Kurt's cell back at the seminary. Kurt had removed the metal cot and put two mattresses one on top of the other, directly on the floor. His room was almost literally wallpapered in posters and he had put a blue colored lightbulb over his sink instead of the typical white one. There were always sticks of incense burning in Kurt's cell. This created an ambience that drew Simon to the place because he felt free to be himself there. It felt safe there.

Kurt's favorite album that summer was the popular song "Grease" written by Barry Gibb and recorded by Frankie Valli. Most of the student monks in the abbey had gone to see the motion picture of the same name that summer. Kurt would play the single over and over in his cell on a beat up phonograph with the volume way up. Simon admired Kurt because the man seemed so sure of himself, unthreatened and unafraid of the authority figures in the abbey. At least this was the impression he gave Simon.

Kurt was a deacon and soon to be ordained a priest. It wasn't prohibited anymore to be in the solemnly professed corridors even if one hadn't yet professed religious vows for life. Simon would often go up to where Kurt's cell was if he heard the song "Grease" booming not too far away from his own cell. Kurt would wave Simon inside and gesture for him to sit on his bed. Meanwhile, Kurt would hold his fist in front of his mouth as if it were a microphone and sing the lyrics of the song Grease.

Simon would lean back against the wall watching Kurt and be in awe of this man who so freely believed it was a "right" to be "who we are", encouraging all of them to do the same, without fear. Kurt would drop to the floor on his knees in front of Simon and belt out the final words, laughing with abandon.

And then, he'd lock eyes with Simon, dropping his arms down and sadly mouth the words of the album.

Thinking back now, Simon reveled in the freedom that those lyrics had given them that late summer before classes resumed at the abbey as they enjoyed themselves at the lake's edge.

Kurt and Aaron, the oldest of the elite band of friends, had decided to scout the area that afternoon and make sure they were free of nosey visitors. Simon noticed how they had joined hands as soon as they entered the dense forest.

+ + + + +

Mark interrupted Simon, "Sounds like you guys were a tight-knit group."

"We were and in our new found freedom, we got bold to the point of being arrogant in the sense that we were somewhat careful but didn't really care what others thought. I already told you we were young and stupid."

"Yeah, I got that. I think that's a given."

"We were so caught up in our little world. It filled us with defiance although I don't think I would have defined us that way. I know it sounds weird but as things unfolded and we lived our charmed life, we were oblivious of the chaos that was quickly gaining momentum. We were lustful in so many ways and finally got to the point of no return. It was that intense."

Mark looked up, "I believe you, dude. I was twenty years old once too."

"Our tight-knit group felt empowered and when we'd get together our conversation often turned to the world outside the abbey. We were filled with curiosity about Stonewall and about how gay men lived. We'd sit and talk about the musical 'Hair' trying to imagine if the nude scenes on stage could really be true. We often wondered what it would be like to go into a gay bar filled with men who felt like us. There were two or three in the group who had

had some experience with this but most of us had not. Most of us were just big kids. As students for the priesthood, we were all in vows and it was strictly forbidden for any of us to visit the pubs that existed around the college down in the town of Leicester. Those pubs were always crowded with college students both male and female. Frat brothers were everywhere and Kurt had told some of us that those guys were always horny and hot. He must have had some experience in attaining that kind of information. It certainly was something to think about, let me tell you. There were no gay bars in Leicester, I mean, it's just a sleepy, tiny college town. Kurt and Aaron had told us that there were plenty of gay bars in Pittsburgh, just a few hours away by car."

"Wait a minute!" Mark interrupted. "Are you going to tell me that some of you guys actually had the balls to leave the abbey and go to a gay bar in Pittsburgh?"

Simon looked at him and said quietly, "Yeah. What I'm talking about now is when four of us finally got the courage to go to a gay bar in Pittsburgh late on a Friday night. I can't remember if it was on Liberty Avenue but I remember clearly that it was called 'The Loose Balloon'. Kurt had said that that's when the place would be wall to wall gay men. Joshua and I went with him and Aaron and we were giddy with nerves thinking about what we would encounter there."

"So Shawn didn't go?"

"Oh, no! Are you nuts? By this point I wouldn't have gone with him to anything like that. He was crowding me too much and I felt nervous being around him. I avoided Shawn quite a bit by then. Just the four of us went. We didn't even tell any of the other guys in our circle of friends. It was too risky, I mean, we were young and stupid but sometimes there were brief instances of clarity and common sense."

Mark smiled, "Yeah, emphasis on the word 'brief'. But explain something because I'm confused. Wasn't Shawn like your 'gay connection' with all those old guys at supper? Proud Mary and the other two?"

"Shawn moved in too fast. I mean, it's like I said, I felt he was crowding me and wanting to control me. He wanted to keep me for himself. By this point in time I had no doubt about his sexual attraction toward me. I wasn't able to see it at first but the night of the Carabinieri boots it became obvious to me. Painfully obvious."

"Fair enough. So did you four guys go to the gay bar in Pittsburgh after all?"

"Oh, yeah. It was quite the adventure. Kurt and Aaron were able to get a car from the abbey because of their clout. The guys getting ready for ordination were given special treatment and had privileges us younger students didn't enjoy. Joshua and I didn't have permission that Friday night to leave the abbey but we snuck in the car anyway. When we got to the bar, it was already close to midnight and the place was packed. Music was blaring and guys dressed only in jockstraps and work boots were dancing on the bar bare-chested and shiny with sweat. Men were dancing with men and kissing while they did so. And some held colorful, laced fans like the ones my grandmother used to hold onto on the front porch when it was unbearably hot except that these men used them to keep to the beat of the music like you'd normally do with a tambourine. Mostly everyone was in shorts and tight white tees or shirtless and it was a sight that had Joshua and me gawking. I took Joshua's hand tightly in my own. I was charged and excited as I was shoved and grabbed by a steady crowd of sweaty gay men trying to get a beer. What mostly impressed me were the hungry, blatant stares from some of the strangers in there. Lots of guys looked really amazing to me, and I was smitten like never before. It all hit me like a charging train when I realized this 'other world' truly existed parallel to our life in the abbey. Some men were older than us but there were a lot of guys our age. I was new to all that lay in front of me but in a way I couldn't possibly explain, I felt that I was a part of it. In an inexplicable way, at that moment, I felt 'at home' among these men. Deep down, I asked myself while I stood there if it could be possible that we were all the same even though I struggled to believe it. I struggled because we had been taught that those of us at the abbey had received a singular call from God. This made us different from other men, elevated and special before God in a way that was logical because of what we would receive as priests. I remembered Father Michael, Father Francis and Father Cornelius. I was called by God to the very same thing they had been called to. I was to receive a grace, an indelible mark on my soul that not every man would ever receive, something that did make me different because of what I would receive. I believed it then and I believe it now but…but in that bar, there was another realization that was desperately trying to break in to my thoughts like never before. Something new and therefore, threatening to me. Could it really be true that those of us standing in that bar on that night were all the same anyway? My attitude that night was challenged to the breaking point and shaken considerably in that crowded bar of sweaty men." He paused. "I remember I was scared to go to the restroom alone, thinking I might get raped. I know it sounds stupid, but that first gay bar experience was all so incredibly beyond anything I could have imagined. I kept thinking that it was a world that actually did exist aside from mine and I couldn't get it out of my head. Toby had been right and this wasn't even New York nor San Francisco! It dawned on me that this wasn't just one, isolated place filled with gay men like me, but that it was a reality that already existed and was growing all over the world. Again, I dared to ask in some distant part of myself if these men and I were the same or if there was enough of a difference based on what we received from God to make us different. I struggled with the question for the very first time that night and dared not wait for an answer."

Simon was astonished to realize how many details he still remembered from those months just before the "Night of the Long Knives". He lay on Mark's worktable wondering what Mark might be thinking about all the things he was telling him. The tattooer was listening and Simon didn't hold back. He remembered and shared another memory from the days just before the iron fist came down on them.

A public event took place in the abbey shortly before that terrible night when the long knives were exposed and fell mercilessly against us. A fund raising supper for the abbey was held in the refectory and every one of the three hundred or so monks who lived there, was expected to attend with our habits on. White, starched tablecloths were laid out on every table and wine goblets had been set at every place for the gala evening. More than fifty seminarians from two nearby seminaries were also there along with priests from the parishes of the diocese. Extra tables had been set up in the vast dining hall to accommodate the wealthy benefactors who had driven in from Pittsburgh, Philadelphia and New York for the event. At the head table sat the Abbot and the Bishop of the diocese along with the entire seminary staff.

The supper was no mere gathering and had been planned for months. It was intended to raise money and secure pledges for the training of future priests at the abbey. Aunt Tessie was asked to organize the sumptuous menu and as the evening wore on, the wine flowed and inhibitions faded. The general happy, festive mood gave way to some raucous laughter among the young men preparing for priesthood and in some corners of the refectory that night, the atmosphere among some of the younger monks, became unashamedly gay and trashy. Most of us students were seated at the tables far from the authorities. Numerous professional men and women, doctors, lawyers and judges, rose to speak in favor of priestly formation and the urgent need to secure priests for the future work of the Church. Simon and his companions knew they were there to impress the benefactors into being generous.

Toward the end of the supper, the key speaker rose to address those in attendance. He was an older Catholic gentleman from New York City, a well-known entrepreneur who was one of the most important laymen connected to the abbey. He sat on the board of trustees and was often mentioned by name in the general prayers at Vespers. His portrait hung in the Chapter Hall right next to those of Abbots and Bishops. Everyone knew that he was one of the most generous benefactors of the abbey.

The distinguished gentleman spoke with eloquence and with the intention of evoking enthusiasm for the works of the abbey but most especially for the formation of future priests. He went out of his way to point to where we students sat, and raising his voice enthusiastically, cried out, "Let's give this wonderful group of young, healthy men a round of applause!" Thunderous applause erupted and boomed in the refectory. He didn't stop there though, and emotionally cried out again, "Let's cheer these boys on and encourage them to become the best priests of their generation!" Again, the assembled crowd dressed in their finery responded energetically. Then the gentleman, carried away by the moment, suddenly roared, "Boys! Boys! That's what we need more of! We need more boys in this seminary! Let's bring many, many more boys here to join these young men!" Many of us student monks and diocesan seminarians had had a great deal of wine that night and the ten or twelve tables where more than a hundred of us seminarians sat, suddenly burst into loud applause and laughter. This caused great excitement in everyone and momentarily, a kind of pandemonium spread like wildfire. The refectory became a carnival. The old gentleman tried to speak but could not be heard over the cries we emitted. "More boys! Send us more boys!" Many of us yelled as we patted each other on the back and held our wine goblets up high. "Boys! Hell, yeah, bring us more boys! Many, many more boys!"

"The Abbot seemed to be enjoying himself and smiling, held up a goblet to the distinguished benefactor and then to the crowd who applauded us. They toasted and drank, oblivious of the double meaning of our words. From where

I sat, I saw that the bishop didn't appear to be quite so happy and pleased as our Abbot and in fact, when our boisterousness finally calmed down, he seemed ill at ease at his place at table. Many other priests who sat there appeared the same. Then it was Father Demetrius' turn to speak. He stood and took the microphone from the distinguished old gentleman who waved at us smiling."

Laughter and screams could still be heard as he moved away from the head table and Father Demetrius suddenly stood at the podium and gazed out at the noisy crowd. A swath of his golden hair had slipped out of place and fell across his face, covering one of his eyes. He threw his head slightly to one side and then jerked it back, causing his hair to shift away from his eyes. He held the microphone in one hand and a goblet full of wine in the other. In that hand, nudged between his index and middle fingers, he held a lit cigarette with a long, twisted ash threatening to break off. Father Demetrius took a great swallow of wine and set his goblet down on the table, then gestured to everyone to quiet down. He took a long drag from the cigarette and dropped it to the floor, stepping on it. In his deep, theatrical voice, he said, "Boys! Oh, yes, let's work on that but let's give a round of applause to our Father, the Lord Abbot." He raised his goblet and unexpectedly toasted, "To Mister Clean!" Everyone roared with laughter as the Abbot stood and ran his hand smoothly from his forehead back across his bald head and smiled playfully. Father Demetrius, feigning embarrassment, put his hand with the microphone briefly over his mouth and corrected himself, "Oh, I'm so sorry, Father Edmund!" The Prior of the abbey looked around the room smiling mischievously, as he said in his best English accent "Well, at least I didn't call him Mister Dirty!" Most everyone rose their goblets to the Abbot laughing and crying out. The evening had turned into a circus of sorts and very soon after Father Demetrius' toast, the bishop leaned over to the Abbot, whispered briefly and rose for the closing prayer. He left immediately and the supper was over. We thought no further about our behavior that night as the guests left and we began to clean up the refectory as was expected.

Now it all seemed like such a faraway time to Simon. All of those events and those people were gone. Mark said nothing when Simon finished speaking. The only sound in the work room was the whining of the needle gun. Simon was lost in his thoughts and without much effort continued telling Mark about the events that led to the "Night of the Long Knives". He was on a roll and the memories spilled out of him easily.

Several weeks after the gala super, Joshua went to Simon's room during study time. He had his woolen cape on over his jeans and white t-shirt and Simon suspected he was coming to ask him to go for a stroll. It was a weeknight. Joshua said excitedly, "Tonight some of the guys are going to see 'The Rocky Horror Picture Show' over at the cinema in Crescent. We're invited. There's like fifteen or twenty guys going."

Simon put down the book he was reading and asked, "What horror show is it?"

"It's not really a horror show, Simon. It's not what you're thinking, it's not a scary movie or anything like that. It's a cult film and always starts at midnight."

Simon was confused, "I'm not sure I understand. You said we're invited to 'The Horror Show' but that it's not a horror movie?"

"It's called 'The Rocky Horror Picture Show', that's the name of the film. The bus is behind the pool, like ready to go at eleven. Some of us are meeting there now, a little earlier for a pre-show libation."

"I dunno, Josh. It's a weeknight. Won't we get caught?"

"Aaron says he'll drive the bus and take us there and wait outside with Kurt until it's over to bring us all back. There's usually a huge crowd and parking is a bitch."

"I don't know." Simon sat back in his chair and took his glasses off. He rubbed his eyes and put the glasses back on. "Look at all this." He gestured to the mess on his desk. "I have two papers I need to turn in by next Friday. Sounds like that movie is gonna end really late if it starts at midnight. I probably shouldn't go. Plus, I'm not really interested in a horror film to be honest. I'll come back here and get freaked out and won't be able to sleep."

"It's not a horror film." Simon thought he recognized an edge in his friend's voice and believed Joshua was getting impatient with him. "It's a cult film," he said flatly. "I know you'll love it." Joshua came over to Simon and rubbed his shoulders. "You're all stressed out. Getting out will do you good. I don't wanna go without you." Joshua rubbed Simon deliberately and kissed the nape of his neck. "I don't wanna go with all those dumps. I want you with me." He slipped his hand inside Simon's t-shirt and squeezed one of his nipples. Simon squirmed and jumped, giggling. Joshua whispered, "I know you'll really get into the audience participation."

"Audience participation?"

"It gets wild, Simon. I've been to it before in Philly. I'll help you with the movie dialogue when it's our time to talk to the screen. Plus, I already have a bag full of the stuff to throw."

"Dialogue and a bag full of stuff to throw?" Simon was lost but more intrigued than he was confused and his imagination soared. "I've never been to anything like that."

"Exactly! You'll love it! Trust me, I know you." Joshua smiled his best, cutest smile for Simon.

"Okay! I'm down." Simon slammed the book shut in front of him. He grabbed his woolen cape and dressed in his jeans and t-shirt as well, left his cell with Joshua.

The small group gathered outside behind the pool building was giggling and laughing wickedly when they got there. A bottle of gin had been passed around as they waited for Aaron and Kurt to bring the bus around. Most of them wore their light woolen capes over jeans and white t-shirts since they really didn't own anything else, except for the cut-offs. Habits were still required for classes and chapel. Large, brown paper bags filled with rice packets, toasted white bread, rolls of toilet paper, bottled water, decks of playing cards, flashlights, confetti and party hats, among other supplies, were at their feet. Simon rubbed up against Joshua, who rubbed back and stuck his hand under Simon's cape. He massaged Simon's back and whispered in his ear, "Yambo, Mamma Luke." Simon loved it when Joshua noticed him that way. It reminded him of when they first met and flirted with each other playfully. He missed that kind of attention which his friend seldom expressed to him anymore unless Joshua had been drinking, like they were now. Things had cooled considerably between them and Simon felt miserable because of it. For the moment, though, he was enjoying Joshua's unexpected attention.

By the time the yellow seminary bus pulled up to where the huddled group waited secretly behind the pool building, they had all acquired a nice buzz. Climbing up into the bus, some of them paired off as they sat down on the narrow bus seats. Simon and Joshua sat together on the skimpy seat meant for two. They covered themselves with the folds of their capes. Underneath, they held hands as the bus lurched forward and sped away into the night toward the nearby, little town of Crescent.

It was a rowdy bunch in the bus that night and everyone joined in as they sang songs from "The Wizard of Oz", "The Patty Duke Show" and "Mary Poppins". Tony sang from "South Pacific", standing up and lowering his impressive mane, all the while acting as if he were shampooing from the scene in the movie, "I'm gonna wash that man right outta my hair!" Everyone cheered and Tony looked up, trying to keep his balance as the bus continued to lurch, singing without restraint, "…and send him on his way…" Then he put his face right up to Simon's, brushing their lips and winking, as he asked seductively with his best imitation of a New York accent, "Get the pick-cha?" Everyone cheered when he finished. Others stood in the bouncing bus, swaying and falling this way and that, as solos from the "Sound of Music" and "West Side Story" were performed. Aaron drove them down the winding country roads to the center square of the town of Crescent and pulled in front of the Bloor Cinema.

Simon was wide-eyed and impressed by the unbridled and boisterous mob that was already gathered under the blaring lights of the entrance awning. Under what seemed to be a myriad of light bulbs, Simon saw the unruly congregation dressed in some form of costume and painted faces. Most of them were college students, male and female, much the same age as them who now descended the bus and joined in the chaos. All of them held on tightly to their brown paper bags and Simon happily accepted an opened bottle of beer from a bare-chested college guy whose face was painted gold and wore only a tight fitting speedo of the same color. On his bare feet were battered Chuck Taylor high tops. Next to one eye he wore a bright red heart to which he pointed and said drunkenly to Simon, "Hey buddy, I've got my 'heart-on' for ya. Get it? I've got my 'hard-on' for ya?" Simon saw that the bottle of beer bore the familiar label from the Abbey of the Most Sacred Heart of Jesus brewery, in Leicester, Pennsylvania, U.S.A. Everyone was yelling for the doors of the cinema to open before midnight and at precisely twenty minutes to show time, the vintage, black lacquered doors of the cinema swung open and the sweaty, lively throng stormed in as one body, amid shrieks and howls of intoxicated joy. Charging forward, the rabble wasted no time in paying for their tickets and grabbing their seats within.

At precisely midnight, the lights were extinguished and the film splashed suddenly across the battered, antiquated screen of the Bloor Cinema. The out of control pack stood and cheered and Simon joined them, fueled by the enthusiasm as well as the gin and beer he had consumed. Everyone sat and quieted and Simon turned to Joshua, wondering what wonderful things would happen next.

The audience of this cult film was in fever pitch by the time it began with the wedding scene. Joshua threw a small bag of rice at Simon and when it was time screamed, "Now!" Rice rained down in the darkened cinema as everyone threw rice. Then it was their turn to scream, "Show us an ear!" at the appropriate time, as well as exclaim, "Dammit, Janet!" Joshua had forewarned Simon, "When you hear the name Brad Majors, you scream like everyone else." Simon waited nervously for the cue and when it came he screamed the thunderous word with the lively audience, "ASSHOLE!"

Joshua reached down into the brown paper bag on the floor between his feet and rummaged. He gave Simon several slices of toasted white bread just before the crowd repeated the words spoken on screen, "A toast!" An incalculable number of slices of toasted bread were leveled at the screen and rained down on everyone amid squeals of laughter. Strangers turned in their seats and hugged each other in the dark as the movie played on. Simon knew that he had to throw water when the raining scene appeared. Joshua had been clear, "Brad and Janet will get caught in the storm. Throw the water then." Simon had asked, "But how will I know when it's 'the' moment?" Joshua had smiled in the darkness, "Oh, you'll know." A deluge of water began to fall on them as the audience produced water pistols and sprayed water on everyone. For their part, they uncapped the plastic bottles of water from the brown bag and splashed out at everyone around them, drenching the squirming crowd, many of whom were now shirtless. Simon was completely swallowed up by the excitement and drank greedily from a warm beer somebody handed him in the dark. When the words from the song, "There's a light" began, they lit their flashlights along with everyone else, some of whom had candles and lighters. They threw confetti during the erotic scene when Rocky and Frank make their way toward the bedroom and squirmed in their seats with delight as the sexually charged scene splashed across the screen. It was dank and humid in the cinema and Simon and Joshua had removed their woolen capes and finally, their soaked t-shirts as well.

At some point, Joshua yelled at Simon to get up and move into the aisle. "It's time for the 'pelvic thrust'," he screamed. They stepped into the aisle, and Simon stood there for an instant trying to figure out what came next. All around him, people were grabbing each other from behind as they threw their heads back howling. A bearded, lanky college student, wearing a stovepipe hat and nothing but a pair of cut-offs, grabbed Simon from behind, putting his hands on Simon's hips and began thrusting up against him obscenely. A kind of mad conga line had formed in the aisle and everyone thrusted into the person in front. It was all highly erotic and Simon was greatly aroused as he thrust his hips, along with the others, barely hanging on to the muscled waist of a sweaty, damp boy in front of him, who turned and smiled and pressed back into Simon.

The movie played on and rolls of toilet paper were then hurled at the screen like festive rolls of paper in a ticker-tape parade. It was at that precise moment when everyone was screaming along with the character, Brad, as he cried out to Doctor Scott, "Great Scott!" They had put on their paper party hats at the dinner scene and thrown their decks of playing cards, when it was time to join in the singing, "cards for sorrow, cards for pain."

When "The Rocky Horror Picture Show" finally came to an end and the lights came on in the house, Simon was taken aback by what he saw. The cinema looked as if a category five hurricane and two tornadoes had passed through it. Plastic water bottles and beer bottles were littered everywhere on the floor. The worn, red velvet seats of the Bloor Cinema were soaking wet and covered with pieces of soggy toilet paper, burned slices of bread and confetti. The aisle was littered with rice, playing cards, wet newspapers and rubber gloves. Simon saw pieces of hot dogs stepped on and pressed into the dirty carpet as well as what looked like squashed, ripe prunes. He hoped they were prunes, in any case. As Joshua held his hand and led them outside, Simon saw underwear briefs and shorts trampled in the aisle and wondered if people had gone home naked. Behind the last row of seats, near heavy, massive velvet curtains, he saw several used condoms strewn about the littered floor. Simon had lost his t-shirt somewhere and wore his cape over his naked torso. His woolen cape was damp and smelled of sweat and beer.

Aaron and Kurt were smoking outside the bus. They had the motor running and were waiting for their friends just outside the cinema. All around them was the charged flood of movie goers shoving against each other and yelling obscenities as they struggled to break free from the stifling mob. As the little band boarded the bus, Aaron threw open a plastic ice chest near his driver's seat and Kurt cheerfully handed each of them a bottle of beer, smiling, "Everyone had a good time, I take it?"

+ + + + +

Mark had straightened up in his stool and had put down the tattoo gun. "Damn, Simon, you guys were out of control. I'm kind of envious, I mean, I did some crazy stuff in college but nothing like you!" He stood, "Hell, I'm jealous of the fun you guys had. And you were supposed to be locked up in a monastery!"

"Yeah. Sometimes I think that maybe I didn't have that much fun when I was young and coming out like other young people who lived in the outside world, but I guess that's not the case."

"Uh, duh! No, I don't think so, bud." Mark had thrown his arms up in the air and stood on the tips of his toes stretching. "I just need to stretch and move a little." He arched his back and cracked his fingers one by one. "None of you guys worried that maybe somebody was watching you or that somebody would eventually rat on you?"

"Well, we didn't really see ourselves as overly wild?"

"Are you fucking serious, dude? I find that hard to believe."

"Most of us were like big kids, Mark. We were in our twenties but we had gone from being under our parent's authority to being under a religious superior. We didn't have much worldly experience. We lived in a sheltered place, in a world that was completely encapsulated. Our hormones were all over the place and our libidos held us captive to say the least. The crazier we got, the more fun we wanted to have. It was like a fever that just grows and grows in intensity late at night. The older guys like Aaron and Kurt had more experience. Some of them had entered the abbey after college. They were wiser. We were dumb like kids." Simon paused and then said gravely, "And then there was Shawn."

"Oh, yeah, that Shawn guy. Where was he in all this? Was he with you guys on the bus when you went to 'Rocky Horror'?" Mark had taken his seat on the swivel stool. He turned on the tattoo gun and continued working.

Simon looked at Mark and rolled his eyes, "Of course not! He was way too sharp for that, Mark. He had other plans. He had great plans for himself. Shawn was a smooth operator. He wasn't about to screw himself by being careless about his behavior like we did. He had all kinds of connections in the abbey and had really pulled the wool over a lot of the older monk's eyes, especially the Abbot, Father Edmund. And yet, even in spite of knowing how he was, and keeping my distance from him, he still had a way of giving me confidence. I felt safe, somehow, when he was in my life. Maybe that was part of my delusion and letting my hair down."

"So you're telling me that you knew this Shawn guy was a player but that you trusted him?" Mark feigned a chuckle and said, "You let him control you even though you knew it was fucked up."

"All I'm saying is that Shawn had clout in the abbey. Possibly I came to realize early on that maybe I didn't really want him as a friend but that I certainly didn't want him as an enemy. Anyway, up until the 'Night of the Long Knives' took place, I kept myself to a safe distance from him."

"I'm kinda confused, Simon, I mean, it sounds from what you've told me that sometimes you were really tight with him and then other times you didn't want to have anything to do with him. Which one was it?"

Simon thought about this and finally said, "Damn, I can't say I totally understood how I related to him. On the one hand, I was drawn to him and respected him because he seemed so sure about everything. On the other hand, I knew he was nothing but trouble. I guess it's fair for me to say that I had periods where I hung out with him and other times when I hid from him. Eventually, though, being honest with you, I think I fell under his spell and embrace."

"I think I know what you mean. But then, when you hid from him, who did you look up to for some kind of guidance and direction? Kurt maybe?"

"Yeah, I looked up to the two older guys in our inner circle. I looked up to Kurt and Aaron. Lorenzo too. They were older and seemed to have their act together. They guided us in a very real way and we trusted them. Whatever direction they indicated, we followed. Kurt actually had a friend in Crescent who owned a bar called 'The Schooner'. Like I said earlier, Kurt was already ordained a deacon. He was a class or two ahead of Shawn. At the time we went to see 'The Rocky Horror Picture Show', Kurt was already approved for ordination to the priesthood, only weeks away. He already had his chalice made and his mother had embroidered the priestly vestments he was to wear for his upcoming First Solemn Mass." Simon continued, "I always thought

Kurt's friend who owned 'The Schooner' was his lover but I really had nothing to base that on. I think they might have messed around together but it wasn't anything serious. I do know Aaron was after Kurt's bones."

Mark looked up and shot Simon a sideways glance and muttered, smiling, "Well, at least one bone in particular."

Simon let out a laugh, saying, "Oh, yeah, that's true enough." Then he added, "A lot of us were after Kurt's bone, I suppose. But I also knew, from Kurt himself, that Aaron wasn't his type and that he didn't interest him sexually. Kurt was a looker and I guess that was a huge part of why folks were attracted to him. He was short in stature but really toned, well put together, just muscular enough to turn heads, with a perfectly curled, thick head of dark hair. He was a jock through and through and he had a terrific personality. Anyone would have been fooled into thinking he was straight. Even though he was a hottie, Kurt wasn't self-absorbed and was really a gentle soul. He never acted haughty but was really kind and patient with everyone, especially the older monks at the abbey who lived in the infirmary corridor. I always thought he was genuine and would be an awesome priest."

"Kurt first introduced a few of us to 'The Schooner' one Saturday night. We even had legitimate permission to go out as a group because Kurt was acting as guardian. The Master of Clerics knew we were going for a few beers. As soon as we got to the bar, everything seemed to fall into place. 'The Schooner' wasn't a gay bar, but rather a local bar like so many in Pennsylvania. Small bars dot just about every corner in most working class towns in the state. But I suppose it sort of became a gay bar whenever our group piled in. After our first visit that Saturday night, more and more of us at the seminary who were out to each other, made every effort we could to return to 'The Schooner' as often as possible. At first, without us, the bar was usually empty. Soon, however, a number of lay college students went there as well and all of us became a close knit group of drinking buddies. A generally faithful group, I might add." Simon thought and then said, "Well, it was more than just being drinking buddies. We enjoyed a real comradery that had a sexually charged undercurrent for many of us."

"How was it sexually charged?" Mark asked.

"Pitchers of beer diminished our inhibitions and conversations became flirtatious. Plus there was a certain amount of pushing and shoving that was definitely homoerotic. We didn't exactly talk about anything gay, but the banter and joking certainly was."

"Did those college dudes know you guys were monks in training to become priests?"

"I would guess some of them knew but we never discussed it. It wasn't something we ever got into." Mark nodded understanding but kept quiet. "We enjoyed our pitchers of beer with one another, drinking and teasing. We hatched all kinds of crazy plans as we sat along those long, chipped, wooden benches painted in glossy enamel colors."

"Sounds like a good time, the kind of drinking hole I would enjoy."

"It really was. As we continued meeting there, friendships were forged and I had my suspicions about some of the college guys I really liked. I never initiated anything but I was really attracted to some of them. The thing was that in time, other guys from the seminary also accompanied us to 'The Schooner'. They weren't really part of our gay, inner group but they seemed to be okay with hanging out with us. When the beer was flowing on any given Friday or Saturday night at 'The Schooner', everybody seemed like a good guy to me. As a result, those of us who went regularly, became less concerned about our behavior at 'The Schooner'. This would ultimately prove to be a bad thing for us. Some of those fringe guys from the abbey who had joined of late, eventually betrayed us to the Abbot and his council. We let those guys in to drink with us and they saw and heard too much from us. Some of us were inclined to put our arms around each other as we drank and our conversation was sometimes brutally honest and campy."

"One night at 'The Schooner', Joshua and I came up with the idea of a 'Gay Nineties' party for the end of the semester in the seminary corridor. It was a custom to have a 'Gaudeamus', as we used to call it in the abbey."

Mark asked, "A Gaudy…what?"

"'Gaudeamus'. It comes from the Latin, 'Gaudeamus igitur'; it literally means 'so let us rejoice'. I guess it's really old abbey-speak. It was a term we used to mean, 'let's have a party', so we'd say 'let's have a Gaudeamus'."

"Did you guys ever say anything in English?" Mark was poking fun now and Simon ignored him. "I mean, fuck, you guys dressed and talked like you were in the Middle Ages! When you weren't wearing robes at dinner you were in capes throwing toast and mumbling gibberish at a movie screen."

"There were vestiges of the Dark Ages, I'll admit. But anyway, the guys on our corridor were only too happy to let Joshua and I organize the whole thing. They couldn't be bothered plus they appreciated our knack for the flamboyant. So, one night while we were drinking there at 'the Schooner', we got the idea for this really fun party and our imaginations soared. As it turned out, the 'Gaudeamus' started really well. The theme for 'The Gay Nineties' evening was well received. We organized Barber Shop Quartets as well as music and costumes from the end of the nineteenth century. We painted huge handlebar moustaches on most of the guys and had bought flat, boater, English straw hats like the kind men used at that time. We had a budget to work with, so there was plenty of food and we got permission to have booze. We invited everyone from the Abbot down to the postulants and we got quite a turnout. I looked that whole night for Shawn but he never showed up. In fact, I would see him in chapel or in the refectory at other tables but it was several weeks before we would speak again. It didn't occur to me that he might have been avoiding me."

"Why do you say that?"

"I dunno, thinking back on it now it seems strange how he stayed away from me. I mean, he was usually looking for me and getting all over me every chance he got. Anyway, the night of the 'Gaudeamus' the Abbot and the authorities didn't stay very long but as the hours passed and the booze flowed, things got way out of hand for those of us who were there. I have a clear recollection of some of us throwing acetate records around the room at each other and other guys dancing wildly on tables as the music roared full blast. At night's end, a couple of guys paired off on their way back to their cells." Simon hesitated but finally admitted, "Me included. I remember Joshua told me he would meet me in his bed but I didn't go to him until first stopping by someone else's cell." Mark was looking intently at Simon. "Yeah, he was this guy a couple of classes behind me who I thought was really hot. I had flirted with him on numerous visits to 'The Schooner' and he had flirted back." Simon was lost in thought as he said, "I swear he was a young version of Robert Goulet."

"Robert who?"

"An actor I was always hot for as a kid during the sixties when I was a little fart. Anyway, this guy and I had never done anything except rub our legs together underneath the table at 'The Schooner' but that night of the party, I went to his cell knowing that he was waiting for me."

"Was he?" Mark asked, his curiosity piqued and obvious.

"You bet he was. I went to his cell, opened the door and slid into bed with him. There was no doubt he was waiting for me and happy when I arrived. I stayed with him until first light, when I got myself dressed and went to Joshua's cell. He was out cold, snoring loudly so I closed his door gently and went to my own bed. The next day was kind of weird."

"How so?"

"Aside from the terrible hangover most of us had, an odd feeling hung in the air. It filled me with dread even though I couldn't tell you why. That afternoon, no one spoke about the party the night before as several of us picked up the mess in the recreation room. There were broken records everywhere along with some leftover food that had been thrown at the walls. There were half-filled glasses with leftover drinks."

Simon chuckled to himself and Mark asked, "What are you remembering?"

"I remember that several weeks later, some of us were assigned to clean out the empty rooms on all three floors of the seminary. We must have found ten or more straw hats from 'The Gay Nineties' party hidden behind drawers or up in the closets. There had been a lot of activity that night." Simon sighed. "Looking back now, I can't believe how blind and stupid we were of the avalanche that was fast approaching. It was coming for us and would take many away. I suppose the long knives were already being carefully sharpened only we couldn't see it."

Mark removed his purple colored nitrile gloves and said in his customary way, "All done here, Simon. You have a perfectly tattooed second pink triangle. Wanna take a look?"

Simon went and stood in front of the large mirror in his underwear and studied his new tattoo. There on his right thigh, red and slightly swollen and raised, was the second pink triangle tattoo. Above it, in bold black, was his prisoner number: 1281956. "Thank you, man. It's perfect."

"Glad you like it. Lay down over here and let me clean that up for you and wrap it in plastic." Simon lay back as Mark applied an antibacterial ointment on the tattoo and said, "I'm wondering about something, Simon. I'm wondering about the 'Night of the Long Knives'." He wrapped Simon's thigh completely around in plastic. "You still haven't told me how it went down."

Simon put his right arm over his eyes as he closed them and sighed loudly without realizing he had done so. "It was real bad, Mark." He paused and then repeated, "It was really…really real bad." He lifted his arm and turned to look at Mark who had sat down on his swivel stool and now stared at him. Simon's eyes stung briefly as they misted over and pathetically, Simon asked the tattooer, "You got some time to hear me out?"

Chapter Twelve
The Night of the Long Knives

Storms make trees take deeper roots.
Dolly Parton

Simon turned away from Mark and with closed eyes recalled for the tattooer all the final events that had led to that awful night. It had been a Saturday night like many other Saturday nights. It was warm and a group of fifteen or so had opted out of supper since it was optional on Saturdays. They had boarded the seminary bus and headed to "The Schooner" for a night of beers, pizza and fun.

The raucous group left "The Schooner" sometime around two o'clock in the morning. They were singing and carrying on as they wound their way through the night, back to the abbey. Joshua had gotten very drunk and nudged Simon insistently, giving him a wicked, sensual look that Simon was familiar with when his friend drank too much. Simon often wondered if Joshua's attentiveness on those occasions were really meant for him or if it could have been anyone else. It hurt Simon to think that it was the latter. And even though Simon couldn't deny that he was relishing in his handsome friend's advances, still, he was also keenly aware that something had indeed gone out between them. As Simon pondered these things, Joshua rested his head on Simon's shoulder. The smell of his friend's damp hair and skin intoxicated Simon and he pushed away the unpleasant conclusions he had just entertained, preferring instead to believe that all was not lost between them. After all, he thought to himself, nothing is ever perfect in a human life. He recalled a conversation he had heard as a boy one evening as he sat on the front steps leading to the porch at home. One of his aunts had been telling his grandmother that, "En este mundo no existe una vida que sea completa. Algo siempre falta." Now, holding Joshua tightly in place next to him as the bus sped ahead in the night, Simon recognized the truth of those words he had overheard long ago, namely, that "In this world, there doesn't exist a life that is complete. Something is always missing." On the last wide turn of the road, as the massive bell tower of the abbey came into view, the singing abruptly ended and the merry band of festive young men froze in their seats because of what they saw ahead. Simon shook Joshua awake and pointed toward the abbey beyond.

Most of the windows belonging to the seminary wings, as well as the majority of windows belonging to the Abbot and his council were brightly lit. Something was terribly wrong and they all knew it. It wasn't until someone meekly spoke up that their trance-like gaze diminished. "Why are all the lights on at this hour?" They sat in silence staring, as the bus made its way past the large metal sign of the abbey and continued under the main arch toward the back, near the pool building. All of them were wide-eyed and no longer cheerful. Simon noticed that even Kurt and Aaron suddenly clearly wore their concern and panic for all to see. It was in their eyes. Dread had overtaken all of them and an unmistakable foreboding gripped their hearts. Simon wondered to himself what was awaiting them inside the abbey.

They left the bus in near silence. Simon could hear the sound of gravel crunching beneath their feet as they headed inside. They slipped into the back of the abbey through the large service door which led into the great kitchen and beyond, the cavernous refectory. All was in darkness as the little band walked on and reached one of the principle corridors. Everything from that point on was brightly lit and at the very end, where thick stone columns held up the vaulted ceiling of the impressive foyer, stood Brother Shawn. He was wearing his black habit and had his arms tightly interlocked across his chest. He stared at them disparagingly with an expression of unadulterated contempt.

Simon approached Shawn and asked cautiously, "Gee, what's going on? It's like...it's like almost two thirty in the morning and this place is lit up like noon." Not one word passed over Shawn's tightly pursed lips and Simon didn't know what else to say. His fellow brothers stood tightly huddled behind him, gawking at Shawn. Finally, Simon found his voice again and spoke up. "I guess we better get over to the switchboard and sign in that we're back home for the night." As he said this, he tried to read Shawn's baleful expression but it was impossible to see anything but the scorn that raged in the portly monk's eyes. Simon sensed that it was best to keep quiet and so as he motioned to his fellow monks, he weakly announced, "Then it's off to bed. It's so late now."

"No need to sign in. No need for any of you to do so." Shawn's voice was haughty and accusatory as he uttered each word deliberately. "By tomorrow afternoon, it won't matter one iota for most of you."

Simon moved in closer to Shawn and asked warily, careful not to incite Shawn's wrath. "Please, Shawn, tell me, what's wrong. Please tell us. What exactly is going on tonight? Everything feels weird and you sure as hell sound and look like it's the end of the world or something."

Shawn didn't bother to answer him directly and instead, he kept looking intently at the group huddled behind Simon. "Looks like the end of the world…or something…does it?" He said this with emphasis, then added, "The bishop was here for a long visit this evening. He left a few hours ago. His Grace spoke with the Abbot and his council and interviewed several professors from the seminary. He sat for more than an hour with the Master of Clerics." Shawn paused for effect and then hissed at the frightened young men clustered together in front of him, "One by one, he sat with them and when I saw His Grace finish with Father Wade, the bishop looked damned pissed. He then spent the better half of an hour behind closed doors with the Abbot again." Shawn gave them all a piercing glance causing most of them to look away. No one remarked on what Shawn had just revealed, not knowing what to say. They knew something bad was going on if the bishop himself had been there. The fact that he looked damned pissed was not good. "All clerics, at every level of priestly formation will sit with the Abbot, even those already approved for ordination. Some have already gone in. The rest tomorrow." Shawn paused again and in a grave voice concluded, "And one by one questions will be answered. Oh, yes. The guilty will answer for their crimes and their treacherous behavior."

"Questions? What questions? What crimes of treachery are you talking about, Shawn? You're scaring me. It all sounds creepy." Simon, in his fear and attempting to dismantle Shawn's dramatic take on what was unfolding, reached out and pushed Shawn's shoulder gently, saying facetiously, "Oh, don't be such a drama queen, Shawn. You're scaring us."

Shawn slanted his eyes and through slits responded sharply. "Drama queen?" Brusquely, he brushed Simon's hand away as if it were something unclean. He glared at Simon and seethed, "Questions, you ask? You should be scared. You should all be scared shitless at this point. There are serious accusations being leveled and I'd say all of you are in very deep, deep shit."

Shawn sneered menacingly at Simon as he said this and wouldn't take his eyes off him. "There's a sign-up list outside the Abbot's office. You all need to get your sorry asses up there and sign up before you get to bed. I don't think the Abbot will be seeing many more clerics tonight but you can bet you'll be sitting squarely in front of him tomorrow." Shawn turned around and walked away down the long corridor.

The little band bolted and dispersed down various corridors. Simon turned to get Joshua's attention but he had already gone. Simon panicked and practically ran to their corridor in the seminary wing. Small groups of students gathered here and there in the corridor even though it was so late by then. Simon tried to gauge the gravity of the situation but couldn't, even though he knew in his heart that the wrath of something deplorable and hateful was about to embrace them. Simon tried to concentrate and not succumb to his worst fears but it was useless to try and do so. Suddenly, an image of Father Chris and Father Wade rose up in his mind's eye. Those two ruthless bastards were like hungry alligators, famished reptiles waiting in the long grass that grows by the still river. Given an opportunity like the one at present, they'd instinctively jump out in a heartbeat and catch you in their powerful jaws, pulling you way down deep into the shadowy river bed. There, they'd tear you apart and eat you up slowly, devouring you so completely that nothing would ever remain to prove that you had ever been there.

Simon saw Seth at his desk and whispered through the open door, "Seth, what's going on?"

Seth looked up and asked, "You don't know anything, do you?" The bell in the great tower sounded three times and momentarily distracted them. "Simon, it's bad."

"Well, what is it? A group of us just got in from Crescent grabbing a few beers and we ran into Shawn who looked and sounded like the Grim Reaper. What an arrogant bastard he can be. It all left me with the impression that the world is coming to an end."

Seth smiled sadly and said, "In a sense, it is ending for some."

"Huh? What does that mean? Gee, everybody is so dramatic here!"

"This has nothing to do with drama. I mean, real life consequences are coming down hard. I have been looking for you everywhere tonight, Simon. I wanted to warn you." He pushed his chair back and said in a whisper, "You know, in a sense I'm not really that surprised that it's all come to this, I mean, some nights our hallway looks pretty busy what with everybody going into everybody's cell and doing each other." He shook his head, saying, "Geez."

Simon was nervous as he entered Seth's cell and sat on the edge of his cot. "What's going on? Tell me. How do you know it's so bad?"

Seth turned toward Simon and moved in closer. In a hushed tone he said, "Look, I know we haven't been real close in a long time and sometimes I feel like you ignore and avoid me." He stared at Simon and said, "I know you prefer the company of Anthony and Noah over me."

"Seth, please, I never intentionally…"

"It's okay! I can live with it. I just want you to know that I consider you a friend and always have since we met in the tower room that first night of postulancy. I want you to know that I care about you and what happens to you." He paused and added, "I've always wished we were closer friends." Simon felt uncomfortable and didn't know what to say. Seth's words had the tone of a farewell speech and this unnerved Simon. "Anyhow, I've been looking for you since suppertime. I noticed you weren't in the refectory."

"Like I just said, a few of us went out for some pizza at 'Jane's', over in Crescent and then hit 'The Schooner' for some beers like we enjoy doing. No harm in any of that."

"Right. Well, late this afternoon, around four or four thirty, the Bishop showed up at the front door of the abbey, unannounced. Poor old Brother Gabriel just about shit himself when he saw who got out of the big, shiny black car and made for the front door. His secretary walked ahead of him and told Brother Gabriel that the Bishop was there to speak with the Abbot immediately. I heard from a few others who were nearby at the switchboard room, that the bishop wasn't his jolly self and that there was no small talk. There were no pleasantries exchanged, instead, he was curt, almost to the point of being rude. Brother Gabriel tried to get the Abbot's secretary and then the Abbot himself directly, but neither answered their phones. He called the Master of Clerics and when Wanda came down stairs, he and the bishop disappeared down the hall and over to the Abbot's office. I heard that when the Abbot finally sat with the bishop, they spent well over an hour behind closed doors. When it was time for supper, everybody was talking about the Bishop's unannounced arrival at the abbey. What made it all worse was that neither the bishop nor the Abbot showed up for supper. The Father Prior said the prayers and supper started the way it does every day."

Simon interrupted Seth, "No one said anything? The Bishop was here and it wasn't publicly announced? That sounds totally fucked."

"Oh, it's totally fucked alright. Not a word from the head table, but it was the only thing everybody was talking about at our table and I would guess at all the other tables. Being Saturday, attendance at supper was low but still, there were enough of us there to surmise that something bad was going on. We could tell because the atmosphere was really heavy and dark. Something like impending doom hung in the air. It was impossible to dismiss." Simon listened as Seth continued, "Then the Abbot appeared toward the end of supper. He seemed preoccupied and he had a drawn expression on his face. He sat down and ate hurriedly as dishes were being picked up all around him. Then he stood for the closing prayer except that before he prayed he said that all clerics in the seminary wing and the deacon's wing, were to sign up to see him personally this evening or tomorrow morning. He also said that no one was to speak to anyone else about any of it upon leaving the interview."

Simon sighed nervously and asked, "That sounds weird and cryptic. What happened next?"

"The Abbot said the prayer and left without another word. He didn't even hang around like he usually does to chit chat with some of the old guys."

"Damn."

"Damn is right. I ran over immediately to his office and sure enough a sign-up sheet was already hanging to one side of the door. I signed up for tomorrow. You better get over there and sign up too." Seth hesitated and then said, "I heard that it's a witch hunt, a purge." He looked painfully at Simon, "I've been hearing guys coming from over there. They're sobbing and shit." He waited and then said, "Your name is being mentioned."

Simon had heard enough. He was beginning to feel sick and it finally dawned on him that what he feared most was actually happening. A deep sense of being hunted overtook him and he got up off Seth's cot and said, "Thanks for filling me in." He couldn't sit there for another second without going insane with fear.

"You need to get in there and plead your case, Simon. You need to think real good about what you're going to say to Father Edmund. You need to choose your words carefully."

Simon walked out of Seth's cell without saying a word and headed toward the Abbot's office. As he walked down the long corridor, he thought he heard muffled crying and hushed voices behind closed doors. He quickened his pace and felt as if his legs wouldn't take him as fast as he needed to go. He felt like he was in some kind of crazy nightmare where you wanted to run but can't because you're in a deadly quagmire and the evil that is coming after you is getting closer. He felt urgency but also dread as he passed a few fellow student monks who simply stared at him and said nothing.

Several sheets of lined papers fastened together, hung next to the closed, massive door of the Abbot's chambers. The instructions at the top of the page stated that everyone was expected to sit in front of the Abbot for one hour. Simon saw that the sign-up list had already swelled to full capacity for that first evening. Since it was so late now, it was apparent that the interviews had ceased for this night and would resume in the morning. He understood that this meant that many of the guys had already sat for their particular interrogation. Suddenly, the door flew open and Kurt walked out. Simon locked eyes with his friend and saw that Kurt's eyes were red and very swollen from crying. He was noticeably distraught but didn't say a word as he closed the door behind him and walked past Simon. Kurt disappeared into the shadows.

Simon hesitated to put his name on the list because he feared what was coming for him but knew he had no choice. He found an empty slot for ten o'clock the next morning, and signed in. He couldn't get Kurt's eyes out of his head as he walked back to his cell. Simon made a stop at the communal lavatory in the middle of the student corridor in the seminary wing. Noah was standing at one of the urinals and Simon approached the urinal next to him. Instinctively, he glanced quickly at what Noah was holding in his hand as he unzipped his own trousers. His friend held himself loosely in his right hand as a heavy flow of urine poured loudly and steadily into the water of the urinal. Simon shifted his gaze at the wall in front of him and said to Noah, "Some crazy shit going on here, huh, Noey? I just got back from doing a few beers. This place looks like they've brought out the guillotine for public executions."

"That's about right, I'd say." Noah smiled to himself as he finished and shook the last drops away. "I'd say that's a pretty fair assessment in this place tonight." Noah stuffed himself back into his baggy jeans as he flushed and turned to Simon. He put his hand on Simon's shoulder and said, "It's not good for us, babe. I fear that it's going to be the end for us. I hear Father Edmund is asking a lot of questions and not beating around the bush. He has obviously been very well informed."

"Informed about what? I mean, to what degree? Relationships and breaking our vows?" Simon was beyond anxious at this point.

"Oh, yeah, at least that, but I'm sure there's way, way more."

"What do you mean?"

"Well, I hear that the Bishop had a list of names and precise accusations. I heard both our names were on that list. I don't know what accusations are being pinned on us but I can well imagine it's anywhere from being 'particular friends' to possibly…" Noah lowered his voiced and said, "to possibly the hidden room down in the root cellar and being 'particular fuck buddies'." He pressed Simon's shoulder and said, "I have nothing concrete but I've been hearing it's nothing less than a witch hunt, plain and simple. Somebody or some guys spilled their guts and ratted on us and it makes me wonder who did that to us?"

"Damn, Noey, you know there's a few closeted guys around who'd love to see us get punished, thrown out even."

"Yeah, but it had to be something big and well planned, not just two or three dizzy nellies screaming 'fire!' or that 'the sky was falling'."

"Do you really think so?"

"Oh, Simon, wake up! Yeah, babe, it's an Inquisition no different than what people got from the Catholic Kings in Spain, centuries ago. Anyone thought to be gay or accused of engaging in sex of any kind with another monk or anyone else for that matter, is ipso facto guilty and will be thrown out and gone by tomorrow. It's not so much a question of proof. That doesn't seem to matter much. It's about being accused. It's all about guilt by association in some cases and I hear the Bishop has demanded that the Abbot clean house by throwing out everyone on that list."

Simon was speechless. "You said guys are gonna get thrown out?"

"Yeah! That's exactly what's going on."

"That's what the sign-up sheets are for? The Abbot is asking questions about all that?" Noah shook his head. It was far worse than Simon had thought. Now he understood why Kurt had come out of the Abbot's office red eyed and stunned. Simon's head spun with fear and he felt exposed and in danger. Noah waited for him to finish at the urinal and then the two friends walked over to the row of white sinks in silence. Simon looked in the mirror and thought that he looked shrunken somehow. Gone were his boldness and his carefree laughter. A heavy pall had come over him and it brought a devastating sense of vulnerability. They had been caught and there was nowhere to hide. In an instant, Simon wondered what he would say to his mother and family if he was thrown out of the abbey the next day. He shuddered to think what God thought of him and if he had finally forfeited the call to serve at the altar. In a flash, he thought of Brother Casimir and knew how he had felt before he had...

He didn't see how the pieces could be put back together and he realized that the Bishop and Abbot were neither fools nor simpletons who could be swayed with an easy argument. Simon dried his hands in silence and saw that Noah was looking at him sadly. How had they been so careless? Why had he thrown everything away so stupidly? All those blatant adventures with his group of buddies now passed before his eyes and his heart sank. Noah took Simon into his arms and hugged him. It wasn't an erotic moment for Simon now as much as it was the union of two broken, frightened souls. They cried quietly and held on tightly, trying to ease the pain of their fear and deep wounds. Noah kissed Simon on his neck and Simon tightened his grip on his friend. Everything was falling apart around them and they had lost control. As he felt Noah's arms around him, he felt that he had no strength to escape the inevitable.

Noah whispered into Simon's ear, "I love you, Simon, for so many reasons. I always have but I think it might be over for us here. I'm not sure about what's going to happen tomorrow to any of us, but I want you to remember what I'm telling you now before everything comes down on us." It seemed to Simon that Noah was carefully choosing his words because he struggled to express himself. "I've never come out and said this to you before until now, but...I really do love you." Simon saw Noah's eyes fill with tears and spill onto his handsome face. "I have always loved you, since you first came to the seminary wing." Simon reached over and wiped away the wetness from Noah's eyes. His friend continued in a very low voice that was barely audible, "And if we...if we have to leave because we are thrown out, I...I could see you and I being together like lovers. We could go somewhere and..." Simon was taken by surprise and had never expected Noah to feel so strongly about him. "I have asked myself many times, 'Would I want Simon as my lover?' And I've said to myself that I would. I've answered 'yes' to this question of mine, to my heart, many times." Noah's lower lip quivered as he looked down at the floor.

Simon was unable to say a word as he tightly clung to him and buried his face in his friend's t-shirt. He breathed in Noah's aroma and tried to process his emotions which seemed to lie somewhere between sorrow and a heightened sense of desire. He could barely deal with the fear that was gripping him as he thought about sitting in front of the Abbot to answer difficult questions. He could barely grasp what he would do if he was expelled. His friend's disclosure was something he had not expected. He was very attracted to Noah and always had been but under the circumstances Simon felt he didn't have the strength to begin to answer him.

Noah interrupted his troubled thoughts by saying, "I know it's a lot to think about. Just keep it in mind for tomorrow." He kissed Simon as he hugged him tightly and whispered, "We could leave together and face whatever comes as a team." Then he added, "As lovers." Noah stepped away from Simon and cleared his throat. Simon didn't answer his friend and Noah crossed his arms over his own chest and asked in a depleted tone of voice, "I haven't seen Tony around at all. Was he on the bus with you tonight?"

Simon lifted his head and, wiping his damp eyes, sighed loudly. There was so much to think about on this terrible night. He answered in an equally exhausted tone, "No, Tony wasn't on the bus. He didn't come with us tonight. I have no idea where he is." Simon felt a rush of emotion and started crying. His tears were hot on his face and he was very close to wailing without control. Noah held him tightly again through his own sobs and the two of them stood that way in the darkened lavatory, two souls, brought together by God's mysterious, painful plans. They faced each other, driven by need and fear. Simon kissed his friend and didn't care that he could distinctly taste Noah's salty, runny nose and tears on his tongue, mingled with his own anguish.

When at long last their tears subsided, Noah said softly, "You need to prepare for the worst tomorrow. That's what I'm doing." Simon let go of him and wiped his own eyes with his t-shirt as he heard his friend say to him, "Don't let the fear eat you up. Be realistic about what could be the worst case scenario and face it. Facing one's fears head on makes us stronger in the long run. Running away weakens us."

"But I don't want to get thrown out!" Simon's tears were threatening to flow again as he mumbled, "I want to be a priest…I don't want…" Simon was sobbing uncontrollably and Noah took Simon's cold hands into his own and pulled him to himself again.

"I know, Simon. I don't want to leave either but in life it's not about what 'we want', it's all about 'what is'. In life we will be happy if we accept what is and move on from there making the best of it. The secret is in what we do with the cards we're handed in life." He led Simon out of the rest room and when they reached Simon's cell door, Noah opened it and said, "You need to get to bed and try and sleep, babe. Tomorrow is another day and will be here before we know it. Nothing you can do now will change God's Will for us." Noah ushered him in and laid him in his cot, removing his shoes gently. He kissed Simon on his forehead and said, "Remember, I love you," and slipped out quietly.

That night, however, there was no sleep and no rest for Simon. Shame and fear of the unknown filled him and he felt terribly alone in the darkness as he had once felt in the cheap, filthy motel room when he was fifteen. He remembered that night long ago when he wondered where God was and why God had abandoned him and seemed so silent in the face of his pain. He could hear his alarm clock ticking behind him and felt the painful pang once again of feeling abandoned by God. Like that night when he had been a boy and that damned, perverted priest snored obscenely near him, it hurt him now to think that God had left him completely alone in his Hell. In the darkness, he curiously remembered the fragment of tragic lyrics from the popular ballad "The Wreck of the Edmund Fitzgerald" by Gordon Lightfoot. It seemed to perfectly fit him now in his anguish. He asked out loud, in a trembling voice, repeating the lyrics of the ballad as he lay in his desolation, wondering where God hides in our very difficult moments. He thought about the squalid motel room and how he had hung on second after second and then, minute after minute and finally, hour after hour, not moving until morning had finally come to free him. He wondered where God had gotten to on that stormy night, when he was abused and raped in the motel room. He thought about the bottomless, green waves that washed over him and how he had almost drowned with Bobby. Where was God when his brother was first swallowed up by the ravenous waters and he himself was abandoned and lost to the same fate? Where was God now? Where was the loving, all-knowing God the nuns had taught him to love and trust? Would God be there with him tomorrow when he faced the Abbot? Would God send him an angel to help him once again as He had done when he was caught in the merciless waves of the sea?

He cried pathetically in his extreme loneliness without making a sound and in his devastated and shattered heart he prayed, "Please God, please don't be so far away from me right now. Please give me another chance!" He slid out of bed and undressed himself. In his complete nakedness he knelt by his cot and held his head in his hands. "Please give me another chance, dear God. Please don't let them throw me out." He cried and sobbed silently, "Please, please, please…" He remained that way for a very long time and at long last, he rose and got under his blanket. "I'm so very sorry for breaking my vows. God, forgive me for forgetting you. In your limitless power, don't forget me, please! Please give me another chance." He thought once more of a blackened, outraged sky long ago that had blown a gale of frigid wind upon his small body, and a churning sea trying to pull him under. He suddenly felt that he was beyond being able to speak and beg any further and the only words that poured out of him, just before he drifted away into sleep, came out almost involuntarily, like the last breath emitted by a dying person, "I'll do anything God, just don't let them throw me out. Tell me what to say tomorrow to Father Edmund. Show me what to do, please, God, please, give me one more chance. Let me be your priest. I'll do anything."

The next morning, his alarm clock rang with gusto at seven thirty. He sat up in his cot and stared at the floor between his feet. He asked himself if the events of last night were true or just some cruel nightmare. He showered and put on his habit. As he dressed and tightened his heavy leather belt around his waist, he wondered to himself sadly if this would be the last time he would wear his beloved religious habit. He made his way to the crypt instead of the refectory, having no stomach for breakfast. He felt completely empty and abandoned as he sat in the musty, damp crypt, surrounded as he was, by so many tombs filled with dust and decaying bones. He wondered what his fate would be as he admired the first shards of purplish light breaking in and filling the shaft of the bell tower. Simon saw the amethyst-colored light gleaming majestically off the massive gold tabernacle at the center of the altar and drenching the sarcophagus of the Prince-Bishop Demetrius, now all aglow in its magnificent radiance. He could not shake the growing sense of emptiness within himself because of his feelings of separation from God. Yet, he understood that God was fully there in the tabernacle. He had no doubts that God was contemplating him at that very moment. He remembered Noah's words the night before: "Don't let the fear eat you up. Be realistic and face it." Simon bowed his head and thought to himself about the scenario that awaited him. What would Father Edmund say to him? What would he ask him? How much did he know? What could he possibly say to the Abbot in his own self defense? Simon felt powerless before such a scenario and allowed his fear to overtake him, hating himself for the mess he had created in his own life.

    The great bell in the soaring tower above him pealed solemnly, nine times. Simon stared at the marvelous light gathered in front of him, not far away and remembered playing under his grandfather's house. He remembered coughing up sea water on the shore and then the droplets of water dripping out slowly from his ear as he lay utterly naked and wounded on a foul, pungent mattress. Simon's thoughts skidded and dug their heels in as the hideous memory opened up before him and displayed the odious scene from his youth. That had been a wretched and appalling motel room. The image of one of its sickly walls splattered and covered in dried, crusty yellow and faded brown drippings left behind by past, faceless patrons never left him. He shuddered as he saw himself in that place, an adolescent boy at the mercy of that corrupt, naked scumbag who took him there. Simon's thoughts dislodged from that painful memory and then, blessedly, Noah's words came to him again, reassuring him. Noey was right, he could face whatever was coming. His and his brother's close brush with death that morning so long ago had been beyond horrific. Simon thought back on it now and still wondered why God had spared Bobby and himself. Why hadn't they perished as he expected? Again, the images of the greedy sea and the obscene motel room came into view. These two recollections circled and circled him in his mind like relentless insects darting about, troublesome blood thirsty mosquitos in the dark of night, intent on having their way. The sea had been so hungry on that long ago morning and had stubbornly refused to give him and Bobby up but God had prevailed. God had certainly prevailed, that much was true. And likewise, he held on to the image of himself emerging from the motel room the next morning, albeit wounded and sullied, but he had emerged all the same and moved on. Simon wondered now if God would save him again from another terrible calamity?

    He knew there was a reason God had spared him on that day in the sea and that night in the motel, even though he couldn't possibly know why. He had come to suspect that God had kept a close eye on him because God had plans. God always had plans for his own. On those awful occasions he now could not get out of his mind, he surmised that he had been given another chance for a reason. As Simon sat in the crypt he realized that it wasn't important to know the reason but that it was fundamental to know that there was one. He had been spared in the sea and at the motel because there was a reason. That was the important piece. He wondered how many other times God had spared him from destruction and catastrophe without his even being aware of it.

Simon stared at the glint and sparkle that emanated from the golden tabernacle on the altar and understood that God had never left him even though God sometimes had a knack for becoming very silent, so silent that He sometimes seemed absent. But God was never absent, was He? Simon had been carefully knitted together, as it were, by God in his mother's womb. Nothing could ever change that. He thought about this as he stared at the tabernacle and let it sink in. So often it seemed that God was silent but being silent is not the same as being absent. He said in a whisper to himself, "It's not the same. Being silent is not the same as being absent." Then he said to God, "You were there all the time, weren't you? You were there, under the house with me, in the sea, in the motel room. He thought about being with Toby and even that time in the root cellar with Joshua. He recalled being prostrate on the cold stone floor just before he received his religious name and habit. All along, you have been there even though you have been silent. You waited for me to act every time. I needed to act on my own because it's my life even though I stray and get lost. That's your gift and curse to me. That part belongs to me. The freedom…" Simon trailed off and then added to his prayer, "You give me freedom but then there are consequences. How have I gotten to where I am now? What will happen to me?" He knew he was at a crossroads in his life. It could go either way for him there at the abbey. Yet, Simon agreed with Noah. He needed to face what was coming and facing it meant doing something when he would sit before the Abbot.

He looked at his watch. It was fifteen minutes to ten. He needed to get to his meeting with Father Edmund. He felt different now, as if he had really and finally understood something basic that had for the most part eluded him until that moment. He had never been alone, God would never leave him even if he had often left God. It seemed to him that God was silent and far away. Even in his sin, even offending God wasn't enough for the Creator to abandon him. He might run from God and wander as he had done but he was not alone. God had always been there and he always would be right there in the moments of grace and in the muck and filth. He was convinced of this and was comforted. He was ready to face whatever was coming and murmured the words spoken by the Prophet Isaias: "I am confident and unafraid."

He stood up, genuflected and left the crypt. As he walked he thought about Joshua and realized that in his anguish the night before he had forgotten to look for him. He mused about where Joshua might be and if he had already met with the Abbot. He walked toward the Abbot's office and arrived just before the bells announced that it was ten o'clock. Suddenly, however, as the moment to actually sit with the Abbot drew near, Simon was less than confident and was filled with great apprehension. The reality of what might happen took hold of him and shook him to his core. The massive wooden door opened and closed. A student monk exited and smiled smugly at Simon as he passed by and winked. He whispered, "Good luck, Simon."

Simon knocked on the door and from within came the no-nonsense voice of Father Edmund, Lord and Father Abbot. "Come." Simon entered the impressive chamber and was terribly frightened. The customary, jovial tone in the Abbot's voice was markedly absent. Father Edmund indicated with a brusque hand gesture that Simon should sit down on the high-backed chair opposite him. He didn't look up. There wasn't even time given to the custom of kissing the Abbot's ring out of respect for his presence.

The present Abbot of the Abbey of the Most Sacred Heart of Jesus sat erect behind the expansive carved wooden desk. He was dressed in the same black habit of the Order that Simon was wearing and the elaborate, gold pectoral cross that the Abbot wore on a thick chain around his neck, swayed gently across his chest. On his completely bald head he wore a skullcap proper to his office. Abbot Edmund seemed exhausted to Simon and the dark circles under his eyes were proof that the Abbot had not slept well. As he removed his glasses and rubbed his eyes slowly Simon admired the ornate ring the Abbot was entitled to wear. The large green emerald at its center gleamed impressively and spoke clearly of the man's authority and rank.

Simon braced for the impending interrogation. He sat nervously thinking about what Father Edmund might ask him. How could he possibly deny that he had engaged in sexual activity? Panic closed in on him as he looked at the Abbot. Simon had no doubts that the stern-looking man sitting behind the desk was well informed and that he was no fool. He figured the Bishop had not visited him unannounced just to make a friendly, afternoon parlor visit without bringing with him plenty of ammunition. Simon tried to concentrate but his mind was a blank and his heart had gone cold with anguish. He knew he had no control in this scenario and didn't have a clue where the Abbot was going to take him.

Finally, Father Edmund cleared his throat and looked at Simon straight on. He replaced his glasses and through them his pale, blue eyes were steady and he did not blink. He tapped loudly with his index finger on a set of papers set out neatly in front of him as he continued to stare at Simon. Without uttering one word, the Abbot stood up and turned away from Simon, facing the large, crucifix that hung between the two tall Gothic windows behind his desk. Sun streamed in through the triangular panes of beveled glass. Simon could see the prisms of light that were held in place and that now bathed the Abbot's thick frame in blinding, white light. Simon knew that the man standing there would determine his future. He was God's representative after all but he was also a man who had a responsibility to uphold the rules. The Abbot necessarily needed to decide if he would send him home in shame as he deserved or if he would allow Simon to remain and continue to study for the priesthood, completely exonerated.

Simon waited for the man to speak. He felt very small and insignificant in the Abbot's chambers. The entire room was paneled in dark oak and lined with bookcases. The ceiling was very high and vaulted and a chandelier hung on an ornate chain that disappeared above into the shadows of the room's ceiling. The wooden floor was covered with a thick padded, intricately woven oriental rug of innumerable colors and geometric designs. Simon was very much aware of an enormous grandfather clock ticking away the minutes behind him and noticed that the only object on top of the desk in front of him was a small, metal lamp. The light it gave was just enough to illuminate the set of papers as well as an open file which Simon assumed was his own. Father Edmund turned around at long last and pulled on the heavy chair next to him. He sat down gracefully behind his desk. He adjusted the pair of wire-rimmed glasses that sat comfortably on the bridge of his nose and shuffled through the papers, moving his lips as he read silently.

Simon thought that the Abbot looked severe and menacing at the moment, unlike his usual self. He had come to appreciate the man's dark sense of humor which often times confused those who did not know him, thinking he was unfriendly and mean. Simon had come to know the Abbot as a sensitive, kind man, who had a very good sense of humor especially about himself, but there wasn't a trace of that in his demeanor now. This was no friendly get together and he knew that the man sitting across from him was his judge and soon to be, his fierce interrogator. Simon not only felt vulnerable but also perverse and dirty sitting in the inner sanctum of the Abbot's chambers. He played nervously with the deep folds of the black habit he wore which had been blessed and represented the life of grace and purity he was called to live. Simon however, felt unworthy and very insignificant as he sat in the spacious room and braced himself for the questions he would soon be asked.

Father Edmund finally looked up and fixed his gaze on Simon. "Brother Simon, have you engaged in any overt sexual activity here in the abbey?" Before Simon could answer, he asked, "Are you aware of any fellow monks who have?"

"No, Father, I have not." Simon felt his face burn with shame. The lie he had uttered stung like a burning coal as it passed over his lips. He had just lied to God's representative.

The Abbot apparently wasn't satisfied with Simon's quick response because he asked, "Are you certain that you are not guilty, Brother? I will repeat my question to you. Have you had any overt sexual experiences here in the abbey?"

"No, Father, I have not."

He paused and then said, "There are serious accusations against you that say otherwise."

Simon barely processed the questions and answered automatically, "No, Father, I am not guilty of doing that." He looked down at his hands, unable to meet the Abbot's piercing, blue eyes.

"His Grace, the Bishop, was here last evening." Once again, the Abbot had removed his glasses and was rubbing his eyes slowly as he spoke. "The Bishop was beside himself about rumors that had reached him in the Chancery regarding some of the clerics here. I must say I was shocked by some of the things he suggested were going on. He also left me with this paperwork." Father Edmund picked up three sheets of typewritten paper. Simon could see the large green coat-of-arms of the Bishop embossed at the very top of the first page. The Abbot replaced his glasses and said, "He gave me this list of names along with these accusations." Father Edmund put them down and picked up a number of other sheets of paper of varying sizes. They appeared to be handwritten. "The bishop also gave me these testimonials from eye witnesses here in the abbey." He set the papers down and sat back in his chair. "They are handwritten by some of your peers, your fellow monks." The clock ticked away and the Abbot waited. He tapped the tips of his fingers on the pile of papers in front of him. "You say otherwise, but your name on this list and in these letters…" His voice trailed off. Simon's blood ran cold. "It says here that you and Brother Joshua are always seen together and that you are inseparable. It states matter-of-factly that it is quite openly known in your inner circles that your relationship is a sexual one. Is it a sexual relationship, Brother? Is this true? Answer me before God. Is it true?" Simon recognized frustration and anger in the Abbot's voice.

"No, Father, it is not true."

"You are further accused in several testimonials of the same thing with several other monks. And then there's the accusation that you are known to drink quite often and get boisterous and unruly." The Abbot shook his head and said in a low, grave tone, "I'm indignant, to be very honest with you. It sickens me beyond words." The Abbot sounded personally offended but maintained control over his emotions. He put his elbows on his desk as he leaned forward. "And there's another thing that disturbs me greatly. You are also accused of having engaged in sexual activity with one of your former classmates, a cleric who has since been dismissed from the abbey. I'm referring to Brother Tobias, Toby as all of you called him. I take it the two of you had also set up house here in the abbey at some point. Is this true or do you deny it as well?"

"Joshua and I are close friends, I won't deny that but nothing improper has ever existed between us, Father. Toby and I were friends too but nothing improper ever happened between us." Simon was shaken and felt that he could not keep up with his responses. His mouth seemed to be in control and far ahead of his brain. He was now in survival mode at full throttle. He knew he had to do whatever it took to survive. This instinct grew in him as he sat there wrestling with the fear that wanted to dominate and crush him. Somewhere in his mind he knew that if he did not survive this ordeal he would never reach the altar as God's priest. Instead, he would be cast out in shame. "I don't know who those 'witnesses' are, but there is no proof for their accusations. Are there photographs or home movies to prove that they are telling the truth?"

"Don't get flippant with me!" The Abbot's raised his voice and snapped at him. "Don't play games with me, son. You are at the center of a very serious scandal. To be very honest with you, the accusations against you and some of your fellow clerics are overwhelming and believable enough for the Bishop himself to have come here personally yesterday and demand an investigation." He sat back and folded his arms across his chest. "I am not sure that I have any choice but to dismiss you and dissolve your vows. The Bishop's take on all of this is to dismiss everyone who appears on that list." He glanced at the papers spread out before him. "Everyone. No exceptions." He stared at Simon. Then the Abbot continued, saying, "The Bishop, of course, cannot make that decision to demote or dismiss anyone here. It's not his call. As monks we are autonomous here in the abbey and I am the sole authority before the Holy See in that regard but according to Canon Law, the Bishop is the one who has jurisdiction over Sacraments. In your case and those others on that list preparing for the priesthood, it means proceeding to ordinations to the deaconate and sacred priesthood are in his hands, not mine. The Bishop trusts in my judgement but if he does not find you worthy for Holy Orders, it doesn't take place, ipso facto. But his decision does rest almost completely on my judgement to present you as a candidate for Orders or to deny you." The clarity of the Abbot's explanation was not lost on Simon who understood perfectly well at that point that he might not survive after all. He thought about Noey's assessment in the darkened bathroom the night before. The Abbot studied Simon carefully without saying a word. His face was not unkind but it bore a stern, unyielding expression that greatly concerned Simon. "I'm not sure how to proceed in your case. I have to say that I have serious doubts about you at this point." He gestured to the open file, "There's a history here that troubles me." He moved the papers closer to himself, saying, "Honestly, it troubles me greatly."

Suddenly, Simon burst into tears and cried out loudly, "No, Father, please!" He begged with every fiber of his being. "Please, let me stay! Please let me continue to pursue God's call to priesthood." Great tears welled up in his large, dark eyes and ran down his cheeks and into his beard. Simon buried his face into his open hands and sobbed. "Please, Father Edmund, please. If you dismiss me, everyone will say that I am being punished because I am guilty of the terrible accusations. Please don't do that to me. Please give me another chance."

The Abbot stared intently at Simon's display of emotion and grief. He asked quietly, "Consider the position I'm in. What am I to do?" Once again he became silent and pensive. Simon thought he recognized a more compassionate inflection in the Abbot's voice. When he spoke again, his tone had definitely softened and was kinder. "Do you assure me that you have not engaged in any overt sexual activity here in the abbey?" The Abbot had looked down and studied his hands. Carefully, he straightened the large ring of his office on his right hand.

Simon looked up and wiped his bleary eyes. "I assure you, Father. I assure you that I have not. Please help me. Please find it in your heart to give me another chance." Since he was a little boy, Simon had learned very early on how important it was to worm and scheme out of difficult situations in order to move ahead and get what he wanted. As a boy of nine or ten years, he had saved his money in a large, empty tin of Folgers Coffee. He refused to spend the large fifty cent silver pieces that bore Benjamin Franklin's image and instead kept the money hidden for a specific purpose. It was meant for difficult situations that might arise like asking his father for permission to go somewhere with his friends or buy a dog at the Humane Society. In those emergency situations, he would dig deep into the tin can. Then he would ask his mother to buy a six-pack of beer and a carton of cigarettes for his father. Armed with those gifts, he would confront his father with confidence and beg him until he got what he wanted.

The delicate situation he now found himself in was not really much different. He knew of course that he couldn't sway the Abbot with offerings of beer and cigarettes. He was no longer a little boy bearing gifts but he realized that he had to draw on every charm he possessed and evoke pity from the Abbot if he was to survive the terrible storm he was presently engaged in. Simon was all too aware that the task at hand was a difficult one, riddled with danger. The Abbot, however, left little to personal interpretation. He had communicated a negative outlook leaving very little to the imagination.

Simon now saw Father Edmund shake his head and speak in a graver tone than before. He did not appeared to be swayed by Simon's obvious anguish and therefore, be easily convinced in his favor. The Abbot looked directly at Simon and said, "I have no real choice, Brother. The accusations are too numerous against you. The Bishop has been crystal-clear with me regarding his decision and my council has also weighed in, especially the Master of Clerics, Father Wade. I must especially listen to the Master of Clerics. I've placed him as my representative with all of you who are student monks. If I go against his recommendations he will rightly feel that I am not giving him his place nor respecting the authority I have conferred upon him. He is adamantly in agreement with the Bishop about dismissing all of you who are accused and on this list." The Abbot pointed to the list again and then raised his finger to Simon, and gently shook it back and forth in the negative. "I have to tell you, son, that he has a very clear idea about you. He wants you out. He specifically named you among the top perpetrators of this mess."

Through tears, Simon continued to beg. "Please, Father Edmund, please reconsider, I beg you. Please give me another chance. You have the authority to do so. Please." For the next several seconds, Simon begged and the Abbot remained silent in his chair not turning his eyes away but listening intently. He looked stern and unforgiving as Simon admitted to him that he was young and inexperienced but certain about God's call to the priesthood. Simon told the Abbot it was all he had ever wanted in his life. He stressed that since he was a very little boy all of his energies had been poured into being a priest and standing one day at God's altar to offer the Sacrifice.

At long last, the Abbot waved his hand in front of Simon. The large emerald stone in his ring caught bits of sunlight that flashed through the room like sparks from a fire. "Enough! Enough…enough." was all that the Abbot said as his voice trailed off. Simon felt that the interview had come to an end. He had had his opportunity to defend himself but now he had the sinking feeling that he had ruined his chances of remaining in the abbey. The room was once again deathly silent except for the ticking clock behind him. Somewhere beyond the massive door, coughing could be heard in the corridor and then the bell in the great tower began to thunder eleven times. The interview was indeed coming to a quick end. Time had run out for him.

The Abbot had been silent and when he finally spoke, he did so in a very low voice, almost to himself and Simon was unsure that he had heard correctly, so he asked "I'm sorry, Father Edmund, what was that you said?"

"Enough, enough of all this mess. I am sickened to my core by it all." He looked at Simon and repeated, "I said I will think about it."

Simon had to control himself not to scream with utter joy. He almost jumped to his feet with emotion and in his enthusiasm blurted out spontaneously, "Oh, Father, thank you! Thank you!" Tears ran down his face. "Thank you so very much!"

The Abbot's reply came swift enough and it was not gracious. "Don't push it, man!" He barked hoarsely, "I haven't said 'yes', I only said I will think about it. You put me in a very difficult position, young man." He closed the file and set it to one side. He reorganized the other papers in front of him. "In any case, our meeting is over. Others are waiting outside. You may go." A great burden was lifted from Simon's heart and the shame that had weighed upon him had ceased, giving way to calm. He had survived. He thought about Tony, Noey and the others. He needed to find Joshua.

The Abbot rose suddenly and said curtly, "Call me tomorrow at one o'clock in the afternoon. I won't be here in the abbey because I have business in Pittsburgh." He handed Simon a small card on which he had written down a phone number. "This is where you can reach me precisely at one. I will have my final response for you then." Then the Abbot said as an afterthought, "I must tell you that there was one written testimonial in your defense. Had it not been included with the other letters, the accusations against you would have been unanimous and a deathblow for you. But I feel that I must tell you this in all honesty. There was also a monk who spoke to me in this room, on your behalf." Simon remembered his conversation with Seth. The Abbot walked around toward the front of his desk and Simon stood up. "You are very young, Brother Simon, but you must learn about the importance of the company you keep and who you associate with. It will ultimately shape you into the man you become. It's very important for you to have good company in your corner. Guilt is often assigned because of bad company. Remember that."

"Yes, Father, thank you. May I have your blessing, Father?" Simon knelt in front of the Abbot who made the sign of the Cross over him and then extended his right hand. Simon took it and kissed the emerald ring that represented his paternal authority in the Church. Simon approached the door and wanted to say something more. He turned briefly as he took the door knob in his hand and saw that the Abbot had already sat down and was opening another file. He thought best about saying anything else. It was clear that the interrogation was over.

Simon stepped out into the corridor where another student monk stood nervously awaiting his turn to enter. The young man wore his panic plainly and looked up as Simon exited the Abbot's office. "Good luck, brother." Simon whispered. But he didn't think that the other monk even heard him as he passed him on his way in.

The crypt floor was cold and damp as Simon knelt gratefully next to the sarcophagus of the Prince-Bishop Demetrius. He still shuddered to think about how close he had come to being expelled from the abbey. Some small part of him still feared that he had misunderstood Father Edmund and that the Abbot had said he was being sent home, that his vows would be dissolved and that he would never become a priest. But he knew that that was not the case. He remained kneeling and glanced up at the altar above him. The tabernacle was in shadows now that it was getting closer to noon. Nearby, a red lamp filled with blessed oil, burned and signaled that the Real Presence of God was only a few feet away from him. It was the red glow of that lamp that now bathed the tabernacle.

Simon prayed, "Thank you, dear Jesus, for hearing my prayer. Thank you for being with me and keeping me close to you." Simon stood and grabbed onto one of the stone angels that surrounded the tomb. He looked around him and lifted the great folds of his habit. Then, carefully balancing himself, he climbed up on a secure ridge at the base of the sarcophagus and contemplated the figure in stone lying peacefully at the top. He leaned over the lifelike marble form of the Prince-Bishop Demetrius and kissed the frigid marble of his ringed hand. It was cold to the tender touch of his warm lips. Simon said softly, "Thank you for helping me." He stepped down, careful not to slip and fall, genuflected toward the tabernacle and made his way out of the crypt. He needed to find Joshua before his friend went in to see the Abbot. He needed to tell Joshua how he should proceed and explain himself in the Abbot's presence. Simon searched the recreation and television rooms and asked for him everywhere but couldn't find Joshua.

Simon then went to the refectory but he wasn't there either. He had not been in the crypt and thought that perhaps he might find him in the abbey church, but again he had no luck. Simon ran to the pool house and searched behind it as well as in the small clearing at the edge of the forest. Joshua wasn't anywhere. He dismissed the top of the bell tower as a possibility for the moment but made a mental note to search there later as well. He was worried that he could not find Joshua before his friend went in to face the charges. Then it occurred to him that he was probably in his cell. He didn't want to think that perhaps Joshua had already seen the Abbot.

The thought troubled him and he made his way to their corridor in anguished haste. It seemed that he had gone everywhere to look for him and not having found him anywhere, decided he might have to search the bell tower after all. Simon wanted desperately to coach Joshua on what to say and how to proceed in his interrogation with the Abbot. If they were accused of wrongdoing because of association, then it would stand to reason that Joshua would also be forgiven and could stay if he knew what to say in his defense. He believed Joshua could survive the purge. Even though they no longer possessed the passion and intimacy they had once enjoyed, Simon still loved his friend even though Joshua had betrayed him. He needed to talk with him now. A part of Simon still hoped to restore what had been damaged between them.

Simon saw that Joshua's cell door was open as he walked down the shadowy corridor. Sunlight poured out into the hall way and Simon was relieved he had finally found him. He approached the cell and running inside, said cheerfully, "Baby, where have you been? I've been searching like everywhere for…" His jaw dropped when he saw the empty room. In cruel fashion, someone had already rolled the mattress on top of the metal cot. In the tiny closet, there was nothing more than a handful of empty hangers. Simon's heart sank when he saw Joshua's black habit draped in a tangled mess over the back of the desk chair and partially on the floor. He bolted out of the room and ran desperately down the hall, hoping that he had not yet left the abbey.

Joshua was indeed outside. He was walking alone at some distance from the abbey proper and had left his two suitcases by the side of the gravel path not far away. Simon ran out to where he was and Joshua saw him approaching and stood waiting. Through bitter tears, Joshua said, "They threw me out, Simon. Those hypocritical bastards! They threw me out like garbage." He looked away. "I'm leaving as soon as my ride gets here to pick me up. I just had to get out of that damned building." Then he hissed, "Those fuckers."

Simon looked at his friend and gasped, "I've been looking for you everywhere since yesterday. Where have you been hiding?"

Joshua didn't answer him but instead said, "You have nothing to worry about, I'm sure. All the really pretty boys seem to have gotten through without much of a scratch…except for me. I guess I'm not their type." He chuckled sarcastically and added, "But then, some of the ugly dumps managed to get thrown out too. It was a swift blade that came down. You got through it, though, but not me." Simon stepped up close to him and wiped the tears streaming down Joshua's face. He held him close for an instant but Joshua squirmed away from him and pushed Simon back, regaining his bitter composure. "The Abbot told me there were letters sent to the Bishop from witnesses and that my name was everywhere in them." He paused and loudly sucked up the mucous in his nose and swallowed. "I didn't try and deny the accusations. I stood my ground and faced all the bullshit hypocrisy. I told him I am gay and that 'yes', I've been enjoying myself fucking with some of the guys." He looked up at Simon and his eyes welled up again as he croaked, "You don't have to worry about what I said about you. I covered for you, Simon. I told him that you and I were only friends and that you were chaste."

"Oh, Joshua, why didn't you…"

"Why didn't I what?" He was angry now. "Why didn't I lie and say it wasn't true? What for? I'm done with all this bullshit. I'm done with hiding and allowing myself to be treated like a fucking leper." He wiped his eyes wildly and pointed his finger at Simon aggressively. "You on the other hand, you have your head up your ass." Simon didn't answer but was hurt by Joshua's bitter words. "I'm done with this religious shit. I'm ready to try the gay scene openly. I've been in touch with Joey up in New York."

Simon's eyes widened and he almost screamed, "Joey! How could you…?"

"Yeah, Joey. Get over it! I know you hate him but he's a really sweet guy. He has friends in the Village that can take me in. That's where I'm headed as soon as I leave this shit-hole and get home for a few days. Joey said I can bring you if you wanna come with me." Simon was stunned and stared at Joshua in disbelief. "Yeah, I figured you'd manage to sweet talk your way into staying here but I would really love it if you came with me. We can set something up." He reached over and took Simon's hand in his own. "I've been thinking, we're both young and creative. We might even meet the right theater people there and begin a new life together." Joshua let go of Simon's hand and said, "We might get hungry but we won't starve, Simon."

"I…I can't, Josh, I mean, I…I don't know how…"

"You can't? Or you won't? Let's start over, you and me. Let's get out of this looney bin now."

Simon whispered, "It's not a looney bin, Josh. Don't call it that."

"It's not? I'd say it's pretty warped and fucked up. Look at the events of the last couple of nights. Look at how many of our friends have been sacrificed because so many others are closeted. It's all hypocrisy, smoke and mirrors. A bunch of vicious closeted queens just covering their own asses. All the way from that Bishop, the Abbot, Wanda and the fuckers who betrayed us."

"You shouldn't talk like that. I get it that…"

"You get what you wanna get!" He was furious now and spittle flew from his mouth. "What the fuck happened to you? What are you now, the repentant whore in the Gospel?"

"I'm being realistic, Josh." Simon spoke slowly, trying to calm his friend. "I'll admit, the witch hunt was merciless and the ones who betrayed us are mostly mean closeted queens, but we did a lot of this to ourselves. We can try and put the blame everywhere else but…" Simon didn't know what else to say. "Did you ever really think the Church would just bless all the wild shit we were doing? We didn't try being careful, we just got in everybody's face."

"I can't believe you! Listen to yourself! Whose side are you on?"

His anger was intensifying and Simon looked around them, worried that their voices would carry, "Shhh, they might hear us."

"I don't care if they hear us! I don't give a flying fuck! They just threw my ass out! You're really disappointing me, Simon. You're proving to me now how you sold yourself like a cheap whore. I can't even begin to imagine how much you must have groveled and kissed their asses!"

Simon felt exposed, "What? Listen, I…"

"You're just bowing down and grabbing your ankles for them. You're giving in. I don't think I know you anymore." Then he said, "I don't think I want to know you anymore."

"Don't say that," Simon felt wounded.

"Joey was right."

At the mention of that name again, Simon felt his anger rise, "Joey was right? What's that supposed to mean? What are you bringing him up for? All he did was come here to break us up and destroy what we had."

"All you're interested in are your little boy dreams and fantasies about getting dressed up and doing all that hocus-pocus at an altar far from the people. You're in Lala-Land, Simon. Wake up and get real. Anyway, all that's changed and good riddance, I say. It's about fucking time! Hopefully, there will be more and more changes and the Church will catch up with the real world. We're still in the Dark Ages here, all caught up with kissing rings, throwing smoke and cookie worship."

Simon was genuinely shocked by Joshua's last two words. "That's blasphemy, Joshua! I can't believe you just said that. You shouldn't speak about the Sacred Host that way. It's Jesus' Body and Blood, Soul and Divinity. It's God's undeniable, Real Presence."

"Yeah, whatever." Joshua looked away. "It doesn't matter a rat's ass to me anyway. I'm outta here." Joshua looked at Simon and shook his head, "You always believed in all this bullshit a lot more than I ever did. You're so weird." He raised his hand and made a swiping movement in Simon's direction, saying, "Go back inside to you spiritual Disneyland, why don't you. It's always carnival-make-believe time in there. Anyhow, it's over for me and you wanna know something, I'm damned happy that it finally is."

Simon looked at him and only managed to swallow as he began crying. He asked angrily, "When were you going to say goodbye to me?" He searched Joshua's face for an answer. "When were you going to at least say goodbye to me? Or were you just going to leave? I thought you loved me."

"What's the point, honestly? You're going to stay here forever, fucking and sucking cock in the shadows, going to confession to another cock sucker and then doing it all over again, hell-bent on ordination to the priesthood. Unlike you, I'm ready to start living in the real world."

"You shouldn't say those things." Tears streamed down his face and Simon didn't bother to wipe them away this time. "The point is I love you. Can't you hear that?"

A small red sports car drove noisily up the gravel path and Simon saw a young man, driving behind the wheel. He honked the horn, waving, and went to where the suitcases were. Joshua's driver put his bags into the tiny car and waited in the driver's seat. Joshua turned to Simon and stuck his hand out, "Well, this is it. My friend from down the road at the college is here. This is where we part the ways. Take care and goodbye."

Simon didn't take his hand but moved in, wanting to hug and kiss his friend. "Don't leave like this, Josh. Let's plan on seeing each other somehow, somewhere. I don't know how but…" He rubbed his eyes nervously. "I can't say goodbye to you. Not yet. Not like this."

Joshua moved back, away from Simon, "Grow up, Simon. Go back inside to your fairy land story. They love you in there." Then he moved up closer and said, "Unless you're ready to come with me now…come with me, I want you to." Simon remained silent with his head down. "You're stuck, man. You want to live in two worlds and you won't admit that it's impossible to do that. Come with me now and we'll live openly as lovers." Joshua didn't wait for an answer or a gesture and walked away toward the waiting car. Simon stood and watched sadly as Joshua got into the vehicle. The tiny red car sped away down the gravel path, creating a great cloud of dust and leaving behind the massive building of towers, turrets and courtyards. Simon waited until Joshua and his friend disappeared beyond the evergreens and firs and the cloud of dust they raised, gently settled and fell back into place.

Joshua was gone. A terrible emptiness bore into Simon's soul. It was something he had felt when Toby had left but this was different. The "Night of the Long Knives" had sent them all running in opposite directions and had pried Joshua away from him. Simon's charmed world was shattered and he felt at that moment that he would never be the same.

The next day, Simon counted the minutes until one o'clock in the afternoon. He had barely been able to eat anything at lunch and felt as if he would vomit at any moment. He went to walk by himself in the courtyard of spices. There among the perfume of lavender, rosemary and so many other plants, he searched for peace and attempted to calm his heart. At the appointed time, Simon put his phone call through to the Abbot. Father Edmund's secretary answered. "Just a moment, Brother Simon. His Grace, the Abbot, will take your call momentarily." Simon was afraid now and feared that the Abbot might have reconsidered. The evidence against him was piled high and he would not be surprised if he was throw out after all.

There was a clicking sound on the other end of the line and Father Edmund's familiar, jovial voice filled his ear, "Brother Simon, good afternoon."

"Yes, Father Edmund. Good afternoon. This is Simon."

"I spoke at length with Father Wade about your situation." He paused and Simon's heart sank in his chest. "My conversation with him was not an easy one and I felt that in all honesty I needed to listen to his valid arguments against you once again." The Abbot stopped speaking, then he cleared his throat and Simon closed his eyes. "Despite Fathers Wade's protests, I have made my decision. You will proceed with your formation and studies here in the abbey for the priesthood as planned. This means, of course, that barring any surprises, you will profess your Solemn Vows soon and become a member of our Order for the rest of your life. Goodbye, dear brother."

The Abbot hung up before Simon had a chance to say a word. He put the phone's receiver back in its cradle but not before saying, "Hello, are you still there, Father?" No one was at the other end.

He had survived the "Night of the Long Knives". God had spared him. So many others had not been so lucky. Of the general number of more than seventy student monks, twenty seven had been accused and were swept up into the witch hunt. Twenty two young men were thrown out, they had gotten the axe. Among them were some of Simon's closest friends, Kurt, Aaron and Joshua. Only five belonging to the inner group had been spared. Tony, Noey, Lorenzo, Shane and himself survived. The ripple effects of that night, however, continued to instill fear and suspicion among them all. That awful night had separated them from one another and their closeness eventually faded and all but disappeared.

+ + + + +

The tattoo shop was very quiet when Simon finally finished. He had lost track of time but was aware that he had been speaking for a long time. It seemed to him that Billy had already left the shop as well as everyone else. Only he and Mark remained there. His mouth was dry and he felt exhausted. Mark cleared his throat loudly and stood up. The wheels of the stool squeaked as he said, "Fuck! That's some mess you guys ended up with."

"I told Joshua that we had brought it upon ourselves. I'm not really sure that at that moment I completely believed that. I think I said it then because I was so grateful to have been spared, but as time passed, I put more of the blame on the guys who had betrayed us. I blamed the unfaithful drinking buddies and the closeted priests who hunted us down like criminals. So many guys got thrown out and it made me feel very insecure. I felt watched by those in authority and came to see many of them as enemies. Not all of them, but many. I never really ever trusted those in authority in the Church again as I had done. I guess that's still true today to some degree. The way we were hunted down has stayed with me my entire life."

Mark nodded, "So that's where this persecution thing comes from. I get it now why you asked for the two pink triangles and the prisoner numbers." He paused and added, "What did you guys expect the outcome to be? I mean, c'mon, from what you told me, you guys were outta control with the booze and the sex." He shook his head, "'The Rocky Horror Picture Show'? Damn."

"I know, I know, but I felt hunted all the same. It was more than just a witch hunt. It tore our lives apart."

"Why do you say that?"

"It was the blind fixation that grew and grew like a fever in some of them that persecuted us and that really angered me. It was the fear and hatred against us who were so bold about our sexuality that drove them to do what they did. I suppose they were afraid it would expose them. Some of those students and priests who persecuted us, came out years later. Do you believe that shit? When they did come out, they were all cool about it because it was now their asses they were considering. Plus, it was already the late eighties. They felt all good about themselves then because the landscape had greatly shifted regarding sexuality." Simon paused and remembered the line the priest had said to him that it's the foot that is stepped on that hurts, not the one doing the stepping. "But on 'The Night of the Long Knives', those bastards who were closeted were doing the stepping, they came at us with blind ferocity like a pack of ferocious wolves. They considered it their duty to stamp out and obliterate any semblance of homosexual activity. So many talented, good people got burned. It was the hypocrisy that was so awful."

"From what you tell me, the Abbot was soft on you after all, wouldn't you say?"

"Yeah, he actually did go against the Bishop and Father Wade and the other bastards whose opinion it was that I should have been thrown out. He was one of the very few I still trusted in the abbey and looked up to until the day he died. I loved Father Edmund very much for sparing me. He was always good to me."

"Do you think there was something to what Joshua said about being a pretty boy?"

"I wouldn't have admitted it then because I didn't believe it. I'm not really sure that's the reason I was spared, at least not completely the reason. It might have helped, I won't deny it but there were plenty of other guys that got thrown out that weren't exactly trolls." Simon thought briefly and added, "I don't think it was the only reason but it might have helped. Still, I realize what you're saying and have to admit that he personally spared me from the axe."

Simon paused. "Years later I clearly found out that being a pretty boy definitely opened doors but I also learned that there was a price tag attached."

"Didn't you ever wonder, though, why the Abbot spared you?"

"I saw it more as God's hand in the sense that Father Edmund, the Abbot, was just an instrument. After the 'Night of the Long Knives' I searched for a lot of answers. I was crushed that some of my closest friends were mostly all gone but I was so grateful that I had been spared. I began to develop all kinds of attitudes that put people into one of two groups. Either you were my friend and protector or you were an enemy not to be trusted. Father Edmund was the first one I considered to be a friend and protector. In the coming years he would help me when I encountered all kinds of difficulties. After the 'Night of the Long Knives' I went deep inside myself and closed myself off from almost everyone, even those around me who had been some of my closest friends. Like I said, even between Noey, Tony, Lorenzo and Shane, something got damaged and it was never the same as it had been. Our group lost the spontaneity it had once possessed. And we dared not be so casual with others about our sexuality."

"You mean you closed yourself off especially from Tony and Noey? It sounded like you three guys were close."

"The three of us had been really close, it's true. But sadly, yeah, well, it sort of happened on its own. Little by little we all sort of drifted apart as I said before. Tony met someone one summer while he was doing a hospital chaplaincy and never returned to the abbey. Noey eventually left and was ordained for a very progressive church that ministered to LGBT people. I really had no one else for a very long time. I kept to myself and set my eyes on the priesthood. I trusted no one at that time but Father Edmund."

Mark sat back down on his stool looking at Simon as he spoke and admired his own work on Simon's skin. Simon already had several tattoos that popped strikingly because of their color. Mark was impressed with how well his tattoos looked. At long last, Simon sat up and dangled his stocking feet as he looked around the room for his jeans and shoes. "I feel like I've been in here an eternity. Is there anyone else in the shop?"

"I think maybe just Billy, up front, but he may have left. Everyone else is gone."

"Sorry I went on and on. Just lots of weird baggage, wouldn't you agree?"

"Incredible life experiences, I'd say. 'Baggage' sounds too negative. The 'stuff' in your life isn't necessarily either good baggage or bad baggage. It's all just 'stuff', its life experiences is all. Just from looking at you, Simon, I'd never guess you had experienced stuff like that. The world you describe inside the abbey is so different from anything I ever experienced." Mark stretched back and yawned. "I gotta say, I'm beginning to understand how you could have felt. There was a lot going on inside of you. It explains a lot about you. Now I can see why you came in here in the first place. I get the persecution angle now but you have to admit something to me."

Simon looked up, "What would that be?"

"You have to admit that you and your buddies were guilty. Did you ever stop to think that maybe you didn't really belong there? Did you ever consider that maybe it was a fantasy for you since you were a little kid, like your friend Joshua pointed out? I mean, maybe as you became a man did you ever think that maybe that kind of a life wasn't for you?"

Simon looked directly into Mark's eyes and without hesitation answered, "Absolutely not. I knew in my heart of hearts that my place was there, in that world. I knew I was born for that. I still believe that even though my situation now is somewhat 'distanced'. I still believe I was called there by God. I have never doubted God's call to the priesthood even now. I guess I just can't figure out why God called me is all. I guess my big question is, why did he make me one way and call me to something that seems to be so contrary?" Simon shrugged and admitted, "In a crazy, roundabout way, the 'Night of the Long Knives' actually helped to clarify that very thing for me. The horrible purge or witch hunt or whatever the fuck you want to call it, helped me to see how wrong I had behaved. After it was over and I was still left standing, I resolved to get back on track and focus on my vocation. It still seemed miraculous to me that I was spared while so many others were not." He added, "I put it right there on my list of miracles."

"Miracles?" Mark sounded intrigued.

"Yeah. I got through what I experienced in the sea, the motel room and then the purge of the 'long knives'."

"Ah, okay. So what you're saying is that the 'Night of the Long Knives' helped you to see more of your real self even though it wasn't a complete picture. I mean, it showed you clearly what you're capable of."

"Yeah, exactly. I was convinced I had a wild, worldly, fleshy side. The purge helped me to admit I had almost completely forgotten my other side, my spiritual side." He looked at his feet and said, "I'm just not sure I went about it the right way."

"Why do you say that?"

"The afternoon that Joshua left, I was devastated and got very depressed. When I walked back inside the abbey I felt empty. Then the next day, like I told you, I spoke with the Abbot on the phone and received a clean slate to start over again in the abbey. That night, I went to bed early and had a dream that was so realistic it shook me to the very root of my soul. Even now as I recall it, I can remember every single detail. It made me realize that I hadn't just survived the purge because I had poured on the charm with the Abbot and made clever arguments on my behalf. No, the dream opened my eyes to much more." Simon swallowed dryly and said, "When I woke up at dawn, after I had had that dream, I was absolutely convinced that God had indeed given me another chance to remain in the abbey for a reason. This realization gave me a new purpose in life and a new set of plans began to unfold in me." Simon locked eyes with the tattooer. "After that dream, I laid in that metal cot, Mark, feeling redeemed and like someone new. Once again I got all those feelings back that I had held onto as a child. Once again, I knew myself to be chosen by God for something specific, for something that only I could do for Him. In those hours while I lay there inert, I chastised myself for having been so irresponsible and negligent."

"Didn't you feel at all that you had also been searching for your true self? I mean, didn't you value your own 'coming out' process as a young adult? As something healthy?"

"What I realized in my cot after the dream was far more than simply coming to terms with my sexuality. I knew I had forgotten God and had put myself in His place. I understood that I had put God's Will to one side in order to do my own will. Lying there I realized I had laid out and followed my plans instead of seeking God's. What the dream did for me was convince me that I was forgiven and completely exonerated. This meant I could really begin again. I had a fresh start."

The tattooer was mesmerized and captivated by what Simon was saying. He simply stared out of curiosity and managed only to ask, "So?"

Simon jumped off the work table and said, "So?" Then as if realizing something, Simon said, "Yeah, I know I need to shut up and let you go home. Sorry for so much chatter. So, I'm outta here."

"Dude! You're fucking killing me! So tell me! What did you dream that could so completely convince you that you could make a clean start after all the stuff you did? I'd have thought you'd be so fucked up in your head that you'd feel like you could never look at God in the eyes again. You schemed and lied and did whatever to get what you wanted. I would have thought you'd be all screwed up with guilt and remorse."

"Oh, I was filled with guilt and remorse from the day Joshua left. Don't doubt that. But the dream did something in me I never expected." Mark hunched his shoulders and held out his hands inquisitively. Simon felt his face burn and tears welled up in his eyes, "After the dream, my guilt and remorse were taken away by God. I understood I could really begin again because God was grateful." Simon looked up at Mark, "God's gratitude took the guilt away."

"Gratitude? I'm not getting it. Explain."

"Yeah, Mark, God's gratitude." Simon had gotten his jeans on and was stepping into his worn-out, black Converse high tops. "God expressed His gratitude to me for returning to Him. It was unlike any dream I've ever had since. It was so realistic and compelling." Simon paused and sat again on the work table recalling the experience. He cleared his throat and wiped his eyes. He hid his hands tightly under his thighs as if to gather courage to tell the dream he had never told a living soul. Then slowly, he recalled the details of his dream for the tattooer.

+ + + + +

"In the dream I could see myself sleeping on the cot in my cell. From a great distance, outside, the faint sound of many trumpets could be heard but coming closer with every passing second and that is what woke me. In the darkness of my space, I realized that the trumpet blasts were getting louder and I understood that whatever it was, it was coming at me. An irresistible desire to look and see what it might be filled me and I got up and cautiously looked out my window. What I saw made me tremble because of its enormity."

Simon continued, "I looked down and could see that I was high up in the abbey, safely in my cell but when I looked to my right, in the direction of the commotion, I began to shake because of what lay before me. A throng too numerous to count had gathered in the far distance. It wasn't a mob but more of a procession which flowed slowly like a great river making its way. Then I began to see the solemn expressions on the people's faces as they drew near. The orderly throng walked without haste and pressed together. The sea of bodies stretched far back on an endless, winding highway for what appeared to be miles and miles. I wondered what this impressive march could be. Instinctively, I crouched down below the window and leaned against the wall as soon as it struck me that it was moving toward me. It seemed that in an instant, a multitude had arrived just under the window of my cell and I could hear hushed voices getting louder by the second. Again, I gave in to the irresistible urge to peer out the window and as I stood up guardedly, I saw the crude, rough-hewn flatbed carriage slowly approaching at a snail's pace, not far away."

Simon looked at Mark and saw that the tattooer had closed his eyes as he listened. "It was a carriage that had no sides to it, just a floor made of long planks, meant to carry crates or barrels. It was a crude thing and was not pulled by horses nor beasts of burden but rather, it was pulled forward by the crowd tugging with great effort on long beams. In this manner, its two wide, wooden wheels moved slowly ahead on its macabre procession. I remember thinking how the people pressed up against it protectively and then it stopped. It was right there. It was suddenly right there under my window and I froze. The trumpets, the chatter and the din filtering upward from the masses below was deafening to me and as soon as I saw them looking up at me and pointing, I slid down against the wall in my cell and felt the cold floor under me. I knew that whatever it was that was out there, it had come for me. My worst fears were confirmed when I heard a man's raspy voice say softly, 'Simon'. He didn't so much call to me in a public voice but rather, I was hearing that voice in my soul. It was a gentle, soothing voice deep within me, like balm. It sounded ancient and fragmented but irresistible and confident. He said my name only once and that's when I realized that the tumult outside had shuffled and moved. Everything had gone completely silent. Twilight was approaching because the light filtering through my windows had shifted."

Simon asked Mark, "Are you following me?" The tattooer simply nodded assent. Simon continued his narrative speaking slowly. "Involuntarily, I got to my feet and looked out the window again. I was no longer three stories up, protected by the fortified walls of the abbey. Instead, my window was on the ground level now and then the window itself just evaporated and I was standing on a paved stone surface outside the abbey with my back to the wall. The silent crowd stared at me and parted, creating a path between me and the primitive flatbed carriage that was slowly approaching and obviously meaning to stop in front of me. I could see a bent figure, perhaps a man, on top of the carriage coming my way. I began to walk through the silent throng pulled by the presence of the man that was now there, visibly bound and exposed for all to see."

Simon cleared his throat. "When I was very close, I saw it was no mere man. I saw Him. I saw the man bound to the rough-hewn gibbet that stuck out rigidly from the floor of the carriage and up into the air. He hung there like a gruesome rag doll, half standing and half suspended, moving from side to side as the carriage began to stop, finally reaching its destination. I could see how His knees didn't touch the floor because thick ropes held His outstretched arms in place above His head. I couldn't take my eyes off the man who had obviously been severely beaten and tortured. His beard was caked with filth and His long, tangled hair was matted with blood and held tightly to His head by a woven cap of long thorns."

"The stench coming from Him was almost unbearable and I saw that excrement had trickled down His inner thighs and gathered in a dark, watery pool beneath His blistered feet. Wounds and open, bloody gashes covered His sweaty torso and I saw that He had cocked His head crookedly to one side in my direction and sort of rested His head on His wounded shoulder in order to lessen His labored breathing. He was completely naked and trembled as He softly moaned in pain. It was beyond clear to me how utterly broken He was in every sense. The tone of His skin, affected by the strange light from the sky at that hour, appeared translucent to me. The tones of His flesh varied between purple bruises of different shades and sickly yellow and blue splotches attesting to the severe beating He had endured."

"I was right up in front of Him now, no further than a foot or two and I could see blood from deep welts, trickling down His back into the boney crevice between His buttocks. His penis dribbled some kind of fluid and His bloody, swollen testicles dangled obscenely between His legs underneath Him, barely swaying, as the carriage swung slightly forward, and then back, finally coming to an abrupt stop in front of me. The tattered man looked at me intently and studied me purposefully. One of His eyes was grotesquely swollen shut and blackened but the other one was open and clear, knowing in its gaze. I saw more than I could ever tell you in that pale, gray green eye that studied me so completely. His eye didn't leave me and I looked away because the sight of Him was so unnerving to me."

"The simple truth was that it was unbearable to look at Him but at the same time His gaze was irresistible and I could not look away any further. I looked at Him again, mesmerized by Him. Then without realizing what I was fully doing, I walked up close to Him and stretched out my hand."

Simon paused. And swallowing, he said, "From somewhere in my dream, I held in my outstretched hand a small, metal cup and I raised it to the man's raw, cracked bloated lips. He drank greedily as I tilted the cup toward His mouth. He never took His knowing eye off me." The memory of the dream kept Simon from speaking any further and he looked at Mark, tears running down his face. He tried to speak but was overtaken by great emotion and when he finally managed to do so, his voice quivered, "He…He…just looked at me with gratitude because I had gone to Him."

Simon swallowed hard at the recollection. "It's the best and only way I can describe it. He looked at me with deep gratitude. In my dream, Mark, I knew I had broken my vows and forgotten my priestly vocation. As I stood in front of the broken man, mere inches from His bloodied flesh and broken body, I feared that I myself had somehow done that to Him and that I would be punished and tortured in the same way. I was expecting to be held responsible for what I had done with the sacred things that had been entrusted to me and that I would have to pay dearly for my transgressions." Simon looked pleadingly at Mark as he said, "But no. There was nothing of that in His gaze. Instead, I only saw gratitude because I had gone to Him. The suffering man was only grateful that I had considered Him and had gone to Him. 'Lord', I whispered when I realized He loved me more than ever before. And then He moved His lips slowly, with difficulty, as He mouthed three words to me, 'Stay with me'."

+ + + + +

Mark sat with his hands in his lap, upright on his swivel stool as Simon concluded. "Then, Mark, when I woke up, I realized God had given me the 'chance' I had begged for. It was bigger than just getting the Abbot's permission to let me stay in the abbey and pursue priesthood. The 'chance' was far broader and the ramifications went deeper than I could possibly imagine. As I came up through heavy, groggy layers of sleep, I knew then that God still considered me worthy to be a priest and to serve the Church as one. I realized that He loved me as I am, 'warts and all' as the expression goes. I lay in my tiny cot aware that a new day was dawning. I studied the first brilliant rays of sunshine breaking into the darkness of my tiny cell and I understood at that moment that I needed to make great changes within myself. I would remain in the Church and prepare, study and serve in order to be God's most faithful priest."

Simon concluded, "I took that dream and made a life out of it. It wasn't until several years later that I wondered to myself if I might have gotten it wrong, not fully understanding the meaning of the Lord's words to me. I wondered then what the Lord's words to me might really have meant. What did He mean when He commanded, 'Stay with me'?"

Chapter Thirteen
Finding One's Voice

It took me quite a long time to develop a voice, and now that I have it, I am not going to be silent.
Madeleine K. Albright

Numerous cardboard boxes filled with old letters and papers were stacked at Simon's bare feet. He sat comfortably in the red, overstuffed chair which was his favorite in the cozy bedroom. The walls had been covered in red damask which he had bought many years before in Rome when he had been a younger man. It was in his bedroom that Simon felt safest. He considered it to be like a guarded womb, a place where he was protected, shielded away from the noise. In this space, he felt invulnerable before everyone who was hostile to him. He could dream as much as he desired in this space like the motto he had seen so many times on the facades of venerable palazzos in Venice: NIHIL ME DOMAT. In this niche and coziness he had created for himself, NOTHING COULD DOMINATE HIM.

He loved glancing at the framed photographs of Pope John Paul II and Pope Benedict XVI as well as one from Archbishop Giovanni Enrico Boccella that hung near his bed. He had collected them over the years and he often read the dedications written on them, to him personally, which he knew by heart. Often, he would read them slowly, out loud, as if it were the first time. On the wall near the fireplace and on its mantel, were several framed documents and photographs, among them those dedicated by Maria Callas, Renata Scotto and Rudolf Nureyev. There was one from Karl Lagerfeld with a caricature of Coco Chanel which the fashion master had himself drawn. Next to his overstuffed chair was a letter written by Sergei Diaghilev from the Savoy in Paris dated 1923 and two other messages, one written by Saint Pope Pius X and two by Pope Pius XII. There were four other letters on the far wall from Giacomo

Puccini with various dates and two messages from the Duke and Duchess of Windsor, along with two letters signed by Queen Victoria taken long ago from a red box. On a small table near a draped window Simon kept a framed envelope with a list of medicines needed at the hospital in Lambarene, in French Equatorial Africa, written in neat penmanship by Dr. Albert Schweitzer. On his writing desk he kept a photograph with a message from Joszef Cardinal Mindszenty, a large photograph of Puccini signed and dated in Bologna 1899 and a sepia cabinet photograph signed and dated, "Nicolas 1894" by the young last Tsar of All the Russias, although yet uncrowned at the time of signing.

Simon believed that these handwritten pieces from the past possessed the unique energy of their authors. To have them in such proximity gave Simon great inspiration and consolation as he reclined, somewhat ruffled by past turbulent memories in the privacy of his bed chamber. Tonight, in his tormented soul, disheveled in spirit as he was, he drew strength once again from these particular souls who had gone before him and whose DNA he believed was still present all around him.

A formidable-sized marble bust of the young Roman emperor, Lucio Cesare sat on a high column of black granite to one side of the fireplace. Above the bust, on the wall, hung an oil painting of a nude young man reclining on one elbow and stretched out on the shore looking out into the distance. Nearby, on a column of polished white stone was a marble bust of Narcissus which he had come across by chance and bought one morning long ago on the Via Della Croce in Rome.

He poured himself a Jack Daniel's and lit the fireplace. Behind him sat the massive carved bed he had inherited from his great grandparents and then his grandparents. Two matching bedside tables completed the set of nineteenth century furniture. His mother never cared for the intricately carved furniture and had gifted Simon with the pieces when his grandmother had died. For him, the antique pieces were an important connection with his past and the people in it, like the letters and photographs near him.

Two candelabra-like lamps with wide, porcelain shades, sat on either side of the bedside tables. They had been given to him by an elderly, forgotten actress friend of his from the golden age of film in Mexico a short time before she had died. Simon had shared a close friendship with the actress for many years even though some family members and close friends had criticized and belittled the relationship. Simon had not cared about their criticism. His friend, Rosario Galvez had understood him perfectly and accepted him with all his eccentricities and sins just as he was. In fact, she had once confided in him that what attracted her to him most of all, was his singular way of doing things and assessing life situations on his own terms.

Oriental rugs he had bought in Turkey many years ago covered the wooden floors of the large bedroom and his three dachshunds lay contentedly on the rugs near him, their eyes closed but not fully asleep. As he lost himself in his thoughts looking at the dancing flames in the fireplace, Simon was aware of his favorite opera by Puccini playing softly on the phonograph. The tragedies in Turandot had always filled him with all kinds of emotions at the same time, melancholy being the most prominent. He identified so much with the Aria "Nessun Dorma" because it addressed the tragedy of having to choose and then be loyal to one's choice. Simon had learned that there was a price you had to pay for the object of your love and desire. The Aria was about to play and Giuseppe di Stefano, Simon's favorite tenor, was ready. Simon formed the words with his mouth as he closed his eyes and gave himself over to his sensibilities.

Simon had always been impressed by those words and had made them his own. Tonight he thought about their meaning, whispering to himself, "But my secret is locked away in me, my name, no one shall ever know." For a long time that had been the case as he lived in several worlds at the same time. He had fooled many people as to who he really was. Yet, all that had changed to a significant degree since he had accepted God's command to be honest with Him, himself and others. Now that he had begun to come clean, his secret was no longer completely locked away and his name, who he really was, would be known by others.

But for tonight, Simon still savored the secrets he held onto and in his gloomy state of mind, he swallowed another generous mouthful of bourbon. For so long he had relished singing those words, giving them his own personal, hidden meaning in the two fundamental worlds he had lived in for most of his life: the sacred and the profane, the spiritual and the flesh. These continued to be the two forces always tugging within him, neither force stubbornly refusing to submit to the other. Two opposite worlds claimed him and he had carefully built his life on both of them, careful to keep each apart, shrouded in secrecy, one from the other. As the Aria came to an end, Simon voiced the final words with di Stefano in barely a whisper:

"Vincero'! Vincero'! Vincero'!"

He said to himself out loud, "I will overcome! I will overcome! I will overcome!" So many memories came to him as he took another long drink and crossed his legs. There were so many things locked away inside of him that no one had ever known until now. Long ago he had resigned himself to keeping it all that way. He had accepted that he would have to live his life within these two worlds. But God had revealed other plans, plans that were radically different from his own. Now, as he sat there, he realized that everything had changed. Like Prince Calaf, alone at night, in the opera Turandot, Simon also felt that he would be victorious over his many demons. His dilemma, however, was that he didn't quite know how or when he would be completely victorious.

He looked at the boxes stacked all around him. He knew the letter he was searching for was somewhere in one of them. A twisted, knotty log crackled in the fireplace and an impressive display of sparks burst loudly in the hearth, flying freely upward, into the chimney. His three weenie dogs opened their eyes at the sound of the crackling and studied him but did they did not move. Finally, one yawned and rolled over and the other two moved closer together in that kind of closeness that is a grace. Simon swallowed another ample gulp of the sour mash whiskey he was so fond of. He was grateful for the liquid warmth that flowed down his throat and spread across his chest warming everything in its path.

He pulled a box up close to him and opened it, continuing to search. He wanted to find the letter and reread it before he took the sketch of his next tattoo to Mark. The next tattoo was simple in design but it was tangled in many emotions and events. He wanted to remember those moments now that he was at a crossroads in his life. He mused to himself once again about the tragedy of having to make choices that later ultimately defines us. How differently his life would have been had he chosen to leave the abbey in order to join the traditional priesthood movement. All of it had so attracted him and given him such a sense of security at the time. It was suddenly possible to regain the faith he so longed for and traditions that had disappeared in the Church. But that was all so long ago and he had been lead elsewhere. He wondered who had lead him elsewhere? Had it been God or himself? Or a little of each, perhaps?

At last, he found what he had been searching for. The square, yellowed envelope containing the letter was still a sacred treasure for him even though he had not framed it like some of the others. For Simon, there were too many bruised memories attached to this letter that were still tender and delicate, and even now, stirred within him. After all the years since he had received it, he still held it with awe thinking about the heroic man who had written it to him personally and who had held it in his own hands. He gently removed the heavy stationary from within the envelope and unfolded the single sheet of paper:

Seminaire Internationel
Saint-Pie-X
Econe, Suisse
My dear Brother Simon,

As I expressed to you in person, it was my pleasure to have met you in April of this year in Pittsburgh, Pennsylvania during my recent journey to America and to have had the opportunity to sit with you and discuss the Priesthood of Jesus Christ and His Reign in Society. It gladdens me to know how serious you are about the call Our Lord Himself has given you and your concerns about the dangers surrounding you.

I am saddened to know that you are confronted with so many difficulties in the abbey to which you belong. The dangers are real and present everywhere within the Church. It is an unfortunate fact that the Church is in great difficulty today. We must all be strong, Brother Simon, if we are to be faithful to the Truth and to Tradition. As I explained to you during our conversation, I will pray for you, asking God and His Tender Mother to guide you in the months ahead. Do not become discouraged in your trials, dear brother.

You impressed me as a serious young man who knows what he is looking for and one day as a priest you will preach Jesus Christ with all your strength, soul, and heart. This is a grace you must take great care of especially because you are surrounded by weakness. The Society of Saint Pius X opens its doors to receive you should the Holy Ghost move you and us in this direction. Feel confident that I understand your predicament completely. I ask you to stay in touch with our priests in the United States of America, as we discussed.

Let us pray one for the other and in this way, sustain the Church in these perilous times. In the Hearts of Jesus and Mary, I embrace you and bless you once again.

\+ Marcel Lefebvre
Econe
13 June, 1983
Feast of Saint Anthony of Padua

Simon kissed the letter and held it close to him. He thought about that day when he had come so close to following a certain path after speaking with the impressive Archbishop. He had been determined then, to be faithful to God's call once again, as he had been as a young boy, no matter the cost and had renewed his vows to God. He would be celibate and resist temptation. He recalled Saint Augustine's struggles and knew he could begin again because God is merciful. His sexual experiences in the abbey had swayed him away from his call but he determined to get back on the right path. Church discipline had loosened substantially and had practically crumbled to the degree that it had left him vulnerable and broken. The laxity had allowed him to drift away into debauchery little by little. His visit with the courageous Archbishop had had to be secret. Simon took a swig of the bourbon and thought how ironic it was that he had had to hide once again. He had gone to the gay bar in Pittsburgh with his friends in secrecy before the "Night of the Long Knives" and then he had gone in secrecy to meet with the saintly, traditional prelate. He had spent most of his life hiding. That much was very clear to him. He felt repulsed by it. Had he been found out by the authorities in the abbey regarding either visit, he would have been in serious trouble and expelled. The persecutions and the hiding never seemed to diminish for him. Toby had been right about this.

Simon looked at the letter in his hand and wondered why God had kept him from joining the traditional priestly Society of Saint Pius X. There, under great discipline and order, he certainly would have flourished in holiness and grace instead of being immersed in sin and rampant licentiousness. He was sure that in that kind of setting he would have changed his ways and repented. But God, it seemed, had other plans for him, plans he himself could not possibly understand. The unbending Will of God took him elsewhere, far from what he thought God wanted for him. Or was it all along what he himself really wanted? He wondered to himself how often he blamed God for his own actions.

Simon had always tried to seek God's Will, but it wasn't a precise science. God wasn't keen on explanations nor revealing concrete plans. He remembered the saying: "If you want to hear Almighty God roar with laughter, tell Him your plans." God's Will had to be prayed for, meditated upon and finally, just submitted to with complete, blind acceptance. This was a fundamental piece of his spirituality that the nuns had taught him as a boy. He remembered with clarity how Sister Mary Agnes had put it to him in high school, "Larry, if you remember anything in your life remember what Dante said, 'Only in His Will, is our peace'. If you seek God's Will and live by it, no matter how strange it may seem to you, no matter how many storms envelope you, you will be okay; you will be strong enough to keep going forward into the light." Simon thought about the nun's words as he contemplated his life's journey. Who can possibly understand God's ways? He remained baffled at each turn.

Simon asked himself out loud, "But how can one ever know the Will of the Almighty?" He looked at the fire burning in the fireplace and asked himself how he could ever really know God's Will with certainty? He still desired to live according to God's Will but it wasn't so simple. He had been taught to seek God's Will as if it were something obvious and effortless to do, yet his experience had showed him otherwise. And then there was his inner struggle between the spirit and the flesh. He knew that he often strayed from the rules and hid from God constantly, many times not knowing what else to do.

Simon sighed and took another drink. God indeed had had different plans for him, that much was evident now. Plans that were way different from anything he could have possibly imagined or schemed for himself. He thought about that faraway time and stared at the flames in the fireplace. It had all begun with an assignment that one summer, to a parish church in Texas which was staffed by monks of the abbey.

Furthermore, events beyond his control came together that summer and fall. Love and vainglory would struggle to the death to win his heart but only one would be victorious. He speculated now what purpose there was in remembering all these things? What was the point if it was all in the past, already done and buried? Was this part of God's Will too? He looked down and stared at the letter he had received from Archbishop Lefebvre. At the time he had received it, he thought the plan was perfectly in place. But it was not. So much for trying to figure out God's plans for him. He kissed the letter once more and carefully put it back into its envelope. Simon finished his bourbon and tried in earnest to push away his troublesome thoughts. He lay his head back in the comfort of his cozy, dimly lit bedroom and allowed the whiskey to tame his remorse. There had been and there continued to be so many loose ends in his life which caused him deep regret. At some point, he simply gave in to sleep, which mercifully freed him from so many disturbing questions.

+ + + + +

A week later in Mark's workroom, Simon took a folded piece of drawing paper from his wallet and handed it to Mark.

"What's this?" asked the tattooer.

"My next tattoo. It's a very simple sketch, man, but it represents one of the most important moments in my life." Mark cocked his head to one side in a questioning manner as he unfolded the paper in his hand. "It's all about a major decision I had to make in my life." Simon paused. "Funny how one decision can change the entire course of your life as it leads you down various paths you never even considered. And while you're making that decision, you aren't even aware of any of it."

"That's how it usually works, my man. There's no blueprint to follow. The key is not to forget the past and repeat bad shit." Mark studied the sketch Simon had given him. "Okay, I'm looking at two tennis rackets crossed over each other and six fiery tennis balls." Mark pointed, saying, "And I'm seeing two initials, 'K.R.', right below everything." He looked up and asked, "What does it all mean, dude?"

"This tattoo is about me looking out from behind the wall I had built around myself after the 'Night of the Long Knives'. It's about someone I met named Kevin who brought me back to life even if for a very short time." Simon felt his guilt rising within him but continued, "It didn't happen all at once but it helped me to look outside myself. I had told myself that God's Will was this one thing and only this one path I had charted for myself. Then Kevin and I crossed paths. I was totally sidetracked from all my plans and best intentions. After I met him I began to reflect on things differently. Things I hadn't thought of before."

"What did you discover?"

"I was forced to admit that I belonged to both the sacred and the profane, to the spiritual and to the flesh. I couldn't explain why I was put together this way but I understood that I couldn't push either completely away nor block either of them out. I understood somewhere deep within myself that it would be impossible to do so. God's call to priesthood weighed heavily upon me. There were times that I told myself that I wanted desperately to identify only with the sacred. Still, this didn't seem to be complete, let alone, a practical decision if I was going to be honest with myself. In any case, it certainly didn't seem to last. At other times I would give myself completely to the profane but again, in time, I would realize that something terribly important was missing in my life."

Mark interrupted him and his question startled Simon. Mark's seeming disinterest in what he had been saying, surprised Simon. "Where are we putting this tattoo?"

"On my right arm, just below my elbow, toward my wrist."

Mark took Simon's arm, twisting it this way and that. "Okay. I got it. Let's get this going." Mark didn't say another word for the moment. It was clear that he wasn't in a talking mood. Simon surrendered his right arm to the tattooer and tried to relax in anticipation of the pain that was soon to come. As he lay there, he wondered what might be on Mark's mind that caused him to be so silent and distant. Simon was thinking about all the things he had talked about last time. Maybe it was just too much to listen to? Yet, Simon had had to talk about it. He couldn't deny that those events that had occurred that night in the seminary had changed everything for him and his tight circle of friends.

As if reading Simon's mind, Mark suddenly spoke up. "How do these two tennis rackets have anything to do with the night of the witch hunt you told me about last time? I mean, since you told me all about it, all that stuff you talked about makes me think that your whole world fell apart."

"Yeah, that's one way to put it."

"I mean, if so many of your buds got kicked out, where was your support group after that? Who did you hang with?"

Simon thought about Noey and Tony first. Right after the "Night of the Long Knives" things had cooled between them. It wasn't illogical because they had all been scared into thinking that they themselves could still be thrown out.

"Well, after that night, the only one who really became my close friend was Seth, of all people."

"The chubby guy in your hall?"

"Yeah. He was, after all, from the original group of us that had entered the postulancy. Out of twenty-four guys who entered, only he and I were left of that class. The fact that we were the only two left out of so many was enough common ground to build on."

Mark studied the sketch again and finally managed to ask, "And Shawn? You were close to him, right?" Simon hesitated and didn't quite know how to respond to the question. Mark put on his purple gloves as he asked, "I mean, what happened between you guys after that night? Wasn't he the instigator in that fiasco that almost got your ass thrown out?"

Simon turned his head and looked at Mark. "Yeah, he was the bastard, alright." Simon paused, then added, "At that point in my life, I'm not really sure where I stood with Shawn, although I was soon to find out." He looked up at the ceiling and remembered Shawn's sudden advances in the cloister of the novitiate and then in Toby's room on that depressing afternoon in the seminary wing. Simon remembered seeing his own mess running off the highly polished boots Shawn had given him that night in Shawn's cell. He continued to look at Mark and repeated the words, "I'm not really sure where I stood with Shawn. The only one that was really there for me after the purge was Seth. After that awful, endless night, he and I became close and we helped each other get through our theology classes and studies."

"Gotta say, I'm kinda surprised, Simon. I thought you and Seth had had some bad shit between you. Didn't you tell me you felt like he was trying to control you? I think I understood you were saying that he was kinda into you, you know, like he was queer for you and jealous of some of your friends?"

Simon chuckled, "Queer for me? Damn, Mark, that's a bit much although who knows what dwells in a man's heart. I had always felt he had a hidden agenda, that's true enough. I don't know, maybe he didn't. I guess I was too involved with my tight circle of friends to bother and find out. I will tell you this, though, after that bad shit went down, he was the only one who drew close to me once the dust settled. And I was grateful, very grateful for his company."

Mark looked at Simon's arm as he said, "I'm just telling you what I think I heard. Anyway, I thought maybe you guys might have had a physical thing."

"I don't think that he would have minded having something physical but I wasn't attracted to him physically. Not at all. Anyway, after the night of the witch hunt, we were all scared out of our wits, and physical attractions were held in check for the time being. At least they were for me." Simon remembered Seth now. "Funny how things in life can throw people together. I had thought Seth to be so completely different than me and afterward he and I became like blood brothers because of our similarities. We were so similar in so many ways."

"Blood brothers?"

"Yeah, honestly. It didn't happen overnight but we became really close until he died unexpectedly."

Mark switched the tattoo gun on and was drawing black ink. He suddenly looked up. "Died?"

"Yeah, he was so young too. But that happened years into the future. Turns out he had a bad heart like his dad and some of his uncles. Anyway, until the terrible night of the purge, Seth wasn't anybody I could say I knew. A few days after everything happened he confessed to me that when he was called to appear before the Abbot it wasn't to defend himself against any accusations leveled at him. He didn't appear on the Bishop's list nor in any of the incriminating letters. Instead, the Abbot had cross-examined him about me." Simon remembered that conversation as if it was this morning. "Yeah, I guess it was one of the things that cemented our relationship."

"How so? What did Seth tell you that made that happen?"

"He told me that he had gone to bat for me and told the Abbot that he had heard rumors about me as well but that they were unfounded. He told the Abbot something like, 'I live across the hall from Simon and I usually keep my cell door open. I've never seen anything out of place.' You know, Mark, after that I began to see him differently and I was of course, eternally grateful for this. I always remembered that conversation with him and as the years passed I could see more and more that he had covered for me because he really loved me."

"Sounds like you were important to him."

"After that awful, shitty night, I became completely celibate again. I spent more and more time in prayer. I would stay sitting on a pew, thinking for hours, just sitting in the dark crypt trying to find my way again. Weeks passed and turned into months and I not only learned to be alone but I sought to be alone. I also learned to endure all the shit I had caused to myself. It wasn't easy to admit. It was something I got used to little by little. I had no choice but to be present to myself without distractions if I ever expected to regain my inner peace again. During that time my prayer life really deepened. I kept a quote from the Prophet Zechariah with me all the time. I would write it out sometimes when I got distracted in my studies: 'Zeal for Thy House consumes me'. I also had a little quote written on top of my desk. It was from something Pope Pius XI had said in a letter to seminarians: 'Faithful Catholics expect much from you'. Every day I prayed for the day of my priestly ordination. In my isolation and loneliness I was comforted by these thoughts. The only person I could share them with was Seth and he always listened and gave me his support. We would take long walks together and this is how I rediscovered God's call to me was still standing. I can't begin to tell you, Mark, how comforted I was by the things I rediscovered inside of me. I knew more than ever that I was called by God to be a priest. Does any of this make sense to you?"

"Not completely, dude, but just keep talking. I'm trying to connect the dots." He chuckled, "I'm from another universe than yours."

"As a way of dealing with my isolation, I took to reading the lives of the saints and began to center myself on spiritual things. You know, Mark, I was amazed to read that the lives of a lot of the saints had been crazy like mine."

"Really?"

"Yeah. It didn't make me feel like I was some kind of exception. I started to make some new friendships among the older, more traditional monks in the abbey. These were the guys I had often seen as thick skinned, kinda hard-assed monks but when I began to know them better, I discovered they were isolated themselves, just like me. I had never given them the time of day and now some of them became my close friends, albeit, different from the close company of friends I had kept before the purge."

Mark chuckled again and said, "Uh, yeah, I'd say there must have been quite a difference."

"There was one older priest, Father Marcellinus. I admired him greatly because he was the kind of priest I wanted to be one day. He was holy and solid in his beliefs, like Father Cornelius had been, as well as Father Francis and Father Michael when I was a boy. Father Marcellinus introduced me to some traditional devotions in the Church I had never even heard of. I discovered a whole new world that restored my sense of tranquility and safety once again. One night after the evening meal, Father Marcellinus and I walked together outside the abbey before Vespers and he told me about waxen discs called 'Agnus Dei'." Simon carefully explained to Mark about the waxen discs.

+ + + + +

After Vespers that evening, Simon followed the priest to his cell. The old monk had several large discs of the thick, yellowed wax which he took carefully from a wooden box that sat squarely in the middle of a small altar covered with a lace altar cloth. Behind the box stood a statue of the Sorrowful Mother about three feet high. The image was of the Mother of God wringing Her hands in exasperated sorrow. At her feet was a bloodied cloth used to wipe the body of Jesus in His terrible agony and death. Simon was captivated by the look on the statue's face of unrestrained sorrow and anguish.

"You won't find this anywhere, anymore, Brother Simon," Father Marcellinus said, as he glanced and pointed to the box with the discs on the small altar. "I have these discs since I was a young monk at the Mother House of the Order in Rome. I had gone to a Solemn Pontifical Mass offered by the pope himself more than sixty or seventy years ago. It was just before the Great War was about to begin." The aged priest squinted his eyes in the darkened room as he continued, "The Holy Father then was Saint Pope Pius X. I can remember him sitting on the 'sedia gestatoria' as they brought him in toward the Papal Throne. I wasn't a priest, then, of course. I was probably a little younger than you are now. The Abbot General of the Order had taken me with him to the ceremony. On that morning, the waxen discs known as 'Agnus Dei' were to be distributed."

Simon asked with great curiosity, "What were the Agnus Dei discs, Father?"

"We were given seven discs that day from the hands of the pope himself. The discs and pieces in this box were part of those discs." Father Marcellinus held the open box close to himself protectively as he spoke. "To be in the presence of Pope Pius X was like being in Heaven, in the presence of an angel. He was elderly then but still possessed such solemnity and grace." The old priest had closed his eyes and Simon could see how tightly he was holding on to the wooden box. Simon felt his skin covered in gooseflesh as he stood silently in awe, listening to this man who had lived in the presence of a saint.

Simon studied the man standing before him. The old priest was the incarnation of class. He wore starched white French cuffs under the black sleeves of his immaculate habit and his snow white hair was combed to perfection. Around his neck was a tall, stiff Roman collar that added to his distinguished appearance. Father Marcellinus finally opened his eyes and took out the largest disc of wax from the box. He held it out for Simon to see. It was about five or six inches in diameter from top to bottom because it was oval in shape. All around the edge were small, raised bead-like forms and in the center was the Lamb of God looking down at the wound on His side. The Lamb held on to the pole of a standard. The Lamb, Jesus Christ, rested on a cushion. All the way around the waxen disc was an inscription in Latin. Father Marcellinus added, "The Agnus Dei wax discs go way back to the fifth century and are one of the oldest sacramentals in the Church. The wax was taken from previous Paschal Candles used at Easter during the Roman Liturgies and Seasons. They were consecrated by the Holy Father himself. He then distributed the discs after the singing of the Agnus Dei at the Sacrifice of the Mass. The cardinals, bishops and other prelates with the honor of wearing the miter would process in order of rank and authority and approach the Holy Father who was seated on his throne. They would kneel in front of the pope, one by one, removing their miter and turning it upside down, the pope would put several consecrated, waxen discs into the open miters." Father Marcellinus cleared his throat. "I accompanied our Abbot General at the time as an acolyte." The old priest inhaled with great emotion, "I'll never forget that moment of sheer and utter splendor, so filled with God and the glories of the Roman Church in the massive Basilica of Saint Peter's."

Simon was in something like rapture, realizing that what the old monk was saying to him belonged to a world that no longer existed. He asked, "Does the pope still consecrate the waxen discs in Rome?"

Father Marcellinus coughed sarcastically, "Oh my, no! The Second Vatican Council and those who pushed it onto us by force, practically shoving things down our throats, made sure that that sublime devotion as well as so many others should be obliterated and forgotten. The last pope to consecrate and distribute the waxen Agnus Dei discs publicly was Pope Pius XII, of blessed memory." Simon listened as the priest continued, "But I was there, Brother Simon. I was there in those days when the Roman Catholic Church was unpolluted. I was there inside Saint Peter's in Rome. It was the year 1910, the seventh year of the glorious pontificate of Saint Pope Pius X." Simon could see how transported Father Marcellinus was now as he whispered, looking down at the large waxen disc in his hand, "I was there."

Simon didn't dare speak and waited for the priest to say something. He thought about Father Michael and Fathers Cornelius and Francis. Standing there in the presence of Father Marcellinus he remembered the priests who had inspired him to become a priest someday. At long last, Father Marcellinus placed the large fragment of wax back in the box and closed it. He looked at Simon through his wire-rimmed glasses and said softly, "I am in my ninety-ninth year now and soon I hope and pray to go to Heaven after my time in Purgatory." He stretched out his hands holding the wooden box, "I want you to have this. I entrust you with the Agnus Dei wax I received because I believe you understand its sacred nature as a sacramental. And I entrust you with it because I can see you love Tradition and will safeguard it."

Simon was taken by surprise and only managed to say, "Oh, Father, I couldn't possibly accept such a treasure, such a responsibility, plus none of us never really knows when we're going to Heaven."

The old priest smiled to himself. "True enough, Brother Simon, but in all probability God already bought my one way ticket way before He will buy yours." He put the box in Simon's hands and said, "Don't be frightened, Brother Simon. I'm more than ready to make my journey back to God. Please accept this and take good care of it."

"But…but why me? Surely there are others who are more worthy." Simon stared at the old monk standing in front of him.

Father Marcellinus paused before speaking further, as if choosing his next words very carefully. He fixed his gaze upon Simon and said, "I've been watching you and see how you pray in the crypt for such long periods of time. I'm impressed how you read the Scriptures out loud when it's your turn in the abbey church during Lauds and Vespers. You speak about not being worthy. None of us are worthy but God calls us to higher things anyway." He tapped Simon lightly on the shoulder, "I have lived long enough to realize that you must have the sins of youth like we all do but I also see that you love God and take Him seriously. I also see that you love Tradition and that you will preserve the old customs and devotions of our True Faith that are disappearing more and more every day. Remember, Brother Simon, that we are what we believe and how we pray is fundamental. Stick to your guns and be true to Tradition. 'Lex orandi, lex credendi', I'm sure you know its meaning."

"Yes, Father. 'The law of how we pray is the law of what we believe'."

Father Marcellinus knowingly nodded. "See, I knew I chose well." Then he looked at the box and Simon followed his gaze, "Prepare them for those who are in need. I can no longer see well enough to prepare them for others."

"How do I prepare them, Father, I'm not sure how they are supposed to be prepared?"

"The Agnus Dei waxen discs were melted together with Sacred Chrism. I hope that they still teach you boys that that means that the oil of Sacred Chrism contains the Holy Ghost. Once that oil is mixed with the wax, it's a special vehicle of the Third Person of the Blessed Trinity. The wax from the discs are used to protect us from sickness, fires, storms, every kind of torment and sudden death. It will help us keep temptation away. It is also given to pregnant women so that they may give birth safely to their child." Father Marcellinus' voice became grave as he said, "This wax has always been used in the Church for centuries, for way more than a thousand years, to protect us against the Enemy, against Satan, against him who the Book of the Apocalypse calls 'The Beast'. Beware of the many legions of demons that the devil has at his beck and call. Never underestimate the power of this wax and the devil's hatred of it."

"Yes, Father. But how do I prepare it. I'm not sure I understand?"

"You take a small piece of the holy wax and put it between two pieces of cloth, preferably two round pieces the size of a fifty cent piece. Then take a needle and thread and sew it all around the edges so that the wax doesn't fall out and is at its center. Leave a space to add a little ribbon or thick twine so that it may be worn around the neck or put in the baby's crib, just above the infant's head."

Simon listened carefully and said, "Yes, Father, I get it now. Thanks for the explanation."

Father Marcellinus put a hand on Simon's shoulder and this gesture caused Simon to look up into the old priest's pale, blue eyes. "Aside from being impressed with your apparent love of God and our timeless traditions, I see something else in you dear brother. And if you will permit me, I'd like to say what it is."

Simon could see, once again, that in pausing, the old man was choosing his words carefully. The silence between the two men in that room, one old and wise and the other young and searching, made Simon nervous and he blurted out, "What is it, Father? What is it that you wish to say to me? What concerns you?" Simon dreaded that somehow, his relationship with Toby and Joshua had reached Father Marcellinus' ears. He shuddered to think that the venerable old monk had heard about 'The Night of the Long Knives' and Simon's share in it. He braced for the embarrassment he was already fearing.

Softly, Father Marcellinus said, "Remember, Brother Simon, that in the beginning, God took the dust of the ground and made clay. And into that clay, He breathed. It became a living creature in God's own Image because God's breath filled it. But without God's breath that dust, that clay, had no real life and never would. It was a dead creature, so to speak. After all, we are the air that we breathe."

Simon was taken off guard. He had anticipated a far different discourse, one that would bring him shame before the man he so respected. He managed to muster a few words, asking, "We're the air that we breathe? I'm not sure I understand you, Father."

"Yes, Brother Simon. Stop and think about that for a moment. We truly are the air that we breathe. It can be the very life-giving breath of God or it can be something else, something nefarious, a breath which is devoid of God, a breath which renders a creature truly dead. I mean to say, the breath of darkness. We become more like God if in our life we breathe into ourselves the air of people who breathe God in, but we become the very worst of humanity when we breathe into ourselves the air of people who breathe in darkness. Both are constantly all around us, wherever we happen to live. One elevates us and the other eventually devastates us."

Simon listened carefully though still not fully comprehending what the monk was saying to him. "Yes, Father."

Father Marcellinus removed his hand from Simon's shoulder and moved in a little closer to him, as he continued, saying gently, "We search in our life for what appears to be good and appealing to us but that which devastates often comes like a wolf dressed in sheep's clothing and we are unaware. This you must be very careful to avoid because otherwise, you will be easily and terribly wounded by it. Never forget that we breathe in what is around us, often times not really very much aware of it."

"Yes, Father." Simon stared at the priest.

Father Marcellinus clasped his hands together as if he were going to pray. He had stopped speaking again and Simon saw how the old monk put his two clasped hands under his chin and had bowed his head in a gesture of reverent supplication. It dawned on Simon, however, in those few seconds of fragile silence that the old man was not going to ask God for anything right now but that Father Marcellinus' gesture of supplication was meant for him. "I see so much piety and good in you, but I need to ask you, to beg you to understand clearly and take to heart very well, what I am saying to you now." The priest extended his clasped hands and placed them on Simon's head in an ancient gesture of transmitting God's presence. "May God make you aware that there are many dangers in the world. There are many thieves of the dark night that will come and approach you with cunning proposals. You must be careful and keep vigilant." He paused again and then he took his hands away and Simon detected a genuinely profound sorrow in the inflection of the old man's voice as he said, "Remember this truth always, dear Brother Simon, that the air that we breathe around us, that is the creature we become."

Not completely understanding everything that the priest had just said to him, Simon nonetheless heard himself say, "Thank you, Father. Yes, I will remember what you have just said to me."

Serenity washed across Father Marcellinus' face and he suddenly announced in a jovial tone, "I thank you for accepting this Agnus Dei wax and the responsibility that comes with preparing it for other souls. I'm too old to thread a needle. My hands shake too much and my eyes are getting dark." Then the old monk suddenly said, without much ceremony, "You'll excuse this old man now, but I need to get to the bathroom. My pipes are old as well and they don't always work as they should." He patted Simon on the back and said, "Thank you again for doing this. I know I have chosen well and my heart is at peace. Remember what I told you about what you breathe around you. Goodbye, Brother Simon."

That night, after Vespers, Simon showed Seth the wooden box with the Agnus Dei discs and the fragments. Seth exclaimed, "Well, bust my balls, I've heard of these but I didn't think they existed anymore." He handled the large disc carefully in his pudgy hands. He looked at Simon and pleaded, "Will you prepare a piece for me?"

"Yeah, absolutely." Simon was touched that his friend understood the value of the sacred wax. He doubted most in the abbey would understand and he feared that they would make fun of it.

Simon was comforted in his isolation during the long hours he spent in his cell alone, preparing the Agnus Dei wax. Usually after study and on weekends, he would sit at his desk and prepare numerous pieces of wax. During those long hours alone he would think about becoming a priest and the dangers that loomed not far away from him. He was now faithful to his vow of celibacy but he often felt tempted by his old sins of the flesh. Images from his past caught him by surprise and he realized the weaknesses were still very much there.

One late night, Simon was sitting at his desk, preparing a piece of Agnus Dei for his sister-in-law who was expecting her first baby. He was exhausted and put everything away and crawled into his metal cot. Sleep didn't come easily and he felt particularly worn down with thoughts he attempted to push away. He remembered Toby and the forest and then Joshua and the root cellar. His body responded easily to those memories and he didn't know how much more he could resist the temptation to pleasure himself because of those memories. He often had these bouts of sexual temptations when memories of Toby's hairy chest and thighs took hold of him and refused to go away. Then intense desires would fill him and he would toss and turn trying his best not to think about the growing tension in his body, particularly, between his legs.

On that night, he fell in and out of fitful sleep and at some point, between sleep and consciousness he realized he was in his cot facing the cinderblock wall. Still groggy, he nonetheless was aware of a presence in his cell. It was so malignant and repulsive that Simon awoke out of pure fear. He was well aware that he was fully awake. He couldn't muster enough courage to turn around and look into the space of the small room behind him.

A voice somewhere in his head or in his heart spoke softly but clearly to him. Simon felt frightened and humiliated by what the voice said. "You pathetic piece of hypocritical shit," the voice began. "Who do you think you're fooling with your pious display and show? Do you really think you're fooling anybody? Everybody in this place knows you're the biggest whore here. You think you're special, that you're God's golden boy, don't you?" Simon could barely breathe and only lay there, rigid and sweating. His limbs hurt, especially his legs, but he didn't stir. "Well, you're probably fooling some of those shit-for-brains in this abbey but I know who you really are. I know you lust after men and long for all the excesses in this world that glitter brightly and put you up on a pedestal above everyone else around you. I've had my eye on you, pretty boy, and know that you're bursting inside most of the time, just to be the worldly whore that you are. I know what you've done with other men. You can't hide any of it from me."

Simon concentrated and whispered what the nuns had taught him as a little boy, "Cease, the Heart of Jesus is with me!" The nuns had said that it was a powerful prayer of exorcism against the devil and his demons. He also prayed the prayer that Father Michael had taught him: "Saint Michael, the Archangel, defend us in battle. Be our protection against the malice and snares of the devil. Restrain him, O God, we humbly pray: and do Thou, O Prince of the heavenly host, by the power of God, cast into hell Satan and all the evil spirits, who roam through the world seeking the ruin of souls. Amen." Simon waited and then repeated the short prayer of exorcism. Then he managed to gather enough courage within himself to slowly sit up and turn around to face the unwanted visitor. The moon was streaming bright, silvery light through the open windows of his cell when Simon first saw the bent figure sitting in his desk chair, and likewise, saw the three heads moving at the same time. He could see the thick serpentine tail slithering on the floor, underneath the desk chair, moving lazily back and forth in a gesture of delight, much like a cat will do when it's more than ready to feed. Simon's heart was lodged in his throat as he did his best to focus in the darkness. Little by little he recognized the bedspread he had draped on the back of his desk chair which had fallen somewhat on the floor and on top of that, his jeans and t-shirt all bundled up.

It took him a long time to get to sleep after that. He understood that in his grogginess and fear, he had mistaken the pile of bedspread and clothes for the figure and presence of the Beast himself or one of his demons sent to torment, frighten and tempt him. Yet, he would never forget the knowing voice that had spoken out to him that night and he had perceived so clearly. He knew in his heart that he had not imagined his humiliation nor his fright. Father Marcellinus had warned him and even though he couldn't explain it, Simon knew what it was that had jeered him that night. The comings and the goings, the unexplainable energies of 'spiritus mundi' were not lost on Simon. The presence of God was real but so was the presence of the other one in His absence and negation.

After that night, therefore, it was increasingly comforting to him to handle the wax and to pray in the crypt for long hours at a time. Both of these gave him a sense of closeness with God. He often thought about his wild past and he felt sincere remorse for having given himself so completely to concupiscence. In his solitude, he thought about Jesus in the desert being tempted by Satan and knew perfectly well what Jesus the man had suffered there. Simon wondered if Jesus had also suffered sexual temptations of the flesh as a man. He concluded that Jesus must certainly have been tempted that way although no one had ever taught him anything so scandalous. Having this thought and entertaining it, made him feel that the evil voice in his room definitely had his number. Simon often remembered the dream of Jesus cruelly bound to the gibbet on the rough-hewn flatbed of the wagon and thanked God for giving him another chance to begin again. It was more than just a second chance. In the dream, the Lord had been grateful to Simon because he had approached Him. And then, God Himself had extended the divine invitation: "stay with me".

The following year, Simon and Seth were up for votations, first for the profession of Solemn Vows and then ordination to the deaconate. Simon had been faithful to his vows since the events of the "Night of the Long Knives". He had no doubts about wanting to be a priest but he was troubled by the laxity he saw all around him. Most of his companions no longer wore their religious habits and the innovations brought about by the Second Vatican Council were now well in place all around him. This was especially true regarding the Sacrifice of the Mass, now commonly referred to in the abbey as simply "The Liturgy of the Eucharist".

The more Simon studied in the seminary and was exposed to many of his professor's and fellow seminarian's new theological views, the more he realized that some fundamental things had completely changed since he was a boy. As a boy he hadn't been exposed to philosophy and theology as he was now in the seminary. The things he understood and believed in since long ago had been unchangeable when he was an altar boy. Those things had fashioned and shaped his desire to answer God's call to priesthood.

Simon now had to face the changes on a daily basis in the chapel. But the discussions about these things were usually heated arguments in class, at table in the refectory and in the recreation room. The greatest change had been a shift away from the understanding of offering "The Sacrifice" on an altar which was meant for the sole adoration of God, at the very foot of the Cross on Calvary. Now, greater emphasis was placed on "The Eucharist", a "perfect thanksgiving" on a table which recalled what Jesus Himself instituted on the night of the Last Supper in the Upper Room in Jerusalem.

All around Simon, there were doubts and questions about what really went on during the daily Mass, the belief in the transubstantiation of the bread and wine and the Real Presence in the consecrated Host. Some argued that the very essence of the theology of those things didn't really change that much in the new Mass but Simon didn't believe that. In time, he was to find out that others didn't believe it either. The term of three words that Archbishop Marcel Lefebvre, the French prelate coined, best explained it. He had said that those in authority in Rome, since the Council ended, had invented "a new religion". The Sacrifice of the Mass was only one change, albeit, the most profound one on a list of a great many other innovations. The old maxim Father Marcellinus had uttered and that he had learned long ago was so true: "lex orandi, lex credendi". The way one prayed was precisely what one believed.

There were, of course, liturgical abuses which went on unhindered and more and more, Simon was beginning to doubt if he belonged in the abbey or if he belonged elsewhere. He was especially bothered by the way a group of students would change the position of the new altar around in the chapel, putting wheels underneath it to facilitate moving it. Sometimes it would be to one side of the chapel completely, at other times it would be in the center of the chapel or toward the back and sometimes they would even wheel it out just before it was needed for the Canon of the Mass. A huge part of him wanted to find security and safety in something more structured and in a traditional place. He knew that Seth felt some of this but that he kept it to himself and never voiced his more traditional leanings because it could draw unwanted animosity. As the time for votation of life-long vows and ordination to the deaconate drew near, Simon understood that if he voiced what he felt, he might be denied both the profession and the ordination. Once again, he felt persecuted for who he was, but now, the persecution wasn't only about sexual orientation and behavior. It was also about what he believed. Great changes had been unleashed in the Church and what had existed previously did not appear to have a chance of returning.

He did his best to keep to himself but the Master of Clerics had been replaced and the new one who had taken his place was extremely progressive in his theology and understanding of religious life. On occasion this new Master of Clerics went out of his way to be cruel to him and never hesitated in ridiculing Simon's traditional spirituality.

+ + + + +

Simon's thoughts were momentarily interrupted as he heard the whining of the tattoo gun in Mark's hand and the tattooer's voice asking, "Why was it such a bad thing to be traditional?" Mark asked as he drew more ink.

"It was just the times. The Church was in renewal and this caused unbelievable turmoil. The time was also ripe in America for more chaos at every level of church life. If you flowed with all the new stuff, you were considered good and reasonable and of course, obedient. You might even be considered exceptionally bright and promising for the new Church that was emerging. But if you resisted and were traditional it was considered backward and you were considered disobedient. The resistance was interpreted as being pig headed and stupid. I know it sounds simplistic but that's basically what the situation was and it was what I experienced."

"Damn." Mark repeated, "Damn." Then he added, "You must have felt like a fish out of water especially since you were doing your best to keep the rules."

"'Damn' is right. That's why I began to have doubts about staying in the abbey. The rules were changing and I was terribly confused and sometimes, even bitter. It was a bit of a curve ball for me as 'being good' and 'behaving' hadn't always been my forte. It would have been easier for me to have well-defined rules rather than rules that were becoming fuzzy and blurred. I often thought I needed God to keep me on a tight leash because of my previous rebellion. But then it all got changed and I felt like God had me on a very loose, long leash. Talk about insecurity and confusion."

"You were so damn close to being ordained a priest, though. Why leave and start all over somewhere else?"

"Well, I wasn't exactly finished with my formation to become a priest. I mean, I still had to be approved and profess Solemn Vows. Then I needed to go out for some parish experience somewhere beyond the abbey. After that, if approved, I would be ordained a deacon and sent out to one of the parishes again, before finally being ordained to the priesthood."

Mark waited for Simon to say something more but Simon was lost in his thoughts. "Well, what did you do? Tell me, dude. Did you fuck around like before and stay and play the game or did you go somewhere else doing your best to be faithful to what you believed? Did that new guy bust your balls completely?"

+ + + + +

Simon closed his eyes. The last few months he was in the abbey just before the votations were at hand were not easy. Simon definitely believed that the homophobic Father Wade had been hell-bent on throwing him out after the "Night of the Long Knives". He also was convinced that Father Wade had told the new Master of Clerics that he believed Simon was completely guilty of breaking his vow of celibacy and was a sneak if ever there was one. Simon had no proof of this, but was convinced of it anyway. He also figured out that Father Wade had made it a point to warn the new man about Simon's traditional bent. In time Simon would feel that the traditional bent was far more odious to the powers at be than almost anything else. Even homophobia seemed to fade and wane and lose its fire in the face of defiant Traditionalism.

Father Wade had disapproved when Simon had gone to the Abbot and begged to preserve several boxes filled with lace albs, birettas and fiddleback vestments that had been used in the abbey for decades and were now destined to be burned in a bonfire scheduled for that purpose. Father Edmund, still the Abbot, had listened to Simon's pleas to preserve the vestments, especially, and had given him permission to keep the contents of the boxes in a locked closet. This had infuriated Father Wade, then Master of Clerics, who had already said no to Simon. At this time in America, and perhaps elsewhere, in many seminaries and religious houses, it had become common place to burn traditional Roman-style vestments made of silk and gold thread in favor of the flowing polyester vestments that were in vogue and ecumenically acceptable.

Simon and Seth disliked the new Master of Clerics and had named him after the matriarchal character in Evelyn Waugh's novel, "Brideshead Revisited". Father John, the new man, was naturally haughty and spoke like one of those great aristocratic ladies of the nineteenth century you'd imagine in an epoch film. He was from an old, wealthy Catholic family from the north and seemed naturally disposed to putting almost everyone down. He had a natural gift for making most of the students feel worthless and beneath his dignity. It was mind boggling to Simon that this man should be homophobic since it was clear to him and Seth that Father John was a closeted, flaming queen. He was extremely effeminate when he spoke and his swish when he walked was far from any kind of manly swagger. They had named him Lady Marchmain because in Waugh's novel the woman was a complete, unloving, utter bitch. Simon was careful not to show his animosity toward Father John to anyone except Seth nor to utter the nickname that they had given the man. When they were alone, Simon would vent his frustration and anger toward this man who constantly belittled him. On those occasions, Simon referred to Father John as "that Supreme Fuckress" and Seth would giggle like a little boy, imitating the priest's haughty, deep voice and effeminate mannerisms.

Simon thought he looked like the creepy guy that was lately all over the news in the evenings. "You know who he looks like?"

Seth was intrigued, "Who?"

"He looks and acts just like Claus von Bulow!"

"He does look like him! Damn, he's the spitting image!" Seth was giddy with laughter. "You better not get near him if he calls you Sunny and wants to see you in his office." They had both laughed heartily at the comparison, recalling the awful crime that was lately in the evening news almost every night.

One afternoon, Seth came looking for Simon all out of breath. Simon's cell door was open and he sat at his desk, wearing his habit as he always did. When Seth entered, he said in a whisper, "Lady Marchmain is looking for you."

"How do you know?" Simon didn't look up from the Biblical textbook he was studying.

"He sent me to tell you." Seth stared at Simon cautiously, unable to read if his friend's heart was fearful or valiant. "He sounded real bitchy."

Simon grunted, "Lady Marchmain always sounds bitchy. It's the nature of the beast." He got up from his desk and straightened out his habit.

"Don't get pissed with me for what I'm going to say, Simon." Seth spoke carefully. "You need to watch what you say to Marchmain. It's probably best if you don't say too much."

Simon looked at his friend, "What are you saying, Seth?"

"I'm just telling you to be careful. I've been hearing lots of shit."

"Lots of…shit? What's that supposed to mean?"

"It's probably nothing. It's probably all bullshit but…I've been hearing that Lady Marchmain is out to get you canned."

The words stung Simon's heart but he said no more. Simon was aware that he had become a marked man. The curious thing was that it no longer had anything to do with sex or breaking the vow of chastity. It was all about his theological views, his isolation and his refusal to blend in, or rather, to bend and play along. He left Seth standing in his cell and walked down the hall in his habit to the office of the Master of Clerics expecting the very worse.

When he arrived, he knocked on the wooden doorframe and said, "Father John, it's me, Simon. I understand you wish to see me."

The door was open and Father John sat with his back to the door, typing away on an old, manual Underwood. He wore a plaid, short-sleeved shirt and beige trousers. He didn't bother to turn around and said curtly, "Shut the door behind you and sit down." Simon sat in one of the chairs that was placed directly in front of the large, gray metal desk. Father John continued typing in silence for several minutes and when he finally pulled out the paper from the typewriter, he turned around and glared at Simon with a scowl. "I'll get right to the point. I won't hide the fact that I have told the Abbot that I believe you don't belong here. Your views and your ecclesiology lead me to believe that you never heard of the Second Vatican Council. The teachings of the Council aren't optional in case you haven't heard. The greatest minds in the Church were assembled there around the pope."

Simon remembered Seth's warning, but couldn't help himself and blurted out, "Oh, yes! I've heard of it and the new religion."

The Master of Clerics rolled his eyes in obvious disgust and responded angrily, "You refuse to fit in with your fellow seminarians and it seems to me that you make it a point to stand out and draw attention to yourself. Do you deny any of this?" He stared and when Simon didn't answer immediately, he huffed and shaking his head dramatically, said, "Ugh! I honestly don't know what to do with you. How did you ever get this far, I ask myself?" Then he added, "Especially when there was sufficient reason to throw you out before."

"I don't think that's fair, Father," Simon said weakly.

"I'm not asking you if you think it's fair, kiddo. I'm stating a fact." He stared again at Simon and then added, "I'll say it again, you should have been expelled with the other perverts who were corrupt. God alone knows how you lied your way out of all that."

Simon stared back and then heard himself say, "It really doesn't matter what you think about what happened, does it? The Abbot, Father Edmund is the only one who ultimately decides, not you. He's the only real authority here. Only his voice counts."

Father John squinted his eyes and shifted slightly in his chair. "Don't get sassy with me, boy. The Abbot isn't going to be Abbot forever. Don't think you can just come in here and disrespect me. I determine who professes Solemn Vows and the Abbot rubber stamps what I give him. Don't you forget that."

"The Abbot determines everything. You simply give him your opinion but he can override it. You are only in your position to serve him and not the other way around." Simon paused and then added, "That's certainly something not to forget." Simon stared back.

The Master of Clerics glared in what seemed to Simon to be almost complete disbelief at his lack of fear and muttered angrily, "You think you're so damn special, don't you? What the hell is wrong with you? You were quite the life of the party some time ago, as I recall. You're singing another tune now but you don't fool me. You're like a rollercoaster. Once in obscene cuff-offs and now all draped up in medieval clothes."

Simon measured his words carefully and said, "I've had time to think and pray. I had a significant experience that helped me understand God's Will for me and…"

Father John suddenly threw his hands up in the air dramatically and looked to one side, as he said in utter scorn, "Oh, please! Stop!"

Simon felt his face go red and hot as he said, "How dare you! That's not fair, the Will of God isn't always so crystal-clear and—"

The man sitting across from him wore a crooked smile as he said, "Dare? I'll tell you what's not fair once and for all. Your childish insistence on being so damned special. I'm not here to hold your hand like the Abbot does. I'm on to you, kiddo and I have plenty of reasons to get you finally thrown out as you deserve." He leaned forward and again Simon noticed how his eyes became slits as he said, "I don't want you here." He opened a file that sat on his desk and said, "The new professor of Mariology, Miss Sullivan, sent me this note." He lifted the sheet of paper and Simon saw a list scratched across it by hand. "She complains that you are disruptive in her class. She's a brilliant, young professor with a PhD in theology and you dare to argue with her!"

Simon knew perfectly well what the genesis of the complaint was. "Sister Sullivan…I mean, Miss Sullivan. She's a feminist and an ex-nun. She spews heresy and radical teachings from her podium. She's far from brilliant. You should sit in some time and you'll see what I mean."

"Don't you lecture me." He looked at the list and pointed, "You practically attacked some of your fellow classmates as well as Miss Sullivan about her views on abortion and her understanding of the so-called virginity of Mary of Nazareth. You came off like a perfect fool."

"They were arguing that Mary was just a simple, Jewish woman of faith. The Church still teaches what it always has and that's that Mary the Mother of God is Mediatrix of all Graces. It's still on the books. Pope Leo XIII defined that at the end of the nineteenth century and the Second Vatican Council you love so dearly, left it in the document 'Lumen Gentium'." Simon stared and added, "But I'm sure you know that last point, Father." The Master of Clerics angrily put the paper down and searched for another one. This one was typed but Simon spoke up before he had a chance to make the next point, "I'm not even going to get into the details of what she said about abortion and what some of my classmates agreed to. But she did manage to say that if Mary had truly been a true woman of courage She might have dared to have an abortion when the angel approached Her with the frightening news. She was referring to the Virgin Birth in terms I've never heard of."

Father John disregarded him. "You argued in Sacraments class with Father Petra about the singular role of a priest in the Church. I suppose you think you know more than your professors?"

"I only said that the Church's traditional teaching regarding the priesthood is all about offering the Sacrifice. Not just a religious celebration that makes people feel welcomed to approach a meal at a table together. I said in Father Petra's class that the Sacrifice of the Mass is a real Sacrifice. I only repeated what I've been taught is truth. The Mass puts us at Calvary again, at the foot of the Cross, where Jesus hangs offering Himself for us. That Sacrifice once offered, puts us there in time and place. It's not a mere reenactment of a past event but the event itself is made present again, entirely." Simon realized he was sitting on the edge of the chair and that he had leaned forward quite a bit. He sat back and said quietly, "The Sacrifice that is offered on the altar is the only one that can be offered for the expiation of our sins. It's about the adoration of God and not men."

"Oh, come on! It says right here that in Father Petra's class you said that the altars should never have been turned around. All the altars have been turned around in this country."

"Yes, I did, because Pope Paul never intended them to be. The altars should have remained facing east, toward Jerusalem, as they have been for centuries, for the priest and the people. Every Sacrifice should be offered 'ad orientem'. The pope didn't intend for the tabernacles to be taken off the center of the altars, either. He admitted to such himself."

Father John held up a third sheet of paper. "Your Spiritual Director has come to me personally and he has expressed grave doubts regarding your suitability to become a priest. He told me quite bluntly that you should never be ordained a priest. He said you live in a fantasy of your own creation and that you're out of touch with where the Church is and where it needs to go in the modern world." Simon had looked down and the Master of Clerics added, "I say that I have to agree with him. You don't have what it takes to be a priest." Simon remembered the Spiritual Director, Father Brad. He had chosen him just before the "Night of the Long Knives" took place. He was a young priest, not a monk of their Order, working on his Doctorate at a university near Pittsburgh and lived at the abbey. He was fun to be around and was not much older than most of them. He never wore his cassock and his long hair was always in a ponytail. Father Brad had invited Simon several times to relax in the saunas with him but Simon had refused, feeling uncomfortable with the vibes he was getting. He finally admitted to Simon one afternoon after Spiritual Direction, that he wanted to have sex with him right then and when Simon refused and left his office, he took the rejection personally. It was then that he had called Simon and said to him that he was not sure he could ever be a suitable priest. He accused Simon of living in his own little world. He even went so far as to say that he would speak negatively about him to the Master of Clerics and could never approve him for ordination. Father Brad had once been his friend, or so Simon had believed, and it had hurt Simon to be rejected solely because he wanted to be celibate. He had tried to find comfort in the passage from the Scriptures in Leviticus that say, "Even my friend in whom I trusted, has raised his heel against me." The young priest eventually received his Doctorate and soon after abandoned the priesthood with a lover he had at the university. Simon had heard that Father Brad's chalice had been found in the wastepaper basket of his room when he had left.

Father John crossed his arms and said smugly, "Don't think I'm not aware of the fact that you've gone on Saturdays to the Cloistered Nun's chapel in town for the Old Latin Mass that they still do there. The Bishop is not in favor of them doing that thing and the priest that goes there doesn't have his permission. He's one of those renegade priests from Philadelphia or New York that belongs to that group founded by that French prelate, Lefebvre." He leaned across the desk and said matter-of-factly, "Your understanding of liturgy is warped."

"We are free to attend Mass wherever we like on Saturdays. Some of my classmates just sleep in and don't even bother going to Mass at all." Simon added, "Others are praised because once in a while they attend services at the Lutheran church in Ottersville and it shows how ecumenically healthy they are. I can't believe you're scolding me for going to the Sacrifice of the Mass that has existed for centuries."

"I wonder if going to a Lutheran service isn't more beneficial than going to that 'hocus-pocus' thing in a language that is dead." Simon stared at the man in complete disbelief. "Don't look at me that way. Honestly, I'm at the end of my rope with you. You don't mingle with the other brothers in formation and only keep to yourself except for Brother Seth. I have no issue with him but then again he's not living in the Dark Ages like you. I can't fathom how he manages to be around you. You rarely take your habit off even when you go into town. Your classmates either wear the clerical shirt when they have to or just street clothes. It's clearly another tactic you've devised to draw attention to yourself." Simon remained silent realizing that there was no sense in trying to defend himself any further. The Master of Clerics sat back and closed the file. He sighed exaggeratedly and said, "I just don't know anymore. You and Seth are up for votations soon and I can't say I'm inclined to vote in your favor to profess vows and proceed to ordination to the deaconate." The words stung Simon's ears and broke his heart but he said nothing. It was time to remain silent. "You just think you can squirm and scheme your way anywhere you want, don't you?" He stared at Simon who looked down and straightened the folds of his habit. Then Father John revealed that he was far from done. "When the two South American theologians came and gave us a private conference here in the abbey, you were noticeably absent."

"I wasn't the only monk who was absent, Father."

"Ha! Right! You and all the old monks were missing. That was an opportunity not to have been missed. Theologians of their stature are privileged minds in the Church today."

Simon could not hold back. "Oh, you mean the two radical priests who came to praise the likes of Father Camilo Torres, the priest who advocated violence as a means to spreading the Gospel of Jesus? You mean Fathers Boff and Segundo? No thanks, Father, I'm not interested in listening to political, Marxist zealots spew their leftist lies. I think I'll just keep passing on that."

"See what I mean? In your arrogance you think you know more than these two learned, brilliant theologians. You truly slay me. You are truly disturbing. You think you know so much. You think you know more than the Pope and the Fathers of the Second Vatican Council." He looked at Simon with repulsion and said, "Let's just admit it. You're not academically gifted. You don't have the capacity for real studies. You can't possibly reach the level of any kind of real, elevated academics. All you think about is a Church that doesn't exist anymore. All you are capable of reflecting on are outdated, silk vestments and pointy hats, recalling the saccharin, silly tales of dead saints and slobbering over relics which are probably no more than dried up chicken or pig bones."

Simon looked up. "Those dead saints you're talking about are enjoying the Beatific Vision right now, as I speak. And can you possibly come up with any reasonable argument for burning the old, silk fiddleback vestments which are at the very least, works of art? It's a new display of iconoclasm you are promoting."

Father John stood. He put his hands behind his back and said haughtily, "Iconoclasm? You smug, pretentious idiot! You think you know so much! I have no more time to waste here. You think you can do as you please because Father Edmund protects you." He seethed and said, "The abbot protects you because that viper, Shawn, has the abbot's ear." He paused, "It's still a total mystery to me how that schemer was approved for vows and then ordained to the deaconate and priesthood. I'd have loved to pluck the feathers from that proud peacock and put him in his place!" Simon saw the spittle gathered at the corners of Father John's crooked mouth when he hissed, "You think you're a pretty boy, too, somebody who can do as he pleases because you have friends in high places. I'm in charge of the clerics in this seminary now." He looked at Simon dramatically up and down and then said, "You think you're untouchable." He pointed in Simon's face just a few inches away. "Well, get this clear in your head: I'm watching you, kiddo. I'm watching you like a hawk. Votations are coming up soon enough in the spring and you best watch yourself. My vote matters big time."

Simon was stunned to hear the Master of Clerics speak that way. He hadn't realized how much the man despised him but was clear about it now. He needed to pray and to think and stay calm. So many things were coming apart for him and the conversation he had just had worried him. Simon felt that his days might indeed be numbered in the abbey if he wasn't careful.

He sat there and stared at Father John wondering if Shawn had actually gone to bat for him during the "Night of the Long Knives" and if any of that really even mattered now? He already knew Seth had helped him but he had forgotten about Shawn since he had distanced himself so much from him. Suddenly Father John left the room without another word. Simon sat stunned by the glacial gesture of the man who should be a guide to him and an instrument of God. Simon could not deny that the interview worried him and was concerned that the priest could very well get him thrown out if he set his mind to it. His opinion did weigh a lot when it came to the votations for vows and Holy Orders. He had put forth a courageous front but deep down he was scared.

That night, Simon didn't sleep well and he finally rose before dawn, washed his face and dressed in his habit. He left his cell and quietly closed his door. He walked through the shadows, down the familiar corridors of the past seven years toward the place he had come to consider his only real sanctuary. There was no one in the crypt at that hour when Simon entered and walked the length of it toward the altar and the tomb of the prince-bishop. He genuflected and knelt on the hard stone floor, barely aware of how cold and damp it was. He felt more alone now than he had ever felt in his adult life. He tried to pray but it seemed that he couldn't organize his thoughts. Everything seemed to be falling apart in his life and he was unsure how much longer he could hold things together. Why hadn't God given him strength to push ahead? Why was he considered unfit to become a priest because he loved the traditions of the Church and wanted to preserve them? Had God not taken notice of his repentance? Didn't God see his struggles with his sexuality and his determination to be celibate as he had promised? Didn't it count for anything in God's heart?

Self-pity overtook him and Simon didn't fight it but gave in completely, grateful for the release that it produced in his soul. It was as if an incalculable weight had been squeezed and pushed out of him. All at once, a valve broke free and a torrent of pain was allowed to gush out and away from him. Simon began to cry in earnest as if he would never be able to stop. He allowed himself to slide forward on the palms of his hands, and he heard the sobbing and the deep rooted pitch of his torment pour forth from the core of his being. He heard the hideous, wounded wail as if from far away and was not completely aware that it had come from within himself. He felt the moist, rough pavement first on his hands and he shivered. Simon was lost in his self-pity and surrendered to his lack of will easily, falling completely sideways in the darkness. He was fully awake but abandoned himself to the agony overwhelming his heart. More than anything else, he felt terribly wounded and broken. His sorrow was beyond description as he lay alone and closed his eyes. Tears poured down his face and he was aware of nothing else but his affliction. He raised his grimy hands to his face and ran his fingers roughly through his hair wondering what would happen to him. He didn't care if anyone heard him in his grief. Simon wondered where God had gotten to? He seemed so silent and at the moment, so utterly hidden from him.

The first rays of sunlight penetrated the crypt in the usual way and Simon was startled by the pealing of the great bell above him at six o'clock that morning. It was the daily call to pray the Angelus and Simon struggled as he rose off the slimy floor of the crypt. He was alert now and remembered entering the crypt earlier before dawn. He found a place on one of the pews and sat there knowing that he had come to a point in his life he had never imagined. He needed to regain his composure but one question burned within the darkness of his soul. What path was he to follow? Before genuflecting and walking out of the crypt, Simon spoke softly as he looked at the tabernacle. "God, I'm completely lost and confused."

In the weeks that followed Simon attended his classes and hours of prayer in the usual way even though his heart was elsewhere. He knew that he couldn't betray himself in the way that the Master of Clerics had proposed and this worried him because the Church that he loved and believed in was almost gone all around him. Simon knew that he would have to face numerous difficulties and challenges once he arrived in the parishes, especially from the pastors and some of the people. From what he had read and heard, things were far different now than when he had been an altar boy in his parish. Why had everything changed so much? It didn't seem possible that the Catholic Church had become something so unrecognizable in such a short time. How was it possible that he was ostracized for upholding and being faithful to the traditions of centuries? Simon was comforted by the support he received from some of the older monks but the reality was that they were at the end of their earthly lives. Plus, they didn't have votations to endure.

One evening after study, Simon went down to the library to read the newspapers and magazines that were kept there. He rarely watched the evening news in the television room but instead liked to read the Pittsburgh papers as well as the Holy See's official newspaper, L'Osservatore Romano, which arrived weekly in its English edition and had all kinds of news from the Vatican. He sat down and had just grabbed one of the magazines near him when he saw a curious photograph in color on its cover. Simon stared at the photograph which pictured a recent Solemn High Mass like the ones he remembered serving as an altar boy. He couldn't believe that the Archbishop who appeared in the photograph was making his way through a handful of cities and towns in the United States and Canada. Simon read about the grateful Catholics who met the French Archbishop who had now become a champion of Tradition and of the Old Latin Mass. Simon was stunned as he read the articles, first in one Catholic magazine and then in two or three others. Who was this Archbishop and where did he live?

As Simon read, he learned from the articles that at first, Archbishop Marcel Lefebvre had restrained himself from taking action. He was practically retired when he was called upon by faithful Catholics, to establish a seminary which he did with their help in Switzerland in order to preserve the traditional priesthood, the Sacrifice of the Mass and Catholic Tradition. The Archbishop spoke about the present Catholic Church as a new religion, forced on Catholics and that the new Mass of 1969 was poisoned. The Archbishop questioned why Catholic spirituality had been forcibly changed and forced upon the Church and he pointed to the growing numbers of priests and faithful Catholics that had apostatized from the Faith. Simon couldn't believe what he was reading. Could it be that he was not alone in his beliefs? In all the articles Simon read that night, it was clear to him that there was a seminary somewhere, even if in faraway Switzerland that still preserved the Roman Catholic faith that he believed in and yearned for. He also read that the Archbishop was taking candidates for the priesthood as he traveled through the U.S. and Canada. There was no one else like this Archbishop in the Church. He was willing to stand up for his beliefs no matter the opposition. He had found his voice and was helping other Catholics to do the same, regardless of personal cost.

It wasn't long before the Archbishop became the center of conversation in the refectory and in and out of classes. Simon kept quiet as he heard the attacks and the smears against the prelate coming from his classmates and some of his fellow monks. Professors openly ridiculed and mocked the movement for Tradition that the Archbishop was awakening in America and Europe. News was that soon pockets in Asia and Africa would respond as well.

Several weeks passed and a seminarian whom Simon knew in Pittsburgh phoned him. They had often discussed the changes in the Church and the hope that the Archbishop roused among traditional Catholics. It was to say that he had heard from a priest there that the Archbishop would certainly be passing briefly through Pittsburgh. It was a given and therefore, very promising. He had said to Simon, "I immediately thought of you. If I can swing a meeting of some kind, would you be interested? It's a rare opportunity."

Simon knew it was dangerous and probably imprudent but he enthusiastically answered "Yeah, of course! Thanks for thinking of me." The Church's doors would be closed to the Archbishop in Pittsburgh but in any case, he was scheduled to offer a Solemn High Mass somewhere and attendance was expected to be overflowing. His friend had pointed out twice that this visit, though brief, would be a singular opportunity to meet the man. Simon needed no encouragement. Simon knew that it would be disastrous to be seen at the Solemn High Mass for obvious reasons but he still expected to be present for it. But mostly, the opportunity to sit with the man was indeed something very special. Simon's friend had said, just before he hung up that it was to be confidential and that he had called Simon only because he knew how much Simon respected the Archbishop. If a meeting could be set up, it would be a one on one interview, in an as yet unknown location.

Simon burned with excitement at the prospect of meeting Archbishop Lefebvre. The only one that he could trust was Seth and one night during study time Simon shared the news of the phone call he had received and what he was planning. He had stood at Seth's door and nervously asked, "Can I talk to you about something?"

"Sure, what's up?" Seth had turned around to face him where he stood at the doorway.

Simon entered and, speaking quietly and plainly, shared his pain with his friend and his doubts about remaining in the abbey. He spoke to him about his steadfast desire to become a priest but wondered if the Church would accept him with his traditional views. "I'm thinking seriously of trying to speak with Archbishop Lefebvre when he arrives in Pittsburgh. He's going to other places as well, but Pittsburgh is really close and an exceptional opportunity for me."

"He's coming through New York, is what I heard. I think almost a dozen places in the U.S. and on to Canada, Toronto, I think, before returning to Europe. Your ass will be so completely thrown out of here if anyone would ever find out you went to see him. Are you sure you understand that fact?"

"I do understand the risk involved. Trust me. But I've been praying since I heard about him and I believe it might be the way for me. I obviously can't make it to Canada nor to New York, but if you help me, I think I can get to Pittsburgh. I need a car…but…not one from here."

"Damn, buddy, I don't know. I've read articles that say he's pushing his luck with the new pope. Pope Paul was old and…"

"I know all that!" Simon didn't want any more opinions. "I just want to know if you can help me set it up, going to meet with the Archbishop. I mean, you have family in Pittsburgh and know some of the priests really well there since you were a kid. You know the older ones who think like we do. It's something I need to do." He pleaded, "Please!" Simon sat on his friend's metal cot.

"How could you possibly land a personal meeting with the Archbishop? I'm sure his schedule is really complicated plus, nobody really knows you in Pittsburgh."

"I have a friend at the major seminary there. We talk every once in a while over the phone and write. He's the one who tipped me off and…" Simon doubted he had already said too much. He was told it was all to be kept strictly confidential or the whole thing could fall apart. "This friend of mine is my connection. He's my 'ticket' if you will. You know deep down that what the Archbishop is saying is true." The two friends spoke late into the night and Seth finally promised to investigate the next day to see what was possible under the strictest confidentiality.

Four days later, Simon was driven to Pittsburgh by one of Seth's uncles before dawn. They drove up to the large, private mansion there and Simon presented himself. It had all been arranged beforehand between his friend's contact who was an elderly monsignor. Simon was welcomed alone inside and after a brief wait, entered a small parlor and met Archbishop Marcel Lefebvre who was making headlines around the world. They spoke in private without haste. When the interview had concluded and the Archbishop had blessed him, Simon left the salon and as he did so, he saw a young man about his own age sitting out in the hallway, waiting to be received. It had been the opportunity of a lifetime and Simon left Pittsburgh impressed by the courageous man of faith and a newfound plan. As he was driven back to Leicester late that afternoon, he felt both exhilarated and full of doubts. He was at a crossroads but he wasn't sure how he should proceed. He promised the Archbishop that he would keep in contact with the priests who belonged to the Society of Saint Pius X in America. Simon gave the Archbishop his mother's address in Tampa so that he could communicate that way with them. Seth was sworn to secrecy and had reminded Simon that he himself was at risk if anyone knew he had helped him.

"I love you, man, but I can never admit having had a part in this if it gets out. You're on your own, ok?" Seth had been clear once Simon had returned. "I've heard that this whole thing is headed down a dangerous path and I intend on staying here at the abbey. You understand?"

"I understand," Simon had said sadly. He had been so impressed by the Archbishop and his vision that he was sure Seth would join him as well. But when he returned from Pittsburgh, Seth had been clear to Simon about his involvement.

Later that night when Simon thanked Seth, his friend admitted his admiration for the preservation of Tradition but repeated that he had no plans to abandon the abbey. "There are all kinds of rumors and what not. I've heard that if things ever got too crazy, you know, like major problems, there might even be an 'Indult of Excommunication' to deal with coming from the Pope himself. I'll admit it's very tempting to regain all the traditions that have been lost in the Church…but to what price?"

Over the phone, sometime after Simon had visited with Archbishop Lefebvre, Simon's mother read him a letter the Archbishop had written to him. More correspondence followed from a priest of the Society of Saint Pius X working in Texas and Simon prayed to know God's Will. Everything in his heart told him what he wanted to do but Simon desired to know what it was that God wanted for him. It wasn't so easy to distinguish between the two. There was so much to consider. The days passed into weeks and Simon was not yet decided.

Spring signaled the end of classes and the period of preparation for final exams. After this, votations would take place for those eligible for vows and ordinations. Simon and Seth were eligible for profession of final vows and ordination to the deaconate. Five deacons were eligible for ordination to the priesthood. It was a time of stress for everyone in the seminary because of the pending exams but more so for those eligible for vows and Holy Orders. Nothing was ever really settled until after votations had occurred. The hurtful things that the Master of Clerics had said to Simon weighed heavy on his mind. His desire to join the Archbishop tugged at his heart and became a source of consolation for him.

Simon had been studying hard for his Christology exam which everyone agreed was going to be particularly difficult. At long last he had turned off his desk lamp and had headed toward the crypt to put everything into God's hands. He prayed for a little while and when he was finished he decided to get a breath of fresh air before trying to sleep. As he walked down the long, dark corridors of the abbey, Simon was lost in thought, greatly impressed by the meeting he had had with the Archbishop in Pittsburg. It seemed like such a fresh start in the right direction for him. Every day he loathed the innovations in the Church more and more even though he no longer voiced any of his oppositions to anyone except Seth. Still, to leave the abbey after so many years was a huge decision to make and there were many things about himself that caused him unrest. Simon was well aware of the two forces that continued to rage within him and pulled him constantly in opposite directions. He also realized that the Abbot was his only protector in the abbey and wondered if he would find another protector like him elsewhere, as in the Society of Saint Pius X. Father Edmund was getting on in years although Simon knew that the man would remain in his post until death.

He opened the door to the cloister where the spices grew and was immediately aware of the strong aromas that filled his nostrils: rosemary, basil, spearmint and tarragon were the ones he immediately recognized although there was also oregano and the heavy scent of gardenias in bloom. The evening was cool and Simon was happy he had decided to get some air before retiring. He walked toward the small fountain in the center of the cloister and saw the moon clearly reflected in the gently moving water there. The pungent perfume of the gardenias monopolized this part of the garden and Simon inhaled the heavy fragrance in the coolness of the tranquil night. He was so caught up by the peaceful stillness and delights of the garden that he failed to see the lone figure that suddenly walked up to him and was momentarily reflected in the water of the fountain.

The familiar voice whispered out of the darkness, "Hello, little, one. I've missed you." Simon recognized the greeting and the voice far too well to have any doubts who it was. A part of him was comforted to hear it even if another part was greatly troubled. "My, my," the voice continued, "What a pleasant surprise this is."

"Shawn!"

"In the flesh, my boy. A long time ago I had thought we would never speak again. It seems you drifted away and became a stranger at some point." Simon could see Shawn smiling in the moonlight as he took another drag from his cigarette. "I was hurt you never asked for my first priestly blessing when I was ordained."

"I'm sorry but after all that happened between us…I mean…and then the witch hunt that came after that…I just didn't…"

"Oh, it's okay, it's okay, little one. I forgive you. I'm just happy we crossed paths again on this dreamy night." Shawn approached Simon and put one arm around him. Simon remembered all of Seth's dire warnings against Shawn and the fact that the Master of Clerics had referred to Shawn as a "viper". However, possibly for the very first time, Simon understood that Shawn was someone he needed to have by his side, particularly now that votations were coming up. Simon knew Shawn had friends in high places within the abbey. After everything that had happened, Simon realized that he had many enemies and very few friends.

He was grateful for Seth and for his friendship but it would not be enough if Simon decided to stay and to profess Solemn Vows, eventually reaching ordination to the priesthood. He knew he needed to be in good standing with the Abbot. Simon didn't forget what the Master of Clerics had said about Shawn going to bat for him on the "Night of the Long Knives". It had been a long time since Simon had had any real communication with Shawn. He looked at the monk standing in front of him, clearer now since his eyes had adjusted to the darkness enveloping him in the garden. Ever since the night of the Carabinieri boots after Aunt Tessie's supper, Simon had avoided Shawn. He had decided that Shawn was not his friend but that he had been manipulating him all along just to have his way with him sexually. Simon still believed all of that but now he was considering something else, something bigger.

For the very first time he was considering Shawn as a necessary protector in his life if he decided to stay. He corrected himself; if God decided for him to stay. Maybe Shawn could fill in the spot of protector in case Father Edmund were to be absent. Perhaps, then, he needed to be in Shawn's good graces and care, rather than apart from him. It was no revelation to Simon, after his conversation with the Master of Clerics, that he could easily be dismissed from the abbey if he wasn't careful. He knew that he eventually needed to talk about this to Shawn. Simon knew that he didn't really want Shawn as a friend even though he might desperately need him at some point but that having him as an enemy would be far worse.

Standing now in the moonlight alone with him, Simon felt awkward in Shawn's overly affectionate touch but did not break away because he realized that he needed him. Simon said apologetically, "I'm sorry I stayed away from you…I've gone through quite a few things. It hasn't been an easy journey for me lately."

"Yes, I would guess it's been turbulent at best." Shawn moved in closer and put his other arm around Simon's waist and pulled him closer to himself so that the two men were now facing each other. "Yes, that damned witch hunt, that purge that was so necessary and so destructive to so many souls. I guess you and I really lost touch after that." Shawn played with the hair that fell on one of Simon's ears.

"I almost got canned, Shawn. I mean…I saw so many of my really close friends get thrown out, especially Joshua." His voice quivered slightly, "I really thought I was next."

Shawn pressed one of his thighs up against Simon's and whispered, "Oh, baby, that arrangement with Joshua was never going to happen. You see, I saw to that personally."

Simon realized now more than ever that what the Master of Clerics had said about Shawn being a viper was true. "You don't know what I went through, Shawn, you have no idea how my whole world shattered in an instant. That night when we got back from the bar in Crescent, my heart sank when I saw all the lights on and then saw the way you stood there. Damn all those bastards that threw me and my companions to the sharks and wrote those letters."

Shawn spoke slowly and Simon could feel the warmth of his breath on his neck. He could also smell the stale aroma of the cigarettes the other man had smoked. "You gay boys got totally out of control. I saw it coming and had to do something. If I hadn't stepped in, somebody else would have like one of those vicious, closeted queens. Wanda for one, would have loved to throw you out just as much as that queen, that new fucker, John! That haughty, proud bitch looks like Claus von Bulow and acts like he'd snuff you out in a minute."

Simon smiled at the mention of von Bulow but suddenly, genuinely surprised, asked, "Wait a minute, you knew the witch hunt was coming? You really did? Are you serious?"

Shawn smiled. "You naïve little boy." He pushed Simon's thick, dark hair away from his forehead and combed it back across his head. "Yeah, I saw it escalating. It was only a matter of time before somebody took matters into their own hands. The Abbot didn't know what the fuck to do until I made my move and—"

Simon interrupted him, "Wait! What are you saying? You started the 'Night of the Long Knives'? You were the architect, the instigator, the creator of that mess?"

"Oh, honey, get a grip. I just threw the match and got the whole thing to explode. You boys created your own mess all by yourselves. It was bound to happen. What I did was steer the whole thing before it got out of control."

"But if you 'threw the match' as you say, then that means you wanted me out. My name was everywhere in the accusations and letters. The Abbot told me as much."

"Yeah, you were deep into everything and didn't have a soul who could save you…except for me. Luckily for you, I'm on your side because I like you."

Simon tried to break away but Shawn held him in place. "I don't understand what you're saying, Shawn. You say you're the one who caused the witch hunt to explode and then you say you did it to save me! I don't get it. I almost got thrown out because of what you did and you…"

"I had to take control and do it all that way in order to keep you here, don't you see that? Getting those spineless, closeted wimps to write accusatory letters, talking to the Abbot, getting the Bishop to hear things at the right time…it was all my orchestration. I gave birth to that fierce beast and then at the perfect moment, when I knew everything was just ripe enough, I let it out of its wretched cage. And they all fell for it just as I planned they would." Shawn smiled when Simon stared at him in disbelief. "Oh, yeah, baby, they opened their mouths and I fed them what they wanted to swallow." He paused and added, "They were eager to take the bait because they had no idea how to tame the storm that was due to arrive if I hadn't taken charge. I gave them direction, a way out, as it were." Simon thought that he couldn't put up with the putrid smell of stale cigarette smoke on Shawn's breath any longer when Shawn said, "You survived the 'Night of the Long Knives'. That's all that's important here. You were always going to survive it no matter what. Didn't I tell you a long time ago, the night I first met you, that I would always be there to protect you? You're young and stupid and you don't listen to me. I'm here to make sure you learn. You kept on falling in love. That's where you fuck up over and over again and are dead wrong. Then the witch hunt made you embrace celibacy again. It rattled your cage until you took notice." He said softly, "A very noble gesture, I'm sure, but not necessary. It's a dead end street for you every time. You want to be celibate for God and that's fine, but you keep falling in love with men. How many times have I gone through this with you before? Love God and have sex with men, but don't love men. Don't confuse the two, separate love and sex if you ever want to become a priest."

"I'm doing my very best to be celibate, it's just that before, with Toby and then Joshua, I just…I just couldn't keep from loving them. It took me away from God, I know, and it almost made me lose everything. I've been on another path lately but I've also been so damned lonely, so isolated." Simon began to sob but kept on trying to speak. Shawn didn't interrupt him and Simon continued, "My head has been spinning for months…I've been trying to…I mean, I want to be a priest with my whole heart and soul. I want God to want me!" He looked up at Shawn and through tears said, "I'm celibate and trying my very best to be chaste because I want God to want me back." Simon fell on Shawn's shoulder and the monk held him up. "All the changes in the Church, all the destruction of Tradition, it's made me wonder if maybe…I don't know, I just don't know if…" Simon trailed off not yet ready to tell Shawn about his plans to possibly leave the abbey and join the traditional movement in the Church.

Shawn waited and when Simon stopped speaking, he said gently, "I know you feel out of place often with your peers. That's what makes Simon, Simon. You're your own man and that's very attractive and sexy in my book. I've seen how you've found your own voice these last number of months and that basically a very good thing. It's okay to be in favor of Tradition but, baby, wake up. That's only going to bring you heartache among a lot of these fuckers here that want any excuse to throw you out. But there's another thing. You just don't seem real happy. Remember that line from Saint Theresa of Avila? 'From silly devotions and sour-faced saints, deliver us, Lord.' Simon, you deserve to be happy. You belong here with us and you will go places in our Order with me at your side but you have to trust me and listen to what I've been trying to teach you. I agree with the Abbot when he says you show great promise. He said to me recently that the promise you show is because you truly do believe in God's call to the priesthood. And I agree. You actually do believe it! Not everyone here has that kind of faith in their own vocation. I say, continue to be your own person, but be smart. Sometimes you have to be cunning and twist and turn a little as you move through life, especially in the Church." Shawn embraced him, and said, "Simon, let go of your pent up fears, doubts and pain. I'm here for you."

As he hung there, supported by Shawn's strong arms, almost like a powerless, immolated boy, Simon began to cry again, saying, "You're the only one who ever seems to care about me for real, you…you…"

Shawn hoarsely said, "Let go, baby, I'm the only one who really cares for you. You're safe now." Shawn hugged him one last time and then left. Simon stayed in the garden of spices for a while and then returned to the crypt. He tried to pray but was unable to concentrate. He stared at the tabernacle and once again, attempted to speak with God but couldn't find the proper words. He thought about everything Shawn had said to him about the "Night of the Long Knives". At that moment, he felt that God was watching him as he had been closely watched once by Him in the forest. He felt comforted in knowing that he was in God's presence and that God had him in His mind. Simon knew then that he had arrived at the moment to make his decision, whether to leave the abbey or remain. He placed himself in the hands of God and under the protection of His Mother, Mary. He would wait to see if he was accepted for the profession of Solemn Vows and for ordination to the deaconate. Tomorrow he would submit three letters to the Abbot. One, to request to profess Solemn Vows and another to request to be ordained to the deaconate. He would also write a third letter requesting to add a name to his religious name. This last letter would certainly be controversial. It would be construed by liberals in the abbey as coming from a traditional-minded spirituality, not in keeping with the spirit of renewal. It was not a popular thing to do but Simon was motivated to make the request in order to place himself under the Virgen Mother's protection. He believed a clear sign would come from the request. If all three requests were fully accepted, he would take it to mean that God wanted him to stay in the abbey. Suddenly, he remembered the dream of the wounded, broken man hanging from the gibbet and the words of gratitude he had heard: "stay with me." Simon stood up and genuflected. He made his way to his cell and sat at his desk. He took three sheets of paper with the letterhead of the abbey and wrote his three letters calmly. Then he undressed and got into his metal cot. Tomorrow he would give the Abbot his letters.

Four days later, exams were over. Simon had submitted his three letters of request and like Seth and his other classmates, had looked with trepidation at the sheets of paper outside the Master of Cleric's office. There, Simon and Seth hugged each other because they had received passing scores on their examinations. Simon wondered what the response would be to his three letters of request from the Abbot.

Another list was posted pending approval to profession of vows. This list contained their summer assignments. If approved, Seth was assigned to a parish in Fargo, North Dakota, and Simon was assigned to a parish in Dallas, Texas. That night, after Vespers was prayed, the Abbot stood up at his place in choir and announced to all the monks of the abbey that the five deacons had passed votations and would be ordained to the sacred priesthood. Applause erupted in the sacred place. Likewise, he let it be known that Simon and Seth had been approved for their profession of Solemn Vows the following week and would return in the fall for their ordination as deacons. "His Grace, the Bishop will be here for the ordinations and we are pleased to announce tonight that our Most Reverend Abbot General from our Mother House in Rome, Father Matteo, has confirmed that he will be in attendance as well. Our Abbot General is making a Canonical Visitation in America and will grace us with his presence." Applause thundered again in the abbey and when it had subsided, the Abbot added, "I must add that following a custom of tradition here in the abbey, one that gives me great joy personally, Brother Simon has requested to add the name of Our Heavenly Mother to his own at the time of his upcoming profession of Solemn Vows, and I have eagerly granted him this permission. Therefore, from now on dear brother monks, Brother Simon shall be known as Brother Simon Maria."

Simon had his answer.

Chapter Fourteen
Kevin

I think...if it is true that there are as many minds as there are heads, then there are as many kinds of love as there are hearts.
Leo Tolstoy

Mark stood stretching and yawned. He looked at Simon and said, "Dude, that's an awful lot of stuff to process." He looked at the sketch Simon had given him and then at the tattoo he had begun, finally asking, "How do you want the colors on those tennis balls?"

Simon sat up, saying, "I'd like them to be the colors of the rainbow flag, I mean, the gay flag; red, orange, yellow, green, blue and purple."

"Cool." Mark took off his purple gloves and added, "I need to take a leak. Then check up on things at the front desk." He winked at Simon, "Make sure Billy hasn't completely fucked things up." With that, Mark left the room. Several minutes later he returned and asked Simon, "Shall we continue? I'm of course very curious to know about what happened to you here in Dallas. Tell me about Kevin."

Simon tried to concentrate on those events from so long ago and finally said out loud, more to himself than to Mark, "Where do I begin?" Mark worked silently as Simon began to speak and remembered his gentle friend, Kevin, the soft spoken man he met so long ago. A part of his heart still ached even though so many years had passed since their paths had crossed and they had shared something of their lives together. That summer of 1983 Simon traveled from the sheltered existence of the abbey in Leicester nestled among the cool shades of firs and various other evergreens and was received by the desert-like, arid heat of Dallas, Texas. He was more than happy for the assignment and was excited about the things that the move would bring. Mostly, he was happy to leave the animosity of the Master of Clerics as well as some of his peers, although he knew that he would especially miss the company of Shawn. In a twisted, complicated way, they had become close again.

+ + + + +

That summer afternoon when Simon arrived in the tiny airport of Love Field he felt as if he had stepped into the blazing heat of an oven. The sky was dark with angry, menacing storm clouds and Father Richard Pazzone, the monk who was pastor at the parish church where he would work, warned him that tornadoes were in the forecast. "We never got to see a twister in Leicester, but oh, boy, we sure get them here and up north in Oklahoma." Father Richard had entered the abbey in Leicester several years before Simon. He seemed to Simon to be a mild tempered man and instantly liked him when he said, "Well, I'm very happy you've come to help us at Saint Sebastian's. You're a breath of fresh air to us here and I am personally grateful to Father Edmund for sending you to us." He winked at Simon and added, "The people will love you if you give yourself to them in pastoral ministry with your whole heart. Especially if you are honest with who you really are. Don't try and be somebody you're not, okay? Just be yourself." He grinned and Simon was pleased that things were off to such a good start. They drove several miles until they reached the church which was nestled under old oak trees. Father Richard was a slender man with a small waistline and of average height. He looked gaunt and skeletal and wore his dark straight hair somewhat long. Simon had heard that he was very liberal in his theology and that it was best to avoid confrontations in this regard.

They arrived and entered the church rectory which was blessedly air conditioned and the priest led the way. He deposited Simon's bags in his room and announced that they would eat supper at 5:30, just like in the abbey in Leicester. "Only difference is, we have Happy Hour here every day at 5:00 pm. Father Michel, the other priest, and possibly a layman friend of mine will join us then. Anyhow, make yourself at home, Simon. You can fix up your room anyway you want. If you need anything just holler." He walked away but returned suddenly. "I put a letter you received on top of the desk there." He pointed to a small wooden desk against the wall.

"Thank you, Father."

"Please, call me Dick, except for when parishioners are around. And one other thing before I forget. Our day off for priests in the diocese is Tuesdays. After Mass in the morning, we close the office and there's nothing until the next morning. Michel and I always meet up with some of the other priests for drinks and supper but that might be boring for you. Still, you're totally invited if you wish to join us. If not, there's plenty to see in Dallas. Laters!"

He shut the door gently and Simon looked around the large, cozy room for the first time. There was a plump lazy-boy chair filled with pillows in front of a television, a stereo player on top of a dresser and a phone on the night table. Simon couldn't believe that there was a phone in his room for his personal use. He picked it up doubting that it really worked and was pleasantly surprised when he heard the dial tone. Wall to wall carpeting made the room feel nice. Simon was happy he had been sent to Texas rather than remain up north as Seth had done. Texas was so different from the rolling green hills and mountains surrounding the abbey in Pennsylvania. Everything here was flat. He felt good about everything so far even though it was all so alien to him. He did prefer the vastness of the abbey buildings in contrast to the tiny rectory that would now be home. But it would only be a matter of months before he returned to Leicester.

Simon threw his small suitcase on the double bed which looked impossibly wide and comfortable to him. This was no narrow, metal cot. He began unpacking the few things he had brought when he remembered that Father Richard, Dick, had said there was a letter for him on the desk. Simon recognized Shawn's handwriting immediately and he excitedly tore open the envelope:

Abbey of the Most Sacred Heart of Jesus
Leicester, Pennsylvania
My little one,

Just wanted this note to be waiting there for you when you arrive. See how I'm thinking about you even though we're far away from each other?

Richard Pazzone, or Dick as he prefers to be called, is a basically good guy, although he can get a bit strange sometimes. Quite a bit strange. Just so you're prepared, don't get nervous if he's really cool one minute and then the evil stepbrother shows up…You can discover it all for yourself. In the abbey we didn't call him "Skitz" for nothing! Of course, as I said, he prefers to go by "Dick" which I suppose is just as appropriate when he acts like one.

Is he still insanely skinny? I haven't seen him in years. I can't imagine him being any skinnier than he was here but I hear he is. He hardly eats anything all day and basically only eats cold asparagus soup right out of the refrigerator at night. He does like his booze, though, so I'm sure you will have plenty of that (lucky you!). He's not a bad guy just be careful and keep your eyes open. When he was still here in the abbey before being ordained, we used to kid about how he always wants to be the center of attention. We used to say that if there was a funeral, Skitz would want to be the dead guy, the cadaver in the middle of the room.

Michel, his sidekick, is harmless and probably won't initiate any friendship with you. He's a strange bird and has been with Skitz for many years. He's smug because he knows that Skitz is needful of him and will always want him around. It's a bizarre arrangement but then again, just another one in a long line of weird shit.

All for now. It will all pass quickly and you'll be back here before you know it to become Reverend Brother Deacon Simon Maria. Wow, that sounds very impressive! I can't believe you're growing up so fast! If you need anything let me know.

Shawn

P.S. Did you remember to take your Royal Copenhagen?

Simon smiled thinking about crazy Shawn and his Royal Copenhagen. Though he knew that Shawn was mostly trouble, Simon appreciated the letter from Shawn. Now that he was far away, he suddenly felt homesick for the abbey. He also admitted, for the very first time, that he needed Shawn. It was a sense of need that he had not fully admitted before.

Simon immersed himself in the tasks he was given and the days soon turned into weeks. He wondered how much more he would be doing as a deacon that he wasn't doing now. Dick was famous for saying to him, "Now don't get all caught up on rubrics and what you can and can't touch at the altar. Give it all your own style. You're a man of faith, a man of God so get into it! Don't be so rigid. I know you can't baptize, preach sermons nor marry folks yet but you can certainly give a meditation on weekdays at Mass instead of the sermon."

Simon had protested, "But isn't that the same as preaching a sermon? I understood that only deacons and priests could preach during Mass."

"Oh, c'mon, Simon. See, there you go again. Don't get caught up on silly rules and details. I'm giving you permission. As pastor I have that power." Simon wondered silently how Father Richard, the infamous Dick, imagined that he had acquired such ample jurisdiction from the local Bishop. "As pastor, I can annul marriages and remarry people right here in my church if I want to without having to ask for permission from anybody." Simon nodded but knew this was pure, unadulterated bullshit.

Simon wasn't great for writing letters. The only time he wrote was to his mother but he had been wanting to write to Shawn for several days, if not weeks. Time passed so quickly in the parish what with so much activity all the time. One afternoon he sat at his desk and wrote:

Saint Sebastian's Catholic Church
Dallas, Texas
Dear Shawn:

I got your letter the very day I arrived. It was waiting for me here and I figured out that you had written it to me a few days before I left, while I was still in the abbey. You always seem to think about everything! Anyway, it was great having your letter here waiting for me.

The people in the parish are super friendly and I seem to get invited to supper every Sunday in somebody's house. Father Richard, rather, Dick, as he insists I call him, never wants to go but tells me that I should, so off I go. Michel never wants to go anywhere.

Dick is great. Anything I need he makes sure I have and gets it himself or has someone taking care of it. I really haven't seen the "evil stepbrother" as you called him. I wonder when he will show his ugly head. Until now, he's great with me and I couldn't possibly complain.

The daily happy hours are fantastic and it's usually just us three monks and a friend of Dick's who usually cooks something exotic. I always remember what you said about Dick not eating and the cold asparagus soup! Yep, there is always a pitcher of the crappy, lime green soup in the refrigerator. Yuck! It looks absolutely disgusting.

There's tons for me to do here in the parish and I'm happy to say that the people respond really well to my more traditional sense. There are plenty of young families with children and lots of older parishioners who have been here their whole lives. Dick hasn't said anything too negative to me about my being old school but some of the people have taken me aside to complain about how liberal he is.

I know this is probably common gossip in every church but I hear things like: "We really enjoy your reverence at the altar because it's so different from Father Pazzone who likes cracking jokes constantly from the pulpit and makes up most of what he does during Mass." I'll be honest with you that it makes me feel good and nervous at the same time. One lady said that it's a holy priest they want and not a clown.

They told me about a weird cemetery he's responsible for but I'll tell you about that later. I just want to do my time here and stay out of trouble. So many storms caught up with me in the abbey as you remember and I'm happy all that's in the past. It's really easy to be faithful to God here.

I'm giving the meditations at daily morning Mass. Dick insists that they aren't sermons. He encourages me and gives me tips on how to preach even though his style is really so different from mine. You ought to see him at the pulpit at Sunday Masses…a song and dance from hell! I'll just leave it at that.

Anyhow, I just wanted to touch base with you and let you know everything is good here in my life. Please answer my letter as soon as you get it!

Simon

P.S. As I said, Father Michel is kinda strange. Yesterday he answered the phone in the front office and went out of his way to be gracious and kind to some lady who called to complain about something. He listened and consoled her, pouring his heart out and saying stuff like, "Yes, I'm so sorry for that," and "You are absolutely right in what you are saying." Then he wished her well and told her God loved her. As soon as he put the receiver on the phone, he leaned down at it and said, "Asshole! Shut the fuck up, you bellyaching bitch!" I thought it was very weird,

P.P.S. I miss you.

Not more than ten days later, the parish secretary came up to Simon holding an envelope in her hand and waving it back and forth in the air. "Brother Simon has a letter from Leicester…"

Simon smiled and caught the envelope excitedly out of her hand saying playfully, "Hey! Gimme that!" They liked each other since the day they had met. Simon heard Dick coming down the hallway, asking what all the noise was up front in the parish office and Simon quickly put the envelope into the pocket hidden in the folds of his black habit. He wasn't sure why he did that but it felt like the right thing to do.

Simon slipped away and got to the safety of his bedroom. He closed the door and laid down on the bed, propping up the pillows first to make sure it would be a comfortable read. He held the envelope in his hands and thought that the really best part of receiving a personal, handwritten letter is to hold it in your hands before actually reading it. It's like planning a trip before actually taking it. He held the letter in his hand and looked at the handwriting. He had to admit that he missed and needed Shawn. He knew he was a schemer, someone to reckon with but he also knew that Shawn was on his side, watching out for him and this was something very important in the abbey. He turned the envelope over and carefully opened it:

Abbey of the Most Sacred Heart of Jesus
Leicester, Pennsylvania
Little One:

I can't tell you how happy I was to get your letter (it even smelled like you! Not Royal Copenhagen, but you!) Truth be told, I miss you too and often wonder during the day what you must be doing down there in the prairies of Texas.

Things here are dreadfully dead as they usually are in summertime. Oh, I wanted to tell you that Little Orphan Annie now has a new masseuse. It was only a matter of time before you got dumped. It happens every cycle. You will soon be ordained for service at the altar where your hands will touch holy things so Annie can't have you rubbing her meaty German white buttocks anymore. As usual, he has chosen well. He's a young, toned little guy from Chicago. Irish and cute. Liam by name.

I'm doing good. I help with Masses at the university in town and there's always a line of confused college kids that need direction and take up most of my time. I'm also working on my Doctorate so after that there's not really a whole lot of time for anything else even though, as I say, there really isn't much to excite us within the walls of this venerable, old place.

I'm glad you're learning to prepare and deliver meditations at Mass. It's going to help you when you have to preach as a deacon and as a priest. After a while, you'll develop your own style and it will come easy.

You will be wise to stay away from bitchy, gossipy church ladies. Don't fall into that especially there at Dick's ranch. You don't want to get on his bad side. What you tell me about Michel totally fits!

All for now as I have some studying to do and it's almost time for supper.

Shawn

P.S. What's the weird cemetery story? I'm intrigued. Pray tell.

Simon put the letter down on his chest and closed his eyes. Everything in the parish was really good but he missed the abbey and the large numbers of monks at prayer and in the refectory. He missed taking walks with the monks before supper, strolling on the gravel walks with a background of a million evergreens, firs and pines. Simon could see in his mind's eye the approaching mist and fog that often came rolling off the blue mountains just beyond the rolling hills and valleys.

He was lost in his musings and felt himself drifting into sleep when a soft knock came to his door. It pulled him back to reality and he sat up, "Yes, who is it?"

It was Father Michel. "Father Richard wants to see you." There was something about the man Simon didn't like. He seemed nosey and inauthentic. The priest looked around the room in one, sweeping glance, then said, "You best hurry, he doesn't like waiting when he's in a mood."

Simon stood and walked down the hall to Father Richard's room. From the doorway Simon could see that it was a combination office, sitting room and bedroom all together. There was a desk piled high with files and paper and in front of it was a small sofa. On the other side of the large room was his bed and dresser. There was also a wicker rocker in front of a huge, wide television screen and next to this was the most complex music system Simon had ever seen, complete with several large speakers that were in every corner of the room and a long black cord that was connected to a large set of earphones. The walls were covered with framed photographs of the pope and local bishop as well as the Abbot in Leicester along with monks and family members. There were posters bearing wise slogans. What most impressed Simon was the grand collection of statues of every size imaginable of Jesus, the Mother of God, the angels and the saints. Religious trinkets were everywhere and on one entire wall there were books.

Simon knocked on the door and Father Richard, sitting at his desk, looked up and said, "Come in, Simon. Please sit down here." He gestured toward the little sofa. Simon sat down nervously wondering why he was there. "I've been meaning to speak to you about something. You're in my care and I'm responsible for you." Simon thought that Dick appeared ill at ease. "I'll just come out with it. I'm not sure you can handle the morning meditations any longer."

Simon was confused. "How's that, Father? I don't understand, I mean, I prepare for them every day and even practice in my room before Mass in the morning."

"Yes, well, the meditations should be about God's Word." He leaned in, over his desk and rested on his elbows. He glared at Simon and said, "It's not about you. Lately, that's what it sounds like. All I seem to hear is 'I did this' and 'I did that' and 'I think this'. People are starting to complain and I can't have that."

Simon was stunned and didn't know how to respond. It took him by surprise because every morning several parishioners went out of their way to say "good morning" to him after Mass and to tell him how much they enjoyed his meditation. Dick never went out to greet the people after Mass during the week. "I'm sorry if I'm not doing it right, I thought…"

"And you need to make your thanksgiving after Mass and get in here to the rectory instead of idle chatter with all those gossiping trouble makers. My God, it sounds like a hen house in the church after daily Mass." Simon felt his face burn and he was terribly embarrassed by the reprimands. He looked down not knowing what to say. "You're here to assist me and not the other way around. Got that?"

"Yes." Simon quickly added, "Yes, Father."

"And there's one more thing, Brother. You're getting too chummy with the secretary in the office. Every time I turn around you two are together giggling like two school girls. I want it stopped now." He sat back and looked at Simon. "You can go ahead and accompany Michel to visit the sick in the hospital on his sick calls this afternoon. I have a funeral later but won't need you." He turned around toward his typewriter and with his back to Simon said, "You can go now."

Simon returned to his room and wanted to scream and cry at the same time. He felt alone and frustrated for the first time since he had arrived. He opened his desk drawer and took out several sheets of paper and an envelope. He still had some time before having to go into town with the other priest for the sick calls at the hospital. He closed his eyes and concentrated before he began:

Saint Sebastian's Catholic Church
Dallas, Texas
Shawn:

Well, I guess I just got my first good look at the evil stepbrother. I can't tell you enough how weird that shit was as it was going down. I had no idea he could be that mean. He called me in and gave me a rash of shit about drawing attention to myself in the morning meditations. He called me on being too friendly with the parish secretary. I really can't believe how he acted.

I'm beginning to get the impression that you know Richard Pazzone, the Dick, pretty well, and I understand completely now why his nickname at the abbey was "Skitz". Take the cemetery thing I mentioned to you in my last letter. Well, it's a weird cemetery he put together overnight here at the parish. Some of the people say it's a loony thing he decided and forced on them. Whenever there's a funeral and the remains have been cremated, the ashes of the dead are simply poured right into the ground next to the church, right under the trees. No markers, no headstones, no cross, no nothing. After the funeral Mass is offered, he invites the family of the deceased to follow him out into his "Garden of Memories" as he calls it. Then he hands them a small garden shovel and tells them to choose the spot they want and just pour their loved one's ashes into that hole.

I didn't believe it until I saw it happen. The family can never really know where the remains of their loved ones are. I've seen squirrels run over that place searching for acorns and digging everything up. And what happens if someday the State of Texas decides to run a highway through the church property? Those tombs are gone forever. I can't imagine my family's tombs lost like that.

I thought about the gladiola bulbs I planted in the backyard when I was a little kid. I would take gladiolas with my grandmother to visit my grandfather's and great grandparent's tombs and put them in copper vases there. What Skitz has done with the cemetery is awful. Someone said to me that they had complained to him about it and that he had gone wild and gotten into a rage and then told them that as pastor of the parish, he had decided it and that was that. He said people knew where they put their dead. Pretty calloused, I think. Then he put a plaque in the back of the church that reads: "Remember to pray for the dead buried in the Garden of Memories". Under this there are smaller plaques with each person's name who's buried there. Somebody told me that the Bishop was pissed when he heard about it but nowadays it's not like before in the Church. The Bishop hasn't done anything about it. I guess he doesn't want to get into a mess with Skitz, Dick, the evil stepbrother or whoever.

This afternoon I'm going with Michel to the hospital to make the rounds of sick calls. I guess I need to get a sandwich now and get ready.

I'm sorry if I sound bitchy and I've written so much. I want to scream.

Remember to keep me in your prayers.

Simon

Simon saw that Father Michel was waiting outside the rectory for him as he passed the parish office and he whispered to the secretary, "Could you mail this for me without Father Richard seeing it?"

She had nodded and put the envelope in her purse. "I'll get it into the post office this afternoon when I leave here. No worries, I understand." She had smiled her best smile for him. Close to two weeks later, she handed him an envelope when no one was around:

Abbey of the Most Sacred Heart of Jesus
Leicester, Pennsylvania
Simon, baby,

Don't sweat that crazy shit down there. I warned you and now you're seeing I was right, as usual. The weeks are passing and when summer is completely gone, you will be back here.

Stay out of Pazzone's path, even when he seems to be happy and not in a mood. I told you he's skitzo. That cemetery story totally defines his erratic behavior but don't get sucked into his crazy tirades. You'll find that from the Bishop down to the last parishioner there, folks wisely stay out of his path for obvious reasons. That's why he's been there so long (and don't quote me but he also keeps the money flowing to the bishop and back to the abbey like few others have done). He screams and threatens and that's how he intimidates. He gets that wild, dark look in his eyes when the crazies flare up in his ugly head and everyone moves away. You'd do well to do the same. It worries me that he's jealous of you with the people. That is so obvious to me in the morning meditation thing. There's no way to change that but hang on. It will all pass.

I will tell you something else and take this as another warning from me: Don't shine too much around Skitz. Actually, don't shine at all. He gets very jealous if he's not the center of everything and receiving everybody's unwavering adulation. If he sees that you outshine him, then you're going to suffer.

Stay clear of him as much as you can. I would guess you are lonely like you say in your letter. I figured you would be. Michel is a boring, empty, harmless queen but not much company. I guess Pazzone doesn't see him as a threat because he's a nonentity and that's why he wants him there. He's his gofer and feel good teddy bear. Sometimes I wonder why we live among such weird and boring people. It seems like they come to religious life because they couldn't make it in the real world. But what does that say about us? Why do we join and stay? We could be successful people anywhere in any walk of life. If you shine even just a little, there's always some sick bastard in the Church that will want to tear you down. I'm not bitter about this, honestly, I just don't think there's an easy answer for why we hang on.

Sorry if I depressed you more with these questions of mine. Hang in there, little one, I'm always watching out for you.

Stay away from going out to Sunday suppers and maybe it's a good idea not to hang around too much after Mass and greet the people. It's a shame but there's no sense in getting burned at this stage of the game. If I were you, don't let him see you with the secretary either and don't seem too happy. It's a stupid game but you need to play it if you're smarter.

Shawn

P.S. On another note, I know that you were close to Father Marcellinus so I want you to hear it from me. He passed away sometime during the night a couple days ago. There was a large manila envelope he left for you with your name on it sitting on top of an altar in his cell. I'll keep it here for you till you get back in a few weeks or so. He was about a week away from turning a hundred years old! I gotta say, he was a classy old guy.

Simon put the letter away safely hidden with the other letters from Shawn. He did his best to work quietly and when Dick's moods did dip from time to time into extreme looney shit, Simon was careful to keep his distance. He attended the daily Happy Hours and tried to appear jovial and at ease. He did everything that was expected of him without drawing too much attention.

One evening after the Happy Hour, the two priests and Simon gathered for supper as they did every day. Father Richard's friend was there as well. It was apparent to everyone that Dick had gotten very drunk during Happy Hour and during the meal asked, "Have…have any…of you noticed…how many ho…homosexuals there are in this parish?" Simon and the other two men looked at each other and no one answered.

"Well…let me tell you a thing or two, because…because I have noticed a thing or two, yes I have boy howdy." He lifted his wine glass and said, "To all the queers of Saint Sebastian's parish. Let's not toast those who prefer the pink hole…" His head fell momentarily to one side and rolled around, finally straightening up again. "No, not the pink hole, not 'g-i-r-l c-u-n-t'." He said it slow and slurring.

Simon felt sick to his stomach and wanted to get up and leave but of course he would have drawn attention to himself and that would have been very bad. "No, I want to toast all the faggots, all those who…who…" For a second he lost track of what he was saying but then suddenly blurted out, "who like and prefer the brown hole to the pink one." He looked around the table and Simon noticed his eyes were bulging, red and wild. "I'm talking about…about 'b-o-y c-u-n-t', oh yeah. The faggots all say boy cunt is better."

It was so unbelievably awkward and obscene that Simon looked down at his plate. He remembered an expression his grandmother always used, "tener vergüenza ajena". Sitting across the table, Simon actually felt shame for the priest's own bizarre, pathetic behavior. Simon filled his wine glass to the brim and without thinking, drank it down like water, hoping to feel more at ease as the wine flowed into him. Dick was unstoppable and said, "Let me tell you about one huge homo in particular belonging to this parish. His mother thinks she's the fucking voice of God." He looked around the table and then looked down at his crossed legs.

It seemed that he had lost his train of thought again but then suddenly said, "I'm talking about Ralph…little Ralphie, the fucking faggot. His damned mother thinks he's a saint because he was an altar boy here and now he's in the seminary." He paused and then said too loudly as he banged his fist on the edge of the table, making the wine glasses momentarily jump on their glass bases, "I don't think he even has a vocation to the priesthood! It's all about her…that stupid bitch. She's the one who—"

Father Michel, trying to sway the conversation in another direction said, "I was so surprised to see how well Sally is doing after her surgery. She looks absolutely—"

"Don't cut me off! Don't you dare patronize me, mister." Dick lifted his fist and tried to bang on the edge of the table again but missed, hitting his knee instead. "I'm not done here, dammit!" Then he said, "Maybe Ralphie does have a vocation after all, I mean…after what he told me this past Saturday in the confessional…" Simon and Michel looked at each other in horror and Simon closed his eyes when Father Richard said, "Do you know what he…he confessed to me? He told me he's a homo, a homosexual. Ralphie told me that he's gay…It was clear to me that he prefers the brown hole…Oh boy…" He laughed to himself, "Oh boy, I'd love to tell his cunting mother that bit of news…and see her fuck up her face." He distorted his features momentarily, giving his listeners a glimpse of what Ralphie's mother's face might look like if he revealed the confessional matter. He stuck his tongue out at her imaginary presence and then lifted his glass into the air and toasted, "To Queerdom and to all the fudge packers here in this parish and beyond!"

Later that night, Simon heard a gentle knock on his door and was roused from sleep. He turned on the small lamp on the bedside table and saw that it was well after midnight. The gentle knock came again and he got up. He approached the door wearing a t-shirt and a white pair of boxers. He opened the door slightly, wondering who it could be. Dick stood there with a strange look on his face and said, "I got way too drunk at Happy Hour today. I need to talk. Can we talk?" He didn't appear to be drunk at all and this surprised Simon.

"Yes, I mean, let me get a robe on and I'll be right over."

"You're fine just like that. Come over a minute? It won't take long."

Simon felt invaded and very frightened to follow him to his room but of course, he couldn't say no to the priest. In any case, he threw his robe over his underwear and walked out. When they sat down together on the little sofa, Dick said, "May I offer you a scotch? Just a drop or two. I can't talk right now without relaxing a bit."

"I…I really don't think…I mean, I'm not sure, Father Richard."

"Dick. Please call me Dick. Oh, it will do you good too. I only wish you were a priest already and could hear my confession. But I'll have to be content with just a fraternal chat between brother monks right now." He went to a little cabinet and Simon heard him pouring the scotch. When he returned, Simon saw that there were two glasses and they were quite full. "Forgive me but the kitchen is too far to go for ice now." He handed a glass to Simon and sat down.

As they drank, Simon heard the story of the man's life. The glasses were filled several times and he lost count but was grateful for the alcohol because of the pathetic things the priest was saying as he opened himself up completely without reserve. He admitted to Simon that he was a closeted homosexual and that that had caused him to drink and sometimes, self-medicate. "I didn't act upon it in the abbey, but I began to soon after I arrived here." He had seen a psychologist in Dallas for several years who really helped him to come to grips with the pain and reality of his homosexuality and his life as a priest. "After my sessions with the shrink, I'd need a drink real bad and I'd go to the gay strip not far from there, on Cedar Springs Road. I'd usually meet someone there or at another, sleazy place called Throckmorton Mining Company where it was easy to pick up a homo. I'd go home with whoever was willing. But the next day I'd be crushed and would drink myself into oblivion…and I'd do pills too. I still do. There's a doctor and a nurse in the parish…" On and on, the man told Simon every sordid detail of his life and his struggle and even in his own drunken state, Simon could begin to understand why the man was so mentally unhinged. He was filled with genuine compassion for the broken man sitting across from him. Simon understood what that kind of pain was like. He remembered Brother Casimir and the abbey bell tower.

The two of them drank late into the night. At one point, Simon got up and brought the bottle to the sofa. He poured the last of the scotch into their glasses as he said, "I understand perfectly what you have suffered, Dick, because…you see, I'm gay too." Dick moved into Simon's space on the small sofa and attempted to kiss Simon for what he had just revealed. Out of a deep and genuinely surge of pity, Simon returned the kiss on the priest's lips. It would not be until the next day that the memory of this moment made him want to vomit for his stupidity and lack of good judgement. He was repulsed but in his heart he knew he had been motivated by compassion because he shared much of the same pain.

It was Simon's turn to speak and he spilled his guts without realizing who it was he was entrusting with the delicate details of his life. He told the priest about his relationship with Toby. He didn't keep much in when he told him about Joshua although he was careful not to mention the root cellar. He shared with him the nights Joshua and he had spent together, safely hidden in the great bell tower. The booze was speaking quite clearly for Simon as he recalled the sexual activity he had been a part of in the abbey and confided his growing desire even now to visit the gay bars and bathhouses in Dallas even though he hadn't had the nerve to do so. At long last, seeing that the priest was ready to pass out, Simon led him carefully toward his bed and tucked him in. The next day, Simon couldn't remember how he had gotten to his room. He was awaken by a cruel and piercing headache that felt as if it could certainly split his skull in two. He felt sick and wondered if he could keep from vomiting. Mostly, he was aware of a gnawing pain in the pit of his stomach, at the very core of his being. He recalled with incredible clarity, everything he had shared with the priest the night before and knew it had been a terrible, foolish mistake. There was no way of taking it back now. He spent that day nursing his hangover and that night in growing panic, penned a brief note:

Saint Sebastian's Catholic Church
Dallas, Texas
Shawn:

It's getting to be late now but I need to tell you something.

It's a long story but I did something stupid and terrible last night. I told Skitz that I'm gay and what's worse, I told him all about Toby and Joshua, etc., etc.

What do you think will happen? Please answer me as soon as you receive this. I'm crazy with panic.

I can't believe that he broke the seal of Confession at supper tonight just like that and didn't seem to be bothered by it then or later. I still can't get over that.

Simon

P.S. I'm so sorry to hear about Father Marcellinus. I know he went straight to Heaven even though he didn't seem to think it would be so easy without doing some time in Purgatory. He was one of the good ones. Yes, please keep the envelope there for me for when I get back.

Several days passed and Simon tried to process all that had transpired that night in Dick's room. It seemed to Simon like an eternity but at long last he received a letter from Leicester:

Abbey of the Most Sacred Heart of Jesus
Leicester, Pennsylvania
Simon,

What in hell could have ever possessed you to give that kind of information to that nut? I can only surmise that alcohol was somehow involved. Otherwise, I can't possibly imagine the events that led you to do it but knowing you, I'm sure you were motivated by truth and compassion. Still, it was very, very stupid. Oh, baby, how are you ever going to survive in this insane world without me by your side?

What is done is done. We need to wait and see what the damage will be but I'm sure he was licking his chops as you poured out your heart. He's a sick fucker if there ever was one.

Listen to me good! Don't get all frightened and crazy. You don't need to panic. If he strikes against you with the information, I will take care of it, okay? You know I will and that I can.

The Abbot and everyone who knows Skitz knows that he's a sicko. I doubt that anyone will listen seriously to anything he could say to attack you. The seal of Confession is something that no mentally sane, faithful priest would ever think of breaking. That's why you're shocked, baby, and that's why Pazzone doesn't care. He's not playing with a full deck of cards. Don't worry about what he does, zero in on keeping yourself above water.

But even if he does trash your name, I will make sure it's ignored like water off a duck's back. Promise me that you'll be careful and don't ever drink alone with him again. Never trust him ever again. He's a mean motherfucker. I am so sorry you got assigned to that looney bin.

Be at peace. I got your back.

Shawn

P.S. The new postulant class arrived a couple days ago. Some real cuties in the group that reminded me of you at that age. The Abbot asked me to accompany him to greet the postulants the next morning and the Beak was pissed because I was there and he couldn't say shit about it. He was definitely in rare but predictable form as he gave his well-rehearsed performance yet again. It was all so insane.

Aside from accompanying Father Michel to the hospitals, the nursing home and the prison, Simon's duties included locking the church doors every evening. He no longer gave the morning meditation at Mass. Each evening, he went to the church and made sure that all the windows were closed, that the votive candles were blown out at the feet of the saints and that all the electric lights and fans were off. It was something he could do quickly because by seven thirty in the evening during the summer months, the church was usually empty. Sometimes, however, a repentant church lady or two would remain behind the others, oblivious to the time, as they beat their breasts in front of the large crucifix over the main altar or knelt in front of the side altar of the Blessed Virgin Mary. Simon really did hate to interrupt them in their prayer but when it would get to be late, he would often give them the fifteen minute grace period as they did in "The Schooner" with the overhead lights to signal that it was closing time and everyone needed to go home.

On an uneventful evening, Simon went to the church to lock up as he always did. He closed windows, put out candles and was about to turn off the lights when he noticed someone sitting toward the front of the church. He saw it was a young man, lost in prayer and obviously lost in thought. He was profoundly bowed down and held his head in the palms of his large hands.

Simon decided to give him a few more minutes before flashing the lights and closing up. He headed to the sacristy and crossed the sanctuary after genuflecting before the Blessed Sacrament in the tabernacle. He laid out the priestly vestments for morning Mass, prepared the missal and the chalice, and made sure that the cruets of wine and water were full. When Simon turned off the lights in the sacristy and returned, he noticed that the young man was gone. He gave the church one last sweeping glance and seeing that no one but God remained, he turned off the lights and locked the doors.

The following evening, Simon went to lock up again. He saw two elderly women praying the rosary. As he approached he heard their Hail Mary's, followed by the announcement of the "second mystery". He knew he had another fifteen minutes or so before they would finish so he went to the sacristy to prepare for Mass for the following day. When he came out, he saw the young man again, this time partially hidden from view by one of the massive granite columns that held up the church roof. He sat upright and was very still. Simon walked near him and could see that his eyes were closed. He heard the two women struggling to their feet as they helped each other out of the pews and down the side aisle.

Simon walked to the back of the church meaning to catch up with the two ladies and say a brief goodbye, but by the time he reached the vestibule, they had already left. He heard soft footsteps approaching behind him and he turned around. Walking toward him was the young man he had seen the last two evenings in church. Simon felt his heart pounding in his ears and a flurry of butterflies exploded in the lower part of his stomach. He waited for him to get closer and then walked up to the young man and said, "Hello, good evening, I'm Brother Simon."

"Hello, I'm Kevin." Simon was struck by the gentleness in his voice, which was timid, and by the piercing gaze in his clear, blue eyes. Simon liked the way he giggled like a self-conscious little boy, a sound that emanated from his throat rather than his mouth. His Texas drawl mesmerized Simon from the start, as he said, "Very pleased to make your acquaintance this evening, sir." They locked eyes and Simon could not look away even if he wanted to, which he did not. Kevin suddenly said, "I saw you here last night, in the church, but

I had to leave before I could say hello." He moved his hands to either side of his torso as he said this and tucked them just under his arm pits protectively, adding, "Sometimes I need to sit in a special place, in a quiet spot, and try and gather the pieces of my life that seemed to have been shattered and dispersed all over the place. I'll find a church or a park and retreat there." Then grinning, he added, "Or a lake nearby."

"I'm glad you chose to come here. Yeah, I remember you." Simon was greatly taken up by the composed and straightforward manner of this handsome stranger and was unaware how easily he was falling under Kevin's sensual spell. Kevin was tall and slender and Simon figured he must spend a fair amount of time in the sun because his toned frame was evenly tanned. The golden hairs on his arms shone like gold in the bright overhead lights of the church vestibule where they stood. His hair was abundant, very long and light blond, almost white where it was tied in a ponytail. His facial hair was somewhere between not having shaved that day and letting his beard grow out, either way, the stubble on his face was seductive. Kevin wore a thick, handlebar moustache that was darker and grew out around his mouth and down his chiseled chin, giving him an air of genuine masculinity. He wore a loose, white t-shirt above tight fitting, faded Wranglers and on his feet were a pair of black cowboy boots. Simon thought that they were both about the same age.

They stood momentarily in an awkward silence and then Kevin said almost in a whisper, "Well, I guess I need to be getting home." He stuck his hand out to Simon and added, "Very nice to meet you, Brother Simon."

Simon protested, "Please, just call me Simon and same here, Kevin. I hope you come back soon." The young man smiled nervously and walked out the church doors, the heels of his boots resonating within Saint Sebastian's. Simon turned out the lights and stepped outside. He heard the motor to his right and saw Kevin in a bright red jeep driving away from the parking lot. He locked the doors of the church and walked toward the rectory. He thought about the envelope Father Marcellinus had addressed to him and wondered what the priest had left him before he died.

Two days later, it was Friday night and the church was packed almost to full capacity. Dick and Michel, accompanied by four other priests from neighboring parishes, were hearing confessions during a penitential service. Simon was required to be present in his habit and lead the recitation of the Sorrowful Mysteries of the Rosary. There would be songs and prayers as the priests continued to hear the sins of the people and absolve them. Simon stood near the altar leading a penitential litany and was delighted when he saw Kevin enter the church. The young man stood nervously by himself at the entrance to the vestibule, his hands tucked into the back of his jeans. As soon as Simon finished leading the litany, the pipe organ in the choir loft began to play the melancholy, ancient French melody of "Let All Mortal Flesh Keep Silence". Simon turned to the tabernacle, genuflected and walked down one of the crowded side aisles to the back of the church. Kevin saw him approach and smiled. Simon smiled back and said in a low voice, "Hey, Kevin. I didn't think I'd see you here so soon. I'm so glad you came back."

"Aw, I never get to church as often as I should but I thought that maybe I'd see you here again." He looked around and with a nod gestured, "I didn't think there'd be so many folks here."

The hymn ended and silence followed. Coughing and sniffles were heard followed by a crying baby. A bell sounded in the distance and a great shuffling noise filled the temple as everyone pulled down the kneelers in front of them and knelt for the final part of the penitential service. The carved doors of the confessionals flew open and the priests came out of them, alerted that it was time for Benediction.

Simon was telling Kevin to stay a few minutes after the service so that they could chat a little longer, when he felt a sudden, aggressive nudge on his shoulder. Simon turned around and saw Dick's angry grimace as he said through clenched teeth, "Brother, it's time for Benediction and you don't seem to me to be ready." Simon blushed and turned and followed the priest to the sacristy. When the service was over, and the priests processed back to the sacristy, Dick came up to Simon and said, "I want you to pick up every booklet left in this church and get things set up for Saturday morning Mass. Snap out of your daze and get working." He turned around and left.

It took Simon over forty minutes to finish everything he had to do and by the time he turned off the lights in the church and locked the doors, everyone was gone. He searched the empty parking lot twice for the red jeep and went all the way around to the other side where the Garden of Memories was but there was no sign of Kevin. He wasn't surprised, of course, because it was late now and he figured that everyone had things to do the next day. That night in his bed, he found it difficult to sleep. Simon thought about Kevin and where he might be at that hour, and decided to put his thoughts on paper for Shawn.

Saint Sebastian's Catholic Church
Dallas, Texas
Shawn:

Even though I can't believe how many weeks I've already been here, still, sometimes it drags. Skitz isn't helping matters and sometimes I feel like I'm never leaving this tiny place. Then when I look at the calendar I can see that I still have so many weeks to go.

I miss the abbey terribly. Don't let this go to your head, but I miss you too. I feel so alone sometimes. There's no one to talk to since I've distanced myself from Sandy, the parish secretary. There is someone who has come by the church sometimes in the evening who's about my age but I've only seen him briefly a couple of times and really didn't get to talk much. He seems so normal and sane, unlike the two here.

Anyhow, nothing more to tell you about from this boring place. We're about ten miles beyond civilization!

Simon

A week later, when Simon returned in late afternoon to the rectory with Michel after visiting the inmates at a nearby maximum security prison, there was a small envelope in his room, on his desk, with a little note next to it which read: "Brother Simon, this came for you today. Sandy." Simon picked up the envelope and saw that it was addressed to "Brother Simon" followed by the church address. He sat on the edge of his bed and opened the envelope. He saw that it was a greeting card. Inside was a sheet of colored paper:

Dallas, Texas
Hey Simon, friend,

I'm sorry for not writing your last name on the envelope but I don't know what it is! And I was too nervous to call the church and ask to speak with you.

I want you to know that I had to leave the other night because it was getting late and I saw that you had chores in the church. I didn't want to stick around and get you in any kind of trouble.

I'm sending you this note to see if you might want to come with me to "Mozart in the Park" this coming Sunday in Fort Worth. It's a real good time and lots of families will be there, some with their kids and even dogs. Everybody sits on blankets spread out on the grass and brings wine sometimes. The music just fills the evening air in such a heavenly way.

I don't really know you much and I don't even know if you can go, so please forgive me if I'm out of line. It's just that I thought that maybe you might like to come with me if you can.

I'll pass by the church on my way to Fort Worth around three o'clock on Sunday afternoon. It starts at four and is over by seven or so. You can just wear shorts and a t-shirt. That's what everybody wears there. Afterward, if you like, maybe we could get a beer or something in Dallas and I can drive you home at a decent hour. If you're outside, around three o'clock, just jump in my jeep and off we go. If you can't and aren't outside, I understand and you don't have to explain anything to me.

Kevin

Simon tried to keep the tears back but they just flowed out, hot and thick, down his cheeks and into his beard. There had been moments in his life when he had felt so alone and abandoned in the rectory that he thought he couldn't bear it. Now the feelings of loneliness he had experienced at Saint Sebastian's had lifted. He was overcome with emotion to think that Kevin was looking for him to invite him to an afternoon and night out. His thoughts, however, turned momentarily dark when he realized he would need Dick's permission to go out at night. He needed to think about how he would ask for permission. He lay back in his bed. There was still time for a nap before supper. He dreaded the thought of the obligatory Happy Hour but was grateful for the alcohol that he would drink. He dozed off easily and when he awoke, he sat at his desk and wrote to his confidant:

Saint Sebastian's Catholic Church
Dallas, Texas
Shawn:

I'm a nervous wreck. I know that this letter will not get to you in time for you to read it and answer me by this coming Saturday night. I guess I'm writing to you because it's the next best thing to being able to sit and talk with you. I don't have anybody here to talk to about this.

You'll remember I wrote you about a guy my age who came a couple of times by the church in the evenings. Well, I finally met him. We didn't really have much time to talk but I just got a note from him and he's inviting me this Saturday to something called "Mozart in the Park".

I still can't believe he remembered me and now invited me to go to something like that. His name is Kevin. My knees get weak just thinking about this cowboy that looks like a Viking and wants to pick me up in his red jeep. Thing is, I need to get Skitz's permission and lately he's been a real mean bitch with me. I'm already beyond fearful just thinking what he might do with everything I told him about myself. And he's the one who will write a report on me of this summer experience in the parish to the Abbot! Shawn, I feel like I'm going to explode. Why did I ever confide in him? I can't believe how stupid I was.

It's time to gather for the farce before supper. I just needed to tell you on paper before I go completely mad.

Simon

Not long after mailing his letter, Simon received word from Leicester:

Abbey of the Most Sacred Heart of Jesus
Leicester, Pennsylvania

Simon:

Honestly, your last letter got me all worked up and I'm more nervous than a whore in church as our Proud Mary would say. I'm crazy curious to know if you got away in that jeep! I want to hear all about the Viking cowboy and how it all went down.

I'm not going to bore you with dire warnings but please remember all the things we've talked about. Enjoy it but be watchful with your emotions, baby. We both know how easily you fall in love. Take advantage of this opportunity for some breathing space to feel normal in that awful, dysfunctional place you're having to live in. But it's like we both know: it will soon be over and you are coming back for ordination and much brighter days.

As soon as you get this, WRITE ME and tell me that you were able to go and that you enjoyed Kevin's company and Mozart's too! Don't be stupid, little one!

Shawn
After that Sunday in the park, Simon sat down and wrote to Shawn:

Saint Sebastian's Catholic Church
Dallas, Texas
Shawn:

Well, my getting to go to the Mozart concert wasn't so difficult as I had feared. I managed to get enough courage to approach Skitz at Happy Hour the very afternoon I wrote you last. I saw that he was high up on his demonic rollercoaster and that I had to act fast before the certain crash. I just said that I was invited to go to a concert called Mozart in the Park and that I was asking him, as my superior and pastor, for permission to attend. He was all happy I recognized his authority (which was my plan of attack) and he said, "Oh? I went to that years ago. It's really fun and family oriented." I told him I was thinking, if it was okay with him, if I left right after the last Mass on Sunday. I could get picked up a little before three in the afternoon. He seemed to be okay with this. He actually told me to enjoy myself and that they would miss me at Happy Hour and Sunday supper. It was way easier than I thought but then again, he was in a blissful fog of his own and doing double Manhattans.

Then it got loony (of course). He was coming into the rectory on Sunday after Masses just as I was going out and he asked me why I was dressed the way I was. I said I was going to Mozart in the Park and he looked confused as if he hadn't the slightest idea of what I was talking about. He said he didn't know anything about that and when I reminded him of the conversation at Happy Hour he just dismissed it saying, "Sure, sure, go ahead, go." He wasn't exactly pissed but he sounded like I pulled a fast one on him.

My ride came a little before three and we got there just before it started. It was just an incredible afternoon and I actually got back late but I didn't see any lights anywhere in the rectory so I slipped into my room unnoticed. So the whole thing was not that eventful and worth so much hand wringing!

It was really nice to get away from the atmosphere in that rectory and be with families and a new friend. He's not Catholic and had questions about my place at Saint Sebastian's, the abbey and so on. I told him I was due back in Leicester at summer's end for ordination to the deaconate and had to explain all of that as well!

Today I'm going with Michel and a man from the parish to the nursing home, so I guess I ought to stop here. More later. Bye.

Simon

Simon was nervous as he reread his letter and didn't want to think what Shawn might read into the previous letter he had sent. He knew he couldn't fool him and that Shawn was very clever. Maybe too clever. He wasn't sure if Shawn would be satisfied with his explanation of what happened on his outing with Kevin. A part of him doubted that he would believe nothing at all had really happened with Kevin. He knew him too well. The truth was that Simon was already in love with Kevin as he had never been before with anyone. The experiences he had had with Toby and Joshua were important to him but they could not compare with what was unfolding now. Simon was lost in love with the gentle cowboy who looked like a Viking and couldn't wait to spend every minute with him.

It had all fallen into place in a way Simon couldn't have planned. From the moment he had locked eyes with Kevin in the church vestibule that one evening, he knew that that man had stolen his heart. Since that first, chance meeting, Simon couldn't keep from thinking about Kevin. In the days since then, he would go early to lock up the church in the evenings, hopeful that his new friend would be there. Instead, on every occasion he got stuck entertaining church ladies who didn't seem to have any rush in getting home to their husbands.

When Kevin's card arrived and Simon had read his note inviting him to the park for music and wine, Simon could not contain his excitement. He was thrilled that of all the people Kevin could have invited, it was him, Simon, whom he had set his eyes on. Simon couldn't sleep at night when he thought about what Kevin's gesture meant. Simon wanted to be with Kevin and believed that it was reciprocal and this belief sent him soaring and keeping him awake late into the night when sleep was all but impossible.

There was no way he was going to tell Shawn about what really happened. He would only scold him and belittle what Simon now held as sacred and untouchable in his heart. Shawn would not want to hear about Simon's love for Kevin and he would sneer at Simon if he attempted to tell him how he knew that he possessed Kevin's heart within his own. Shawn had drilled into him that he should not ever, under any circumstances, fall in love again. His brain completely understood Shawn's arguments and accepted the logic. But Simon's heart refused to be bound by such hardened, glacial prohibitions. The love that flowed easily in his heart was carefully hidden within Simon, not wanting anyone, especially Shawn, to know how perfectly it held him. Simon could not deny to himself his real intentions. It started with a glance and was cemented in a jeep ride. It swelled and took root on a summer evening in a park, when the waning sun bathed everything in perfect light. The gift God had given Mozart centuries before had been meant for the two of them, Kevin and Simon, on that magical afternoon. Their fragile souls had danced cautiously around each other until finally, with mutual consent, each had naturally and easily penetrated the heart of the other.

Simon propped up some pillows and lay back on his bed. He tucked his hands behind his head and thought about Kevin and himself. Simon had been nervous as he waited for Kevin outside the church that Sunday afternoon. He had hidden himself behind a great oak tree so that no one would see him and come up to strike a casual conversation. He continually searched the road for Kevin's red jeep as he waited anxiously. He was a willing prisoner of the deep emotions stirring unchecked within him and the pounding of his heart in his ears didn't help him relax in the least. When at last he saw the red jeep approaching, he waved at Kevin excitedly. Kevin waved back and Simon saw that he was wearing cut-offs and a sleeveless t-shirt that exposed the thick bush of blond hair under each arm. Simon climbed in and spontaneously hugged Kevin without thinking. Kevin had giggled in his boyish, throaty way as they awkwardly hugged each other for the first time. They drove away in high spirits, Kevin's ponytail flapping behind him in the wind and Simon turning in his seat to have a better view of the man beside him.

They found a spot under a low growing Japanese maple that spread it's limbs and red foliage over them like an ornate canopy. Simon sat down next to Kevin on the old, worn blanket the latter had brought. Kevin took out a bottle of red wine and two paper cups and they toasted their new found friendship. "To you, Simon. Thank you so much for accepting to come, friend."

"To Kevin!" Simon held up his paper cup. "To you, my friend who invited me!" They tapped their cups together and sipped the dry, red wine slowly. Simon didn't want that precise moment to ever end and fiercely held on to it.

He looked at Kevin's tanned, furry legs and was embarrassed when Kevin kidded him, asking, "What you staring at, Latin boy? You looking at my legs?" Simon blushed and Kevin giggled, "Aw, I'm sorry, Simon, I'm just messing with you." He reached over and playfully messed up Simon's hair.

Simon laughed out loud as he rearranged his hair with his hands and said, "Guess I'm busted. I was just admiring your body. Do you do a lot of exercise?"

"I'm so glad you noticed!" Kevin was pouring them more wine and Simon held both their cups. "My passion in life is tennis. I play any chance I get. I don't really get out anywhere and I live pretty much alone these days. Any chance I get, I go and play tennis. It's a great sport because you just have to keep moving and that gets you lean."

"I can see that." The wine was giving Simon a buzz and he stretched his legs out next to Kevin's and moved in closer. Their legs slightly touched and rubbed together, "I wish I was as toned as you."

"You look pretty great to me." He lifted his paper cup to Simon. "I love the dark hair on your legs, by the way." Simon rubbed his leg against Kevin's and they both laughed.

"It comes with the suit. My dad was Cuban and my mom is Spanish, so I guess I have no choice but to be a hair ball in this life." He looked at Kevin's legs, "How about you? You sound like a Texas cowboy but you look like a Viking to me."

"A Viking?" Kevin threw his head back laughing and Simon was lost to the lust that blossomed in his heart as he admired Kevin's pronounced Adam's apple. "Simon, I have been called any number of things but never that. I will tell you though, my family does come from Sweden so I guess that explains the Nordic features." He pushed playfully into Simon and repeated, as if to himself, "Viking. I like that" Then he said, "I may look like a cowboy but I'm not Texan. I was born in Kansas but I guess I've been in Dallas so long I probably look and sound like I'm a Texan."

When the concert was over it wasn't quite six thirty and the light was still very good. Kevin asked Simon if he was up to a beer back in Dallas. "Sure, I'd love that." The two happy friends picked up the blanket and the empty wine bottle and paper cups and headed to the jeep.

They sped down the highway toward Dallas and after a short time, the unique tall buildings of the city appeared in the distance. They talked about their work and Kevin was fascinated by the fact that Simon was a monk. "I don't know much about the Catholic Church but you sure don't look like any of the monks I've seen in pictures! And you sure as hell don't act like one."

"You're not looking at enough pictures," Simon joked playfully. "In the fall, once I leave Dallas and return to the abbey in Pennsylvania, I'll be ordained a deacon. After that, I'll go to a parish for a few months before being ordained a priest." Simon could see that Kevin was trying to understand all this information. "Not really clear is it?"

"Nope, not really." He turned and looked at Simon as he drove and then looked ahead, saying, "And will you come back as a deacon and then as a priest to this church here, where you are now?"

"That doesn't depend on me. It's where the superiors want to send me." Simon thought that Kevin suddenly looked sad when he heard this and he added, "But you never know. I could end up here again!"

"I sure hope so."

At long last, they left the highway and drove through several neighborhoods. Simon saw that they had turned on Cedar Springs Road and remembered that Skitz had mentioned it on the night they had had their drunken talk. Simon asked Kevin, "Is this the gay strip? I mean, are the gay bars here?"

Kevin slowed the jeep down and said, "Yes it is. Is it okay for you to be here?" He looked at Simon and said, "I'm so sorry, I didn't think to ask you. I'm really so sorry. We can go to another part of town if you like. I didn't think that maybe it's not a good idea for you to be seen down here, I mean, with your church work and all. It's where I only hang out and I stupidly thought…"

"It'll be okay." Simon was excited about this unexpected adventure. "I've actually wanted to come down here but I was scared to by myself because I don't know anyone here." He reach over and punched Kevin's partially bare shoulder, "But all that's changed now, hasn't it?"

Kevin giggled softly and smiled, "Yes, it has, sir."

They found a parking space and went in to a bar. It was dark and cool and filled to the doors. Kevin took Simon's hand and held it tightly. It was the first time they had held hands and Simon liked the way it felt. He told himself he liked feeling like he was Kevin's. They ordered a couple of beers and went to a tight space by the door where they could lean up against the wall. Behind them was a large window. Much as they tried to share some conversation, it was impossible because the music was blaring as Fine Young Cannibals were declaring, "She Drives Me Crazy". Simon managed to shout, "The beer is as it should be."

"How's that, Simon?"

"Like a friend of mine would say, 'It's stupidly cold'."

Kevin shouted back, "Wanna get out of this noise and get to somewhere quieter?" Simon nodded assent and they downed their beers and set them on the ledge of the window behind them. Again Kevin took the initiative and grabbed Simon's hand as he led them both out of J.R.'s Bar and Grill. Once outside, their ears adjusted and Kevin said, "Let's go into the Mining Company, okay?"

"Sure." Simon had no idea where they were going until they walked just a few paces and Kevin led him into another bar. The sign outside read: 'Throckmorton Mining Company' and as soon as they entered it got very dark. There were small orange colored lanterns hanging from the curved, rough ceiling and everything was made to look like a tunnel in a mine shaft. In fact, Simon was amused when Kevin turned and said, "Lower your head a little," and they passed down a dark, winding tunnel that opened up into a cavernous space which was the main bar and dance floor. The music was loud, of course, but nothing like J.R.'s. Simon could see that there was a spacious, second floor balcony. It seemed to Simon that there were shirtless men everywhere, and as they walked up a ramp, Simon saw an endless line up of men standing there. He figured out that those men were there, looking to hook up. Was this the place Skitz had told him about? Was it here where he had come and hooked up with strangers?

They had a beer and walked around. Simon was fascinated by the place because it was so dark and erotic. It was filled with some of the sexiest men Simon had ever seen. He looked at Kevin in the shadows and admired his friend's handsome face and athletic build. His thick moustache stuck out impressively under his perfect nose and Simon murmured something, smiling broadly. Kevin looked at him and cocked his head slightly to one side inquisitively, "What is it?"

"I said, you really are a Viking, aren't you?"

Kevin was coy and laughed easily, "Oh, right! If you say so. I'll be anything you want, mister." Then he put his hands on Simon's shoulders and drew him affectionately to himself. He looked at Simon with his extraordinary blue eyes and Simon thought he saw weariness and sorrow in them. "I can be anything you want me to be for you." Then he bent down a little in order to reach Simon's lips. They kissed gently for the briefest second and after that first kiss, they hugged each other tightly. Simon sensed that Kevin would probably never let go of him if he was allowed to stay that way. At long last they came up for air and Kevin winked at Simon. "If I'm your Viking, then you're my mad monk." They laughed like two fools. "Another beer and we get out of here?"

"Deal!" They drank their beers and Simon leaned back against his statuesque friend. Kevin put one arm around him and held him by the waist as Simon glanced at the men near them. He saw how other men passed by and stared at them and Simon felt exhilarated because he knew at that moment that he belonged to Kevin. The thought filled him with a sense of completion he had not known for a very long time. He leaned back further into Kevin and put his back squarely into Kevin's chest. Kevin wrapped both his arms around him and held him close. He kissed the top of Simon's head and rested his chin there. Kevin towered above Simon and he squeezed Simon as he bent down and kissed him on the side of his neck. He felt the handlebar moustache graze his skin as well as the stubble on Kevin's unshaven face. Simon immersed himself in that moment of splendor and nothing else could have felt so sublime. Gone were his tortured feelings of loneliness, frustration and self-pity. All the madness he had to endure on a daily basis at the hands of Dick faded significantly as he reveled in Kevin's arms. They finished their beers and Kevin led the way out of the bar, once again taking Simon's hand tightly into his own.

Once outside, he asked Simon, "Do you want me to take you back to the church now? I mean, do you need to get back now? It's getting to be eight o'clock." Simon didn't want to think about leaving Kevin and struggled to come up with an answer. "Or can I suggest something? If you like…" Kevin paused and was hesitant. "I don't know if maybe…you would like…to come over to my apartment. It's not far from here, just a couple of streets. I have some cold beer in the fridge and its quiet there. I can put some soft music on."

Simon was more than ready to accept Kevin's invitation and said, "Really? I'd love to see your place."

In his excitement, Kevin put his arms around Simon and held him close. The evening crowd was growing and the street was full of men eyeing each other. Simon could feel the crowd bumping into them as they stood hugging each other in the middle of the sidewalk. At last, Kevin stood back and said, "It's a real small place. Just me. I live alone there." He smiled and took Simon's face into his two large hands. Then he kissed Simon on his forehead and said, "C'mon, baby, come home with me." They held hands as they walked to the jeep and drove two blocks away, to a quiet shady street with no exit.

Walking arm in arm, they made their way up a flight of exterior stairs and reached Kevin's apartment. He unlocked the door and stepped back to let Simon go in first. "Thanks," was all that Simon could manage to say in his heightened state of expectations.

"Welcome to my little pad." The wall that met Simon to his left was covered with several picture frames displaying numerous newspaper clippings from the Dallas Morning News. Next to these were framed photographs taken at a beach and amusement park. Another photograph showed Kevin hugging a young man as he blew out the candles on a cake. There were other photographs but it was too dark in the apartment hallway to see much of anything. Simon made some kind of mental note in the back of his head to ask Kevin later what they were about.

Kevin pressed himself into Simon's back and Simon could feel Kevin's excitement at the small of his back as he was ushered down a hallway and into a bedroom. A full mattress was on the floor in the center of the room. The bed was unmade and a tangled blanket lay partway on the floor. Tall bookshelves served as a headboard and they were filled mostly with picture frames, knickknacks, and a digital radio alarm clock that was softly playing The Police's latest song, "Every Breath You Take". Simon read the bright red digital numbers that told him it was eight twelve in the evening.

They breathed nervously and kissed each other not needing to say a word. Silently they helped each other to undress and when Simon saw all of Kevin's sleek, athletic body, he realized that Kevin looked like a Greek god descended for him from Mount Olympus. Kevin caressed him and guided Simon onto the mattress. They shared their pent up passion for each other with such intensity, that when they erupted, it was with loud groans and peals of laughter. They were slick with sweat as they lay close together afterward in each other's arms. Simon was intoxicated by the aroma of sex that permeated the room. They lay facing each other, each lost in the gaze of the other. Simon could feel Kevin's profound need to be held and loved. Kevin's need was palpable to Simon in the small bedroom and out of instinct, Simon hugged the man he barely knew.

"I love you, Kevin. I know it must sound weird because we only really just met." He kissed Kevin's face and tasted with pleasure, the salty sheen that covered it. He kissed Kevin's eyes and then his nose. Slowly he kissed every inch of his forehead before finally reaching his lips. Kevin sighed with closed eyes and returned the kisses in the glow that followed their lovemaking. They remained that way in the darkness, unwilling to part and before long, when their labored breathing had calmed, they fell asleep together, wrapped in the arms and legs of each other.

Simon woke up and tried to adjust his vision in the darkness. He reached out but Kevin wasn't next to him. He looked up behind him and saw that it was ten o'clock. He heard muffled noises down the hall and rolled off the mattress aware that he was naked. Simon followed the smell of food that wafted toward him and he suddenly realized he was famished. He entered the hallway and saw that lights were on in the living room. It smelled like pizza to him and he looked for the kitchen.

There was Kevin, tall, lean and tanned, wearing nothing but an apron over his well-toned torso and compact waist. Simon stared at him without being able to utter a word. The pale white of Kevin's butt cheeks accentuated them in contrast to the golden brown skin of his strong, furry thighs. Kevin's muscular back was evenly tanned. It was obvious to Simon that Kevin played tennis completely shirtless and had no difficulty imagining the sight.

Kevin was busy pulling something out of a small oven when Simon snuck up behind him and put the palms of his hands on Kevin's furry, perfectly round backside, massaging him gently. Kevin didn't even flinch but instead emitted that boyish giggle that Simon was getting to love more and more. "You silly guy," Kevin said, without turning around and holding a large pizza on a tray. "I saw you coming up behind me. I saw your reflection on the glass of the oven door." Kevin put the pizza down on top of the stove and turned around. He saw Simon's excitement growing and reached for it. "Ouch!" Kevin said loudly, pulling his hand away and making believe that he had burned himself, "That thing's way hot!" Simon laughed like a little kid and realized all at once, how singularly happy and satisfied he was at that very moment.

They ate the pizza sitting on the living room floor and drank cold beer from the bottles as they watched television. They remained naked as they enjoyed being together, relaxed in each other's company. Simon admired how Kevin had trimmed the hair on his chest and how the golden treasure trail that winded down and over his bellybutton grew into a sumptuous mass of very dark blond hair. There, in its center, his formidable manhood was nestled. Simon ran his hand over Kevin's chest and said, "You're so incredibly beautiful."

Kevin giggled softly and responded, "And I love that you don't trim your chest," he said, running his hands through the hair on Simon's chest. "You're so damn hairy everywhere and I love it." He said softly, "I love you. I honestly do and it sounds weird to me too because we just met. Still, it's like we belong together."

They reached for each other and made love on the floor, kicking beer bottles in every direction and not caring where they landed. Afterward, picking up the fallen beer bottles all over the room, they laughed together like lunatics, giving in completely to the chemistry they shared and possessed. Simon didn't want to leave but knew that Skitz would be watching and waiting back at the rectory. The mere thought of leaving Kevin and returning to the rectory depressed and unnerved him.

Chapter Fifteen
"Stay with Me"

Believe me, every man has his secret sorrows
which the world knows not; and often
times we call a man cold when he is
only sad.
Henry Wadsworth Longfellow

Simon knew that he needed to get back to Saint Sebastian's and the shitty existence that awaited him in the rectory. "I guess I need to go, Kevin. I don't want to, but I'll be in some deep shit if I don't go now."

"I understand. I'll drive you over now. I don't want you to get in any kind of trouble." His eyes misted and he asked in an uneven voice, "Can I see you again? Can we get together again? Today was just…" His voice broke and he inhaled with exhausted emotion. He looked at Simon and smiled wistfully, "It was just perfect today. Completely perfect."

When they drove up to the church property, Simon was worried that Skitz might be spying on him. "You can just leave me over by the church and I'll walk over to the house. This isn't exactly a safe place for me." They kissed and hugged in the darkness and said goodnight.

They had agreed to meet outside the church the following Tuesday. Kevin picked Simon up at the agreed upon time and they drove together in Kevin's jeep to a section of Dallas that Simon had never visited. "I want you to meet a friend of mine who's having a cook out and some of his friends over. I've met some of them before. It's nothing fancy but I think you'll have a good time. They're all just a bunch of silly queens but good guys." Kevin said, "If it gets too boring we can leave early and go somewhere but there is a pool there."

"A pool? I'd love that. What about swim trunks?" Simon asked. "I didn't know we'd be going swimming."

Kevin giggled his best giggle and looked at Simon mischievously like a naughty boy, "It's a skinny dip party and nude cookout." Then he asked Simon, "Is that okay? I forgot to mention it to you. Maybe you're not into that."

"What? That is super okay with me!" Simon cheered. "An afternoon in the pool naked with you is just what I need! I'm looking forward to this! Thanks for the invite." As it turned out, everyone at the cook out was fun and laidback. He and Kevin had plenty of time in the pool together alone. Everyone there was paired off and he and Kevin had an incredible time in the water. It was a perfect afternoon and Simon enjoyed the intimate time he had with Kevin and the overall vibe of the place.

It was getting to be about ten on that Tuesday evening when Simon found his shorts and t-shirt and dressed himself. While he tied his worn Converse high tops, he asked Kevin, "When can we get together again?"

Kevin answered, "I was thinking the same thing."

"I can't really get away whenever I want. But I do have the free day like today. Are you free next Tuesday?"

Kevin stood and dressed himself. "I'm thinking about something." He smiled to himself.

"What are you thinking, Viking-man? I'm hearing gears and shit grinding in that handsome head of yours and I'm liking it. Should I be liking it? What are you planning?"

"Well, if you really wanna know…?" Kevin asked playfully.

Simon pushed into him. "I do, you bitch! Tell me."

They laughed together and Kevin finally said, "Well, I do have some accumulated time off. Fuck, I haven't missed a day at work in ages and just let my vacation accumulate."

"So?" Simon was beyond curious.

"So, I'm thinking that maybe next Tuesday I take off and I pick you up like really early…maybe ten o'clock in the morning? We can do two things and really stretch the day."

"I totally wanna stretch things with you, Kevin." They both laughed at Simon's sexual innuendo. Simon dramatically cleared his throat in a theatrical way. "Anyway, having said that, that would be great as the priests announced that they're leaving the rectory around nine in the morning to go…wherever." Simon put a hand on one hip and asked playfully, "But what are you thinking about for us? Where are you planning on taking us?" As Simon said this he momentarily lost his balance and fell against Kevin's bare chest. The smell of him was galvanizing and Simon literally was breathless. He hugged Kevin and said, "I really don't want to leave you ever. The more time we spend together, the more I want to be with you."

Kevin answered, "I know. I feel exactly the same. I don't want you to go anywhere away from me."

"So next Tuesday you pick me up at ten?"

"Yep. It's a date!" Kevin giggled.

"And where are you taking us to?"

"Well, hell, mister monk, it's just going to have to be a surprise, ok?"

Simon was beside himself with love for the hunky man God had sent him. Simon combed his hair with his hands as best he could and thrashed out the water from his beard. Kevin shook his mane of white blond hair. They looked at each other as only lovers can do and held on to each other without needing to say another word. At long last, they said goodbye to Kevin's friend and the other guests and left in Kevin's jeep.

As they neared the church, Kevin nudged Simon and asked, "Out by the church a good place to drop you off, correct?" Simon smiled and nodded. They sat speaking for a little while in Kevin's jeep and finally said goodnight, hugging each other and not wanting to let go. Kissing each other in the shadows was always the perfect end to a perfect day together for them.

Simon met Kevin the following Tuesday near the church as planned at almost exactly ten o'clock in the morning. The heat was rising and it promised to be another scorching Texas day.

Simon couldn't contain his curiosity and blurted out, "So where are you taking us so early?"

Kevin giggled and said, "Look behind your seat."

Simon turned and looked. He found a small canvas bag and pulling it out, asked, "This?"

"Yep, that's it. Open it."

Simon smiled and opened the bag. "What the fuck…?" He pulled out two towels and two small spandex suits. "Damn, these are speedos!" He held them up. "Are these really speedos?"

Kevin was giggling and laughing and beating the palm of his hand on the steering wheel. "They are authentic, Simon I bought them this week thinking of you…of us!"

"Well, where are we going?" Simon was lost in his thoughts. "Damn, I've always wanted to wear one of these."

"First to 'Captain Nemo's Wild Adventure Family Water Park'! It's up the road on I-30, near Arlington. It's an awesome water park. Huge slides and awesome places to cool off. Plus…truth be told…I'm totally down to see you in that black speedo!"

Simon screamed. He literally forgot decorum and screamed out of excitement. "I've seen that place driving by and so wanted to go." Then he added, "You're gonna make everybody horny, men and women, wearing this red speedo! Starting with me!" He held up the tiny red swimsuit. Kevin giggled.

Simon and Kevin spent the better part of the day at the water park. At long last, in late afternoon, they dried themselves with their towels and bare-chested and in their speedos, at Simon's insistence, they drove back to Kevin's neighborhood, deciding on the way to order Chinese takeout. Armed with supper, they drove back to Kevin's apartment, got naked and spent the rest of the early evening in Kevin's bed. They fed each other, mouth to mouth and drank beer and devoured every bit of the Chinese fare. All around them in bed, were the remains of white, oil stained food containers and bits of fried rice. They were dizzy with love and lust for each other and finally fell asleep in each other's arms after such an active day. Simon and Kevin woke up several hours later and held each other in the dark, neither wanting to speak as if a fragile, marvelous spell might be broken if they did so. Their need for each other grew that night and their intimacy deepened noticeably. In those delicate hours together, they satisfied their own carnal hunger but also gave each other the pleasure that they sensed the other longed for. Simon was 26 almost 27 years old and Kevin was 27.

It wasn't quite half past twelve that evening when Simon opened the door to Kevin's apartment and stepped outside. He turned around meaning to finally ask Kevin about the newspaper clippings and photographs framed and hanging on the wall but then felt it wasn't the moment to do so. He would have to remember next Tuesday to ask him. Kevin was dressing himself and standing half hidden behind the door, and Simon stood on the landing admiring his friend. It wasn't just Kevin's body that attracted him. It was his whole boyish manner, his unspoiled, almost innocent spirit that captivated him. Kevin was masculine and butch, but he was also gentle and fragile. Simon felt that there was something in Kevin's life that filled him with a noticeable sorrow and it was also this aspect that drew him to Kevin. Simon wanted to love him and heal his wounds, he wanted to hold him and comfort him, take care of him and protect him. Simon keenly felt the need for someone like Kevin to love him as well, someone who would heal him and keep him safe. Kevin was already that man who held him in that way. He felt in his heart that Kevin was capable of understanding him and loving him as he was. In some deep part of his heart, Simon understood that Kevin and he shared deep wounds and that wounds were wounds and that everything else about them were simply details.

As they approached the rectory, Kevin drove Simon near the church again. Simon didn't see any lights on at the rectory and assumed everyone was asleep but he didn't want to press his luck. Maybe Skitz could still be up and about in the darkness drinking, popping pills and spying. Everything and anything was possible in that cursed house. It was almost one o'clock in the morning when Simon carefully closed the door to his bedroom. He fell asleep easily not fully realizing that it was because he felt so very loved.

When Kevin had dropped Simon off that night, they had agreed to see each other on the following Tuesday again. Simon had said to Kevin, "But this time you don't need to come pick me up. The priests are going in one car next Tuesday to some priest gathering outside Dallas so I have the use of the other car in the rectory. I just need you to draw me a map so I know how to get to your place and back."

Simon counted the days to being with Kevin again and finally, on Tuesday, Simon drove to Kevin's apartment using the map Kevin had drawn for him. He was excited on many levels knowing that he would see Kevin and couldn't wait to be with him. When he had found a parking space, he climbed the steps two at a time and knocked on Kevin's door.

"Hey, beautiful monk," Kevin said. "C'mon in." Simon walked in and as soon as Kevin closed the door, they were in each other's arms holding on to each other once again. Since late Tuesday night when he had last seen Kevin, it had felt like a lifetime to Simon since he had been this way with him.

"I was thinking we could go for a swim," Kevin said. "There's a pool downstairs that belongs to the apartments."

"I'd love to get in the pool! It's so hot out there." Then Simon asked, "You still got those speedos handy?"

"I think I might have that black speedo that fit you like a glove." They undressed each other slowly and in silence and finally managed to get their swim trunks on. Simon laughed nervously because his erection wouldn't fit in the black speedo Kevin had given him. Kevin's own erection stuck out ridiculously as he tried to put himself inside and under the spandex of his tight red speedo. After playfully pushing each other around in the living room, and sharing a beer, they finally headed to the pool. Each held a frosty bottle of Coors beer in one hand, as they held each other by the waist with the other, and both sported a towel on their bare shoulders.

It was a typical, stifling, Texas afternoon when they got there and the pool was an oasis which they enjoyed together. When they came upstairs, Kevin suggested that Simon shower while he prepared sandwiches. When Simon was done, Kevin showered and afterward, they sat together naked on the sofa eating and drinking beer. Kevin was intrigued by Simon's life in the abbey and full of questions. Simon shared his boyhood dreams of the priesthood with Kevin trying to explain how the vows of poverty, chastity and obedience worked. Kevin listened in amazement and admitted that he had never known anyone who was going to be a Catholic priest or monk. Simon finally asked, "What about you, Kevin? I know you're from Kansas but what else?" He kidded, "You're…like this…tall, blond stranger."

Kevin sat up nervously and spread out his long, tanned legs in front of him. He lifted his arms over his head and cracked his knuckles loudly. "Not really a whole lot to tell. I love tennis. It's my passion, but I think I already told you that." He shifted and sat cross-legged. He became silent and said, "My dream is to one day travel to Wimbledon and experience it in person." He was silent again as if hesitating. Then he said, "Really, there's not a whole lot to tell. I get to work early in the morning and come home. I'm pretty much a hermit. It's been a long time since I was at the bars, I mean, the other day with you…it's been awhile." He turned and looked at Simon with misty eyes, "It was magical being there with you. Holding you like that and letting everybody know that we were together. I loved the look on some of those guy's faces! It was pure envy. We look so good together." He stared out into the room, away from Simon's gaze.

Simon wasn't content with Kevin's answer because it seemed to him that Kevin was evading his questions. He couldn't imagine that such a handsome guy like Kevin would lead the solitary life of a hermit, only going out to work and then return home. After all, Simon was the real monk and he certainly didn't live that way. He figured that there was more, so he pressed on and asked Kevin, "May I ask you about something?"

Kevin faced him and asked cautiously, "Sure, Simon, what about?"

"Since I came over that first Sunday, I've been wondering about the framed newspaper clippings you have at the entrance to your apartment. What's all that about? I saw them among the photographs you have there as well."

Kevin looked away again and the silence that followed in the apartment told Simon that it wasn't good. At last Kevin said in a low voice, "The clippings are about Cory. He was my lover of seven years...my baby." Kevin swallowed dryly and pushed on, talking into the room rather than facing Simon. "He was beat up badly, viciously, and murdered about seven months ago on his way home here one night. Those fuckers that did that followed him home and bashed him, cut him really bad. The police said it looked like the work of several people." He stopped and added sadly, "People is the wrong word. I'd say animals. Monsters. They stabbed him in the chest and in his abs but he was able to get away and somehow managed to dragged himself in here." Kevin gestured toward a corner of the room near a window with a tilt of his head, "I can't figure out how he had the strength to do it. I mean, he had to climb those steps..." Kevin trailed off and swallowed hard. "I...I think he was looking for me to protect him but he couldn't find me." Again he paused. "I wasn't home. He finally collapsed over there." Again he gestured and sighed, speaking unevenly, "I was out and when I got home I was out of my mind to see the blood on the steps outside and the landing. The door of the apartment was all messed up with bloody hand prints and was wide open. The ceiling lights were off and I couldn't see much until I switched on the lights. I walked in here never expecting to see...what I did see." He suddenly faced Simon and said, "The mess of blood I saw led to a dark pool where Cory was." Kevin turned away and closed his eyes tightly as he continued, "There was so much blood everywhere. He was lying on the floor, face down. He was barely alive when I took him into my arms and gently turned his head, calling out to him. I couldn't stop kissing him. But I knew it was too late. His eyes were already glassed over."

Kevin turned and looked at Simon through red, tear-filled eyes and as Simon took Kevin's hands into his own, he only managed to say, "Oh, Kevin, I'm so sorry."

Kevin's square chin quivered and he spoke so softly that Simon moved closer and put his arm around his friend's neck as he listened. "I called the police and an ambulance arrived but by that time, he was dead." Kevin fell onto Simon's chest repeating through sobs, "My Cory was dead. My beautiful baby…was gone. Just like that." Simon held him for a long time and when Kevin was ready to speak again, he said, "He died a senseless death. It was so violent and hate-filled. The police weren't very interested in pursuing the case because it involved homosexuals and we don't really count, do we? Even though I phoned the police station almost every day and went there myself several times, nothing was ever done. Those savages that did that weren't ever searched for and never paid for what they did. The Dallas Morning News followed the story in those clippings I keep on the wall there, but that was it. It never went anywhere. All I ever had left were those clippings…" Kevin took a deep breath and looked up at Simon. He wasn't crying now but the tone of his voice revealed to Simon, the breadth and depth of Kevin's pain and loss. "I keep the newspaper clippings by the door so that I'll never forget my friend, my lover…my Cory. He was my life, honestly, he was my whole life." Even though the two of them were naked and Simon touched Kevin very slowly and deliberately, the moment wasn't erotic as it had been before. The cause of the pain that Simon had seen in Kevin's eyes had now finally been revealed. Simon caressed Kevin's face and wiped away his tears, kissing his eyes and his forehead. He caressed his hair gently and massaged Kevin's shoulders and chest and little by little Kevin calmed down and relaxed. He fell asleep with his head in Simon's lap and his left arm wrapped around Simon's waist. He held his right hand in a tight fist under his own chin. As Kevin snored quietly, Simon thought about everything Kevin had just told him. Simon loved the man he had only just barely met and yet, he held Kevin close to him as if he had known him his entire life. He imagined holding him every day and every night just like this, forever.

As the shadows of late afternoon began to fill the small living room of the apartment, Kevin stirred in Simon's lap and kissed Simon on his abdomen but didn't get up. He laid his head down again. Simon kissed him and held on to him. He undid Kevin's ponytail and spread out his long hair on his own thighs, not wanting to ever leave the guy. The two men remained that way on the sofa for a very long time.

Finally, as the sun disappeared almost completely on that late afternoon, twilight took over and began to fill the room with its dreamy, waning light. Kevin finally stirred and rubbed his eyes. He looked up and said with a steady voice, "I love you, Simon. I really do."

"I love you too, Kevin. I can't lie to you. I've fallen in love with you in such a short span of time. I feel so blessed."

Kevin turned over and nestled the back of his head in Simon's lap. He stared up at Simon and then looked at the ceiling saying, "Since Cory died, I haven't left this apartment except to go to work and to get food. I rarely play tennis anymore like I used to. Sometimes I need to get out just to clear my head. Going to the bars hurt too much after he died. That's why I was in your church. It's on my way home from work and even though I'm not Catholic nor religious, I go there in the afternoons or evenings sometimes, to try and make sense of the whole awful mess." He closed his eyes and winced, "And to try and deal with my loneliness and sadness. Sometimes I feel like I'm drowning in a bottomless, black sea of dull pain. I can't understand why he was taken from me and why it had to be so violent." Kevin looked into Simon's eyes. "You were like a dove coming out of Heaven, flying out to save me when I first met you that night in the church. I've been drowning ever since Cory died and then, all of a sudden, you were right there. You flew to me and I stretched out my arm and stopped drowning. I felt it the minute we first talked."

Simon remembered how he had been filled with lust when he first spoke with Kevin in the vestibule of the church and when they had been together on Sunday in the park and later, in the bars. He was still very much physically attracted to Kevin but now something had shifted significantly and he couldn't shake what he was feeling in his heart. He felt a profound, needful love for Kevin and it was in every nerve of his body. He bent down and kissed Kevin on the lips saying, "I love you." Simon struggled with his emotions because he knew that it was not simply sex he wanted with Kevin. He remembered Shawn's dire admonitions and pushed them easily away as he sat there with Kevin in his lap. At that moment Simon knew that he could not live as Shawn said that he should. He loved the man he now cradled way too much for that. It had happened so fast and yet, it felt so utterly perfect.

Simon wasn't sure what time it was but he knew that he needed to get back to the rectory. It was getting dark outside and he was afraid of getting lost on his return to Saint Sebastian's. Holding Kevin close to him, after hearing everything he had said, made Simon wonder how he was going to go out the door and leave Kevin behind. He desperately wanted to stay and sleep all night with this man in his arms and wake up next to him. He wondered if loving someone with this much intensity was a common, everyday thing or if it was rare and unique. It wasn't like the feelings of young love he had strongly felt with Toby and Joshua. That had been real but this went deeper and was very different. Then Kevin said, "Stay with me." He sat up and looked at Simon, "Won't you stay with me, Simon?"

Simon couldn't believe the words he had just heard and stared at Kevin. Those words were the same ones that were once put to him long ago in a dream. He thought he knew then what the shattered, broken man hanging from the gibbet had meant. Hearing those same words now pierced his heart terribly. Could it be the same command? Simon had not anticipated hearing those words now from Kevin. He looked down at Kevin and saw the pleading look in his lover's eyes and the needful expression on his beautiful face. He wanted to say so many things to Kevin but didn't know how. Everything had seemed so simple and uncomplicated that night when they first met but now…now it was getting terribly complex and tangled. How was he to answer the request of these two broken men? Shifting and squirming in his place on the sofa, Simon rose as he had from the dream in the abbey and only managed to say weakly once he was on his feet, "Actually, I think I need to be getting back to the rectory. It's getting dark and I'm afraid…"

Kevin had sat up and taken Simon's hands into his own. "I didn't mean tonight, I meant forever. Won't you stay with me here? It makes such perfect sense for us to be together. I can't help but keep telling you that I love you, I really do." He looked at Simon. "I never thought that I'd be able to say that again to anyone, but it's true. I love you. And I feel that you love me."

Simon sat back down next to Kevin and realized that he didn't want to live without him either. He realized that in time, he'd know that he couldn't live without Kevin. For some mysterious reason unknown to him, God had thrown them together. Simon thought about the loveless, horrid life at Saint Sebastian's and the loneliness he struggled with at the abbey. That kind of loveless scenario among men appeared to be part of the consecrated life. He suspected that it was the same in all religious houses. The same sordid, loveless, empty experience was the norm. He felt caught in a terrible dilemma.

He still wanted to be a priest with his whole heart and soul, but he knew he couldn't live without love, no matter what Shawn said about sex without love.

What he felt for Kevin at that very moment wasn't something frivolous or just something shallow and transitory, borne out of lust for a sexy man. It wasn't just sex but it was far more sacred to him than that. Simon could sense God's presence in Kevin and in himself when they were together, like they were now. He felt like nothing was missing. No one but Kevin and he could understand what they had come to experience together. Maybe it was because he was older now and had matured, but the connection he felt with Kevin was different than anything he had ever felt with Toby and Joshua. He did know one thing and it was that he didn't want to lose Kevin. His mind was racing as he considered his dilemma. He eventually had to return to the parish and ultimately to the abbey but he also wanted to stay with Kevin. He leaned into Kevin's bare chest and not being able to look into his eyes, Simon said, "I love you too, Kevin. I won't say no to you. But I need to get back to the parish. And beyond that, I need to return to the abbey in Pennsylvania. I need to take care of things if I can come back to you. I'm in vows and there's a process I need to put into action. At the very least, I need to talk to the Abbot and tell him that I'm leaving." Simon thought about the Solemn Vows he had just professed and felt guilty as he spoke about leaving the abbey and joining Kevin for a life together with him. He had professed vows for his whole life but he had not counted on this love. Why did God put these things in his path and make him this way?

Kevin lifted Simon up and hugged him. Then he cupped Simon's face in his hands and asked, "Are you sure you'll come and stay with me? Is that what you're saying?"

Simon looked at Kevin and could not hold back any longer. He opened his heart and allowed it to take over and when he opened his mouth, he said, "Yes, Kevin. I will. I want to be with you. I want us to be together. It's just that…I just need to get back to Pennsylvania soon…I just need to get back to the abbey and see the Abbot. I was only sent here for the summer and the assignment is almost over. I leave in a few days. I had no idea that I would meet you and that I'd fall in love with you." He dropped his head on Kevin's shoulder. "And I had no idea that you would fall in love with me."

"Stay then. Don't go back. Just give them your two weeks' notice from here. I'm afraid that if you leave and return to Pennsylvania, you won't come back. From what you've said to me, becoming a priest is what you've always wanted and once you go back there, to them, you won't come back. You'll choose them over me. You'll stay there."

"I can't stay now. It's not that easy. I need to take care of it." Simon knew that what Kevin was saying had a great element of truth to it. He hesitated to say what he was thinking because he didn't know how it would sound. He searched desperately within himself for any easy way to say it. "Maybe it would be easier if I was ordained a priest and sent down here. I could ask to come down here and we could still see each other and be together."

"What?" Kevin sat back and looked at Simon. "How could that be? Maybe they'd never send you here. But even if they did and you stayed in the Church, you and I couldn't live together openly as lovers, could we? It would always be something hidden as if it was wrong to love each other, as if we were doing something forbidden."

Simon remembered Toby's similar words and felt himself cornered. He said weakly, "It would be hidden but we could make a life together somehow." Kevin didn't answer and Simon realized how shallow his argument was. At that moment, he hated himself for not being honest with Kevin nor himself. He hated himself for wanting two things at the same time and not being able to choose. He admitted, "What I just said was stupid, Kevin, I'm sorry. It's a fucking game I play with myself because I want two things that can't exist at the same time." At that moment, when he looked into Kevin's eyes, something clicked in Simon like the wheels and cogs of a complex lock opening and beginning to move together and he realized that he stood at a crossroads. He believed the moment demanded a decision and that he could no longer fool himself and others. He said, "Leaving all of that world in the abbey and not reaching priesthood won't be easy for me but…I'll do it." Without warning, hot tears ran down his face as he realized that he was caught in a mixture of emotions. It was about his love for Kevin and his own deep need of him but also fear and doubt about the future that lay ahead. The thought of giving up and losing priesthood was just too much to endure at that moment and Simon pushed the horrid thought away. The emotions were just too great for him to bear any longer and he heard himself say, "I'll do it…I'll leave all of that behind in order to be with you my whole life. I don't want to live without you. I can't live without you. I love you, man. I really do and it's you I want to spend my life with." He kissed Kevin who returned his kiss. "I don't want to live a life without your love. I just need to put things in place. I can be back here in the fall or sooner." As soon as Simon said the word *fall*, he remembered the upcoming ordination to the deaconate and his heart sank. He was almost finished with his studies. So many long years preparing. Everything was ready for ordination and now he had crossed paths with Kevin. He had to stop playing the awful game that was tearing him apart.

"I really need to run, Kevin." Simon stood up and Kevin got to his feet as well. They dressed and Simon said, "I'll be back, Kevin." Their lips met and they held on to each other for a long time, not wanting to let go.

Kevin said softly almost in a whisper, "Stay with me now." He wiped his tears away with his hands and cleared his throat. He looked at Simon and said, "You can't do it now, can you? I wish you could but I can see…" Kevin stood back and put his hands under his arm pits timidly, saying, "I'll be here, if you come back."

"I WILL come back, I just told you I will. I love you and I want to live my life with you. I want to wake up next to you every day and belong to you and on one else. I don't want to be alone anymore. Not now. Not after being with you and knowing now what really loving another person feels like."

Kevin stood staring at Simon as tears once again ran freely down his face. "I'll be here waiting for you." Simon turned and passed the wall with the framed newspaper clippings and photographs of happier times. He now understood that it was Cory in the photographs next to the clippings. Frozen in time were sunny, carefree days at the beach and wild, rollercoaster rides full of mindless laughter at an amusement park. Lost in the cobwebs of memory was the celebration of life around a birthday cake, now long gone. These grim trophies hung on the wall as a somber reminder of the brutality of lost and shattered dreams. It was a cruel monument to the twisted and gnarled paths that are assigned to all of us and that we cannot escape but absolutely must trod. Simon had often wondered about the argument for free will that he had been taught and it briefly crossed his mind now. Do we really ever have free will, he wondered to himself? Does God really allow us to roam and wander about as we wish or are things already set in place without our knowledge or consent? Do we decide which way to go or are things already set for us? He knew there were philosophical and theological considerations that made sense in this regard, after all, he had studied them for many long years in the seminary. But his heart questioned all of this now.

Simon opened Kevin's front door and felt Kevin's strong hands suddenly hold him in place by the waist and draw him to himself. Simon felt and smelled Kevin's proximity and wanted to slam the door shut in front of him, turn around and just stay. Kevin sounded desperate as he persisted one last time, insistent and almost begging, "Stay with me now, Simon. Don't leave."

Simon moved forward and dared not turn around. "I can't now, Kevin, honestly, I can't, but I'll be back. I don't want to live my life from now on without you." Simon pressed further back into Kevin's embrace for a moment and then it was Kevin who let go. Simon walked out the door and stepped outside into the stifling night. He turned around, fully expecting Kevin to follow him and say goodbye at the car. Instead, to Simon's surprise, Kevin slowly closed the door as he looked at Simon through tears. Simon heard the door being locked from within. Kevin had stepped back into his solitude of wounds and unhealed pain, past the newspaper clippings. Past photographs capturing blissful moments from once upon a time. Again, as before, Kevin was all alone. He had stepped back into the loneliness he knew only too well.

In five days Simon was to leave the parish to return to the abbey, and the people of the parish got together and prepared a going away luncheon for Simon. It was Saturday and almost everyone in the parish had come. Aside from a splendid array of dishes and desserts, there were also gifts and speeches of gratitude for his presence that summer. They even gave him a felt, black cowboy hat with a silver buckle. Father Richard Pazzone was there at the beginning with his arms wrapped tightly across his chest. He looked angry and out of place, standing far from the festive crowd. At his side was faithful Father Michel, looking to Simon like a dutiful nurse standing next to a patient at a mental sanatorium. By the time the speeches of praise began, and the farewell cake was cut and served, the two had left without saying a word.

Dick was decidedly drunk and in a foul mood all during the Happy Hour that evening. Simon didn't need to be told that his farewell luncheon might explain the reason for Skitz's dark mood. When they moved into the dining room, the atmosphere was tense and conversation was in low supply. Simon was disheartened to leave on such a negative note but he realized that he couldn't change the reality of the place nor the two priests who lived in the rectory. The fact that he was leaving the next day made him care less about the whole thing.

Simon was relieved, therefore, when Skitz stood up suddenly, just after dessert and thankfully, said supper was over. He was alarmed, however, when, just as he was about to go to his room and finish packing, Dick hissed at him, "You will come to my office now. Don't make me wait."

Simon tried to make eye contact with Michel but the priest looked away and made for the kitchen with the dirty dishes. Afterward, Michel disappeared into his room and closed the door. Simon approached Skitz's room and knocked on the door. "Come." The voice from within was curt and unfriendly.

"You wanted to see me now?"

"Sit down." He was sitting at his desk and Simon noticed several bottles of opened pills. "It doesn't matter that your assignment here ends tomorrow. As far as I'm concerned, you should have been dismissed before now." He glared at Simon and said, "If I had had my way, you would never have stayed so long." He paused and repeated, "Your departure is way overdue." Simon did not answer and waited for the tirade to be over. Skitz momentarily appeared to be distracted, as if he had forgotten the reason for calling Simon. He waited but the priest said nothing even though he sat staring at him wearing a blank expression on his weary face.

"Did you want to see me about anything else?" Simon asked impatiently. "I would think you want to say something to me if you called me in here."

"Don't you get wise with me, you little spoiled bitch. I saw you today, showing off with all the people." Spittle drooled out of a corner of his mouth as he said, "Don't think you can fool everyone. You can fool all those candied-ass, pious idiots out there who think you're so spiritual and singularly gifted but not me. I have your number. I certainly do." He pointed a finger at Simon, "I know all about you, don't I?" He smiled, "All the gory details from you personally." Then he said sarcastically, "Don't think I haven't put two and two together in regards to what's going on between you and that hunky cowboy friend of yours. I can see what's going on and you can be sure I'm going to raise my voice to the four corners of Heaven and Hell if I decide to. Don't think I don't know about it. Michel has informed me on two occasions after I sent him to sit out by the church at night. And I've seen it myself once." He licked his lips obscenely and said, "Oh, yes, Michel was out there on my behalf and reported to me what I myself have seen. Such an affectionate farewell on so many nights when your stud man dropped you off by the far side of the church. Such a display of romantic hugs and passionate kisses in the dark by the light of the moon."

"What?" Simon had no response to the enormity that he had just heard.

"You heard me you fucking brat, you little homo. I've suspected and I've done my homework, you horny little slut. You think you're going to be ordained a deacon in the fall, do you? You think you can run to Father Edmund and everything will just be hunky dory for you? Well, when I finish…"

Simon stood and bellowed, "When you finish what, you pathetic sick fuck? You drunk! You fucking drug addict! You have no right to threaten me and treat me like this. I'm in Solemn Vows, don't you forget that. I'm not some kind of novice off the street. I'm almost done with formation and thank God, I'll soon be free of this looney bin." Simon stood and hissed, "And what a pathetic sidekick that Michel is. It's sickening to me that such a man should cater to your sickness. It only tells me that he's just as fucked as you are." Simon turned and marched out the door, weary of the summer's senseless scenarios.

As he made his way to his room Simon could hear Dick going on and on. The pathetic man kept screaming and threatening wildly at him from his desk down the darkened corridor, "You get back here! You get back here and show me some respect or you'll be sorry, you proud bastard!" Simon was happy that finally tomorrow he was leaving Saint Sebastian's and returning to the abbey in Leicester.

Shawn was waiting for him at the airport and they drove from Pittsburgh to Leicester. As they got into the car, Shawn said, "We can stop at The Lamplighter for drinks and supper and catch up." He had hugged Simon in the car several times. "I'm so happy you're back!" Then he smiled and said sarcastically, "I can see you had the time of your life in Skitz's little Texas ranch."

Simon rolled his eyes in disgust and sighed dramatically, "Oh, yeah! I had the fucking time of my life with that sick loon, Dick, and his pathetic sidekick, Michel." They drove down the hilly roads away from Pittsburgh and Simon noticed a large, yellowed envelope on the seat next to him. Written across the front, in large, carefully scripted handwriting was his own name. "Is this for me?"

Shawn looked sideways as he drove. "Oh, yeah, I almost forgot. That's the envelope Father Marcellinus left for you." He looked ahead at the road. "I brought it along because I think it's fitting for you to have it, now that the priesthood is so close for you." He added, "I thought you might want to open it along the way to the abbey." Shawn smiled, "I felt it up and down, and I think I know what it is."

Simon was intrigued and took the envelope in his hands and stared at the handwriting. He felt a pang of sadness knowing that he would not see the old priest at the abbey anymore. He opened the envelope carefully and pulled out a small bundle wrapped in yellowed tissue paper. Around it was a note, attached with a faded, red rubber band:

Dearest Brother Simon Maria:

By the time you read this I will be in Purgatory getting ready for the joyful entrance into Heaven.

I want you to have this for the day of your ordination to the sacred priesthood. Sadly, they are not part of the ritual anymore. It is, of course, unused and I know it was meant for you all along. It belonged to someone I knew and cared for very much, but who did not make it to the altar before his ordination. Now it belongs to you. Thankfully, our Diocesan Bishop is of the old school and I am sure he will place it on you on the day you become a priest forever, if you petition him.

Pray for me on the day of your First Solemn High Mass that I may be in Heaven just as soon as possible.

Father Marcellinus

Simon unwrapped the aged tissue paper and held the elongated, white linen cloth in his hands. It had three raised, gold crosses embroidered across the top's length and two slender strips at each end. "What is it?"

"It's called a maniturgium. Marcellinus is right, they took them out of the ritual. It's unfortunate but hey, you have one!"

"What is it for?"

"On the day you are ordained a priest, the bishop, after he has imposed his hands on your head and transmitted the priesthood to you, will ask you to stay kneeling. He will consecrate your hands with the Sacred Chrism oil and then clasp your hands together. At that point, he will use the maniturgium to tie your hands together. It's a sign that your hands have been sealed, consecrated forever, in order to touch the Body and Blood, Soul and Divinity of Jesus. The maniturgium is also practical because any of the Sacred Chrism oil that runs off, will be soaked up by the linen. Then you go to the sacristy and take it off and a deacon with help you wash your hands with lemon, bread and water. The maniturgium you will save for your mother."

"Save it for my mother?" Simon wasn't quite sure he understood.

"Yeah, that's the second use the priest's maniturgium has. On the day your mom dies, her hands will be clasped together and tied in the same way yours were on the day you became a priest forever. It's an ancient sign that she takes to Heaven to prove that she was the mother of a priest. It shows she gave the Church a priest to offer the Sacrifice on earth."

Simon was taken up by the explanation and only managed to say, "Wow, that's a beautiful symbol." Sadness filled Simon's heart knowing that he would not ever use the maniturgium because he was leaving everything to be with Kevin.

"Lucky you, you have friends who look out for you. Now it's not used and unfortunately, no one gave me a maniturgium for my ordination day. Marcellinus must have been keeping that for most of his life."

In the days that followed, Simon dared not speak with Shawn about Kevin. He knew that if he told him he was seriously thinking of leaving the abbey for Kevin, there would be trouble. Big ass trouble. Simon, in fact, understood that if he was going to really leave, he couldn't tell a soul except for the Abbot when the time came. If he did leave, his announcement and departure from the abbey would not be received well. He wondered how he would tell his mother and family if he did leave in order to go with Kevin. He knew that he would be vilified. He spent his days in the crypt struggling for a clear answer. He thought about Kevin every minute of every day and wondered where he was and what he was doing. He asked God if his thinking was clear. He begged God to show him if he was finally being honest and making a decision that corresponded with the Divine Will and the nature God had given him at conception. "Please, dear God, show me what I must do. Show me the path to take. You hold everything in your hands. You have called me to priesthood since I was so young. But you also made me gay and you've given me a sexual appetite and a desire to be loved as a man and to love another man. Please show me what I must do." But God was silent in His Heaven and in His tabernacle and Simon felt that he was left to decide for himself. He missed Kevin terribly and wished they were together.

Meanwhile in the abbey there was a whirlwind of activity. Ordinations to the deaconate and the priesthood were coming up as well as the anticipated visit of the special guest from Rome. Everything was highly anticipated and there was a festive spirit in the abbey. Simon had asked Shawn one afternoon when they walked outside before supper, "Who is the Abbot General, anyway and why is he coming? I'm not sure I got all that."

"All the abbeys in the world enjoy autonomy for the most part, as you know, but the Abbot General is assigned by the Vatican, well, by the Holy See in the pope's name, to oversee everything, in all the abbeys. His seat is in Rome, in an ancient abbey located in the very heart of the Roman Forum. The monks who have gone and lived there say it's a formidable abbey. Many parts of it date back to the Emperor Vespasian and that's like the middle of the first century AD, so you get the picture. It houses a number of archives dating back centuries and the Abbot General is the visible head of our Order to the Holy See."

"Wow, and he's coming here for ordinations?" Simon chuckled, "Does anybody even know we exist in this tiny hamlet called Leicester?"

"Yes, little one. The Vatican knows and sees everything. It turns out the Abbot General is visiting several abbeys in the States and ours is one of them. Eddie invited him to be present for the ordinations and he said 'yes'." Shawn shoved Simon playfully to one side, "Imagine your clout! The Abbot General in attendance at your ordination as a deacon! That's certainly a feather in your hat!" Simon smiled but said nothing. Shawn looked at him, "Are you okay, baby? I'm not seeing you jump for joy. Is everything okay with you? Normally, you'd eat this shit up."

"Yeah, sure, why wouldn't everything be okay?" Shawn narrowed his eyes and looked at Simon. Simon narrowed his eyes back at Shawn exaggeratedly and stuck out his tongue.

Simon wanted desperately to speak with Kevin on the phone and hear his voice, but phone calls were strictly limited and for the most part prohibited for those who were not yet priests. He missed his friend and lover terribly since he had returned and even though it was a consolation to be back in the abbey, he didn't feel the same about being back within its familiar walls. Something in him had definitely changed. Having met Kevin had changed so many things in him. He still wanted to be a priest and ordination to the deaconate was the last step before becoming a priest. Yet, he had to admit that he felt empty and lonely without Kevin because he needed him. A piece of his heart had stayed with Kevin in Dallas, there was no doubt about that.

Simon thought about taking a walk to clear his head but he was too restless to do so. Instead, he knew that what he wanted was to be with Kevin. Writing a note to Kevin was his only option. He sat at his desk and took a sheet of abbey stationary. His heart swelled with desire and love for the man in Dallas he wished to be with:

Abbey of the Most Sacred Heart of Jesus
Leicester, Pennsylvania
Kevin,

I want and need so much to hear your voice! More than that, I need to be with you. I miss you. I miss our rides in your jeep, your cooking! I miss our speedos and our time together. I miss your bed.

I wanted to call you so many times since I got back but I don't have a phone available to me. I decided to write to you. It's the best I can do to feel close to you and I hope when you receive this you'll know how much I love you and need you in my life. Soon enough I hope that we will be together in Dallas. My heart feels like somebody's squeezing it and it hurts, every time I realize we are so far apart from each other right now.

This morning I decided I'm going to speak with the Abbot to let him know I am determined to leave the abbey and will no longer pursue my preparation for priesthood. I will ask for the dispensation from my Solemn Vows. Once I fix all of that, we will be in each other's arms and continue our life together. I say "continue" because our life together has already begun.

I love you more than I can express in words. What I feel for you can only be expressed in person. I love you.

Simon

He reread his letter and put it down. Simon needed to speak with the Abbot as soon as possible. It would be wrong to wait till just before ordinations to say he had chosen to leave. At that very moment, he felt that the time had finally come to speak with Father Edmund. He shouldn't wait any longer and torture himself as he was doing with his indecision. He mustered all the courage he could and walked down the corridors to the Abbot's office. He knocked on the heavy oak door of Father Edmund's chambers. He received no answer. He knocked again, but louder this time and still received no answer. Then he saw the memo on the clip next to the door. It read: Dear brothers, I am in Pittsburgh all week for meetings of the Board. I will return next week just before ordinations. Abbot Edmund.

What could he do now? Simon was disappointed and frustrated at the same time. He was prohibited from speaking with Kevin and now also with the Abbot. He had tried to speak with God but it didn't seem to him that there was any possible communication there either. He knew that he couldn't mention anything to Shawn. Simon knew that there was a serious danger looming very close by and it had to do with him quickly losing his resolve. He needed to speak with someone about what he was planning to do, and he needed to do it now. For the moment, he needed to clear his head. He returned to his cell and stretched out on his metal cot. It didn't take long for him to slip away into sleep.

Shawn burst into Simon's cell, holding a small sheet of paper with what looked like handwritten notes. He slammed the door behind him. Simon jumped in bed and his first thought was that his letter to Kevin was sitting on his desk.

"There you are, baby. I've been looking for you." He glanced with little interest at the handwritten letter on Simon's desk.

"Oh? What's up?" Simon got up and sat at his desk chair. He turned the letter over.

"Letter to Mommie?" Shawn sat on his cot uninvited.

"Yeah, right. So what's going on?"

"I had a phone call from Pittsburgh. The Abbot called me. He needed to consult something serious with me."

"Really?" Simon was genuinely surprised. "What are you now, his principal confidant?"

"Well, actually…something like that, yes, at least in this matter I am. The Abbot General, Father Matteo, asked Edmund if he could borrow Father Bruno, Eddie's secretary, while he's making the rounds here in America. Seems that the Abbot General doesn't have anyone to fill that post, so he asked

Edmund to help him out. It appears the man's English is quite limited." Shawn crossed his legs and put his hands behind him, palms down, on Simon's mattress. "Eddie asked me to be his secretary while Bruno is away with Father Matteo as interpreter and translator." He smiled broadly as he said this. "I'm finding out about all kinds of shit I surmised but now fully know."

"Wow, you're acting-secretary for Father Edmund while the Abbot General is here?"

"Yeah, how about that?"

"You're moving up the ladder, mister fancy pants!"

"At a snail's pace, unfortunately, but I was happy to be asked. It's something…crumbs, but something." Shawn looked at Simon. "So I had a call from Pittsburgh, from the Abbot. It was about you." He held up the small piece of paper and glanced at it.

"About me?" Simon heard the alarm in his own voice. "What was it about?"

"Seems your friend Skitz, the Dick, down in the prairies of the great west called him yesterday and kept him on the phone for quite a while." Shawn cleared his throat, "The abbot was all upset about the call and I had to calm him down before I finally understood what the beef was." Simon stared at him at the mention of Richard Pazzone's nickname but said nothing. "Basically Skitz told the Abbot in no uncertain terms that 'a', you're a queer pervert, 'b', you're a vile, disobedient monk, and 'c' you go to gay bars and bath houses in Dallas." Shawn stared directly into Simon's eyes, adding, "He also told the Abbot that before you left the parish, you found a lover at a concert in a park and that you were sneaking away constantly to live with him. He said you set up house with him already."

Simon was literally unable to respond, given the magnitude of the hypocrisy and breach of confidence. He simply stared at Shawn, his mouth slightly open, uttering, "What?"

"What's going on, baby. In every rumor I've ever heard, there's some strand of truth." Simon stared at Shawn. "I told you to be careful with Skitz. He's a mean, sick motherfucker. I guess we both know what he decided to do with the things you told him about yourself."

Slowly, Simon's head cleared and he said, "Yeah…that was stupid on my part. I trusted him." Simon was thinking about that drunken night. "I was so stupid…no, I was beyond stupid. I had no idea he would betray me like that."

"Oh, he's a nut job alright. A vicious sick fuck of a nut job. Has been since he came here to these hallowed halls." Shawn looked at Simon and uncrossed his legs. He sat up and said, "Look at me." Simon looked at Shawn. "I'm not concerned about what nutsy said to the Abbot in his phone call. After all, I calmed the Abbot quite easily. Everybody knows Skitz is loony and has a mean streak in him straight out of the putrid bowels of Hell. And he's not exactly a candidate for 'mister macho of the year', being an obvious queen, so any of his accusations of other's sexuality falls apart from the get-go." He paused and then said, "No, baby, I'm not worried about that. I already covered for you with the Abbot and he's dismissed it completely, so don't you worry about that part."

Through tears that were more from frustration than from fear, Simon whispered hoarsely, "Thanks." Then he asked, already knowing in his heart what it was, "What's the other part?"

"I'm concerned about something else. I'm very concerned about something else, baby." Shawn moved closer on the cot to where Simon was. He grabbed the legs of the desk chair and pulled Simon toward himself. He took his hands into his own and said, "I didn't like those letters you wrote me about meeting that guy Kevin. You said your knees got weak thinking about your 'cowboy that looks like a Viking', that's how you wrote it, or something very close to that." Simon sat upright not saying a word. "I also didn't like that when you wrote to tell me about the concert in the park, you avoided mentioning anything else about him. And then…silence." He squeezed Simon's hands. "Baby, c'mon, I know you better than that. What's going on? What happened with this guy Kevin that got Skitz black balling you on the phone with Eddie? Dick is a sick fuck, we all know that, but Eddie said that Skitz had sent Michel to spy on you. What's all that about?"

Simon thought about denying everything Shawn had just said but suddenly he let go of the tension that had been building within him and had gripped his heart like a thick, wire vise. He put his head down and his shoulders slouched noticeably. He couldn't hide what he was carrying in his soul. He honestly didn't want to hide anything anymore. He looked up at Shawn and simply said, "I had sex with Kevin. Several times at his place, but that was it."

Shawn sighed and dropped Simon's hands. He laid the palms of his hands on Simon's knees and said, "Don't bullshit me, little one." Sternly, he said in a low voice, "Don't you ever bullshit me like that again. Don't lie to a liar and don't bullshit a bull-shitter." He took his hands again and asked slowly, "What happened with this Kevin fellow? The real truth, not the sorry bullshit story you just tried to feed me."

"I…I…" Simon began to cry now and was shaking in his chair as all the emotions he had pent up within himself over the summer, came pouring forth. "I had amazing sex with Kevin. He's a beautiful masculine man. Not a confused boy, but a man. He does look like a cowboy-Viking, but…but…it was more than that. I am in love with Kevin and I want to leave the abbey to go live with him. To spend my life with him. I've decided and want to tell the Abbot as soon as he returns." He sobbed loudly now, not caring who heard. Shawn simply sat there, showing no emotion.

He waited for Simon to calm down and said, "Baby. What the fuck am I going to do with you? Won't you ever fucking learn what I've been saying to you over and over? First Toby and then Joshua…"

"Will you shut the fuck up? Will you please just shut the fuck up and respect me for once! I'm not some little boy! I'm a man. This is different from Toby and Joshua and root cellars! Kevin is different, what I feel for him…the connection we have…"

"Stop it! Stop that! It's the same damn thing over and over and all you're doing is hurting yourself and setting yourself up for a life of shit, of pure misery."

Simon sat back. He wiped his eyes and pulled out his handkerchief and blew his nose. He stared at Shawn and said, "No, you stop it. I love Kevin and I'm leaving the abbey. I've decided. There's really no more for me to say and quite honestly, I don't owe you a fucking explanation. You got that? You may think you have the entire world by its fucking balls but you don't." Shawn sat back and was speechless. "As soon as the Abbot gets back from Pittsburgh, I'm out of here. It's not easy for me, believe me. I've struggled day and night with this decision and I still want to be a priest but I'm in love with Kevin and I've chosen. Right or wrong, I've chosen. The only one I need to explain myself to is the Abbot." He paused, "And I'll not be asking Father Edmund for his permission. It's my life, dammit."

Simon saw how Shawn's demeanor suddenly relaxed, saying quietly, "But you're so close to priesthood, baby, you're…"

"I've decided. You can tell that to the Abbot if he calls you again." Simon stood, indicating he was done. Shawn didn't move and an awkward silence wedged itself between them. At long last, seeing that he wasn't moving, Simon said, "Excuse me but I need to get some air." He picked up his letter to Kevin and walked to the door of his cell. Simon didn't look back at Shawn but opened the door and walked out, not bothering to close it behind him. Simon was done explaining himself to Shawn. He was taking command of his life now.

Very late that same afternoon, after walking outside for what seemed forever, Simon was in the crypt thinking and trying in vain to pray, gathering his thoughts in order to speak with the Abbot that evening. He felt terribly sad knowing that he wouldn't be ordained a deacon and subsequently, never be on the altar as a priest. It hurt him to think that he would never offer the Sacrifice. Maybe he had finally arrived at some degree of maturity and accepted that he couldn't have everything he wanted at the same time. He had resolved to go to Kevin.

He heard foot steps behind him as the bluish shadows of the crypt began to gather. The individual coughed several times and then Simon heard the unmistakable sounds of someone genuflecting and then settling on the pew kneeler. The kneeler creaked in the damp vastness of the dark crypt. Simon thought about Kevin and it eased the pain that had gripped his heart. He was sad to leave the abbey and the future priesthood that it promised. It wouldn't be easy for him to put an end to all his plans and boyhood dreams. But thinking about Kevin made his heart lightened up. He thought about the two of them creating a life together and he thought especially about not feeling alone and afraid anymore. Simon knew that it was costing him to leave the abbey but he knew that his loneliness would be addressed. He and Kevin would find their way together. They would face their fears and pain, their disappointments, hand in hand. He would help Kevin deal with his sorrow and Kevin would help him deal with his.

Simon was lost in these thoughts and didn't notice the monk who walked past him and toward the tomb of the Prince-Bishop Demetrius. When he was finally aware of the other man, Simon saw him touching the sarcophagus with temerity and wondered who the man might be.

The monk Simon was seeing wore the black robes of their Order. He wasn't tall and Simon figured he must be a man of no more than fifty five or sixty years. His hair was jet black except for a bit of gray on the temples and his features were definitely Latin. He was shaven but Simon saw that he had a thick under-beard and would probably have a daily five o'clock shadow by four in the afternoon. He had never seen the monk before and was ready to close his eyes and lose himself in his thoughts again when the afternoon sun gleamed off the large, gold pectoral cross he was wearing. Likewise, the heavy gold chain around his neck that held the cross caught all the light in the dark place. Simon was momentarily surprised to see it, but then noticed that on his right hand the monk wore an impressive gold ring with a large, oval amethyst at its center. Simon realized who the monk must be and he felt himself drawn to him. He rose and genuflected and made his way toward the tomb of the prince-bishop.

"Hello, Father, my name is Brother Simon."

The monk turned around, startled by the greeting and smiled expansively at Simon. With his left hand he held on to the pectoral cross that hung around his neck on the thick, gold chain Simon had seen. He extended his right hand for Simon to kiss the ring in respect, which Simon did. "Oh! I am Father Matteo, the Abbot General." He took Simon's hand and squeezed it, then said apologetically, "I am sorry and please forgive my bad English. It's not so good. I am from Spain."

Simon said excitedly, "So are my grandparents! My family comes from the north, from Santillana del Mar and the Basque Provinces."

The monk's face lit up. "Entonces, hablas Español?"

"Si, Reverendisimo Padre!" Simon was impressed to be in the presence of the Abbot General from Rome. "I'm very pleased to meet you. I heard that you were coming to visit us but honestly I didn't know when you'd be arriving. I hope your trip here was good."

"Por favor! Por favor! En Español! No entendí nada." The priest held his hands up to the sides of his head mockingly. He explained in Spanish that it had been weeks since he had found a soul who spoke his native tongue and that since he had arrived in the abbey, he barely understood much of what was said to him. He continued in Spanish, saying, "It's such a blessing to hear my language! This is why I'm looking for a secretary. I simply can't continue this way, always in the dark about everything when I travel outside of Italy and Spain." He laughed, saying, "In English, there's a different word for every word in Spanish! Obvio!"

"Yes, I hear that you don't have a secretary at the moment and that Father Bruno is accompanying you during your official visitation."

The gentleman continued in Spanish, "Bruno, yes. He's from this abbey. He's a good monk but he is too old and set in his ways. He speaks Italian and he understands Spanish but the two languages are not the same. He belongs here, in this abbey among the mountains and pines. I am grateful to Abbot Edmund for loaning him to me but I need someone younger and more energetic, someone who speaks Spanish fluently!" They both laughed softly as they walked around the crypt searching for an exit door.

Simon explained in Spanish who the prince-bishop was and a bit of the history surrounding the abbey. At the Abbot General's suggestion, Simon led him around the crypt and then they walked upstairs and out into the waning, late afternoon sun.

The Abbot General from Rome asked Simon many questions. He wanted to know everything about him: where he was from, what he was doing, where was he assigned for the deaconate months and what would he do after ordination to the priesthood. Simon explained that he was one of the two monks designated to be ordained deacon the next day but that they still didn't know where they would be sent. He struggled as he spoke, knowing that his conversation was a complete farce.

"Then you will probably go to a parish until ordination to the priesthood?"

"The deacons are sent out after ordination, yes, Father. Usually a couple of months after that, they are ordained a priest."

"Where will you be assigned once you are ordained a priest?" Simon's head was spinning at this point because there he was speaking with the highest authority of the Order and he didn't know how to say that he was actually leaving the abbey to go to Dallas to live with the man he loved. "Actually, Father Matteo, I—"

The Abbot General cut him off, "I am thinking about something that is extraordinary right now, at this very minute. It just now comes to me! This is something that only God Himself could have devised. Only the Holy Spirit." Simon was startled by what he was hearing when the prelate monk asked, "Why not come to Rome when you finish your internship as a deacon? Come to Rome and be ordained a priest there. Then you can remain and be my personal secretary?" Simon was beyond stunned. "I am looking for a secretary and you speak English and Spanish perfectly. It would be easy for you to learn Italian. These are the three fundamental languages that we use in the administration at the Mother House. You would be perfect! What do you think?"

Simon could hear something like the roar of the ocean in his head and his heart began to pound wildly in his chest. He was completely taken by surprise at that moment and could only think of one thing: he was being asked to go to Rome. To Rome! The emotions that raged inside him were many but instead of being chaotic, they made him understand clearly that this was not a simple, everyday opportunity but instead, a life-changing one. Was God finally speaking up and saying something to him? He shivered to think that he had almost gone to the Abbot days before to tell him of his decision to leave the abbey. His heart hurt and stung thinking about Kevin, waiting for him so many miles away.

Since the day he almost drowned with his brother, Bobby, he felt in his bones that this was the closest he had come again to an undeniable experience of divine interception. Why had God sent him to Dallas and allowed him to fall in love with Kevin? He could barely say a word to the man standing in front of him. The most he could manage was, "Oh, Father, it would be such an honor to serve you in Rome, but something has changed my plans in a way I never expected and actually, I've already decided…"

The Abbot General waved his hand, "None of that talk of 'serving' and no 'buts', please. You will come to Rome to work 'with' me, at my side. You and I will create wonderful things together for the good of the Church. We must speak of this further after I speak with Abbot Edmund tonight." Then he added, "I do ask you, please, to be very prudent and say nothing of this to anyone until I have spoken with your Abbot. He and I need to discuss it first and then it will be officially settled and announced publicly."

"Yes, of course, Father." Everything was moving too fast for Simon, in a direction he had not thought of previously. As they walked ahead, toward the abbey entrance, the reality of Rome began to sink in.

The Abbot General excused himself and Simon was grateful for the space. He had much to think about. He remembered as far back as when he was a little boy, being captivated by colorful books of kings, tsars and popes living in palaces in the great cities of Europe. He and his mother had poured over such books and his imagination had soared. Now that same imagination had been suddenly, abruptly roused from sleep. He had often fantasized about the privilege, the pomp and self-satisfaction that he imagined existed in those lofty places. He asked himself what it must be like to live in that world, above most other people, knowing you held a singular position, unlike the masses.

Simon loved and needed Kevin and was determined to leave the abbey in order to go to him. He longed to join Kevin and build a life together, but now this had taken place. Simon realized that an unexpected door had just blown wide open in front of him. Was it even real, or had he dreamed the whole thing? Shawn had warned him over and over again about the dangers of falling in love and for a split second Simon now doubted his decision to leave the abbey. He was approved to be ordained a deacon the next day and now, as God would have it, he was being invited out of the blue, to go to Rome after his ordination to serve at the side of one of the highest authorities in the Church, at his personal invitation no less.

Father Edmund was his protector but now it seemed a more powerful one had crossed his path and come into the picture. It dawned on Simon that the opportunity that lay before him was a life changer. It wasn't something that just happened every day. Unaware, he whispered to himself, "Neither is love. It doesn't just come every day." Yet, his thoughts slid back easily to the incredible invitation he had received from the august visitor from Rome. The Abbot General could promote him to the heights of an ecclesiastical career unlike anything he could ever have imagined for himself. The man was inviting him to Rome, where the Pope himself lived in the Apostolic Palace and cardinals and bishops strolled without haste in the piazzas of the ancient city. To live there and to work, to rub shoulders with the men who made things happen in the Church, this is what the whole thing was about, wasn't it?. This was no mere job opportunity and Simon realized he had to rethink all of his plans and he had to do so very quickly. There was very little time to decide the course he would take. Sister Mary Agnes had once said to him in school. 'Remember, Larry, God doesn't call us when we're ready. Oh, no, God calls us when it's time'.

A great part of his heart already belonged to Kevin and now his heart reminded him of this truth. He was keenly aware that it went way beyond anything he had said or promised Kevin. It wasn't so much about keeping his word as it was about what he had given Kevin and received from him. His heart was ready to go to Kevin. That part had been clear because to Simon it belonged to the realm of the sacred. But that was before he met the Abbot General in the crypt. All of it was before God had thrown him the massive, proverbial curve ball he had just received. That chance meeting in the crypt changed everything now and once again, Simon knew that he had to choose. Was it a chance meeting or was it all part of God's plan? Simon simply didn't know. What he did know was that a deep sorrow was gripping his heart regardless of what he chose. To decide Kevin over Rome or Rome over Kevin would leave a great part of his heart in shambles, tattered and torn. Separately, both situations were wonderful and joyful but he couldn't have them both. And to have to choose and keep only one weighed terribly upon him and filled his heart with anguish and sorrow.

If he chose Kevin over Rome, he would have his love with him and create a life with the man who loved him but he would lose a singular life-changing opportunity as a priest. He had received that call as far back as he could remember. One could say it had started way before he ever crawled under his grandfather's house, digging in the dirt. Simon believed the call had come to him in his mother's womb. If he chose Rome over Kevin, he would be at the threshold of a promising ecclesiastical career, surrounded by history, where the power and the glory was. This was no mere assignment to a backwater parish like Saint Sebastian's but would affect his future life in a singular way. E.E. Cummings' words sprung up in Simon's mind: 'be of love a little more careful than of everything'. If he chose Rome over Kevin he knew that he would betray and lose love again. It would be even worse, this time, he admitted to himself because he understood love much better than before. His thoughts came and went like this uncontrollably, thrashing wildly within his heart. In the heightened state of excitement that Simon now found himself, he failed to think about loneliness and not having Kevin next to him in Rome. He failed to ponder the reality of another abbey on the other side of the world and the men who lived there. True, they would be important individuals but most probably they would be unloving and empty men, much like in the abbey in Leicester. He was sure that those men had had to sacrifice many things in order to rise to the top. Is that what he wanted? Was he willing to pay that price for personal glory? He failed to think that there would be no one there to love him as Kevin loved him. There would be no one with whom he could share his bed. What had taken place for him in the crypt with the Abbot General was too huge for Simon to easily wrap his brain around and all these considerations weighed upon him. There was Rome squarely in his path, within his reach. And it was bigger than everything else.

Simon returned to his cell. Given the interruption with Shawn and then everything that had taken place in the crypt afterward, he had not yet sent Kevin the letter he had penned earlier. It was in his pocket and he reread it now, holding the letter in his hand. He crossed his arms on his desk and laid his head down. He sat in that position for a long time, trying to decide what he should do. At some point, after the sun had set, without going to prayers or supper, he undressed and crawled wearily into his cot. He tossed and turned knowing that he only had a few hours to choose. In that way he fell asleep. Finally, before day break, without having slept all night, he sat at his desk and wrote Kevin a new letter:

Abbey of the Most Sacred Heart of Jesus
Leicester, Pennsylvania
Kevin, my love:

Where do I begin? Everything would be so much easier if we were face to face or at least if I could hear your voice and speak with you on the phone. But neither of those are a possibility for me. I know that my words will not serve me well now.

Everything here has shifted in a way I can't even explain very well. I had decided to tell the Abbot I was leaving the abbey in order to be with you. I had decided it was time. I walked to his office but he wasn't here because he was away in Pittsburgh.

Then I met the Abbot General. He's the highest ranking man in our Order. He asked me to come to Rome to be his personal secretary and it is something that has changed everything.

I love you more than I can possibly express and want to share my life with you, but my whole life has been in preparation for the priesthood. I can't have it both ways even though my heart is breaking at his moment.

After a really bad night, I have decided to accept the position in Rome and will be ordained a deacon this morning. Forgive me. I'm so sorry but I can't come to you as I promised. I feel worse than awful and can understand it if you despise me.

I will always love you, always, even though I am sure you doubt that now.

Simon

At ten o'clock that morning, in the splendor of the Gothic, abbey church, Seth and Simon were ordained deacons by the local Bishop in a solemn ceremony. In attendance were the Abbot, Father Edmund and the Abbot General, Father Matteo.

After the ceremony Shawn came up to Simon and hugged him tightly, "You can't imagine how happy I am that you chose to stay here in the abbey. It would have been such a mistake if you had left. Do you know where you're being assigned to as a deacon?"

"Yes, I'm going to Pittsburgh. My assignment begins effective the first Sunday of Advent, so I still have a couple of weeks here."

"Pittsburgh? That's great news, baby! You'll be close by! I will definitely come see you there." Then he added, "I got bumped from my secretarial career by Bruno who has been returned. The Abbot General leaves for Rome after tomorrow. Bruno tells me Father Matteo already found a secretary but it's all top secret." He sighed, "Lamentably, I think my climb to the top just came to a screeching halt."

Simon made sure he didn't show the slightest sign of knowing anything. "Well, you'll get your Doctorate soon. That's something to celebrate. Then you can teach."

"Teach? Hell no, I don't want to teach." Shawn hugged him again, "I'm so happy for you! When this is all over and you're settled in Pittsburgh, I'll come over and we'll go out to dinner some place nice to celebrate your ordination." He went to leave but then turned around again and winked at Simon, saying softly, "You can wear your Carabinieri boots then."

Several days before Simon was to leave for Pittsburgh, he received a letter from Dallas with the initials "K.R." on the return address. He took the envelope to the crypt and opened it there. It was a card with a colorful scene of churning waves under a dark, stormy sky. Coming out of the water was an outstretched arm and hand. Flying above it was a white dove, flapping its wings. Simon could see Kevin had drawn it himself. Next to the outstretched arm was written "Kevin" and next to the flying white dove was written "Simon". Inside was a folded letter. Simon held it for a moment in his trembling hands and hated himself for having betrayed Kevin and his love. He unfolded the letter:

Dallas, Texas

My beautiful, mad monk, Simon,

I knew that if you went back there to them I would lose you and you would never come back to me. And see, that's exactly what happened. I told you.

The days that we spent together here are like a dream now except that the bottles of beer we drank are still lined up against the wall and I know it was real. I haven't moved them, waiting for you to come into my arms again.

Why didn't you just come back like you said you would? You were really that dove from Heaven that came to save me when I was drowning but now you're just far away. You flew away from me, far, far away and the drowning is really awful now.

If ever you change your mind, I will be here waiting for you. I love you still and I will always love you.

Kevin

PS How could I ever despise you? I love you more than you realize.

Simon put the letter back in the card and into the envelope. He sat there, thinking about his life and where his recent decision was taking him. He felt in his heart that God indeed had a plan but that it was all very unclear to him. Things had seemed to go one way for a minute and he had fallen in love. Then they had completely gone somewhere else, way beyond the stretch of anyone's imagination. What had he been expected to do?

He felt miserable about betraying Kevin and realized that what Shawn had taught him must have finally sunk in. It was okay to have sex but completely stupid to fall in love. But his heart told him that that was pure bullshit. He thought to himself that if he hadn't fallen in love with Kevin it wouldn't have been so damn painful and messy, plus he wouldn't have hurt Kevin. His heart sprung up and reminded him of the love they had shared together. It wasn't a phase nor was it some childish game but something real. His heart reprimanded him in the fiercest manner: how could you betray something so perfect, so pure, so divine? How could he ever forgive himself for his betrayal of love? But all that was history now, it was all in the past. He had done that and the die was cast. How could he have possibly known about this new piece in God's strange and complicated puzzle?

He had had to choose and he chose. There was no way out of it and no going back. He had new things coming in his life and in a very short time he would finally be ordained a priest and go to Rome. His brain told him that this was definitely cause for celebration. Even his heart had to agree to this. How fast it had all happened! He chose the Church, the priesthood and his future over everything. He had chosen all of it over love and realized he had had to sacrifice Kevin in the process. It was all less than perfect but he was forced to decide and he did. Simon stood, and suddenly the words from the Christ in the dream came rushing into him. They were the same words Kevin had uttered pleading: "Stay with me." He sat back down and dared to wonder what the words to him really meant. Had he interpreted them correctly or had he misunderstood completely? Was it to remain in the Church as a priest, which is what he wanted, or was it a command to let go and leave that behind and immerse himself in the love of another person? Had he obeyed the Christ to perfection by remaining at the abbey and continue toward priesthood or had he disobeyed Him completely, not understanding? Simon bowed his head not knowing the answer and then, standing, genuflected and left the crypt.

+++++

Mark, the tattooer, had turned the tattoo gun off and sat in his swivel chair staring incredulously at Simon. Dryly he said, "You can look at your tattoo now." But then he stood, indignant and said, "You fucking left that guy, Kevin? After you promised to love him and move in with him but then you backed out? That poor guy…you lead him on." Simon thought his tone was judgemental. "What were you thinking, dude? How could you do that? Fuck, in my book that makes you a huge piece of shit."

Simon looked at Mark sadly, "I guess it was glory, man. 'Sic transit Gloria mundi'." He repeated, "I didn't remember that ancient warning."

"Huh? What the fuck does that mean?"

"In Roman times, when the emperor or his generals returned from battle, victorious, they rode in on a chariot before the cheering crowds. There would be two slaves standing right behind him in the chariot. One held a gold wreath over his head while the other whispered in his ear: 'Sic transit Gloria mundi' which means 'the glories of this world are passing'. The popes later on used this in their own crowning ceremonies as well. It was actually said as part of the ritual for the crowning. It was always a reminder that the glories, power and honor of this life are passing. All of it crumbles and disappears eventually." Simon paused and admitted, "I forgot the warning of those ancient words..." He repeated, "I forgot the warning." Then he added sadly, "I didn't understand what 'Stay with me' meant because I couldn't say no to Rome and what it seemed to me to promise."

Mark dismissed Simon's attitude and explanation, "Bullshit! That's all bookish bullshit to me, man. What you did to Kevin...fuck me! Its unforgiveable, dude. You told him you'd be there for him. You promised Kevin that you'd go back and live with him! You fucking promised and he was waiting for you. After all the stuff he told you about his life. What was going on with you, Simon? Fuck, you were that dove he mentioned. That's no mere thing, dammit." Mark sighed as he got up. He seemed disoriented to Simon or better yet, not focused on what he was doing because the tattooer appeared distracted. He finally said, "'Stay with me'...those were the words of the Lord in the dream, right?" Simon nodded. "You'd have to be some self-centered, unloving bastard not to know what that meant. He wasn't telling you to stay in a loveless institution no matter how glorious and secure it might mean, you stupid fuck. The Christ was commanding you to 'stay in love', to stay with Him. From the very little...very little I know..." Mark's eyes had misted over and his voice quivered. "From the very little I know, I've heard that somewhere it says that where there is love, that's where God is, way before Him being in churches and rituals. If there's no love, dude, God just isn't there. You don't have to be a fucking Einstein to understand that. In that dream you had, the Lord wasn't telling you to keep sticking to the institution of the Church to become powerful and gather up as many fucking titles as you could just to fulfill a childhood dream! And when those same words crossed over Kevin's lips to you, the Lord wasn't telling you to run from and betray a man who loved you, and who you loved. He was telling you to stay with Him, to really be in His company and that meant to give yourself to love when it came to you. Kevin was put in your path for that. Loving Kevin was to be in God's presence. Without love, there is no presence of God. God desperately wanted to be with you and Kevin."

It felt to Simon at that moment that God was speaking to him through the tattooer. Hadn't Simon figured out that that had been God's plan from the beginning of this whole tattoo-thing? Wasn't it just a divine ploy to get Simon to face his shit head-on without excuses? Simon turned away from Mark. It was all too much to bear at the moment. He needed to get home and his drink. He needed to think and accept and take responsibility. Simon finally exhaled and said, "You're absolutely right, Mark. I betrayed love when I betrayed Kevin…I betrayed God because of my lust for glory and power. The glories and honors of this world were suddenly laid out in front of me, glittering and perfectly within my reach and I couldn't and wouldn't see anything else. Once it was held out to me, I just couldn't say no. That's what happened, Mark. That's what fucking happened in a nutshell." Bitterly, Simon admitted, "I reached only for that. It was all I could see at the time. Nothing else mattered at that point, really. Sadly, nothing else."

Mark looked at Simon and said softly, "Sorry I busted your balls, but you needed to hear it. You need to face it." Then Mark got closer to Simon and said gently, "You see, Kevin needed you terribly but you needed him just as terribly. You think God didn't see that?"

"Yeah, I know that now." The tattooer put antibacterial on the tattoo and wrapped Simon up in plastic. As he was ready to leave, Simon turned to the tattooer and said, "I'll be back soon, Mark. I'm not done yet."

"No, I wouldn't think you're done yet, you're not nearly done yet. There's Rome." Mark was cleaning up his work space and did not look up. "And was it worth it? Was betraying the Christ by betraying Kevin worth it to you? Did it ultimately make you a really happy, fulfilled man or did it mercilessly strip you bare and plunge you into unimaginable sorrow and emptiness?"

Simon stood at the door of the room, saying, "Tough questions, Mark. Very tough questions. Yeah, there's still Rome to talk about. I chose Rome and that's where I paid the price for the betrayal. I exchanged love for so many other things I thought were more important." Simon hesitated and then added, "The path God lays out for each of us…there are a lot of foggy patches along the way." He muttered to himself as he walked away from the room, "And it often takes us to places we couldn't have imagined in our wildest dreams."

Epilogue

With trepidation, Ashmedai, the king of demons, crept out from the shadows in which he had ensconced himself and barely managed to whisper to the Almighty, "I must say, if I am going to be completely honest, that I'm somewhat perplexed by the narrative I've just heard. What I don't understand is why You said that the hideous nightmare HAD to take place for Simon." Then he added, "And for that matter, I would surmise that You're of the opinion that so many other things HAD to take place for him as well. Things that I think could have easily been avoided in his best interest."

Bore Olam opened His eyes and focused on the demon squatting obscenely on the pavement before Him. "Yes, that's correct. Things had to happen, regardless of what you may think or surmise."

A cunning expression blossomed on the demon's middle, most human-like countenance. "With all due respect, Domine, I can't say that it makes any sense to me. Are You suggesting that hideous events must take place in every human life? Are You saying that You're responsible for sending them because they are necessary and unavoidable?" As he concluded his interrogation, the demon appeared pleased with himself and his observations. Ashmedai extended his arms gracefully to either side of himself, palms upward. Then he bowed down in a dramatic gesture reminiscent of the grace of the French court of young King Louis XVI in which, centuries before, he had so completely enjoyed himself.

The Creator of the Universe looked down from His throne above the cherubim and said, "Let me put it to you this way. Things that are ALSO painful and hideous DO happen in every human life for a specific purpose. A purpose only I'm aware of. Events and experiences that are not always understood, are meant to take place. It's all part of an intelligent design, a Divine Scheme if you will. Every leaf that falls to the ground and every tear that is shed, eventually has a redemptive purpose."

The demon straightened up and said, "Hashem, do forgive me for saying so, but that sounds heartless and cruel to me. I mean, to cause pain and to purposefully send suffering to mortals—"

Bore Olam corrected the demon, "I don't send suffering but I do permit pain and suffering, yes, that's correct. It may not seem fair nor loving, but it is."

Ashmedai shook his three monstrous heads from side to side in a manner that suggested negation. "No, I certainly do not understand Your reasoning. It makes no sense to me why You allow suffering. Take Your golden boy Simon, for example. You've seen what it's done to him. You know how much it has unraveled him."

The Creator responded softly, "Do you think for a moment that I desire for him to get hurt? But it must happen. He must endure suffering and hardship because he's on his life's journey. He's in the thick of it. This is the reason it's gotten messy and painful. It's the way I have fashioned it."

The demon, however, persisted, "Oh Adonai, You've sat back and allowed him to get tangled in his confusion which has lead him to get really hurt. And in the process, You can't deny that that has spilled over and that he's necessarily hurt others. Is that Your inexplicable Divine Plan?"

The Almighty considered the demon's words and said, "It's part of it, yes. Out of blind, mindless chaos and rebellion, My Will is still carried out. It is always motivated by love."

"But Master, from the story of Simon's life You just shared with me, he's broken and he's gotten himself very badly bruised and wounded, not in the physical sense, but emotionally. You seem to have approved and never had any intention of keeping it from happening. And then there's Your apparent silence when things seem to get worse…honestly."

"Wounds and bruises, deceptions and disappointments, even shattered dreams, can lead a soul to genuine strength and deep self-understanding. Even the misinformed perception of my apparent silence has a reason. This is ultimately what will catapult souls to become what they were created to be." The Eternal Father then added, "This, precisely, has always been My desire for Simon."

With exaggerated fanfare, the demon bowed low, once more, and cried out, "Kyrios! Oh, great Theos! You hold every card, I admit, but with all due respect, I simply can't agree. It makes no sense to me. The story You've just shared with me proves completely otherwise. Simon is a soul filled with a deep, personal desire to serve You. Yet, You allow him to wander away from You when he's easily swayed and tossed about by his unbridled concupiscence and lust of every kind." The demon emphatically repeated, "It makes no sense! The outcome that I see is far from him gaining any strength and even less do I detect any kind of deep understanding of self in him."

"I mean, c'mon, he betrayed his first love and then, knowing better, Simon betrayed Kevin because of his intense vainglory. Is that what he's supposed to become? Is this the perfect product of Your intelligent design? Is he destined to become a loveless, deceitful creature like myself? I say that what took place in that squalid motel room, made him into a frightened, self-seeking individual, trusting no one except himself. He became determined after that, hell-bent on getting his way, taking all that he could for himself without any thought for anyone else, come hell or high water, as the old saying goes."

The Almighty studied the demon closely. "I don't deny that it frightened him terribly breaking him to the point of feeling completely abandoned by Me. I'm sure that he even questioned My love for him. But you must accept that it's all a process. The lessons he learned in that dreadful motel room served him well later on, whether he was aware of it or not. Sure, there are moments in a human life when suffering souls can become quite paralyzed in their fear and brokenness. Their sorrow must never be denied nor deemed to be trivial. But it doesn't all come to a screeching halt for that soul. Good times and bad times are really just stepping stones along the journey, they are just 'times', neither good nor bad. Ultimately, My Divine Plan comes full circle and will never be outdone no matter the circumstances surrounding it."

Ashmedai folded his deformed arms tightly around his corpulent chest and concluded, "Well, You'll have to pardon me but the story You've just told me proves nothing of what You say. Simon was a regular kid, albeit a horny, clever one, who managed to wheel and deal in order to get himself ordained a priest of the Holy Church of Rome. He betrayed others shamefully, and rightly suffered the consequences in the process." The demon shrugged, admitting, "I just don't get it. To me, it doesn't prove anything about strength or self-understanding and acceptance."

The Creator smiled knowingly and said, "I realize you're bitter and cynical, after all, look at what you've become for all eternity. But I haven't finished telling you the story of Simon. You don't know the full story yet. There's so much more to tell. That's why your conclusions are flawed and you insist that there are holes in my arguments." Then the Almighty paused deliberately and added, "You're forgetting something, aren't you? There's still Rome to talk about. Immediately after his ordination to the priesthood in Leicester, he went to Rome."

The demon's interest was suddenly piqued. "Oh, yes, that's right! I'd almost forgotten! Rome! You did mention Rome in your narrative, didn't you?" The demon became pensive as he looked out into the vast chambers of time and space. He fixed his gaze beyond the realms of the past and the expanse of eternity which opened up before him. He appeared quite mesmerized, perhaps due to personal recollections of Rome. He seemed to be genuinely transported in thought, by centuries upon centuries of vivid memories of the Eternal City.

"Ah, Rome," he said more to himself than to anyone in particular, as he smacked his lips without shame and said, "That deliciously ancient, decadent playground of mine and my demons. I'm so very fond of Rome, both the ancient days and ever since the Church of Rome was established and took root there. That singular venue has afforded me so much diversion and pleasure."

END OF BOOK ONE